The Glister Journals

Book 1

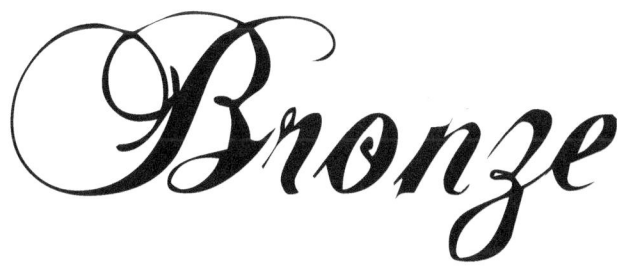

Bronze

B B Shepherd

China Blue Publishing
San Jose

Printed in the United States of America

The Glister Journals

series is dedicated to:

my dear family:
thank you for your love, patience, and encouragement;
and for making me laugh so much!

youth equestrian athletes everywhere:
my most profound respect.

Dr. Craig H. Russell:
amazing educator

Contents

Prologue

Chapter One   Break the Spell   3.

Chapter Two   Confused   13.

Chapter Three   Tongue-Tied   25.

Chapter Four   All In My Head   36.

Chapter Five   Right Between the Eyes   50.

Chapter Six   Just Falling   65.

Chapter Seven   A Wanted Man   83.

Chapter Eight   Leading Me   99.

Chapter Nine   Dreams Exploding   115.

Chapter Ten   I Don't Really Mind   129.

Chapter Eleven   Let It Out   147.

Chapter Twelve   Not Real   166.

Chapter Thirteen   Never Forget   183.

Chapter Fourteen   A Little Ride   199.

Chapter Fifteen   One Thing I Know   215.

Chapter Sixteen   A Mean Cycle   233.

Chapter Seventeen   Deep Breath   248.

Chapter Eighteen	Waking Up	266.
Chapter Nineteen	Wish I Had A Clue	282.
Chapter Twenty	Clipped	299.
Chapter Twenty-One	So Close	321.
Chapter Twenty-Two	No Escape	354.
Chapter Twenty-Three	Not Always	378.
Chapter Twenty-Four	I'll Find You	395.
Chapter Twenty-Five	If You Need A Friend	417.
Chapter Twenty-Six	Don't Let Go	446.
Chapter Twenty-Seven	Getting Nowhere	465.
Chapter Twenty-Eight	Smile On My Face	487.
Chapter Twenty-Nine	Going Under	501.
Chapter Thirty	Tangled Up	536.
Chapter Thirty-One	Upside Down	561.

The Glister Journals

"All that glitters is not gold" usually means things may look more valuable or important than they are. It's from *The Merchant of Venice* by William Shakespeare but, as a dear friend pointed out to me, it's a misquote. The original is "All that *glisters* is not gold." A fine distinction, perhaps, but sometimes the smallest difference or detail can completely change your perception of something.

I prefer to think it means that things aren't always what they appear to be, for better *or* worse. Sometimes they're just different. I also prefer the word *glister*. "Glitter" reminds me of cheap jewelry, tiny pieces of metallicized paper, and glam rock and disco. Not that there's anything wrong with glam rock or disco, of course.

"Glister" makes me think of dew sparkling on grass and spider webs early on a summer morning; water shimmering off the back of a dolphin leaping joyfully out of the ocean; light reflecting off the hair of the ones I love.

Everyone knows we shouldn't evaluate people by appearance, their situation in life, the labels others give them, or even the things they do in some cases. But I guess that's easier said than done. We all make assumptions every day. Some more important than others. Some more damaging than others. And things, very often, are not at all what they seem.

Chapter One

Break the Spell

Douglas, Northern California
August 2009

First days are probably hard for everyone. They're worse if you've just moved to a new town and don't know anyone. The absolute worst if it also happens to be your first day of high school, you have a history of not fitting in, and you have no expectations that anything will be different—like me.

But before that first day two events occurred; omens of changes to come. *Huge* changes.

Change wasn't something I'd thought about before then. My appearance hadn't changed much. On the skinny side, my arms and legs looked long and made skirts seem shorter than they'd probably look on someone else. There wasn't much difference between my waist and hips; I hadn't developed the noticeable curves most of my female classmates already had last year. I thought I looked nondescript and awkward, but I'd never been very concerned about my appearance.

For as long as I could remember, I'd worn my hair in one braid. Left unbound it was straight and long enough for me to sit on. An indistinct shade, it wasn't what anyone in their right mind would call blond but lacked the depth of hue that could be considered brown. Dirty and dishwater were adjectives I'd heard used. Those descriptions always made me feel guilty, as if I'd neglected an important task that could prove vital to something like world peace or the environment.

Makeup wasn't allowed at my previous school and hadn't been forced on me by my mother or one close friend, so I didn't dwell much on my face. Its presiding feature was my glasses and that didn't bother me. I'd worn them most of my life; one more thing that hadn't changed. The braces were gone though, and I was thankful for that. Maybe I'd take up the clarinet again. Maybe not.

Clothes were suddenly an issue. My previous school, which I'd gone to since first grade, had required a uniform, so I'd never had to choose what to wear. Like a lot of other things in my life, it had been decided for me. I suppose it's strange that I'd been okay with that, but I had and probably still would have been if I were continuing at the same school.

Mom and I wrangled a little when we went clothes shopping, but she got her way most of the time. My tastes tended toward conservative colors and comfortable styles, but I suspected she watched too much television. Hollywood's idea of high school fashions might look great on other girls, but they seemed designed to highlight my deficiencies.

"Try this on."

"I don't really like that color."

"But it's pink. You like pink."

The skirt was bright enough to scare away the most adventurous of wasps. "Not *that* pink."

"Well, try this shirt on. It'll look cute on you."

"It has lace."

"You don't like lace?"

"Um . . . I don't think I'd feel comfortable wearing it." I'd rather have more substantial material covering my body.

I let her get away with skirts that seemed too short, tops that made me want to wear another shirt under or over them, even clothes with—*horrors*—ruffles. But I was adamant about my shoes. I wasn't sure what Mom was thinking when it came to the girly clothes, but I refused to wear anything with heels. Being one of the tallest girls in class last year was bad enough; no need to accentuate the problem. I finally got my way with two pairs of flats and my first pair of Converse. The Converse were a major win as Mom thought they were too boyish, but I used logic on her and she had to admit

that our new neighborhood required different fashion sensibilities. I compromised by getting gray instead of black.

As for our neighborhood, we both felt completely out of our element since moving from West Los Angeles to the northern Sierra Nevada foothills. Things had changed so quickly my head was still spinning, and I wasn't sure how I felt about it.

On the one hand, I'd left everything I'd known: traffic, smog, concrete, apartments, mostly mild weather, fairly easy access to the beach, shopping and restaurants, endless media, and my best friend, Brenda. Mom had left the same including her family, all of whom had always lived in the Los Angeles area.

One of the biggest differences we noticed right away was noise. It had never occurred to me that I lived surrounded by almost constant though mostly background noise: televisions, stereos, sirens, dogs barking, even occasional helicopters. And that was just at night. During the day, it mostly blended with the sound of traffic in a symphony of white.

Here, there was a remarkable absence of noise, which only became very noticeable when the occasional—probably lost—large truck rumbled down the road. I loved the quiet. Daytime sounds were provided mostly by my mother and the wide variety of birds outside. Nighttime cricket noise was another matter altogether. It was also much darker at night here. Constant glow from countless city lights no longer interfered with the amazing display of stars. I didn't miss the noise but, all in all, I had some habitat and culture shock going on.

On the other hand, moving here felt like an adventure, something I'd rarely experienced. We'd never had to guess much about the weather in Los Angeles. So far it had been unbearably hot here, but we'd been assured that not only would there be ample rain to turn the brown countryside green, but we could expect ice too, and snow close by. That was rather exciting. And unnerving. Adventure and dealing with the unknown wasn't something I sought out. No, not at all.

"What happens if we get snowed in?" All I knew about snow was what I'd seen on television.

"I guess we'll just have to wait it out and hope someone rescues us," said Mom, solemnly.

"Really? What if we run out of food? Or water?"

"We can melt snow for water, I suppose." She still appeared very serious. I must have looked concerned as she laughed and said, "We won't get snowed in. It's not supposed to snow right here. But it'll be very cold. I'm sure we'll be able to use the fireplace."

We'd never had a fireplace before. "Where will we get wood?"

"We could chop it up ourselves," said Mom, trying to look serious again. "There are plenty of trees around here. That could be one of your new chores. Make your bed. Tidy your room. Chop the firewood. Maybe we can hunt for food too. Wouldn't that be fun?"

I knew she was joking, but that was going too far. "Could we start a fire now?"

"It's almost a hundred degrees outside!" she said, looking shocked.

Now I laughed at her.

Even exploring my new home was unsettling; not the house itself, but the surrounding territory. And that's what it felt like—*territory*. This was the first real house I'd ever lived in, with a staircase inside and everything. But apart from that and the size of it—much larger than any apartment I'd ever lived in—the house was normal enough.

It was the property itself that both fascinated and somewhat terrified me; a whole new world that made me feel a little Lewis-and-Clarkish. The front yard had no landscaping to speak of. Mom had plans to fix that. The main driveway led straight to the garage, but a dirt road on the south side went far back behind the house. I hadn't followed it to its end. The back yard spread out for acres.

Though spanning some distance, most of the property at the back was visible from the window over the kitchen sink. I hadn't actually gone far from the house but wandered about in my mind every time I did the dishes. I might have explored sooner in reality if my imaginary explorations didn't always encounter indistinct natural hazards and unknown creatures, particularly of reptilian and, well, *buggish* descent.

In spite of my lack of intrepidness, the things that happened before the first day of school were out of the ordinary and probably fueled my foolish hope of intervening magic. Not that the incidences were unusual in any normal sense, but they certainly weren't typical for me.

The first occurred while I washed dishes one evening. We'd been there about a week. Mom was in the living room on the phone with my aunt. She

spent quite a bit of time on the phone these days, talking to family and friends in Los Angeles and talking to Dad, who was still there too.

Beyond a lawn, currently brown from neglect, the acres sloped gently away and became gradually more covered with long grasses, low bushes, and occasional oak trees until meeting a small stream. I hadn't *seen* the stream but had been told it was there. Beyond that were hills. Somewhere beyond the unknown eastern boundary lay government land.

The sun was still shining brightly and my inner adventurer was enjoying a ramble down by the imagined stream when a sudden glint between the trees and underbrush on a far hillside caught my eye. I watched the spot for a while and, just as I had decided that I'd imagined it, I saw it again. A definite—*glint*. I couldn't think of another word for it; more than a sparkle but not quite a flash, just a hint of something bright.

And it had moved, shifting to the left of where it had been. I watched for some time hoping to see it move, but it just disappeared again; one moment it was there, the next it wasn't. I wondered if it was something reflecting sunlight or if it had its own source of light. I continued watching until the shadows behind the house had become long and dark. I didn't think to tell my mother about what I'd seen—or thought I'd seen.

Finding many excuses to look out the kitchen window or just sit in the shade of the back porch, I scanned the back hills for signs of light. But it wasn't until I was washing dishes again a few evenings later that a similar sight occurred. The glints lasted a shorter length of time, but I was sure I'd seen them.

I offered to do the dishes every night. "No, really, Mom. I *want* to do them."

Mom looked surprised. I never minded being asked to do things but rarely thought to volunteer.

"You know, you're welcome to do the laundry and vacuuming any time you want, too."

"Thanks, Mom," I said, trying to sound equally serious.

Another week passed and I didn't catch a glimpse of the—whatever it was. I came up with all kinds of theories, of course, from the mundane to the ridiculous. Among the latter were aliens, though why they'd be glinting didn't seem important, and smugglers moving gold bars, from where to where seemed likewise immaterial. The most obvious explanation was that the sun had reflected off metallic litter of some kind, in two separate places at two different times, disappearing as the sun moved. Still, it seemed odd that the reflections looked distinctly golden and hadn't lasted longer.

A week later I had stopped scanning the far hills as there were no more occurrences of the light. It was awkward to get out of dish duty now though, so I did them anyway. I was almost convinced that I'd imagined the whole thing until late one afternoon. I was moving sprinklers on the lawn that Mom was determined to bring back from the dead. Looking toward the southeast, an area of dense trees, I was surprised to see a patch of gold matching nothing in the surrounding green and brown vegetation. I froze, watching intently to see if it faded or moved. After about a minute, it seemed to glide to the left and then was gone. I stood indecisively for a few moments. Investigating the unknown had never held any allure for me, but it would probably bother me later if I didn't at least try to have a closer look.

If I'd been capable of it, I would have run, but I had a tendency to sprain my ankles whenever I tried, so I avoided it as much as possible. The further I got from the house, the thicker the shrubby plants dotting the gentle downward slope became. This hadn't been obvious from the house and my shorts did nothing to protect my skin from the dry and apparently thorny bushes.

It seemed like I had walked for a long time and I could no longer see the house when I finally heard the stream. I saw no fences and assumed our property must continue for some way into the hills. Surely there would be some man-made physical boundary between our land and that of our neighbors, government or otherwise. I hesitated to go further. Not only were my legs bare but my feet felt very exposed in flip-flops. I began to think of snakes and the other vaguely imagined creepy-crawly things that had kept me from exploring before now.

A sudden loud rustling, as if something large moved through bushes just beyond the thick trees, made my mind up for me. I headed back up the hillside as quickly as my weak ankles and weaker footwear allowed, my heart pounding and threatening to jump out of my throat.

As the house came back into view, I saw my mother on the back steps looking concerned.

"Taking a walk?" she asked, dubiously. Mom knows me pretty well.

"Um . . . yes. I just thought I'd see where the stream was." There still didn't seem to be much point in mentioning my sightings.

"Well, be careful. There's a lot of wildlife here."

In spite of my recent fright, I felt like laughing. *What an understatement!*

The second incident happened the same week, just days before school started. Though probably less strange or mysterious to anyone else, it was just as unsettling to me.

Already feeling nervous about school—meeting new people was right up there with unfamiliar surroundings and creepy-crawlies—I was finding it difficult to keep my mind sufficiently occupied to not think about the dreaded first day.

I'd spent a lot of time outside and was sunburned. Except for occasional beach trips, which I loved, I'd spent so little time outdoors in the past that I rarely got tanned, even in summer. But these last few weeks had been unusual and we'd spent our time differently. Not that I'd watched that much television before, but I didn't even have that distraction, or the Internet. YouTube was always a surefire way to kill an hour or two. There was currently no cable in our area, so we were catching up on movies we'd missed by renting them. But otherwise the TV stayed off.

Mom talked on the phone quite a bit, as I've said, but apart from talking to Dad when he wasn't out of the country, Brenda was the only one I considered calling. She had called me every day when we'd first moved here, but her school in Los Angeles had started already and now she said she was too busy doing homework if I called her during the week.

Mom and I also painted the interior of most of our house, which had kept us busy. My bedroom walls were now a soft gray with a dusky rose and white trim. I really liked it. I had reread almost all the books I owned and all of Mom's that even slightly interested me. There was probably a library in town, but we hadn't gone to it. One day we had driven south to Sacramento, just to look around and see the capitol building, and another we drove into the mountains for the scenery, but Mom didn't enjoy driving the mountain roads.

Drawing and listening to music occupied most of my time, but even that became boring sometimes. I had thought about journaling and even had a leather volume with parchment-like paper—a gift last Christmas from Aunt Audrey, Mom's younger sister. But my actual existence up until now had been unremarkable and I had no motivation to chronicle anything imaginary. So I often spent time sitting on the front or back porch steps, in the sun if it wasn't too hot, letting my mind wander, sketching, and listening to music through earphones.

This particular afternoon was stifling hot even though I sat in the shade, the sun creeping relentlessly toward my bare toes, so far still shaded by the roof of the house. I had been doodling randomly in my sketchbook when I caught movement in my peripheral vision. Looking up, I was surprised to see a medium sized Australian Shepherd—mostly gray with spots of tan and black, and white face, chest, and legs—observing me from near the road.

We regarded each other respectfully and silently for at least a minute. Then it began walking, nose to the ground but watching me closely. While timid about the thought of wild creatures and downright chicken when it came to creepy things, I'd never been nervous of other animals. I had often wanted to get a cat or puppy, but Mom was allergic to cat dander and our apartments hadn't allowed dogs. It had always been out of the question.

I slowly put the sketchbook down, took the earphones out, and turned my full attention to the dog. It likewise faced me and stood panting, as if waiting for a cue.

"Come here," I said in a soft voice, patting my leg encouragingly.

The dog looked up and stopped panting for a moment. Its ears twitched forward as if to encourage me in return. I continued to talk in a quiet voice, telling it how pretty it was and wouldn't it like to come and see me? It hopped through the split-rail fence at the edge of the yard and walked warily toward me. As it got closer it began wriggling, its stub of tail seeming to wag its whole body. I was struck by its beautiful pale blue eyes.

"Who are you?"

I waited for it to sniff my hand, resting against my knee, and then slowly reached toward the top of its head and scratched. It tried to lick my face and I laughed, scratching more roughly around its ears and neck. We sat together for quite some time, me stroking and scratching the lovely soft fur and the dog obviously basking in the attention. It occasionally licked my hand and leg and continued to try to lick my face if I bent too close.

It was leaning contentedly against my leg as I stroked it, and I was wondering where it could have come from, when the dog's ears perked up and its shoulders tensed. It didn't move, but its attention turned toward the south end of the street. After a moment, a high, uneven revving approached.

A rider on a motorcycle came into view around the hill. As he drew closer, the engine dropped to a lower, even drone. He looked from side to side, ahead, and sometimes behind as he rode. He had almost passed the house when he caught sight of me, looked away, then quickly looked back. Circling in the middle of the road, he came to a stop and sat staring in my direction, legs to the ground, bike idling.

I realized it was the sight of the dog that had caught his attention and not me, of course, but that didn't stop my cheeks feeling like they had burst into flames. It wasn't a response I was used to. I hoped it wasn't noticeable from that far away or that my sunburn covered it.

I thought he was the most attractive boy I'd ever seen. It was difficult to tell how tall he was, but the one visible jeans-clad leg looked long and slim. The brown arms holding the handlebars were very well-muscled for someone who didn't look much older than I was. I guessed he was probably about sixteen but could have been older. I would be turning fifteen in January but I thought I looked about twelve.

The boy's hair was a medium brown but even at this distance I could see highlights of a lighter shade. It was wavy and a little on the long side; longer than most of the boys I'd gone to school with. His face looked very tanned, too, and while I couldn't tell the color of his eyes, his brows were dark and finely shaped. From what I could tell, at this distance and with my imperfect vision, he looked *really* cute.

My mind was racing. *Should I just sit here?* Maybe he was waiting for me to do something. *Should I stand up?* Not a good idea. Long expanses of skinny burned flesh with welts and scratches from my ramble the other day could hardly be attractive. He probably wouldn't see them from the road, but I knew they were there. *Should I talk to him?*

"Um . . . hello . . . is this your dog?" Of course it was his dog. Why else would he even be looking over here? That would sound way too stupid.

"Um . . . nice dog. What's its name?" I'd have to yell if I wanted him to really hear me. I didn't like yelling. My voice always cracked and squeaked if I tried to talk too loudly.

The boy gave a loud, high-pitched whistle—I was impressed that he didn't have to put his fingers in his mouth to do it—then revved his engine twice and sped back the way he had come. Though the dog had been watching the boy the whole time, it hadn't shown any inclination to move until hearing the shrill sound. Now it didn't hesitate or look back at me but tore after the boy and disappeared.

For some reason, I shuddered violently—then mentally slapped myself. I was such a wimp. Brenda was always telling me so. Sometimes I was a dork and a couple of times I had thought her on the verge of calling me a loser, but she was right. I had no social skills to speak of and absolutely zero experience with boys. Prospects for change didn't look good.

So on the first day of school, I stood checking myself out in my antique mirror. The depressing truth was that I thought I looked exactly the same as I had in middle school. And I had a suspicion that, except for a change in vertical dimension, I looked much the same as I had in elementary. I tried not to feel devastated, but it was very disappointing that the magic I'd vaguely hoped for had not mystically transfigured me before now.

Or maybe I had it wrong. Perhaps I was under a spell, a curse, which decreed I would never grow out of this gangly, mousy phase. I knew where none of my classes were and would know nobody. And I was sure I still looked about twelve.

The spell hadn't been broken.

Mom called from the foot of the stairs. "Allison! Hurry or you'll be late!"

"Coming, Mom."

I left the mirror convinced I went to my certain doom.

Chapter Two

Confused

My mother dropped me off at the front of the school. I smiled heroically for her sake as, armed with a new backpack, my class schedule, and a map of the school, I set off in search of my first class. As public high schools go, Douglas High was probably small, but it was still larger than the school I had attended before, and the layout was more confusing.

A few people glanced at me curiously but most were either too busy reconnecting with friends or looking lost like me. My clothes had me feeling self-conscious; I felt overdressed, though I was far from the only girl wearing a skirt—possibly just the dorkiest. My school uniform had been mostly blue and white, and everyone had blended together, which had suited me just fine. Here the majority of clothing seemed to be black with varying shades of gray, white, a lot of denim, and occasional pastel or bright splashes of color. The variety was nice, but I wished I wasn't one of the splashes.

The corridors cleared, people moving as if by some unheard signal, and I was soon one of the only students still looking for their first class. I found it just as the bell rang and twenty-something pairs of eyes zeroed in on me as I entered. I felt like sinking through the floor and kept my eyes fixed on the linoleum. There were only two seats left in the middle front. I slid into the closest one.

The teacher talked nonstop as if giving a well-memorized speech he'd recited for a hundred years about classroom behavior, work expectations, no bathroom passes—I'd have to remember that one—and a list of dos and don'ts for his class and the school at large. Today would mostly consist of teachers making sure they had saturated us thoroughly in the rules of their individual classes and the doctrine of the school. We would attend shortened versions of all eight periods and commence our block schedule tomorrow.

As he talked, the teacher walked around the room placing worksheets in front of each of us. He barely paused for breath before launching into an assessment of our math skills and showed us a copy of the depressingly thick Algebra textbook awaiting us in the library. As math was one of my weakest subjects, the day wasn't off to an auspicious beginning.

It was some time before I felt the color in my face return to normal. I didn't raise my eyes until I did and hoped the remains of my sunburn covered the despicable blush. Finally daring to look around, I noticed a girl looking at me, her head tilted to one side as if sizing me up the way the tough girls at my old school used to. She had wild coppery red curls hanging to her shoulders and incredibly bright eyes. There were a few freckles across her nose and cheeks—which she had inexpertly tried to cover with makeup—and a smudge of dirt on her chin. More interesting to me were the beat up jeans and black sneakers she wore. She looked so comfortable, like she couldn't care less what anyone thought of her. It impressed me greatly. I finally realized I'd been staring at her and that she was now glaring at me in a very unfriendly way. Looking down quickly, I began working on the worksheet.

In Science, we were told we would acquire two more textbooks, several notebooks, and a binder. Obviously I was going to need my locker. I eventually found it just as the bell was ringing for PE, my next class. So far the three textbooks promised to us would fit in my backpack, but I'd have to make drops at my locker if I acquired many more.

PE was relatively harmless, the classes combined for today and gathered in the gym. I sat inconspicuously among other freshmen, many of whom didn't seem to know anyone either. I was relieved we weren't expected to perform in any way on this first day, but the coaches warned us that we'd need full PE kit for the next day and forgetting wasn't an option. Something about fitness training and early track tryouts was mentioned too, but as PE was my least favorite subject, I only tuned in to what I absolutely had to know while surreptitiously looking around. I tried to look behind me once, to the top of the bleachers, but there was a large group there who all seemed

to notice me turn around. After my experience with the red-haired girl in Algebra, I felt very self-conscious so turned back quickly and kept my eyes focused straight ahead.

Health followed with the promise of another thick textbook and glares from the red-haired girl, who was also in this class. I carefully kept my gaze from wandering to that side of the room. Determined to not only find my locker again but actually get inside it, I headed that way at lunch. I tried the combination at least a dozen times with no success. Hunger finally sent me in search of the cafeteria.

Several people from classes I'd had that morning were there, but I didn't feel confident in approaching them so sat at the end of a table near the back. I was brooding—hoping the rest of my day would be no worse than the morning and wondering whether I should go to the office about my locker—when I became aware of a girl limping toward my table. She wore a dress that modestly flattered her well-developed figure and had a cast on her lower leg. But that's not what caught my attention. The dress looked so natural on her as if it would be absurd to see her in anything else, and in spite of the limp, her movement was graceful. Her shoulder-length hair was thick, wavy, and rich brown—exactly the kind of hair I wished I had. A silver heart-shaped locket lay in the middle of the V-neck of her dress. She was elegantly attractive, her face truly pretty. She looked like a magazine model; the way you like to imagine yourself until you're brought back to reality by a mirror. I was sure she must be a senior.

"Do you mind if I sit here?" she asked.

It took me a moment to respond. I was surprised someone like her even acknowledged my existence. "Sure," I said. I watched her face as she sat down across from me. "What happened to your leg?" I asked, then felt like sinking below the table, afraid I sounded rude.

"Oh, just a clumsy accident." She began eating and I waited for her to continue, but she didn't.

Feeling awkward, I thought I should try starting a conversation, but I just wasn't any good at it. I wanted to know more about her but, while she seemed friendly in a quiet sort of way, she kept her eyes down and her thoughts to herself.

When the bell rang, I began to leave but turned back to the girl. I don't know what gave me the courage—she seemed so much older, why would she care what I thought? But something about her caused me to take a chance.

"I hope your leg feels better," I said.

She looked at me then and smiled the most beautiful smile. "Thank you," she said, sincerely.

I smiled back and left for my next class.

I was good at English and nobody seemed to take an instant dislike to me, so I hoped I could do well in that class. History would probably also be relatively easy, and the book didn't look too enormous. Seventh period was a universal study hall in our first-period rooms, which meant avoiding my red-haired nemesis once more.

I was sure my last class would be my favorite: Art. As it was close to my algebra/study hall room, I was one of the first there and grabbed a seat toward the back. To my surprise, the girl I had met at lunch came through the door and looked around the room. I gave her a smile and she returned it, walking with a slight limp to the seat next to me.

"You're taking Art too?" I asked, immediately realizing how inane it sounded. "I mean . . . I would have thought you'd be in a more advanced class. Or something."

The girl smiled and said, "No, we have to take this one first. I hope to continue with the more advanced classes, though."

Frowning, I asked, "What year are you?" then worried I might be sounding rude again.

"I'm a freshman," she said. "I missed most of the year in seventh grade and had to repeat it, so I'm a year behind age-wise."

I didn't know what to say, so I just said, lamely, "Oh." I was curious to know why she'd missed so much school but didn't want to ask. I was just glad she was there.

"I'm Melanie," she said. "Are you a freshman too?"

I nodded. "I'm Allison. I just moved here."

"Mmm. I didn't think I'd seen you before. But students come from different middle schools around here."

The class started at that point, and we had no more opportunity to talk. At the end of class, she smiled and said, "See you tomorrow."

I waved goodbye and headed for the library to get my textbooks. My heart sank as I rounded the corner and saw a line stretching all the way down the corridor and out the building. This was going to take a while. Mom would be waiting for me, so I decided to find her first. The last thing I wanted was for my mother to go wandering around the school looking for me.

Sure enough, she was there in the parking lot, wanting to know how my first day had been and looking both worried and hopeful. I avoided the question by explaining the situation: getting textbooks was going to take a while. Did she want to go shopping or get coffee or something? She didn't look happy but agreed to be back in an hour.

"Wait here, Mom," I warned. "I'll find *you*, okay?"

She gave me a knowing look but agreed.

After getting my books, I decided to try my locker again. Lugging heavy books around wasn't something I wanted to do if I didn't have to. I had tried the combination a few times and was letting failure get to me when I realized I was being observed. I turned to see the red-haired girl leaning against a far set of lockers surrounded by other similarly dressed kids. There was an amused look on her face, but the expression disappeared immediately. She turned away to talk to one of her companions.

I took a deep breath. Today I'd made a new friend, apparently already found an enemy, and let a storage receptacle get the better of me. Feeling that I'd accomplished enough for one day, I sighed again, gave up on the locker, and made my way to the parking lot to find my mother. She was waiting with a frappuccino for me and didn't ask any more questions. I was incredibly grateful.

That evening I sat on the back porch watching the far hillside and surrounding area for signs of reflection, but I saw nothing. I called Brenda after dinner, but she seemed very distracted and not inclined to talk. Mom and I watched *The Princess Bride* on DVD and then I went to bed. I lay there thinking that this first day hadn't been *too* bad. If I could get through this first week without any major catastrophes, life might not be unbearable. The dork spell hadn't been broken, but perhaps I could rise above it.

The next morning I dressed with care, trying to walk the tenuous line between what wouldn't upset my mom—she had, after all, invested in the new clothes—and what might blend in a little better at school. I thought about the well-worn jeans and high tops of the red-haired girl and sighed. Even if

I'd owned such apparel—and I didn't think my gray Converse counted—I'd never have gotten past the front door. I just wasn't the type to fight with my mom over clothing. Opting for a soft pink skirt Mom had bought and an older plain white shirt I'd had for a year or so, I hoped to look less conspicuous than the day before.

Block schedule started today, which meant two classes with the red-haired girl. My general plan for the day was to fly under her radar as much as possible. I also hoped to see Melanie again. I went early to the office about my locker, but there was a line of kids before me. By the time I got up to the counter, it was almost time for class. The lady there wasn't very encouraging when I told her my problem. There were no spare lockers, others were having the same difficulty, and the custodians' workloads would keep them busy for weeks. Uncooperative lockers were not high on the priority list. I was coming to the conclusion that I was just going to have to tote the books around. *If nothing else, maybe I'll gain some muscles this year.*

Algebra passed without incident. During role call, I discovered that the red-haired girl's name was Robin Cowell, and though I never once looked in that direction, I could see her in my peripheral vision. Otherwise, I ignored her.

Melanie was in my PE class, which I was thrilled about, but she didn't dress out. She sat on a bench at one side of the field. All I could do was smile and wave to her.

I was very thankful that the girls were at one end of the field while the boys were at the other. Although I knew none of them, it would have been more intimidating if the boys were closer. Even so, I felt awkward during the class. People seemed to be looking at me and whispering to each other, but as nobody said anything out loud, I had no idea what the problem was. We were doing simple stretches and fitness tests, which I was able to do without making a fool of myself, so I ignored the whispers. I was hoping to catch Melanie before lunch to see if we could eat together, but she had already gone by the time I changed.

I considered trying my locker again—*you never know, one of these times it might just magically open*—but instead went to the cafeteria. I got a sandwich and some milk and sat where I had yesterday. When I saw Melanie approaching, I smiled broadly at her, happy that she was joining me.

"How much longer will you have to wear a cast?" I asked. That seemed like a safe question.

She wrinkled her nose slightly. I was beginning to see that she used understated expressions and gestures. It was going to take careful observation to read her.

"One more week. It was just a bad sprain, not broken. But it's badly bruised and they wanted to make sure it's completely immobilized, so they put a cast on."

I still wasn't satisfied so tried my original question again. "How did you sprain it?"

Not answering right away, she looked at me thoughtfully as if trying to gauge something about me. She absently touched the heart locket around her neck as she thought.

"It was just a freak accident. I was grooming my mare and she spooked badly for no apparent reason, knocking me over and stepping on me. She's never done anything like it before." She was watching me closely and I realized I was gawking at her, my mouth open.

"You have a horse?" I asked, quite awed.

She looked self-conscious for a moment and laughed gently. "Yes. I have two, but one of them isn't really mine." I didn't comprehend this last statement so ignored it.

"You're so lucky!" I breathed.

She chuckled again. "You really aren't from around here, are you?"

I shook my head, trying to picture my new friend in the situation she'd described. "I'm from Los Angeles. You don't see a lot of horses there."

"Mmm," she said, looking at me in a slightly speculative way as she continued to eat.

"I have an aunt in Colorado who has horses," I offered, "but I only went there for a little while when I was six."

"Really? I had a friend who moved to Colorado, but I've never been myself." This was said rather wistfully.

She changed the subject then, asking me about my other classes, and we talked until the bell rang. We waved goodbye and I went to my English class followed by study hall. There, I was able to get a lot of my algebra done and avoided looking at Robin. I glanced at her once out of curiosity. Surprised to see her regarding me with what looked like similar interest, I looked away quickly and didn't see whether her expression changed or not.

I was relieved to get home and relax. Day two down and I had survived, quite admirably I thought. Barring unanticipated disasters, I could do this. The only thing I wasn't looking forward to was picture day on Friday, but I was sure I would even live through that.

Deciding to play it *very* safe and make sure to escape my mother's censure on Friday, I wore new clothes the next two days. If I didn't make an attempt to wear what she had bought me, I knew I was going to hear about it and I didn't want to get stuck on picture day wearing something I would regret the rest of the year, maybe the rest of my life. Choosing my least favorite, a dress in a conservative dark blue ruined by inappropriate ruffles, I comforted myself that Melanie would probably wear a dress too. The only other problem was that my backpack looked incongruous with the dress. I swapped it for a small bag and carried the three hefty books I needed for Science and Health in my arms. *Small price to pay.*

A shock awaited me in Health. The teacher announced our first assignment: a report to be worked on with a partner. It would have been bad enough if I'd had to choose someone to work with, but she had assigned partners. She told us to raise our hands as she said our names. Sure enough, my name was called with Robin's. I looked around at her; she was looking at me with the same disbelief I felt. This was going to be interesting.

She left class without giving me another glance, and I escaped to the cafeteria where I waited hopefully for Melanie, but she never showed. I was very disappointed, not only because I could have used the reassurance of a friendly face but also because I was curious to find out more about her. I enjoyed Art even though Melanie wasn't there. I wondered if she was all right. Once at home, I started to fret about approaching Robin regarding our collaboration, then firmly pushed the thought away, deciding tomorrow was plenty early enough to worry about it.

A vague sense of dread oppressed me as I awoke the next day. It didn't take long to remember the cause. I chose to wear a light yellow dress that

I didn't think would stand out too badly. I actually liked it and thought it made me look a little older. Grabbing my algebra and English books, I had almost made it through the door when I thought better of it and went back for my health book. It was annoying that I'd have to carry all three books around, but hopefully I'd be able to get a start on our report in study hall, with or without Robin.

I awaited her arrival in Algebra with a kind of hopeful apprehension, but she made it into the room just as the bell rang, glanced at me quickly, and then looked away. I couldn't read anything into the brief contact and tried to think the best. I looked once more during class, but she was frowning as she wrote.

Frowning over the work or over having to talk to me? I didn't find out, but she came over to my desk at the end of class.

"So, I guess we have to work together," she said. Her words were gruff, but her expression looked indecisive.

"I guess so," I said, equally noncommittal. I'd let her lead the way on how we would proceed.

Her face twisted, seemingly further proof of her uncertainty, but she said, with what seemed like a generous spirit, "Well, let's meet in study hall. I'll bring my book."

I nodded and held mine up.

She looked surprised as if she hadn't expected that much from me.

"Okay. See you later, I guess." With that, she bounced out of the room.

Melanie still wasn't back, so I took my time changing after PE. I was on my way to lunch when Robin walked up beside me.

"So, did you dress like that at your last school?" she asked abruptly. I couldn't tell if she was trying to pick a fight or was just curious.

I wasn't a fighter.

"I wore a uniform," I said, cautiously. I looked at her. She looked back with a blank expression. "You know . . . everyone wears the same thing? It was a private school."

A look of understanding crossed her face, and she nodded once slowly but looked wary again.

"Don't you want to put those in your locker?" she asked, indicating the books in my arms with a tilt of her chin.

"I'd love to, but I can't get it open." I felt like I'd just admitted to something pathetic.

She snorted once, obviously finding it funny. "Do you eat in the cafeteria?" she asked.

We were almost there. My immediate response was to say yes, but she gave such a look of revulsion that I literally bit my tongue. Unlike Melanie, there was nothing subtle about Robin.

"We eat over there," she said, indicating with a jerk of her head a couple of tables on the grass, close to the lower field.

"Are we allowed to eat there?" I asked, quite sure I'd heard otherwise.

She arched an eyebrow and gave me an odd little smile. Then she shrugged and laughed, leading the way. Spread out over and around the two tables, I recognized some of the kids she'd been with that day by the lockers, plus at least six or seven more—mostly boys.

Leaning back on his elbows in the middle of the group and watching steadily as we approached was the boy I'd seen on the motorcycle. Two girls were talking animatedly to him, one on either side, but his face was expressionless as if he didn't hear them. As we got closer, I realized I wasn't wrong in my previous assessment: he was remarkably good-looking. I became aware of my heart thumping hard in my chest—just my natural reaction to the prospect of meeting so many new people, I was sure.

"Hey," said Robin in greeting.

Almost everyone looked up and a few of them responded back, but the brown-haired boy continued to regard us impassively. I didn't realize I was staring at him—actually at the strange highlights in his hair—until he moved, slowly getting off the table and walking unhurriedly up to us.

Well, actually, up to *me*. Right in front of me.

I swallowed hard.

"Dave, meet Allison," said Robin, standing next to me.

Now that he was up close, I could tell he was about my height. It only added to my growing discomfort. *Why couldn't I be shorter?*

I couldn't bring myself to look him in the eyes at first so wasn't sure of his expression, but the next thing I knew, my glasses were slowly lifted away. I looked at him then, startled.

He regarded my face with a look of appraisal that did nothing to make me feel more comfortable. Without my glasses, everything was a little fuzzy

and misshapen, but I could tell an expressive eyebrow went up, very slightly, and his mouth quirked, almost imperceptibly. I recognized the look immediately. It was more subtle and natural on him.

He looked back toward the table. "Hey, Chris, come here," he called.

A boy I hadn't noticed before looked over his shoulder at us. He had been facing the field and reclining on the table directly behind where Dave had sat. I didn't notice anything in particular about him as he came to stand next to the first boy. Looking away, I desperately tried to control my embarrassment and its effects on me, but I was sure my face was scarlet. It didn't help that everything was blurry.

"What do you think?" asked the boy named Dave.

I looked back to the two boys now standing right in front of me. I was squinting a little, feeling really annoyed, somewhat intrigued, and very determined to hold my ground and not let my knees buckle in fright. Despite being denied my glasses, I could tell there was a twinkle in Dave's eyes matching the slight smirk on his lips. I looked away quickly toward the newcomer.

He was several inches taller than Dave and had longer, blonder, slightly less wavy hair. At first there was a familiarity about him that struck me, but then all other thoughts were driven out of my head. For a few moments our eyes met, and what I saw in his unnerved me, though I couldn't have said why. An odd sensation washed over me or through me or both—I wasn't sure—and I saw something register, as if he'd felt it too. Strange emotions moved there in his eyes, for just those moments: searching, sad, hopeful, hurt, other things less definable—and even with impaired vision, I was sure I'd seen it. Then it was gone. The look in his eyes hardened and a scowl descended on his dark brows. He seemed angry and looked away as if disgusted. I felt like I'd been caressed and then slapped.

"You're an idiot," he said in a low voice and turned his back on me, hands jammed in his pockets.

I assumed he was talking to Dave, but I knew my cheeks were flaming even more. I felt thoroughly humiliated.

Dave grinned and then set my glasses gently back on my face as naturally as if he did it every day. His attention turned from my face to my overall appearance, standing back, appraising once more. I looked at Robin, hoping she would come to my rescue, bail me out somehow, but she just stood a little to the side looking amused.

Great. What on earth have I got myself into now? Is this one of those bully gangs that like to pick on the dorky kids? Are they going to try to get me to do stupid, degrading things to prove my worth? I'd had more than a little experience with that. I gritted my teeth and started to get mad, still trying to keep my knees from shaking.

"What's with the clothes?" Dave asked, a slightly puzzled look on his face. Unfortunately, it just made him look cuter. I couldn't tell if he was asking me, Robin, or Chris, whose back was still turned to us.

I had no idea what to say, but Robin answered for me. "She used to go to private school." Dave looked surprised but not sure what it had to do with anything. Robin clarified, "They wore uniforms."

Comprehension slowly spread over his face, a wicked gleam coming into his eyes, his smile matching the unholy amusement in them. "That would be interesting," he said slowly. He turned to the other boy. "Don't you think?"

Chris didn't move at first. He looked at Dave, still scowling, and stalked off back toward the quad. Dave watched him go, eyes narrowed, and then turned back to me.

"Doesn't she have a locker?" he asked, nodding toward the books I was still carrying.

It took a moment to realize he had asked Robin instead of me, and I wasn't sure whether to be affronted at the rudeness or relieved that I didn't have to answer.

"Won't open," said Robin.

"Hmm," he murmured. He abruptly walked away, following Chris. He turned once, that slight smirk on his face as he continued backward, then turned again and kept walking.

Feeling absurd and bewildered, I looked uncertainly at Robin. Her eyes were laughing as she let me stew for a moment. Then she laughed out loud and came over to take a couple of the books I held.

"He likes you," she said. She grinned and walked off as the bell rang.

I followed after her, still feeling absurd and even more bewildered than before.

Chapter Three

Tongue-Tied

Robin and I were able to decide on a topic for our report and got some ideas for content from our textbook. She suggested we research online Friday after school, and I happily agreed.

"Do you want to do it at your house?" she said.

"We don't have access to the Internet right now." She looked disappointed, so I said, "Maybe we could use the library here at school?"

She frowned and wrinkled her nose. "We can go to my house, I guess. Our internet service isn't very fast, though. I usually go to Dave's house to do important stuff but. . . ."

She looked away and didn't finish. I was glad as I didn't want to respond to that.

"Your house is fine," I said. I still wasn't sure how Robin really felt about me, but we appeared to be allies, at least for the time being. *Allies can turn into real friends, can't they?*

After class, I started to say goodbye, but she grabbed my arm and pulled me in the opposite direction, away from the parking lot. I soon saw we were heading toward our lockers, and then specifically toward *my* locker. Suddenly Dave was walking next to me, holding his hand out. I looked at it dumbly until Robin whispered, "Combination."

I stopped and struggled with my books, trying to get in my bag, aware I was blushing. Dave reached over, wordlessly, and took the books from me. I blushed harder. Finding the combination, I held it out to him and he swapped my books for it. I couldn't bring myself to look directly into his eyes, afraid my strength of will would fail.

Looking briefly at the paper, he turned to my locker, his fingers deftly dialing the numbers. He tried the latch. It didn't move but hitting a specific spot with the side of his fist made it pop open like magic.

Robin and I both laughed. Then he turned to me. Now I couldn't avoid looking into his face. He looked pleased with himself, his eyes twinkling like before. Still without a word, he handed back the slip of paper, smiled, and walked off.

My brain went blank for a moment, my heart beating stupidly fast. Then I managed to stutter loudly, "Th . . . th . . . thank you!"

He must have heard me though he didn't indicate it, and I couldn't decide if he was really that cool or just insufferably arrogant. From the way my pulse behaved around him, it didn't matter which it was.

Keeping the algebra textbook out so I could start on homework, I put two books in the locker, then hesitated. Would I be able to get it open again? Robin was watching me, her head tilted a little to one side. Smiling at her, I closed the door with a show of much more confidence than I felt. I'd deal with it tomorrow. We said, "See you," and walked our separate ways, I toward the parking lot and she toward the front of the school.

Mom and I had to wait in a line of cars to get to the exit, and I saw Robin walking along the sidewalk in the distance. She was heading toward town and I wondered if we should stop to offer her a ride. As we finally turned onto the street, I saw a big black Chevy truck swerve suddenly in toward the curb right beside her and come to an abrupt stop. She looked up and smiled. The passenger door opened and Dave jumped out. I saw Robin begin to climb in and then we were passing them. Chris was driving. His head turned in our direction just as we passed, but I didn't know if he saw or recognized me.

I was pondering about certain people you couldn't help admiring for their air of self-assurance—attractive, arrogant, moody, or otherwise—when my mother voiced concern over my preoccupation.

"Is everything all right?"

I looked at her, surprised. "Sure, Mom."

"You seem very quiet and far away."

"I'm fine. Really," I assured her. "Actually, I'm planning on going over to someone's house after school tomorrow. We have a report to do together. She says the internet's slow at her house so it may take a while. Can I call you to pick me up when we're done?"

Mom brightened immediately. "That's great, sweetheart! I'm glad you've made a friend already! Does she live close to school?"

I thought it might be a little too soon to call Robin *friend*, though I had to admit, the locker incident almost had me convinced. I didn't know whether she had instigated that or Dave. And if it was Dave, what did *that* mean? As to where she lived, I didn't have a clue. When I saw her walking, I assumed she lived reasonably close by, but if rides from Chris were routine, maybe not.

"I'm not sure," I said after a few moments. "I guess I'll find out tomorrow."

Mom looked at me a couple of times and then said, "Well, call me if you need a ride to her house or anything."

I smiled and tried to be conversational the rest of the way home and during dinner. Later, I mostly hid out in my room on the pretext of doing homework, though much of that time I caught myself staring into space. I had so many questions about the new people I'd met, but they weren't questions I felt comfortable asking. I'd gotten into trouble in the past for asking the wrong questions. Time would tell, I supposed.

Friday morning brought with it a growing sense of anticipation—for what, I wasn't sure. My stomach felt fluttery and nervous, but I also felt light-hearted *and* a little light-headed. The combination was a new experience for me. I thought I liked it but wasn't sure about that either. I dressed practically, keeping in mind that it was picture day and wanting to avoid any discussion over clothes with my mother, but also wanting to be comfortable all day.

I chose older pants that fit me well, my gray sneakers, and a new top that I thought would look okay. Then I stood in front of the mirror for several minutes, checking out every angle and wondering what Dave saw when he looked at me. I saw a dork. But I saw a more *hopeful* dork than I had seen Monday morning. Things were looking up.

Sighing, I grabbed my books, crammed them into my backpack, and headed downstairs. Mom looked at me critically. She opened her mouth to say something but apparently thought better of it. I was glad. I might actually have put up some sort of fight if she had wanted me to change my clothes, but I didn't want to. I also didn't want to feel more self-conscious than I already did.

Needing to retrieve my Health book, I headed to my locker first. A couple of people I vaguely recognized as being friends of Robin and Dave called out, saying, "Hi." At first I thought they must be talking to someone else. Too late to respond, I realized they really were talking to me.

I dialed the numbers on my locker and tentatively tried the lock. It didn't move. I balled my fist and struck the door in the same spot Dave had, but it didn't open.

Then *he* was beside me, reaching over to twirl the dial and reenter the numbers. He banged the door just like before and it popped open. I looked at him, pretty much eye to eye. His eyes were beautiful: deep, soft brown with a seemingly ever-present twinkle.

I gulped.

He grinned.

"See you at lunch?" he asked.

I thought my heart was going to stop at the sound of his voice, so soft and close. I was sure I could feel his breath on my face. Unable to say a word, I nodded. He smiled slightly and walked away.

Looking down the corridor, I saw Robin at her locker. She smiled and waved. I waved back. I was starting to believe in magic after all, or something very like it. Either that or a cruel and extensive practical joke was being played on me. I had seen some movies with plots like that and was determined to be on my guard. In the meantime, I would try to assume the best and enjoy my inexplicable good fortune and seeming popularity. Besides, while I didn't want to read too much into his sudden attention, I just didn't want to imagine that Dave could be that mean.

The morning passed in a distracted blur. Pictures were being taken in the gym and were scheduled during our Health class. Robin stood next to me, asking questions and trying to engage me in conversation—not my strongest ability at the best of times—but it was even harder to focus than normal. Dave was there, sitting on the bleachers and waiting with the rest of his class. Suddenly feeling all arms and legs and terribly exposed, I turned my back toward him as if I hadn't seen him while Robin made silly faces in

that direction. I was curious to know if he was making faces back—I somehow couldn't imagine that—but resolutely kept my shoulder turned.

I went before Robin, sitting on the stool, angling the way they told me to, and looking slightly to the right. Big mistake. Dave and one of his friends had now positioned themselves there, Dave leaning on the slightly taller boy's shoulder, an improbably benign expression on his face. An immediate flush crept up my cheeks.

My attention was called back to the camera and the picture taken before I could think. Now I felt even more nervous and dreaded how it would turn out.

Grateful to get off the stool and away from the camera, I stood to the side, waiting for Robin. As she sat down, Dave wolf-whistled and called out something more befitting a construction worker. Robin wasn't fazed. She looked straight at him, stuck her tongue out in a childish way, and then tossed her copper curls defiantly as she turned back to the camera. Her eyes were bright and her lips curved in an uncharacteristically prim smile. I watched the photographer grin as he took the picture. It would be a good one. That figured; Dave was there to discompose Robin, but *I* was the one affected adversely.

What a dork. Hopefully, I can get a retake.

A teacher shooed the boys away, and I headed back to Health with Robin. Once there, we made a rough outline for what we would research later.

"I was thinking," she said, abruptly. "We should go to the library in town. Their internet's much faster than mine. We might find some books, too."

"Okay," I said, willing to go along with whatever she wanted to do but surprised and a little disappointed. I wondered if she just didn't want to take me to her house.

"We can stop and get coffee or something too," she added.

That definitely sounded good. I couldn't believe it when the bell rang; the morning had disappeared so fast and it was lunch already. Suddenly there were butterflies in my stomach and I felt unbalanced. I'd never felt like this before and didn't know what I was more uneasy about—Chris' apparent dislike of me, Robin's change of heart, or Dave's very existence. I wasn't sure if it mattered whether Chris liked me or not, except that he and Dave seemed to be close. I was starting to like Robin and hoped we could be real friends. And then there was Dave. I certainly liked him but was completely unsure of his feelings or motives regarding me. I didn't want to be too paranoid, but I didn't feel like I was standing on solid ground with any of these new friends, if that's what they were.

Then I thought of Melanie. Had she missed me eating with her yesterday? Was she going to the cafeteria now? I almost wished I hadn't agreed to eat with Dave's crowd. *Almost.* And I felt a little guilty for eating with them instead of Melanie today. *A little.* I decided to compromise, telling Robin I'd go to the cafeteria to buy a sandwich first and then meet her out at the tables. I didn't know why I wanted to keep Melanie to myself, but I felt too unsure of the others. Playing it safe for a while just seemed like a good idea.

I bought lunch and went back to the table where I'd met her. After about five minutes, she joined me.

"Did you get your picture taken?" she asked quietly, rolling her eyes slightly. It was the drollest and most exaggerated expression I'd seen her make.

"Yes," I said, trying to wrinkle my nose the way I'd seen Robin do. "But I know it's going to be awful. I just hope they'll give me a do-over."

"Oh, I'm sure it'll be fine," she said.

I shook my head. "No, you have no idea. I was very . . . distracted."

Melanie was obviously curious but just smiled.

"Actually, I'm going to have to leave right now," I said, feeling the need to extricate myself before we got too deeply into conversation. I felt so at ease with her; it would be easy just to stay and talk. But the thought of Dave considering, for even a second, that I might not want to join them—join *him*—made me feel horrible. "I just wanted to say hi. I agreed to have lunch with someone today. We're working on a report together." It was only bending the truth a little. "I'll see you in Art, though. Okay?"

Melanie's smile held no hint of reproof, and I was grateful. "Okay. See you then," she said. Her pleasant manner left me looking forward to seeing her later in the day.

The butterflies came back as I made my way to the tables near the field. Even worse than approaching them for the first time with Robin, was approaching all by myself. She shouted to me when she saw me and all eyes turned my way. I concentrated on not tripping over my own feet, which I felt likely to do just because everyone was watching, and sat down next to her.

Chris was directly across from me and I braved glancing at him. Familiarity struck me again—something about his eyes—but he looked away immediately and then turned, facing away from me. I tried not to take it

personally. After all, what reason did he have to dislike me? Unless he just thought I was ugly. While it wasn't a pleasant thought, it didn't grieve me too much. I really only cared what Dave thought. I'm sure that was pathetic, but this was my first real crush on someone; I didn't know what to do, think, or expect in return.

Hanging out with a group wasn't something I had ever done either, and while I normally would have shunned the idea, it had unexpected benefits. For instance, I didn't have to talk at all unless someone spoke directly to me. This gave me perquisite two: being able to observe my new acquaintances without drawing attention to myself, especially if they were the ones talking.

Today I noticed more about the others in the group, and that the individuals varied somewhat from day to day. Today there were thirteen kids arranged around the tables. I thought I recognized some of them from before, but a few of them I was sure I didn't. Most were average, normal-looking kids, guys and girls—a few very attractive and a few others somewhat less so, first impressions and personal preference speaking, of course. Many were dressed similarly, but it didn't seem to be a requirement. There was no obvious outward unifying factor, though most of the kids were White, a reflection of the school and Douglas in general; very different from my old Los Angeles neighborhood. But no single demographic was represented beyond a certain age group. I was glad that it didn't seem to be exclusive in any obvious, external way. But everything appeared to revolve around the two boys I'd met, and only Dave seemed to care or be aware of it.

The main topic of conversation was sports, primarily soccer and basketball, and my listening focused a little more when talk turned to the early track tryouts taking place during PE next week. Something had been said about it on the first day of school. Apparently Douglas High was known for track and field and took it very seriously, training athletes early in the year to compete in the spring.

Someone said, "I wonder what Legs can do?" and, looking up, I found everyone regarding me with interest and obvious speculation.

I was horrified. Now I also remembered the whispers and glances in the gym. Did they really assume that because my limbs looked long, somehow that translated to athletic ability? I started to feel sick and couldn't help looking at Chris and then Dave. Chris had turned his head and I could now see his profile. He was frowning. When I looked at Dave, he had a questioning look in his eyes. Then he seemed to frown slightly too. And then he looked downright annoyed.

"Her name is Allison," he said in a low voice.

My head swam and a wave of nausea washed over me. *They think I'm going to be some kind of track star? Is that why they're so friendly? What should I do? Deny it now and suffer the consequences immediately, whatever those might be? Or wait until next week when it would become pitifully clear to everyone that I had no physical abilities at all?*

As I wrestled with whether and how to respond, Chris surprised me by saying, quite loudly and firmly, "What does it matter?"

He hadn't moved, still facing away from everyone, still frowning. I had only heard his voice the one time yesterday and got the distinct impression he used words sparingly, but his opinion apparently carried weight.

It became very quiet for a moment. Then someone changed the subject. I was glad and surprised at Chris' intervention at first. Then I realized, instead of meaning that it didn't matter whether I was athletic or not, he could just as easily mean that *I* didn't matter. The second option seemed more likely. I tried to shrug it off.

Robin and I had agreed to meet after school by our lockers, so I decided I might as well give mine another try. I looked around and, recognizing no one close by, dialed the numbers. My effort met with the same lack of success as before, but this time I felt someone behind me, reaching forward over my shoulder to dial again. I could feel the warmth from his body on my back, even though it was a very warm day, and I knew how my cheeks must look. I half turned to look behind me and got a severe shock.

It was Chris.

Of course, it couldn't be Dave. He isn't tall enough to reach over me like that.

I looked up at his face, but he avoided looking at me. The locker door popped open, and I tried to gather my scattered wits enough to say, "Thank you," but my mouth just hung open. The proverbial feather could have sent me flying. He walked off without saying a word.

Robin joined me then. She must have seen Chris open my locker but made no comment. I dropped off everything I didn't need, then followed her out to the front of the school. Across the street, I saw Melanie standing with a tall, dark-haired boy. He looked like he was probably a senior. She saw me

and waved and I waved back.

Robin noticed. "Friend of yours?"

"We have Art together," I replied. "She's really nice. You don't know her?"

"No, but she looks familiar." She said this as if it were a bad thing. "She probably went to Douglas Middle. I went to Foothill. I know the guy, though. Roger. He's a real snob."

I looked at her uncertainly and then looked back at Melanie and the boy. They were both attractive, well-dressed people. While Melanie was undeniably pretty—and that was an understatement—the boy wasn't what I would call really handsome, at least not in the way I thought Dave was. But there was an air about him that drew your attention. Something in the way he carried himself, in the set of his shoulders and the way he stood. He was what my mother would call clean-cut, like someone in the military or a politician. He reminded me of a lot of the boys that had gone to my old school; boys who would now probably be seriously involved in sports, advanced placement classes, or leadership activities. Robin lost interest as we headed down the street, but I saw the Mercedes that picked them both up.

Tires squealed suddenly right next to us making me jump sideways and bump into Robin. It was the big black truck I'd seen yesterday, and Dave was leaning out of the passenger window, smiling.

"You ladies need a ride?"

"Nope," said Robin. She linked her arm in mine and pulled me forward, her nose tipped in the air.

"Hey," called Dave, "that's not very friendly." The truck moved ahead slowly as we walked. "Are you going home?"

"Nope," said Robin again, trying to keep a straight face.

Dave sighed loudly. "Where are you going?"

"None of your business," said Robin, but now she was smiling.

A parked car made forward motion impossible for the truck. It pulled out and drove away.

"Sheesh," said Robin. "He can be so annoying sometimes."

The relationship between these two puzzled me exceedingly. For my own peace of mind, I had to ask, "Are you two going out?"

She looked as if I'd asked if she were dating a llama. Her eyes crinkled at the corners and she laughed loudly.

"Me . . . and Dave? Hardly. He's like a brother to me . . . I guess. I don't have any brothers so I'm not sure. Besides, Dave doesn't go out with girls."

Shocked, I stared at her as visions of Chris' face, words, and frowns jumped to mind.

Robin's eyes went wide and she laughed again.

"No, no, no! I just mean he never pays any real attention to girls. I'm sure he likes them. You know, *likes* them. But he's never dated anyone. He just likes them around." She looked thoughtful for a moment. "Maybe it's because he didn't really grow up with any." She shrugged her shoulders and kept walking.

My heart sank. I guessed that answered one question at least, and my mind was too preoccupied again to process her last statement. He no doubt made everyone feel the way I did, important and special somehow. He probably didn't even have a clue he was doing it; he was just being himself. A part of me was relieved. I wasn't sure what to do with the feelings I was having for him. An even bigger part was terribly disappointed. I was very curious to find out what to do with those feelings and had so hoped he was feeling them too. I sighed loudly.

Robin looked at me suspiciously. "You weren't thinking—" she started, but I pulled myself together quickly and smiled back at her.

"Have you known him a long time?" I was quite practiced at taking emotional blows, hiding my feelings, and moving on. Changing the subject was a tactic that usually worked.

She rolled her eyes dramatically. "Forever. I remember him from kindergarten! It seems like we've always been in the same class, in the same school."

"Wow," I said, impressed. "You've been friends a long time." Added to my other social difficulties, making let alone keeping friends had always been difficult.

Robin's face screwed up. "We haven't always been exactly *friends*," she said. "When we were little he used to tease me . . . a lot . . . about my freckles and red hair and being a girl. You know, regular bratty little boy stuff. It used to make me cry, though. And then around third grade he got *really* mean, and not just to me either. But I guess he was used to teasing me, so it just got a lot worse." She frowned and was quiet a moment, obviously remembering. She brightened suddenly. "And then one day, he wasn't."

"Wasn't?"

"Mean. He just wasn't mean anymore. Whoa . . . I haven't thought of that in a long time. But we've been best friends ever since. And now he kind of looks out for people, you know? Like you."

She looked at me and I felt my color change again, though this time I probably went pale.

So that confirmed it; he was paying attention to me, helping me, because he was like that to everybody. If anything, he just felt sorry for me. My heart suddenly felt made of lead. I'd never felt so disappointed about anything in my life. I'd been trying so hard not to think the worst of him, but also thought I hadn't allowed myself to get my hopes up. I was wrong.

"So, Dave is a freshman?" I asked, swallowing hard, trying to clear the lump in my throat. This had just occurred to me and hopefully covered my reaction. I had thought he was at least a year older. It seemed strange that we had no classes together in such a small school.

"Yeah," said Robin. "He'll turn fifteen in October, so I guess he started school a little later than some. But then, Chris is seventeen already and only a junior."

"Chris is seventeen?" I was surprised. I had been sure they were about the same age, in spite of Chris' height.

"Mmhmm," she affirmed. "He just had his birthday earlier this month."

"Have they been friends long?" I asked, wondering what drew a junior to a freshman. They could barely have known each other in middle school.

Robin stopped and looked at me in obvious amazement. "You're sort of clueless sometimes, aren't you?" She continued to stare at me as if expecting a light bulb to go on over my head. She finally laughed and said, "Dave and Chris are brothers."

Chapter Four

All In My Head

The question wasn't uttered in a demeaning way, but I flushed anyway. I knew it was true.

Duh. Of course they're brothers. That's why Chris looks familiar.

They didn't really look that much alike, but there was something similar. Something about their eyes.

"Coffee first, I think," said Robin. "Get some caffeine in us."

I nodded enthusiastically. It wasn't so much caffeine as the distraction that I wanted. The best coffee place was apparently in the "new" strip mall, which wasn't new at all but newer compared to most of the town. A lot of the buildings in Douglas, especially on the eastern Old Town side, probably qualified as historic sites and were quaint in a rough and ready, old-westy sort of way. Driving through that side of town with Mom always felt surreal, as if we had stepped back in time a hundred years.

It took us a while to get to the shopping area, but we weren't in a hurry. The parking lot was enormous, most of it vacant. At the far end was an abandoned gas station and car wash. A few cars were parked near the station with a lot of kids hanging out, most of them on skateboards. Many were doing tricks using the curbs and pavement. A few used the far embankments to do, or at least attempt, even more. The embankment formed a large *V* at the corner of the lot and was paved over in concrete, probably to prevent erosion into the car wash area.

We bought iced drinks and found seats outside the coffee shop in the shade of a large umbrella. Watching the kids at the far end of the parking lot, I thought I recognized some people by their general build and clothing. I was looking for one in particular.

I realized I was frowning and squinting when Robin said, "Yeah, they're here sometimes when they don't have to be somewhere else after school. They hang out at different places . . . kind of move around so they don't get into too much trouble in any one place."

"Trouble?" I asked, a little concerned.

"Yeah, you know . . . people afraid of lawsuits if someone gets hurt or thinking there's drugs. Maybe just not wanting kids to have fun." She shrugged. "The Calderas don't care much if they get in trouble, but they kind of watch out for others, like I said."

"Caldera?" I asked, knowing exactly who she meant.

Robin nodded. "Their family owns a huge ranch. You know . . . cattle. They're pretty well-known around here and get away with a lot of. . . ." Her eyes slid sideways to my face, and I got the feeling she was amending her vocabulary. "Stuff. But still, they don't like getting others in . . . trouble."

I already thought I recognized Dave, but I now saw Chris on the embankment and wondered where his truck was. He skated down the steep ramp then shot up the other side and seemed to hang in the air at least two feet above it for a moment. He caught the end of his board, came back down, jumped onto a railing, slid for several feet, and lifted off again, spinning his board beneath him before landing. I'd never seen anything like it except maybe on television; not done by someone I knew. Dave tried to copy the stunt, making it onto the railing but unable to keep his balance. His board shot out from under his feet and he fell hard on his back. I gasped when I realized what was happening and jumped up when I saw him hit the ground.

"Don't worry," said Robin, grinning. "I swear they're made out of rubber or something. They do all kinds of crazy things and never seem to get hurt . . . much." She grinned again.

I relaxed a little when I saw Dave get up and brush himself off, laughing. I'd never heard him laugh and wondered what it sounded like. A couple of other boys tried the trick but didn't have enough momentum to lift onto the railing. They jumped clear and landed on their feet while their boards shot through or just fell to the ground. It was fun to watch, but I winced every time someone fell. I never saw Chris fall. Each time Dave did—often, as he was always trying something ridiculous—I tensed and held my breath till he got up again. I tried not to be obvious, but Robin noticed.

"He's such a show-off," she said. "You're going to be nervous all the time if you hang out with us. Dave'll do anything he's dared to and he'll try to top anything anyone else does. He's very competitive. And reckless. Chris is even worse." She became serious for a moment. "Actually, Chris is a little scary sometimes. He doesn't even show off. Dave does things for fun, for laughs, you know? But Chris," she frowned as if trying to find the right words, "is different."

"He takes it more seriously?" I offered.

She shook her head. "No, not really. He's not competitive in the way Dave is. If he competes, it's like he's competing against himself. He doesn't seem to care what anyone else does or thinks. At all."

"Has he always been like that?" I asked, just curious. It seemed strange that the brothers were so completely different. "He's so . . . quiet." I was going to say something more along the lines of *angsty, moody,* even *creepy* but changed my mind. I didn't know any of them well enough to use words that strong.

Robin considered my question and shrugged. "He's been like that ever since I can remember, but I've really only been around him the past couple of years. That's when he started hanging out with us more, even though he was in high school and we were still in middle school. I don't remember him around much before that. But that's when I started going over to Dave's house more, too. I know Chris had a girlfriend all through middle school, but something happened—she dumped him or something—but I'm not sure. He never talks about it. But then, he doesn't really talk about anything, at least not when I'm around."

I thought that was interesting and tried to picture the belligerent Chris with a girlfriend. It was difficult.

Over on the other side of the lot, Dave was talking to Chris and looking in our direction. He and another boy left the group and coasted over to us on their boards. Chris bumped fists with a couple of other guys and followed, walking and carrying his skateboard. I lost interest in him as the other two boys drew close. They stepped off and popped their boards up, catching them, and then came to sit at the table with us.

I was wriggling inside. I couldn't help it. Just being able to be around Dave, the fact that he noticed me at all, was better than any dream I'd ever had. I didn't want to wake up.

"Coffee, huh? This is the big secret?"

"No secret," said Robin.

She sounded like she didn't care what he thought, though I doubted she could be completely resistant to his charm. Either way, she obviously liked annoying him. I was pretty sure it went both ways and couldn't help being amused and envious. I wished I knew him well enough to joke and be at ease around him like she was.

The other boy was the one Dave had been leaning on in the gym earlier; I thought his name was Matthew. He was a good looking boy with dark brown hair and eyes, but it was difficult to notice him much next to Dave, the one the sun rose and set on—at least in my world. In fact, I found it hard to keep my eyes off him and he seemed okay with that. He sat partly in the sun which reflected a strange, light, almost pink glow on the ends of his hair. I'd noticed it before.

A couple of girls walked up the pavement toward the door, both smiling and saying, "Hi, Dave!" They waved at Matthew too, but the smiles were obviously for Dave.

He acknowledged them with a return smile and, "Hey," but immediately turned his attention back to us. "What're you doing after this?" he asked.

Robin glanced at me, her eyes dancing a little, and said, "Homework."

"Homework? It's Friday! Why do you want to do homework?"

" 'Cause it beats doing it at eleven o'clock on Sunday night like you do," she said.

"Ow!" said Matthew and laughed.

Robin licked her finger and drew a line in the air. I couldn't help laughing a little too, drawing the attention of both boys. They seemed to expect me to add to the conversation, so I swallowed and said, "We have a report to do together."

At this moment Chris strolled up and stood regarding his brother. "I'm going to work," he said without enthusiasm.

"Hey!" said Dave, his eyes lighting up. "Why don't you come to my house? You need the Internet right?" This last was said to me, his teeth flashing in a wide smile.

"Right," Robin drew the word out slowly, "because we'd get so much work done there." She rolled her eyes. "You'd get bored and make Allison play video games with you or something, and—"

"Halo!" the two sitting boys said at the same time, nodding and smiling at each other.

"*And*," continued Robin, "I'd end up doing it all by myself. No, thank you!"

I took exception to that and said, "I wouldn't do that to you!"

"Oh, come on," said Dave. "Chris can drive us and we can take you home later." He looked over at me. "I know where you *both* live."

So he *did* recognize me from that first day! I could so easily picture him on his motorcycle looking dusty and hot—in more ways than one. Matthew was the only one who looked surprised at what Dave had said.

"Make your own way home." Chris looked and sounded even more sullen. "I'm leaving."

Without a backward glance, he dropped his board, stepped on, and effortlessly glided away. If Dave was cool—which he undoubtedly was as far as I was concerned—then Chris was frozen. I preferred the warmer climate around Dave and wasn't sad that Chris had left. I had never known anyone who seemed so isolated, even when he was around others.

"Where's his truck?" I couldn't help being curious.

"Back near where he works," said Dave. "It's better if we don't park too close to where we're," he smirked a little, "having fun."

"Clean getaways are preferable," agreed Matthew with mock severity. "Especially when they appear chaotic." Both boys grinned.

Dave misread my questioning look. "He works at the hardware store, further up on Main."

I acknowledged the information. I *had* been curious, as I was about Chris in general, but only because of Dave.

"So, where to?" he asked.

Robin sighed and rolled her eyes dramatically again. "Library. And you're *not* invited."

"Oh, come on. We can help," he said. "You wouldn't condemn me to being bored with Matt, would you?"

"Nice," said Matthew, his mouth twisting wryly.

Robin looked genuinely annoyed as we gathered our things and then began walking back the way we had come. Matthew skated ahead while

Dave walked on the other side of Robin, carrying his board. They bantered all the way to the library, tucked up a narrow side street and a much smaller building than I was expecting.

"So, what are we researching?" asked Dave, holding the door as we entered.

The lady behind the desk glared at us. Then I saw she was focused on the boys' skateboards. "You can't bring those in here," she said, as if expecting a fight.

"Is it all right if we leave them near the door?" asked Dave politely, flashing a smile at her.

She seemed to melt a little—I would have been amazed if she hadn't—and said she supposed it would be all right. He beamed at her and her face cracked into a reluctant smile. I wondered again if Dave's power of enchantment could truly be natural and genuine, or was it just a well-practiced act, a way of getting what he wanted? I still wasn't sure it even mattered.

He and Robin each appropriated a computer. Matthew leaned back against a table, watching me for some reason.

"I'm going to go check for books," I said, feeling awkward and pointing over my shoulder.

"Hey, I don't have a password," said Dave. He looked expectantly at me. "Allison, give me your library card."

"I . . . I don't have one . . . yet," I said, feeling flustered and wishing like mad that I *did* have one just so I could give it to him. "I only have one from Santa Monica, and I doubt if that would work."

Matthew reached in his pocket for his wallet then pulled out a card and handed it to Dave.

Dave looked at Matthew in wonder. "Dude. You read books?"

Matthew laughed easily. "I have been known to crack open a tome or two, amazing though it may seem."

I smiled, feeling less awkward, pointed to the stacks again, and retreated into them. I was surprised when I found Matthew following me around.

"So," he said, "we're looking for . . . ?"

I felt a little shy; I didn't know him at all but was willing to be friendly. "We're looking for information on the effect pets have on people, especially as it relates to physical health, emotional stability, and longevity."

My glasses had slipped down my nose from looking at a low shelf and I pushed them back up as I spoke. Then it occurred to me what an incredible nerd I must seem. His eyes crinkled a little as if he would smile, but instead he made a face indicating he thought it a worthy topic. I still felt he was laughing at me, but I wasn't sure in what way. We wandered around until we found the "health" section, which was woefully small.

"This doesn't look too promising, does it? Maybe you should do a report on the evils of smoking or drugs instead, like everyone else is probably doing."

He held up a book titled, *Smoking: Seeing Through the Haze*. It wasn't a humorous topic, but the title made me laugh. He laughed too.

"What about this one?" I asked, showing him a book titled, *Women Who Love Men Who Hate Women*. We made scared faces at each other but then had to laugh again.

"What's going on?" a soft voice asked. It made me jump and I turned to find Dave close by, looking past me and regarding Matthew very steadily. It was kind of weird.

Matthew shrugged his shoulders, his eyebrows raised. He took a step backward. "Just looking for books," he said, "and not having much luck."

"Except for finding a few disturbing titles," I said, trying to ease the odd tension I felt in the air. Dave's eyes rested on mine briefly but effectively, my knees turning jellyish and my breath catching slightly. He almost smiled at me, smirked at Matthew, turned, and walked away.

I looked at Matthew and he smiled too, looking sheepish. "I guess we should focus."

What was that all about? I'd never thought myself completely devoid of simple understanding when it came to other people, but I was beginning to seriously doubt that I understood them at all. Why did everything lately— from Dave's odd attention to me, to his brother's apparent malevolence, to his friendship with Robin, to the weird vibe with Matthew just now—perplex me so? Was it all overactive imagination?

I was still musing on this when Matthew waved his hand near my face.

"I've looked at everything from *Alzheimer's* to *Violence* but don't see anything pertinent," he said. "Maybe we should be looking in *Animals*."

"Good idea," I said, embarrassed at being caught so off task. I was beginning to see why Robin hadn't wanted Dave to come with us—and he wasn't even *trying* to distract me.

We perused the shelves in the animal and pet section, coming out with a couple of books at least mentioning positive effects of owning pets. Then we headed back to the computer stations. Robin was on her feet behind Dave, arms crossed and looking irritable. Dave sat slumped down comfortably in his chair, scrolling through a motorcycle website.

"I see you're being productive," said Matthew.

Dave looked up at him as if he couldn't imagine what he was talking about. Then he walked slowly to the closest printer.

" 'Studies find that people who don't have a cat are thirty to forty percent more likely to die of heart disease or stroke than those who do'," he quoted smugly, removing a small stack of paper from the printer tray and handing it to me. There were about ten pages from at least six different sites; more than enough. "I started on about the eighth page of the search, so probably didn't repeat anything Robin has."

"You think you're so smart," Robin said, taking the pages from me and comparing them to what she had. I could see by her face that he was right. It just seemed to annoy her even more. "Well, I guess we're done. I've got to get home."

She handed the pages back to me and took the books from Matthew, checking them out while the boys got their boards and went outside.

"I'll call my mom," I said, feeling sad and wishing I could drag this time out. But Robin really did seem to just want to go home. I stepped outside and called my mother, wondering where the boys had gone. Had they—had *he*—just left without saying goodbye? *Sure, why shouldn't he?*

Robin joined me outside. We sat on a low wall and could see the guys doing flip kicks at the end of the small parking lot.

"Hey," I said, remembering something I'd been too preoccupied lately to think about. "What kinds of wild animals are around here? Like, in the hills."

Robin looked thoughtful. "Coyotes, foxes . . . deer and rabbits. Boar. Mountain lions, I guess. I've never seen one, but I've heard of them. And bobcats. Some say there's bears too, especially further up in the mountains. Why?"

I tried to look unconcerned. "Oh, I was just wondering. My mom was afraid of me wandering too far from the house."

Just then my mother pulled into the parking lot. Robin followed me to the car to meet her. I looked toward the guys, hoping—and dreading—that they might come over too, but they kept their distance.

"Mom, this is Robin," I said.

Robin waved, seeming a little unsure, and said, "Hi."

"Nice to meet you, Robin," said Mom. "Did you girls get what you needed?"

"Yes," we both answered.

"For now," I added.

"Do you need a ride home, Robin?" asked Mom.

"Oh, no," said Robin, quickly and firmly. "I'm fine. It's not far. I walk all the time."

"Are you sure?" pursued Mom. "It's very hot today."

"Yeah, I'm fine. Really."

She handed me one of the books we'd found and we said, "See you Monday," as I got in the car.

Mom turned the car around and then we were pulling out of the lot. I looked back a couple of times toward the boys, now standing still and watching us leave. I wanted to wave but it felt stupid. I also felt bad. I hadn't even thanked them for their help. Mom noticed my glances in their direction.

"Do you know those boys?" she asked, obviously very interested.

"Huh?" I stalled. "Oh, yes. They go to school with us. They're good friends of Robin and helped us get information."

"That's nice of them," said Mom, a little archly I thought. "Good-looking boys."

"Hmm? Oh . . . yes, I suppose so." I tried to sound as if I hadn't noticed.

I looked sideways, carefully, back at the guys again. They—*he*—was walking with Robin and seemed to have already forgotten me. Monday seemed a *terribly* long way away.

My mother had done the dishes all week since my return to school, but I insisted on doing them this night. I felt in desperate need of debriefing and hoped time alone doing something mundane would help. The world turned to dusk as I stood at the sink and watched out the window. Something pulled at my memory, but I was too distracted by other thoughts and it eluded me.

I used to ignore the things that bothered me and, in so doing, deflate their importance to me. But honestly, up until now those things had been

relatively trivial to start with. I had never been the kind of person to carry the weight of the world on my shoulders but, in this case, I didn't think ignoring my concerns would make them disappear. And I was pretty sure I didn't want them to disappear. It was a confusing situation for me. Having spent my life more or less invisible to the world had suited me just fine. It made life easy, uncomplicated. And isolated. And—lonely, I guess, though I hadn't thought much about it before. Now suddenly people were noticing me for some obscure reason and, perplexing though it was, I thought I liked it. If it was real. And that was part of the whole problem. *Or I could be worrying for nothing.*

It would have been great to be able to talk to someone, to get an outside perspective, but my options seemed pitifully limited. My mother would have loved for me to confide in her, I'm sure, and the little girl in me wanted to avail herself of her mother's experience and wisdom. But that could come with a price I didn't want to pay. I loved my mother and everything, but these feelings were too new, too confused, and much too vulnerable to allow someone so otherwise intimately acquainted with me to have access to them. And once in the open at home they might be fair game for all manner of analyzing, interpretation, and interference.

If she found out how I felt about Dave, regardless of what she thought about it, I could imagine her betraying me the first time she met him. Images of her beaming at him like a fifties TV show mom and forcing fresh-baked cookies on him. Or cornering him in a public place and giving him the third degree regarding his life plans and future prospects. Images no doubt completely unfair to my mother, but the thought alone was enough to prevent any rash gut-spilling in the near future.

Robin would have been the next likely candidate, but I didn't have her phone number and it was potentially worse than talking to Mom. It was becoming evident that anything Robin knew became appropriated by or conveyed to Dave immediately or soon thereafter. Maybe they were telepathic. They certainly didn't appear to have any difficulty communicating. If I admitted to liking Dave, which she probably suspected already, he'd be the first to know. That *could* be a good thing, but what if it wasn't? So far, all I really knew about him was that he seemed to enjoy championing underdogs, and apparently I fit that description. Hardly flattering. No, talking to Robin about anything that serious and personal was definitely out.

I wished that I knew Melanie better. If I'd had *her* number, I might actually have called. Of course, I hardly knew her either, but I had no reason to distrust her. She seemed like the kind of person I could talk to.

The only other person was Brenda. She had never dated but was always interested in one boy or another with varying degrees of success, so she had way more experience than I did. At least she must have dealt with the emotions, right? Our relationship had always pretty much relied on her both supplying the topics of conversation and steering them, and she was very accomplished at both. Now I actually had something *I* wanted to talk about.

Mom and I had agreed earlier to watch a movie together that night, and I knew she'd be disappointed if I backed out. She had said how lonely it seemed at home now that I was back at school and that she needed to find something to do with all her spare time. I never knowingly did anything to keep her occupied or entertained, but I knew she appreciated my company. In fact, that seemed to define my existence. On my tombstone would be engraved, '*We didn't know her very well, but we liked having her around.*' I sighed. Now I was becoming morose.

I finished the dishes, dried my hands, and went upstairs. Taking my phone out of my backpack, I pulled up Brenda's number and sat with my thumb poised over the call button but didn't push it. Lately she had cut calls short, saying she had homework to do. It was true that she had started school when I had not, but if she had wanted to talk to me, wouldn't she have made some effort? Not sure I wanted to risk rejection right now, I put the phone on my dresser. Perhaps Brenda wasn't the best person anyway. Sighing, I resigned myself to Mom and a movie. Dave and the despicable doubts would have to wait.

Later, my room wasn't the refuge I had hoped it would be. I couldn't bear seeing myself in either of my mirrors. The reflections there gave irrefutable proof of my lack of elegance, style, grace, sex appeal—anything that could remotely be expected to attract someone as exceptional as Dave. I sat at my desk listening to music and doodling, but the random squiggles always ended up looking suspiciously like an already beloved first or recently learned last name.

Even listening to my music was difficult; the well-known lyrics all seemed to take on new meaning. Some of my favorites now felt like knives stuck in my heart—or maybe my stomach, I wasn't sure which—and twisted, even though the words had perhaps meant little to me before.

I thought I might as well try to do something constructive so decided to compile a list. Lists were orderly, dispassionate, safe. If I organized the events of the week and my thoughts about them on paper, and thereby hopefully my feelings too, perhaps I could sort through what was fact and what was merely wishful thinking.

Writing only what I thought I knew for sure about Dave, I came up with this:

Brown hair, brown eyes, ~~cute handsome~~ hot!

Rides a motorcycle

Skateboards

Likes dogs (assumed)

Can whistle really loud (not sure of practical use, but it's cool)

Knows where I live

Apparently popular in school (big surprise)—likes to have a lot of people around

Messed up my school picture (on purpose?)

Very good friends with Robin (but not dating her)

Sense of humor (very important)

Inquisitive (very)

Helpful: locker, giving rides, report research, invited / expected at lunch, invited to his house (sort of)

Champion: for noticing me at all, reprimanded friend about my name

Interested in what we're doing (both of us or just Robin?)

Charming (and knows how to use it?)

Good at Internet research (useful skill)

Reviewing the list was not as reassuring as I had hoped it would be. Leaving off his appearance and other personal attributes, which obviously affected the way I felt about him more than how he behaved, everything could be explained either by my sudden close alliance with his best friend or by his own nature. Nothing pointed to any other motivation on his part for paying attention to me except for one thing: his odd behavior in the library with Matthew. He hadn't said a word or moved a muscle that I had been aware of, yet Matthew had definitely backed off. And Matthew hadn't been doing anything except helping me.

To *Champion*, I added: *protective/possessive? (Why?)*

That was puzzling but was the only thing not immediately explainable. I gave up thinking about it and went to bed, hoping the morning would bring more clarity, but it was a long time before I finally slept.

The morning brought a little too much clarity. I felt so foolish and wondered if my infatuation was obvious to the whole world. I had a feeling it *was* obvious to the one person that mattered and his closest friends. I pulled my pillow out from under my head and tried to smother myself. No luck.

Dave dominated my thoughts completely. How was I going to make it through the weekend without seeing him? And then wouldn't it be even worse on Monday when I *did* see him?

It was early still, not my usual Saturday midday wake-up time, but I also knew I'd never be able to get back to sleep. Getting up, I crossed to my back window and opened the curtains. Though it was barely seven o'clock, sunlight lit the eastern sky behind the hills and now filled my room. The hillsides were still shadowed, but patches of light could be seen where the ground wasn't covered with brush or trees. I put my glasses on and surveyed the landscape, now much more well-defined. Immediately, movement toward the base of the far hill caught my attention—something dark moving through the brush. Something large.

I dressed hastily—pants and sneakers this time—and rushed quietly down the stairs. Stealthily creeping out the back door, I walked quickly to the dirt road heading to the back of the property. I kept my eyes on the hill, but from this vantage point, I could see nothing but trees and undergrowth. Keeping to the dirt road, I walked until I came to a cattle guard crossing the stream. It was nowhere near where I had seen the movement, but I wanted to see where it led anyway. Ahead were steep hills and to the right I could make out a barbed wire fence. I assumed this was the southern border of

our property. To my left, the stream meandered through dense brush and trees. The road curved around and disappeared beyond that.

Continuing to follow the road, I was surprised to find an open space beyond the line of trees and underbrush. A large enclosure was bordered on three sides by the impenetrable brush and on the fourth, closest to the road, by pole fencing. There was no gate in the wide opening of the fence. I walked to the center and looked around. It was certainly an old abandoned pen or corral of some sort, with the creek running through the northwest corner, but otherwise there was nothing there.

I left the enclosure and followed the road a little farther north. There was a sudden rustling beyond a clump of high bushes and I froze in my tracks. *Maybe this wasn't such a good idea. . . .*

Thoughts of bears, boar, and mountain lions invaded my mind and caused my heart to thump heavily. Another rustle brought a large tawny head, shoulders, and forelegs out from the edge of the foliage. Now I was frozen in awe. My heart sped up; not in fear but excitement.

Standing before me, not ten yards away, was a large horse, its long, light-colored mane twisted and full of twigs and debris. Its tawny coat was mostly covered in dirt, and its legs were caked with brown as if it had been playing in mud. It was beautiful.

"Hi," I said softly.

The horse regarded me calmly then took a few more steps as if I weren't there. I could now see his tail. It was so long it dragged on the ground but was in a pitiable condition, even dirtier and more tangled than his mane. I knew nothing about horses, but I thought he probably looked very nice underneath all the dirt. He also looked very thin, his ribs showing slightly through the yellowish hide of his flank, but otherwise he looked healthy to me. I felt oddly relieved by his existence. This, at least, was *not* just in my head.

"Where do you belong, huh?" I asked, only just beginning to wonder if I should be worried at all about my safety.

I reached my hand slowly toward him, but he snorted loudly, trotted away, and clambered up the steep side of the hill.

He was gone.

Chapter Five

Right Between the Eyes

To say that I was preoccupied the rest of the day would be putting it mildly. My mother was cooking breakfast when I got back to the house. She looked up in surprise as I came in.

"I thought you were still in bed," she said.

"I couldn't sleep." I almost told her right away about the horse, but something held me back. "I went for a walk." Mom looked at me skeptically. "I found the stream." She feigned interest. I thought about telling her of the corral but decided against that, too, until I knew more. "Do you know who lived here before us?"

"Well," said Mom, frowning in thought, "the house has been here quite a few years but is otherwise new. No one's ever lived in it. I believe the land was part of a larger cattle ranch that was sold off in pieces, like most of the area around here. In fact, I'm not exactly sure who lives closest to us." She sighed. "I miss having neighbors."

I didn't miss having neighbors one bit, but my mother was a sociable person. Being out here on her own probably wasn't easy for her.

"Maybe you could join something," I offered. "You know, like a club."

"Maybe," she agreed, putting a plate of pancakes and bacon in front of me. I wasn't hungry but ate as much as I could.

My internal energy for the rest of the day was split between thinking and puzzling over Dave and the horse I'd seen, Dave winning out most of

the time. Mom wanted help with projects around the house—general cleaning and hanging new drapes in the living room—which took up the whole morning and part of the afternoon. We quit when it got so hot even the air conditioner couldn't cool the house completely.

"At times like this I really miss being close to the beach," said Mom as we both collapsed on the couch. "I almost wish we had a pool."

"But then we'd have to clean it," I said. I'd had to help clean my cousins' pools before.

"Oh no, *dahling!* The pool boy would do it, of course," she said in a lofty, upper-crusty kind of voice.

"Well then, we should have one installed *immediately!* I don't know *why* we've waited so long!" I said, trying to match her tone but not quite managing it. It wasn't one of my talents.

Mom laughed and then looked excited, her eyes lighting up. *Uh oh, Mom's had an idea.*

"We should go!" she said. "To the pool in town!" She looked at me expectantly. "We could cool off and, you never know, you might see someone you know there."

Swimming was one of the things I was actually good at. For a moment, I was tempted to join in her enthusiasm. But then the thought of me, *in a bathing suit . . . in public . . . in a town where someone like Dave exists*, quickly changed my mind. The part of my brain that was still rational realized that Dave probably wouldn't be caught dead at a public pool. But the other, apparently now larger part insisted, *But what if he was there? What if he saw you?* I wished we lived closer to the beach, too. I would have gone in a heartbeat.

"Why don't you go, Mom? I think I just want to hang out here and relax."

This was true. And apart from all the useless thinking that would undoubtedly take place, there were things I wanted to do. A couple of things had occurred to me this morning and I acted on the first as soon as Mom finally made up her mind to go by herself.

As soon as she'd pulled out of the driveway, I jumped into the shower then dressed with care but practicality. It seemed like I was doing a lot of that lately. I wanted to look decent but needed to feel comfortable too. I left my hair loose to dry, slipped my glasses on, and headed out the front door.

It was a scorching hot late August day with no hint of a breeze, the air constricting my throat and burning my eyes as soon as I stepped outdoors. I walked south along the grassy shoulder of the road, heading deeper into the hills—the direction Dave had ridden from that first day I'd seen him. I hadn't thought of it before, but a few things had occurred to me as we'd worked this morning.

I had thought it very cool that he'd been riding a motorcycle but, at the time, I had also assumed he was much older. The fact that he was only a few months older than me meant that he couldn't have his driver's license yet. Not that I'd have put it past him to drive wherever he wanted to without one. I was getting the impression that the Calderas, although probably not lawless, pretty much did as they pleased. But it seemed more reasonable to assume that he lived nearby. He hadn't been wearing a helmet, as if he'd jumped on his bike and taken off quickly without thinking about it, knowing he wasn't going far. And it was a dirt bike he'd been riding, not a street bike. Then there was the dog. It couldn't have wandered too far, could it? So Dave must have come from somewhere down this road.

And I'm just going for a little walk . . . in the heat of the day . . . with no particular destination or purpose in mind. . . .

My face and arms were burning as I walked along the grassy shoulder. Then the road narrowed, the hills closed in, and trees shaded both sides of the road. The first driveway I came to led to a large house easily seen from the road and set off in an open field with dense trees and shrubbery behind it. It didn't look like a "large cattle ranch." It was a few minutes before I reached the next driveway, winding away through trees that I couldn't see beyond. But the sign near the road said, "The O'Dell's." That obviously wasn't it either.

I kept walking but was beginning to think about turning back when a truck rumbled down to the end of a narrow lane on the other side of the road ahead. It stopped, then turned left toward me. It was an older truck, dull red, and the driver was a man wearing a cowboy hat. He drove very slowly toward me then stopped. Waiting until I had reached him, he said out the open passenger window, "Are you walking far?"

All the cautions about not talking to strangers occurred to me, of course, but he had such an open, friendly face and sounded concerned and respectful. I stopped and answered him, "No, I was just exploring a little."

"Well, be careful," he said. "People drive pretty fast down this road." He smiled and did something I'd never seen someone do in real life. He tipped his hat to me. The truck rumbled and rattled on down the road and disappeared around a hill.

Curious, I walked farther until I could see up the lane. About fifty feet from the street a large wooden sign spanned the width of the road. It said:

BAR 8 RANCH

The only other thing visible before the road curved around the hill was a smaller sign saying, "Slow—Horses," with a horse and rider silhouette. I knew nothing about cattle ranches and couldn't begin to guess whether this could be where Dave lived, but it seemed possible.

I stood indecisively. A narrow dirt road continued across from the lane, on my side, but it also quickly wound around trees and out of sight. A sign close to the main road prohibited motorized vehicles. Walking farther on the main road would take me deeper and higher into the hills. But the ranch was obviously private property. I certainly had no excuse to explore there.

Besides, if it did turn out to be his home, that would make me a stalker, wouldn't it? It would be an *attempted* stalking, at least. That was just pathetic and creepy. I couldn't imagine Dave stalking anyone. I was sure he would be more direct. If he liked someone, he'd just let them know. *Of course he would. If he liked them, he'd just let them* know.

I didn't want to think about that anymore. My hair was already completely dry and it was hotter than ever. I headed home.

It didn't surprise me that my mother wasn't there yet. I was sure she was enjoying the cool water and social atmosphere of the pool and was glad of it. It also gave me time to prepare to act on my second revelation of the morning.

It was probably too early; I'd need to wait a little longer to go hunting. It had occurred to me this morning that, if the horse was indeed the mysterious reflection of the past couple of weeks, it had always appeared in the early evening as the sun went down. I suspected the creek was its objective as it had been in that area this morning also. I was assuming it came, morning and evening, to drink. There probably weren't many other sources of water available.

I searched the refrigerator hoping to find regular carrots but only found packages of baby ones. The fruit bowl was full, though, so I took an apple. I didn't much care for fruit, but Mom liked it. I put the treats in a lunch bag and sat on the back porch, waiting for the shadows to lengthen.

I thought about the horse and what its story might be. When I'd first seen it, I'd thought it might have been left behind by the previous tenants. But if no one had lived here before us—at least, not in the near past and as the property existed today—that didn't seem likely at all. If it had been left behind, then it was from many years ago when this had been part of a cattle ranch. And if that were true, then the horse was feral; more or less wild.

Or perhaps it *was* wild. I knew wild horses existed. I vaguely remembered my aunt in Colorado saying something about them when I was small. Could this be a mustang? I had no idea what they looked like or if they could be found around here, but I knew who probably would.

I considered that it might have escaped from a neighboring property, but this didn't seem likely. From its general appearance, it had been loose for more than a few weeks. Surely they would have found it by now.

I continued to watch the far hillsides and saw no large movement or reflection, but the sun was now getting low. In the hills around here, it became dark quickly. Leaving a note that I'd gone for a walk, I headed toward the hidden enclosure, trying to think of a good excuse for all my recent exercise. My mother might become suspicious about my sudden proclivity for taking walks, and I was feeling vaguely guilty about not telling her the real reason. I wasn't used to keeping things from her and now there were two rather important things I was keeping secret.

The enclosure was almost completely in the shade by the time I got there. It felt deliciously cool and very peaceful, just the gurgling of the stream breaking the stillness. I left the road and picked my way carefully toward the creek beyond the corral, close to where I thought I had seen the reflections before. The trees and brush grew close together there, making visibility difficult and walking quietly almost impossible.

I thought I was doing well when I caught a glimpse of tawny hide between large bushes some way ahead. Walking as slowly and quietly as I could, I moved toward the bushes until I could see the horse clearly through them. It stood facing my direction, its ears turned toward me and nostrils gently flaring. It seemed neither alarmed nor aggravated, simply curious. I couldn't tell whether it could see me, but it obviously heard and smelled me. Did it remember me from this morning?

We regarded each other for several long moments. Its ears occasionally swiveled sideways and backward but always came back to point directly at me. Its head finally dropped, lips gently nibbling delicate shoots of grass in the moist soil near the creek, the movement of its ears the only indication that it was still aware of or interested in my presence. Apparently I was no threat. I walked slowly out from behind the bush so we could plainly see each other. He continued his browsing, unconcerned.

I was captivated. Scruffy and dirty though he was, I still found something regal and exquisitely attractive about him. I couldn't put it into words and I had nothing to compare him to, but he seemed special. His head was big but beautifully shaped, his eyes large and dark. In spite of his ribs showing slightly, he seemed powerfully built, his neck thick, his haunches and shoulders well-muscled. I wondered how he'd look cleaned up and well fed. I was sure he would be gorgeous and already wanted to make him so.

I slowly opened the bag that held my bait; more like an offering of worship now. Pulling the apple out, I stood with it in my extended hand. He watched me, never once pausing in his leisurely browsing. As he moved forward, I moved with him. I wondered if I changed my position, would he be more responsive? I squatted down to be at the same level as his head; he continued to watch me, unimpressed. He moved again, and I started to rise to also move but lost my balance and fell over in the dirt. He looked up and snorted softly at me. I felt he was laughing at me and told him so. Following him but still keeping a respectful distance, I talked to him in a low, quiet voice.

I told him how I'd been seeing him, the light reflecting off his sides and back, like now, the sun filtering through the trees and sparkling with a golden gleam in the areas not completely covered in dirt. I told him how pretty I thought he was, how I would love to see him cleaned up and a little fatter.

"You know, not *too* fat, but healthy. . . ." And I probably spoke a great deal of nonsense. He listened politely but unemotionally, always moving farther away from the stream and finding less and less to nibble.

It was getting dark so I left my offerings for him. I was sure he wasn't going to come near me anyway. I set the apple down and poured the carrots out next to it. Then I walked home.

Mom had made dinner and looked a little concerned when I came in.

"Did you have a good time?" I asked.

"Yes!" she answered. "It felt wonderful, and there are a lot of really nice people there."

"That's great, Mom," I said and meant it. I knew she'd been bored and lonely since we'd moved here. Perhaps this would be one outlet for her. I thought I might have found one of my own.

"How was your walk?" She looked at me searchingly.

I had to think quickly. She, of course, knew nothing about the walk before this, and there was no need to tell her.

Well you see, I went looking for a boy I have a crush on, and then there's this horse on our land that I'm trying to get to know. . . .

No, probably not a good idea. Being an only child of protective parents suddenly seemed harsh. It hadn't occurred to me before, but this might prove difficult. After all, I'd barely been allowed to have a bicycle. What would they say to a horse? And I had no idea what the climate would be like regarding boys but had a feeling it would be challenging. *Good thing that's not likely to be an issue in the near future.*

Not allowing myself to dwell on that negative thought, I said, "I'm just enjoying the cool mornings and evenings. I don't go very far, but it's fun to explore a little."

Mom seemed to accept that. "Well, just be careful."

"I will, Mom," I said, not sure if I meant it. I had been careful all my life, but I was starting to feel like I hadn't been truly aware of things going on around me. My world was starting to open up and come alive, like a part of me was awakening for the first time. I wasn't sure, but as much as it worried and frightened me a little, I thought I liked it. *Careful* was once absolute in my life. I had a feeling it was going to be relative from now on.

I avoided thinking about Dave all evening and went to bed determined to *not* think of him at all. It took me a long time to get to sleep.

Morning seemed to come extra early again. Wasting no time lingering in bed or debating the pros and cons of my inevitable action, I went downstairs through the quiet, still cool house, grabbed an apple from the bowl, and headed out the back door. A sense of excitement gripped me, twisting my stomach and making my heart beat faster. It felt like I was on my way to a clandestine rendezvous with a secret lover, so of course Dave immediately leaped to mind. *Right . . . in your dreams.*

Pushing Dave as firmly to the back of my mind as I could, I continued to where I'd last seen my new friend. The food was gone; that was a good

sign. The creek burbled and splashed gently, and I went to stand as close to the water as I could without getting wet. Too wide to step over, I might have been able to jump over it with a running start—if I were any good at running.

I crouched down, experimentally sticking my finger in the water. It was freezing. I didn't know where the flow originated, but I would have assumed nothing could be that cold in this heat. I set a leaf on the water and watched it race away downstream. Then another. The air smelled and felt fresh, and it was incredibly peaceful here, just the sound of the creek and a few little birds rustling in the undergrowth.

I'd almost forgotten why I'd come when movement and sound to my right startled me. Upstream, the horse drank, ears constantly swiveling. He didn't look at me at all but seemed to gaze at something far across the stream.

"Hi," I said in the soft, low voice I had adopted for him. "I brought something for you."

I held the apple up. He continued to drink, but his eye swept over me briefly, then looked back over the stream as if he had more important things to think about. Something that had bothered me yesterday struck me again. A familiarity. Not quite *deja vu* but like a vague memory almost remembered. But that didn't make sense; I didn't know any horses, and I'd never been in a situation like this before.

When he finished drinking, his head lifted and he stood tall and aloof, gazing calmly at me as a king might take slight notice of an unknown, groveling peon.

"Did you like the apple and carrots?" I asked quietly, still holding out the apple I'd just brought.

He stretched his head out very slightly and moved his nose in my direction. Then he took a step toward me. My heart almost leaped out of my chest. He made the odd, almost beckoning movement again and took another step.

"What?" I asked, as if he would speak and answer me. "Do you want me to get up? Do you want me to roll the apple to you?" I stood up slowly and took a step toward him. He took a step back and turned his head away as if indicating his intention to leave. I stood still and he slowly turned back toward me. "What?" I asked again and laughed.

This time he definitely nodded his head. He wanted the apple, I was sure of it, but he wouldn't tolerate the peon to come close. The offering must be left like yesterday.

"Okay," I said, setting the apple on the ground, "but this is no way to treat an admirer."

He watched as I backed away. It became apparent that he wasn't going to make a move as long as I observed him, so I promised to see him later and walked home.

I spent most of the day working on the report and trying not to think too much about the horse. I tried to not think at all about Dave. The first two I accomplished quite successfully. The last—not so much. The printed pages I took notes from had been found by him. The book was from the library where he'd come to check on me in the stacks. Worst of all, my eyes kept straying to the list I'd made, still sitting on my desk.

Stupid list. It was a source of both delight and despair. Seen in an optimistic light, I could *almost* persuade myself that *maybe* he really liked me. You know, *liked* me. But then reality—who I was and my relation to the rest of the world—would invade and burst the happy, almost rose-colored bubble. Then I'd catch myself practically wallowing in dejection and looking for even more ways to put myself down. That just wasn't healthy, even if the things I thought about myself were true.

I was thinking something had to give when my phone rang, buzzing and threatening to leap off the dresser where I'd left it. My first ridiculous hope, of course, was that Dave had somehow acquired my number for some unfathomable reason. That proved my pitiful state of mind. I had mixed feelings when I saw Brenda's name.

"Hello?"

"Allison! It's Brenda! What are you doing?"

"Working on a report," I said, thinking the familiar voice was oddly disquieting, not comforting as I had thought it would be. "I'm just about done, though."

"Ugh, homework has been the worst ever, right?"

"Well, actually I haven't—"

"Have you made any friends yet?"

"Yes," I said enthusiastically. "There are some really nice—"

"Me too! I can't believe it. Well, I guess I can. I mean, we have so much in common. They're so cool and everyone knows them. We've already done so much together, like shopping, and almost every day after school we go somewhere different. " She chatted on and on for what seemed an eternity.

I got the distinct impression that these friends of hers were what Robin would probably call snobs—girls that cared mainly about popularity and one-upping each other with their parents' credit cards. I couldn't see Brenda quite fitting in with that kind of crowd, though I knew she had always admired people like that. She had also left the private school we'd both attended and now went to one of the more affluent high schools in westside Los Angeles. From what I was hearing, I didn't think it was a good move.

"...And there's this boy. He really likes me and asked me out on Friday. He said he'd been watching me since the start of school. Can you believe it? I almost can't! His name's Trevor. He's a sophomore on the football team. He's so good looking. And he drives!" She went on to describe her date in great detail, which involved her going to the movies with him and a bunch of other kids after school, and then getting pizza. It sounded like fun, but I wasn't jealous. "I'll e-mail you a picture when I get one. Is your Internet working yet?"

"No, not yet, but Mom says—"

"So, are there any cute guys in Hicksville?"

I wasn't offended by her constantly cutting me off; she was just being Brenda. Nothing new there. She'd never been very interested in anything I'd had to say. But something about her tone of voice and the assumption it implied, along with the derogatory name, made me angry. Images of my new school, my teachers, my town, and most importantly, the people I now hoped were my friends, passed through my mind. I seethed in silence.

"Allison?" She sounded almost worried at my lack of response. "I'm not too surprised if there's not. I mean, after all—"

"Brenda," I said, loudly and firmly, and waited until she was quiet. Then I continued in my normal voice, "Why did you say that? And the name of our town is Douglas. It's really nice here."

She was quiet for a moment, obviously surprised I would voice my feelings like that. I was surprised, too. "So, it sounds like you *do* like someone," she said.

"Maybe."

"Does he like you? Is he cute? How old is he? Does he play football or drive?"

"We're just friends," I said, carefully, "but he's very . . . attractive."

I suddenly realized I didn't want to discuss him. He wasn't just an object for comparison to me. How could she understand?

"Attractive, huh?" she said, sounding dubious.

I could picture her face as she tried to wrap her mind around the kind of guy she thought I might find attractive. Now I didn't want her to know exactly how cute he was.

"Is he into sports?" she asked.

I didn't even know. "He's pretty good at skateboarding. I think he might be into soccer. And track."

"Hmm. . . ." I pictured her eyes narrowing as she sized this up against her football player. "What does his dad do? Trevor's dad is a financial planner. He has some famous clients. I haven't been to his house . . . yet . . . but he described it and it sounds amazing."

"Dave's family owns a large cattle ranch," I said, thinking this should impress her, and then was mad at myself for even trying to.

"So he's, like, a cowboy?" she asked.

"Um, no . . . I mean . . . not really . . . at least . . ." I didn't know what to say. I'd never considered it before. I knew so little about him. Still, I didn't like the way she had said it. *And what if he is? That's pretty cool, right?*

"Does he drive?" she asked. She was starting to sound patronizing.

"He rides a motorcycle," I said with deep satisfaction. Let her make of that what she would.

"Hmm," she said, obviously comparing all the facts. I could imagine it wasn't as easy as she would like, my information being outside the box she was familiar with.

After a moment of silence, she asked, "So has he asked you out?"

"I told you . . . we're just friends." *At least, I think we qualify as friends.* I knew I sounded defensive but was unable to keep the edge out of my voice.

I wanted this conversation to end.

"So, basically, he doesn't really know you exist," she said, and I caught my breath at the meanness I thought I heard behind the words. "I mean, as a girl . . . you know. . . ."

Bam! Mean but true. She had made her last words sound lighter, but the damage was done. She had only voiced what I'd been saying over and over to myself and still not wanted to believe. I just hadn't put it into those

exact words. I felt myself shutting down in a way I never had before. Still, I felt I owed her, if not for real friendship, then at least for companionship when I'd had no other. I wouldn't be purposely rude to her.

"You may be right," I said, quietly.

"Don't feel bad, Allison. I'm sure you'll find someone, someday." This was said in a much kinder tone but still felt patronizing. "Maybe you just need to hang out with different people."

"Maybe," I said, not wanting to elaborate further with her.

There was no way she could understand. Our values were too different. I don't know why I'd never noticed it before. I didn't want to hear my new town and friends disrespected by anyone, especially someone who'd never seen or met them. But beyond that, though her opinion had been important to me once, now I didn't much care what she thought. Was I just fickle? Swept along with the closest current? Or was I, perhaps, actually developing a mind of my own? I wasn't sure, but the fact that I was even considering it was a good sign. It was unfortunate that along with the more individualistic thinking came this heightened awareness of my social deficiencies.

"Well, I better go. I've got stuff to get ready for tomorrow," she said, back to her normal Brenda tone.

"Yes, me too," I said, glad to end the call.

"Talk to you later then," she said. "Bye."

"Bye."

I sat thinking over our exchange. So much was different, I couldn't quite process it. At one time I would have agreed, almost unthinkingly, with anything she said, would even have changed my own preferences to conform to hers. But no longer. I was starting to like my new town, school, and home very much. And the new people in my life were, I suspected, a positive influence on me. I was noticing and thinking about things in a way I never had before and, in spite of the angst it added to my life, I was beginning to think it was a good thing.

But I also felt she was probably right about one thing. Dave couldn't be interested in me; not the way I wanted him to be. He couldn't think of me as I thought of him. It seemed idiotic to even consider it. Perhaps I was getting a little more attention than some of the other girls in his entourage, but that was probably due to my being new and hanging out with Robin. If I wasn't there, I doubted that he would miss me.

My eyes fell on the list again. Folding it closed, I shoved it in the bottom drawer of my desk. I was going to have to do something drastic to remove myself from this group I'd fallen into, and with it, Dave's presence. If I didn't, I was sure I would end up hurt even more and would look like a complete fool. I probably already did.

I wasn't even sure why it mattered. I'd never cared much about what I looked like to others, and I was used to being thought nothing, a mouse, a dork at best. It wasn't that I hadn't cared what people thought, but that I'd lived beyond it, refused to think about it, and not let it hurt or affect me emotionally too much. At least, not since elementary school. I certainly couldn't remember ever blushing, a new and unwanted development.

It was unfortunate that most of my knowledge of social interaction had come from movies and television. But the only scenarios I'd ever seen like the one I found myself in now, always ended badly: the dowdy, "different" girl gets taken advantage of and purposely hurt, or she unintentionally makes a complete fool of herself and still gets hurt. I didn't want to be either of those girls. I was more certain than ever that Dave would be very up-front about it if he liked someone, or if he wanted to deal with somebody, he'd be in their face. The best thing for me, probably, would be to avoid him completely. It would only drive me crazy to be around him; I wouldn't be able to stop wishing.

Coming to terms with this idea was difficult though. Dave was important. How I felt about him was important. What *he* thought was vitally important. And it mattered so much to me that my throat constricted, and my eyes filled with tears just thinking about him. It hurt to think of not being around him, of not being close enough to see the sun reflecting off his hair, of not hearing his gentle voice when he talked to me, of not feeling his soft brown eyes resting on me or looking into mine—however disinterested he really was. But it would hurt even more to be nothing to him and have no chance of being more. It would hurt too much when, inevitably, he'd lose interest in the dorky new girl and his attention would turn to someone else.

I came to a decision. It wouldn't be easy, physically or emotionally, but my resolve was building. I would avoid him. Completely. I mostly saw him at lunch or if I went to my locker. I could live without my locker; I'd just carry everything. At lunch, I'd eat in the cafeteria with Melanie and get to know her better, as I wanted. And no loitering after school. It could be done, and

he'd probably barely notice. After a couple of days, he'd probably forget all about me.

By this time tears were streaming down my cheeks and I wiped at them angrily. Feeling sorry for myself wasn't going to help. The pearl-gray walls of my room, which usually made it feel light and airy, seemed to close in around me. So even though it was still early afternoon, I went downstairs, grabbed a bag of carrots, and told my mother I was going for a walk. I managed to do it without her seeing my face.

The heat hit me as soon as I stepped outside—stifling, smothering—then again full force as I stepped off the back porch and into the sun. Shade was scarce along the dirt road, so I walked as quickly as I could, past the enclosure and into the shade of the trees along the stream. Here I sat and rested my forehead on my knees, my eyes closed. In a moment, I was sobbing into my arms crossed over my knees. And I didn't care. It took me by surprise but felt good too, so I let the floodgates burst open. There was no one there to hear me, see me, or think me the foolish, hopeless dork I thought myself.

When the tears finally subsided, I felt very calm. A small breeze had begun blowing, cooling my hot, wet face, stirring the loose strands of hair around it, and making the surrounding leaves rustle slightly. I didn't want to think about why I had cried or what it meant. I couldn't even remember the last time I had really cried like that. I never felt that strongly about anything. Or maybe I just hadn't allowed myself to feel that strongly, until now. I was different than before, even if my mother couldn't see it or Brenda hear it on the phone. The barriers I'd had in place—holding things, people, feelings at a distance, enforcing a sense of indifference on myself—were falling. I was beginning to see how much my life had lacked because I hadn't wanted or was afraid to feel. I wasn't sure I could handle it. What if I burst into tears when I *wasn't* alone? I was already dreading the embarrassment.

I tried to relax and turn my suddenly overactive imagination off, to enjoy the breeze and soft sounds around me. I found it soothing, comforting, and I wondered at myself. One short week ago I would have been too afraid of the unknown to wander this far.

I don't know how long I sat there. It had probably been a long time, but I didn't want to abandon my little parallel universe, this place where I unexpectedly felt at peace, at home, and where anything seemed possible.

Then I heard a rustle and there he was: salvation. He stood about five yards away, an expectant expression on his beautiful face. My heart lifted and I smiled.

Magical.

Chapter Six

Just Falling

"You're early," I said

He came no closer but lowered his head, his upper lip moving through the leaves and loose debris on the ground as if looking for something. His ears angled toward me, only occasionally flicking in other directions, and he watched me closely. I couldn't help laughing. He looked like he was pretending to do one thing while wanting to do something else.

"You don't fool me," I said more severely. "I know what you want."

I opened the little bag of carrots and threw one toward him. He took a step and lifted it delicately, crunched, and then looked expectantly at me again. I put a few in my hand and held it out toward him. His nose reached toward me, his nostrils flaring gently, but he wouldn't come any closer.

"Fine," I said. "We can do it your way . . . for now."

This strange relationship was so surprising and pleasant; it was okay if we continued in this way. It seemed like we had all the time in the world. I wished I felt the same way about Dave, content to just be somewhere in his general vicinity. But I didn't. I didn't want to be just another satellite orbiting around him, a peripheral connection at best. That revelation surprised me too. Was I now thinking too highly of myself? Confusion and misery threatened to take over again and I wiped at my eyes.

"Here you go," I said through tears I couldn't stop. I poured the rest of the carrots on the ground and backed away. "See you tomorrow."

I'd been gone a long time. It was almost dark and Mom voiced her concern. Then she saw my face and asked if I was all right.

"Of course." I wondered why she asked.

"Okay," she said, still looking anxious. "Well, you better get cleaned up for dinner."

My reflection in the bathroom mirror gave me a shock. Not only were my eyes red but my hair was a mess and my face was filthy from dirt smeared through tears. I looked like a little kid who'd been roughed up on the playground. I got cleaned up and rejoined my mother.

"Your eyes are all red," she said. "Have you been crying? What's going on?"

"Nothing, Mom," I lied. "I just got some soap in my eyes. I'm fine."

She obviously wasn't convinced but didn't pursue it.

I tried to keep my mind off the subject torturing me, off the words Brenda had said, and off what I thought I knew to be true. Before, I had wondered how I'd get through the weekend, waiting until Monday to see Dave again. Now I wished that Monday would never come so I wouldn't have to deal with him at all—seeing or *not* seeing him.

I was able to avoid my locker first thing Monday morning. I didn't want Dave or his brother to help me.

Robin said, "Hey," when she came into class and took the seat across from me. The boy who'd sat there before gave her an odd look as he entered but took her vacated seat instead. She asked if I had worked on the report and we talked about it until class started. We'd have to get together sometime to organize our information, but I didn't want to risk any more chance meetings at public places.

"Why don't you come over to my house tomorrow?" I asked. "We don't have Internet service, but our computer's good."

Robin looked very pleased and agreed. I was sure Mom would be happy too.

A shock awaited me in PE. Everyone was talking excitedly about track testing, which began today. A few people stopped talking when they saw me and there was some whispering again. A thick wave of dread dragged over

me and I felt like crawling out of the locker room toward the field. *How on earth had I forgotten? See . . . that's what comes of being obsessed with—*

No! I refused to let my mind go there.

The boys were gathered on one side of the track while the girls were on the other. Apparently we were starting with the thing I was worst at—running. *Good. We'll get this disappointment over right away. Then they'll realize I have no skills and I can be invisible again.*

Coach had us stretching and warming up our muscles. This I could do. If warm-ups had been an event, I could have competed with the best of them. I waved at Melanie, sitting on the lowest seat of the closest bleachers. She waved back and I think she smiled, but it was hard to tell without my glasses. At least I could look forward to lunch with her today.

The track circled the football and soccer field. Girls were running the hundred-meter first while the boys ran the two-hundred. We stood in rough lines of five abreast and took our turns sprinting down the track. I managed to position myself in the middle of the center line.

As the people in front of me drew closer and closer to the starting line, I felt sicker and sicker. I hated doing anything that caused me to stand out or be watched. Just watching the other girls made me feel nervous, and it was better to pretend the boys weren't there at all, though their loud prompting, jeering, and cheering was hard to block out. At least I was sure nobody on that side of the field would be watching me.

The girls all seemed so confident and ran as if they'd been training for the Olympics. When my turn came, I felt defeated before I'd started. My brain wrestled with instructing my legs to pump faster, my feet to push myself forward harder, my arms to *just stay out of the way, darn it!*—while the gap between myself and the other runners widened and widened.

By the time I reached the finish line, the others had lost interest in my progress. I felt humiliated and this was the shortest race! How much worse was it going to be as the distances lengthened?

There were different girls to run against by the time I returned to the lines. They were all shorter than me, which wasn't unusual, but a couple of them looked at least *potentially* as nonathletic as me. At first I actually pulled ahead of those girls, and I was beginning to think I might come out of this one not looking too bad. Then the inevitable happened. I don't know whether in midair or upon landing, but something gave in my ankle and I almost went to the ground, just barely catching my balance. The other girls ran past me and I limped off the track.

Coach came over and asked, "Do you need ice?"

"No, I think I just have weak ankles."

She looked a little disgusted but told me to go sit out the remainder of the class. I gratefully headed toward Melanie, not far away.

"What happened?"

"I can't run," I said, matter-of-factly. "I never have been able to. My ankles twist easily."

We talked for a couple of minutes, my gaze finally wandering toward where the boys were. Everything was a bit fuzzy without my glasses. I wasn't comfortable wearing them during strenuous activities, and though I was mostly farsighted, my astigmatism caused a general blurriness anyway. Even so, my attention was caught by a figure taking his place at the starting line. The signal sounded and he sprinted down the track.

No way! My eyes were glued to him as he easily took the lead and won his heat. He began the walk back to the start and seemed to be scanning the track as if looking for something—or some*one*.

A chill ran down my spine and I desperately wished I was invisible. Then I chastised myself for even imagining he would notice me. I was trying to look away, but my eyes insisted on turning back to him. He was looking around now in earnest as if he had actually lost something. I was vaguely aware of Melanie asking a question, but I didn't hear her. Dave, looking amazing to me—in spite of blurriness and PE clothes—had turned again and now appeared to be looking directly at us. I looked away.

"Do you know that boy?" asked Melanie, having noticed the object of my preoccupation and his apparent focus on us.

"No. That is," I amended, not wanting to lie to her, "not really."

I was determined to downplay any connection for my own sake. My resolve was fixed. I was quite sure it was. Whatever his interest over here was, it couldn't really be me. I was thankful that the shower bell rang just then and that the girls' locker room was close by.

"Are you eating in the cafeteria today?" I asked.

Melanie laughed gently. "Every day. I'll wait while you change," she said, following me into the locker room.

I was nervous as we limped out together. I looked around quickly to make sure the coast was clear, but Dave was nowhere in sight. I was both relieved and despondent.

See, I told you.

My ankle was already feeling better, but I couldn't completely put my weight on it. Melanie and I found that we were limping in rhythm and were giggling about it by the time we joined the cafeteria line.

My radar immediately picked up on Dave, walking across the quad with two pretty blond girls I had seen in the lunch group before. I wasn't sure of their names, but he was talking and they were hanging on every word. I didn't think he'd seen me and was sighing with mixed relief and grief again when he looked straight at me. I turned away quickly, back to Melanie, knowing I was blushing. My stomach was tying in knots. From her expression, I was pretty sure she had caught the exchange, but she said nothing. Again I appreciated her quiet, unassuming nature and tried to focus on buying lunch, though I doubted I could eat.

I grabbed some milk and an apple, putting the latter in my backpack for later. It wasn't for me. I tried to hold up my side of the conversation but found myself woefully preoccupied with the fact that I needed to empty my locker before the next class. Without help, I wasn't going to get into it, but I wouldn't ask for any. My stomach was churning more and more until I finally excused myself, wanting to get there well before the bell rang.

There was no sign of Dave as I struggled with the combination and lock several times. Then someone was standing next to me, startling me so much it made me jump.

"Are you all right?" Chris asked, sounding surly, trademark scowl firmly in place.

"Yes. Fine. Thanks." I tried to sound happy.

He wasn't looking at me, as usual, but the scowl deepened. His eyes flitted to mine once, then immediately away as he opened the locker door. Then he walked away, as enigmatic as ever. I couldn't help shaking my head a little.

What a confusing guy! Was he asking out of general curiosity? Or because I hadn't been at the tables at lunch? Had someone noticed my limp? Or had his brother said something? I was still sure that Dave wasn't the kind of person to send someone else to do or ask things for him. But why would Chris care? I was convinced that he wasn't that observant.

At least everything was out of my locker; I wouldn't need their help with it anymore. Idiotically, tears welled up and I walked quickly to English, glad I didn't see anyone I knew on the way.

Later as I sat down in Study Hall, Robin said, "Hey, where were you at lunch?"

"I was eating with Melanie," I said, trying to sound normal. "You know, that girl from Friday after school." Robin looked at me blankly. Apparently she didn't remember. "I don't think she knows a lot of people, so I want to eat with her sometimes."

Robin seemed to accept that, and I was determined to say nothing more even if she didn't. Where and with whom I ate lunch was my business, right? *This is me, being assertive. Amazing.*

We said goodbye after class and I retreated hastily to the parking lot. I avoided looking around. I'd had all the chance encounters I could handle for one day and I couldn't let Dave's—or Chris'—curiosity foster any ridiculous fantasies. Hopefully tomorrow would be easier. The less time I had to think and brood the better.

At home, the distraction of intermittent conversation and the motion and noise of my mother busy around the kitchen helped to keep my mind focused away from what was tormenting me while I did homework. It would have been harder to work in my room, where my thoughts would more likely dwell on the forbidden.

Mom was in a really good mood, having gone to the public pool again before picking me up. She had met a couple of women there also waiting to pick kids up from school, and she had enjoyed their company. She was also pleased when I asked about Robin coming after school the next day, as I had thought she would be. I was looking forward to it too. I was considering telling Robin about the horse but hadn't quite made up my mind. There was still the issue of information winding up in Dave's possession and, now more than ever, I didn't want that happening.

"Why don't you invite her to dinner too," said Mom. "Then we can take her home later."

"Sounds great," I said, and then tried to concentrate on algebra.

When she began preparing dinner, I said I was going to take a break, grabbed the apple I'd put in my backpack without her seeing, and slipped out the back door. It was still early, but I needed to get out of the house to move my body and clear my mind. After I'd crossed the cattle guard and walked around the corral, I stopped, amazed. Past the enclosure the dirt road turned into more of a wide trail, and there stood the horse right in the middle of it as if waiting for me. He looked almost anxious, the folds above his eyes drawn in as if in worry.

"What's the matter?" I asked softly. "Did you think I wasn't coming?"

It occurred to me that I'd seen him—and brought him treats—the past two mornings. Had he been disappointed when I didn't come this morning? Had he missed me? Had he been waiting for me all day? We stood regarding each other for a while as if waiting for the other to make the first move. I was holding the apple behind my back and I didn't think he had seen it.

"Will you let me get closer?" I finally asked, slowly taking a step toward him.

He stood his ground.

Another step.

Still there.

Two steps.

He bobbed his head a couple of times as if saying, "Get on with it!"

Two more steps. He was just as skinny as the first day I'd seen him, but more gold gleamed through the dusty patches of his coat where the sun touched him. He turned and took two steps away. He was now almost sideways as I faced him. Stepping forward, I reached toward his shoulder. He moved away again but then stopped and turned his head, looking at me.

This continued for a while, I reaching toward him, itching to touch his tawny coat, but he always stayed one step ahead, just barely out of reach. It was like a game of chess, the king teasing and staying one step ahead of a pawn. He had moved into the trees now, closer to the stream, the sun dappling his coat where it filtered through. I wondered if he was leading me there for a purpose or just circling back to more familiar territory. Or was he actually playing some sort of game with me? He no longer looked worried.

I finally stood still and held the apple out to him. He seemed to consider for a moment, then bobbed his head as he had done before.

"Okay fine, Your Highness," I said, setting the apple at my feet.

I backed away about five feet and waited. He waited too, looking at me as if he expected me to do something more.

"I don't know what you want, but I'm going home now, okay? I'll see you tomorrow."

I began walking away, but about ten feet farther I looked back. He walked casually forward, picking up and crunching the apple. Bits of fruit dribbled out the sides of his mouth and I laughed. He looked so cute. I continued to walk away, looking back until I could no longer see him.

On the way back to the house, my heart felt considerably lighter than it had on the walk out to see him. I tried to hold on to the feeling through the evening, forcing myself to picture his beautiful face every time another, even more adored visage came to mind. I still found it hard to eat and fall asleep.

Tuesday was horrible. I managed to avoid Dave, but it seemed like light had gone out of my life. I felt dull and listless all day, barely able to keep up gentle conversation with Melanie at lunch and feeling awkward around Robin during Health. She seemed to be watching me, waiting for me to say something, which didn't help. It surprised me that she didn't confront me in some way as reserve and restraint didn't seem her style, but if she wondered about anything, she kept it to herself.

The only time I saw Dave was while walking to the car after school. Unfortunately, Mom had parked in the same vicinity as Chris and it would have been hard to miss him. He stood by the open passenger door of Chris' truck, looking in our direction. Chris stood on the other side leaning against the truck's bed and talking to a couple of other guys. I managed to keep my gaze from lingering but caught the nods exchanged between Dave and Robin. Then they were in the truck and pulling away. My stomach was one big knot and it didn't go away all evening.

Robin and I worked well together. She had a mind for organizing facts and a no-nonsense approach that kept us on track. I had the more creative task of layout, illustrations, and text editing. Robin loved our computer and wanted to make colored graphs and charts. I told her to go for it, glad that it kept her attention off me. When we had everything ready to put together, we took a break. Mom had made iced tea so we took some out onto the back porch. I still hadn't made up my mind about disclosing my secret.

We sat in companionable silence for a while, then she said, "Are you all right?"

I was a little startled. Someone else had just asked that. "Of course. Why?"

"You just seem kind of sad and, I don't know . . . out of it."

"No, I'm fine. Really," I said, trying to sound and look sincere. This was one topic not open to discussion. Time to redirect. "Hey, do you know if there are any wild horses around here?"

Her brows rose. "You mean like mustangs?"

"Yes, exactly."

"No," she said. "Not that I've ever heard of. But I guess there could be. Why?"

I looked at her then looked away, deliberating. Did I dare? Thursday we'd be completely done with our report. Were we real friends or just project buddies? The way things stood, I couldn't plan on spending much time with her at school, except in class, as she would probably be with Dave. But I couldn't tell her that. I had severe doubts about trusting her with anything, but without a show of trust would our friendship survive? I decided it was worth taking the risk. I really liked her and didn't want to lose her.

"Remember the first day of school," I asked. "In Algebra?"

She looked wary. "Yeah."

"You didn't like me."

"You were staring at me," she said, defensively.

"I thought you looked really cool," I said. "I didn't mean to stare."

She looked a little self-conscious. "Seriously?"

"Yes. What did you think of me?"

Now she looked *very* self-conscious. "I thought you were a soc. A snob."

"I'm not sure what you mean, but why did you think that?"

She shrugged. "The way you were dressed. The way you looked. The way you were looking at me, or the way I *thought* you were looking at me. I thought you were one of those country club bi—" I could see her mentally changing gears again, "girls." I was surprised at her admission and reasoning but let it go.

"What made you change your mind?"

"Dave," she said, looking sidelong at me as if to gauge my reaction.

That took me completely by surprise and my heart skipped a beat at the sound of his name. Though I felt it was wandering perilously close to forbidden territory, I had to know. "How?"

"After we got paired up in Health, I was complaining about it and he asked me to point you out. He said he thought you were okay and that I should give you a chance." She shrugged again. "Then he wanted to meet you."

I wanted to ask why, but I was already blushing so badly and didn't trust how it might sound. Besides, I already knew why. *He likes to help the underdog. He just feels sorry for me. He recognized me for the friendless dork I am . . . was . . . whatever. Shut up and don't think about it anymore.*

"Yes, I've noticed that you're close. You seem to tell each other everything," I said carefully. I avoided her eyes for now, trying to will my color to normalize and my voice to not betray me.

She looked a little smug. "Yeah, that's true. We've been best friends since third grade. I told you that, didn't I?"

"Yes, you did," I said, smiling. "What do you think of me now?" I asked, not as shyly as I would have done just a few days ago. I really wanted to know.

She gave me a playful look. "I think you're kind of weird . . . but you're growing on me."

Then she smiled and laughed as I hadn't seen her do before. A warm glow spread through me. I felt happy in a way I couldn't ever remember feeling. *A real friend? Another first.*

"I wanted to tell you something, but I don't want anyone else to know." I looked back and held her eyes with mine. "Not *anyone.*"

She looked uncomfortable as if I might ask her to do something life-threatening or illegal. She finally said, "Okay."

"I think I should show you," I said. "Wait a sec."

I jumped up and went into the kitchen. My mother wasn't around, so I grabbed an apple from the bowl and returned to Robin.

"Come on," I said, stepping off the porch and waving her to follow.

We walked down the dirt road, over the cattle guard, and around the corral.

"Whoa," said Robin, stopping in her tracks as she noticed the enclosure. "What's that for?"

"I don't know. It's been here a long time, I think." I put my finger to my lips and waved her on again. We made our way down to the stream and found a place to wait.

"What are we waiting for?" she whispered.

"You'll see . . . I think," I answered. I wondered whether the presence of another person would matter. I hoped not.

We didn't have to wait long. A slight rustle of trees and there he was. He acknowledged our presence with a bob of his head then proceeded to the stream. I waited for Robin's reaction. It never occurred to me that she would see anything other than what I saw.

Her mouth hung open for a moment, then she looked at me, her eyebrows raised. "Wow. That's a really ugly horse."

I felt stunned. "What? How on earth can you say that he's ugly?"

She shrugged her shoulders. "I think he's ugly. His head's too big, his neck's too thick, and he's a mess. I don't think his conformation's very good."

"Con-fer . . . what?"

"The way he's put together. He's too big in some places and too small in others. Where'd he come from?"

"That's the thing . . . I don't know. He won't let me get too near him, but he's not afraid of me."

Robin was quiet as she contemplated the horse. "Who else knows about him? Your mom?"

I shook my head. "You're the only person I've told, so I doubt if anyone else knows. Or if they do, I guess they don't care. He looks like he's been loose for a while."

"We should tell Dave and Chris," she said bluntly.

"No! I mean . . . *please* don't," I pleaded with her.

She frowned disapprovingly. "Why not? I don't understand."

"You promised!" I threw at her, a little more vehemently than I meant to. She looked surprised. Then, more controlled, "I trusted you."

She was still frowning but shrugged. "Definitely weird," she muttered.

"Thanks," I said, feeling a little of the earlier glow return.

She rolled her eyes and shook her head.

"We should probably head back," I said, standing up and placing the day's offering at my feet. The horse raised his head and looked at us, water dribbling from his mouth.

"Do you really think he's ugly?" I asked as we walked back.

Robin laughed, shaking her head again.

We had dinner, finished putting our display board together, and printed out the report.

"What time do you have to be home, Robin?" asked Mom. "We can take you whenever you need us to."

"Oh . . . thanks, but I have a ride," she answered.

I froze. "You have a ride?"

"Yeah. Chris is picking me up when he gets off work at seven. Is that okay?"

My heart started beating rather fast and my mouth went dry, but as her words sank in I forced myself to relax. "Does he know where I live?" I asked as casually as I could.

"Oh, I'm sure Dave told him where it is," she said. I noticed Mom's curious glance. "He'll call if he's not sure."

This was not that comforting to me. About half an hour later we heard someone pull into the driveway. She picked up the printed report and thanked my mother for letting her come over and for dinner.

Mom smiled and said, warmly, "Anytime, Robin."

Leaving the poster board on the dining room table—it would be my task to bring it to school on Thursday—I followed her to the door, my heart thumping a little too hard. But my fears were unfounded; Chris was alone.

"Robin," I said, loud enough for her to hear as she approached the truck, "remember . . . you promised."

She looked back over her shoulder and rolled her eyes.

Wednesday I awoke feeling not quite myself, though I was beginning to doubt I knew who I was anymore. At school, I went straight to Algebra and waited nervously by the locked door until the teacher allowed me to go in.

PE was a nightmare. We had to choose at least three field events to attempt and be assessed at and run the four-hundred-meter. Boys and girls took turns running heats for the latter and lined up in two ragged lines inside the track. The field events, except the long jump, were being held on the lower fields where the baseball diamonds were. I didn't see Dave there anywhere and assumed he was running, so chose the field to avoid him. Deciding to attempt what I thought would be the least hazardous events, at least to myself, I chose javelin, high jump, and long jump. The latter was by the track, so I stayed away from that for now.

Javelin was kind of fun, and I was able to propel the thing away from me. I doubted whether I would have been able to do that with the shot, and I was afraid I might have killed someone with the discus. In spite of comments

from my now disenchanted classmates like, "You throw like a girl"—*Duh*—I at least acquitted myself without profound embarrassment. The high jump was easy. I just jumped, knocking the bar down easily all three times. That *was* the object, right?

Having no excuse to linger on the lower fields, I headed up to the track and joined the group waiting for the long jump. I hoped I could also fail this relatively quickly and harmlessly. Trying to keep my eyes and as much of my mind as possible on the event before me, I watched how the others prepared and approached the jump, and struggled to not think about where Dave might be.

Melanie, sitting on the bleachers as before, no longer wore a cast. I pointed to my leg and then pointed at her. She nodded, smiling. Then she picked up the crutches lying beside her and frowned—something I'd never seen her do.

The line for the jump was fairly short and in no time it was my turn. I hoped the bell would ring, allowing me to postpone the inevitable for two more days, but no such luck. I tried to judge my distance and keep my feet forward, but I still jumped too soon and landed badly without covering much ground at all. I fell hard onto my knees then down onto my chest. The sand was much softer than the surrounding ground would have been, I'm sure, but it still knocked all the air out of me. I was just glad my face hadn't slammed into it as well.

It took me a few moments to collect myself and push myself upright. When I did, scuffed but expensive-looking running shoes attached to deeply tanned and leanly muscular legs stood right in front of me.

No! Please, no!

I didn't dare look up any farther, a familiar reaction already making my scalp tingle. A brown, strong-looking, and oddly calloused hand was held open in front of my face, and I felt I had to accept it though I knew it was going to cost me dearly.

Clambering gracelessly to my feet with the offered help, I had to look, just to ascertain that it was, indeed, who I thought it was. My eyes met soft brown. I thought he looked concerned but a spark of humor lurked, as if waiting to see how I would react to my humiliation and ready to laugh if I was.

I wasn't. In fact, I could barely mumble, "Thank you," and look away before tears clouded my eyes. Anything else that might have been done or said between us was denied by the shower bell, and I walked sadly and gratefully away, not daring to look at him again.

What's the matter with me? I was seriously considering the possibility of mental illness because of my growing instability. More than ever I was convinced that being around Dave was going to mean personal pain and depression, and that it was getting harder and harder to hide it. I didn't think I could change the way I felt about him, but I was equally sure he'd never change how he felt about me either. He was always going to see me as a klutz or a weakling that he could give aid to. And that was always going to hurt.

Brenda was right. I needed to hang out with people more like myself. *Now if I could just find some.*

The rest of the day was like moving through a dense fog. The fact that it was incessantly sunny didn't help my mood at all. It was hard to pretend that I was all right. I spent lunchtime with Melanie. She acted as if she didn't notice and, though she was normally so quiet, kept the conversation going in such a way that I rarely had to actively participate. Later I couldn't remember what she'd said but was convinced that her strategy was for my benefit. And, as Robin had seemed so forthright so far, I was amazed that she tolerated my abstraction and didn't demand to know what was wrong. She looked at me oddly in study hall a few times, though.

My mother dropped a bombshell on me later. She was so excited that she blurted it out as soon as I got in the car. She had been going to the pool every day for an hour or two before picking me up and had become acquainted with the afternoon lifeguard. That lady, Jasmine, was pregnant—*very* pregnant—and needed to take leave sooner than she had thought. She had noticed how well Mom swam, that she seemed to enjoy being there every day, and had discovered that she had been a pool lifeguard when I was younger. She asked Mom if she would come to work there.

"It would give me something to do and people to talk to. What do you think?"

"That's great, Mom," I said absently.

"The thing is, it means I would be working when you get off school." She hesitated and glanced at me. "I wouldn't get home until after six o'clock. You'd have to take the school bus home unless you want to walk to the pool."

"That's fine. I can take the bus." My brain was barely processing the information.

Whatever. I'm glad she's got something to look forward to.

When we got home, I retreated to my daily tryst as soon as possible. The sound of the stream soothed me and a cool breeze caressed my skin as I waited. I allowed myself to think about *him*—perhaps I could get it out of my system and behave normally tonight—but refused to let myself cry, much as I wanted to. I was actually pretty fed up with and ashamed of myself but seemed unable to help it. I was honestly doing the best I could.

When the horse showed up, I was relieved. I'd begun to think of him as *Gold*, but when I spoke to him, I usually called him something sarcastic like *Your Lordship* or *Your Highness* as that's how he seemed to behave. We played our game of almost-tag again, I moving toward him and he staying just out of reach like a mirage, a skyline never quite reached. As he moved in and out of the shade, the sun glittered and glowed off the cleaner patches of his body. I still thought he was gorgeous.

It was difficult to eat at all that night and in spite of being physically and emotionally exhausted, I couldn't sleep.

Thursday was a marathon of torture. Our Health class presentation went okay, though I found it hard to concentrate. Robin saved us by taking charge and doing most of the talking—not exactly how we had planned it. Several times during class she looked like she wanted to say or ask something of me but didn't. I never once caught sight of Dave but was nervous about it all day, which caused a knot in the pit of my stomach. I did see Chris as I walked to the cafeteria at lunch. I couldn't begin to interpret how he looked at me, but I pretended I hadn't seen him, feeling like a traitor.

Adding insult to injury, I had to take the bus home. I was jostled, poked, and stared at by all manner of kids. And someone screamed in my ear, causing the driver to stop the bus and glare at me as she delivered a lecture on bus rules. By the time we reached the end of my road, I felt raw.

I went straight out to find Gold. Finding a dry place near the stream, I sat down to wait for him, and though it was almost impossible to keep tears from welling up, I refused to give in to them completely.

I didn't feel like playing when he finally showed up but was comforted by his presence. At one point he seemed to get annoyed or perhaps worried that I had neither played our game nor given him his treat, and he stepped close enough to touch my head with his nose. I held my breath as he towered over me, blowing softly, and remained sitting with my arms around my legs and my forehead on my knees. I figured, if he trampled me, at least I'd be out of my misery. Instead, he pushed me sideways just hard enough to knock me over into the dirt. Now I was covered in dust but unhurt.

"Hey. Not so rough! Is this what you want, sir?" I held out the apple I'd brought for him.

He then amazed me by reaching forward and gently taking it from my hand. I stayed with him for a while but was back at the house by the time my mother got home. She took one look at me and insisted I tell her what the matter was.

"How did you get so dirty?" she asked, sounding cross. "And you need to eat more than apples and carrots to stay healthy and have energy, you know, though I'm glad you're at least eating those."

I had no clue how to respond so I said nothing. Unfortunately, she misread my silence as petulance and jumped to conclusions.

"Look, I'm sorry if you're unhappy that I'm working and that you had to ride the bus. I can always quit the job. We don't really need the money."

She looked very unhappy and I realized she was feeling guilty. Now I felt even more guilty than before.

"It's okay, Mom. Really!" I assured her. "I don't mind you working. I think it's great. And riding the bus isn't so bad. I've just . . ." I was dangerously close to tears again. "I've had a really hard couple of days."

Trying to stay focused and calm, I related my PE experiences to her—without mentioning Dave, of course. I figured it would suffice to explain my mood, and she did seem mollified. She knew I wasn't athletic. She even apologized for being short with me, but it just made me feel guilty again. I claimed weariness and retired for the night as soon as I could.

Friday, I woke up feeling like I'd just gone to sleep. I was tired and felt physically ill and emotionally drained. I considered staying home, but I knew I had to finish my jumps and run the four-hundred-meter. If I didn't do it today with everyone else, I'd be doing it next week. I decided I would rather fail these abysmally today than next week all by myself. *May as well get it over with. Then maybe I'll be able to get on with my life.*

The trouble was, I didn't believe that was possible. I was positive my feelings would never change. That thought settled depression squarely in place for the day, and I was sure things could only get worse. I also wondered if Robin would begin avoiding me now that our forced collaboration had ended. But she smiled as she came into Algebra, though she wasn't as chatty as she usually was.

Dave was nowhere to be seen by the track during PE, so I assumed he was on the lower fields. Both of my remaining attempts at the long jump ended in falls, and I felt irrationally sad that no strong, calloused hand appeared to help me up. Running the 400 seemed to take forever, and I wasn't surprised that I came in a solid last, holding my side and limping from a slightly turned ankle. When the bell rang, I was incredibly relieved and eventually joined Melanie in the relative safety of the cafeteria. Two classes to go until I could relax or fall to pieces, whichever it was going to be.

By the time I approached study hall, I was so exhausted and wrapped up in my own thoughts and misery that I was aware of absolutely nothing else. I was glad—yes, I was definitely *quite* sure I was *very* glad—that Dave seemed to have forgotten me. Hopefully by Monday I would have recovered my equilibrium somewhat and his lovely Quixotic gestures would find a new, more worthy and outwardly appreciative target. But I was desperately miserable too and prayed that no one would even try to talk to me. I didn't think I could hold it together without a concerted, uninterrupted effort.

I didn't realize my eyes were glued to the ground about a foot in front of my feet until I walked right into an arm barring entrance to the room. It startled me so badly that I immediately looked up, my heart hammering against my ribs.

"You should watch where you're going or you might get hurt," said a beloved voice.

No, no, no, no, no! my brain screamed. *Go bother someone else!* I didn't dare look into his eyes.

He took me by the upper arm and gently pulled me aside, away from the classroom.

No! Leave me alone! The words just weren't making it past my lips. I allowed myself to be led around the edge of the building, my pulse's speed undiminished.

"What the hell's going on?" His terminology was actually harsher than that, and I winced a little, but he'd said it gently. He continued, even more softly, "Why are you avoiding me? Are you mad at me? Did I do something that hurt you?"

That made me look up and my breath caught at his expression: such a mixture of concern, hurt, and confusion that I began to feel like I was melting.

At that moment I officially gave up the ghost of my resistance. He had won, and I finally admitted to myself exactly what was wrong. I had fallen a lot this week and had the scrapes and bruises to prove it, but this was the hardest fall of them all. I couldn't run and hide, and I wouldn't try to avoid it anymore. The bell rang and I did the only thing I was capable of doing at that moment.

I burst into tears.

Chapter Seven

A Wanted Man

I was too embarrassed to look at his face again, afraid to see disgust in his expression, but I was very aware of his whole body tensing as if ready to run. I wasn't surprised. If I were him, I'd want to run too.

"I'm sorry!" I managed to gasp, wishing I could keep my renegade emotions in check. My whole body was quivering, partly from emotional overload but also from just being so close to him, the focus of his attention.

"What the hell," he said, a little under his breath, then, "Hey . . . *Hey!*" softly but with some urgency. "People will think I'm being mean to you or something. What the . . . *heck's* the matter?"

"I'm sorry!" I breathed again, taking my glasses off and wiping my eyes. I didn't care what anybody besides Dave thought of me, but his words made me look around.

The bell had rung and the corridors were clear—except for Chris. He was leaning back against a wall not too far away. Had Dave brought him for moral support? That didn't seem likely. He met my gaze briefly, then looked away, scowl in place, jaw clenching.

He knows!

He pushed away from the wall and stalked off. If Dave really didn't know what was going on, would Chris tell him?

"I'm sorry," I said, finally getting a handle on the tears but not the shaking. "I've had a hard week. I guess I'm just," I looked at him, not connecting too deeply with his eyes in case he could read the truth in mine, "stressed out."

"I guess!" He laughed gently and sounded relieved. "Seems like you fell a little bit, huh?"

You have no idea. I knew he was referring to the physical realm, though, so I pretended to examine my knees and elbows, which bore proof of my ineptitude.

"A bit," I said.

He suddenly seemed to feel awkward—very uncharacteristically—and reached out as if to touch my arm again. Instead, he shoved both hands finger deep in the front pockets of his jeans.

"Uh . . . so . . . you're okay?"

I *was* okay. The tears had subsided and I wiped again at my face, but the shivering remained. Sheer nerves, probably.

"Yes, I'm okay."

"So . . . friends, right?" He sounded like he really wanted to be reassured.

I looked into his eyes—a fatal mistake. My shaking began to disappear as the melting progressed. Friendship it would be since that was what he offered. I would try to be satisfied with that and learn to live with disappointment. *Did friends drool over each other? I might have to watch that . . . probably a dead giveaway.*

"Yes, friends," I replied, trying to smile and putting my glasses back on.

"You better go to class," he said softly. "You're late."

I was able to laugh a little. "So are you."

He grinned and started to back away from me. "Hey, wait for me after class, okay?"

I was about to say, "Okay," when I remembered the bus. I'd been told it didn't wait for anybody. "I can't."

"Why not?" he asked, still moving backward.

I shook my head and moved toward my class. "I just can't," I said.

I couldn't bring myself to tell him I was riding the bus. I hadn't even told Robin, though I wasn't sure why.

Reaching the closed door, I remembered what I'd looked like the last time I'd given in to tears and decided to head for the nearest restroom instead. My face wasn't streaked with dirt but looked blotchy, and my eyes were a bit red.

Wonderful. At least he's seen you at your worst and still wants to know you. It could be worse.

I splashed cold water on my face and cleaned up the best I could, then headed back to class, glad it was just study hall.

"Miss Anderson," Mr. Payne said. "Thank you for deciding to join us this fine Friday afternoon. We thought you must have found something more enjoyable to do."

Every eye in the room was now firmly on me. I was sure my reaction was appropriate.

Note to self: find a way to circumvent blush response. Soon!

Robin's eyebrow quirked as I sat down next to her.

"Sooooo . . . ?" she whispered—an all-encompassing question.

"Sooooo . . . what?" I whispered back. I wasn't sure what to say.

"Look, something's been wrong with both of you all week. Did you get it worked out?"

I smiled, my heart skipping a beat or two. *Both* of us? He'd been affected too? Thinking of Dave now—what he had said and how he had looked—caused the amazing warm glow to spread through me again. Acceptance. Friendship. *Definitely magical.* I smiled again.

Robin's eyes opened wide. "Oh my god!" she almost hissed. "He asked you out, didn't he?"

"Don't be silly," I whispered back. "Dave doesn't date girls. Remember?"

She caught her breath and for a moment I thought she looked a little sick. "He *did*, didn't he?" she breathed.

I felt bad for making her doubt.

"No. Really, no. We had a . . . a misunderstanding. That's all. Friends. Just friends."

She looked relieved and shook her head. "Good. That would just be weird."

I wasn't sure whether to feel worried or offended. "Mmm . . . probably. Would *you* go out with him?" It seemed like a fair question.

"Hell, no" she whispered back. "That would be even weirder."

Good. I wanted to ask why but still felt emotionally shaky; it might be better not knowing.

After class I was torn: stay and wait for Dave and figure out how to get home later, or chicken out and make a dash for the bus? A part of me was in denial that our *tête-à-tête* had actually taken place. I couldn't quite believe that after all my agonizing and depression this week, I could suddenly feel so lighthearted and hopeful. *And I want to see him again already, but. . . .*

When the bell rang, I found out what a coward I was. I grabbed my stuff, said, "See you Monday," to Robin, and left. Once on the bus, I felt like an idiot and tried to talk myself into getting back off. It was safety versus adventure and I kicked myself the rest of the day for not having the guts to face him. Even so, my disgust at this weakness didn't diminish the glow I still felt. I *would* see him again, and I *could* wait until Monday.

I gushed to Gold about my unexpected afternoon, but he appeared completely unmoved. He did, however, move close enough to let me touch his nose. A shiver ran up my arm. Then his lips moved and I had a stab of fear that he might bite. Instead, he rubbed the back of my hand with his mobile upper lip, making me laugh. I stroked the velvet skin around his nostrils and he allowed it for a moment, then stepped away. When I brought the apple out from behind my back, he stepped back toward me and accepted it quite politely. I tried to stroke his neck, but he turned and stepped out of my reach again.

I sat in the shade and watched him for a while but was back in the house when Mom got home. I asked how her day was and listened without having to pretend interest. She noticed the difference.

"You seem to be feeling better. Did you have a good day?"

I thought for a moment and then smiled. My day had been awful until just before last period. "I had a *great* day."

I had planned on sleeping in on Saturday. Mom left early for a Red Cross class in Sacramento and wouldn't be home until late afternoon. I didn't even set my alarm, so I was startled awake when the front doorbell rang around eight-thirty. I thought about not answering but whoever it was, they were stubborn.

Pulling a sweatshirt over my tank top, I went downstairs and peeked through the curtains in the dining room. My stomach flip-flopped on seeing Chris' truck in the driveway.

I'm really still in bed, dreaming. No . . . nightmare! Then I stifled a cry of pain. I'd stubbed my little toe on a dining room chair in my haste to back away from the window. *No, definitely awake. This is so not fair.*

Now very nervous and suddenly concerned about how messy my loose hair might be, I crept to the door, took a deep breath, and slowly opened it.

Dave.

Dave . . . on my doorstep. Mind blown.

I couldn't form a single word. He didn't speak right away either, looking at me oddly for a moment.

Then he said, "Hey, sleepyhead," obviously taking in my stylish apparel and tousled unbound hair. He addressed the truck loudly, "She's here."

Robin and Chris got out of the vehicle and walked toward us. Robin was dressed similarly to Dave in jeans and boots.

"You ditched me yesterday. Nobody had your phone number, so this is your own fault."

"My own fault?"

"That I woke you up," he said, evincing not a shred of remorse.

"Yeah, and me too," said Robin.

"Well, it would be hard to get here without Chris," said Dave.

"And Chris wouldn't let him come without me," said Robin, yawning.

Chris looked uncomfortable, like he wanted neither credit nor censure for anything his brother decided to do.

"So you went to all this trouble just to get my phone number?" I didn't quite buy that, much as I wanted to.

"Well, since we're here . . ." Dave looked at Robin as if expecting something from her. The response was subtle for Robin, but I caught her reluctant glance back. He continued, "Can you come with us to our friends' place?"

I looked back at Dave. "My mom's not home," I said, shivering though it wasn't that cold. "But I can try to call her, I guess." I stood back and opened the door wider. "Come in. I . . . better get dressed."

They followed me into the house and I ran upstairs to make myself more presentable, my hands shaking the whole time. When I came back down, they were in the kitchen, sitting at the table and whispering. I was starting to feel suspicious but not sure why.

"Where are we going? I'll need to tell my mom."

"Tom's," said Dave. "He owns a guest ranch further up the road."

Memory stirred. "Guest ranch?"

"Yeah. Like a hotel, or resort. With horses," he said.

"Horses?" I repeated. This was getting interesting.

"You sound like an echo," said Robin.

"Sorry. It's just, I talked to someone last Saturday coming from a place just up the street . . ." I almost said more but didn't want to reveal too much. Instead I said, "He was driving an old red truck."

They all nodded and said, "Tom," at the same time.

"He's a good friend of ours," said Dave. "The ranch used to be a lot bigger, way back, but got divided up and pieces of it were sold off. This whole area was probably part of it."

"I had been wondering who had owned this place before," I said, thoughtfully.

"Well, that would have been a long time ago. Way before Tom's time. I guess the last people who owned this place built the house, but I don't think anyone ever lived here. Anyway, Tom has plenty of help in the summer, college students mostly, but in winter we sometimes help out. He and my dad have been friends a long time."

Talk of horses reminded me that I hadn't gone to see Gold yet. I was convinced he was about to let me get really close. Should I tell Dave about him? Dave *and* Chris, since he was here as well? Since we were officially friends now and he was sitting right here in my kitchen, my reasons for not telling him were irrelevant.

"Um . . . there's something I'd like to tell you . . . ask you . . . tell you about."

It might have been my imagination, but the atmosphere in the room suddenly changed. Chris had kept his eyes on the back of a cereal box on the table, but he now looked at Robin. Dave looked quickly at Robin too, then back at me. I thought she might be blushing a little but wasn't sure. Dave continued to look at me expectantly.

"Um . . . there's a horse loose . . . on our land . . . out back."

I felt more and more awkward. It was sinking in that Dave was sitting here, right now, almost right next to me, at my kitchen table of all places. He had seen me more or less in my pajamas! In spite of the presence of his brother and Robin, the situation seemed so intimate that I started to shiver nervously again. And then it hit me how funny it was too, and weird, and amazing. And I was going to bore him with concerns over a horse?

"Can we see him?" Dave said eagerly.

"You want to see him?" I asked, reaffirming what I thought I'd heard.

Chris looked at me now, something as close to interest as I'd ever seen on his face. His gaze shifted quickly back to the cereal box, but his leg started to bounce nervously like he was impatient to leave. *He's so weird. . . .*

I looked at the kitchen clock. "It's a little late, but we can go and look."

"Good!" said Dave, jumping up. The others got up quickly too.

"Hold on," I said.

I had asked my mother to get some normal carrots, she warning me not to eat too many as it would turn my skin orange. Taking a couple from the refrigerator, I led the way out toward our regular rendezvous spot. I was still having trouble accepting the fact that Dave was really here and kept stealing quick looks at his face. What would he think of Gold? What *did* he think of *me*?

Try not to think of that—it just makes you more useless than usual.

"That's nice," he said, noticing the corral. "Shame it's so far from the house. You could keep a horse in it."

I could keep a horse in it. *Keep a horse?* That, oddly, was another new concept. I'd think it through later.

"It needs a gate," said Chris. They were the first words I'd heard him speak today.

Okay. You get points for observation.

I indicated they should be quiet and continued toward the creek. I had begun to assume we were too late when I rounded a bush and there he stood as if waiting. His eyes were bright and his ears pricked forward as if he sensed something was different. Then he startled violently. Robin and the boys had walked into his line of sight. It was the first time I'd ever seen him show anything resembling fear.

Then he did something very strange. He reared up onto his hind legs slightly and lunged toward us, slamming his front hooves together into the ground, snorting loudly and making a strange groaning sound. He immediately wheeled around, pivoting on his hind legs, and galloped away through the trees and brush. His movement had been so dynamic, it had taken only a moment. Dust settling through the air was all that remained behind.

"That was weird," I said. "He's never done anything like that before."

"We must have scared him," said Robin.

"He was angry, not scared," said Chris, quietly. "He was warning us."

"About what? Angry about what?" I said, confused and a little shaken.

"Did he act that way with you?" Dave asked, looking at Robin.

"No, he was fine . . ." I had started to answer, still shocked by Gold's behavior, when what he had asked sank in.

So, she *had* told him. Why was I even surprised? Was that the real reason he was here? Robin and Chris both looked sheepish.

I decided to act like I hadn't caught the slip. "He's always very calm but hasn't let me get too close. He let me stroke his nose last time, though. I was hoping I could get closer today. That's probably not going to happen," I said, sadly.

"Did you see the way he moved?" Dave asked his brother excitedly, as if he hadn't heard me.

"Do you think he's a mustang?" asked Robin, looking from one brother to the other.

"He trusts you," said Chris, apparently to me, though he was still looking in the direction Gold had gone. "I'm sure you'll regain his trust when we're not here."

"Why would he have acted like that?" I asked. "He didn't mind Robin."

"I bet he can turn on a dime," said Dave, obviously still pursuing his own thoughts.

"I still think he's ugly," said Robin. "And he sure is dirty."

"I think we should try to catch him," said Chris, "but you're probably the only one who can."

"Man, I'd sure like to see how he handles cattle," said Dave.

Chris shook his head slightly and I thought he almost smiled.

"You have a one-track mind," said Robin.

Dave looked surprised as if he didn't know what she was talking about.

"Riding, cutting . . . horses and cattle," she said to me. "That's all he really cares about."

This was interesting. Horses and riding again—I could fit everything I knew about both on one of those tiny sticky notes.

"Cutting?"

"You don't know?" Dave asked, then grinned. "Hmm. We'll have to show her."

We walked back the way we had come. Chris detoured, walking over to the opening in the corral and pacing between the posts. Then he ran to rejoin us.

"And I care about other things," said Dave to Robin.

"Oh yeah? Like what?" she asked.

"Like my motorcycle," he said, grinning. "And my truck."

Robin rolled her eyes. "You can't even drive it yet."

"Sure I can. I just can't get my *license* yet." He grinned again.

"You're not convincing anybody," she said with a superior air.

"I care about lots of," he looked at me and smiled, "stuff."

My heart skipped a beat or two. *Don't be an idiot. And don't read any-thing into the things he says. Or does.*

Robin and Dave continued to banter back and forth and Chris fell into step beside me.

"If we rig up a gate for that corral, could you work toward catching him?" he asked, never once looking at me.

I was a little nonplussed. It was the most I'd ever heard him say, and I couldn't help noticing how similar his normal, non-grouchy voice was to his brother's.

"I don't know."

"It might take some patience, but you've gotten this far with him. See if you can coax him toward the corral."

"O . . . kay," I said, bemused. *What was that? Almost a conversation?*

"I care about soccer," said Dave. "And surfing . . ."

"Don't you think his head was too big?" asked Robin.

I looked at Chris. He glanced back and I could have sworn I saw a smirk, but it disappeared immediately and he looked away again.

When we got back to the house, I tried to call my mother but she didn't answer. I left her a message and ran upstairs to get my key. Chris led the way out and I locked the door behind me.

Chris' truck was big but had a regular-sized cab. He went to the driver side and Dave opened the passenger door. Robin got to the truck before me, but she stepped aside, indicating I should get in first. I didn't think that was fair but couldn't think of a viable reason to switch places. I hoped Dave might intervene, but I'm sure he never gave it a thought. I sighed and climbed in.

As the engine turned on, the CD Chris was listening to began to play. It sounded familiar and angsty. I liked it. Robin and I shared the center seat belt, squished together so tightly it was impossible to not be almost sitting on Chris. I felt very awkward; he looked even more uncomfortable.

Dave reached over Robin and switched the CD player to the radio, and then pushed the presets until he found what he wanted: a hard rock station. Robin rolled her eyes as Dave really got into the track playing, and I couldn't help laughing. He knew the song very well, singing slightly off-key and drumming on the outside of the door. It affected me oddly. I spent the trip trying to control my feelings and trying not to lean on Chris any more than I could help.

We drove in the direction I had walked just one short week ago. How long ago it seemed! And I didn't think I had walked that far. As we turned onto the lane, I noticed the horse sign again and another, a little farther on saying, "CAUTION – 15 MPH." I was surprised Chris kept to the slow speed, but the reason for the sign and his care became apparent as the road curved.

A group of riders walked down a trail just off the shoulder on our right. The first rider was a guy who looked in his early twenties. He and Chris exchanged nods and slight gestures of acknowledgment. The twelve or so riders following him were mostly older with a couple of helmeted children. The rear was brought up by two girls, who also looked college age. They smiled broadly as we approached.

"Hi, Dave!" they called brightly. "Hi, Chris." This had a different ring. I wasn't sure whether they sounded shy or respectful or just wary.

Dave called back to them, "Hey! You guys still here?"

"Two more weeks," they laughed. "You gonna be here when we get back?" Their voices now came from behind the truck.

Dave stuck his head and shoulders out the window. "Probably!"

"College girls." Robin sounded disgruntled. "They think Dave is so cute."

"Ow!" he said loudly. Robin had jabbed him hard in the ribs with her elbow. "I can't help it if I'm friendly." The smirk on his face said he was quite comfortable with the attention, both inside the cab and out.

"Yeah, you just think you're all that."

"Maybe I am," he said, obviously trying to sound arrogant.

"Oh, puh-*lease*," said Robin, rolling her eyes. "You know they like Chris better anyway."

Dave grinned but didn't agree with or deny her claim. Chris continued to frown at the road ahead.

I had assumed that our destination would be on the other side of the hill, or the next, but we kept driving and driving around one hill after another

with nothing coming into view. We finally drove into a small valley with many large structures, several smaller buildings, and fences and enclosures of all kinds. And horses. Lots of horses. A warm, slightly sweet, very pungent aroma permeated the truck. I was amazed that there was a property like this so close to my home, though it would probably take a long time to walk there.

"I'll drop you guys here," said Chris, quietly. He had stopped at the edge of a walkway in front of a huge Victorian house. "I'll be back after two."

Dave looked at me. "Is that okay?"

"Yes, I think so," I said. "If my mom calls me back and doesn't want me to be here, I can always walk home."

Robin grimaced and Dave looked skeptical but said nothing. He opened the truck door, hopped out, and held it open for Robin and me. He grabbed a black hat from behind his seat, then leaned back in. Whatever Chris was saying was in too low a voice for us to hear.

Robin said, "Come on," and started walking in the direction of a smaller house. "That's the guest house," she said, indicating the larger house we were circumventing, "but Tom and Cheryl live back here."

The guest house was a very large three-storied house, painted dark gray with white and brick red trim. It had a huge covered porch, large bay windows on the first and second floors, and a tower on the third. Behind it stretched a large back yard shaded by tall trees. There were flower borders and a spacious green lawn with redwood garden furniture set out. On one side was a large pergola covered with vines, and a seat swing hung at the far end of it. It seemed like an oasis in the otherwise dusty, brown environment.

The smaller house obviously hadn't been painted anywhere near as recently as the guest house, but it looked just as quaint, though from a later era. It was shingled in dark gray to match the guest house, with brick red and federal blue trim, but also had some brick and stone work. We walked through a small gate, up between porch pillars cobbled in smooth river rocks, to the large red front door. Robin knocked three times and went right in. I followed, already feeling shy.

"Cheryl?" Robin called.

A loud squeal erupted from somewhere down a short hallway and a very small, tow-headed child of indeterminate gender immediately ran out of a doorway, down the hall, and threw itself around Robin's legs. I guessed that it was a boy, but it was difficult to tell. The little jeans and plaid flannel shirt hinted at masculinity, but the shoulder-length curls and cherubic features could easily have been a girl's.

"Cody!" laughed Robin.

A pretty, petite woman came out of the same room carrying a toddler astride her hip. "Robin!" she said with obvious pleasure. "I haven't seen you since the beginning of summer. And who's this?"

Dave came through the door before Robin could answer, postponing the introduction.

"Hey, gorgeous," said the woman, walking up to him and giving him a side hug with her free arm. "Where's that handsome brother of yours?"

Dave grinned at her. "Hey, Cheryl. Chris went to work. They let him have some time off this morning." He glanced at me and actually looked a little embarrassed. "He'll be back around two. Have you met Allison? She's new around here. We were going to hang out and show her around if that's okay."

Cheryl suddenly regarded me with a lot more interest.

"It's nice to meet you," I said, quietly.

"Well, it's nice to meet you, too," she said, giving me a speculative look I seemed to be getting a lot lately. "Always a pleasure to meet friends of these guys. Be careful, though, or you'll get put to work. And don't let this one," she indicated Dave with a bump against him, "lead you into trouble."

"Hey!" said Dave indignantly.

I smiled. That actually sounded like a lot of fun—both the possible work and especially the potential trouble.

"Do you ride, Allison?" she asked. She had a gruff voice and down to earth manner in spite of her appearance. I was sure I was going to like her.

"No," I responded truthfully.

She looked at Robin and said, "Guess you're going to have to do something about that," but she bumped Dave again as she said it.

I thought I'd been doing well so far, considering everything, but my cheeks began to burn. Dave looked at me, a distinct look of mischief on his face. It disturbed me that Robin wore a similar expression.

"You guys are practically neighbors," said Dave. "She just lives over on Brookside."

"Really?" said Cheryl. "Ever done any babysitting?"

I probably looked shocked. "Just my cousins, but they're a lot older."

"Hmm," she said, a smile playing around her lips. "Well, you should go show her around and find Tom. I think he's here, probably around the barns. I'm sure we can set you up with a mount." She smiled again. "You'll have to ride if you want to keep up with these guys."

A thrill shot through me at the thought, though I had no clue why. Even with my recent adventures with Gold, the thought of actually riding him simply hadn't entered my head.

Once outside, Dave put the hat on, took the jacket off and looked—yummy. I thought of Brenda and smiled. *Cowboy, huh? If you only knew!*

He led the way toward two long, low buildings. "These are the main barns where most of the horses for guests are kept. This one," he said as we walked toward the first barn, "is mostly for guests who bring their own horses. Bar 8 hosts different events during the year, especially in summer, and a lot of people come here on vacation bringing their horses. They get to relax, their horses are taken care of, and they can participate in events, work in the arenas, or go trail riding. And people who don't have horses come too, of course." He looked into the first barn as we passed it, then pointed toward the second.

I couldn't think of anything else to say besides, "Cool."

"We'll take you up to the big house later," said Robin. "You should meet Gloria. She's the manager."

"And they have *really* good food," said Dave.

Robin agreed enthusiastically.

"Everyone likes Tom and Cheryl. On event days, they barbecue and people from town come and hang out. It's a lot quieter in winter, though. We sometimes help and keep them company."

"Especially Cheryl," said Robin. "It's really quiet when most of the college kids go back to school. They sometimes come out on weekends, but otherwise it's pretty dead."

"What are the pens for?"

"They're turnouts for the stalled horses. They get a little exercise that way. But most of the ranch horses are kept at pasture, especially in the winter. The big guys are out all year."

"Big guys?"

"The draft horses," said Robin, pointing toward a field beyond the parking lot. There were three horses, two large grays and a much smaller, mostly tan colored horse.

"They're beautiful," I breathed.

"Yeah, just don't ever let one step on you!" said Dave, as if he had first-hand experience.

We had entered the second, older-looking barn. There were six stalls on each side of the building facing each other. Several horses watched us with varying degrees of interest over their gnawed doors, and country music played from somewhere nearby. The pungent odor I'd smelled was certainly more concentrated here, though not overwhelming. I actually liked it. I didn't like the flies.

Wooden plaques with brief names like Stormy, Hero, and Pearl hung beside each stall door. I walked cautiously up to a pretty black and white face expecting it to avoid my touch as Gold did, but it stood unconcerned, its eyes half closed.

"Tom's horses are all really gentle," said Robin encouragingly.

I straightened the horse's forelock. I had started shivering again in spite of the heat. Very odd.

"Hey." A tall man leading a brown horse had entered the other end of the barn.

"Hey, Tom," said Dave and Robin, walking toward him.

"What're you guys up to?" Tom asked, cheerfully. He led the horse into a stall and reappeared with just a halter in his hand. "How's school going?"

"School's great," said Dave.

"School sucks," said Robin at the same time.

Tom laughed. "I believe we've already met," he said, extending his hand toward me. I shook it shyly. "Welcome to Bar 8."

"This is Allison," said Dave.

"She doesn't ride," said Robin.

"Yet," added Dave.

"Well, we'll have to change that," said Tom. "You know the beginners' horses. Saddle one up for her."

"What?" I said, alarmed.

"No time like the present," said Dave.

"Gotta start somewhere," added Robin.

"It's a conspiracy," I muttered.

"No, more of an intervention," said Dave, shaking his head. "You need help."

The next few hours were the most fun I'd ever had in my life. Dave and Robin showed me how to halter, lead, and tie a horse, and took turns working with me and the paint horse I'd been petting, Flash, and another horse named Fritz. The country music came from a large radio on the tack room floor.

"I've tried switching channels a couple of times," said Dave, "but I get threatened."

I laughed. I hadn't listened to much country music, but it suited our surroundings perfectly.

They got brushes from the tack room and showed me the basics of grooming, then got saddles, saddle pads, and bridles out. Dave saddled the paint horse first, then unsaddled her and supervised me as I tried to do it. Apparently I didn't do it quite right, so he adjusted and tightened the girth more. I might have been able to learn better if he hadn't been standing so near me the whole time, bumping into me as he showed me this or redid that. Robin had Fritz saddled already and showed me how to bridle Flash.

When the two horses were ready, I led Flash to a small arena nearby. Here Robin took over again, demonstrating how to mount while Dave stood next to me explaining what she was doing. Then it was my turn. The shivering I had experienced earlier hadn't exactly gone away and had been exacerbated by Dave's closeness, but now I was noticeably shaking, my teeth almost chattering.

"Are you all right?" asked Dave.

"Yes," I managed to say. Excitement, fear, joy, and wonder coursed through me in about equal measure. I shuddered violently and said again, "Yes, I'm fine."

Dave held Flash as I mounted. Robin, on Fritz, spent the next half hour or so just walking around the small arena with me, showing and explaining how to rein, stop, and then walk again. Dave looked on from the ground. Then he and Robin changed places, and he taught me how to make the horse jog and come back to a walk using my seat, legs, and hands. I bounced a little at first, but Flash's gait was smooth and I was soon able to relax into her rhythm. Dave seemed genuinely pleased with my progress, which thrilled me. They were both very patient and seemed to have done this kind of thing a lot.

"Are you hungry?" Dave asked after a while.

I found that I was and nodded. We walked the horses back to the barn. Dave seemed to throw himself off Fritz and was by my side before I could attempt dismounting by myself. Flash stood still enough, but my legs were unexpectedly wobbly. I almost fell, but Dave grabbed my arm to steady me.

"Careful," he said. "I thought you might be a little shaky. Beginners usually are. Let's put the horses back and go up to the house."

Shivering again, I nodded and watched as Dave unsaddled Fritz, copying every move he made. Robin watched and gave help when I needed it. After stabling the horses, we left the barn and I looked toward the field.

"Could we go see the draft horses?" I asked.

"Sure, but let's go after lunch 'cause I'm starving," said Robin and gave Dave a dirty look. "I didn't get any breakfast this morning."

Chapter Eight

Leading Me

We returned to the guest house, up some steps to the back of the huge porch and a side door. This opened into an enormous kitchen. Bustling around and fussing over two much younger women was a very large lady in a white apron. We tried to stay out of the way until she noticed us.

"I suppose you'll be wanting lunch?" she said, gruffly.

Immediately feeling guilty, as if I had actually asked for something completely unreasonable, I wanted to disclaim any such expectations. After all, we weren't guests and I had no money with me. The aroma hanging in the kitchen caused my stomach to rumble, though, and I heard Robin's do the same.

"Trail riders are just coming back. Go help with the horses and come back for lunch. We *might* have something left."

"Thanks, Phyllis," said Dave, grinning at her. As we hustled back out the door, he said, "She's always like that, but she loves to feed people."

"I . . . I don't have any money," I said.

"It's on me," he said. I must have looked reluctant as he added, "Really!"

"Get real," said Robin. "Don't listen to him. They never charge us for lunch."

I was still feeling funny about it as Dave led me over to a small, sleepy-looking horse led by one of the girl wranglers. The small boy riding it looked like he was clinging to the saddle horn for dear life.

"He got nervous on the trail," said the girl, smiling warmly at Dave. "Leading him made him feel a little more secure."

"Here, I'll take him," said Dave, returning her smile and taking the lead rope. He smiled at the boy, then raised his voice enough for all the riders to hear him. "Phyllis says to go in and eat. We'll take care of the horses."

The wranglers and guests made grateful comments.

"Ready to get down?" Dave asked the boy, smiling and lowering his voice to a softer, more familiar level. The little boy solemnly nodded his head. "Do you want to get down by yourself? Or do you want me to help you?"

The boy seemed to deliberate, then reached both arms toward him. Dave reached up slightly and lifted the boy easily, setting him firmly on the ground and helping him take off his little helmet. The interaction was almost unbearably sweet.

"There you go, buddy," he said as the parents walked up.

"Say thank you," said the boy's mother.

"Thank you," the boy said, smiling shyly at Dave.

"You're welcome!" Dave replied heartily, beaming at him.

I was impressed with how gently yet confidently Dave had handled the little guy, as if he did it all the time. I didn't have much experience with small children except for my cousins. When I was little, I'd find something to do by myself at family gatherings, like playing with the dog, or drawing. Now that my cousins were older it was easier to interact with them. As the oldest cousin, it often fell to me to keep an eye on them, but I didn't think I did it very well. I loved them and enjoyed them in small doses, but then I'd get away by myself. When Cheryl had mentioned babysitting, it had really unnerved me.

I realized Dave was looking at me patiently and that I had, as I often did when thinking of him, gone off into my own world. *It's pretty bad if I do it when he's standing right here!*

"Going into a hunger coma?" he asked.

I laughed, embarrassed.

"Come on. You take care of Sugar here, and I'll get this guy," he said, patting the horse next to us.

Sugar was small in comparison and appeared very gentle and quiet, dozing the whole time I unsaddled her.

"I'll unsaddle if you put away," said Dave. And he did, working so fast it was hard for us to keep up with him.

We finished putting the tack away and then helped Dave give the horses a quick brush. He and Robin checked their feet before leading them back to their stalls. I led Sugar while Robin and Dave both led two horses at the same time. I envied their abilities and promised myself that I would feel as at ease around horses one day. Back at the rail, Robin pointed to another relatively small horse. This one was more of a handful and obviously wanted to get back to the barn.

"Don't let him lead you," called Dave, following me and leading two more horses. "Show him who's boss or he'll walk all over you. If he starts pulling ahead, stop and make him back, or walk him in a circle. He's just trying to take advantage of you."

He was right. The horse would walk for a couple of steps then begin pulling ahead of me.

"Lead him back this way a few steps," called Robin, following Dave with another two horses.

The closer we got to the barn, the stronger the horse pulled. I stopped a couple of times, making him walk backward with me a few steps as Dave had said. I was glad he was fairly small, but leading him still made me nervous. If he had really decided to give me a fight, I knew who was going to win, though I wasn't going to give up without one.

"He's being a brat," said Dave, now walking in front of us. "Just get behind us and he'll settle down."

He was right again. I'm sure he would have run to the barn if he could, but he followed the other horses with something close to resignation. On entering the barn, he relaxed and calmly went into his stall.

"Nice work," said Robin, smiling at me as she walked over. "He can be such a little booger."

I laughed but was relieved to be done with him.

Dave and Robin went back to put the last three horses away. A horse in one of the paddocks caught my attention and I wandered over to him to wait. He was medium height, comparatively, and a soft brown unlike the other brownish and reddish horses there.

In fact, it was his color that drew me to him. A strange glow reflected off his glossy coat; a pinkish patina reminding me strongly of Dave's hair when sunlight hit it just right. The horse walked over to me right away as if glad at the prospect of company. He came right up to the rails and I reached through to stroke his nose, his cheek, his forehead. He had a white diamond shape in the center of his broad brow but was otherwise solid-colored. Moving sideways, he allowed me to stroke his sleek neck, the way I had been hoping Gold would. I liked him.

"I see you've met Remmy," said Dave, walking up close beside me. He stroked the horse's neck also, and his hand accidentally brushed against mine a couple of times.

I shivered and tried to keep from blushing again. *Maybe if I counted to ten. It's supposed to work for tempers, right?*

"How you doin' old man?" he said affectionately.

I marveled at how close the color of their hair was with the sun shining on it: a soft brown with highlights that were more pink than gold.

"Is he really old?" I asked as Robin joined us.

Dave said, "He's thirteen. That's not really old for a horse, but I've known him ever since I can remember. He was born on our ranch. My dad gave him to me when I was nine."

"He's yours?" I asked, surprised.

"Used to be," he answered. "He's sort of semi-retired, I guess. He was my first real cutting horse. I have a younger horse now."

"Dave's dad raises cutting horses as well as cattle," said Robin.

"Mostly cattle," said Dave. "He's got partners in the quarter horses, but they're still bred and raised on our ranch. It's more like an expensive hobby. Then there's the other stock horses, like Remmy. He's part mustang."

I felt another "wow" coming and stifled it. They already knew I was painfully ignorant on such topics and easily impressed; no need to rub it in. I tried to think of something halfway intelligent to say.

"So why is he here?" That would have to do. I wanted to ask, *"So, where do you live?"* but held back, like I did with so much regarding him. I thought it might sound stalkerish, though I couldn't think why he would mind telling me. We were friends, right? That's all. In spite of the fact that my body insisted on reacting to his proximity. I wondered if I would get used to it if we spent a lot of time together, but just the thought made me shiver again.

"Convenience," he said.

I panicked, struggling to remember what his answer was in response to.

He paused and grinned, eyes twinkling as if he could see the mad tap dance going on inside my head. "I ride him when I'm here, and Tom uses him whenever he wants." He seemed to consider for a moment. "He'd be a good horse for you when you feel a little more confident. He's fun but well-behaved. Aren't you, boy?" He scratched Remmy around his ears. "Come on, I'm starving!"

We walked back to the large kitchen, Dave taking his hat off as he went in. A small table in an alcove was set with three places for us. Robin looked at me, wagging her eyebrows and grinning. Dave was grinning too. He was reaching for a plate when Phyllis bustled into the room. Spotting us, she stopped, fists on hips.

"Did you wash your hands?" she asked severely.

I was embarrassed. The others looked uncomfortable too.

"Why don't you show Allison where the restrooms are, here in the house?" said Dave. "I'll go to the bunkhouse."

Robin looked disapproving for some reason but nodded. She dragged me past the formidable form of Phyllis, through a swinging door, and into the dining room where guests and wranglers were enjoying a large meal. The room was decorated beautifully with papered walls and lots of brass, brocade, and dark wood. Robin had me peek into a couple of other rooms: a large sitting room designated as the "Parlor" and a smaller room with two desks and a wall lined with bookcases as the "Library." Both were decorated similarly to the dining room.

"There are ten bedrooms. One belongs to Gloria, the housekeeper. I'm not sure where she is right now. Anyway, the rooms are decorated really pretty but all different, you know? People that don't book a room in the guest house get cabins. Things slow down in the winter, but it's always booked up through the summer season. And a lot of people like to stay here in winter. It's quieter and they can ride but still be close to the mountains for skiing."

Dave met us back in the dining room, holding plates for us. On the long sideboard were fried chicken, sliced roast beef, and an Italian-looking casserole that smelled wonderful. There were baked and mashed potatoes, cooked vegetables, and fixings to make your own sandwich or salad. At the end was a large bowl of fruit, small bowls of Jello, an upside down cake, and individual pastries of various shapes and flavors. The whole room smelled amazing.

I took some chicken and a baked potato, sure it would be enough. I'd never had a huge appetite, but the stress of the past couple of weeks had caused it to diminish even more, though I felt ravenous at the moment. Robin and I went back to the alcove in the kitchen and sat down. When Dave came back, his plate twice as full as ours, he put a pastry on the table in front of me.

"You've got to at least try it," he said. "Get in good with Phyllis."

"You could stand to gain weight, too," said Robin severely. "I bet you didn't eat all last week."

I felt Dave's gaze resting on me and refused to look at him. Evasive tactics were in order.

"Is this where you'd been . . . when I first saw you?" I didn't want to reveal too much, but the answer was either yes or no and I really wanted to know.

Dave looked at me, slyly I thought, and smirked as if at a private joke. "Yeah," he said. "Merle went missing, so I was looking for her."

"Merle is your dog?" I asked.

"Merle is Chris' dog," corrected Robin.

"Oh," I said, my assumptions of that day continuing to evolve. It was easy to recall Dave on the motorcycle, looking dangerous and much older than I now knew him to be. I still thought he was probably at least *slightly* dangerous, one way or another. "She's a very nice dog," I said, mainly because I couldn't think of anything else to say. "She's so pretty and . . . and friendly."

Robin stopped in mid-chew and looked as if I had said something bizarre. "Merle? Friendly?"

Dave was still smirking.

"What?" Robin sounded annoyed.

"Merle apparently likes Allison," said Dave.

"No way," said Robin, looking at me as if I were an alien.

"Truth," countered Dave. "Chris doesn't believe it either, but I saw what I saw."

"Merle doesn't normally like strangers?" I guessed.

"Strangers, family members, *lifelong friends*," this last Robin said with venomous emphasis.

"She likes *me*," said Dave.

"Well, we all know how special *you* are," growled Robin.

"Darn right," he replied.

Before I could tell what she was going to do, Robin had lobbed a fork full of mashed potatoes at him, but Dave was still faster, raising his arm to ward off the blow.

A white linen wall appeared suddenly next to the table and we all looked up into the stern face of Phyllis. She didn't say a word but looked at us with a baleful eye, especially Dave. He licked the potato off his forearm.

"Excellent as always, Phyllis!" he said, giving her his most charming smile.

She *humphed* and, appearing completely unmoved, said, "There will be no food fights or there will be no more food for you."

"Yes, ma'am," said Dave, meekly but still smiling.

I tried to look like the innocent bystander I was and began eating the pastry. It truly was delicious and I slowly ate the whole thing, though I was already full. Phyllis watched as if reserving judgment on me.

When I was done, we bussed our dishes and wandered back out and around to the front of the house. People were sitting and talking in the shade of the huge porch. Sounds of laughter and splashing came from the other side of the house. I hadn't noticed before, but a pool area ran the length of the yard and about half the length of the house, shielded from the yard by a tall vine-covered trellis and at the front by espaliered trees. It was open on the east side where a long row of small cabins sat. Beyond them, another low building lay. A chain link fence encircled the entire pool area.

"That's the bunk house," said Robin, indicating the farthest building. "The girls live closest to the road, and the guys are at the other end."

"They don't get paid a whole lot," added Dave, "but room and board are free. It works out well for the ones that can't go home for school breaks and holidays, and a few stay on part-time throughout the year. Hey, what time is it?"

Robin said, "I think it's about one, one-thirty."

"Let's go for a short ride," said Dave.

"We don't have time to go far," said Robin. "Not if we're taking Allison home when Chris gets here. And we can't run or she'll fall off!"

"Yeah, I know. We won't go far. We could just walk, but it would be more fun to ride, right? Besides, she needs all the practice she can get."

"Where are we going?" asked Robin, looking confused.

"You'll see. I just want to show her something."

"Oh," said Robin as if she'd guessed.

"Let me check with Tom." He started walking toward the barn, then turned and continued backward. "Saddle Flash and Fritz. I'll be there in a minute."

The thought of riding again made me feel a little anxious, but I definitely wanted to. I haltered and led Flash out with as much confidence as I could, though they seemed to have picked the perfect horse for me. Robin was at the rail with Fritz when we got there, and I followed her into the tack room. When we came back, Dave was there riding Remmy without a saddle.

"Hurry up, would ya?" he said with mock severity.

"Shut up, cheater," said Robin.

I laughed but was impressed with how at ease Dave looked. I wouldn't want to be on a horse without the horn of the saddle to hang on to. I was even more impressed with how attractive he looked on Remmy; they looked made for each other.

I felt nervous about mounting Flash by myself. Either it was apparent or he just wanted to help as Dave jumped down from Remmy in one fluid movement, draped his reins over the rail, and walked over to me.

"Remember what we did before?" he said, standing very close—too close—just behind me.

I closed my eyes and started counting, but it didn't help much; the shivering was back. *Perhaps if I counted backward?*

I tried to follow Dave's simple instructions. The first parts were accomplished with no problem. But either because my legs were still wobbly from earlier or, more likely, my natural clumsiness was asserting itself, I just couldn't get enough momentum to push myself off the ground. Flash had been patient, but now I had trouble holding her still. This made my innate lack of balance even more evident.

"Wait a minute," said Dave, laughing a little. "Let's do this differently."

He held the reins for a moment while I awkwardly extricated myself from the stirrup. Then he told me to take the reins in my left hand again.

"Now face me a little," he said, "put your foot in my hands and be ready to swing your other leg over."

I knew I was already red in the face, both from embarrassment and exertion. Now I had to step in his hands? It didn't help that it had turned into another very hot day. Maybe he wouldn't notice.

He reached down, but before I could do what he'd said, he abruptly straightened again, took his hat off, and placed it on my head. It was too big and the brim pushed the tops of my ears down.

"We're going to have to get you a hat. You're sunburned already."

Darn. I guess the counting doesn't work either.

"You need some boots too," Robin added. "It's safer to ride with a heel on your shoe and boots are best, especially for trail riding."

Hat. Boots. Ample layers of sunscreen. Got it.

Dave bent over slightly again as if bowing to me, his hands cupped for my foot. I was seized with a desire to reach out and touch the top of his head, to touch his hair, but I shook it off. What kind of weirdo would he think me if I ever allowed myself to do something like that? Instead, I complied. I had barely put my foot down when I was practically thrown into the air. I had the presence of mind to swing my leg over the saddle quickly as instructed and caught myself before slamming down onto Flash's back.

"There you go," said Dave, grinning. Then he patted my calf before reaching for Remmy's reins.

Still blushing hard, I realized he meant nothing by it and was just treating me the way he had treated the little boy earlier. I couldn't help it if it affected me differently. Dave gathered Remmy's reins and a little mane in his left hand and, even though Remmy began moving forward, effortlessly threw his leg over the horse and settled lightly onto his back.

I bet the high jump is nothing to him.

Dave led the way between the barns and small arenas, closer to where the draft horses were.

"Oh my gosh," I breathed as I began to get an idea of their actual size. "They're *really* big!"

"They're both eighteen hands," said Robin proudly, as if responsible for their stature. "That's tall, even for Shires."

"What do you mean by 'hands'?" I asked.

Dave, who I was having a hard time keeping my eyes off of, in spite of the impressive Shires, dropped his reins and half turned to face us. He held one hand out as if to shake someone's hand, then alternately stacked one hand on the other. Remmy continued to walk calmly forward.

"It's four inches," said Robin. "He's just showing off because Remmy's so well-behaved."

"I heard that," said Dave, still riding without holding the reins.

I couldn't help watching him, his body moving in easy rhythm with Remmy's stride, the sun causing a pink glow around his head and reflecting off the smooth, glossy hind quarters of the horse.

We rode along a dirt road between the low hills to the south of the barns. Horses dotted the upper slopes of the dry pastures on either side. Most of them stopped grazing and watched as we approached and passed them. Then a couple began running down to the fence. The rest followed, setting off the horses on the opposite hill. My anxiety returned as Fritz began prancing next to us. Flash's head came up a little higher, but she watched the other horses with relatively calm interest. Robin held Fritz in pretty tightly. Dave picked his reins up as Remmy's nostrils flared, and he carried his head higher than before but still behaved himself.

"How're you doin'?" Dave asked, twisting around to look back at me.

"Okay," I said, smiling and trying to look more confident than I felt.

"Good," he said and faced forward again.

"Where are we going?" I asked Robin in a low voice.

"You'll see," was all she'd say.

We continued, leaving the pastured horses behind. The road was extremely dusty but deep gullies showed where rain from previous seasons had worn through it. There were hoof prints and tire tracks all along it.

Dave eventually led us toward a barbed wire fence to another large pasture. I didn't even see the gate until he made Remmy sidestep up to it. He pulled some wire up to release a post, then lifted the whole thing up and rode to the side, opening a gap for us to ride through. I was struck again by the ease and grace with which he rode, Remmy seeming to move on his own as they reversed the procedure to close the gate behind us.

I looked at Robin, sure it couldn't have the same effect on her as it had on me. I was right. She was giving me the sparrow look again: head tilted, small smile, eyes ready to laugh.

"What?" Dave asked as he rejoined us farther inside the pasture.

"Allison's impressed," she said brattily.

Blush.

Dave frowned and made a sound something like *pffff.* "You'll be doing that kind of stuff in no time. It's just trail riding." He turned his mount and continued leading the way.

Sure, easy for you to say. You were apparently born on horseback. Or maybe you're part horse. . . .

I remembered reading somewhere that a source of centaur stories might have occurred when early Greeks saw horses for the first time, ridden by nomads. The riders, probably hunters from the east, were so aligned with their horses that the Greeks assumed they were one creature. Apparently the Aztecs experienced something similar when conquistadors, bringing horses from Spain, invaded their lands. Watching Dave and Remmy, I could believe it.

Especially if those riders rode without saddles or—

"Earth to Allison," Robin's voice interrupted my reverie. "Flash is mellow, but you're being lazy. Hold the reins like *this*," she demonstrated what she had taught me in the corral earlier, "and for heaven's sake let go of the saddle horn!"

Dave and Remmy waited for us to catch up and we continued, riding abreast with me in the middle. The hills were covered in long, dry grass and were relatively small compared to the tree covered foothills farther east. But they were still rather steep, requiring us to lean forward going up and to zigzag slightly going back down.

"One more rise," said Dave as we started up another hill.

When we got to the top, I caught my breath. Spread out before us was an amazing panorama. To the northwest were the comparatively crowded rooftops of what must be our town, Douglas. I was surprised at how far away it looked. I could just make out the Catholic church spire at the west side of town, the Presbyterian spire in the center, and the top tower of the old fire house in the east—the only three-story building in town.

"See that green roof over there?" said Dave, pointing northwest. "That's the roof of the gym at school. It's on the same road that leads out here. That dirt road we were on leads to the same road further south. You can get to my place from there." I looked at him and he smiled back, then raised his arm and pointed again, this time to the south. "Pretty much everything you can see from here in that direction is our ranch."

My jaw dropped. Spreading south from Douglas were many rooftops, private homes. The foothills continued north and east far beyond that. But to the south of us lay gently undulating land dotted with large live oaks, most of it as brown as the ground we now stood on. Smaller dark dots I assumed were cattle. Farther south were bigger hills. Farther west were green fields.

Dave followed my gaze. "We grow most of our own alfalfa. That's the flatter, cultivated land you see over there to the west. But most of our ranch lies beyond these hills, so we can't see it from here." His arm swept across the landscape.

Then he pointed to the steeper, wooded hills closer on our left, lying south and east; the same range of hills that lay behind my house and led, eventually, into the mountains. "My house is that way. We take a short cut across our land and up that dirt road when we come directly here," Dave continued. "Today we went all the way around: into town to get Robin, through town to your place, and up the back road." He smiled again.

I couldn't think of anything to say. I was beyond amazed and wondered what it meant; why he had shown me this. Or did it mean anything at all? He hadn't shown it in a boastful way, nor had he seemed to want to impress me. It was more as if, having agreed to be his friend, he thought I should see this, an integral part and extension of himself.

"Next weekend is Labor Day. We always have a big barbecue. Can you come?"

The question seemed to come out of the blue and took me by surprise. Dave was inviting me to do something? At his home? My heart beat faster. It didn't matter that an unknown horde of other people were probably invited as well.

"It's really fun," said Robin. "Everybody goes."

That's what I suspected.

"Well, not *everybody*," said Dave, giving her a meaningful look.

"True. But our friends go. The Calderas host a play day and have a lot of events."

This sounded very interesting and I had a lot of questions. But before I could formulate one clearly, Dave said, "We'd better get back. Chris is probably there."

On the way back, they talked animatedly about past Labor Day play days and the events included for their guests. Cutting classes as well as interesting sounding activities like pole bending and barrel racing were discussed and explained to me though I had trouble imagining them.

As we rode back through the grassy hills, a couple of the pastured horses neighed as we came into view. Fritz made an effort to respond, but otherwise everyone remained calm. I could see Chris' truck parked near Tom and Cheryl's house. Something lay in the bed and over the cab.

Dave jumped lightly down from Remmy as soon as we reached the rail and stood by in case I needed help, but I dismounted from my trusty steed without assistance. This time my legs felt horribly shaky and I stood very still, trying to maintain my equilibrium like I'd been at sea and needed to regain my land legs.

"You're doing great!" Dave said, beaming. Robin smiled over at me too. "We'll have you running barrels in no time."

"What?" I exclaimed, startled and not sure what he was talking about.

"You're a natural. I can tell already," he said.

Very sweet, but I think you're too optimistic.

"I . . . I don't know." I hoped he really was just joking.

He laughed. "Well, one thing at a time, maybe."

I nodded, relieved.

Chris joined us then. "It's almost three," he said matter-of-factly.

I was shocked that it was so late. Dave nodded and led Remmy away, but Chris caught up and exchanged words with him. Dave nodded again and went on his way while Chris returned to us. I was in the process of unsaddling Flash as the others had taught me. Chris watched, critically I thought.

"Need help?" he asked as if he expected me to say yes.

Something about that rankled and I put my chin up a little. "No, I'm fine." As an afterthought, I added, "Thanks." I didn't mean to be rude to him.

I took the saddle off and set it on the rail.

"I'll put tack away," he said loudly enough for Robin to hear as well.

I almost objected, then realized he could just as easily have said that he'd put the horses away. I would much rather do that myself.

"Thanks, Chris," said Robin sincerely.

"Thanks," I said again, thinking he was probably just trying to hurry us along. So far today he'd had to bring Dave and Robin to my house, hang out there with us, bring us here, go to work, and now he'd have to take me home. I was sure he must want to be done with us—me especially—and go do whatever he did on his time off.

Both Chris and Dave were already back by the time we'd put the horses away and we walked together to the guest house. My legs were definitely wobbly.

Cheryl stood up as we approached the porch, baby Zoe in her arms. Cody ran to the top of the steps and wiggled his fingers at us.

"Robin, could you watch the little ones for me? Gloria needs something from town and I was going to go with her." She looked fondly at Cody but then grimaced at Robin, whispering, "I could use a break, too."

"Oh," said Robin, looking at me uncertainly. "I think we have to take Allison home right now."

"We can take her and come back for you. We may as well come back this way anyway," said Dave, but Chris looked as unsure as Robin.

"Yeah . . . okay," said Robin. "If that's okay?"

I shrugged. I didn't know why it wouldn't be. Then it occurred to me that without Robin there, there was nothing to keep me from sitting next to Dave in the truck. *Yes, I like this plan!*

"That's fine," I said, trying not to sound too enthusiastic.

"Thanks, guys," said Cheryl, and I thought I saw a trace of humor in her eyes. "It was nice to meet you, Allison," she said, smiling at me. "You're welcome here anytime. I'm sure Dave can always find a horse for you." Here she actually winked at him.

"Th . . . thank you," I said, a little overwhelmed with the friendly offer.

"We'd better go," said Chris, quietly.

Robin put her arms out for Zoe as she reached the top of the steps and then took Cody by the hand. "Wave b'bye," she told him and he wiggled his fingers at us again.

Dave grinned and I laughed, waving back. Cody was *so* cute.

"See you Monday," Robin called after me.

"Okay!" I called back as we reached the truck.

Now I could see that there were two poles resting in the long bed of Chris' truck, secured by rope.

"Chris got you a gate," Dave grinned, holding the door open for me.

Today had been one surprise after another and this one completely caught me off guard. I glanced at Chris as I got into the truck, but he avoided looking at me, as usual. Dave climbed in after me and we started back the way we had originally come. But enjoyment in sitting next to Dave was tempered by my grudging curiosity regarding Chris and his interest in catching Gold. Was he just being helpful? Was he concerned about the horse? Or did he have

some ulterior motive of his own? He said nothing the whole trip except to remind me to put my seatbelt on.

Dave seemed happy and untroubled by anything, singing and drumming to the radio all the way back to my house, and I began thinking about what this day meant to me. I had friends; *real* friends, I was sure of it. The heartbreak I'd suffered all week seemed insignificant in the light of this.

And the awkwardness I felt around these boys, while hardly dissipated, either wasn't that noticeable or didn't bother them. Either way, I hoped that the next time I saw them, at least Dave, I might begin to feel more comfortable around him. Like Robin. They bantered so easily with each other, their words almost sounding mean sometimes, but they obviously cared about each other. I wanted to feel that way too.

When we got to my house, Chris pulled into the dirt driveway. But instead of continuing toward the cattle guard, he parked near the side of the house.

"Let's walk down in case the horse is around. We don't want to spook him if we can help it."

"Good idea," said Dave, getting out of the truck.

Then he turned and held his hand out toward me. It reminded me strongly of the day he had helped me up after my failed long jump and a host of attendant feelings washed over me. I didn't really need his help; Chris' Chevy wasn't exactly a monster truck and I had got out by myself just fine at the ranch in spite of the relatively high lift. Blushing furiously, I took Dave's hand anyway, allowing him to be chivalrous. I thought he held my hand longer than necessary and I struggled to keep a grip on reality.

Chris had put leather gloves on and was noisily and, I thought, a little violently releasing the poles from the truck. He reached into the bed, pulled out another pair of gloves, and threw them at his brother. Dave frowned at him and dropped my hand, laughing a little. Together they pulled the poles out and started toward the corral, Chris in the lead with Dave at the other end. I felt awkward again as if I should be helping somehow, but I figured I'd just get in the way so walked along silently behind them.

When we got to the enclosure, they fitted the ends of the poles through the posts on one side of the opening in the fence and let the other ends rest on the ground.

"See if you can coax him in," said Chris. "Lift the top pole and run it through the other side of the fence first. Then you can run the bottom one through. If you catch him, you need to let us know right away. There's water for him there," he pointed to the corner of the corral where the stream ran through, "but we'll need to feed him. The sooner we start, the better off he'll be." He began walking away, then stopped and spoke without looking directly at me. "And be careful. You've established some trust with him, but if you catch him, get out of there right away, just in case."

"Okay," was all I could say. I was feeling overwhelmed again. Could this day possibly contain any more surprises?

We walked without talking back up to the house, the boys following me to the back door. Now I felt *really* awkward. How to say goodbye? *'See ya.' No, too familiar. 'Later.' Too brief. 'Thanks for the amazing day.' Too gushy.*

I opened the back door and they followed me in. Should I offer them a drink? It had felt weird for them to be in my home at all; it would be even weirder alone with just me. Then I got the biggest shock of the day.

"Allison?"

"Daddy!"

Chapter Nine

Dreams Exploding

Startled looks all around. Dave and Chris had come to a stop, one on either side of me, Chris moving slightly to the front. I looked quickly at their faces. On Chris' I read surprise, wariness—concern? It was hard to tell; all his expressions looked pretty much the same. Dave looked surprised—and *intense*—standing very straight with feet planted as if ready for a fight.

Their reactions were nothing compared to my dad's consternation. He was standing at the kitchen counter with his back turned to us when we entered the house. Now I could see that he was preparing food. He must have decided to cook dinner for Mom. He did stuff like that.

"What's going on? Where have you been? And who is this?" he asked quietly, looking from Chris, to me, to Dave, to Chris, to Dave, and waving the knife in his hand slightly as he talked.

"I tried calling Mom," I said, not wanting to sound defensive but failing miserably. "I left her a message."

"And she tried to call you back," he said, trying to sound calm and reasonable and not quite accomplishing it either. "But you didn't answer."

"I never—" I checked my front pocket but felt nothing. *Oops. I think I might be in trouble. . . .*

"I'd like to know what's going on," Dad said, still trying to remain calm. "Mom said something about you going with a *girl* named Robin to a friend of *hers.*" He was looking pointedly at the boys indicating that neither of them looked remotely girlish.

"Oh," I said, the real awkwardness of the situation finally beginning to dawn on me. "This is Dave . . . Dave Caldera . . . and this is Chris . . . Caldera. They're friends too. We all went to their friend Tom's. Robin's still there watching the kids. They," I looked at the boys in turn, "just brought me home."

Dave stepped forward at that moment, his hand almost fiercely thrust toward my dad.

"I'm sorry, sir, for the confusion," he said, politely but firmly, shaking my dad's tentatively offered hand.

The grip looked strong and I couldn't help notice Dave's bicep tighten under his t-shirt sleeve. My dad's face tensed slightly as he returned the handshake, reluctantly it seemed.

Dave continued, "It's really nice to meet you. It's my fault. We were going to visit our friend Tom and his wife Cheryl up the road, and I thought Allison might want to go as well."

Is that what happened? I don't exactly remember it that way.

"This is my brother, Chris."

Chris stepped forward and shook hands with Dad, just a little less forcefully. They locked eyes, something I'd never seen Chris do with anyone, and something appeared to pass between them. It didn't seem to make Dad feel any better.

"Well, we'll talk about this when your mother gets home," Dad said to me. "Thank you for bringing Allison home—" He shook his head. "How exactly did you get here?"

"My brother drives, sir. He's seventeen." Dad looked completely unconvinced that this was in any way comforting, and Dave hastily added, "He's a really good driver."

"I'm sure he is," said Dad, sounding even less convinced.

"Um . . . I guess I'll see you Monday at school?" I said, turning to Dave.

The best thing right now seemed to be to get these guys out of the fire. I'd have to work at getting myself out later. I didn't want Dad scaring Dave off completely, though to be fair to him, Dave hardly looked scared and I doubted there was much in the world that *could* scare him. That was a comforting thought.

"Yeah, okay," said Dave, smiling at me.

"I'll . . . I'll walk back to the truck with you," I said, glancing back at my dad, my nervousness growing again.

A host of odd thoughts ran through my head. It had felt so weird to have Dave in my house this morning, turning up on my doorstep like that before I was even dressed properly. Then the Gold incident and everything that happened at Bar 8. Now this. I felt guilty as if I'd done something illicit. And here we were, heading back to the truck and I wished I knew what Dave was thinking and feeling. Did any of this affect him the way it did me? *Probably not.*

"I hope we didn't get you in trouble," said Dave, a little apologetically, but like he now thought the situation funny.

"We?" Chris said under his breath.

"Oh . . . no. Just a . . . a misunderstanding," I said, trying to seem like I was shrugging it off. "I guess I'd forgotten my dad was coming home today."

"We didn't even know you had a dad," said Dave, looking more serious.

That seemed a strange thing to say. "Not have a dad? Everyone has a dad."

"No, not really," said Chris quietly, then opened the truck door and climbed in.

His meaning hit me hard and I felt like a complete, insensitive idiot. *But you guys have a dad. I've heard you talk about him.*

"Hey," Dave said to Chris. "You got a pen in there?"

Chris picked something up from within the cab and tossed it out the open door. Dave caught it then stepped directly in front of me, taking my left hand. I caught my breath.

"Call me and let me know what happens with the horse, okay?" he said, writing on my palm.

"Okay," I said, rather breathlessly.

"And be careful," said Chris, not looking at me, his trademark scowl in place.

I nodded my head, but he probably didn't see.

Chris started the truck as Dave went to the passenger side and climbed in. It wasn't until they had driven away and I turned back to the house that I realized I was still wearing Dave's hat. Why hadn't he asked for it back? The thought of wearing something of his in front of my dad made me blush for some reason, so I took it off. Immediately I felt deprived, but I could still feel the pressure of his hand on mine. I closed it in a fist and held it close to me. I'd have to remember to keep my hand closed until I could transfer the number to my phone and wash my hand.

I walked slowly back to the door, trying to sort through the events of the day to see if there was anything I needed to be wary of and not wanting to go into lengthy explanations. That made me feel guilty too, even thinking about keeping anything from Dad. But apart from the obvious—the existence of Gold and my true feelings for Dave, which I was already keeping from my mother anyway—I couldn't think of anything else to be concerned about. Not the basics anyway; embarrassing details could probably be avoided. Diverted and shocked by this uncharacteristic thought pattern, I reentered the kitchen and met Dad's raised brows and questioning eyes.

"What's going on, Allie?" he asked, too quietly. Just the tone of his voice made me feel guilty like I had grossly disappointed him somehow.

"Nothing, Dad," I said but knew that answer wasn't going to suffice. "Dave and Robin are my friends at school, and Chris is Dave's brother, so I guess he's kind of a friend too. They were going to Bar 8. It's just up the road." I continued more enthusiastically, actually glad to be able to tell someone about my adventure. "It's a guest ranch and it's amazing. They have so many horses! Tom and Cheryl own it and are friends of Dave and Chris and their family. Robin and Dave were teaching me how to ride!"

Dad had been listening with a patient look on his face, but at this he looked stern. "You were riding? Horses?" I couldn't tell if he was just incredibly surprised or angry. He looked thoughtful for a few moments. "Well, we'll have to talk about this later when Mom gets home."

"Okay," I said meekly, turning to leave the room, my inscribed hand fisted tightly at my side. Then I stopped and returned to give him a big hug. "I'm glad you're home, Daddy," I said and meant it.

"Me too," he said, hugging me back.

I went to my room and shut the door. I knew this subject was far from closed, but I had a respite until my mother got home. I sat at my desk; my knees pulled up and my chin resting on them as I slowly opened my hand. *Dave wrote on my hand! His phone number! For me!*

I couldn't get over it. What an unbelievable day! The daze hadn't worn off yet; I was on some kind of high, and it was going to take more than over-protective parents to bring me down. I probably could have brought myself crashing down if I'd thought too much—after all, I still felt I knew my place

in the world, and it wasn't on the same plane as someone like Dave—but I firmly decided not to. I'd suffered badly this past week; why not bask in the glow of Dave's attention, however transitory it might prove to be?

Picking up my cell phone—on my desk where I'd placed it after calling Mom this morning—I saw that I'd missed not one but three calls, all from my mother. *Oh dear. That means she's going to be really worried as well as annoyed.* That was never good. And with Dad home too. Bad timing.

Between Dave and Gold and the mostly downward-tilted roller-coaster I'd been on all week, then this incredible high at the end, I guess it hadn't registered that Dad was coming home. Four or five years ago, when Dad had a regular job, he left in the mornings, came home at dinner, and was almost always home on weekends. Now he was home for a week or more and then gone; sometimes a few days, sometimes a few weeks.

I didn't understand the specifics of what his company did or the details of his job. But I knew that he and a friend, Robert, had developed a computer system for use in industry and manufacturing—anything that used automated or robotic systems. They had started their business while working in unrelated jobs and now had their own company. This had been based in Los Angeles, but they'd decided to keep an office there and move the main business north. Costs were the main reason for moving the company, but we knew Dad wanted to get us out of the city for other reasons.

Robert had a baby and two small children, so Dad did most of the traveling, especially internationally. He often went to South America and Asia, not only marketing but helping to set up new systems and training people to make the best use of them. And that's about all I knew, except that, for the past three or four years, my dad was often gone. Now that the main facilities were being set up close to Sacramento, Dad might be home more—or traveling less—as he was needed to help organize and direct things there. I had mixed feelings about that.

Since we'd moved here, he'd been gone almost the whole time, busy with his company's move as well as conducting business abroad. I usually missed him badly, but during this absence I'd barely thought of him, especially since school started. That realization made me feel guilty again. It seemed I'd had little thought to spare for either my mom or my dad, but it wasn't like I'd done anything *wrong.*

I looked at my palm, at the irregular shape of the numerals, and marveled again. I carefully entered them into my phone.

Then I thought of Gold. Would he be there this evening? Would I even be able to check? I wanted him to be there if only to have an excuse to call Dave. I also suddenly realized that keeping Gold's existence a secret might be tricky with Dad home. Mom wasn't a problem. Dad was more likely to go exploring.

I toyed again with the idea of just telling my parents about Gold but resisted it. After all, Dad had grown up on a ranch, though he seldom talked about it. I wasn't ready to have things completely change, and I was convinced they would. My time spent with Gold had been precious and meaningful to me. And I felt he was the strongest link I now had to Dave.

These thoughts occupied my mind until my mother came home. I could hear my parents talking downstairs, then heard my name called.

Uh-oh. Here we go.

I hadn't washed Dave's number off my palm yet. Closing that hand firmly, I could still remember the pressure of his hand holding mine while he wrote it and imagined him holding it again as I descended the stairs, preparing to mount my defense. Although I thought they were overprotective, I'd never knowingly given my parents cause to doubt or worry about me. That had to count for something.

Walking into the kitchen, I tried to exude a confident righteousness I was far from feeling. I couldn't help noticing that Dad sat where Dave had this morning.

"Sit down, Allison," he said.

Mom looked at me strangely as if she was nervous and worried, but she said nothing.

Dad continued, "Do you understand why we're . . . well, a little upset?"

I almost responded with a reflexive yes but stopped myself. Instead, I tried to understand *why* they were upset. I didn't. After a few moments of thought, I answered, "No."

Dad raised his eyebrows as if he couldn't believe his one and only offspring could be so obtuse, though I doubt if he meant to. Mom looked even more worried.

"Allison, you were gone all day, we didn't understand where to, or with whom, and right after I get home you come through the back door with two

strange, older boys. What were they doing here? And what were you thinking?" Dad's voice was getting louder and higher pitched, which hardly ever happened and never because of me.

Now I was feeling *really* nervous, but something about what he'd said needed addressing. "They're not *that* strange," I said seriously, thinking of Chris, who I actually thought was pretty weird.

Dad looked surprised and exasperated. I wasn't trying to be funny, but I could see a different side than my parents did. I tightened my left hand.

"Why don't you tell us what happened today?" said my mom softly, I think more to give my dad a chance to calm down than to give me an opportunity to explain.

"I was going to sleep late and stay home," I began, outlining my best intentions, "but they came over—"

"Who are 'they'?" Mom asked, and Dad nodded his head.

Dave was the first name to spring to mind, but I caught it in time.

"Robin," I said judiciously, knowing at least Mom approved of her, "and Dave and his brother Chris. They're friends from school. We just hang out together. You know, eat lunch and . . . stuff. And I don't think Dave is much older than I am. Remember the boys who helped us with our health project at the library, Mom?" I asked enthusiastically. I thought she'd be more receptive with even a slight connection to them.

"Yes, I remember *seeing* them," Mom said cautiously. "From a distance."

"Well, Dave was one of them, and Chris is his older brother. They're like brothers to Robin. They . . . watch out for her. And they seem to have adopted me too. They wanted to show me their friends' ranch and introduce me to them since they live so close. We're kind of like neighbors, really. You said you missed knowing who our neighbors are. Remember, Mom?" Okay, I knew this was playing dirty, but it *was* true. "They came over because they didn't have my phone number. I tried to call you. I really did. And I didn't mean to leave my phone here. I was just in a hurry to get ready. I thought it would be okay. And then, I guess I was having so much fun, I didn't even realize I didn't have my phone."

Mom and Dad looked at each other and were quiet for a minute. "So, this 'Chris' drove you somewhere?" asked Dad, not yielding one iota.

"Just up the street," I said, trying to sound reassuring. "He was really careful. We just went to Bar 8 Ranch. It's so cool. They've got so many horses.

And a pool. And the people are so nice. We helped to put the horses away that the guests were riding and had a really good lunch . . ." I had been speaking very quickly but realized if I kept going I'd be rambling. I finished in a slower, softer voice, "They know Dave and Robin really well, and it was *really* fun."

"I didn't see a girl with you," said Dad, sternly, "and I still don't understand why boys were coming into the house if you thought we weren't home."

"Greg," said Mom quietly, laying her hand on Dad's arm.

"I told you," I said, trying to be patient, "Robin stayed at Bar 8 to babysit for Cheryl while she went to town. The guys . . . we had just looked around outside a little," I improvised. "They followed me into the house because . . . I offered them a drink of water." I felt squirmy inside, knowing that wasn't completely truthful. It was the first time I had ever prevaricated to my Dad, and I had a feeling he could tell.

"I'm a little speechless, Allison," he said, shaking his head. "I guess I can't assume you understand things you apparently don't. I think we're going to have to set some pretty firm boundaries here."

His voice and expression were so serious that I began to really worry. I also thought that he wasn't speechless at all.

"First of all, we need to know you'll come straight home from school. Alone. And no rides from people we don't know. In fact, *anything* unplanned needs to be okayed *before* you do it. Understand?"

I understood, but I knew I was frowning. What on earth did they think I was going to do?

"And *no one*,"—I understood him to mean *no boy*—"is allowed in the house without permission from Mom or me. Is that clear?"

I was still frowning. What on earth did they think the boys were going to do? *Get real, please!* I was starting to feel rebellious. Another first.

"So . . . I'm not allowed to have friends?" I asked quietly, trying to sound reasonable.

"That's not what we're saying, Allison," said Mom, looking from Dad to me and still looking worried. "We don't know these new friends of yours. And we're concerned about . . ." Her eyes darted to Dad. I assumed she was trying to change what she'd say.

"So, if they come to the door, I tell them they're not welcome here?" I tried to control my voice and expression, but I felt hurt and angry.

"We need to know you understand and respect our rules," said Dad. "I need to know that you're not getting into some kind of trouble when I'm away." He didn't define *getting into trouble*, but the parameters seemed drawn. Dad's expression softened and his voice lowered as he said, "You know, it's going to take some adjusting for all of us, to our move and the fact that you're in high school now. There will be difficult choices in the future, and we want to help you learn to make the best ones."

I opened my mouth to comment back—something to the effect that I didn't think I had demonstrated any lack of good decision-making skills so far—but he held his hand up, stopping me from speaking.

"So," he said in an authoritative let's-wrap-this-meeting-up kind of voice, "until further notice, you will remain at home except for school. And you'll come straight home unless you have specific permission first to do something else. If Mom's working, I'll pick you up if I'm home. Otherwise, you'll ride the bus. Is it understood?"

The dutiful daughter, Daddy's little girl, wanted to capitulate and say yes immediately with no demur. But that part of me that was awakening to a new sense of self wouldn't allow it.

"No, I don't understand," I said quietly. "What have I ever done to make you mistrust me? And you haven't even really met Dave or his brother. They would *never* hurt me. I'm absolutely sure of it."

"You've just met them, Allison," said my mother, gently. "And we haven't met them at all. We just feel you're too young to be dating or anything."

I was dumbstruck for a moment and looked at my parents in amazement. "Dating?" I almost laughed at the leap they had made. "I'm not *dating* anyone."

"Well, hanging out alone with boys is not acceptable right now, Allison," said Dad firmly. "You're not even fifteen yet. I think there's a lot you just don't understand."

I felt like throwing that back in his face, but I didn't. My face was burning, but it wasn't from embarrassment or even anger—just an overwhelming sense of helplessness, completely convinced of the unfairness of the situation. For the first time in my life, I seriously considered rebelling. But two things held me back.

The main thing tempering my instinctive response was an overriding sense of immense relief. As unhappy as I was with this laying down of the law, I knew that I'd see Dave at school and that my friendship seemed important to him. That meant more than anything in the world to me. As long as I wasn't prevented from seeing him, I could bear this. I would see him Monday, would spend what time I could near him, and would be treated as a friend. I wasn't asking for or expecting more than that. The memories I already had would sustain me in between. He had seemed strangely perturbed that my father actually existed, but I didn't think that would change our friendship. I hoped not. This interference, intervention, meddling—I could think of worse words for it—made me unhappy, but nothing compared to the agony I had been in this past week. I could handle this.

The other thing that prevented me from reacting badly was, trying to see the situation through my parents' eyes, I *could* understand their concern, however misplaced I was sure it was. They thought I was completely naive, and perhaps I was a little, not having experienced a lot of things. But not *completely*. There were those movies I'd seen after all, mostly with Brenda; I *knew* what my parents were concerned about. I also knew they were wrong. I was positive they were. Still, I was glad later, when I had calmly thought through everything, that I hadn't caused a fuss. It probably would have made the situation worse.

"I understand that you're concerned," I said as calmly and diplomatically as I could, "but I don't 'hang out alone' with them. Robin was with us all day. She just stayed at Bar 8 while they brought me home. *They* were the ones concerned that I get home early so I didn't get in trouble." Thinking back, I thought it was Dave who had voiced those concerns and arranged our timeline, but they had all made a point of keeping to it.

A new concern occurred to me: this was going to be tricky. In spite of trying to stay cool, everything came out in a rush. "There's a barbecue next weekend, on Labor Day. Dave invited me. It's a big deal around here with horse . . . games. Or something. It's at their ranch. It sounds like so much fun. There'll be a lot of people there from town and school. They're really well-known around here." I stopped to catch my breath and calm down again. "Please . . . can I go?"

They looked at each other, then Dad simply said, "No."

I felt the blood drain from my face as I realized how serious he was, but I knew there was nothing I could do. Mom on her own was usually reasonable and accommodating, not that I had ever put her to the test. But I was beginning to see a side of my father I'd never seen before. A part of me wanted

to fight back, but I knew they were doing what they were convinced, for the time being, was right for me. And I had a feeling the keyword was *time*.

I swallowed hard and remained as impassive as I could, then turned and left the kitchen. I had planned to go to my room, but my parents' voices reached me on the stairs. I stopped and sat down near the top landing.

It was true I hadn't known Dave or his brother long and didn't know much about them at all. But everything I'd learned so far made me feel safe with them, even with Chris, who I didn't think liked me very much. And not only safe by association with Robin but actively protected for my own sake. I hadn't thought that through before. It added to my returning sense of well-being and certainty of their goodwill.

"You don't think we're being a little harsh?"

Yay, Mom!

It was silent for a moment. I could picture my mother and father reading each others' faces.

"No, I really don't." Dad sounded tired and very gruff. "Seeing her with those boys gave me the shock of my life. It never occurred to me something like this could happen. I can't help wondering what could have been going on in those kids' heads, and what *might* have happened if I hadn't been here. It was obvious they never expected to see *me*."

"I'm sure there was nothing *wrong*," said Mom, her voice lowered.

"You didn't see the boys," said Dad. "These are tough kids. I thought the little guy was going to try to fight me or something. And the taller one . . ." Dad's voice trailed off. Either his voice lowered too much for me to hear or he didn't finish the thought aloud. "What they could want with Allison unless they thought they could get away with something, is beyond me. She's just a little girl."

My cheeks were flaming with indignation on all counts, but Dad's logic hit me hard too.

"Oh dear," said Mom, so softly I almost didn't hear her. "She's been so unhappy lately and wouldn't talk about anything. She's been acting so differently, almost since the first day of school. I'm wondering if these boys have anything to do with it?"

Oh, crud.

"I noticed it as soon as she started talking to me," said Dad, equally softly. "I don't think these people are good for her. What could be going on to change her so suddenly?"

"She's growing up, Greg. I don't think we should assume the worst and jump to conclusions. She may have had a lapse in judgment, but she hasn't *done* anything. At least, I'm very sure she hasn't. And either have the boys, to our knowledge. I'd like to meet them."

Yay Mom again!

"I don't know," Dad said, and I could picture him shaking his head. "And then there's the whole horse issue. I don't know why it didn't occur to me that she might get mixed up with horses, living around here. I guess I assumed that, since she's never really been exposed to them, it wouldn't be something that would attract her. I moved here to protect my family, to be able to afford a home in a decent place, and try to raise my daughter away from the things happening in the city. Hah!" he exclaimed mirthlessly. "Out of the frying pan, into the fire?"

"This *is* a good place, Greg. Just give it a little more time. As for the horses, it was just a day at a ranch. Is it so bad?" Mom's championing of our new home surprised me a little. I guess she was really starting to like it here. "Allison is going to grow up regardless of where we live, and there will be problems and temptations wherever we are. Let's give it a chance."

It was quiet again for a few moments.

"I'm just worried about her," said Dad. "I guess I didn't think boys would be an issue. Not yet. Not for a while. I'd pictured a very different situation . . . and type of boy. And horses. You know why I'm troubled about that."

I don't! What's wrong with horses?

"Well, we can probably keep her away from horses, but we can't choose her friends for her. And Greg, at least she *has* friends here. Robin seems like a nice girl and she's told me of another girl at school. As for the boys, I'm worried too. But we can't lock her up or prevent her from seeing them at school. You know she's a good girl. We need to trust her."

"Maybe I've just lost touch with reality. I've been gone so much, I suddenly feel like I don't know my own daughter. She looks the same, but something's different and it worries me. And boys like *that*. Why aren't they hanging out with . . . I don't know . . . cheerleaders or something?"

So Dad was worried enough to automatically *not* trust my friends or me, and Mom was inclined to give us all the benefit of the doubt. My dad was right about at least one thing: I was different. I hadn't changed the way I looked; it hadn't even occurred to me to try. I doubted much could be done to help me anyway. I certainly didn't have any ambition to look like the kind of girl that would attract "boys like *that*." At least, not the kind Dad seemed to have in mind. And I'd never seen them trying to hang out with the kind of girl I assumed Dad meant. Though to be honest, a lot of the girls who did hang out around the Calderas were attractive and might be *just* like that.

It was true that I was different on the inside, though. Things I'd never thought of before were now very important to me, and I was feeling things I'd never even imagined. How could I not be different? But these were things my father had no knowledge of and wasn't going to if I could help it. I could imagine being sent off to an all girls' school or something. I was glad he loved me enough to be concerned, but I was hardly flattered by his opinion of my lack of allure, accurate though it might be. And I *was* almost fifteen— almost old enough to start driver's training and get a job. Only a little over three years away from being able to vote on important issues concerning the governing of our country.

My parents had been quiet for a few minutes, then I heard dinner being prepared. Their conversation turned to things less critical to me. I sighed unhappily and retreated to my room, closing the door quietly. I half expected my mother to come and find me, but she apparently thought I needed to sort through this on my own. *Right again, Mom.* It was looking like she was potentially my best ally in these matters. I began looking forward to—and dreading—her meeting Dave.

I went downstairs later and ate calmly enough. Though I still felt pretty upset, it didn't seem like a good idea to exhibit it. I'd never been a chatty person so I hoped they didn't notice. After dinner, I couldn't handle the pretense anymore so said I was very tired and went back to my room.

It was true; I was exhausted. It had been a busy day in the sun, and muscles I hadn't known existed were beginning to complain. But the emotional strain was starting to wear on me again too, and I needed to sort through it all. I had managed to avoid emotional fireworks with my parents, but the feelings in my heart whenever I thought of Dave or any attempt to keep him out of my life were just as explosive. A long, hot bath eased my aches, washed the dust off, and helped my mind relax. Then I curled up on my bed with the lights off. After a moment, I got up and reached for Dave's hat, sitting on my desk, then lay down again.

It's funny how an aroma can evoke sights and sounds and feelings. The hat possessed a light but complex fragrance that reminded me immediately of Dave—probably from whatever shampoo he used—but also of sun and horses and leather. It was a good smell and made me feel warm and happy. The black felt was soft and smooth to the touch but more unyielding than it looked. It obviously wasn't a cheap hat.

I couldn't help smiling. What would Dave think if he knew I was sleeping with it?

What a dork.

Chapter Ten

I Don't Really Mind

I awoke early, Dave's hat clutched in one arm. At least I hadn't completely crushed it during the night. That might have proved awkward to explain. Yesterday's occurrences swept through my mind, overloading it and leaving me feeling disoriented at first, not sure if they were all from actual events or dreams.

Having the hat helped to bring the memories into focus and chronological order. The aroma still clinging to it brought vivid images of Dave and corresponding sensations back to me. Dave at my front door, sitting at my kitchen table, and right behind or beside me around the horses. My temptation to touch his sunlit hair as he bent before me. His riding as if one with Remmy and showing me his domain. In the truck on the way home, his leg and arm touching mine. Him standing firm before my father, strongly gripping his hand. Dave, holding *my* hand as I got out of the truck and as he wrote his phone number on it.

I was glad that he wasn't like some of the boys I remembered from middle school who drenched themselves in cheap cologne. I'd never been aware of anything but a light, sometimes warm and musky but attractive smell when I was very near him, which lately seemed to be pretty often. I embraced the hat and was comforted by the warm scent, my disorientation replaced with resolve. I hadn't thought much about doubt before, but there were now two things—new, intoxicating things—that I was completely sure of in my life, and I would tenaciously cling to them.

No, three things. . . .

I thought about my parents' conversation with me and then with each other, and felt the same mix of indignation and grudging acquiescence filter up. I had already judged myself unworthy of Dave so many times I'd lost count, and Brenda hadn't helped, but to hear my *parents* do it! Did they think me so completely undesirable? Or did they just think a boy like him incapable of offering real friendship to a girl like me?

Get real! If all he wanted was to mess around, there's a herd of pretty girls that seem ready to oblige him.

I would never believe him pathetic enough to take advantage of someone just because they were weak or stupid or both, and a social misfit like me thrown in for good measure. A universe that allowed that wouldn't be worth living in. I tossed the thought aside easily, my confidence in him completely unshaken. That was one of the things I was sure of. Let them say and think what they would about me. I knew what I knew and it would sustain me.

It was barely light, but I got up, grabbed my glasses, dressed, and braided my hair as quietly as I could. Grabbing Dave's hat, I sneaked downstairs, took an apple from the bowl in the kitchen, and crept out of the house. I ran as fast as I could, feeling buoyed up by my pep talk and willing myself to not sprain my ankle, all the way to the cattle guard.

Once out of sight of the house, I walked quietly to the shady part of the stream where I'd first met Gold. I thought about my dad and wondered about his reasons for being anxious about horses. I was starting to feel like I wasn't going to be allowed to do *anything*.

I waited until the sun had crept to the top of the eastern hills, but I didn't want my dad to come looking for me. Disappointed but still feeling empowered and full of resolution, I left the apple where I had first left food for Gold and walked home. No one was in the kitchen and I was hungry, so I laid Dave's hat on the table and began cooking ham and eggs.

"Can I get some of that?" Dad asked from the doorway.

I turned and smiled. "Sure! How many eggs would you like?"

He looked surprised, as if he thought I might have held a grudge, but he smiled back. His eyes took in the hat and his mouth opened, probably to ask where it had come from, but the answer was so obvious that he quickly

shut it again. I don't think he wanted to hear it out loud. I couldn't help hiding a smile, not because of Dad's discomfort, but because of the absurd contentment having the hat made me feel. I doubted Dave had purposefully left it with me, but I was glad he did! And who knew why Dave did anything, except perhaps his brother, an enigma himself.

"Hey, we should go out to dinner," said Dad, dragging his eyes away from the hat. "There must be somewhere good to eat in town, right? It's been a long time since we ate out together."

I smiled but didn't know. Mom and I had only had take-out Mexican and pizza a couple of times since we'd moved here. I finished cooking our breakfast and gave a plate to my dad. I sat down by the hat and felt smug, as if I had some kind of invisible protection. Dad cleared his throat and began eating, but he seemed a little twitchy.

I spent most of the day in my room, leaving the door open so my parents wouldn't think I was sulking. I got all my homework done and spent the rest of the day happily daydreaming, drawing, and listening to music. Tomorrow was Monday. I smiled and touched the soft felt of the hat, sitting on my desk within easy reach. My hand still bore a slight shadow of numbers. I'm sure nobody else would be able to tell what it signified.

I smiled again, then frowned. I had hoped that Gold would show up this morning. Then I would have had a reason—no, an *obligation*—to call Dave. I had thought about calling him anyway to ask whether he wanted me to bring his hat tomorrow, but it seemed like such a slim excuse. Girls probably called him all the time, and I didn't want to be just one more. The last thing I wanted was to annoy him. No, I was content to wait until tomorrow. I'd see him one way or another.

My room was darkening when my dad stood in the doorway and asked if I was ready to go. I felt no need to dress up so put everything aside and followed him downstairs. He seemed to be back to his usual self, joking and keeping us entertained until we reached the steakhouse in town. He always had interesting stories of his travels and knew how to give a funny twist to them most of the time.

We didn't have to wait long to be seated. It was dark there; it had an intimate feeling, and everyone seemed to be talking in hushed tones, unlike most restaurants I'd been in where the noise level sometimes overwhelmed me.

My dad asked me about school and I tried to think of positive, interesting things to tell him. But almost everything that came to mind included a certain brown haired boy I thought I shouldn't bring up too often, so I had to get a little creative and embellish some otherwise mundane events. I told him about the track tryouts, trying to make them sound funny and making light of my mishaps. Dad knew I wasn't exactly Olympic material. *All's well that ends well* seemed to apply, so I stayed calm and tried not to think about the Dave aspect of those episodes in case I got careless. I happily told him about Melanie, making a point of mentioning that she rode and had horses—conveniently leaving out the part about her getting hurt—and describing the things we were doing in Art.

"And then there's Robin," I said. "She rides too. At least, at the guest ranch she did. We got an A on the Health project we did together. Of course, we had some help." Dad cared about grades, so I didn't want to miss the chance to give my friends a favorable mention.

I became aware of someone walking in our direction and looked up just as he reached our table. "Hey," he said, friendly as ever.

"Hi!" I said, surprised but glad to see him.

Matthew was the kind of guy who obviously cared about his appearance. Not that he seemed vain but, even dressed for school, he always looked neat. He looked especially nice this evening: dark pants and light-colored, buttoned shirt, every hair seemingly in place. He looked different, though; nothing of the usual skater boy appeared tonight. It made me feel underdressed.

Sheesh. It's just a steakhouse.

He acknowledged my awareness by rolling his eyes slightly, and I almost laughed. Looking at each of my parents in turn and then back to me, he raised his straight brows as if expecting something.

"Oh," I said self-consciously. "Mom, Dad, this is Matthew, another friend from school."

Matthew reached over, shaking hands first with my dad then my mom. I couldn't help comparing the interaction with the ones that had occurred yesterday in my kitchen. I had a feeling my dad was doing the same. Both my parents greeted him with open, friendly expressions.

"It's really nice to meet you," Matthew said politely, smiling at them in turn. Then he looked back to me and shrugged. "I just thought I'd come say hi. You didn't eat with us all week. I wondered if everything was okay."

"Ye . . . yes . . . of course," I said, squirming a little and hoping I didn't blush, especially with my parents watching with such interest. "Everything's fine. I was hanging out with a friend who got hurt . . . and . . . stuff."

"Oh," he said, nodding his head slowly. "That's cool. Well, I'd better get back. It was a pleasure to meet you," he said again to my parents, then looked back at me. "See you tomorrow?"

I think he looked hopeful.

"Definitely," I said happily, thinking it was nice to have friends but also thinking of the company I expected Matthew to be in.

"He seems like a very nice boy," whispered Mom as Matthew walked away, presumably back to his family.

"*All* my friends are very nice," I said.

"Was he one of the boys who helped you at the library?" she asked, ignoring my tone.

My mind raced, wondering how to answer her. I could have played it safe and just said yes, but that wasn't good enough.

"Yes, he and Dave Caldera," I said, trying not to sound too deliberate but feeling the need to make it clear. "Actually, Dave did most of the helping, but Matthew's really nice too."

The mood at our table abruptly changed. I pretended not to notice. On our way out, we passed the table where Matthew was sitting. We waved at each other. He appeared to be there with his parents and two older girls and a younger boy that I assumed were his siblings. His parents smiled and looked at me with interest.

The ride home felt subdued, but I had already retreated to a place in my head where I could be alone with my own thoughts and opinions. Everything else kind of rolled off me. It bothered me that my parents were so easily impressed by Matthew and so willing to mistrust Dave, but I wasn't going to let it upset me. I still knew what I knew and was comforted by it.

When we got home, I watched a movie with my parents like we always did when Dad was home, and I tried to act as I thought they wanted me to. I would rather have just gone to my room. I had hoped to look for Gold this evening, but it was already dark. I'd have to get up early instead.

I woke up before my alarm went off, even though I had set it for an hour earlier than normal. Nervous and expectant, I hoped that Gold would be around, but I looked forward even more to getting to school. All the way down to the stream I wondered when I'd see Dave, how would he act, how would I react and feel, and then chastised myself for making such a big deal of it.

Quit thinking about it or you won't be able to function. Or you'll get your hopes up too high and be shot down. There. A good dose of reality.

The apple that I had left the previous morning was gone, but plenty of other creatures could have eaten it. I wandered around a little but finally left the day's offering in the same place. There was little edible vegetation left near the stream. I feared he might have moved on to greener pastures. Literally.

Dad offered to drive me to school and said he'd pick me up later too. I thought it best to ask him to drop me off and pick me up at the front of the school instead of in the parking lot.

Dave appeared out of nowhere as I made my way to my locker, answering the question of how I was going to put my books back in it. "You didn't call me," he said, a quizzical look in his eye.

"I didn't see Gold," I said, my heart beating so hard I was sure he must be able to hear it.

"Who?"

"The horse. You . . . you said to call and let you know what happened with him. I didn't see him again."

"You could have called me anyway," he said, opening my locker.

My cheeks felt hot. I kept the books I would need for the day and closed the door as the bell rang.

"See you at lunch?" he asked, backing away from me.

Still blushing, I nodded. He grinned and went on his way.

I thought about Melanie at lunchtime but walked out to the tables with Robin without hesitation. Dave watched our approach and smiled, not once faltering in conversation with the kids around him.

They were discussing soccer and the scrimmage game scheduled for the next day. I was able to ascertain that practice had been going on after school most of last week and that Dave and a few of the other boys were players. The older guys were giving each other a hard time about past blunders and gloating over moments of glory. They were also giving Dave and another boy a hard time about being "punk JV" when Matthew arrived. He was dressed as

I was used to seeing him: T-shirt and shorts, his cropped curly hair ungelled. He walked straight to where Robin and I sat at the end of one of the tables.

"Hey!" he said

"Hey," said Robin.

"Hi," I said and scooted over so he could sit down.

"It was nice to meet your parents last night," he said, quite loudly.

I almost choked on a mouth full of sandwich or I would have said something back immediately. Instead, I tried to smile and nodded acknowledgment. I noticed the other end of the table had grown quiet and Dave regarded us with slightly knit brows. He must have heard.

I needed to say something. "Do you and your family go to that restaurant often?"

"Yeah," said Matthew. "Just about every week."

Dave smirked. Matthew smiled and shook his head. I pondered.

I had no direct contact with Dave during lunch but couldn't help studying the girls gathered in his general vicinity. There was no single type represented and I was glad again that there didn't appear to be a requirement for being a member of this group. It also provided further proof to me that my father was very wrong about Dave. Not that I needed it, of course.

When the bell rang, Robin and Matthew got up and walked off together. I had resigned myself to waiting until the next day to see and talk to Dave again when he appeared beside me.

"Where's your phone?" he asked.

"My phone?"

He held out his hand. I set my backpack on the table, opened the front pocket, found my phone and handed it to him. It didn't matter what he wanted it for; he asked for it, he would get it. I had a feeling that would be true with anything.

He took the phone and shouldered my backpack. As we walked, he keyed in numbers. When we reached my building, he handed the phone and my backpack back. Then he took a phone out of his pocket, looked at it, and waved it slightly in my face. He now had my number. Grinning and walking backward a few steps, he then turned and walked away. I walked on clouds to my next class.

I found myself smiling most of the afternoon, so much so that Melanie noticed in Art. I told her that I kept remembering something funny and asked if I could meet her for lunch tomorrow. It was going to be hard to stay away from Dave, but I was determined to spend time with Melanie too.

"Of course," she said, happily. "You know where to find me."

Homework was kicking in with a vengeance, and I needed both of my big textbooks at home so didn't bother with my locker. I knew I should make another trip to the office about it, but I didn't want to deprive myself of this link to Dave. As I was thinking this and walking up to the car, my phone buzzed. Dad smiled and opened the door for me. I got in and quickly dug my phone out of my backpack.

'Need your locker?'

Dad looked like he was trying to not look like he wondered who it was. I typed, *'Not now. Thanks!'*

There was no further response, but I sat back feeling content and happy. Dad looked at me a couple of times, obviously curious, but he didn't ask.

The next morning I rose extra early again, took a couple of carrots from the refrigerator, and headed determinedly out toward the stream. I had grabbed Dave's hat at the last moment and put it on. It was getting harder to notice a distinctive fragrance on it, but it still made me feel connected to him. I was wrestling with whether to bring it to school or not when I came around a bush and saw Gold. He stood as if waiting for me and nickered softly as I came into view.

"You're here!" I cried, throat constricting, eyes burning.

I thought I was prepared to never see him again. But here he was, eyes bright, ears pricked forward, looking as regal yet scruffy as he had before and even more attractive to me. I wanted to run and throw my arms around his neck but controlled myself. Warning words—*Be careful*—came to mind. I didn't believe they were necessary but heeded them anyway. I stepped a little closer, tucking one of the carrots in my back pocket out of sight and holding the other out invitingly.

"What have you been up to, huh?" I asked him softly, sniffling a little. "I missed you!"

He looked to the side as if thinking for a moment, then stepped close enough to lip the carrot. I drew back a fraction and he followed another step closer. He took the offered end of it in his teeth, but I held on, causing him

to bite through. He munched for a minute and then stepped even closer for the remainder of the carrot. Now I could easily stroke his nose. I could have reached out to stroke his neck but decided not to. Instead, I stepped back to see if he would follow.

He looked at me, eyes gentle, demeanor relaxed. I pulled the other carrot out and took another couple of steps back. He stepped toward me slowly and took the end again. I let him bite through it. I was tempted to step back more but didn't want to be too obvious, even to a horse. If I could get him to come to me at all, I might eventually persuade him to follow me to the corral. I gave him the rest of the carrot, stroking his cheek and the soft skin around his nostrils.

"I have to go," I said, "but I'll see you later. Okay?"

He stood munching but didn't follow as I backed away from him.

I considered calling Dave but decided I would rather have something to talk to him about in person. I still felt so nervous around him. I wondered again if that would ever change.

When Dad dropped me off, I saw Dave talking to several kids, mostly girls, near the closest corridor. My heart skipped a few beats. I'd never seen him near the front of the school before. I looked at Dad as the car came to a stop. Hopefully he wouldn't notice and Dave wouldn't draw attention to himself. He couldn't be there for me anyway. *Duh.*

"See you after school, sweetheart," said Dad, smiling at me.

"Okay." I closed the door and stepped back, but stayed near the curb with my back to the school until he pulled away. When I turned around, Dave was right there and it startled me.

"Jumpy," he said.

"You weren't there a second ago."

"Yeah, I'm sneaky like that," he grinned. "Locker?"

We began walking. The girls he'd been talking to a moment before watched us and looked offended as we went by, but he didn't seem to notice.

"Um, no, I'm okay," I said, "but I wanted to let you know I saw G— the horse . . . this morning."

"Cool," he said, nodding his head. "How did he seem?"

"Fine," I said. "He acted the same as before with me. I got him to follow me a little, but it might take a while to get him all the way to the corral."

We had reached my homeroom. I hadn't even noticed we were walking that way. He stopped and turned to me, hands in his pockets.

"So . . . you haven't told your folks about him?"

"Um, no. I . . . I don't want to do that . . . yet."

He shrugged his shoulders as if to say, *Whatever.*

"See you at lunch," he said and began walking away.

I remembered Melanie. "Oh! I'm eating in the cafeteria today."

He turned and gave me a funny look, then smirked and continued walking away.

Algebra, like the rest of my classes lately, left me loaded down with homework, and Robin and I complained about it until the bell rang.

"We should do it together," she said. "Want to go to the library after school?"

I did but was quite sure I wouldn't be allowed to. I didn't even want to ask. After all, my dad didn't know that *certain* people wouldn't even be around due to soccer games and other unspecified "stuff," and I doubted if making a point of telling him would make a difference. Then I had a flash of genius.

"Why don't you come over tomorrow?" I asked. "You can have dinner with us. You haven't met my dad yet, and I want him to meet you." That was very true.

"Okay," she said, nodding and looking like she thought it was a good idea. "I'm sure it's fine."

We went our separate ways and I wondered about her family. She never mentioned them, but that wasn't unusual. Nobody talked about their families.

Melanie walked almost normally now and dressed for PE but was excused from doing anything strenuous. Coach had her manning a stopwatch for the people still making up running times. I was thankful I had finished last week.

Everyone else was working on soccer skills: learning to dribble, pass, and shoot the ball. This was actually fun though I wasn't good at it. The girls were on the lower field while the boys took the football field. I felt envious of Melanie as, if I'd been in her position, I would have been able to watch Dave.

At lunch, I noticed her silver locket again, and it reminded me of something I wanted to ask her. The question didn't seem as urgent now, but I was still curious.

"Have you ever liked someone, but not known how they feel back?"

Melanie looked at me curiously and smiled slightly. "Liked, like . . . *liked*?" she asked, humor lighting her eyes.

I could feel the pink creeping up my cheeks. "I mean . . . somebody who's friendly, but . . . you're not sure exactly how they feel about you?"

She looked wistful and played absentmindedly with her locket. "You mean whether they're real friends?" She had a far-away look in her eyes now and I wondered what she was thinking.

"Not exactly," I said, afraid of revealing too much. "I mean, they seem to be your friend and everything, but you don't know why."

"You mean, you think they might be more than friends?" she asked, looking at me a little too perceptively.

No, that's ridiculous, there's no way. I frowned. It was difficult to put into words exactly *what* I was thinking without sounding, well, ridiculous.

"I don't know. It's confusing. Sometimes it seems like . . ." *Sometimes it seems like he cares a little too much, pays a little too much attention for just a friend. But that's where it ends. There doesn't seem to be anything more to it. There's nothing . . . more. There. I've answered my own question.* I sighed loudly and Melanie smiled.

"I knew someone once," she said. "I thought he cared about me. You know, *really* cared. I was convinced of it. Everything he did and said led me to believe it. And then one day it just wasn't the same anymore." She looked sad but smiled her pretty smile and shrugged slightly. I felt devastated, but I wasn't sure if it was for her sake or mine. "I think . . . I think you should enjoy the friendship. I'm sure your story is different from mine."

It seemed like such a mature thing to say that it scared me. Whoever had hurt her was an idiot, that was for sure. Still, I needed to be careful. Wishful thinking was too likely to make me see and read things that couldn't be there, and that would only mean hurt later. Right? Feeling very mature myself for such reasoning, I picked up my tray and stood to leave, only to find Dave standing at the edge of the table.

I gulped and sat back down, maturity thrown out the window in favor of pure, unadulterated adoration.

"Hey," he said, smiling at me and looking at Melanie with curiosity.

"Hi," I choked out, then cleared my throat. "This is my friend, Melanie. Melanie, Dave." My cheeks burned and not just because he was standing so close; I was sure Melanie could make the obvious connection to my previous questions.

Dave's eyes narrowed as he looked at her. "You look familiar," he said. "Have we met before?"

"No," said Melanie, her eyes steadily on his. "You've probably just seen me . . . around."

Dave looked unconvinced but seemed to shrug it off. Scanning the lunch room as if he'd never seen it before—which he probably hadn't—he seemed to wonder what the allure of the place was. He looked at me and tipped his head toward the door. I waved at Melanie as I got up, disposed of my tray, and followed him outside.

"Why do you want to eat in there?"

"Because I want to eat with Melanie and that's where she eats," I said logically.

"Yeah, but . . . why?"

I didn't have an answer I wanted to share so tried redirection. "I still have your hat."

The abrupt change of subject seemed to amuse him, his eyes crinkling up as he smiled. "Bring it on Monday."

"Monday?" I asked, wondering why he wanted me to wait so long and calculating exactly how long that meant I got to keep it.

"The barbecue," he said, still looking amused. "Did you forget?"

"Oh, right," I said, suddenly even more nervous. "Um . . . I can't go . . . to the barbecue."

Now he had an odd look on his face. *Incredulous?* "Can't go? Do you just need a ride or something? I'm sure we can get you there—"

"No," I said, starting to feel a little desperate. *My parents don't like you. They don't know you, but they don't trust you.* What could I say? "Um . . . I think we already have plans . . . or something . . . that I can't get out of."

He looked thoughtful and made a noise like *hnh* as if such a possibility had never occurred to him.

"I . . . I've got to go," I said, pointing toward the door of my next class. He always led the way, yet we always arrived at *my* classroom. Just another of those really confusing things.

"Yeah," he said as if preoccupied with something. "See ya." He turned and walked away.

"Bye," I said and sighed.

I didn't need to go to my locker after school, but Dave's expression had left me worried, so I went anyway. If he thought I didn't care about the things he cared about, would his interest in me diminish? And this barbecue seemed to be important. I stood regarding my locker, wondering what I would say to him. I couldn't wait long.

Suddenly Chris was beside me, and I shivered. It seemed to happen when he appeared suddenly like that, not because I was afraid of him or didn't like him—at least, not really. I thought it might be because, of my close acquaintance, he was one of the few people significantly taller than me—him and Matthew. I looked up at his face and realized that I hadn't noticed him around for a couple of days. That didn't mean he hadn't been there. I felt a little guilty.

"He had to leave early for a game," he said, apparently thinking he was answering an unspoken question. I hadn't even thought it yet.

"Oh . . . right. Thanks," I said as he walked off.

Gold was waiting for me Wednesday morning and obligingly stepped toward me when I held out the carrot. He crunched it in two, but I held onto the second half, letting my hand fall to my side, away from him. When he had finished munching, I stood my ground but held the carrot away from me a little. He hesitated, then stepped right up to me to take the remaining piece.

I reached out to stroke his thick neck, my heart beating fast and a shiver running down my spine as I smoothed his dirty coat. A quiver shook the skin where I touched him and then on his shoulder where my hand came to rest. Then he shook himself and stepped forward beyond me, a cloud of dust surrounding him. I'd never seen a horse shake itself like that and I laughed. He looked back at me, seeming reproachful, an improbable mix of cute and noble.

I still held an apple and he eyed it expectantly. Holding it up enticingly, I took a bite.

He turned as if he would step back to me, but I walked forward instead, past him and toward the road. He followed me for a few steps as if not thinking, then stopped, raised his head and looked more alert.

I took another bite of the apple. "Mmm . . . yummy!" I said as if he could be convinced that way.

It actually seemed to work. He took another few steps and was almost within reach, but I turned and moved away again. He seemed to deliberate, then moved two steps closer. Then he stopped. Apparently he'd reached his limit of being manipulated for the morning.

"Okay, you win." I walked back and held the apple out to him, not wanting him to lose interest.

Instead of taking the whole thing, he bit into it and I brought my hands together to catch the residue. I held my hands still until he finished what he'd left behind. Then he licked my hand. A thrill ran through me and I couldn't help smiling. It felt like we had reached a new level of—something. Trust? Something Chris had said came to mind. Gold let me reach forward and stroke his neck and shoulder again, and the same shiver ran through me. He was so big and strong. It amazed me that I could just pet him like this.

"I'll see you tomorrow," I said softly and headed home.

At school, I was disappointed to see Chris waiting by my locker but smiled, grateful anyway. His expression stayed neutral as he opened the door and watched me exchange books.

"Did you get into trouble the other day?" he asked suddenly.

It startled me and I looked at him a little wide-eyed. "What?"

"Saturday. Did you get in trouble?"

"Oh," I said, trying to gather my thoughts. *Let's see . . . my dad found me alone with two boys. What do you think?* "No. Of course not. There was just a little . . . misunderstanding . . . about where I was. It's fine."

He was frowning—nothing unusual there—but I got the distinct impression he wasn't buying it. He walked off without another word.

There was a loud buzz of conversation at lunch, and it all seemed centered around Dave. For the first time, I wasn't sure he even noticed Robin and me as we walked to our usual end of the table and sat down. Matthew was already there. Chris sat next to him but faced away from everyone, looking off across the field.

"I assume we're all talking about The Game," said Robin, waving her hands and rolling her eyes.

"Of course," said Matthew between mouthfuls of his sandwich. "We won't be hearing the last of it for a while, I'm sure."

I looked toward Dave, surrounded by his friends and more girls than usual, some I'd never seen before. I looked back at Robin inquiringly.

"Varsity played a scrimmage game yesterday after JV. JV team members shouldn't have played in it, but one of the players got hurt right before halftime and instead of sending a regular replacement in, they let Dave play. He made three goals in the second half."

"Chris made four," said Matthew.

"In the whole game," Chris added quietly as if accuracy was important.

"The team wants Dave to play varsity this year, even though he's a freshman," continued Matthew. "But Coach says he wants him to play JV so we have a chance at having two winning teams this year. Then he can play varsity next year."

I found that I was blushing for no reason I could account for. I *did* feel proud of him, though I knew nothing about soccer.

"Next year will be incredible," said a boy farther along the table. "Both Calderas on one team and Shane and probably Matthew as well. And *me,* of course." Everyone laughed as if he'd made a joke. "I bet we'll be unbeatable."

I noticed Chris get up, throw something away, and stalk off.

"It's up to what Dave wants to do. I guess that's pretty unheard of," said Robin, looking at me, "so it's kind of a big deal."

Several of the girls in Dave's vicinity giggled loudly, though he didn't seem to be contributing much to the conversation. I sighed. I doubted that he would notice me at all today.

The rest of the day dragged by, even Art, which I usually enjoyed.

"Is everything okay?" asked Melanie, perceptively.

"Of course," I said, shaking off my blues and smiling. I was going to have to be careful how I acted around her; she knew too much. At least I was sure she wouldn't be spilling everything to the object of my affection.

I was tempted to go to my locker but didn't want to be disappointed. Chris was making me feel more than a little uncomfortable, too. For someone I didn't give much credit for observation to, he sometimes got *extra* points.

I decided to compromise by trying to catch Robin at her locker instead of at the front of the school like we'd planned. I found her there, but no one seemed to be near mine. I felt stupidly dejected.

"Are you ready?" she asked. "You don't need to go to your locker?"

"No." I took one last look in that direction. I guessed I'd live until tomorrow.

Dad was waiting.

"This is my friend Robin," I said as we got in the back seat.

"Hi," smiled Robin.

"Hi there," said Dad, smiling back at her and then at me. "So, I thought a stop for something cold might be in order?"

We both agreed that cold beverages were indeed definitely in order.

That pretty much set the tone for the evening. We finished our math homework much sooner than I would have done on my own and probably more accurately too, and we quizzed each other on the Health chapter we'd be tested about on Friday. Dad hummed in the kitchen as we worked. He seemed very happy, and he and Mom joked and laughed a lot while they prepared dinner together after she got home. A couple of times I caught Robin looking thoughtful, almost sad. She always smiled when she noticed me looking at her though.

Just before dinner, she asked, "Could I use your phone?"

"Sure, it's over there," I said, pointing toward the kitchen door. She didn't say much and was off within a couple of minutes. It wasn't until much later that it struck me as odd that she hadn't either used her own phone or borrowed mine.

We spent the time after dinner in my room, Robin perusing my CDs and making fun of the eclectic nature of my collection. I didn't mind. At one point she grabbed Dave's hat, which was sitting on my desk, and set it on her head. It seemed to prompt her to tell me stories of hanging out with Dave and Chris, and I had no desire to stop her. I hoped that understanding her relationship with them a little more would help me get a handle on my own. It was still a complete mystery to me.

"Sometimes I spend weekend days and holidays with them if they're not off somewhere else. And even then, sometimes they take me along." This obviously made her extremely happy. "They work hard and do a lot of other stuff too . . . skateboarding, dirt biking, surfing. School sports. I usually go to the home games. And they ride, of course."

I couldn't imagine being even half that busy.

"Your folks don't mind you hanging out with them?"

She frowned as if it was a non-issue. "Naw. The Calderas are like . . . family. You know?"

She took the hat off and set it back on my desk without ever commenting on it. About seven-thirty we went back downstairs.

"Do you need a ride, Robin?" asked Dad, just as I heard a familiar vehicle pulling up outside.

"That's my ride now," she said, smiling. "Thanks for dinner. It was really nice to meet you, Mr. Anderson. Goodbye, Mrs. Anderson. See you tomorrow, Allison."

I stepped outside after her and watched as she walked up to the black truck in the gathering dusk. Chris opened the door for her from the inside. She climbed in and waved as they backed out of the driveway. Then I noticed Dad standing behind me.

"Her brother?" he asked, squinting through his glasses and sounding a little concerned.

"Kind of," I said lightly. "Dave's brother. You met him on Saturday, remember?" I smiled at him and went back into the house.

Feeling a little dejected but not hopeless, I held Dave's hat as I fell asleep.

I woke up late and rushed down to the creek. Gold was waiting by the road close to where I had left him the previous morning. I didn't have time to play any games so I walked within a few steps of him and waited for him to come the rest of the way. When he did, I gave him the apple I had brought and he let me pet around his face and stroke his neck again. When I turned to leave, he followed me almost to the edge of the corral. There he stopped and watched me walk away. I thought again of Chris' words, that I could regain his trust. It looked like he was right. I might be able to catch him after all.

I wanted to talk to Dave so badly, to tell him what was going on with Gold and, well, just to talk to him. I almost messaged him but still felt reluctant to bother him. I believed, *hoped*, that he would contact or seek me out when he wanted to. I didn't own him and he certainly owed me nothing. It was unreasonable to expect more than that. Still, it was difficult going through the day without seeing him.

I had thought I might catch a glimpse of him in PE, but girls and boys were still on different fields. Melanie got to play with us today which made the class more fun and made the time go a little faster. I hoped Dave would seek me out in the cafeteria again, but he didn't. I didn't even see Chris anywhere and was starting to feel a little shaky by the end of the day.

Had I offended him? Did he think I didn't want to be around him, go to his house, to the barbecue? My intellect, what I had of it anyway, reminded me that Dave didn't seem to get discouraged easily and that he was probably just occupied with other things. My emotions, however, were threatening another meltdown.

Robin acted as if everything was normal and I couldn't think of a subtle way to ask what Dave was up to. I guess what I really wanted to know was, had he even thought of me in the past two days? I kept an eye on my phone, hoping to see the light and icon that indicated a message, but it stayed dark and quiet.

I was subdued on the way home and couldn't force myself to eat much at dinner. Mom had been telling a story about something that had happened that day, though I wasn't really paying attention, when the phone rang. It startled me; we rarely received calls on our home phone. Dad got up and answered it.

"Hello?" he said, looking at Mom and shrugging. "This is he. Uh, why, yes. Right now? Uh, yes. Yes, that would be fine. Goodbye." He looked perplexed as he put the phone down.

"That was—" The sound of the doorbell cut him short and he stood looking like a deer caught in the headlights of an oncoming semi.

"Is everything all right?" asked Mom, plainly alarmed.

Dad seemed to snap out of it as he moved toward the front door. "Yes, I think so. . . ."

He opened the door and I held my breath.

"Mr. Anderson?" said a deep, masculine voice. "Thank you for letting me stop to see you. I am Alejandro Caldera. I believe you have met my sons?"

Chapter Eleven

Let It Out

It took a moment to realize who was there. Mom and I could see the door from the dining table but, because it opened toward us, he was still hidden.

"Uh, yes, of course. Please, come in." Dad made a real effort to be courteous, but I could tell he felt off balance. He opened the door wider and, as the unexpected visitor stepped through, I remembered to breathe.

He was shorter than my dad but more powerfully built, his shoulders wide and his chest broad under the tailored jacket. Something about him immediately commanded attention. Although his apparel was western in style, he looked businesslike, almost formal from the quality of his clothes and the way he wore them. He held a black hat in his left hand and held his right out in greeting to my father. Dad automatically reached forward to complete the clasp, brief but firm.

When he looked our way, I felt a physical jolt and I think this time Mom stopped breathing. Mr. Caldera was a very handsome man even though he was quite a bit older than my dad, his deeply tanned face showing some creases around his eyes and mouth, and silver glinting in the dark brown hair at his temples.

"Please forgive me for interrupting your dinner," he said. "My sons wanted me to call, but it occurred to me that a personal visit might be more . . . credible . . . under the circumstances. I hope you will forgive them. You see, they have no sisters at home, and there are things,"—he seemed to choose his words carefully again—"they do not take into account."

He had a deep, rich voice, rather hypnotic to listen to, and though he didn't exactly have an accent, his diction was very precise. He had pronounced our last name oddly, too, the suffix of our name and the word "sons" sounding more like *sohns* than *suns*.

My mother stood up and said, smiling, "Please, come and sit down. We've just finished. Would you like some coffee?"

He held his hand up and said politely, "Thank you, but no. Another time, perhaps. I am on my way to a meeting, but I promised to clear up any . . . misunderstandings . . . or concerns you might have. I wish to vouch for the good intentions of my sons."

On this last word, his eyes rested on me and I felt my cheeks grow warm. To say that Dave looked just like his dad would be a stretch, but there was a definite resemblance, though Dave's features were more refined. His eyes and the curve of his dark, expressive brows were similar. Chris also had the brows and eyes, though otherwise not as strong a likeness.

"You must be Allison," he said, pronouncing the last part of my name with the same odd inflection. "My boys are concerned that it may be their fault that you cannot come to our little gathering on Labor Day. David, especially, would like you to come."

Now I truly was blushing, both from embarrassment and a thrill of pleasure. I looked quickly at my mother and father to gauge their reaction to these words. Dad looked unsure and a little severe. Mom looked at me and widened her eyes just enough for me to notice. I noticed that Dave's name was pronounced differently too. Though Mr. Caldera said it quickly, it sounded like "Dah-*veed*" rather than, what I assumed, "*Day*-vid."

"I would like to personally invite you. It is a tradition here, a community party of sorts. I understand you are new to this area. It would be an excellent opportunity to meet people and get to know us all a little better. It is very festive with music . . . and food, of course. And we have riding competitions and rodeo events for the riders. Mostly for the youngsters, but many adults enjoy participating."

I could tell Mom was all for it and seemed to be holding her tongue with great effort. I had a feeling I wouldn't have to say a thing; Mom would fight this battle for me.

Dad appeared to be struggling with what to say and how to feel, so Mom stood up again and said, "We appreciate you taking the time to come and meet us. And we look forward to meeting your family, Mr. Caldera. Thank you so much for the invitation."

"Please, call me Alex. And it is my sincere pleasure," he said and seemed to really mean it.

My heart skipped a little at the possible implications of his visit. He crossed the few steps separating us to shake my mother's hand and then turned to me. I wasn't used to shaking hands with anyone, let alone someone who was already starting to take on the status of a celebrity to me. He shook my hand gently and I glanced quickly into his eyes. I was reassured by what I read as approval there. I had been afraid he might be the kind of person to tease, but his attitude was kind and respectful. I looked forward to seeing more of him.

More of him? And his 'sohn'!

To my father, he said, "Thank you, Mr. Anderson, for your time and . . . understanding." Then he turned toward the door. "I hope to see you all on Monday. Good evening!"

With that, he left. We all remained silent, rather stunned by the whole interlude. Dad opened his mouth, then closed it again.

"A rather impressive gentleman," said Mom.

"Mmm," said Dad.

"It sounds like fun. And it would be rude not to go, now that we've been so particularly invited."

At this, my dad looked stern again and said, "Hmph. We'll see."

A smile played on my mother's mouth. I was confident Mom had the situation under control. If she wanted to go, he'd have a hard time finding a reason not to. And it was obvious her curiosity was piqued.

I looked at the clock—almost seven. Should I call Dave? I was pretty sure he'd been playing soccer, but he might be done by now.

I helped with the dishes then went upstairs and sat on my bed with my phone in my lap, trying to decide whether a call was appropriate under the circumstances—or not. On the one hand, I was pretty sure it was Chris who had initiated concern over *why* I wasn't going; I had no idea what his motivation could be, though. On the other, Mr. Caldera had made a point of letting me know that it was Dave—Dah-*veed*—that *especially* wanted me to go. I couldn't keep a silly grin from my face.

See? You were worried for nothing again.

My phone suddenly buzzed and vibrated in my lap. It startled me so much that I dropped it, then kicked it across the room in my haste to pick it up. When I finally did, I was thrilled and very gratified to see *Dave.*

Gulping, I answered. "He . . . hello?"

"Hey," said the soft voice on the other end. Every sense suddenly heightened and my stomach did little flips.

"Hi," I almost whispered.

"We just got home," he said. "Both our teams won."

"Congratulations." I tried to say it calmly, but I was practically jumping out of my skin and wanting to squeal like a fanatic. It was a new impulse and I struggled to restrain myself. "So, you decided to play JV?" I asked, trying to sound knowledgeable.

He laughed gently. "Yeah. You know, let my brother be best on his team one more year and everything." He was still laughing, which kept him from sounding arrogant. "I was wondering if my dad had called." Uncertainty had crept into his voice. "He said he'd talk to your parents about Monday."

"Oh . . . yes. He came by," I said lightly.

"What?" he exclaimed loudly. "You're kidding! I never thought he'd do *that.*" He was quiet and I wondered if I should try to fill the silence. Then, "What did he say?"

"Um . . . he just told my parents about the barbecue and invited them to come." I didn't mention the apology. I hadn't thought one was necessary.

"And?"

"I . . . think we're going," I said, trying to sound calm and accomplishing it quite well.

"So, are you glad?" His assured tone belied any real question.

I felt like I was going to explode, but held it in and was able to say, very calmly, "Sure."

"Good," he said. I could imagine him smiling. "You'll have fun. I promise."

I had absolutely nothing to say to that so responded lamely, "Okay."

"So, I'll see you tomorrow."

"Yes."

"Bye."

"Bye."

Cloud Nine.

I woke up extra early, having slept like a log. When I was ready, I grabbed Dave's hat, took a carrot from the refrigerator, and headed out to see Gold. He was near the creek and I was able to coax him to follow me as far as the road. There he stopped and seemed to wonder why he was following me. I stepped back and he moved close enough to break off half the carrot. I stroked his neck as he munched, then backed toward the corral, talking softly to him the whole time.

He watched me but made no move to follow. I held the carrot out and reminded him how yummy it was, but he wasn't buying it. I considered what to do. I was instinctively trying to avoid anything negative in our interactions.

I finally walked back to him, smoothed the hair on his face, and gave the carrot to him. He accepted it with grace and very loud crunching. Then he shoved me with his head, catching me off balance, and I fell on my backside.

"Hey! That was uncalled for!"

I was completely unhurt, but now my clothes, especially my rear, were all dusty. I hurried back to the house and changed.

I was hoping that Dad would say something about the barbecue on the way to school, but he didn't, and I didn't want to bring it up. Robin and Dave were both waiting for me; they seemed to be hanging out near the closest exterior corridor. I turned to say goodbye to my dad and could see that he saw them too. I couldn't read his expression but was glad Robin was there, not just Dave.

"So, you can come?" Robin asked as I approached them.

"I'm not sure yet, but I *am* sure my mom wants to go," I said.

They both looked satisfied with this and we walked around until the bell rang.

Lunch conversation was mostly about the soccer games and how both Varsity and JV "slaughtered" their competition. This seemed to be viewed as a good omen for the season. People around the tables had certainly multiplied since the first days of school and kids were now spilling off the edges and either standing nearby or sitting on the grass of the field next to them.

I wished I wasn't wearing a skirt as Robin chose to sit on the grass, but we were able to find a patch that was neither wet nor too dry and prickly. At first I was disappointed and felt almost demoted in the ranks of the Caldera followers, but Dave sat as if keeping an eye on us and several times smiled our way. I realized that I could observe him better from this new vantage point. I could also see Chris in his usual place, his back to the table and facing the field, so now mostly facing us. Apparently sitting that way really was just more of an unsociable quirk than an antipathetic attitude to anyone in particular—like me. I was surprised I even cared.

Having just met their dad, I couldn't help comparing both boys to him. Dave resembled him more, from his hair color and the general shape of his face to his bearing—the confident set of his shoulders and self-assured body language. I thought Dave was much better looking than his father, of course, but he did have youth on his side.

As well as much lighter hair color, Chris' face was a different shape, but his eyes were very similar. At one point, they simultaneously looked our way and I was struck by it, though Dave's gaze lingered while Chris' was fleeting, as usual. His physical attitude was also quite different. While I wouldn't say he had bad posture, there was something introverted about his demeanor—an indifferent slouch. It came across as negligent confidence. His expression varied little, even while talking to people. I had thought I'd seen glimpses of more, both in expression and demeanor, but he always quickly stifled or disguised it. At best he seemed abstracted and slightly impatient. At worst he appeared self-absorbed, annoyed, and completely disassociated.

I was sure that if he weren't Dave's brother, I would have avoided him or not noticed him. And that appeared to be what he wanted, but he was Dave's family—I couldn't help being curious about him. His cold manner was enough to keep most people at least somewhat at bay. Today was very unusual in the number of girls vying for his attention; at least as many as there were for Dave's.

"I'm assuming Chris owned the game yesterday," said Robin, watching the girls near him. His reactions to them seemed to have a narrow range of cool politeness to absolute disregard; nothing to surprise there. Other guys were trying to engage the girls' attention without much success.

Dave was attentive to everyone around him, guys and girls alike, and they looked like a happy, sociable circle of friends. The area around Chris

looked deceptively lively. I found myself reluctantly more intrigued by this than in watching Dave. Chris was like the eye of a storm—calm, his expression blank—while all around him was chaotic and loud. The expressions of the kids near him seemed to lack confidence, their laughter sounding harsh and forced.

"Like moths to a flame," Robin said.

"What?"

"Some people are just drawn to what they can't have, I guess. He's so obviously *not* into them, yet he poses some kind of challenge . . . the 'lure of the unattainable,' or something. Dave, I can understand. He makes people feel special, important. He's a challenge, too," her eyes danced as she smiled, " 'cause he flirts outrageously but never asks anyone out. But Chris," she shook her head slowly, "I don't think anyone knows what he thinks or feels, not even Dave. You kind of have to take him as he is, you know?"

I remembered what Robin had said about Chris before and wondered again about his history and why he was like this, so different from his popular and likable brother. She had mentioned a girlfriend. Was she the key to his disposition? But it had been a couple of years ago. Surely that was a long time to carry a torch. Then again, I couldn't imagine ever not loving Dave. I knew I would love him forever. Even so, if Chris had been serious about that girl, that was no excuse to treat the world as an enemy, was it? *Was* it? *Could he really just be pining for a lost love?*

At that moment, he seemed to notice me; I had been staring at him while I mused. He frowned deeply as if even more annoyed than he already was by the fawning fangirls. Extricating himself ungraciously from the surrounding bodies, he jammed his hands in his pockets and walked away. I felt shaken, as if I had unknowingly done something heinous and couldn't undo it. That was ridiculous, but I felt bad anyway.

"Are all of these kids into sports?" I asked, trying to divert myself.

"Mmm . . . some. Others, I don't recognize at all. They'll get tired of being ignored and eventually go away. Seems like this happens at the beginning of every season; the groupies emerge but eventually most crawl back to their holes."

This seemed harsh and I inwardly squirmed. After all, wasn't I really just a groupie too? Isn't that what Chris probably thought? I had a feeling that when he looked at me, he saw a parasitic creature. It would explain a lot.

Robin began indicating certain kids. "The two girls sitting closest to Dave are Stacie and Jessie. We've known them forever. They've had a crush on him since at least middle school, but. . . ." She made a face and shrugged her shoulders. They were both pretty blondes that I'd seen hanging out with him before. "They want to play girls' soccer, but they're better at softball, so we'll see. They ride and show too.

"Dave plays soccer, obviously, and he'll probably do track in the spring. Chris plays soccer too, of course, and he's really good, but he plays basketball like. . . ." She shook her head slowly. "I went to a couple of games with the Calderas last year. Chris was MVP for the school team both freshman and sophomore years, and for the whole league last year. That's kind of crazy. He's sure to get a scholarship for college. I heard that scouts were noticing him already last year. The weird thing is that he doesn't seem to enjoy it; he's just good at it. Now, Dave and soccer . . . you watch him play and you *know* he absolutely loves it. It just kind of comes naturally to him, like riding, and working cattle.

"Matthew's playing soccer now too, but I don't know what his plans are for the rest of the year. He usually does the same as Dave. They've been friends a long time too. I think they were in Little League together or something, but I've never seen Dave play baseball. I think Matt swims too, so maybe he'll be on the school team."

Matthew noticed we were looking his way and grinned at us. Robin put her hand to my ear, pretending to talk about him. He got the attention of the boy next to him and did the same, all the while watching us. The two boys continued the sly looks and lowered voices for a moment and then laughed loudly, as if at a really funny joke. Robin stuck her tongue out at them.

"That's Kyle," she said, her head close to mine, voice lowered conspiratorially. He and Matthew were watching us with exaggerated suspicion. Kyle was one of the few Black kids in our grade. He appeared to be shorter and sturdier than his buddy. "I think maybe he's playing football. And that's Tanner." She nodded toward a slightly scruffy boy behind them, goofing around with some girls. His face and arms were tanned, like most of the boys. "He's funny. A real dork. Kinda like you, only not as quiet." She smiled and elbowed me in the ribs. I didn't mind. "He's athletic too, so I'm sure he'll be doing something."

Dave was regarding us again, looking thoughtful.

"I play softball in the spring. I'd love to do track as well, but I doubt if I can do both, especially with spring shows and whatnot." She frowned suddenly and said, "Transportation is an issue, too."

I was curious about this but not sure what to say, so instead said, "Wow, everyone's so athletic. I don't really fit in, do I?"

Robin grinned and said, "Nope, not at all," just as Dave joined us.

He looked toward his left shoulder, as if to look behind him, but smirked instead and sat down on the grass in front of us.

"Allison thinks she's a misfit," said Robin, brutally.

He immediately said, "Of course she is," but his eyes were laughing.

The smirk turned into a real smile and I couldn't help smiling back. Then I noticed Matthew looking at the table in front of him, smiling a little and shaking his head. I thought it odd as he was no longer talking to Kyle.

"Hey," said Dave. "Why don't you hang out with us after school? It's Friday. No homework. No practice."

I felt a pang of disappointment but hoped it didn't show. "I . . . don't think I can," I said, absolutely sure I couldn't. Dad had been clear about that.

"Can't you call and ask?" Dave was frowning.

I couldn't think of a good way to explain the situation without embarrassing implications. Calling to ask unfortunately wasn't an option.

"I'm sure I have to go straight home today." Hopefully, he'd leave it at that.

"Oh well," he said, shrugging his shoulders.

My heart sank a little; he obviously wasn't as disappointed as me.

They talked, mostly bantered, for a few minutes before the bell rang. A few times I tried to think of something clever to add but failed. It wasn't the first time intellect had deserted me around Dave. I was sure it wouldn't be the last. Words always fled when I wanted them most and I felt I lacked any kind of real charm capable of retaining his attention.

Would I ever be able to express myself honestly to him? Would I ever be able to say something that would give a clue as to how I felt about him, perhaps something that could prompt a similar response in return? I could picture myself old and wrinkled with a long gray braid and thick glasses making me look like an owl, and *still* stuttering and trying to get up the courage to declare my feelings.

"Locker after school?" Dave asked as he stood to leave.

"Huh?" I asked, startled. "Oh, ye . . . yes . . . please."

He smiled and walked away with Robin.

The weekend was going to seem very long and I wasn't guaranteed to see Dave on Monday, but at least I'd see him one more time today. In Art, Melanie asked if I was doing anything special over the holiday.

"I might be going to a barbecue on Monday," I said, enthusiastically. "At least, I *hope* I'm going."

"At a friend's?" she asked lightly, but she looked at me knowingly.

"Um . . . yes." I realized I had opened a subject I didn't want open. "What about you?"

"Horse show." She seemed neither excited nor unhappy, just used to it. She was playing with her silver locket again. "I'll be at a friends' house all weekend too. I doubt if my mother can go, so it makes it easier on everybody."

"Wow," I said, not having a clue what any of that signified but impressed anyway. "I'd love to watch you ride sometime."

"Really?"

"Of course! I've only just started riding, but I'm very interested. I think," I said, not sure I wanted to broach the subject again, "I *think* there's a show at the barbecue."

She looked like she knew way more than she was letting on. It made me curious and uncomfortable. She appeared to also struggle with whether to say anything, then said, "You're talking about the Calderas' ranch, right?"

I blushed furiously. Why couldn't I just tell her? She apparently knew who Dave was and seemed to have me figured out already. Something in me just didn't want to voice it. I didn't want to be seen as a pathetic girl with a hopeless crush that everyone knows and laughs about behind her back or, even worse, pities. I had admitted my feelings to myself. That was as far as I was willing to go.

"Yes. I have other friends going so it would be fun to hang out with them there and . . . stuff."

"Of course," she said seriously, but I had a feeling she was just being kind or was practiced at hiding her feelings; possibly both.

When the bell rang, I put materials away as quickly as I could but it took several minutes. We walked together toward the front of the school, separating near my locker and wishing each other a fun weekend.

Robin and Dave were waiting for me.

"We wondered if you'd left already," said Robin, looking annoyed.

"Sorry," I said, hoping Dave wasn't annoyed too.

He didn't appear to be. "No big deal," he said, popping my locker open.

"Oh, Robin!" I switched books and then handed her my phone. "Can I have your number?"

She appeared mollified. "Of course. I need yours too." She put her number in and handed it back. "Call me when you find out about Monday, okay?"

"No, call *me*," said Dave. "I'm more important."

"No, you're not," said Robin. "Your head is just bigger. You'd better call me before you call *him*. He's becoming obnoxious."

"*I'm* obnoxious?" he said, raising his beautiful brows at her.

"I . . . I have to . . . go . . ." I said, laughing and indicating the front of the school. I hated leaving.

"Okay," said Robin. "Call me later." She waved and walked away.

Dave walked backward beside her long enough to shake his head and point to himself, mouthing, "*Call me.*"

Dad was waiting. "You're a little late," he said.

"Sorry. I had to clean up in Art and then stop at my locker." This was true. The moment I clicked my seatbelt, my phone buzzed in my hand.

"Don't wear shorts or a skirt." It was Dave.

"Don't wear—" I stopped and looked sideways at Dad.

"Not that I don't like shorts and skirts on you," he continued. "You're kind of cute in shorts and skirts. Of course, I guess you'll have to wear *something*—. Ow!" Apparently someone had hit him.

Now I was blushing and hoping dad wouldn't notice. He was showing way too much interest in who might be on the other end of my phone. I covered the phone and said, "It's Robin reminding me of some homework."

This, obviously, was not true; just one more lie to add to my list of recent iniquities. How many exactly was that now? I briefly wondered if God cut teenagers any slack in the lying department. Lying wasn't easy for me. If the last few weeks were any indication, the next few years were going to be rough.

Dave chuckled on the other end. "That bad, huh?"

"Mmm. Maybe."

"Looks like we'll have to do some serious damage control."

I liked that he'd said we. That seemed to include me, one way or another.

"I'm open to ideas," I said, unable to keep from smiling.

"I'll have to think about it. I'll keep you in the loop."

I laughed. It sure was easier talking to him on the phone, just imagining him, than in person when his presence kept me mostly discombobulated.

We were passing a large group of kids walking down the street, including Robin and Matthew talking together. I wished I was with them. Then I saw Dave. He was ahead of the others by himself, coasting sideways on his skateboard, phone at his ear and unabashedly aware of us. Our eyes connected as we passed. I blushed hard again.

Argh! Why does he do that to me?

"So," he said as if there had been no awkward pause or eye contact during it, "wear jeans at the barbecue."

"Um . . . I'll try. But why?"

"So you can ride, of course."

"Oh, I don't know about that." I couldn't say more under the circumstances.

"Call me. Tomorrow. Tomorrow *night*," he amended. "And call me *first*."

I laughed. "All right."

"See ya," he said.

"Bye."

"Robin seems like a nice girl," said Dad, glancing at me as he drove. Was he suspicious?

"Yes, she's great," I said as lightly as I could. "I've made a lot of friends here. Good friends."

"Are you happy, Allie?" he asked.

"Yes, Daddy," I said, truthfully. "Very happy."

A feeling I was recognizing with growing familiarity had wrapped around me. I couldn't keep a silly grin off my face.

"I have a surprise for you when we get home."

"Oh?" I asked, hardly listening. "Okay."

At home, Dad made me sit on the couch and then put the remote in my hand. I looked at him in question.

"Turn it on!"

I pushed the power button. Any doubt as to the surprise was put to rest by an obnoxious commercial.

"We have TV," I said, trying to sound happy. I hadn't thought about television since some time before I'd first seen Dave and Gold. My imagination was sufficient for me now, for better or worse. "We have cable?"

"No. If we were living over on the west side of town, we'd have it. There's a huge new development planned over there with a whole new country club. Those places will probably be a better long-term investment than this house. We could still move—"

"No!"

He looked shocked at my intensity. I was too, but I didn't want to move. It wasn't because of the house but the neighborhood; magical things happened here.

"I . . . don't want to move," I said more calmly.

"Okay. No moving."

"How do we have TV?"

"Satellite!" Obviously excited, he took the remote back and started flipping through channels.

I started to get up, wanting to get to my room to daydream.

"So, tomorrow," he said, and I sat down again, "I thought we'd go into town and get some fencing to put around the dish. And I thought I'd look into putting a fence around the whole yard." He looked sideways at me. "So we can get a . . . puppy!"

He looked so expectant, so sure I'd be excited. But I felt deflated. For a second, I thought he was going to say *pony*.

"A puppy?"

His face fell. "I seem to remember talking about getting a dog once we'd moved."

"Oh. Did we?"

He looked like he suspected I was an alien doppelganger. Maybe I was.

"Um . . . I'm going to my room." I headed toward the stairs but turned back, feeling a little sympathetic. "I'll help with dinner if you want."

He nodded absently.

He brought it up again later while we ate. Mom exhibited surprise just as I had.

Looking perturbed, he said, "Am I the only one who remembers the conversations about getting a dog?"

"I remember, sweetheart," said Mom, "but is now the best time?"

I silently agreed.

After I'd gone upstairs, I remembered that we had talked longingly of having a puppy one day. It might even have crossed my mind when we first moved here. But that was *before*—before Dave, before Gold, before horses and friends in general. I didn't want the responsibility right now, and I was pretty sure it would fall on me. In fact, I suspected it was a *let's-keep-Allison-busy* tactic.

"You're not going to be here all the time," Mom continued, "and I'm working too, at least until they change the hours or Jasmine has her baby and comes back. Allison is the one who would take care of it, so it should be her decision."

They both looked at me. Not what I was hoping for.

"Um . . . I don't know," I stalled. "I'll have to think about it."

Dad looked disappointed again, but Mom gave me an understanding smile. Just what she understood, exactly, I don't know, but she could see that having a dog wasn't high on my priority list.

If I'd had to choose something, besides a horse, I would much rather have had a cat. But with my mother's allergies, that wouldn't happen. Still, I went to bed feeling happy, with plenty of new memories of what Dave had said and done to dream about, and looking forward hopefully to Monday.

On Saturday morning I got up at my regular time—no sleeping in now—and headed out wearing Dave's hat and carrying three carrots. Rather than searching for Gold, or doing what he wanted me to do, I decided to try to take control of the situation. Taking a stand on the road not far from the corral, I called to him. Of course, I realized that Gold couldn't be his real name, but I hoped the sound of my voice would draw him out.

I didn't have long to wait. He came around some bushes and stood regarding me as if deciding whether or not to go farther. I stood my ground and called again, holding a carrot out. When he got close enough, I let him bite off half the carrot and then backed up closer to the corral. I thought he watched me calmly but shrewdly. Again he approached and I let him have the rest of the carrot. I spent some time talking to him, adoring him, and playing my fingers in his forelock and around his ears. There was no doubt that he liked the attention, and I was in awe that I'd gotten this far with him. Still, I had a goal and we weren't there yet.

I tried to entice him toward the opening of the corral with another carrot. He waited much longer this time, almost like he was trying to please me without compromising himself. I flushed with pleasure when he stepped close once more and, instead of taking the carrot, rubbed his face on my chest, almost knocking me down again.

"Hey! Enough of that," I laughed, thrilled at the progress it seemed we had made. "Will you come a little farther?"

I took the few remaining steps to the opening. The poles were still as the guys had left them. I had almost given up when he stepped all the way up to me, close enough to touch the post with his nose—and he did. He didn't seem nervous but was more on his guard. I tried to give him the rest of the carrot, but he ignored it, a faraway look in his eyes.

We had come this far so I decided to push the boundary a little further. Stepping through the opening, I walked to the center of the paddock and watched him. He watched me in return. After about ten minutes, I set the remains of the two carrots down in the center of the corral and walked back to him. I stroked him and talked softly to him for several more minutes. Then I said goodbye. I hoped he would make his way into the corral to feed on the grasses there.

Later that day, Dad wanted me to run errands in town with him while Mom was at work. He was leaving again for about a week but wanted to get the satellite dish fenced before he left. We made a few stops first and then went to the coffee shop before heading back.

"Hey, Allison," a familiar voice said as we entered. Matthew and his dad stood at the pick-up end of the counter.

"Oh . . . hi!"

"We bump into each other everywhere, huh?"

"It seems like it," I agreed.

They walked over to us when they had their drinks.

"Dad, this is Allison . . . and her dad," he said. "Remember? We saw them at the restaurant. They're new in town."

Matthew's father was a well-built man with dark brown curly hair like his son—a nice looking man.

"Zachery Morris," he said, reaching for Dad's already extended hand. "Nice to meet you."

"Greg Anderson," said Dad, smiling. "Likewise."

"Are you coming on Monday? You know, to the barbecue?" asked Matthew.

I could have hugged him—like a brother, of course. I resisted giving Dad a pleading look and just said, "I don't know yet."

"Well, we'll look for you there," said Mr. Morris. "Hope you can come."

We said goodbye and I worked at containing myself. Matthew would never know how helpful he'd just been, but there was no doubt that my dad was already inclined to be generous in his judgment of him and his father. The odds of going just got better.

After getting our drinks, we continued back through town to our last stop. It hadn't occurred to me that the lumber and hardware stores would be the same. A familiar black truck was parked on the street close by. We parked in the small lot. I thought about staying in the car, but I was doing my best to just be Dad's little girl right now, which I figured meant doing what he did and what I thought he wanted. I got out of the car and followed him into the store.

He was looking around, getting a feel for the place before asking for help, as Mom would have done in a clothing or cosmetics store. I looked around until I saw something that caught my attention. On the end of an aisle was a display of decorative light switch plates. I'd never given any thought to them before, but some of these were very pretty. The one in my room didn't match at all since we'd painted. I liked a soft gray one with dusky pink-colored roses around the edges. I took it off the hook, trying to imagine what it would look like on my wall.

"Hey," said a soft voice just behind me.

I jumped and almost dropped the switch plate. If I hadn't already assumed that Chris was here, I would have sworn the voice was his brother's. I tried to put the switch plate back on the hook but couldn't get it on properly, and then I *did* drop it, making me feel completely inept. I picked it up quickly, feeling like an idiot.

"Here, let me get that for you." Chris took it gently from my hand. "Any luck yet?" he asked, easily returning the plate to its hook.

"Yes, I think so. My dad hasn't said anything for sure, but I think we're going."

He looked half amused, half annoyed. "No, I mean any luck with the horse?"

"Oh, of course. . . ."

Oh. Of course. What on earth made me think you would possibly be interested in whether I can go to the family barbecue?

"Actually," I said, lowering my voice and making sure my dad wasn't near, "I've got him up to the corral, but he's suspicious. I can tell." It occurred to me that this remark sounded fanciful, but he nodded as if he wasn't surprised.

"Chris!"

A man in a brown apron walked down the aisle toward us followed by my dad. It was obvious that Dad recognized Chris, and Chris seemed tense. *Awkward!*

"Excuse me, miss," the man in the apron said, apologetically. "Perhaps I can help you. Chris, would you help this gentleman with fencing material? I can help the young lady."

I couldn't help giggling. "Oh, that's okay. I'm with him. That is, we're together."

The two older men looked confused.

Blush. *Way more awkward!*

"That's my dad," I said, pointing at him.

"Oh . . . I see!" said the man, jovially. "Well, I'll let you go together then!"

"If you'll come this way, sir," said Chris tonelessly, leading the way out to the yard, his expression blank.

Dad followed him rather stiffly and I brought up the rear, feeling guilty for no reason and resentful for it. Dad purchased what he wanted and Chris was coolly polite.

"Would you like this delivered to your home, Mr. Anderson?" Chris asked.

I'm sure he had to ask that of everyone, but Dad seemed to take exception to it. His mouth smiled, but his eyes didn't.

"No, I've got it. If you'd just put everything in the back of the car, I'll go and pay. We'll be fine."

I followed my dad back inside and had a sudden epiphany. *Chris . . . lumber store . . . corral poles. Duh.* Chris must have paid for the poles too. In spite of his unsociable nature, I didn't think he'd be the type to steal. But I didn't get another chance to talk to him; he had loaded the car and disappeared back into the lumber yard.

I didn't dare ask Dad about the barbecue on the way home, but Mom brought it up at dinner.

"Have you made a decision about Monday?" she asked. "People were talking about it today at the pool. It's quite a big deal apparently . . . one of the highlights of the year."

It was plain Dad didn't want anything to do with it. He opened his mouth and I thought he was going to say, "No," without further discussion. But he looked at us in turn and closed his mouth again. "I guess we can go for at least a little while."

I squealed. I couldn't help it. Mom clapped her hands. I think she wanted to go almost as much as I did. I couldn't wait to call Dave. Now I *did* have a good excuse!

"Allison." The sound of his soft voice in my ear, saying my name, made me feel like melting.

"Hi." I was already forgetting why I'd called.

It was quiet on the other end. Then, "So . . . what's going on?"

"Oh . . . um . . . it looks like we're going. Monday. I . . . just thought I'd tell you." I was feeling awkward again. "You said . . . you wanted me to call you."

"Yeah," he said, but I thought he sounded a little preoccupied. Somebody shouted and then laughed loudly in the background. "Yeah, that's great. So you know how to get here?"

"Not really." He'd given me an idea at Bar 8, but I wasn't sure.

"Okay. It's easy. Head through town and turn up by the high school and keep driving for a while. You'll eventually pass the main entrance to Bar 8 on your left and then the dirt road we rode on. Just keep driving. It's about another five miles. You'll see it. Just come in the main gate and drive up near the house. I'll be pretty busy, but we'll watch for you." He yelled to someone on his side of the phone, "Watch out for—" a word I didn't recognize. Then he seemed to be talking to me again. "Okay?"

"Okay," I said. "I guess I'll see you Monday."

"Yeah, see you then."

That was kind of weird. Just when I start feeling, I don't know, maybe a little special, his manner jerks me back to reality. Just as well, I suppose.

I called Robin right away. She sounded happy that we were going.

"I've been over there all day and I'm exhausted. We've been painting and moving stuff . . . just getting the place ready. It's a lot of work. You should have come."

"Maybe next time," I said, sadly. "What time are you going?"

"Oh, I'll be there early. Chris is coming to get me about six."

"Six!" I exclaimed.

"There are some early events I'm riding in. We took Gali over there today."

"Gali?" I asked.

"Oh, that's right. You've never met him. Gali's my horse. His real name's Galahad, but that's not what I call him. You can see him Monday."

"I can't wait!" I said, realizing again how little I really knew about her.

Sunday morning I went to meet Gold as usual, calling him from the corner of the corral. When he appeared, I walked straight into the center, sat down, and then waited to see what he would do. I was surprised the carrot pieces were still there. I had cut up an apple today, just for a change. After a few moments, he ambled up to the gate opening.

I called to him but he showed no inclination to join me, instead looking around, ears flicking forward and back and nostrils gently flaring as if assessing the likelihood of entrapment. Eventually I gave in, bringing the apple and carrot pieces to him in my cupped hands. He took a piece to munch but seemed listless, which worried me. He needed to get fed properly.

The rest of the day dragged by. Dad worked on his fencing project, and I helped him a little, trying to keep him happy and pass the time. The backyard was starting to show signs of life, green shoots showing through the brown. One day it would be nice just to sit out there, perhaps with friends. Mom was home too and seemed in a very good mood. She was probably thinking about Monday, like I was, and I thought Dad was starting to relent. It had been a long time since we'd done anything fun together as a family.

It was difficult to fall asleep. I finally got up and got Dave's hat. Though I couldn't discern his scent anymore, it still reassured me and I eventually slept.

Chapter Twelve

Not Real

On Labor Day I was up even earlier than what had become normal for the past week. While I got the feeling that Gold wasn't fooled regarding the corral and was, in fact, simply playing along, I hoped it was just a matter of time before he gave in.

Up, dressed, braided, glasses on, hat, carrots, out the door, and down to the corral; it had become my morning routine. I was as quiet as I could be, reasonably sure my parents would sleep late since Mom wasn't working, and I doubted my dad was in a hurry to go.

Gold was waiting on the road and I called for him to come to me. Only hesitating a moment, he ambled over and took a bite of the carrot I held, delicately but without enthusiasm. It seemed almost as if he did it for my sake. He had been taking the treats with less and less relish. That wasn't good. If I couldn't catch him soon, we'd have to call in professional horse catchers—or something.

"Come on, boy," I said, holding out another carrot and walking toward the corral.

He walked along just behind me until I reached the gate opening, but then he stopped. I didn't. I walked to the center of the enclosure and sat down. The ground was hard-packed earth with sparse, dry vegetation, but the stream ran across the corner and was flanked by greener grasses. It wasn't a lot but better than nothing.

I continued to talk to Gold, saying nonsensical things until he looked like he was dozing off, eyes closed, a hind leg resting. Then I sat and just watched him for a while. My parents would have to know about him soon. If I caught him, it was going to be impossible to keep him a secret anyway. If I didn't catch him, somebody had to. He needed looking after, not just an affectionate admirer.

The sun rose higher. I clapped my hands softly and beckoned him to come as if he were the puppy my dad wanted us to get. I kept calling as I broke the remaining carrots into pieces. He finally raised his head and walked slowly to where I sat. He nosed around Dave's hat, then knocked it off and blew gently on my face. I held my hands out with the carrot pieces and he ate them obligingly.

"See, it's not so bad here, is it?" I asked him softly. "If you stay here, we can feed you and take care of you."

I got up and stroked his face. He remained standing in the center of the corral and watched as I walked out but made no move to follow. I made no attempt to close the gate. After a moment, he moved unhurriedly toward the stream and began grazing. I watched him for a little while before heading back up to the house, feeling very excited and relieved for his sake. If he could be comfortable here, I was sure we could catch him when we wanted to and feed him. *And then . . . we'll get you cleaned up. And then . . . and then . . .*

I couldn't think further than that, but I couldn't wait to tell Dave.

The house was still quiet on my return and I started breakfast, the one culinary thing I really knew how to do. Dad soon appeared. He seemed to be in his customary lighthearted mood, apparently reconciled to the day's agenda. He gazed out the window as he sipped his coffee.

"We should go exploring," he said. "We could go for a hike. There's reserve land just over those hills."

I chose to stay mute on the subject.

Mom joined us then and the morning sped by pleasantly. My parents joked with each other and seemed relaxed and happy. This boded well. I eventually left them to get ready to go. Since the only real jeans I had weren't quite right for riding, I wore the same pants I'd worn to Bar 8, a relatively new shirt, and my Converse. Not terribly stylish, perhaps, but I'd be comfortable. Then I grabbed Dave's hat and went downstairs.

My mother looked surprised. "Don't you want to wear shorts? Maybe a tank top? It's going to be hot today."

"Oh, no, this is okay," I said as if I hadn't given it much thought.

"She looks fine," Dad approved.

I gave my parents the simple directions Dave had given me and we set out for the Caldera Ranch soon after twelve.

I was more than usually nervous about seeing Dave today but excited to be going to his home. I had a mental picture of this, what I imagined a cattle ranch looked like: something between Bar 8, vague childish impressions of my aunt's ranch in Colorado, and ranches of old Westerns I'd watched with Dad and Grandpa. I was even more nervous about my parents meeting Dave. Mom had seen him from a distance without knowing who he was. That didn't count. And Dad's introduction to him had hardly been positive. Hopefully he'd form a more favorable impression today.

We drove to town and then south past the high school. As we continued driving, houses and small properties gradually became farther apart and included fields and pastures of varying sizes. Many contained cattle, horses, and other farm animals.

Soon the properties to our right became even more spread out, the houses often hidden by large stands of shade trees. On our left, open pastures became more hilly, and we passed a sign saying "Bar 8 Ranch" with an arrow pointing east up a side road. The rest of the road was hidden by hills. Much farther on, we passed an unmarked dirt road on the left. It must be the end of the road Dave, Robin, and I had ridden along.

The land on our right was now open, grassy hills sparsely dotted with live oaks. We occasionally saw animals in the distance, I assumed groups of cattle, but otherwise the landscape was empty. Eventually white fenced pastures appeared on our right as we curved southeast toward the steeper foothills. The road came to a fork, the left continuing into the hills, the right becoming a paved drive between pretty poplars. Two large, white gates stood open invitingly. Also white but looking hundreds of years old and suspended from the wide archway:

CALDERA

"Oh my," my mother said softly.

This was understandable as the scope of not just the property but the "little gathering," as Mr. Caldera had called it, became clearer. The pasture on the left was alive and crowded with trucks, horse trailers, people, and horses. The pasture on the right was full of cars.

"I guess this is where we park," said Dad, pausing before the pasture gate.

"Dave said to park up by the house," I offered.

Dad looked at me, then up the driveway. There was no sign of a house, but tons of people and horses milling around. He looked back at me with an *"I don't think so"* expression and pulled into the pasture. Mom's eyes were bright with interest, but Dad's mouth looked grim.

On the other side of the long drive, there appeared to be a wide dirt track with a large oval paddock just beyond. There were riders on the track, often in pairs, and also inside the large paddock while people sat on some small bleachers, watching. Beyond this was something even bigger, but all we could see was the back of much larger bleachers.

Beyond where the cars were parked, an area was set up for young children. It was like a little carnival with small motorized rides and a couple of bounce castles. At the end farthest away from the parking area, ponies were led around a rope corral, ridden by small children.

We walked farther up the road toward a wide space filled with booths and seating areas, some covered by canopies, some in the sun. A stage had been set up and a few people were getting sound equipment and instruments ready. An incredible aroma caused both of my parents to comment on it. There were several barbecue stations with other food stands nearby, and dotted around and between the booths, stage, and seating areas were art displays.

Looking back toward the horse trailer parking, we could see that the larger structure was a full sized arena. An announcer's booth and two large sections of bleachers occupied the farthest side. Two metal structures with a maze of fencing behind them were on one of the shorter sides. Dust was being kicked up inside the arena and spectators watched from the stands and the ground around the fence. We couldn't see what was actually happening, but we could hear occasional exclamations and applause from the spectators. The whole place, from the horse trailers to the seating and stage area, was busy and noisy.

Poplars continued in a curve along the driveway uphill to our right. I looked that way and caught my breath. My mother looked to see what had surprised me and did the same.

Standing above and apart from the activity surrounding us was a house. Castle more like! Not that it really looked like a castle—the walls weren't crenelated and there was no portcullis or moat. Tall trees concealed most of it from where we stood, but it appeared to be huge. A large paved area in the front had a big piece of statuary in the center of it. The driveway continued around the right side of the house and I could clearly see Chris' truck under the trees. A second truck, smaller, lighter in color, and obviously older, was parked next to it. The house itself, what we could see of it, looked like it should be overlooking the Mediterranean. It was *really* huge.

I gulped. *Unreal!*

I could tell my dad was already interested in whatever food was available, and my mom looked like she'd be content to linger around the artwork and connect with people she recognized from her job. I was sure everything and everybody I was interested in could be found somewhere in the vicinity of the horses and riders.

"I'm going to go down there, okay?" I said, indicating the arena behind us.

"Oh, let's all go," said my mom.

Dad agreed easily, which surprised me. I would rather have gone by myself. I scanned every rider and every person standing around the fence of the large arena, but so many people dressed similarly—blue jeans, boots, hats, long-sleeved shirts—that I couldn't recognize anyone. My radar was tuned primarily to find Dave, of course, but I needed to find Robin first for completely selfish reasons; I'd feel less out of place with her and my parents already knew her. *And she's not likely to be too far from Dave. . . .*

We made our way to the bleachers closest to the road and climbed to about the third row where there was plenty of room. I looked around and saw some kids that I thought I'd seen at school, but I didn't actually know them. Judging by their clothing, they weren't here to ride.

A group of cattle were loose at one end of the arena with three riders moving among them. A smaller pen stood at the other end. The object seemed to be to get certain cows into the pen, but I wasn't paying attention too closely; I was looking for someone.

Across the arena, at the far corner near where the main entrance appeared to be, I saw someone that could have been Chris. He was on horseback, though the horse was difficult to see clearly. It looked light in color. The guy had on a light-colored shirt, tan gloves, and a light colored hat that covered his eyes and most of his face as he talked with a man standing on the ground next to him. I caught glimpses of longish blond hair when he turned his head.

I was still staring at him when he finally looked my way. He froze for a moment then turned to the person on horseback on the other side of him. It was a girl, but I didn't recognize her at first because her hair was pulled back beneath her hat. He pointed toward me and the girl looked my way, then waved. It was Robin. She dismounted and handed her reins to Chris, and then made her way to where my parents and I sat.

"You're here!" she said happily when she finally reached us. "We've been watching for you. How'd you slip by us? Did you park by the house?"

I looked in that direction and realized why Dave had said to park there. Any car driving all the way up the drive would be easily seen from down here. My dad looked a little sheepish but pretended to be very interested in the ongoing event.

"No, we weren't sure where it was," I said, "so we parked where everyone else did."

"What's happening here, Robin?" asked my mom.

"This is a team penning event. Beginner's level. Later on they'll have events that I'll ride in. Mr. Caldera likes to make this a real family event, so they have all kinds of things for different levels of riders. Over there." She pointed in the direction of the smaller arena we had seen when we'd first arrived. "They have easier classes for less experienced riders. Modified gymkhana games and stuff. I think there's a trail class going on over there right now.

"In a little while, they'll be doing advanced pole bending and speed barrels here. I ride in those." She grinned widely and was obviously looking forward to it. I was looking forward to watching her. "Later on they have the advanced events, though nobody's professional. The playday's an open event the Calderas hold every year. It's purely for fun and practice. And to raise money for charities and groups."

More and more interesting. Even Dad looked curious.

"How does that work?" he asked.

"Well, everyone that enters a class pays an entry fee. It's different for each event, but the winning riders get cash prizes and the rest goes to the charity or group it's benefiting. For instance, I know the money for the gymkhana classes is going to the animal shelter because there are more events and they tend to be easier. More people enter them, but the entry fees are smaller. It's getting the largest percentage of money because they rescue large and small animals, and wild animals too. It takes a lot to keep it going. The events like penning, reining, and cutting—the working horse classes—mostly go to the local 4H and FFA clubs. The more advanced rodeo events go to cancer research. There are fewer events and entries for that, but the entry fees are higher. The riders do it mostly for practice and, well, to show off, you know? And people who aren't riding make donations too. So it's cool and makes a lot of money."

"Wow," said mom, looking impressed. "I had no idea. This is amazing. No wonder there is such a good turnout."

Robin smiled widely. "Yeah, they've been doing it forever. I think Dave's great-grandfather or someone started it, and it's been a community tradition ever since. Even the food makes money for charity. Mr. Caldera donates the beef and some of the other food too, so all the profit of that goes to charity. Then there's stuff like the art exhibits. A percentage of anything sold goes to specific charities."

My dad had a thoughtful look on his face, which I took to be a good thing. How could he not feel favorably toward a family that did something like this?

"Does Dave compete too?" I asked hopefully. I would love to have an excuse to cheer him on in something, but right now I just wanted to know where he was.

"The Calderas don't compete for prizes, for obvious reasons, but they sometimes ride for fun. People don't mind. They're giving up their time and they're so good at what they do. They mostly just work. I was helping this morning too. Dave's manning the gate right now."

I forgot all about trying to be cool about him around my parents and almost got whiplash turning my head. At first I didn't see him. The three riders that had been in the arena a moment before had exited and three more were entering. The long gate was swinging closed behind the last rider and then I saw him, climbing up to sit on the gate with several other guys, all dressed similarly. He wore a light-colored hat low over his eyes and a long-sleeved light blue collared shirt. He looked like a cowboy.

Duh.

"Let's go get him," said Robin. "He's been working all morning. I'm sure he'd love to be rescued."

"We'll be right back, okay?" I said to my parents, not waiting for a reply but following Robin out of the bleachers and over to where Dave was.

We passed behind the rider I had thought rightly was Chris; he turned to look our way just long enough to show he had noticed us, but it gave me an odd jolt. He looked very different and terribly grown up but more at ease than I think I'd ever seen him. With the hat on he looked more like Dave, too. His horse was an attractive palomino, lighter than Gold with more of a cream colored mane and tail. She was tall and long-bodied and stood dozing, resting one hind foot as Chris sat with one leg hooked over the saddle horn.

The man standing next to him noticed Chris' attention turned to us and also looked our way. He was very professional looking, maybe in his early thirties, and although he was dressed similarly to the others, he didn't look like he was going to compete.

"That's Dr. James . . . James Emory. He's a new veterinarian working with Dr. Simons, our regular vet who usually comes to this event. But I think Dr. James offered his services for free. He's here in case he's needed. There's a medical team on call too, to be on the safe side."

"Hey, take your nag," said Chris as we approached. He tossed the end of the reins of a small horse to Robin.

"Don't call him a nag," she pouted, but she said it without any heat. "Allison, meet Galahad, my baby."

He was a pretty little horse, a lovely dark gunmetal gray all over with black mane, tail, and legs. Galahad's eyes and ears were very alert and he stood as if ready to run. I reached forward to stroke his nose. He allowed it but wasn't really paying attention to me.

"He gets a little worked up at shows, but he's a *good boy*." The last two words were said in a funny baby voice that I would never have imagined Robin using. It made me smile.

By the time we reached the gate, Dave had finally noticed us.

"Hey, take over for me, would you?" he said to the guy next to him.

The other boy nodded absently and Dave jumped down to join us.

"I was beginning to think you weren't coming," he said to me, smiling.

"Um . . . my parents . . . they weren't in a big hurry to leave. I mean . . . they were just kind of relaxing this morning."

He grinned and leaned in, holding my gaze, his face close to mine. "It's okay," he said softly, then smiled widely and leaned away again. I supposed he didn't want me to think he was angry. "Come on, we'll show you around. You hungry?"

"Um . . . I better go back to my parents first. They won't know where I've gone."

"Great idea!" he said exuberantly. "Let's go get your parents."

Robin and I exchanged glances. I wasn't sure how much she knew about my parents' lack of enthusiasm towards the Caldera brothers so far, but her eyes twinkled and I suspected she had probably guessed at or been told a lot.

"Um . . . I . . . brought your hat," I said, holding it out to him and feeling stupidly shy. I'd never seen him so dressed up, though he seemed supremely unconscious of looking any different than normal.

"Oh, thanks! My lucky hat!" he said, taking the light-colored one off and reaching for the black. Then he changed his mind, frowning. He placed the light one back on his head and set the black on mine. "Hold on to it for me a little longer, okay?"

I nodded, blushing of course.

"Hey, Chris!" he yelled as we passed behind his brother, still sitting reclined on his mount. "Where's Henry?"

Chris looked around halfheartedly, then shrugged and went back to watching the arena.

"Big help," muttered Dave to himself. Then to us, "Come on. I'll find him later."

"I'm going to go put Gali up for a while . . . let him rest before the barrels," said Robin. "I'll catch up with you." She led Gali off, away from the arena.

Dave and I walked over to where my parents were sitting. He turned a couple of times to smile at me as if reassuring me. Did he guess how nervous I felt about this? I hoped he wouldn't feel awkward around them, though I shouldn't have worried. He never looked like he felt awkward and I was beginning to think him incapable of it.

"Mr. and Mrs. Anderson! I'm really glad you were able to come today," he said heartily and, I thought, very graciously under the circumstances.

"You must be Dave," said my mom warmly, her eyes bright with curiosity and what looked like a certain amount of admiration. That didn't surprise me; how could she not admire him? She had reached out to shake his extended hand, which he returned enthusiastically.

"Mr. Anderson," he said, extending his hand to my father. Dad hesitated only a second before responding. The grip they exchanged certainly seemed firm but lacked the intensity of their first encounter. "I'd like to apologize in case I seemed rude when we first met. We were unfamiliar with Allison's family situation and didn't know you were her father. It took us by surprise and . . . I guess made us feel a little, you know, protective."

My father looked him in the eye with an expression that had an *"I bet it did"* quality to it, but he just nodded, apparently withholding judgment.

"Let me show you around," Dave continued in a very friendly tone. "We should head toward the food and beat the crowd. When this event is over there'll be a break while they drag the arena for the next events." He smiled his most winning smile for my mother, then looked respectfully at my dad and nodded as if requesting him to take the lead. Subtlety might not be his *forte*, but I had yet to see his charm, when turned on, fail its purpose.

Dave positioned himself between my mother and father as we walked back toward the plaza. I tagged along a little behind, still feeling nervous for several reasons and trying to overhear their conversation.

"How often do you have events like this?" Mom asked politely. "This is amazing. Much more elaborate than I imagined."

Dave smiled his best teeth-sparkling smile at her.

Okay, you can tone it down. You've won her over already!

"Once a year is enough," he laughed. "The rest of the year is pretty dull. We use the arenas for work and training, and other people come in and do the same but nothing on this level. Sometimes we bring cattle in for tagging and immunizations instead of doing it at pasture, maybe twice a year. But most of the time this whole place," he indicated the crowded plaza we were entering, "is empty. We're not even home on weekends a lot of the time."

It didn't look like he was going to elaborate, and I was dying to ask why, but Mom's curiosity came through.

"What do you do on the weekends?" she asked.

Dave grinned and looked over his shoulder at me as if to let me know he was still aware of me. "We have a lot of . . . hobbies. Surfing. Skating. Motocross. And we show a lot. Cattle and horses. Stuff like that."

"Do you work?" asked my dad. It was hard to tell whether he was just interested or implying something.

Dave looked at my dad—shrewdly, I thought—and said, seriously, "Every day. Before school. After school. Weekend mornings and nights. Holidays. Animals always need care. Things need to be cleaned. Stuff needs to be fixed. We have Miguel, our ranch manager, who oversees everything. He makes sure the big things around here get done and helps Dad with finances. Our foreman, Nick, oversees our stock and land; and ranch workers help with daily and seasonal jobs. But there's always more to do. We all have our regular chores plus whatever gets thrown at us. Like this," he grinned, spreading his arms wide.

"When we have any spare time, especially in the winter when things slow down a little, we help our friends too. Like Tom and Cheryl over at Bar 8." He stopped and smiled at me again. "I wanted to get a job in town this year, like my brother, but Dad wouldn't let me. Said, since it's my first year of high school, I needed to concentrate on it. You know." He shrugged.

"Allison says you're not in any of her classes," said Mom, out of the blue, taking me completely by surprise. "That seems strange in a high school so small."

Dave's eyes rested on me a moment, just enough to reactivate my blush. Then he said, confidently, "Yeah, it seems a little strange. We have PE at the same time, but I guess we're just taking different classes. We probably wouldn't even have met if it weren't for Robin."

Robin was just walking up. "What did I do now?" she asked suspiciously.

Dave grinned and Mom laughed. "Just made sure Allison made some wonderful new friends," she said warmly, and I looked at her gratefully. *Now if she'd just quit with the searching questions, even if I'm dying to know the answers myself.*

As Dave brought us over to a huge iron barbecue, I became aware of his father. He was sitting nearby at a shaded table and talking with a couple of men and a woman, but he recognized my parents and stood up, waving us over.

"Mr. and Mrs. Anderson," he said in his rich, distinctive voice. "Please, won't you join us? We are just enjoying a late luncheon. Or perhaps early

dinner?" He smiled widely at us and then his seated guests. "Please, join us when you have your meal." He looked over at the man who was tending the vast quantities of meat on the grill and spoke to him in Spanish. "Your meal is on the house," he said, turning to us again. "Please, get whatever you would like."

My mother looked very gratified and Dad looked pleased too. He nodded to one of the men sitting down and I realized it was Matthew's father. The woman was his mom, though I probably wouldn't have recognized her by herself.

Good. People my parents can talk to. Maybe this will keep them occupied for a while.

Dave was solicitous, helping my parents get the food they wanted. Along with ribs and steaks and roasts, there were French and sourdough breads, baked potatoes, corn on the cob, and several types of beans, all cooking over aromatic wood. Nearby, tables held salads and desserts. Robin followed, loading up her plate with ribs and bread. I hated myself for it but wasn't hungry. I took some bread and a couple of slices of meat. We followed my parents to the table while Dave got a plate for himself. As they sat down at two of the three empty chairs, Mr. Caldera made introductions.

"Mr. and Mrs. Anderson, have you met Chief Morris and his wife, Patricia?"

"*Chief* Morris?" asked my dad, smiling and reaching to shake the other man's hand. "Police?"

"Fire," said Mr. Morris, smiling. "You can call me Zach."

"Ah," said Dad, nodding. "I'm Greg. This is my wife, Jen, and you've met my daughter, Allison."

"I don't believe you've met Dr. Simons," said Mr. Caldera, indicating the older gentleman sitting at the table. "He has been our veterinarian for a long time. He is a highly valued doctor in our community and a close personal friend." He said this warmly and sincerely, but I thought I detected a little gallantry, as if he were flattering the older man for some reason.

Dave walked up, his plate practically spilling over with food. "Dad, have you seen Henry?"

His dad looked amused and said, "No, I have not seen *Henry*. I wish you very good luck in tracking him down, however."

This seemed such a strange response that I almost couldn't resist asking who this Henry was anyway, but Dave threw me off balance by frowning heavily at my plate. It made his brows curve and draw together in that dangerous look that never failed to make my knees feel rubbery.

"Is that all you're going to eat?"

"What?" I gazed at him dumbly.

"You need to eat more. You're too skinny. Come on. We'll eat up here." I turned to follow him, but my father spoke up.

"Check in with us a little later, Allie. Okay?"

"Okay," I said.

Turning back to Dave, I saw a familiar glint in his eye as he began backing away.

" 'Allie,' huh? Well, come on *Allie*, there's someone who wants to meet you."

I looked at Robin. She grinned at me and began following, already eating from her plate. I was impressed. I doubted I was coordinated enough to walk and eat at the same time.

"What?" she said as if suddenly annoyed.

"Nothing!" I said, not meaning to make her feel scrutinized.

"I have to ride soon and I'm starving, okay?"

"It's fine," I said, on the defensive myself. I was suddenly worried that I'd really offended her.

"What's your problem?" asked Dave, laughing.

"You, of course," said Robin, but there didn't seem to be any animosity involved. They were just their normal quarrelsome selves.

"She's just nervous," he said, turning to look back at me again, "and she gets grouchy when she's hungry . . . which is *all* the time."

"Look who's talking! At least my food fits on my plate."

"Hey, I'm a growing guy and I haven't eaten for at least two hours," he said, laughing.

Entertaining though they were, it hadn't escaped my attention that we were proceeding up the hill toward the house. As we drew closer, the dimensions and shape became clearer, and it was just as big as I had originally thought, though not quite as imposing.

It had a definite aristocratic Old World Mediterranean look to it, but it also looked physically old and artistically warm. Inlaid brick covered the

open courtyard, but it had oil stains here and there. The statue in the center of it was a person, perhaps an angel. It stood on a pedestal in an empty basin. Dave and Robin both walked past without looking at it.

Apart from the statue, some shrubbery along the front walls, and wrought iron, the house had little outward ornamentation. It had many sections and odd angles as if it had been constructed like haphazardly stacked boxes or had rooms added randomly over time, and looked designed to be functional rather than consciously artistic.

The many roof surfaces were covered with red clay tile, but there didn't appear to be any symmetry involved, even in window size and placement. A few second-storied windows had elegantly simple wrought iron across the bottom two-thirds, and there was a balcony with wrought iron railing. Apart from that, it was quite plain.

The austerity was softened immensely by its color, however. It seemed to be painted several graded hues of soft buttery yellow-gold, in places appearing light cream, in others almost pink. It occurred to me that it could be just one color affected by light and shadows. The overall visual effect on me was physically tangible and very sensual, like a strong, savory flavor, or a warm, sweet aroma; like the colors and movement of a Van Gogh. I thought it was amazingly beautiful.

"Are you all right?"

Dave was peering in my face and looking a little perplexed—such a cute expression on him—and I realized I had stopped walking, totally zoning out.

"Oh . . . yes. Fine. You have . . . a beautiful home," I whispered, still feeling strangely moved.

He looked at the façade of his home as if he'd never thought about it. "Uh . . . yeah. Thanks."

He looked at me oddly again, giving Robin a sideways look as if he wasn't sure of my mental balance. He'd lived here all his life so understandably took it for granted. Robin also seemed to be immune to its simple beauty.

Putting his finger to his lips, Dave quietly opened the huge arched double door. He motioned for us to go in first then closed the door silently. I vaguely wondered why we needed to be so quiet, but I was too busy trying to process everything that I had seen and felt so far today and dealing with the fact that Dave was so close and attentive.

The anteroom we stepped into was dimly lit and cool; an immediate relief from the bright, hot afternoon sun. I'd been holding up pretty well without thinking about it, but the sudden cool made me feel like collapsing somewhere.

The only furnishings were two large, ornately carved wooden chairs against one wall and a wooden chest covered with a brightly colored, tasseled shawl on the other. On the latter sat a beautiful bronze sculpture of a bucking horse. At the end of the small room, an open archway adorned around its edge with decorative tile led into an even darker room. I could barely make out a long table stretching toward a wide, open doorway overhung with foliage and leading back into diffused daylight. A cool breeze and the sound of gently burbling water came from somewhere just beyond.

I wanted to explore there and take a closer look at the bronze, too. But after hanging his hat on a wall hook, Dave grinned and signaled silence again before leading us down a dim corridor to the left. Robin and I left our hats on hooks and followed him, tip-toeing.

The short corridor opened to an amazing space. The floor, as it was in the entryway, was a rich red-brown glazed tile. To our left was one of the biggest kitchens I had ever seen, almost completely open to the enormous living area on our right. The only thing separating the two rooms was a long counter. The kitchen was brightly lit and cheery with an interesting mix of modern and rustic looking décor and fixtures. It was difficult to take everything in at once, but I was struck again by the warm, sensual colors. It felt very homey in spite of its size.

What I could see of the living area looked functional and comfortable. Several overhead fans circled slowly and silently, but the lights were off. Straight ahead, a curved staircase led upstairs to an open corridor and balcony running the width of the downstairs room. Both the stairs and balcony were contained by elaborate wrought iron. The balcony seemed to be open to a large space just above the kitchen. Corridors disappeared between walls to either side of it. I thought I could hear a television or something on.

Dave had entered the living room as if stalking someone not there at the moment. A noise somewhere behind the staircase caused him to motion us back into the shadows again. He set his plate on the counter and lay in wait under the staircase.

A door closed somewhere just beyond him and a short, plump woman in a dark dress appeared carrying a large bowl full of items. Her face was pleasant and her hair was dark brown with a hint of gray, pulled back into an old-fashioned bun. A sharp click, click, click on the tile floor followed her and I recognized the dog from the first day I'd seen Dave. That seemed so long ago! My heart clenched a little and I shivered, remembering how he had looked—how hopelessly unapproachable. And here I was, in his house. He considered me a friend!

And I'm still not used to him. He's even more wonderful to me now.

I shook a little and my eyes got blurry. The day was definitely becoming more surreal and unbelievable as it progressed. *Good grief . . . get a grip!*

"Angel!" Dave stepped forward into the light, startling the woman so badly it made her jump. "Here, let me take that for you," he said, taking the bowl before she could drop it.

"You are bad!" the woman said, slapping his arm and following him into the kitchen. She laid her hand dramatically over her heart but didn't really look phased at all. I had a feeling this kind of thing happened a lot.

Dave laughed and then said, "I brought someone to meet you."

I was still in a daze and Robin looked at me severely, as if she thought she might need to slap me.

"Go ahead and sit down," he said to us as he set the bowl on the lower side of the counter. "Angel, this is Allison. *Allie*," he said, looking back at me, a twinkle in his eye, "this is Angel. She makes sure we get fed and beats us up when we're bad. She hardly speaks *any* English, though, so you'll never understand her." But he said this with such an evil look on his face I knew at once he was kidding.

The lady in question exclaimed and play-slapped him on the stomach. "*Aiee! Eensufferable!*" she said with relish, as if it was a favorite word that she found plenty of use for. She turned to me and said, politely and distinctly, "Eet ees a grreat playshure to mee' chou."

"It's a pleasure to meet you, too," I said shyly.

"See, I told you she was cute," Dave said to Angel, the wicked look still on his face.

I felt a telltale scalp prickle.

"You are *bad!*" she said again. "You embarrass her!"

"He has to practice to stay good at it," said Robin dispassionately and still eating. "He can't embarrass me anymore, so Allison's fair game."

"Don' chou let heem mek you fill . . ." she looked at a loss for the word, then waved her hands in the air as if it would help her remember it, ". . . *that* way. You must eegnore heem."

"Don't tell her that!" Dave exclaimed, grinning.

As if that could ever be possible.

"Angel, have you seen Henry?" he asked her.

"I don' know," she said, shaking her head. "Esteban, he ees upstairs. Maybe also Quique." She shrugged as if it was not her assigned duty to keep track of the elusive Henry.

I couldn't stand it anymore.

"Who's Henry?"

Chapter Thirteen

Never Forget

They all froze wearing the same expression. Dave looked beyond Robin and me, seemingly into the empty room behind us, and yelled, "Henry?"

"What!" a voice yelled back from somewhere upstairs.

"*Aiee!* No yelling eenside, *por favor!*" hissed Angel.

"Get down here," said Dave, sternly.

It was quiet for a few moments, then a muffled voice said something. Finally a boy, about eight years old, appeared behind the balcony railing; Robin and I could see him from where we sat.

I caught my breath. Dave looked a lot like his dad, but he was also quite different. This boy, at first sight, looked just like Dave. *Exactly* like Dave. I looked at Robin in wonder. She was looking smug even as she continued to eat.

"What?" the boy said, frowning his little Dave frown and sounding persecuted.

"Get down here," Dave said again.

The boy huffed loudly and stomped down the stairs in stockinged feet. He had probably started the day dressed as nicely as his big brothers, but his jeans were now filthy, his shirt had dirty streaks and was half untucked, and his face and hair looked like they had been wet, got dirty, then dried.

"You're supposed to be outside helping," said Dave.

"I was," said Henry, eyeing me with wary interest.

"I haven't seen you most of the morning. Where've you been?"

"I was helping with the ponies until Bret showed up."

"Who's Bret?" asked Dave, frowning and starting to sound a little exasperated.

"A kid from school."

"What's he got to do with anything?"

"I don't like him."

"So?" The exasperation was growing.

"He doesn't like me either."

Dave sighed in frustration. "You still haven't told me why you're not outside helping somewhere."

"I was going to beat him up."

"What?" Dave exclaimed.

Angel threw up her hands and muttered something in Spanish, and Robin was choking on her food from sudden laughter.

"You can't beat him up! He's a guest here. Dad would kill you."

"I *know*. That's why I came up here."

The logic was clear to me and I couldn't help smiling at him. He regarded me intensely in return.

"Who's that?" he said, pointing at me.

"That's our friend, Allie, and it's not polite to point. Allie, meet Henry."

"It's nice to meet you, Henry," I said, feeling all warm and fuzzy inside.

A change came over Henry's face as he cocked his head to one side and smirked in a very familiar fashion, then gave me a leisurely top-to-toe and back again. If some other guy had done that to me, I would have been disgusted and felt dirty. If it had been Dave, I'd feel I'd died and gone to heaven. It appeared to be a skill that Henry was currently cultivating and it completely enthralled me. I was in love.

"She looks—" Henry began, but Dave raised a pointed finger at him. "Hey!"

Henry frowned at him indignantly, his little dark brows curving in together even more, just like those of his older brothers. "You said it wasn't polite to point."

"It's even less polite to say rude things, and you'd better be *really* careful what you say to my friends." Dave wore an expression I'd only seen a couple of times. Both instances had included Matthew.

Henry seemed to consider and decided to hold his tongue.

"Have you eaten?" Dave asked.

"Yeah. I ate *out*side, but then Bret found me, so I came *in*side."

"Okay," said Dave. "I guess you did the right thing, but you can't hide in here."

"I ain't hiding! I can whoop him easy. I've done it before."

"Henry!" from more than one voice.

"He was *askin'* for it. *Geez!*"

Dave turned away at that point, unable to smother a smile. I suspected he was secretly tickled pink that his younger brother was such a little hellion.

"No family resemblance. *At all*," said Robin, under her breath. She avoided a glare from Dave, then said, "Hey Henry, where's Stevey?"

"Upstairs."

"Stevey?" said Dave in a slightly louder than normal voice. "Are you up there?"

There was no answer, but a slight noise made Robin and me look up. A little boy, probably at least a couple of years younger than Henry, stood looking down at us through the railing.

"Is he there?" asked Dave quietly.

I couldn't speak but nodded my head slowly.

"Hey, Stevey!" said Robin in a bright voice. "Come down and say hi."

Stevey let his hand drag along the railing as he slowly and quietly walked down the stairs. Henry had lost interest in us and went to one of the large refrigerators.

Robin pulled the stool next to her out and patted the top. "Come and sit down."

Stevey slowly obliged, looking at me solemnly once he'd climbed up.

"This is Allison," said Robin, turning toward me. "She's a new friend. Say, 'Hi.' "

He didn't seem interested in speaking, continuing to regard me without expression, but raised his little hand in a brief wave.

I was still speechless. The world as I knew it was being reinvented yet again. I would never have imagined a person like Dave before I'd met him. I doubt I was capable of imagining anyone so perfect, nor had I had reason to. And to become a part of his world was still keeping me reeling. That two more beings existed, possibly incorporating even *parts* of who he was, was completely blowing my mind.

I lifted my hand and returned the wave. Then I gulped. My throat grew tight and my heart hurt, but I didn't know why. He looked almost exactly like both of his brothers standing nearby, without the rough edge of his father's rugged handsomeness. There was a softer contour in the shape of his face, in the line of his brow and jaw.

Dave had started eating quickly and looked at me frowning. "You'd better eat. We've got to get back."

I hadn't even started.

"What do you think, Angel? Think we can get Allie to eat more?"

"I remember leettle Rohbeen, she would never eat," Angel sighed and shook her head. "She ees steel too skeeny, but she eats!"

Dave grinned and Robin rolled her eyes.

"Be careful," Robin said to me, "or they'll fatten you up by Christmas. Angel's food is way too good."

"*Si!*" Angel exclaimed, "And I am to make more, so you must all make an end. *Váyanse!*" She continued to scold us in Spanish and began spreading out the items she had brought out earlier on the island counter.

"Henry, go get Sam ready," said Dave.

I wondered whether this was another mini-Dave waiting to slay my heart or something less dangerous. Henry turned from his perusal of the refrigerator contents, frowning and looking mutinous.

"We talked about it this morning, remember?" said Dave, still eating but looking steadily at his brother.

Henry's mouth slid sideways in thought, then after a moment he said, "Fine!" He shut the refrigerator door with more force than necessary and stalked away, disappearing into the short corridor behind the stairs.

Robin licked her fingers as she got up to dispose of her paper plate, then washed her hands in the sink. "Do I have barbecue sauce on my face?"

"No," said Dave, straight-faced.

"A little," I said truthfully.

Her hand flew out as she walked past Dave, catching him hard in the ribs and making him grunt.

"Thank you, Allison," she said with great dignity, reaching for Dave's napkin and wiping the spot I mirrored on my own face. "It sure is nice having *you* around!"

She raised her brows in question and I nodded, the offending smudge having been wiped away.

"I'm going," she said. "I've got to get Gali warmed up and I don't want to miss my ride."

"See you down there," said Dave, finishing his last rib.

I was embarrassed that I still hadn't finished eating. There had been too much distraction. Taking a couple of hasty bites, I got to my feet. Chris' dog, Merle, had been lying spread-eagle on the floor in the corridor, enjoying the cool tile against her tummy, but now stood up and moved cautiously out of Robin's way. Then she moved toward me, wagging her stump of a tail. I squatted down to greet her, happy that she seemed to remember me.

Robin stopped, her mouth hanging open. "What the heck?"

"What?" Dave hadn't seen the dog's movements and stepped around the counter. "Oh. Told you."

"Sheesh," said Robin as she turned to walk away. "Chris is gonna freak."

Dave reached over for my plate and frowned disdainfully at it, shaking his head.

"You'd better get something else to eat later. There's plenty of food all day. You can always come up here too. Right, Angel?"

She agreed readily.

"Oh, and if you need to, you know, use the bathroom, don't use the portables out there. We only rent them for the day. You should come in the house. There's a bathroom right over here." He stepped past me, into the dark corridor beyond the stairs. There was a door to either side, both closed. He opened the left door to reveal a large, clean, though surprisingly spartan bathroom. There was no tub, but a large self-contained shower occupied most of the far end.

"Okay," I said, meekly. "Thanks."

I had wondered where restrooms were and was embarrassed but glad he was thoughtful enough to mention it. I hated portables. He noticed me look at the other door, though I was trying hard not to appear nosy.

"This is the mud room," he said, opening the door. "It's mostly storage and stuff. You know . . . extra food for the hungry hordes. But if we get too dirty, which is pretty often," his teeth flashed, "we just hose off in here first."

The room contained two large freezers and many cupboards. In the far corners were two open, tiled stalls with coiled hoses. A door stood between them, apparently leading outside. Boots, all types and sizes, lay semi-neatly along one wall below hooks hung with outerwear.

"We usually come into the house through there," he said, nodding to the far door, "to help keep the house clean. But you're a first-time guest, so you get to use the front door. At least for today."

I could tell he was laughing at me but felt completely humbled anyway. He could have no idea how privileged I felt. I bet a lot of people got to come through the front door, but how many got to see the mud room?

He held the door open and called, "Merle!" She responded immediately, her nails clicking on the tile as she trotted obediently into the room. "Stevey, why don't you come with us now? Come and get your boots."

Stevey climbed down from his stool and walked silently through the door. He found a small, dusty pair of boots and pulled them on.

"Where's your hat?" Dave asked.

Stevey looked around the room carefully, as if it were completely cluttered instead of almost empty. *Adorable.*

"Is it upstairs? Go look. And turn everything off up there, okay?"

Stevey marched out the door and I let my breath out. I guess I'd been holding it again.

"He's so cute!" I breathed.

"Yeah," said Dave, his eyes soft and a smirk on his face. "He's my little buddy."

I was hoping he would say more—there seemed to be much more to say—but he just told Merle to stay, closed the door, and led the way back to the kitchen. Stevey came back downstairs, a little cream colored hat just like Dave's in his hand.

"I'll give you a real tour another time, but we better get going," Dave said. "See you later, Angel."

"It was nice to meet you," I said to her.

"Eet was *very* nice to mee chou alsoh! You must come again, yes?"

If I'm invited! Who knows what will happen tomorrow? I just smiled and nodded.

We grabbed our hats at the door and walked toward the drive leading back to the plaza. This time I noticed more about the statue. The pedestal was actually a basin and set of tiers. It looked like it was or had been a working fountain and appeared much older than the statue itself. And it

was indeed an angel, its wings folded close to its back like a bird content to remain, however briefly, on the ground. As we walked beyond it, I could see that it was female, hands folded one on top of the other over her chest, and her eyes and finely featured face focused heavenward. She was beautiful.

I wanted to ask Dave about it but was distracted by Stevey taking his hand. He looked up into his big brother's face. Dave looked down at him and smiled. Too cute! Then Stevey stretched toward me, pulling Dave with him, and took my hand. I had thought I might explode from happiness before, overwhelmed with Dave's flattering attention and an overload of cute from his little brothers. Apparently I was wrong. I *could* stand even more, though when I thought about the indirect hand-holding with Dave I could barely focus on how to walk.

This family is going to be the end of me. I just know it!

I thought about that first day I'd met Dave at school, of my early interactions with Robin and observations of Chris, and how I had feared that their motives might be less than friendly. And then later, I'd even worried that their positive attention to me could be an elaborate joke. Those thoughts now seemed so foolish, though I'd had good reason to consider it from past experiences. I hadn't thought about those old wounds much before meeting them. I thought I'd blocked the memories out. Now I realized that they were still there and had never really healed. Maybe they could disappear. *As much as scars ever really disappear.*

Amplified twangs and feedback were coming from the stage area, and there were even more people around than before. I noticed many of them wearing little pink ribbons indicating their chosen charity and thought again how cool it was that the Calderas had such an event at their home.

We skirted the plaza, effectively avoiding my parents, which didn't bother me at all. The dirt path was dry and dusty and led past the despised portables toward fairly large, long buildings just up the hill from the main arena.

"Those are our workers' quarters," said Dave. He was pointing to a building just visible, close to the hillside and surrounded by shade trees. "And that's the stallion barn," he said indicating the building closest to it.

We kept walking toward the closest barn. Stevey let go of our hands and ran toward Henry, now leading a paint horse toward us, brown and white instead of Flash's black and white.

"Meet Sam," said Dave, taking the reins. Henry stood back, arms across his chest, looking disdainful. "He's the gentlest horse in the world. You can ride him anywhere and I'd bet my life that he would never get you in trouble. He's even older than Chris. We all rode him growing up. He's mainly a companion for our stallions now. They enjoy his company when they're turned out for exercise and he keeps them sociable. He lives in their barn too. Seems to keep them calm and happy to know he's there. Anyway, he's yours for today."

My heart beat fast. When Dave had mentioned riding, I had pictured something along the lines of Bar 8, not this crowded, busy, huge—*thing*. I felt nervous on so many levels, but I trusted Dave's judgment in these matters and wouldn't have dreamed of demurring.

Shaking, I let Dave give me a boost up as he had done on that other day, and tried to settle lightly into the saddle. The stirrups were much too short so he quickly adjusted them, then stood back with a questioning look.

"Okay?" he asked.

I nodded.

"Good. Wait here and I'll be back in a minute. Henry, you'd better go back to doing something or go find Dad."

Henry gave us both insolent looks, snorted loudly, and sauntered off toward the plaza.

Dave watched him go, his eyes narrowed, but then he turned to me and said, "Be right back," and walked off around the barn, Stevey following and trotting to keep up.

I spent the waiting time trying to calm my nerves, stroking Sam's neck and talking to him. When Dave reappeared, my heart sped up again. He had donned black chaps and led a glossy, black horse. Stevey sat in the saddle holding the horn.

"All right?" he asked.

"Yes!"

He swung up behind Stevey and said, "Good. Come on, we'll walk around. I need to warm him up a little," he said, patting his horse's rump. "Let's find Robin. She'll be down there somewhere."

We walked the horses toward the wide dirt track that encircled both arenas, then proceeded on it with Sam and me next to the inside rail. From this side, I could see how the paddocks led into long, fenced corridors in

sections that connected to an opening in the large arena, near the main rider's entrance.

Three barrels had been set up inside that arena now. As the opening chords of the first song came from the stage, back at the plaza, the announcer alerted barrel racers to be ready. Dave explained that this event was for advanced riders, mostly girls who competed at rodeo level, but the more advanced gymkhana riders, male and female, could enter too. Then there'd be team roping, and he'd ride in that. They didn't allow professional competitors to enter, though many, like Dave and his family, actually worked cattle for a living.

"I'm not too good at roping," he confided. "It's not something I take the time to practice. I'm good at other things, though."

He gave me his most wicked smile, and I felt my face grow very warm in spite of the shade of his hat. I was sure he referred to sporting endeavors, but he could have just wanted to see me blush. It was becoming clear he loved to tease and while I was glad he seemed to be treating me more as he did Robin, I doubted he understood how differently I felt about him. My mind had started running along much more dangerous lines.

"Hey," said Robin as she pulled Gali up beside Dave. She looked over at me. "How're you doing?"

I couldn't help beaming at her. What could I say? *"I'm in seventh heaven!"* They'd probably ask what heavens one through six could possibly be. *"It's the best day of my life!"* So lame. Before today, last Saturday had been the best. I'd never experienced anything like these past few weeks. I would remember it forever. And I couldn't articulate how much I appreciated them, how much their friendship meant to me, and how full my heart was. Old, ugly experiences from my past seemed far away and inconsequential, if not completely forgotten.

"Great!" I said as enthusiastically as I dared.

"Good!" said Robin, looking pleased. "I'll walk with you a little until I need to go."

We continued together around the huge track. Dave's horse was lively and occasionally seemed to want to break into a run, but Sam walked along calmly, never even twitching. Many other riders passed us going in both directions, always saying, "Hi," or waving. I realized it was just because everyone probably knew who Dave was. *It must be like being in the company of a celebrity.* But I didn't care about that. In fact, I wished it was just Dave and me.

"Allison!" my father's voice cut through my abstraction.

We had reached the far side of the track and were starting to head toward the road. We stopped the horses and turned to face the group walking down from the plaza.

My parents looked concerned. My father actually looked a bit angry. Mr. Caldera and Dr. Simons followed behind with a couple of adults I had never seen before, and Tom and Cheryl were there with their children, too. I smiled and lifted my hand. They smiled and waved back.

"What are you doing?" my father asked unnecessarily. I knew he knew what I was doing. And I knew that he wasn't happy about it, just like I had known he wouldn't be. What I didn't know was why.

Nobody seemed to know what to say. Mr. Caldera walked up beside my dad while the other adults continued toward the bleachers.

"I assure you, Greg, she is perfectly safe. Sam has been the first horse of all my sons."

I noticed our parents were on first name terms. I hoped that was a good sign.

"But she doesn't ride," said my dad, missing the point.

"But I want to!" I blurted out, my heart beating wildly.

If he was to deny me right now, I didn't know what I'd do. I probably wouldn't disobey him outright or say anything against his decision, but I felt instinctively that I would have lost an important battle.

I was prepared to be obstinate. I didn't want to cause a scene but also didn't want to give up this opportunity.

"Please, Dad. I'm okay. Really!"

"Sam's completely safe, sir," said Dave, earnestly. "Even Stevey here can ride him all by himself."

Mom laid her hand on Dad's arm and said, "Greg, she does appear to be fine."

Dad looked unconvinced and started to say something—something negative, I could tell—but stopped. He looked at Mom, then at me.

"No running," he said. Then he looked directly at Dave and commanded, very seriously, "You watch out for her."

Without hesitation, Dave responded "Always." Chills ran down my spine at the implication of that single word. "We won't leave her alone around the horses for a second."

They regarded each other solemnly for a few moments longer, then Dad nodded. Mom looked relieved and Mr. Caldera smiled, looking at his son with a satisfied expression.

"Come, Greg and Jen," he said, leading my parents away. "I believe our Robin will ride soon."

Robin grinned as she watched them leave. She looked at me, her eyes wide, and wiped her hand dramatically across her brow. "Whew! Why doesn't your dad like horses?"

"I don't know," I said. "He grew up on a horse ranch, too."

"Seriously?" asked Dave, frowning and watching my father's retreating figure.

We continued in our original direction. I was feeling embarrassed by the episode but was still thinking mostly about the ramifications of that one word, "Always."

"Always" as in, "for the rest of the day"? "Always" as in, "under these circumstances"? "Always" as in—

"Allison?" Robin was looking at me with raised brows. Dave was too.

"Hmm?" Blush.

She smirked. Dave looked away so I couldn't see his expression, but I had my suspicions.

"I'm riding ahead," said Robin. "I need to be near the gate when I'm called. I'll stay with you later, though. Okay?"

"Sure," I said, feeling awkward again. "You don't have to babysit me, though. My dad just worries too much."

"We're not babysitting," said Robin, seriously.

"Yeah," added Dave. "We're 'Allie-sitting.' Completely different."

Stevey seemed to think this was funny and giggled—an adorable sound.

"Besides," Dave continued, suddenly serious, "I promised."

"Thanks," I said, determined to not let my mind wander around this last statement or the way he'd said it. *Stay focused!*

"See ya!" said Robin.

She rode around the short side of the track and disappeared behind the bleachers. We walked around the smaller arena where a reining class was in progress, and Dave explained what was involved. So many types of events. So many seemingly different ways to ride! I was fascinated by them all.

"So," he said, after a few moments of silence. "Do you think we can convince your dad to let you learn?"

"Reining?"

He looked amused. "Eventually. I was thinking of more basic skills. First things first. Even Stevey knows how to ride, right buddy? Here, I'm tired. You hold the reins for a while, okay?"

Stevey took the reins. Dave's horse still looked very aware of his surroundings—his ears twitching to catch every sound, his head on the move, his bright eyes taking in everything—but otherwise he seemed more relaxed. Dave looked at me, his eyes twinkling. My heart melted—again. How amazing it would be to have a brother like him! *Still, it would be even better—*

No! Focus!

"Well?"

Darn! He must think I'm a total airhead. What were we talking about? "Um . . . oh! I don't know. He's just . . . protective."

"Yeah, I *get* that," he said, looking at me sideways but smiling.

We were passing a row of small pens on the outside of the track, most of them occupied by large cattle. I grabbed at the distraction. "What are they?"

"Those are bucking bulls. You'll see them later. They're mostly from contractors, but a few are owned around here. The contractors bring young, inexperienced bulls. See that big red speckled guy?" I looked in the direction he was pointing and nodded. "He belongs to Chris. Mean sucker. I mean the bull. I've never been able to cover him." He saw my clueless expression and added, "Ride him the whole eight seconds. Chris plans to sell him when he gets a good enough offer. The one next to him? The black Brangus?" He pointed again. "Big black bull with kind of a hump? He's mine. We've raised them since they were yearlings. Chris' bull is older, but I started younger than he did, so mine's only a year younger than his." His face twisted wryly. "He rides better than me, though."

"Are you going to ride? Today?" I asked hopefully.

"Of course," he said. "If I get a chance. We only have ten bulls, including ours, and they only get ridden once. So the guys that entered will ride first—you know, 'money for charity' and all—and if there're any bulls left, we get to try 'em." He looked like he fervently hoped for this. "As of this

morning, there were. The other guys know which bulls they're riding, but we have to wait and see. Makes it more interesting anyway. Dad used to ride when he was younger. He followed the pro circuit for a while before taking over from Grampa here, but he says he doesn't miss it. And he doesn't want us to pursue it professionally. We ride in youth events. That's all. Still," he said, his eyes lighting up, "it's a hell of a lot of fun!"

I suspected he might have some judgmental impairment and was tempted to ask if he'd ever fallen on his head. He gave me a sidelong look and laughed, as if reading my mind.

"This section of the track gets closed off when we bring the bulls and horses through," he said. We were passing an area where long gates could open across the track on both sides. "After all the open events, we close the track and open the gates." He pointed to a narrow alley between fencing. "That leads into the return going to the arena. The chutes are at the end. We only have two, so it takes a while to switch out animals. But there usually aren't that many people entered to ride in the bucking events anyway."

More enclosures on the outside of the track contained horses.

"Bucking horses," he said. "You'll see them later, too. Hey, do you feel up to walking faster?"

"Sure," I said, feeling comfortable and confident on Sam.

"Cool," he said. Then talking to Stevey, "Hey, buddy, can I take the reins back now?" Stevey shook his head but was smiling slightly. "Thanks, Stevey," Dave said, though Stevey hadn't relinquished them. "Can I have them now?" he asked again. This time, Stevey let Dave slide his hand over his to take the reins. Then Dave looked at me. "Remember how to use your legs?"

I urged Sam on and he moved forward easily. Dave appeared to be holding his horse back. We had made a complete circuit of the track, now skirting the main entrance to the arena and the many horses and riders assembled there. We found a place along the fence where there was room for our horses and we could see everything going on in the arena. A blonde girl on a brown horse was in the middle of her run. Parts of her horse's tack seemed to be color coordinated with her own outfit, and I commented on it.

"Yeah . . . it's a girl thing, I guess." He smirked and shrugged. "That's Jessie."

I recognized her now as she left the arena. Next up was Robin, galloping through the starting line. I'd never seen her ride like that before and was extremely impressed. Dirt went flying as she rounded the barrels, but Gali never faltered at all. They tore back through to the finish line and we both shouted and whooped for her.

"I want to do that!" I said, without thinking.

"Yeah?" asked Dave, his eyes shining.

"Yes!" I said, realizing that I really did. I'd give anything to be able to ride like that.

"Well, we'll see what we can do." He smiled.

I smiled back. Stevey looked upside down at Dave's face and smiled too. Robin joined us after a few moments.

"How'd we do?" she asked. "I didn't even hear the time."

"13.903," said Dave.

I was impressed. I hadn't heard the time announced either.

Robin's face twisted. "Probably not fast enough. Jessie just got 13.895 and Lori's *always* faster than her. I'm gonna go walk him out a little," she said, patting Gali's neck. "I'll be back."

We continued to watch the barrel racing, Stevey clapping his hands happily whenever the crowd did. Robin came back after a while and positioned herself to Dave's left. There were probably about twenty-five different riders, but I became a little distracted by watching Dave and Robin's horses nuzzling each other. They seemed on very good terms. In between riders, I mentioned this.

"They're brothers," said Dave. "They grew up together, pretty much."

"Half-brothers," corrected Robin. Dave shrugged. "They have the same sire, Barbed Defender," she said, proudly.

"Def, for short," said Dave, grinning.

"Yeah," Robin agreed. "He's a black mustang and a fantastic cutting horse. They breed him to quarter mares sometimes, and the foals make great barrel horses."

"Cutting horses," corrected Dave, still grinning.

"Both," conceded Robin. "They're great at everything really."

"Remmy's a half-brother too," said Dave. "He's just older."

I guess that explained why the horses were so similar in build.

"What is your horse's name?" I asked Dave, a little shyly.

"His real name? Or what I call him?"

"Either," I said.

"I call him Tee," he said.

"His full name's Caldera's Barbed Trouble," said Robin, proudly. "His mama's name is Caldera's Double Trouble."

"I'd better get going," Dave said, looking around as if he'd lost something. "Matt and I are up second for roping, I think."

I assumed he was looking for Matthew, but then I saw him focus on Chris, just riding up between himself and Robin. "I was hoping you'd show up. When are you riding?"

"There're about six teams before us," said Chris.

"Well, I promised Allie's dad we'd keep her safe. And you better take Stevey."

Chris looked away but gave a sharp nod.

"Okay, buddy?" Dave said gently but firmly. "Go to Chris, okay?"

Stevey had been leaning back against Dave, looking very comfortable and idly hanging on to the loose end of one of two ropes tied to Dave's saddle. He looked at Chris and then looked at me. He completely surprised everyone by reaching his little arms toward me.

"You want to sit with Allie?" Dave asked. He looked at Chris, who was frowning—no surprise there—then looked at me. "What do you think?" Dave seemed to be asking both of us.

"He wants to come to me?" I asked, gratified but feeling a little unsure whether I could handle the responsibility on horseback.

"I'll watch them," said Chris, not looking at us at all but watching a tractor rake around where the barrels had stood moments before.

"Okay?" Dave asked me again.

I probably looked a little nervous. "I guess. . . ."

Dave hopped down on the off side between our horses, then reached up for Stevey. He lifted his brother from Tee and passed him up to me, waiting for him to swing his leg over the saddle horn and making sure he was steady. It reminded me strongly of how he had handled the little boy at Bar 8. Now I knew why he was so good with little kids.

"There you go. Be back in a few." He flashed a smile and backed Tee out from between us, then swung back into the saddle and rode out onto the track. There he let Tee run.

Chris never said a word or looked in my direction, but he made his horse sidestep until he was right next to me. In spite of his unsociable manner,

I was glad he was close. Robin made me feel even better by riding over to my other side.

Stevey sighed deeply—contentedly, I thought. He leaned back against me and began playing with the saddle strings. His little hat was in the way a bit, but after a while, I didn't notice it much. I held him close with my right arm, not because he wasn't securely nestled on my lap, but because I wanted to. I had a growing sense of something I'd never felt. Protective? Yes . . . and something more. I wanted to take his hat off and bury my nose in his hair. I wanted to brush my cheek softly against his. *Is that creepy?* I wasn't sure but thought I'd better resist.

The team roping began and I watched, fascinated in the fast action taking place in the arena. Robin explained as we watched.

"Does it hurt the cow?" I asked.

"Steer," corrected Robin, "and no, not usually. The whole point is to restrain the animal so, theoretically, they can brand or tag it or treat it medically. Cowboys would never purposely hurt their cattle—that would be stupid. They don't always do things this way anymore, but they used to and sometimes still need to. Okay, Dave and Matt are next," she said, and we waited expectantly to see them.

Chapter Fourteen

A Little Ride

The atmosphere around the arena had certainly changed. The stands were much more crowded than they'd been before and the band playing behind us at the plaza added to the general noise and excitement.

"Matthew Morris and David Caldera, riding for no score," was announced, and everyone whistled and called approval, including us. Even Chris whistled loudly.

A black and white speckled steer ran into the arena from a small chute. Matthew rode out on a tall brown horse right behind on its left and Dave on Tee a little further behind to its right, both swinging their ropes. Matthew cast his rope and caught the steer around its horns, then bore left. Dave loosed his rope also and caught the steer by the foot. A groan went up from the crowd. The ropes pulled tight for a moment, and I thought the steer would topple over, but then the ropes relaxed and it ran off. Two other riders on the sideline drove it toward the exit.

"What happened?" I asked.

"He missed the throw. Only got one leg. That's a five-second penalty. But they still did really well."

I began to watch for Dave to return, but he and Matthew remained near the steer's exit. Then the next team came in, the heeler missing the hind legs on the first throw and trying again.

"They get a second try, but it takes too long to make a good time. Dave and Matt's would be better than that if they got to keep their score."

Matthew and Dave followed the steer out. After a while, we saw Matthew coming toward us, but there was no sign of Dave.

"Hey, L—" I thought he was going to say "Legs," and I felt kind of funny. But instead he finished, "LA! Look at you, all riding and everything."

He was smiling broadly, but his eyes flicked past me a couple of times. I turned to see Chris looking at him steadily. He rode his horse in alongside Robin and greeted her.

"Nice ride," said Robin.

"Thanks," he said. "We almost had him perfectly. Our time was good, but the penalty would have hurt. Oh well, can't be perfect at everything, right?"

"I don't know," said Robin. "You guys are pretty close to it. I'm surprised all the time that your heads don't just explode. Speaking of big heads, where is he?"

Matthew laughed. "He's back there talking to people. There were girls ready to pounce." Matthew said this as if no more needed to be said, which was true.

They continued to chat. Chris watched the roping, looking almost content. Stevey yawned and wriggled.

"Are you getting tired, Stevey?" I whispered just beneath his hat. He shook his head. "Okay," I said. I was quite happy to remain as I was. Sam was calm and Stevey content. So was I, though I was looking forward to Dave coming back. There was only one other thing—

"Um," I said, just loud enough for Chris to hear, "I need to get down . . . for a while. Could you take Stevey?"

Chris looked at me questioningly, then seemed to catch my meaning and nodded.

"Hey Stevey, come sit with me for a while, okay?" He made no move to take him but sat waiting. Stevey didn't move. "You haven't ridden Goonie for a while, have you? Come sit with me." He held his hand out but didn't grab his brother. After a moment, Stevey slipped sideways and almost fell into his hands. It scared me until I heard his tinkling laughter as Chris caught and cradled him in both arms for a moment. His hat hid most of his face as he looked down at his little brother, but I saw his mouth widen in a smile—a real smile—the first I'd ever seen.

At that moment Dave rode up. "What's up? How're you doing?" His eyes swept the area, seeming to take note of everything to see what he'd missed.

"Fine," I smiled, thrilled he hadn't become completely diverted. "But . . . I kind of need to . . . you know." I pointed up the hill.

"Yeah," he said immediately, "I saw Stevey changing hands. But don't dismount here. I made a promise, remember?" Matthew and Chris both looked at him oddly. Chris lost interest first and Matthew looked thoughtful. "Can't have your dad mad at me, right?"

"Right," I agreed easily, though I was sure our motivations weren't the same. Still, he'd been watching!

"Come on, let's ride up the road a ways."

I agreed. I managed to back Sam adequately if inexpertly away from the fence and we walked side by side in the direction of the house.

"We'd better stop here," he said as we reached the edge of the plaza and the curve of the driveway. "Dad doesn't like the horses too close to the designated pedestrian areas."

I hadn't noticed before, but there were signs posted: horse and rider silhouettes with the universal NO symbol over them. It struck me as funny and I laughed. His eyes twinkled.

"Take your time. Get something to eat. It'll be a while before the pole bending. Robin's riding in that. Then there'll be another break before the bull and bronc riding. Do you still want to ride?"

"Yes!" I said and nodded enthusiastically.

"Okay," said Dave, his eyes crinkling at the corners as they seemed to do when he was really pleased. "I'll keep Sam for you."

I dismounted and handed him the reins. We waved and he headed back toward the arena. I took a deep breath and began the climb toward the house. It felt strange to walk up there alone. The shadows were lengthening as the early evening drew in, casting even more interesting colors across the huge house. The lightest shade was now the color of butternut squash with shadows looking varying shades of peach, salmon, and the deepest, almost blue. Perhaps not everyone would immediately see the beauty of the house, but it was charming to me—in an oversize kind of way.

It felt even stranger to enter the house alone, the cool hitting me so hard this time I felt like collapsing on the spot. I'd been so distracted that I hadn't noticed the heat too much, but now that I was here, I could imagine not wanting to go back out at all. I walked through to the kitchen where Angel was still working.

"Um . . ." I said, causing Angel look up and smile. "I just need to go. . . ." I pointed in the direction of the bathroom.

"*Si!* Yes, yes, you go!"

I did. When I came back out, I asked, "Um . . . do you need any help?"

"Oh!" exclaimed Angel. "You want to help? *Bueno! Gracias! Si*, you can help. *Aqui*," she said, showing me a large pan filled with cooked potatoes. "You can eslice these . . . soh, and soh, and soh." She showed me how she wanted them cut, then put the pieces into another large, deep pot. "Soh many people! Every year eet gets more and more," she said proudly. "Which means more and more food, no?"

I smiled and continued cutting.

"I was *soh* happy to know Rohbeen, she has a new friend," she continued conversationally. "A girl! I had told these boys, and Alejandro alsoh, 'She ees getting older. She talks and acts like a boy. She needs a girl to talk to. *No hombres* all the time!' I was soh happy when Dah-veed, he tell me abou' chou," she said. "Alejandro, he is very pleased alsoh. No girls een the family, you understand? They have, how do you say, *primas?*" She thought for a moment. "Cohseens. But they are no close by here. Eet is good for them to be around girls. Like *hermana* . . . seester, no?" She reached over and covered one of my hands with one of her own, then patted it gently. "I am very happy you are here."

I smiled and blushed from her confession, happy to please but feeling funny about it. Honestly? "Sister" was not my ambition. But to be in Dave's life under any circumstances was more than I had ever hoped for. So the struggle would be to control my wandering thoughts. *Just think of Dave as a brother. How hard can that be?*

Since she seemed inclined to talk, I asked a question that had been bothering me for at least a couple of hours. "Is Mrs. Caldera around?"

It seemed like a reasonable, innocent enough question, but Angel's whole demeanor changed abruptly. She had been cutting up eggs and other ingredients and adding them to the large pot, but she now clicked her tongue unhappily and turned away as if to do something else at the sink. I could have sworn she crossed herself. She then reverted to Spanish that I couldn't follow at all, and suddenly became terribly interested in how the potatoes were coming along.

"Le's get thees feeneeshed, no?" she said, all businesslike, helping me cut up the last few potatoes. She then took a large bowl filled with a white, creamy substance and poured it over everything. "Thees ees the esecret! The mayonnaise! *Home*made!" she said and began stirring.

"It smells delicious!" I said sincerely, but I was also trying to get back in her good graces.

"*Si!*" she said, happily. "*Es muy delicioso!*"

Here she lapsed into incomprehensible Spanish again as she took the huge pot in both hands and went to one of the refrigerators. I got there ahead of her and opened the door.

"*Gracias*," she said warmly, sliding the pot onto an empty shelf. There would obviously be no more information today, but she didn't seem to be holding anything against me. "You go back now, no? Enjoy!"

"Okay," I said, smiling.

"*Espera, un momento!*" she said, catching my attention. "You must eat more! You are too skeeny! You must get some food!"

"*Si!*" I said, smiling.

She laughed and smiled back.

Now feeling hungry, I wandered over to the plaza. There was plenty to tempt me, but I didn't want to take too long—I was already missing Dave and wondering what I was missing at the arena. I settled on corn on the cob. Luckily Miguel remembered me. He tried to get me to take some ribs, but I laughingly declined.

I saw a lot of kids I thought I recognized from school and waved back to the ones who acknowledged me, but I didn't want to stop to talk to anyone. They seemed to look at me strangely, as if seeing me for the first time. Most of them had never paid attention to me before. I tried to eat the corn as I walked but had barely managed to land a couple of bites before Dave approached, leading the horses.

"I was thinking of organizing a search party," he said, smirking. "I'm glad you got something to eat, though. You are going to eat that, right?"

"Yes, of course," I said. *As soon as I'm not moving.* "I was helping Angel a little. Sorry it took so long."

"I was just kidding," he said. "Here, let me give you a boost."

Mounting and holding on to my corn was a little tricky, even with Dave's help, but I accomplished it and we headed back to the arena. I looked around for Stevey and Chris.

"Where's Stevey?" I asked.

"Chris had to ride," said Robin, "and Stevey was getting tired, so I took him over to his dad."

She pointed toward the far side of the arena where I could just make out Mr. Caldera with Stevey, my parents, and quite a few other adults and children all sitting together. They all seemed very happy, talking and laughing. *Excellent!*

"You missed it," she continued. "Chris and Shane had the perfect ride, but it was just for practice, you know, so they didn't win. And Dave and Matt would have come in third except for the same reason. They're getting ready for the senior pole bending right now."

Matthew had been joined by a small group of other riders a little distance from Robin. Chris was on the ground in the arena with several other people, kicking clods of earth around and setting up poles several yards away from each other in a straight line. This—the pole bending—looked like it would be interesting too. Robin left us as soon as the event was announced. I watched closely as rider after rider set their horses down the line of poles at a dead run. Turning around the end, they came back, weaving in and out, down and back, and galloped over the finish line. It was very exciting.

"Do you think I could learn that too?" I asked, unable to contain myself. They made it look so easy, though the thought of riding that fast was scary. I hadn't ridden faster than a slow trot yet.

"Of course!" said Dave, looking pleased. "In fact . . ."

He never finished what he was saying but looked thoughtful. I couldn't help wondering what he was thinking, but I was distracted soon enough just by his presence. It was thrilling to be able to watch the events from horseback like this, with him "keeping an eye on me." Tee didn't seem to want to stand still, though, sometimes getting too close. Dave always moved him away, but I wouldn't have minded him closer.

Robin's name was announced and she appeared at the entrance of the arena. I thought she rode like a mad woman, but she was obviously always in control. Gali's movements were tight and fast and he looked like he could have run it without a rider, but Dave pointed out how she used her seat, legs,

and hand to direct him. They seemed so perfectly in sync with each other. Unfortunately, they got too close to one pole and knocked it down, causing a huge groan to go up from everyone watching. She didn't return right away but eventually rode back to us.

"I know, I know," she said, shaking her head. "Don't even tell me what I did wrong."

"I wasn't going to say anything," said Dave, looking benign. "I wouldn't dream of rubbing your nose in the fact that you dropped him coming out of the third pole on the way back, or that you weren't looking where you were going."

"Thanks so much," said Robin, sarcastically. "I can always count on you."

"Hey, it's a trainer's job to find fault with his pupil," he said.

Robin rolled her eyes.

"You trained her?" I asked, feeling shy. Would he teach me? I wasn't going to ask—not right now anyway—but it was something more to add to my daydreams.

"Taught her everything she knows!" he said with a self-satisfied smirk. "Everything she does *right* anyway."

"No, just how to ride." countered Robin.

We watched the rest of the pole bending, two of the girls they knew well, Stacie and Jessie, coming in first and third respectively.

"Bull riding's next," said Dave. He smiled what I was starting to think of as his wicked smile; more than a smirk, it never failed to make my heart skip beats. "Time to do battle," he said. "When Chris gets here, I must leave you, fair maidens, and I'll be busy for a while."

Robin gave me a long-suffering look. Dave waited until Chris reappeared, leading his horse.

"Here we go," he said, backing Tee away. Then he frowned at me and rode up close again. "I'll be needing that back," he said. "It's my lucky hat."

I'd forgotten all about it, but I was still wearing his black hat.

"No doubt that's why you missed your throw earlier," said Robin sarcastically.

Dave shook his head. "No excuses. Still, I'd rather have my lucky hat for this ride." I took the hat off and held it out to him. He took it, smiling. "Could you hold this one for me? I wouldn't wear it, though." He wrinkled his nose as he passed the white one to me.

"Sure," I said but felt a little sad. I'd become quite attached to the black one.

"See you later," he said, raising the hat toward his head and then stopping. He sniffed lightly at the hat, then looked at me and grinned. I felt the red spread upward on my face like a thermometer rising. I remembered how the hat had smelled of him a week ago, but I'd been wearing it so much that apparently it now smelled like me.

"Extra lucky," he said provocatively, settling the hat on his head. Tee seemed to dance away.

Robin made a face and shrugged her shoulders but didn't say anything. Chris stood next to me on the ground, making it even more unlikely that we'd share conversation. Then I noticed that he was talking to the same man he'd been talking to before, the veterinarian, but I couldn't hear much of what they said.

The announcer thanked the band, a group of high school students, for playing through the afternoon. I had thought they were pretty good. Another local band would be playing classic rock during the last two events and would continue into the evening. The music was now coming over the loudspeaker too. They said the barbecue would keep going for another two hours and adult beverages would be available. Then they thanked a list of local businesses for supporting the event both physically and financially.

"It's really cool," I said to Robin, "how the whole town is involved in this."

"Yeah," said Robin, looking proud again, "though not *everyone* gets involved. All of Old Town loves it, of course, and most of the downtown businesses get involved by donating money or physically helping and promoting it. It's a pretty important event. The only thing bigger is the county fair, and that happens before school starts. This is kind of the final blowout before winter, you know? But clean-up's a b—" she stopped and finished primly, "a bother. It takes them at least a week to get everything back to normal."

The announcers were now talking about who had provided the bulls, who was going to ride, and who the judges were. It sounded very official, but Robin said it was all amateur, just a chance to get a good practice ride and for the bull owners to see how their prospects would perform. Mr. Caldera would be one of the judges.

Our attention was drawn to the metal chutes at the far end of the arena and the judging and rules were explained for those of us who didn't know.

Robin added her own comments to what they were saying, which often clarified but sometimes just confused me more.

"Just watch," she said as the first rider prepared. "Dave'll help the riders get ready and he usually helps in the arena too. Those guys over there?" she said, pointing to two oddly dressed men. "They're bull fighters. It's their job to distract the bulls once the rider is off."

"Distract?" I asked, wondering what a bull would need to be distracted from.

"Yeah. So it doesn't try to trample or hook the rider. You know . . . if it has horns? That's why they're so careful who they let ride. They have to show proof of their ability, like scores from previous open bull riding."

Chris mounted his horse next to me and I watched Dr. James head toward the chute area.

"James'll stand by," said Chris, "ready in case an animal is hurt at all, but it rarely happens. The riders on the other hand. . . ."

I was starting to have a really bad feeling about this. I guess it was obvious.

"There's an EMT right here, just in case," said Robin. "Don't worry so much."

"Are you going to ride?" I asked Chris. I was glad he was close, almost close enough to reach out and touch me. Not that he would ever want to do that, of course, but his presence was oddly comforting. I think I would have felt even better if he were near his brother.

"Not the bulls. Not today," he said tonelessly, and I couldn't tell if he was unhappy about it or not. He seemed to pick up on my cause of concern and added, "My brother can take care of himself . . . at least, when it comes to riding." This had an edge to it and he looked directly at me for a moment. It chilled me. *What was* that *supposed to mean?*

I didn't want to let him get away with making me feel bad, so after a moment I asked, "Goonie?"

His eyes were hidden by the brim of his hat, but I saw his lips twitch for just a second. "Laguna," he said. "Her name's Laguna, but Stevey calls her 'Goonie.' "

I smiled, satisfied that some kind of equilibrium was restored between us. He was so weird.

For the next thirty minutes or so my fingernails dug into my palms, even my reining hand, and my shoulders began to hurt from the tension I felt by the time the last entered rider had finished. Only three riders out of the eight had managed to ride the full eight seconds. The first rider had only lasted two. Two of the riders landed badly, and one was stomped on and had to be carried off. Another had been chased by his bull until distracted by the bull fighters. I caught sight of Dave a few times, opening the chute gates or closing the exit gate after the bulls. Lastly, it was his turn to ride.

"Are you okay?" asked Robin. "You look a little green."

Chris regarded me steadily for a moment.

"Shouldn't you be there too?" I said, a little desperately.

"Nope," He turned away with what seemed like callous unconcern.

I couldn't say anything more; I just wanted it to be over. I didn't really want to watch either, but it was impossible to drag my eyes away once I'd caught sight of Dave's black hat in the chute. The announcer called his name and the name of the bull he was riding, then the gate swung open. The bull was a huge yellow monster. It looked way bigger than any of the other bulls had been, but Dave was probably the smallest guy, too. Still, he looked amazing. His body moved in easy response to the bull's, his legs slapping tight against its sides even though the animal changed direction a number of times and completely left the ground several more. It was the longest eight seconds ever.

When the buzzer rang, he allowed himself to be catapulted away from the bucking animal and miraculously landed on his feet. He was obviously very happy about that, jumping in the air and striking out with his fist while the crowd roared. The announcers made a fuss about "Alex's kid," what a great bull and ride it had been, and wasn't it a shame he couldn't be scored. The men around the chutes were all slapping him on the back and shaking his hand as he left the arena.

Nonsensically, I felt relieved and proud and furious all at the same time. I realized there were tears running down my face and tried to brush them away before anyone saw. But Robin and Chris turned to each other and started speaking and, as I was in between, they couldn't help seeing. They both shut their mouths again and looked floored.

"What's your problem?" asked Robin, sharply.

"Nothing," I answered, crossly.

"Geez," she said, looking appalled. "I told you a long time ago, if you're going to hang with us. . . ."

I glanced at Chris, but he was looking away again and seemed disinterested. *Small mercy.*

The arena was being prepared for the bareback bronc riding, the tractor once more dragging the dirt to even out the footing. Dave soon returned to us, receiving congratulations and returning waves from almost everyone he passed. Chris backed away as Dave placed himself between Robin and me.

"Nice ride," Chris said in passing, as if it was no big deal.

"Deepest thanks," Dave replied solemnly, folding his right arm over his chest and bowing his head. "Go and do likewise, my brother."

Robin snorted. Dave grinned at her then looked at me, his smile quickly fading.

"Are you okay?"

"She was worried about you," said Robin.

"I'm fine," I said, feeling as annoyed with myself as I was with her.

"Seriously?" Dave asked, his eyes wide. "I'm touched." Then he frowned deeply and turned back to me. "Unless that means you didn't think I could do it."

He narrowed his eyes at me and pretended to look mad. It made me laugh. I tried to relax but still felt very tense. *I guess I'm not going to be a big fan of bull riding.*

"Let's walk the horses, okay?" Dave said, and Robin and I both agreed. We'd been in the same spot for quite a while.

"So, the next event is like the bull riding?" I asked, wanting to redeem myself, but not sure I was going to like it either.

"Sort of . . . but not really," said Dave. "The ride's different."

"And no horns," added Robin.

"Are . . . are you riding in that too?" I asked, hoping he'd say no.

"Not today, but I usually do. Chris is riding."

"They decided to take turns so one of them would be able to keep an eye on you," said Robin, and it sounded like she was accusing me.

I felt horrible. I didn't want to be a headache to Dave, a cause of trouble or someone that dragged him down. *And* Chris. I was already indebted to him and felt uncomfortable about it.

"Robin!" Dave sounded reproachful. "Don't worry about it, Allie. It's no big deal. We want you to have a good time. And feel safe. And not make your dad mad."

I tried to smile but had trouble regaining my composure. And I was still tense from the bull riding.

Our attention was claimed once again by the announcers and Robin and Dave talked animatedly about the different riders they knew: Matthew, Tanner, Shane, Kyle, and Tom from Bar 8. And Chris, of course, but he wouldn't be scored. Apparently Chris preferred bull riding, but for some reason he was content to let his brother ride today. We found another place near the fence where we could watch.

The action was certainly fast and crazy and I felt the same tension gripping my shoulders and creeping down my spine. Dave was so wound up I could tell he wanted to be out there riding, but I was glad he was next to me, close as Chris had been. Safe.

I had to admit, it was very exciting to watch. Dave told me about some things to watch for: the rider's free arm, his leg motion, the horse's high kicks and body twists, all making it almost impossible for the rider to stay on. Shane and Kyle were bucked off before the time was up, but Matthew and Tanner lasted the whole eight seconds. Dave said Tanner's ride was better, and he did get a better score. Apparently Matthew's horse bucked too rhythmically and basically moved in a straight line, not considered as difficult as Tanner's, who twisted and jerked and changed direction every other buck. Tom was bucked off right before the buzzer sounded.

"Girl's next," said Dave. "Colby Swift drew her."

"This should be fun," said Robin, her eyes laughing.

I looked at them both, uncomprehending.

"Dancing Medicine Girl is Tom's. We just call her 'Girl.' You saw her at Bar 8."

I still felt in the dark, but Robin was starting to be able to read me well and said, "She stays in the pasture with the Shires."

Understanding dawned as a rather small tan and white paint sprang violently out of the chute, not giving the rider a chance at all. She twisted and threw herself around so wildly I wasn't surprised when the man, just barely maintaining his balance as she twisted one way, came to grief as she immediately twisted in the opposite direction. He fell hard as she continued to kick

out until a rider in the arena released the strap. She seemed to enjoy leaping and kicking up her heels a few more times until the riders herded her out.

"She sure loves to buck," said Robin.

"Tom's gotten a lot of offers for her," said Dave, grinning and shaking his head, "but he really loves her. She's as gentle as a kitten on the ground, and loves the big horses, but she's feisty and tends to cause trouble with the riding horses, so she gets special treatment. He loans her out sometimes, just to give her a chance to do what she's really good at, but he doesn't want to sell her. She's more of a pet than anything else."

That had been the last scheduled ride. Dave explained that normally scores would be averaged over at least a couple of days, but today was just high score wins. The winner was a man I didn't know, but Tanner won third place which seemed very impressive against some of the older, more experienced riders. The very last rider for the day would be Chris.

"I'm curious to see which horse he chose," said Dave, straining to see far enough to tell. "There were three he could have chosen from, but there was a big, black mare that is supposed to be wicked hard. He probably chose her." He was grinning, a little grimly I thought, but he looked proud all the same.

When Chris' ride was announced, cheering and whistling broke out around us and all the way through the stands. He was obviously very well known. They said the name of the horse and Dave nodded.

The horse exploded out of the chute like Girl had. Although she was huge, she was fast and violent, her movements quick and jerky, her kicks high and wild. She seemed to spend a lot of time either suspended in the air or spinning around in one direction then the other. I was surprised to find my heart beating in my throat again, both my hands gripping the horn of my saddle as if I could somehow hold on for Chris, and my back as tense as it had been earlier. Chris might be weird and might not think very highly of me, but I would hate for him to be hurt.

My worry was wasted. He somehow stuck to the horse like glue and instead of being jerked back and forth, his body seemed to bend almost gracefully as she whipped about. Only once did it look like he might be in trouble. The horse twirled wildly to its right, then bucked hard, jumping forward and rearing, almost falling sideways from the momentum. For a second, it looked like Chris might fall in the opposite direction. But his hand on the strap stayed tight and so did his legs, and though his upper body got snapped sideways, he somehow kept his balance. He remained on until the buzzer rang. The horse had bucked twice more before Chris saw a chance to swing his leg over its lowered head and jump clear, landing in much the same manner as Dave had after his bull ride.

The crowd went wild and the announcers shouted excitedly. I relaxed and started breathing again, feeling exhausted. I wished my eyesight was better or that I had been a little closer, as I wondered whether Chris had smiled at all at his successful ride. *At all?* I supposed I'd never know. He walked calmly out of the arena, head bowed and face hidden.

People started leaving the stands, returning to the plaza or heading toward the parking area. Several riders came over to talk to Dave and Robin. They tended to give me strange looks, even the ones that recognized me, and I felt like a complete impostor.

The sun hadn't set but was sinking low enough to cast long shadows. I figured it must be about seven o'clock. I saw my parents approaching and Dad had his determined look on—a look I was becoming more and more acquainted with. But Mom was smiling, bright-eyed and curious.

"We're going to be leaving, Allie," said Dad. I think he was trying not to sound too stern but was looking it all the same.

I felt embarrassed, not sure how to respond in front of so many people. I didn't want to just leave, not having a chance to properly say goodbye. And then I remembered. Gold! I hadn't told them about Gold at all! This was important and I would dig my heels in if I had to, figuratively speaking of course.

"Let me take Sam back," I said, reaching forward to pat his neck. "I can meet you at the car."

Dad looked like he was going to utter a decisive no, but Mom said, "Why don't you meet us in a minute at the plaza. We'll go listen to the band."

She smiled at my dad, who frowned back but thankfully must have realized how embarrassing it would be to argue with his wife and daughter in front of so many people, young though they were.

"I'll be right there," I assured them, then looked apologetically to Dave and Robin. I hadn't meant to break up their conversation, but I did need to talk to them.

"Yeah," said Robin, picking up on something she either heard in my voice or saw on my face. "We should go put the horses away so we can start

helping somewhere." She turned Gali toward the barn and I followed her. After a minute, she turned and yelled, "Hey, Caldera! You comin'?"

Apparently Dave hadn't sensed any urgency in the situation and was still talking. Robin and I were just dismounting as Dave rode up.

"Gold came into the corral today! I almost forgot to tell you, but he followed me in, and when I left he was still there. I'm pretty sure I can catch him anytime. What should I do?"

Dave thought for a minute while they unsaddled the horses. "You should close him in, for sure. We need to tell Chris. He's around somewhere, but we've got to get the horses put away first. Robin, take Tee and turn him out for me. I'll put Sam away. We can groom them later. Allie, you should go with Robin."

I would have argued that, as I had ridden Sam, I should go with him to put Sam away, but he had said it in such an authoritative manner, I felt it best not to. Dave walked with Sam in the opposite direction, toward the smaller barn. I held the horses for Robin as she unsaddled them, then she opened the gate to a large paddock and led both horses in, took their bridles off, then returned to close the gate behind her.

"They can play for a while," she grinned. Gali was already on the ground preparing to roll as Tee looked on.

"I should probably get back to my parents," I said hesitantly.

"They don't trust you, do they?" she said.

"It's not that," I said, not wanting her to think them too strict. "They just . . . worry. Especially my dad. He's gone a lot and . . . I think I'm growing up too fast for him." I smiled but realized that I had probably nailed it. It wasn't me that he didn't trust, exactly, but my age. *And everyone else my age!*

Dave joined us then, but I repeated, "I should go."

"I'll go with you," said Robin. "I'm the chaperone!" She slipped her arm through mine and turned me toward the plaza, but I stopped and turned back to Dave.

"Thank you," I said, feeling awkward, "for everything. Thank Chris too . . . please. And say bye to Stevey and Henry for me."

Dave just grinned and nodded before turning to walk down toward the arena.

Robin walked with me toward the plaza. I was sad that I had to go, but I was tired and it had been an amazing, enlightening and, as usual when the Calderas were involved, rather confusing day. Robin, in spite of her occasional fits of impatience and annoyance with me, seemed to appreciate me being around. I was feeling more and more as if we had the potential to be good friends. All in all, a very satisfactory day.

My parents smiled at Robin returning with me. Dad was probably glad that Dave wasn't with us, but that was okay—for now. They said goodbye to Cheryl and the kids and the Morrises, who they had been talking to, and we walked toward the parking lot. As we reached the long driveway, Chris loped up on Laguna, Dave sitting up behind him.

"Allie!" he called. Then he gave me a thumbs up.

I looked at them both. *Was that for what I thought it was for?* Dave nodded and waved a brief goodbye. I nodded and waved back. Chris didn't do anything, his face mostly hidden beneath the brim of his hat.

Chapter Fifteen

One Thing I Know

On the way home, I was content to gaze out the window into the darkening dusk, completely wrapped up in my own thoughts. Dad was apparently occupied likewise. But Mom wanted to talk.

"Well!" she said, turning so she could see both Dad and me. "They have a lovely place, don't they?"

"Mmhmm," I agreed dreamily.

"I suppose I was expecting something like. . . ." She looked at Dad. "Something like Isabel's. But it's quite different, isn't it?"

Isabel is my dad's sister in Colorado. The ranch used to be referred to as "Granddad's" before he passed away. Now it was "Isabel's." Dad never referred to it as "home." In fact, he never referred to it at all.

Dad focused on the dark road ahead and pretended it was demanding all of his attention. "Pretty different," was all he said.

"Did you have any idea it would be such a grand affair?" she asked me.

I couldn't help thinking that was a silly question.

"Um . . . no."

"Well, I was impressed by the generosity and cordiality of Mr. Caldera. He expressed the hope of seeing much more of us, but I'm sure that was directed mostly toward you."

"Mmm," I said, not sure what would be considered an appropriate response. *"Maybe I could live there?"* probably wouldn't go over well. It felt like she was leading up to something.

"He seemed so pleased that you've become friends with his sons and especially Robin."

I nodded and tried to smile, not wanting to comment.

"I didn't get to meet the older brother—what's his name?"

"Chris," I supplied.

"Yes, Chris. He certainly knows how to ride, I guess!" Even in the gloom, I could see her eyes were bright and appreciative. "Dave seems very nice," she continued, a little too casually. "Apparently he and Matthew have been friends a long time?"

"Apparently," I agreed, not wanting to sound terse, but not sure where this was going or what to add. If the adults had been talking about their kids this afternoon, and that seemed likely, she probably knew way more than I did. That was disconcerting in itself.

"And he and Robin also? I got the feeling they're close."

Now I felt the edges of the real issue were being poked. I did my best impression of *"Allison's not really that concerned with this but finds it interesting,"* and said, "They've been friends since third grade. They're like brother and sister. Even Angel said so. And I guess I've been adopted too. I think . . ."

I was going to say something about the Calderas "watching out" for her, but changed my mind. There was too much I didn't know. It also suddenly occurred to me that it would imply that they thought I needed looking after too, which had been true. Now, however, they knew I was very well—no, *too* well—protected but still seemed to want me around. This made me ecstatically happy, even if it was only to be a female companion for Robin. I would have liked to be more, of course, but I could live with it.

"You think . . . ?" Mom prompted patiently.

"Hmm? Oh . . . I don't remember."

"Well, I'm so happy that you've made such good friends," said Mom, pointedly. I doubted that she was subtle enough to ever make a good salesperson, but I appreciated the effort, and her influence with Dad was certainly greater than mine.

After a few quiet minutes, she said, "So, do you think Dave is in reme-dial classes?"

"What?" I exclaimed. The abruptness of the question startled me.

"He's obviously a very physical boy. I've heard that sometimes children who excel at sports don't do as well in the classroom. It just seems strange that he's in none of your academic classes. And he does seem to be kept extremely busy. I'm sure it must be very good for him in general. Probably keeps an active boy like him out of trouble. I understand his brother is already seventeen and only a junior, too. Right? And he's working at the hardware store in town?" This was obviously rhetorical and she left it hanging as if the implication was clear.

And there she was: the mother I had pictured cornering my adored one to drill him for personal qualifications. I was thankful she hadn't actually done that and hoped she wouldn't do it in the future. My cheeks were burn-ing but only partly in mortification at my mother's audacious remarks. The rest was in shame. I had wondered and thought the very same things myself.

And so what if it's true? It doesn't change how I feel about him. It doesn't change who he is.

"All your friends ride, don't they?" she observed.

I was glad she was changing the subject, but in light of the day's activi-ties, this also seemed like a very silly question. This one, however, I was more than happy to play along with.

"Yes, all of them. Even Melanie. You haven't met her yet," I said. I was sure they'd love Melanie.

"She wasn't there today?" asked Mom.

"No, she was at a different horse show all weekend."

"Do you like riding, dear?" she asked softly.

The air around us felt suddenly stiff and we were all obviously aware of it. I felt my mother was purposely walking a tightrope for me right now. I could easily forgive all her probing from before.

"Yes!" I breathed passionately. "I *really* want to learn. May I? Please?"

Mom looked at Dad, who had remained silent all this time.

He negotiated the turn to go back through town, then said, "We'll see."

Mom glanced at me and smiled. The subject had been broached and half of the parental unit appeared to be in my favor. It was enough for now. The remainder of the trip home was accomplished in relative silence.

I felt completely exhausted though it wasn't that late. Dad made straight for the television and Mom asked if he wanted anything on her way to the kitchen. I moved to the stairs but stopped and turned back.

"Thank you," I said. Mom and Dad looked curious. "Thank you for letting us go today." I didn't want to be too effusive. It wasn't necessary that they understood how *much* I appreciated it. Understatement can be a very good thing.

Mom looked pleased, said, "You're welcome, dear. We had a really nice time too," and continued to the kitchen.

Dad regarded me for a moment, then smiled, relenting. I smiled calmly in return. He turned back to the TV, but he wasn't looking at it. He looked thoughtful. I continued upstairs but left my door open. I wanted time to think by myself but also wanted to listen for any pertinent conversation.

There wasn't much. I sat near the door with my sketchbook, my back against my nightstand. There were so many things to mull over. Dave's little brothers—what a surprise they had been! Henry was going to bear watching, obviously, but what was the story with Stevey? I didn't know much about small children, but he seemed to act much younger than his apparent age. I certainly had never been around one so—quiet. Maybe he was just shy, though he didn't seem to be.

What about Robin's family? Somewhere in the back of my mind, I'd expected to meet them today, but they were never mentioned. And Dave's mother? I had tried to imagine what she would look like and had definitely expected to meet her, but she had not appeared and Angel's reaction to my one question had not invited more. I wanted to ask Dave directly, but the memory of Chris' reproof on the day they met my dad prevented me. I didn't want to seem rude or be snubbed again. It was difficult not knowing these things, though. It made me feel that I had to be even more careful of what I said around my friends, especially if it concerned family.

Downstairs, Mom had returned from the kitchen and joined my dad. Their voices were quite low, but the TV's volume was down too. I could just hear them.

"What do you think?" asked Mom.

"About?" he asked.

Oh, come on! Even I know what she's talking about.

"About everything. Especially about Allison riding."

"You know how I feel," he said, dully.

"But what about how *she* feels?" *Yay, Mom!* "She looked more confident and happy today than I can ever remember." *Really?*

Dad was quiet. I knew he truly *wanted* what was best for me, but I didn't think he necessarily *knew* what was best for me, namely, being allowed to *really* ride.

"It'll be difficult for her if she's not allowed to do the things her friends are involved in."

Great point, Mom!

"And you know I have good reasons for my sentiments on the subject," countered Dad.

I don't! Please elaborate!

It was quiet for a couple of minutes. Then Dad said, "Look, when I come home again, we'll discuss it, but I'm not prepared to make a positive decision on this right now."

"Well," said Mom, so softly I could barely hear her, "what about her friends? Is she still not allowed to spend time with them?"

I held my breath. Ultimately, this was even more important.

There was a long pause before Dad spoke again. "Robin seems like a nice girl; I don't mind Allie spending time specifically with her. But I don't feel comfortable with her hanging out with boys, especially those Caldera kids, no matter how influential their family is."

Quiet again. Then Mom, softly, "That seems unfair, Greg. I'm sure Allison doesn't care about that. Sooner or later—"

"Can you honestly tell me that you're completely okay with her involvement with these boys? That you have no concerns?"

I held my breath again and strained to hear Mom's answer. It never came.

"Well, until I'm more convinced, I say 'later.' Let's wait and see."

Disappointed, I went to bed.

I had set my alarm to wake me up extra early. I hurried down to the corral expecting to go looking for Gold but was surprised to see him inside the corral, eating something. He looked up and regarded me, chewing; I approached the fence, confused. The food was in a heap near the closest corner of the enclosure. *Some type of hay?*

Realizing this might be my only chance, I calmly walked to the gate, lifted the top pole, and slowly and quietly slid it through the topmost slot in the opposite post. He raised his head again, interested but apparently content to remain where he was. I lifted the bottom pole, closing him in. Then I approached him, very slowly.

"Be careful." Funny how when somebody doesn't say much, you remember everything they *do* say.

I walked up to within an arm's length of Gold and stopped. He continued to munch complacently, relaxed, his eye calm. I was sure he was aware that I had closed his one exit, but he seemed resigned to his capture. I was becoming convinced he wasn't wild at all and wondered even more what his story was.

I spent a while talking to him, then went home to get ready for school. This time I was determined to tell Dave about Gold first thing. No getting distracted! Dad dropped me off at school and said goodbye a little sadly; he'd be gone all week. Dave and Robin were waiting nearby again.

"I caught him!" I said as I joined them and we walked in the direction of our lockers.

"Really?" Robin's eyes lit up.

"Any trouble?" Dave asked.

"None," I said. I was still surprised about that myself. "There was some food there. It looked like some kind of straw or hay."

"Hmm," murmured Dave, frowning. "We need to talk to Chris. See you at lunch?"

"Yes!" I said happily.

Robin and I walked together to Algebra and the class sped by. I thought a couple of kids looked at me strangely, but when I whispered my observation to Robin, she looked around, pouted a little, and shrugged her shoulders.

By the time I had changed for PE, I knew something was up. The lowered voices and covert glances I had encountered at the beginning of the year was nothing to this. A few girls glared at me in outright hostility or looked down their noses at me as if I were a worm they were considering stepping on. At the end of the class, a sophomore I'd never had anything to do with purposely tripped me and I fell, scraping my knee. Her friends laughed.

"Ooh," she said, looking at me blandly and moving her extended leg back slowly. "You'd better watch what you're doing." It sounded like a threat.

What on earth?

Melanie helped me get up. "What was that about?"

"I have no idea," I said, shaking my head but starting to feel a familiar dread that made me feel sick. I knew this behavior; I'd been treated like this many times before, but it had been a long time ago. At least, it had been *feeling* like a long time ago. Why was this happening now?

"Did . . . did anything happen over the weekend? Were you able to go to the . . . barbecue?"

She seemed to want to ask something more specific but didn't. Of course, I now realized that to call the Caldera event simply a barbecue was like calling Disneyland a carnival, but I knew she was just being diplomatic.

"No . . . and yes. I mean, yes we went, but otherwise . . ."

I frowned, considering the other part of her question. What *had* happened? I had become even more aware of my growing feelings for Dave and had allowed myself to enjoy being close to him. I felt I had even more reason to trust him now, and wanted to, though deep down I knew I still had fears and was still questioning. *Was there a problem because I had been near him all day? Were people saying that I needed him somehow? I couldn't deny that; I had already come to that conclusion myself. Did it matter what they thought?*

"Happen like what?" I asked.

I let Melanie's clear eyes search mine for a moment, then she smiled and said, "Oh, nothing. I was just trying to think if you could have done something, maybe even unknowingly. It doesn't make sense." She smiled again. "Are you coming to the cafeteria today?"

It suddenly hit me that it was Tuesday, not Monday, a day I normally would have eaten with her. "Oh! I forgot! Sorry, I . . . I promised to meet someone at lunch, but I'll eat with you tomorrow for sure, okay?"

A shadow passed across her face. Doubt? Concern? I didn't think it was like her to be jealous or anything. It must be something else.

"I'm really sorry!" I said again.

"Don't be silly. It's fine. Really! I'll see you tomorrow, okay?" She smiled, her expression calm and clear once more.

"See you tomorrow," I agreed.

I was hyper aware of attention as I approached the tables. Some looks were sneaky, making them even harder to read. Most appeared very curious or stormily malevolent, the latter exclusively from girls in the group. For someone who preferred to blend into the background, I had received way too much attention since coming to this school. What on earth was it now?

Robin and Dave were standing apart from the main group. Dave looked like he was trying to convince her of something. She looked unsure and even more so as I approached. I hated interrupting them, but the hostile aura around the tables kept me from joining that group.

"Hey," they both said.

"Hi," I answered, feeling like I was on shaky ground. Everything had been normal this morning, but would they now treat me like everyone else was doing? What had I done?

Dave gave Robin a meaningful look and she glared back at him as if saying, '*Okay!*' but said nothing. Then Dave called to Chris who was sitting where he usually did, a darker than normal scowl on his brow. He seemed almost relieved to be able to walk away from those that had gathered around him, and they watched as he walked over to us. Unnerving.

"Allie caught the horse," Dave said to Chris. "There was hay. You?"

His brother still had a deep frown on his face, as if thinking of something unpleasant, but nodded his head. "I went over early this morning. I left some oat hay; it'll be better for him for a while, and then we can add more alfalfa and stuff. He hasn't had enough to eat for a long time. I'm concerned that he doesn't get sick from too much too quickly."

It sounded like he knew what he was talking about and I was more than happy for him to do what he thought best, even if he was talking as if I weren't there. I was also impressed that he must have come over very early this morning and walked all the way from the street or we would have heard his truck. That would have been awkward to explain to my parents.

"Can we come over after school to see him?" asked Dave.

"Well," I said, thinking it through, "Dad was supposed to go to Los Angeles and my mom's working. I just need to make sure Dad . . ." I suddenly felt guilty—I hated feeling like I was doing something wrong, "make sure my dad's not home."

"We both have games," said Chris. "They're local, but we'll have to move quickly."

"We could give you a ride home," said Dave.

"Um . . . I . . . I can't do that," I said, feeling very uncomfortable with

the temptation to say, "Yes, *please!*" but also knowing I had to draw a line somewhere. "I have to take the bus."

"Oh . . . yeah." He looked disappointed, maybe annoyed.

"Give Dave a call when you get home," said Chris, quietly. "Let us know if we can come over. The horse needs to be fed at least twice a day. I have bales in the truck."

I was impressed again. Chris sure knew how to mobilize when he was motivated by something.

"Yes, of course," I said eagerly, wanting to do anything I could without going against the letter of my dad's law. I wasn't inclined to worry too much about the spirit of it. I had been told to take the bus and not have people in the house. I could do that. As for "hanging out with boys," that's not exactly what I'd be doing. We had a mission. It wasn't just hanging out. This was one of those fine distinctions I was starting to feel justified in making.

"Dave," Chris said quietly, indicating with a slight tilt of his head that he wanted to talk to him.

The two of them walked several paces away where no one would overhear them. I couldn't help watching them, even when Robin began talking to me.

As the guys stepped away, she said, hesitantly, "So . . . Dave was thinking . . ." She seemed to rethink her approach. "*We* were wondering . . ."

Chris had said something that Dave apparently found humorous but perhaps difficult to believe. He was looking at the ground as he listened, a frowning smile on his face.

". . . if maybe, since your mom is working and your dad is gone a lot, they would let you come over to my house after school. You could say we're doing homework . . ."

A deeper frown had replaced the smile on Dave's face. His mouth opened slightly as if something surprised him and he looked at his brother with an almost angry, questioning expression.

". . . and we could do that too, of course . . . but I could give you lessons on Gali to help you learn to ride."

Dave turned his head and looked directly at me, still frowning.

Oh God . . . what on earth did I do? Now I was feeling sick, suddenly afraid, and my head felt like it was spinning.

He turned back to Chris and they talked together some more, looking serious. They were both quiet for a minute, then Chris said something and, after another couple of moments, Dave nodded his head, a look of resignation on his face. I looked at Robin, feeling numb, my mind blank.

"Well?" she said, giving me her Earth-to-Allison look.

"Something's wrong," I said quietly, "but I don't know what it is." Tears were starting to prickle behind my nose, making my eyes water, but I was determined not to cry.

"What?" asked Robin.

Chris walked away, not rejoining the kids at the tables. They were still watching us with undisguised interest as if trying to interpret something— just as I was. Robin appeared to be the only one oblivious to the little scene. Dave walked back to us and seemed to force a smile. He looked to Robin questioningly.

"I don't know," she said. "She's spacing out again."

"Sorry," I said, trying to gather my thoughts and calm myself.

I had started shaking slightly, and Dave was regarding me with suspicion. No matter what the problem, crying was not an option!

"Um . . . let me ask my mom. But," I tried to smile, though I think it was wobbly, "I'm pretty sure she'll say yes." Then I looked earnestly at them both and blurted, "Thank you! Thank you both for thinking of me!" I didn't know what was going on, but I didn't want either of them to be in any doubt that I appreciated their friendship.

Robin looked embarrassed, but Dave's expression completely softened, his smile gentle and his eyes twinkling. A warm glow soothed my rattled nerves, and I began to feel a little better. Whatever the problem was, Dave didn't seem to be mad at *me*. For now, that was all that mattered.

"Yeah . . ." said Robin, looking at Dave as if looking for help. "Sure . . ."

"I've got to go . . . take care of something," said Dave, seeming distracted, "but I'll see you later, okay?"

"Okay," I said.

Robin looked confused as she watched him walk away. "I have a bad feeling you're rubbing off on him." She turned back to me, a comical look on her face. "I don't know if I can handle that."

I was able to laugh, more delighted than she could guess.

Continuing to feel the object of observation all afternoon, I stayed as far away as possible from anyone appearing to give me the evil eye and tried to ignore everyone else. Whatever it was, it would probably either die a speedy

death and be forgotten, as I'd observed drama from my old school always had, or it would be brought to light and dealt with. Cowardly by nature, I was hoping for the first option. At least Robin seemed to be ignorant of my problem. It made me feel it couldn't be anything too important after all.

I was disappointed that it was Chris that met me at my locker after school. But he acted as he normally did, simply saying, "Remember to call as soon as you get home," before walking away without ever looking directly at me.

The bus ride home seemed interminable, butterflies in my stomach making me feel ill at ease and the jolting of the bus adding to feelings of nausea. I felt better once I'd been dropped off and I started up Brookside.

The interior of the house was dark, cool, and silent, but I called, "I'm home!" anyway. No answer. Dumping my backpack on the kitchen table, I dug my cell phone out. I was surprised to see that Brenda had called—yesterday, apparently, while I was out—and had left a message. I'd listen to it later. I called Dave as I went out the back door to double check the garage. No cars.

"Hey," Dave answered immediately.

"There's no one home," I said, feeling a twinge of guilt but suppressing it fairly easily.

"We're at Tom's, so we'll just be a few minutes," he said.

"Okay. I'm going down there and make sure he's all right."

"Good. We'll meet you there," he said.

I had to clear the front corner of the corral before I saw Gold dozing in the shade of the trees and shrubbery near the back. I could tell he had heard me coming from the movement of his ears, but he didn't bestir himself. I was glad he felt so comfortable.

"Hey," I called softly to him, climbing through the rails and walking slowly toward him. I realized I hadn't brought anything to give him, but he didn't seem expectant. I also noticed there was little evidence left of the hay. He remained relaxed and sleepy-eyed as I approached and stroked his neck, then his cheek. He moved his head enough to bump me gently, acknowledging my attention, but he remained where he was.

"Are you all right?" I asked. "Is this okay here? You don't mind too much?" I played with his long forelock as I talked to him, trying to work some of the tangles out with my fingers. He seemed so calm and content; I wondered if he actually liked being in the corral.

For no reason I could detect, he suddenly became alert, his ears swiveling, his eyes fully open, and no longer resting a hind leg. After a moment, I heard a slight distant rattling, growing louder, and then the truck engine. Gold moved away, plainly apprehensive.

As the truck came into view, he became much more restless, pacing with long strides along the far side of the corral. I wasn't too surprised by this behavior but was completely unprepared for his violent reaction as the boys got out. The nervous pacing was replaced by loud snorts and odd turns with short spurts of speed as if seeking a means of escape. He looked angry, his ears mostly turned back. Chris and Dave didn't move from their places by the truck, and both looked concerned.

"Allison," Chris said evenly, just loud enough for me to hear him, "back away slowly and get out of there."

I didn't feel in danger but did what he said without arguing. I didn't believe Gold would purposefully hurt me. Still, I was learning to trust Chris' judgment if not his temperament and motives. I backed toward the fence and slipped back through the rails. Both boys visibly relaxed. Gold remained extremely agitated.

"Let's get this done," said Chris, moving quickly toward the back of the truck and lowering the tailgate.

He pulled out a heavy tarp as Dave climbed into the truck bed and grabbed the nearest bale of hay. The bales looked heavy. Together they positioned them side by side on half the tarp, out of Gold's reach. Cris cut the wires holding the bales together.

"Feed him one flake each of alfalfa and oat every morning and one of oat every night," said Chris. He pulled off a chunk of each to show me what a flake was, then put one of them through the fence where I'd seen Gold eating that morning.

Dave went back to the truck and pulled out a small black bucket and a halter and lead rope. "I brought some brushes, just in case. If he settles down and lets you, it's a good way to continue to build trust."

Frowning as if in thought, Cris said, "He isn't feral, but he is a stallion. He might be unpredictable and potentially dangerous. He's also probably valuable and somebody, somewhere, wants him back." For a few moments, they both watched Gold, still alternately pacing and half bolting on the far side of the corral. "He doesn't like us, but the fact that he didn't mind Robin makes me think he might have bad experiences with men. I think I should tell James . . . ask him to look at him. Would you mind?"

"The veterinarian?" I asked, remembering the name.

"Yeah," said Chris. "He's a good friend. He might have some ideas."

"Yes. Sure. Could he come before my mom gets home?" I felt funny asking that, but Chris didn't seem to mind.

"He probably would." Chris looked back at Gold again. "Don't go near him unless you feel completely safe. Okay?"

"Okay," I said, "but I really don't think he'd hurt me."

Chris was silent a few moments more, and then said, "Promise."

"What?" I asked, confused.

A muscle twitched in his jaw as if he was clenching his teeth. I'd seen him do that before. "Promise," he said again.

"Okay." I wasn't sure what to make of his insistence. "I promise."

"We've got to go or we'll be running laps," he said to Dave, then abruptly went back to the truck.

Dave stepped closer to me but watched his brother. "The games," he said with a small smile. He looked pensive for some reason then continued, "Look . . . you might not see me around too much for a while, at school and stuff. But I don't want you to worry, okay?"

My head felt funny. My heart too. What was he saying? I just stared at him, hoping for enlightenment.

"We're going to be pretty busy after school, what with games and stuff, and track training is starting." He looked me in the eyes but seemed uncomfortable for some reason. "I'm just telling you 'cause, you know, you got worried . . . before. . . ."

"Oh." Warmth spread up my face at the memory.

"We're friends, right? Nothing's going to change that. Okay?"

I looked in his eyes and melted. *Yes. Of course. Whatever you say.*

"Yes." I hadn't meant to whisper, but the moment felt so solemn. I had no idea what was going on but chose to trust him about it. I was sure I would find out sooner or later, and no matter how horrible, I would remember this moment and be comforted.

I was able to smile. He looked relieved and smiled back.

Chris was turning the truck around. "Today!" he called.

"Gotta go," said Dave. "Want a ride back up?"

"No. I'm fine," I said.

"Okay. See ya!" With that, he ran to the truck and jumped in. It rumbled up the road leaving a trailing cloud of dust behind.

My mind and feelings were very confused, but once again Dave had assured me of his goodwill and, all in all, I was happy. I stepped close to the fence and watched Gold. He eventually began to relax and came to stand in the middle of the paddock, facing me. I didn't talk to him. I was actually wrapped up in thoughts completely unrelated to him, but as he calmly regarded me, I finally broke the silence.

"Are you done now?" I tried to sound sarcastic like Robin. He looked sheepish and I laughed. "Come here, silly."

I continued to call to him softly, and he finally lowered his head and walked over, not quite all the way to the fence but close enough to reach out and sniff the hay. He seemed reluctant to take anything that had been touched by the guys, but hunger won out; he bit deeply into the hay and began munching. I watched as he ate, talking to him as the shadows lengthened, but I didn't enter the paddock or reach out to him. I wanted him to know that I would never hurt him, but I wasn't going to force it. The morning was soon enough to test our friendship.

Mom was tired when she got home and I offered to help with dinner. As I peeled potatoes, I asked, "Mom, why does Dad hate horses so much?"

She seemed startled by the question and a little worried. "I don't think he hates horses, Allison. It's . . . complicated."

"I know he grew up with them. It seems like he'd like them. Or at least not mind them."

"Well, I suppose it's time you heard this. It might help you understand Daddy a little better." Mom smiled and looked out the back window as if seeing something far away. "I remember when I first met him. Have I told you about that?"

"Several times, Mom," I said, knowing she would tell me again anyway. And she did.

"We were at college together . . . UCLA. He was a computer science major and I was a liberal arts student. It's a miracle we ever met, really. I had just finished high school. It was my freshman year. His too, but he'd been working on his family's ranch in Colorado for a few years. He would never tell me much about it. I was taking one of those required computer classes

and was having so much trouble. I used the computer lab and wasn't doing well until your dad noticed me and offered to help. He worked part-time there." She stopped to look at me, smiling. "He later told me he thought I was cute . . . and hopeless."

She still seemed far away. I was trying not to blush, her words reminding me of something. *No, it's not the same. Not at all. I can't even afford to draw comparisons. . . .*

"Your father was a computer genius even then, of course, so he helped me get through the rest of my class with flying colors. We got along so well and always had something to laugh and talk about. After that quarter, he tried to take classes with me, but after about the first year, there wasn't much left he could take without wasting time. But that first year we studied together, hung out with friends together, and finally, he asked me out on a real date."

Here she looked at me self-consciously. "But I've told you about all that before, I know. It was some time after that he told me about his family and his home. He'd been expected to stay on the ranch and help run it after high school. Your granddad had been injured years before, kicked by a horse, his back broken. He was in a wheelchair after that. Then his brother Dan was badly hurt in a riding accident. His leg never healed quite right, so he walks with a limp to this day."

I had vague memories of meeting Uncle Dan when I was six but couldn't remember anything specific.

"As soon as Dan graduated, he moved away, not wanting to live on the ranch anymore. So Daddy was left with his two sisters, Emily and Isabel, and his mom and dad. He stayed and continued to work on the ranch for two years after Dan left, but he eventually admitted to himself that he didn't want to be there either. He had become nervous around the horses and just didn't really care. He loved computers and was good at thinking of ways to improve the way they and different programs worked. He knew he wanted to start his own business one day. Unfortunately, his family wasn't supportive of him going away to college the way he wanted to, but he ended up leaving anyway. Emily left as soon as she graduated too. They blamed your dad for that. Isabel was unhappy that she was the only one still at home and became angry at your dad."

Mom was looking sad now. I had never heard this part of the story before. "What happened?" I asked.

"Well, Daddy and I fell in love, obviously, and just before we graduated, he took me to Colorado to meet his family. Dan had moved to Denver to work . . . he had gone to a city college for accounting . . . and Emily had already gotten married and was living a few towns away. But they were all there to meet me. That's when he asked me to marry him. And, of course, I said yes.

"Once again his family expected him to move back to the ranch and take over. They began talking about what that would be like, how I'd fit in, what new ideas they had. Then Daddy told them that we were not moving there but would be staying in Los Angeles, where he already had a good job lined up and could start fully developing his own ideas. And, of course, that's where *my* family was.

"The Andersons weren't happy and, I'm afraid, seemed to blame me for keeping Daddy away. They never quite understood that your dad needed to do other things. He loved them dearly, but he had to make a decision regarding his own future. And once decided, he couldn't turn away from it. When we got married, Dan, Emily, and Grandma came out for the wedding, but Isabel stayed with Granddad at the ranch.

"A couple of years later you were born," she smiled at me again, "and Daddy was working hard at his day job, then working on his own business at night. We went back to see the family for Christmas the year that you were born, but it was very awkward. I felt bad knowing that they thought I was responsible for keeping Daddy away, and that made him mad, even though I didn't want it to. He and Isabel fought almost the whole time we were there which made everyone else unhappy. We ended up leaving earlier than we had planned, just to restore peace."

Mom sighed and looked so sad that I felt bad for her—*and* Dad. Though I had no siblings, I could imagine how horrible it would be to have such strife in your family, with the people you love most in the world.

"We didn't see them again until Grandma's funeral when you were six years old. That's why we went back there, but you might not remember. We didn't talk about it that much. You had never met her, so we didn't want you worrying about it. But the whole 'moving back to the ranch' proposal came up again, of course. Now that Grandma was gone, and Granddad was not doing too well, they really did expect Daddy to leave everything he'd worked so hard for behind. But," she shook her head, "even if it had been possible, your dad just didn't want to go back.

"He took a couple of trips back there on his own to help Isabel with business matters, but otherwise, he didn't see them. Then four years ago, your grandfather died. Daddy and Robert were just beginning to get their own business going with their first international presentation scheduled. Your father was the only one who could do it. He chose not to postpone the meeting. It wasn't just his future at stake, but his partner's and their employees. Aunt Isabel never forgave him for not going back for the funeral."

Dinner was ready and we sat down to eat. I was trying to sort through what my mother had told me and relate it to my dad's attitude toward horses, but it was confusing.

"I guess I can see why he'd be . . . cautious . . . about me and horses," I said, "but what does it have to do with Aunt Isabel and him being mad at each other?"

"Daddy is worried most of all for your safety. His father and brother were physically hurt badly, and I know it doesn't seem fair, but I think the bitterness that those injuries caused is, well, influencing his judgment." Then she said, gently, "There are other things he's concerned about, too."

"I know," I admitted.

"Let's just see what happens, okay?"

"Okay. Oh!" I remembered Robin's odd conversation with me. "Robin was wondering . . . instead of taking the bus home when you're working, could I sometimes walk home with her? We can do homework until you can pick me up. Or I can walk to the pool. Please? I *really* hate riding the bus."

Mom smiled. "That sounds like a great idea. Tomorrow?"

I almost said yes, then remembered the other conversation. I should probably come straight home tomorrow. "Maybe Thursday?"

"Okay, Thursday." Mom looked at me, then reached her hand out to cover and hold one of mine on the table. "Allison, you know I'm proud of you, right?"

"You're proud of me?" I asked, very confused.

"Yes, I am. I've been watching you deal with some difficult situations, with your dad and with your friends, though I might not fully understand. And you've been very mature and upright about them. I know that everything's not easy, but you know you can talk to me, right?"

I looked at her wide-eyed, hoping I looked as mature and "upright" as she apparently thought me.

"Sure, Mom," I said. *There were no boys here this afternoon. Horse? What horse? Yeah . . . homework . . . with Robin. Mmhmm.* Were those burning coals I felt on my head?

I retired early, feeling depressed. The only thing worse than lying to someone you love is when they make a big deal about trusting you. And when the person you like most says you won't see them much for a while for a reason you can't comprehend, well, that's *completely* depressing.

Chapter Sixteen

A Mean Cycle

Gold was waiting at the corner of the corral looking adorably sweet as if nothing disturbing had happened the day before, and as if he were saying, *"Please may I have some more hay. Please?"*

I couldn't help laughing as I tossed the hay through the fence. He immediately began eating hungrily, which I took as a good sign. I picked up the rubber curry comb Dave had brought and approached him slowly. He seemed very calm so I reached out and brushed along his neck and shoulder, loosening some of the built up dirt and mud. His skin quivered at the touch of the hard brush, but he remained relaxed, munching steadily on his hay. I went to work with a will, determined to make headway through the dirt and improve his appearance.

I found the physical exertion oddly mesmerizing and lost track of time, suddenly panicking that I might be late. I'd taken a shower last night but now needed another—badly. It seemed like all the dirt I had brushed off Gold, and there had been a lot of it, was now on me. I managed to slip into my bedroom for clean clothes before Mom came out of her room.

"Allison," she called through the door and knocked. "Are you up?"

"Yes, Mom," I called back, hoping she wouldn't come in.

She stuck her head in and asked, "Do you want breakfast?"

"No, thanks," I answered, now hoping she wouldn't notice the clothes I was wearing. She could be so darn observant.

"You really should eat something before school, you know."

"I know," I answered.

"Okay," she said, resignedly. "Well, we leave in twenty minutes, right?"

"Okay," I said.

As soon as she closed the door I grabbed a clean shirt and a skirt and ducked into the bathroom, fastening my braid as high as I could. I smiled, thinking of Robin. I thought I understood why she sometimes looked less than spotlessly groomed and occasionally had smudges of dirt in odd places, even first thing in the morning.

She was waiting for me at school, but there was no sign of Dave. It must have been obvious that I was looking for him, as she said, "He had an early track meeting. Coach is starting them running in the mornings, especially while the weather's still hot."

"Oh," I said, disappointed that I wouldn't see him. Is that what Dave had been referring to?

Chris stood at my open locker. "James said he could come over after three. Would that be okay?"

I nodded.

"We'll see you later then," he said and walked away.

We? As in he and the vet and *Dave? I hoped so.*

"Dr. James is going to see Gold?" asked Robin.

"Yes. I'm glad he can come. I guess we need to figure out what to do with him now that we've caught him," I said, though I knew exactly what I wanted to do with him. "Oh . . . my Mom says I can come over after school sometimes. So, tomorrow?"

"Great!" said Robin, smiling, but I thought she looked a little doubtful. "Well, I'll see you in Health, okay?"

"Okay," I said, closing my locker and waving to her.

I was conscious of many dirty looks cast my way, but nobody tried to trip me again or anything. I took that as a positive sign but continued to avoid everybody. One thing happened at lunch that disturbed me. Though I desperately wanted to see Dave, I was on my way to meet Melanie when a group of five girls crossed my path. They stared at me as they walked—glaring, frowning, sneering, or some combination of these.

"I don't get it," one said loudly. "There's no way. . . ."

"Seriously! She's such a freak," said another.

I kept walking until I joined the lunch line, keeping my eyes on the ground, then bought a sandwich and found Melanie. My discomfort must have shown as she looked concerned and asked, "Is everything all right?"

I tried to shrug it off. "Yes, fine."

She looked disappointed, which I thought was odd. A change of subject seemed in order. "You never told me about your weekend. How was your show?"

She smiled and told me of her long weekend eventing. Though she tried to explain it to me, I had a hard time imagining it. She also used a lot of words that meant absolutely nothing to me, but I was too embarrassed at my ignorance to ask her to explain. I thought I had learned a thing or two about horses and the people who rode them, but she seemed to be speaking a different language than my other friends. All I really understood was that, while most of the people I knew rode strictly Western, Melanie rode English, and that they dressed differently and had different saddles. But beyond that, the nuances were obscure to me.

After a few quiet moments, I noticed a slight frown between her brows. She played absently with her silver locket—a sure sign something was troubling her.

"What's the matter?" I asked gently.

Her eyes had been lowered, but she looked up at that. "You know you can talk to me, don't you?" She seemed a little embarrassed. "I mean, if something was bothering you. I just wanted you to know in case you needed to. Talk to someone, that is," she added, and I got worried all over again.

"Okay," I said, appreciative but confused. "Thanks." I didn't know what else to say. Then I remembered when I might have called her to talk if I'd had her number. "Can I have your phone number?"

"Sure," she said, looking pleased but still embarrassed. "I can give you my home number, but I don't have a cell."

"Okay." I entered the number she told me and then gave her mine, which she wrote down in a notebook. "I want my parents to meet you," I said. "Maybe you could come over some time."

She blushed slightly but still looked pleased. "That would be nice."

By the time we parted, I had almost forgotten the comments the girls had made earlier and was trying to look forward to the rest of the day. I liked my computer class. It was easy and I didn't have to worry about interacting with anyone, giving me plenty of time to think and daydream. Then I'd go to Art, my favorite class, where I'd see Melanie again. It should have been a nice afternoon.

Hopes for that ended when I reached my regular seat in the computer lab. Someone had written one word on a pink sticky note and stuck it on the monitor screen for me to find.

SLUT.

My cheeks burned and my heartbeat sounded too loud in my ears. My first impulse was to look around the room to see if anyone was gloating, but I caught myself. Much as a part of me wanted to know who had put it there, another part didn't. If I knew, I might react outwardly in some way and I definitely didn't want to do that. Nor did I want to give them the satisfaction of knowing their objective was achieved.

I took the note off the monitor—trying to appear calm, though my hand was shaking—and crumpled it as I sat down, leaving it on the back of the table. I didn't want it in my backpack and I knew I wasn't resolute enough to make it to the trash can and back unruffled. I pretended to assume it was for someone else. They wouldn't see the tears beginning to sting behind my eyes and nose. With everything else going on, I knew it was for me, I just didn't know *why*—except that it must have something to do with the Calderas.

That was a whole other issue. I thought that I would have put up with anything for them—for Dave especially. But whatever the problem was, it might be preventing me from seeing him, and that was way more than I had bargained for. The only thing that kept me focused and somewhat positive was the hope of Dave coming to my house later. That would make up for a lot.

During the class, I heard snickering and the odd word or two said extra loudly for my benefit coming from three girls who were also in my math and English classes. I'd seen them occasionally at the tables, especially since soccer had started, but otherwise hadn't had any contact with them. They seemed to be hanging behind after class, watching me with scornful expressions.

"So pathetic," said one, loudly. I assumed she referred to me, but I wouldn't turn to look.

"Seriously . . . *as if* . . . right?"

They all laughed at this cryptic remark. I passed them and reached the door.

"Where on *earth* do you think she gets her clothes?" asked the third. "I mean, look at her skirt!"

"Very attractive," said the first. "Early eighties Goodwill, I think."

Giggles.

They were following me. What on earth had I done to them? What, exactly, was I being judged and punished for? This felt like early middle school all over again, only worse. Surely people should outgrow this kind of petty persecution by high school. They didn't even *know* me. Why tyrannize a stranger? I took a deep breath and kept walking. Their muffled laughter, vague disparagements, and denigrating epithets similar to the one left on the monitor remained too loud to ignore but offered no clues to their specific cause.

Melanie gave me a concerned smile when I entered the Art room but said nothing until instructions had been given and we began mixing paint. As usual, she saw the unhappiness I tried to conceal.

"What's going on?" she asked quietly.

I looked at her, wanting someone to confide in but still uncomfortable trusting anyone. "Oh . . . apparently I've offended someone." I tried to shrug it off, but the recent abuse bothered me much more than I wanted to admit. "I just don't know what I did."

Melanie looked as if she wanted to say something but wasn't sure if she should. It occurred to me that she might actually know. I wanted to know too.

"Do you?" I asked.

She still looked uncomfortable but finally said, in a hushed voice, "There are . . . rumors. Look, I'm sure at least half the school knows who the Calderas are, even the kids who went to Douglas Middle like me. The rumors are that either you are secretly dating one of them," here she looked apologetic and said in an even softer voice, "or that you are trying to maneuver yourself into that position."

"What!"

I was shocked, my loud exclamation making everyone in the room stare at me. But the fog was beginning to clear a little. I tried to think it through quickly, but my brain was refusing to grapple with it. Everything had seemed okay until after the Caldera event. People hadn't been falling over each other to get to know me, but I'd been tolerated pretty well. Or ignored. I remembered even Melanie had asked a searching question about it yesterday, as if she already knew something.

"Do you think that?" I asked in a whisper.

She was quiet for a moment, then looked at me in a kindly way.

"Allison, I don't know you very well yet, and I wouldn't think less of you if either circumstance were true, but you haven't impressed me as the kind of person that would be devious or dishonest or . . . I don't know . . . calculating in any way. Honestly, I don't know why it's anyone else's business. But I know that the Calderas have reputations, based on truth or not, and that Dave might just be the most popular person in this school. That affects people in a lot of different ways." She became quiet again, then said, "There probably aren't too many people who don't like the Calderas, or at least admire them, one way or another. Still . . . they *do* exist. And the ones that *really* like them . . ."

She didn't finish the thought, but I understood. So this was all about jealousy? That the ill-favored, upstart dork could possibly think herself worthy of the most perfect creature on the planet—in my admittedly infatuated opinion—or even worse, that *he* might actually think it? Both ideas were so preposterous, I should have laughed. Dave's warning words to me ensured the opposite.

I remembered the private conversation he'd had with his brother. What had Chris said? And what had Dave said in return? It had obviously concerned whatever was going on. Then I'm told that I might not see him for a while. Even at the time, something about the way he'd said it told me "might not" meant "would not." And what did *that* mean? Was he just protecting his reputation? Melanie seemed to be implying that was possible. It seemed obvious to me now that Chris had put him on his guard.

My throat was tightening and the prickling that had threatened behind my eyes and nose all afternoon were making me sniffle.

"We're just friends," I whispered. "Um . . . I'll be right back."

I left her side without looking around the room and got permission from Miss Laski, our art teacher, to go to the restroom. Having locked myself in a stall, I struggled to regain my calm, chastising myself all the while.

Why was I so upset? This wasn't the first time in my life that I'd been targeted as someone to despise and then been abused accordingly. Had Dave or even Chris hurt me? No. I was just reacting to the apparent jealousies, insecurities, and assumptions of others. That had to be a first. Why let it bother me now? This time I at least had an idea why it was happening. Was

I going to be just as bad as everyone else and doubt the Calderas? After everything I'd already gone through? After all the undeniable kindness and concern they'd shown me? *Good grief! Haven't we learned that lesson yet?*

I willed myself to think calmly, rationally. I was shocked at how easily the feelings of despair I'd experienced just a couple of weeks ago—*was it really that recently?*—had come back like a flood, threatening to overwhelm me. But I couldn't, I *wouldn't*, let that happen.

I thought of the day Dave confronted me about avoiding him. I remembered what he'd said, how he'd looked, and how he had seemed disturbed by my distress, even if he hadn't understood it. Even Robin had said that he'd been affected by it. What reason would he have to fake something like that? I remembered the day we'd spent at Bar 8, his kind attention at his home, everything in between. I couldn't believe him capricious in this; he was *not* abandoning me. I had to trust that there were good reasons, honest reasons, for his avoiding me, if that's even what was happening.

Suddenly feeling very tired, I rubbed at my forehead and eyes. What was my deal anyway? It wasn't like he was my boyfriend or anything. I didn't own him. I had no claims on him at all. We were just friends.

And you're okay with that, remember? He told you not to worry. Remember?

That made me feel better. He *had* told me not to worry. He remembered the last time there was misunderstanding between us. That made me feel *way* better.

It bothered me a little that Melanie thought it might have something to do with reputations. And what if he *did* feel he had a reputation to uphold? A reputation for what? I wasn't even sure what that was supposed to mean. A reputation as a flirt because he liked girls and enjoyed their company? A reputation as "hard to get" because he didn't or *hadn't* dated anyone? A reputation for being reckless? A reputation for befriending dorks? I couldn't imagine him caring about any of these things, let alone make efforts to maintain or deny them. Perhaps there was something else I wasn't aware of. So what? Should that matter to me?

Once again I was left asking myself, *Do you trust him? Do you trust his friendship? His character?*

A deep shuddering breath later, I made the decision that I did. I *did* trust him. And I *would* trust him. I would try very hard. That warm glow

I'd first felt with Robin, and now every time Dave smiled at me or paid attention to me, was pushing out the hopelessness I'd been threatened by a few moments before.

The attention he'd shown me at the event must have been closely observed and resented by quite a few. Not surprising I supposed, but that was their problem. Maybe I was going to have to toughen up. Being Dave's friend was hardly going to make me popular or make my life easy. I was no longer invisible because of it, but I was resolved to remain open and loyal to him. At all costs. It was inconceivable to me that he could be proven unworthy of that. I'd made progress, though. It had taken me much less time to figure it out this time.

Feeling much better, I splashed my face with water, dried it, and returned to class, even able to smile at Melanie as I rejoined her.

"Are you okay?" she whispered, questioning my serenity.

I still felt wrapped in Dave memories and smiled calmly again.

"Absolutely."

My loud outburst and hasty exit from the room guaranteed that my classmates were watching me now, but I didn't care. I dug deeply into my avoidance skills and ignored everyone quite successfully. With Melanie, I stuck to conversation limited to the assignment at hand.

Circumventing my locker, I headed directly toward my bus, cutting through the Language Arts building. I was still aware of people watching me, and at one point three tall and solidly built boys seemed to be barring my way. They appeared to be sophomores, maybe even juniors, and were all dressed in casual but expensive looking clothes. A couple of them wore varsity jackets. I came to an abrupt halt. The corridor was eerily empty now except for them. All three faced my direction, standing abreast and filling the hallway. I wasn't aware of ever having seen them before. Three pairs of eyes regarded me and three mouths seemed to sneer. If their imposing presence alone hadn't intimidated me, their expressions would have.

Not sure what to do, my mind raced with choices. Turn back and walk another way to the bus? Walk up closer and say, "Excuse me, please?" Wait them out and see what happened? A fourth option, head back to my locker and hope that Dave or even Chris was there, occurred to me but was immediately discarded. I couldn't, *wouldn't*, play maiden in distress. Not after all this. I needed to stick up for myself, at least a little. By the time I'd come to

this conclusion, they had apparently lost interest, walking past me so close I had to jump from side to side quickly to avoid being knocked over.

When they'd passed, I hurried to my bus, breathing a sigh of relief and resting my forehead against the window as I sat in the relative safety of the hated vehicle. *Too much weirdness!*

I focused out the window all the way to my stop, listening to the rattle and engine drone of the bus and blocking out the low hum of voices. I had better things to think of. Like Dave. I hadn't seen him all day. Would he come today? Or did he have something to do after school? Or was he really avoiding me? I couldn't help wondering. I wished I knew for sure what was going on, then realized that, no, I really didn't. Not knowing would allow at least some fantasies to remain intact. Knowing might destroy them all. *Ignorance is bliss . . . I think.*

And Gold. I was looking forward to seeing him, feeding him, and grooming him. If I could brush him once or twice a day, I could get him looking decent quite quickly, I was sure. *And then what?* All plans ended there. I could think no further.

At home, I changed back into the clothes I'd worn that morning and then grabbed an apple and hurried down to the corral, hoping to have some time with Gold before distractions arrived. I brought my phone along, just in case, though I wasn't expecting any calls. Gold was waiting at the nearest corner, close to the tarp-covered hay, his eyes bright and ears pricked forward. He made a funny noise that sounded like *"hurhurhurhur"* when he saw me—the first time he'd ever done that.

" *'Hurhurhurhur'* right back at cha," I laughed, walking over to stroke him.

He nuzzled me over the fence and I let him take a bite out of the apple before giving the whole thing to him. Then I gave him his hay. I'd been brushing him for quite some time while he contentedly ate, when he raised his head and looked in the direction of the cattle guard, though we couldn't see it. A few moments later, I heard someone walking across it, then down the road. Gold became restless, moving away from me, the hay, and the fence. Then Chris appeared—alone. Gold looked unhappy, pacing on the far side of the paddock near the stream. I ducked back through the fence.

"How is he?" asked Chris in a soft voice, his eyes following Gold's movements.

"He's fine. He doesn't seem to mind being here at all. Just . . ." I wasn't sure how to say it.

"Just that he doesn't like me. Guys." His mouth quirked in a grim line that could almost have been a smile if his eyes had reflected it. They didn't.

"Apparently," I said, feeling apologetic for some absurd reason.

"James should be here in a minute. I figured I'd walk. Try to keep him as calm as possible."

I nodded, not sure what else to say. The following silence between us made me feel uncomfortable, my experiences from earlier in the day—and yesterday, too—and the possible causes of them nudging my memory. The sound of an approaching vehicle saved me from trying to make conversation.

A large white truck with a compartmentalized bed came into view, then stopped near us. I thought I'd seen it before. Dr. Emory had an open, handsome face and was about the same height as Chris, though of a more mature build. He extended his hand to me and I shook it shyly.

"You must be Allison," he said with a pleasant smile. "We haven't been properly introduced, but I've heard a lot about you and this horse of yours." He indicated Gold. "How is he doing?"

He seemed to be asking either Chris or myself, but Chris showed no inclination to answer.

"Um . . . I think he's doing better," I said, not sure specifically what "doing" encompassed.

"He's eating all right? His appetite seems good?"

"Yes!" I admitted happily. "He loves the hay and eats all of it."

"Good. He looks like he's in pretty good shape, apart from being a little malnourished. To be honest, I was expecting a lot worse. There certainly isn't much food to be found in these hills right now." He walked back to the truck and opened a compartment, removing a pair of latex gloves from what looked like a tissue box, and some other articles, then proceeded to the fence. "Let's get a little closer look," he said, stepping through the rails.

"Um . . ." I said nervously, not knowing how much Chris had told him, "he doesn't seem to . . . um . . . like . . ."

"It's okay, Chris explained his preferences. Can't say I blame him," he said, smiling.

I smiled too, relieved at his confidence.

Gold's reaction was immediate. Snorting loudly, he galloped to the opposite front end of the corral then pressed against the rails near the gate, as

if he would push them down. I wondered if he could. He ran back the length of the fence, then back again to the far front corner, gathering himself right before the fence. I thought he was going to jump and wondered if he'd be able to do *that*. Instead of trying, he came to a stop and leaned his weight on the fence again. It creaked painfully and I winced at the sound, but it held.

Dr. Emory walked to the center of the paddock and stood still and quiet. Gold paced back and forth near the corner, keeping a wary eye—and ear—on the vet, but made no more attempts to lean on the fence. After a moment Dr. Emory pulled on the gloves, squatted down, and appeared to gather something into a small plastic bag.

"Did he just . . . ?" I wasn't sure I had seen right.

"Manure," said Chris. "He'll test it for parasites. Worms."

"Worms!"

He looked at me briefly, obviously noting my appalled expression. "All horses have worms. It's a fact of life. But it's important to know what kind and how badly infested they are."

Dr. Emory walked back to us. "I'd love to get a closer look at him, but that seems impossible right now without stressing him more or tranquilizing him. How long has it been since you first saw him?"

I did the math in my head. "About seven weeks, I think."

"Hmm," he said. "Well, he's obviously been foraging for himself for quite a while. I'd estimate him to be about five or six years old. He could be younger. He's also obviously of Iberian breeding, perhaps Lusitano. You were right about that," he said, looking at Chris. "I would say Andalusian from his general build, but I've never heard of one that color."

"Apparently it's rare. Usually mixed breeding," said Chris. I looked at him in wonder, his knowledge impressing me greatly. He looked a little self-conscious and shrugged slightly. "I looked it up."

"Well, I'd say two things are certain. This is a valuable horse and someone is missing him." Dr. Emory looked thoughtful, then said, as if to himself, "It seems strange that we've had no official alerts to be on the watch for such an animal." Chris and I looked at him inquiringly and he explained. "Usually, if an animal is reported missing in the area, especially a large, valuable animal, we're notified to keep our eyes open for it, or to at least to be aware of possible leads. But I haven't heard anything."

Chris was starting to look restless and finally said, "I've got to go. I was supposed to be at work a while ago."

I felt bad, as if I'd made him late. But I felt even worse when the vet said, "You know, if we're going to work with him at all, it's going to be really difficult that he won't let men near. We might need to call in a woman vet. Chris, what do you say about trying to spend some time with him? If his breeding is what we think it is, he's got intelligence and good temperament on his side. He must have had bad experiences fairly recently. Maybe we can change his mind?"

Chris appeared slightly perturbed and looked briefly at me as if to gauge my reaction. I didn't have one. "Whatever," he said, not sounding or looking as indifferent as the expression implied. "I . . . gotta go," he said again. He turned and headed back up the road.

"I understand that you haven't told your parents about him?" said Dr. Emory.

My mind had wandered off and his words startled and confused me. "What?"

"The horse. Your parents don't know he's here?"

"Oh . . . no . . . not yet."

"Well, you should probably tell them. Soon. I doubt if it'll take long to find his owner. We should also improve his living arrangements a little. It's a shame this enclosure is so far from the house because otherwise it's quite adequate. I'm a little concerned about his drinking from the stream, but I suppose it can't be helped for now, and apparently he's been doing it for some while without adverse effects. I'd like to get his food off the ground, though. That could cause problems. And you need to have some way to clean the manure out of the corral. Once you've told your parents, I'd be happy to talk to them about him."

I agreed that would be a good idea, but said my father wouldn't be home until Saturday. I didn't mention what his reaction was likely to be.

On the way back to the house, I tried to think of the best way to broach the subject with my mother. On the one hand, I was glad Dad wasn't home. I knew Mom was likely to be more sympathetic, especially now that I somewhat understood Dad's prejudices. On the other hand, it meant dealing with my duplicity twice; once now and again when Dad got home.

"Hey Mom, do you remember when you thought I was eating all those carrots?"

"I bet you thought it was weird that I suddenly liked going for walks, didn't you?"

"Mom, you know that day that Dad came home and Dave and Chris were here?" I actually *wanted* to explain that one.

When my mother finally got home, I realized "a picture is worth a thousand words" probably applied to my situation.

"Mom, can I show you something?"

"Of course, dear. What is it?"

"It's outside. Just come with me, okay?"

Mom smiled and her eyes twinkled conspiratorially. "A secret, huh?"

"Um . . . yes. So far."

She walked along with me quietly at first, though she looked at me a few times and I could tell that she was dying to talk. After a couple of minutes, she suddenly asked, "Is everything all right at school?"

I was unsettled by her question and searched her face for signs of comprehension but read none. It must have been one of those generic "mom" questions.

"Yes. Sure," I said, not feeling that I was lying. *All right* was surely just a matter of perception and comparison.

"Have you been able to spend much time with Dave at school?"

This shook me too, and I could tell it was *not* generic at all.

"No . . . not much," I said truthfully. "He's . . . really busy."

She tried to read my expression, but deadpan was one of the skills I had honed over the years and I thought I did a pretty good job of it now.

When we came within sight of the corral, she looked surprised to see it and started to say, "I didn't know . . ." but stopped as Gold stepped into view.

He gave us his low, rumbly greeting, and I walked up to the fence to stroke him.

"Oh my," said Mom. She was silent for several moments, watching me pet Gold's face and neck. He had mostly finished the hay and appeared happy and relaxed. Finally, she said, "What's happening here, Allison? Whose horse is this? Where did it come from?"

I discarded all the preambles I had practiced earlier and launched into a precise history of my experiences with Gold, with only a few unimportant omissions concerning my state of mind and emotions, and the cause thereof during that time. I made sure she understood how helpful, careful, and unselfish the Caldera brothers had been and how gentle Gold had been around me. I finished with Dr. Emory's visit and conclusions, including his suggestion that Chris try to spend time with him and why.

Mom looked overwhelmed. Unlike my father, she had grown up in the city and, to my knowledge at least, had little experience with or interest in horses.

"I don't know what to say," she said at last, but I could see that she wasn't happy. "You might not see it this way, sweetheart, but keeping all this from us is really the same as lying. How do you think I feel about that?" She put her palms to her cheeks and added, "And *what* is your father going to say?"

She was right. I didn't exactly see it as lying but felt guilty anyway. And what my dad was going to say, and more importantly what he'd do, was my primary concern at the moment. I knew Mom would forgive me and probably sooner than later fall in love with Gold too. Dad, on the other hand, might put a stop to everything—*everything*—as soon as he found out about it.

"Pet his nose, Mom," I said, shamelessly redirecting her attention. "It's so soft right here. He's kind of dirty right now, but I'm working on him."

My mother still looked unhappy and unsure, but after a moment she sighed deeply and reached out. Gold stood quietly, his eyes closing. Mom stroked his nose and then his cheek.

"Is he really safe?" she asked.

"He's been perfectly safe with me," I said. "He just *really* doesn't like boys." I couldn't help smiling.

After a moment, she laughed and I laughed too.

"Oh dear," she said, sighing again. "I'm afraid even that quality isn't going to endear him to your father. You know he's worried about you already. And the fact that the boys have secretly been helping isn't going to be in either your *or* their favor." She reached out and stroked Gold's nose again. He wiggled his upper lip over the back of her hand and she laughed. "He *is* lovely, though."

"He is, isn't he? Dr. Emory is going to try to find his owner. I want to keep him until then. Can we try to talk Dad into it?"

I was afraid this was being manipulative—a quality I despised in others and for which I was apparently being accused in other matters—and I was unhappy about it, but just a *tiny* bit. There was so much at stake. Right now it felt like my whole life.

"I don't know," said Mom, shaking her head and looking doubtful. "One

thing's for sure. I'm not saying anything until he gets home, but that's for *his* sake, not yours." She looked at me severely. "I don't want him to drop everything and rush home. Until he *is* home, I'm not giving permission for anything. You can do what's necessary to take care of him, but the boys shouldn't be here without your dad's express approval. Especially after the misunderstanding before."

"Okay," I said, resigned but very relieved that she now knew.

Chapter Seventeen

Deep Breath

Robin met me at school the next day and I walked with her to her locker. I had decided to avoid mine but could see Chris leaning against the wall nearby. I felt bad and wasn't sure what to do, but he must have read something in my body language as he walked away. I was going to have to see about getting that stupid locker fixed.

"So, are you coming after school?" asked Robin. She seemed uneasy.

"Yes. Mom said it was fine. I was afraid she'd change her mind after I told her about Gold."

"You told her?" She sounded surprised.

"I wanted her to know before Dad gets home." I told her about Dr. Emory's visit and the following meeting with my mother. "Thinking about telling my dad is scary. I'm not sure how he'll take it or what he'll do. Even my mom's nervous." Robin pretended to bite her nails and I said, "Exactly."

The school day passed without incident—mostly. I was aware of but ignored the glances and whispers that still seemed to follow me. As I spent my first class with Robin, and then a class and lunch with Melanie, I was able to focus on my friends and not on any periphery nonsense.

The only truly unsettling moment occurred as I walked toward the other side of the quad where my English class was. As I progressed down an exterior corridor, I became aware of several guys watching me. I would have ignored them except that two of them were the same ones that had barred

my way the day before. I stopped in my tracks and for the first time in my life felt a real fight or flight response. It wasn't pleasant.

"Making friends I see," said a familiar voice, quietly and right behind me. "I don't think they're your type, though."

An arm circled my shoulders and I thought I'd cry with relief. Matthew, now beside me, smiled calmly and steered me in another direction. "Let's find another way, shall we? You don't want to mess with them. Very unpleasant fellows. No sense of humor whatsoever."

"Who are they?" I asked, really curious. "And what do they want with me?"

"They are nobodies who think they are somebodies, my dear. And you don't want to know. They just want to cause trouble. We shall foil them." He smiled again and I was grateful.

We skirted a couple of buildings to take us around a different way to my English class. The bell rang just as we reached the door.

"I'm so sorry!" I said. "You're going to be late!"

He shrugged and smiled, and went on his way. I felt a pang of guilt that, as I hadn't seen Dave, I hadn't seen Matthew either, yet had not missed him at all. But thinking of him now, a little warm glow helped me brave through the relative loneliness of my class. Then I was with Robin again.

After study hall, we began walking toward the front of the school, the way that Robin usually went. This involved crossing the quad and lunch area near the cafeteria, always crowded with students before school and during breaks but now mostly deserted. The only students around were hanging out by lockers or obviously on their way somewhere. Except for the group of guys by the caged vending machines. The mostly big guys. The big guys who now noticed us and included one of the same big guys that had been in the two previous groups of big guys. He knocked elbows with one of his pals and said something that made the other guy sneer, then they walked toward us.

I began to panic, but Robin seemed oblivious, continuing her one-sided conversation—I didn't even know about what. I hoped the guys would just pass us by but they split up to pass us on either side, and two purposely walked between us, jostling and dividing us. One, an attractive blond boy dressed and groomed conservatively and looking nothing like what I would think a bully would look like, gently pushed me into the chest of the same boy who seemed intent on harassing me. That boy wrapped his arms across my stomach.

His voice, loud and sarcastically polite, said, "Careful now. You don't want to get hurt."

But then he pressed his face to my head and whispered in my ear. The embrace and voice made me shudder violently. And although the words he used were not themselves overtly nasty or threatening, taken in the context he most certainly meant them and under present circumstances, they chilled me and caused my heart to throb uncomfortably in my throat. Nobody had ever talked to me that way, and I couldn't for the life of me understand why this boy would do so now. He let me go just as suddenly and walked away.

"*What* is your problem?" said Robin, catching her balance. "Go find some Neanderthal chicks to pick on, would ya? Geez! What jerks," she said, coming close to me again. Then she noticed my face. "You're as white as a ghost! Did that jerk say something to you?"

I didn't answer. I didn't want to repeat what he had said under any circumstances, but I was too shocked to call on any deflective skills. I was finding it difficult to think at all. My mind and heart repeated a name over and over like a mantra.

"He did, didn't he? What did he say?" she asked sharply.

I had no doubt that if I told her, she would march straight after them and take them to task one way or another. Grateful but definitely not wanting her to get involved, I tried to laugh it off. "He was just being a jerk, like you said. It was nothing."

Her expression changed, now looking concerned. "You look like you're gonna pass out. Or puke. Are you okay?"

I took a deep breath, nodded, and grabbed her sleeve. "Yes, I'm fine. Come on, let's go."

Robin still looked suspicious and we continued for quite a while in silence—very unusual for her. Finally she said, "Oh . . . Dave says to say 'Hi.'"

That was nice but disappointing. I had hoped that he might join us after school.

"Where is he?" I asked, trying not to sound too desperately curious but really wanting to know. I hadn't seen him all day, not even in PE.

"He left early for a game. Somewhere near Sacramento, I think. Hey, we should go to a home game sometime."

I agreed that would be great and we talked about several things before I decided to ask the question that had been bothering me all week. "Robin, is there some kind of rumor going around about me?"

She looked at me almost accusingly as if I had asked her something unreasonable. "Don't worry about it. People are stupid. You've seen the way some of the girls are. It just shows how stupid they are that they think you're competition or something."

Was that supposed to make me feel better? "Right," I said, but I felt shaky.

Robin laughed. "I didn't mean it like that, silly. I mean, they just can't comprehend a guy simply liking a girl, you know? As a friend. Not someone like Dave anyway. Or Chris either I guess. From what I hear, the girls in both camps are pretty mad at you. They're watching for any sign of . . . well . . . *more* than friendship, I guess. They'll figure it out eventually. Then they'll leave you alone."

I wished that made me feel better, but it just left me feeling hollow. I couldn't help wondering again if that's why Dave was avoiding me, so people wouldn't assume he really liked me. Did it bother him that much for people to think he could possibly like someone like me? Did it bother Chris that people thought that of his brother? I sighed deeply. Life would go on, right?

We walked along Main Street toward the strip mall but soon detoured up a side road just past the street the library was on. We continued for quite some way until the normal yards of houses became fields and pastures. Robin seemed to grow more and more nervous the farther we walked. Then I realized she was actually nervous about me going to her home. I remembered how awkward she had seemed when inviting me, and apparently had only done so because Dave had convinced her to. I wondered what she was worried about.

We eventually walked up the dirt driveway of an old, wood-sided bungalow surrounded by dense trees and shrubbery. There was a small front yard, neatly maintained but mostly brown. Robin smiled nervously at me.

"I'm gonna give Gali a snack before we go in," she said, bypassing the front door and walking to the rear of the house. "He'll be happier if he eats a little first. Then we'll get something to eat too. And we can finish our math."

"Okay," I said, happy to do whatever she wanted.

The backyard had a small paddock housing Galahad and a larger one with barrels set up in the now familiar triangle. A wooden shelter offered

Gali afternoon shade and probably afforded some protection in the colder months too. Gali whinnied loudly when he saw Robin.

"Hi sweetie," she said in the baby voice I'd heard her use before. "We're gonna play with Allie today, 'kay? And you're going to be a good boy and not buck her off." She dropped her backpack on the ground and said, "Wait here." Then she ran to the garage. After a moment, she returned carrying a small bucket. Gali followed her over to the hay rack and the contents of the bucket pinged and rattled noisily going in. Gali eagerly buried his nose in it.

"It's just a supplement, but he loves it," she smiled, patting his glossy neck. "Okay. Let's go in."

She had seemed her normal self around her horse but now appeared nervous again. She led the way in through the back door, calling out, "Gran? Are you awake?"

The house was dark inside and comparatively cool, shaded by the trees and large shrubs surrounding it. We entered through the kitchen and left our backpacks on the table. Then she led me into an even darker living room.

"Gran?" she said quietly, approaching an armchair.

The person sitting in it startled badly. "Robin?"

"Hi, Gran," Robin said softly. She leaned over her grandmother, planted a kiss on her cheek, then reached up over her head to turn a lamp on. "You fell asleep in the dark again."

"Oh!" Her grandmother chuckled self-consciously and tried to straighten herself in her chair. "Just a little nap."

She smiled sleepily as she looked up at Robin. She was a very plump lady, probably a little shorter than her granddaughter, with wild iron gray hair escaping from a wide, loose chignon.

"Gran, this is Allison. I told you she'd be coming over."

"Yes, of course. It's so nice to meet you, Allison. Please forgive me for not being awake when you arrived."

I responded to her hand held out toward me, but instead of shaking it, she put hers in mine in a quaint, trusting gesture.

"It's nice to meet you too," I said.

"Please, call me Fiona. Now . . . I'd better make some tea," she said. She *humphed* slightly, getting out of her chair with the aid of a stout, old-fashioned walking stick, and then made her way toward the kitchen slowly with a slightly rolling walk.

"She falls asleep in the afternoon sometimes," said Robin, looking an odd mix of apology and defiance.

"She's wonderful," I said sincerely. "I miss my grandmother. We used to see her and Grandpa a lot, but I haven't seen them since we moved. And I never got to meet my other grandmother. She died a long time ago."

Robin nodded. "I've never met my other grandmother either," she admitted, then looked as if she regretted saying it. "But Gran and I get along really well."

I smiled. She seemed more relaxed, but I felt she didn't want me to ask questions. I was curious but had no intention of interrogating her. I had always felt uncomfortable asking people personal questions, even though I had never really minded being asked them myself. I figure people usually tell you what you need to know when the time is right. Robin was just one on a growing list of people I was curious about. People I cared about. I had never had anything that personal for people to find out, but that was also changing rapidly. I was starting to understand not wanting to be asked.

Robin watched me, warily I thought, but I smiled again and looked around the room. It was still dark, even with the lamp on, and the wall-papered walls and general sense of clutter made the room seem small and extra cozy. Apart from Fiona's chair, there was a small couch and another armchair. All had cloth throw covers on them and looked like you could curl up and read in them very comfortably. An old, medium sized television was the only piece of technology in the room. The rest of the furnishings were books, pictures, and knickknacks. I thought it would be a wonderful room to sit in on a quiet, rainy day, but right now it felt warm and claustrophobic.

"You want a sandwich?" asked Robin.

"Sure," I said and followed her out to the kitchen.

I hadn't felt hungry at lunch and hadn't eaten much. If I was going to ride, eating was probably a good idea. There was no sign of her grandmother, but a kettle had been put on to boil and was just starting to whistle.

"Grab that teapot over there, would you?" Robin asked, indicating a large, brown teapot on the counter near the sink. I did and watched with interest as she poured boiling water in, swirled it around, then poured it out again. Something in my expression made her laugh. "Warming the pot," she said, her eyes twinkling. "It brings out the flavor of the tea."

I nodded as if it made perfect sense, though it appeared merely ritualistic to me. She put several spoonfuls of loose black tea from a square tin into the teapot, then filled it up with boiling water.

"Haven't you ever had tea before?" she asked, skeptically.

"Iced tea," I said. "And my aunt used to make me drink herbal tea, but—" I realized the rest of my comment might be ill-timed.

"But you didn't like it?" she asked, her eyes still twinkling.

"It tasted nasty."

"Well, you'll like this. I can almost guarantee it," she said.

Fiona came slowly back into the kitchen and began to ask polite, fairly noninvasive questions like, "How long have you lived in Douglas?" and "Where did you move from?" and "Do you have any brothers and sisters?" and I was happy to answer them. Robin made peanut butter and grape jelly sandwiches while we waited for the tea to brew, then Fiona poured it for us. Robin took my cup and added milk and sugar, then gave it to me. I tasted it gingerly, expecting the same taste I'd experienced before, but my eyes grew wide at the unexpectedly delicious flavor. Robin laughed and led the way down a short hallway to her room.

It was the most cluttered room I'd ever seen and I couldn't restrain a gasp of awe as I looked around, almost on sensory overload. It made my bedroom seem as austere as a monk's cell by comparison. Posters and photographs covered almost every inch of blank wall: horses and fluffy baby animals with funny captions next to rock bands; contemplative inspirational posters next to various cartoon characters and one of Teenage Mutant Ninja Turtles. I couldn't help giggling at this last one. I hadn't figured Robin as a TMNT fan.

She followed my gaze and smiled ruefully. "Dave gave that to me for Christmas in, like, fifth grade. He thought it was really cool, I guess. I haven't even thought about it in . . . forever." She looked suddenly self-conscious. "I guess I should take it down."

"No!" I blurted, more vehemently than I meant to. Now I was blushing. "I mean . . . he gave it to you. You should keep it. You should keep *all* of them."

Robin looked unsure, but she was the one blushing now.

Her room was small with barely enough room for the furnishings. A twin bed was partly covered in pillows and old stuffed animals. A small desk had just enough room for the monitor and keyboard of her computer. Two small dressers held clothes trying to escape from every drawer. A small

bookcase supported a CD player and a modest stack of CDs on the top shelf. Shelves occupied one wall.

Every surface was completely covered with stuff: books, magazines, Breyer models and My Little Ponies, little plastic toys and china figurines, various other objects that were undefinable without closer inspection. And candles—candles everywhere. Some were apparently so special they would never be lit, but others were well-used, burned down to a stub with copious amounts of melted wax around them. The holders ranged from antique-looking silver to chunky glass and wood, and some were simple china saucers.

"You like candles." I knew I was stating the obvious, but I felt compelled to say it.

"Yeah," she said and smiled. "It comes in handy when the power goes out in the winter. But I just like candles. Gran and I watch TV at night together—it's kind of our thing, you know? But she goes to bed pretty early. So I light my candles and do my homework, or read, or watch videos on my computer. I like the way they make me feel . . . kind of warm. And not lonely." Her voice had become soft and an introspective look rested on her face. I'd never seen her look that way. She always seemed so fiercely self-reliant. Her mood changed abruptly. "Do you like candles?"

"I guess," I said. "I've never had any, so I'm not sure."

"Hmm," she said.

We sat on the rug by her bed, eating sandwiches and drinking tea while we worked on math. Most of it had been done in study hall so it wasn't long before we'd finished. We washed our dishes in the kitchen and then went outside. The sun had descended just enough to cool the air slightly, and Gali appeared bright-eyed and interested in whatever we had planned. I followed Robin into the garage and was surprised to see an old Mustang parked there. She noticed my surprise, I'm sure, but chose not to say anything. Instead, she took a halter and bridle down from a hook, lifted her saddle from a wooden saw horse by the wall, and asked me to grab a couple of brushes from a shelf.

Gali obviously enjoyed the attention from both of us. Robin taught me how to gently separate the hair of his tail with the dandy brush, which I couldn't wait to try on Gold, though I knew it would be a major undertaking. Gali graciously allowed me to mount and ride him around for a while, Robin giving me instructions and encouragement as well as scolding when I was doing something wrong or "being lazy."

Gali seemed to get fed up with the slow pace after a while and became difficult to handle. Robin called a halt at that point and switched places with me. I climbed up onto the top rail of the corral fence while she rode Gali and demonstrated lead changes, roll backs, and sidestepping. I was very impressed and looked forward to being able to communicate with a horse as well as my friends did. Then she ran the barrels a couple of times, finally walking him out around the paddock as we talked.

"When I get good enough, will you teach me that?" I asked.

"Barrels? Sure. When your seat's more secure."

That was something to look forward to.

My phone buzzed in my pocket and my heart leaped; I thought it might be Dave. He'd probably be done with his game about now. But it was only my mother, calling to find out where Robin lived so she could come and pick me up. I gave her directions to the house as Robin unsaddled Galahad and gave him another quick brush. Then we returned to the house to wash our hands and wait for her. When she arrived, Fiona insisted on her coming in and she would make more tea.

"It's really good, Mom," I whispered, and Mom accepted the invitation. "Come and see Robin's horse," I encouraged her, not sure if it was a good idea or not, but wanting to remind her that my friends were all horse people. I had every intention of being horsey too.

We led her out to see Gali, who was more than willing to receive more attention. Mom admired and petted him and said how nice it must be to be able to keep him at her house. Then she seemed to realize something and became quiet. She looked around and noticed the barrels in the next corral but said nothing, as did I.

When we went back into the house, Fiona had prepared tea on a large tray. She had Robin carry it into the sitting room, as she called it. Fiona sat in her chair, pulling a small table in front of herself and on which Robin placed the tray, then poured out a cup of tea for each of us. Mom was going to have hers plain, but I insisted she have it as Robin had prepared it for me. She liked it too. Fiona and my mother began talking comfortably together, and Robin and I went to gather up my things.

"Here, you should have this," she said, holding a candle out to me. It was a soft rose color, about two inches in diameter and five inches tall. It had

never been lit. "I'm not into pink," she said. "I don't even remember where I got this one. It'll go with your room, though."

She was right. She held a little box of matches up with a questioning look. "Thanks," I said, sincerely.

When we came back into the sitting room, we found the conversation had taken a predictable turn.

"So, they gave Robin the horse?" Mom was asking politely, but I thought I could hear a different question in her voice.

"Yes, for her twelfth birthday. At first she kept him at the ranch until she was used to riding him. He was a bit of a handful for her. Dave had taught her to ride years before, of course, but on a much older horse."

Here Robin looked at me and mouthed "Sam." I smiled and nodded.

"But then she wanted to be able to ride more often and couldn't always get all the way out there. So Tom and Cheryl took him for a while until the boys got a place ready for him here. Now she can ride whenever she wants, and they transport the horse to shows and suchlike."

"They seem like very generous people," said my mother, and I could tell she was hoping Fiona would keep talking.

I thought it was time to leave.

"Oh, yes," said Fiona. "Of course, they have their faults like everyone else, but they've been very good to us. The boys come and keep the yard under control and help in lots of ways, and Alex, their father you know, has been terribly helpful. They've been like family to us for a long while now."

Robin was looking as panicked as I was beginning to feel. It looked like we both wanted this conversation to end, though I doubted our reasons could be the same.

"Mom, I should probably get home," I said tentatively, not wanting to seem rude. "There's that thing I have to do, remember?" Robin raised her brows at me and I mouthed, "Gold."

Mom looked at me uncomprehendingly for a moment, then shook her head as if waking up and said, "Oh, yes. Right. I almost forgot all about . . . that. It's been so nice to meet you, Fiona," she said warmly to Robin's Gran, giving her hand a squeeze. "I look forward to seeing you again."

"You are welcome anytime, dear. And Allison is welcome here whenever she wants. It's nice to have another girl around."

I smiled and thanked her for the tea.

Mom was unusually quiet on the way home. I was afraid that she might begin asking me questions I either couldn't or didn't want to answer, or that she would make suppositions I would have to acknowledge, deny, or just endure. But she didn't. It was an uncomfortable silence, but I was glad for it. When we got home, I changed quickly into clothes that were already Gold-dusty and had started to head out the back door when I stopped and turned back.

"Do you want to come, Mom?" I asked. She had been getting something out of the freezer and looked very tired.

I thought she'd say no, but she looked at me calmly for a moment and said, "Yes, I do."

Grabbing an apple from the bowl, I held it out to her. She took it and smiled, but it wasn't her normal easy-going expression. She was obviously preoccupied.

Gold looked his usual mix of regal and adorable when we reached the paddock. He made his throaty *hurhurhur* sound.

"Good evening yourself, Your Lordship," I replied, and Mom laughed.

She looked at me and held up the apple. I nodded and she stepped forward to give it to him. While she did, I picked up the halter and lead rope Dave had brought and slipped through the rails.

"Let's see if he'll let me put this on," I said, holding it ready and approaching him slowly.

Mom gave him the rest of the apple and then stroked his neck as I lifted the halter over his nose and slowly tried to buckle it. Gold lowered his head as if to help me, then rubbed against my chest, almost making me drop the halter.

"Hey, cut that out," I said, not really scolding and thrilled that he seemed to have no issues with halters.

I led him around in the enclosure and he was a perfect gentleman, his head by my side, very relaxed but matching my movements exactly. I didn't know much, but it was easy to see that he'd been very well trained. Remembering the horse that had pulled me so badly at Bar 8, I appreciated Gold's quiet manners and wondered if he would also be a brat if he were returning to his stall after a long ride. I wondered what he'd be like to actually ride and hoped one day I'd find out. Had he even been ridden before? I guessed there was only one way to find out and I wasn't the best person to attempt it.

Mom came in and held him while I gave him a quick brush. He was starting to look more presentable except for his mane and tail, which were a horrible disgrace. It would take a major investment of time and effort to make a dent in the damage there. I took the hoof pick and went to lift a foreleg the way Robin had shown me, but he lifted the leg with barely a touch, allowing me to hold his hoof. I traced the lines of the frog and the circumference of the hoof, even though they were quite clean, and checked his other feet. Then I took the halter off and fed him, giving him a final pat.

"Every day we seem to accomplish something more," I said enthusiastically to my mother as we walked back to the house in the gathering dusk. "See how gentle he is? He's obviously well trained."

"Mmhmm," said Mom, but she sounded noncommittal.

Something was bothering her, I could tell. It occurred to me that by taking her into my confidence, I had actually made her my accomplice in crime, though that certainly hadn't been my intention. I hoped if Dad were angry, he'd only be mad at me, and not at Mom. I wondered if she was thinking the same thing.

I helped her make a quick dinner, did the dishes afterward while she went to change her clothes and relax, and watched television with her for a while. When I got up to go to my room, I asked, "Can I wait for you at Robin's again tomorrow?"

"Mmhmm," said Mom again, watching the television screen. Then she looked at me searchingly. "You're just going to Robin's, right?"

"Right," I said, seriously. "We might get coffee first. Is that okay?"

My mother continued to look intently at me but nodded her head.

"Oh," I said, remembering something important. "Can I go to school early tomorrow?"

"Okay," said Mom, but she continued to look at me inquiringly.

"I need to go to the office about my locker," I said. "It's been stuck and . . . well . . . Dave and Chris have been helping me open it, but . . . I don't want to keep on bothering them." Although this was only partly true, I thought it would at least sound good under the circumstances. "I went at the beginning of school, but they were too busy and it never got fixed."

Mom still had that preoccupied, slightly worried look on her face, but she nodded. As I turned to go, she said, "Allison," and I turned back. She looked as if she was going to say something serious at first, but then her face relaxed. She smiled a little and said, "Good night."

"Good night, Mom." I assumed her unspoken concerns had to do with trust, and she was choosing to trust me. I loved her for it but felt disturbed and annoyed too.

After my shower, I put a CD on and found the candle and matches Robin had given me. Using the back of an old sketchbook to put the candle on, I set it on my bedside table and lit it. Then I turned off my light and sat cross-legged on my bed, watching the little flame flicker and dance. The small glow caused the gray walls of my room to look decidedly dark blue. The way I felt.

I sighed deeply. I thought about what Robin had said; how the candles helped her feel less alone. I guess I didn't understand. I'd spent almost every minute of the day with either Robin, Melanie, or my mom, and yet I still felt lonely. I couldn't believe I hadn't caught even one glimpse of Dave in two days. It left me feeling empty in spite of attention from people who cared about me. I thought I must be a very selfish, ungrateful person.

And now I'm feeling sorry for myself for getting mad at myself for feeling sorry for myself. What a loser.

I blew out the candle and tried to sleep.

I had waited for fifteen minutes in the school office before a lady came out from an interior room to help me. She assured me that the custodian should be able to see to it within a day or two; to come back next week if the problem had not been rectified. I thanked her and left. It was still early and my curiosity got the better of me. I found myself wandering down toward the track.

Sure enough, about twenty students were gathered there, mostly boys but some girls too, milling around close to the coach as if waiting for some sort of signal. Even with my impaired vision, I recognized Dave, Matthew, and Tanner in the group. A couple of the girls might have been ones who liked to hang out at the tables, but I wasn't sure.

Dave stopped and gazed in my direction. He looked like he would have walked over, but another boy got his attention. He looked back at me once, then turned and left the track with the others. I felt a little happier. At least I had seen him, and he had definitely noticed me. And he really was busy.

I walked slowly to class. As I sat down at my desk, I heard my phone buzz. Very unusual. I stealthily took it out.

"I saw you."

Dave.

I wrote back, *"I saw you too."*

": B"

I laughed. *":)"*

The bell rang and I put the phone away. I was being watched, but I didn't care. My world was looking a little brighter at the moment and that's all that mattered. I felt butterflies at the prospect of at least seeing him at lunch. I hadn't been near the tables since Tuesday. I hadn't been near him since then either. I also fervently hoped he would join us after school. After all, it was Friday. No games. No practices—I hoped.

My silly exchange with him kept me happy all morning. While I couldn't help wondering if he'd even thought of me in the last couple of days, at least he'd looked like he wanted to come and say hi this morning. And he had bothered to acknowledge me with a message. That was a lot. And I had every expectation of seeing him at lunch. Yes, I was going to go to the tables and brave whatever reception I got from the crowd there.

Robin and I walked together after Health. I thought I could see Dave's familiar frame sitting in his regular spot on one of the tables. But before we were close enough to be sure he had seen us, he walked off across the field toward the gym with five other boys, including Matthew. It felt like my heart had fallen somewhere down around my knees. Robin looked as disappointed as I felt, her mouth set in a firm line, but she looked at me and shrugged.

"He told me in Carter's class this morning that he'd hang with us after school," she said.

My heart revived somewhat. That would have to get me through my afternoon classes. I was curious, though; apparently Robin and he had at least one class together.

"Carter's class?"

"Ag. Science," said Robin.

"Ag. Science," I repeated. I'd never heard of it. I didn't think it existed in Los Angeles.

Robin rolled her eyes and sighed. "You're such a city girl," she said. "Ag. Science is for people interested in farming and ranching, food production, and animal science, or if they're just more interested in it than regular science. Some people take it because they think it'll be easier, but we still have to learn basic chemistry and a lot more biology, plus environmental science and some business and stuff. I think some people took it this year just because Dave did. I bet over half the girls couldn't care less about crops or animals. It's so annoying. Our class is huge!"

This I understood; I would have taken the class too! We had reached the tables and there didn't appear to be much room left, even though six boys had left. Chris was there but barely acknowledged that he saw us, and nobody seemed inclined to make room so we sat on the grass. It seemed a little strange that Chris should ignore us. I thought he might at least want to know about Gold; get an update or something. Perhaps he felt he also needed to keep his distance from me, though it seemed unlikely. Then again, maybe his not caring what people thought was just an act. I was beginning to feel diseased or contaminated or something.

My afternoon classes passed by without incident. I never looked at the girls in the computer lab, but they didn't go out of their way to make me aware of them either. Melanie seemed happy to see me in Art and didn't ask any more questions. I was pretty preoccupied, anticipating seeing Dave and actually getting to spend some time with him. Unfortunately, things didn't work out that way.

"He said he had something he had to take care of," said Robin when I ventured to ask if Dave was going to hang out as he'd said.

You've got to be kidding me! It was hard not to be acutely disappointed.

"Do you want to go get coffee?" she asked. "Or we could just go home and have tea with Gran."

"Coffee sounds good," I said, though I was really just hoping that somehow Dave would show up at the coffee shop.

We chatted about the horses all the way there. She told me stories of Galahad: how she had been rather scared of him until she got used to him and her riding improved; how mellow he was now compared to back then. I told her about being able to halter Gold and lead him around, how well-behaved he was, and how easily he lifted his feet for me to clean. She seemed genuinely impressed, which was quite gratifying. It seemed as if at least something was going right.

"So . . . now you've just got to face your dad, right?"

I grimaced and nodded, sipping my drink. "I really don't want to think about it right now."

She nodded. "By the way, why didn't you tell me you'd had trouble with those guys before?"

The question completely caught me off guard, but I couldn't pretend to misunderstand who she meant or which incidents she was referring to, though I thought about trying. Of course, there had actually been two other incidents, but only the one she could know of.

"I told Dave about what happened after school yesterday, and Matthew was there and told us about what happened before. You should have said something. You can't let anyone bully you, especially guys like that. What did that jerk say to you anyway?"

I shook my head.

"It had something to do with the Calderas, right?"

I said nothing but couldn't deny it.

"Well, Dave was really mad. Mad about the guys, of course, but mad at you, too, for not telling him. He even told me to tell you so. I hate it when he really gets mad."

My cheeks were burning. On the one hand, no one likes to get scolded, even second hand. On the other, I couldn't help feeling a little relieved that he knew and very pleased that he cared. I just wished that he'd told me—and scolded me—in person.

We sat outside in the shade, as we had that first time, but it just wasn't the same. There were no vehicles near the abandoned gas station and the only skaters looked like a couple of inexpert middle school kids. Robin seemed to be thinking the same as she sighed loudly and said, "It's going to be so boring this weekend. The guys are going surfing. And they won't take me with them."

"Do you surf?" I asked, curious.

"No, but I would if they'd teach me. But they won't." Her face expressed her opinion of that. "They only take me if the whole family's going to the beach, just for the day. Most often just Dave and Chris go with their dad. They rough it, camping wherever they can and following the waves. I guess the forecast is generally good for this weekend." She shrugged and looked off into the distance. "Maybe they're getting ready right now, or leaving really early or something, and that's why Dave couldn't hang out."

We both sighed heavily and decided to leave.

Doing homework didn't seem that crucial when we got to her house. It looked like we'd both have plenty of time to do it over the weekend. Robin spent some time "taking the edge off" Gali first, and then let me ride him around—walking and jogging, turning and backing—until I was starting to feel quite comfortable on him. After an hour or so, we settled him for the night, and then went into the house to wash up and have tea with Fiona. When Mom arrived, I ran out to the car so she couldn't stay and talk, but I promised to call Robin over the weekend.

Mom and I were subdued all evening. I went to see Gold when we got home, led him around a little, and fed and groomed him, but Mom stayed at the house. She seemed really tired. Neither of us mentioned Gold or the Calderas or Dad, but all those topics weighed heavily on my mind and I assumed were troubling Mom too. I knew Dad would be leaving Los Angeles late this evening and wouldn't be home until very early in the morning, but I chose to go to bed fairly early for a Friday. I didn't know if Mom would say anything to him tonight and didn't want to be awake if she did.

I repeated my little ritual of the night before, lighting the candle and sitting in the near dark listening to music. Tomorrow would probably decide the fate of Gold, and with it, possibly the fate of my friendship with Dave. Dad would probably be angry that I had in effect lied, as my mother had said, and would no doubt feel compelled to punish me, something he'd rarely had to do. I was too old for spanking and being confined to my room would never have worked as a punishment for me. It seemed more likely that something important would be denied to me. There were only two things that important.

I remembered my list and retrieved it from the bottom drawer of my desk. Reading it now, there was nothing to suggest any extraordinary attachment to me, nothing beyond a certain thoughtfulness. Still, I couldn't resist. I picked up a pen and thought about what I could add to it.

Was unhappy when I avoided him (missed me?)

Helpful with Gold (still not sure of motive)

Wanted me to hang out at Bar 8; wanted to show me his ranch (sharing nature)

Invited me to his home for barbecue and show; took care of me; thoughtful all day

Angry that I was bullied (he cares!)

Angry that I didn't tell him I was bullied (wants me to confide in him?)

This was a little more encouraging and at least indicated a particular friendship. Especially remembering the first and last situations. I'd have to hang on to those when I began to doubt. I still felt terribly lonely, and thinking of Dave just brought tears to my eyes. I already seemed to be prevented from seeing him at school. Would I also be banned from seeing him outside it?

My hope seemed as fragile as the candlelight barely illuminating my room. I sat and watched the flame dance for a while through bleary eyes, but finally blew it out and went to sleep.

Chapter Eighteen

Waking Up

I slept badly, waking several times from bad dreams. At least twice I dreamed that Gold was taken away from me. What was weird was *how* he was taken away: at least once by train and once by airplane. I quickly returned to sleep each time, so I wasn't exactly sure how many times I dreamed the same thing. Each time I was left yelling, trying to run and go with him but being held back by someone I couldn't see. One time I woke up actually crying and feeling an acute sense of loss, but I wasn't able to completely remember the dream. After this last time, it was a long while before I could go back to sleep as, once awake and reasonably calm again, my mind automatically turned to Dave and the worry of what might happen next.

When I did at last fully wake up, it was much later than I'd planned. I bolted out of bed, threw my clothes on, and barely took the time to grab my glasses. My hair remained loose, but it didn't matter. I needed to see Gold and feed him before my dad was awake. No one was up yet, so I crept downstairs and ran as fast as I could to the corral.

Gold rumbled at me accusingly and moved back and forth a few steps by the fence where he normally got fed.

"I'm sorry! I'm sorry!" I apologized, feeding him as quickly as possible. "It's all your own fault, you know. Giving me bad dreams!"

Unrepentant, he tore hungrily into his hay. I gave his body a quick brush then moved to his tail, trying to carefully separate a small section of the very

long hair as I had seen Robin do to the much shorter tail of Gali. But it was impossible. The ends would have to be brushed out first. I worked hard on it, finally quitting when I had gotten about ten inches done. I'd have to work halfway up his tail before I'd be able to completely separate it into sections. I thought I might be able to accomplish it this weekend; the rest of his tail and his mane would have to wait for now, though. I needed to get back to the house and get the coming ordeal over.

Mom was up and drinking coffee by herself in the kitchen. She looked exhausted, like she'd gotten even less sleep than me. I sat down at the table with her and remained silent as she regarded the liquid in her cup.

Finally, she spoke, very quietly. "We're going to let Daddy sleep as long as he wants to. Then we're going to fix him a nice breakfast and let him drink his coffee. Then you're going to tell him everything. *Everything*. And you need to be as honest as you can, especially about how the boys are involved. I don't know exactly how upset he'll be, but I'm sure he won't be happy. And if you care anything about what the next few years are going to be like, you will accept any decisions he makes regarding the horse *and* your friends. Do you agree?"

Whoa!

I gulped—audibly. It was the most solemn and stern I could ever remember my mother being with me. If she was this serious, what would my dad be like? I nodded a vigorous assent. I was quaking in my boots already—without the boots. But I knew she was right. Mom was trusting me. Dad would probably take more convincing, and how I handled this situation now might set the tone for the rest of my adolescence. That was depressing, but I was sure it was true. Dad was very traditional when it came to morals and ethics and character and all that, and securing his trust seemed like the most vital thing I could undertake for the foreseeable future.

"You don't think—" I debated about whether to finish the thought. I really wanted to know her opinion and I was starting to get very worried about it, so I asked, "You don't think Daddy'll make us move back to LA, do you?"

"Allison. . . ." Mom said warningly.

We continued to sit in silence, savoring what felt like the calm before the storm, until we heard Dad coming down the stairs. Then Mom and I sprang into action. I got the eggs and bacon out and started cooking while Mom fixed his coffee the way he liked it and started a fresh pot.

Dad arrived in the kitchen looking a little groggy and disheveled but smiling and obviously happy to be home. I'd been feeling lonely all week even though in the company of family and friends most of the time. It occurred to me that Mom and Dad must have been feeling the same way—missing each other. Why had I never considered that before? But that prompted more selfish thoughts, wondering if I'd been in Dave's thoughts at all beyond yesterday morning. I shook my head, angry at myself. Now was certainly *not* the time to become morose. I needed all the positive energy I could muster.

Mom and I nibbled on bacon and sipped coffee while Dad told us about his week, the things he'd accomplished, or not, and the people he'd seen. I tried to look interested but wasn't processing much of what he said, waiting for the appropriate moment to say my piece. Dad himself provided the perfect segue into my confession.

"So, what have you girls been up to?"

Mom looked at me meaningfully. I took a deep breath before speaking.

"Daddy, there's something I need to tell you about."

"Okay," he said, looking happy and expectant at first, then dubious when I didn't begin to talk immediately.

I tried to speak slowly and calmly. "You know after we moved and everything, and then you weren't here for a long time?"

I waited for my father to respond. He raised his brows and widened his eyes, wanting me to get to the point. He was looking much more guarded now, and my palms were getting sweaty.

"Well, I started seeing this . . . light . . . or what I thought was a light, or reflection, or something . . . over in the hills," I said, pointing in that general direction.

Dad waited patiently.

"I saw it several times and then started school and other stuff happened and then I sort of forgot about it . . ." I was talking fast and knew I needed to slow down and stay very focused to say only the things I wanted to say, and not slip up and say something I didn't. "Then I saw it again early one morning, so I tried to find it, to see what it was."

When I didn't continue right away, he said, "And. . . ."

"It was a horse."

"A horse," he repeated.

"Yes, a horse. At first I wasn't sure if it was on our land. I thought it might be a neighbor's. Then I thought it might be wild."

"I suppose it *could* be wild," he said, frowning in consideration.

"Well," I continued, "I started bringing it carrots and apples and was able to get closer and closer to it—"

Here Dad interrupted, sounding exasperated. "I don't suppose it occurred to you that you could get hurt?"

"Um . . . maybe . . . at first," I reluctantly admitted. "But then I was able to get closer, and he started expecting me. He was really hungry."

"Did it occur to you that you should at least tell your mother?"

I tried to keep any expression that could be construed as guilt off my face. "Well, not at first. I just thought it was weird that there was a horse wandering around. And then . . . well, I was kind of unhappy, and he was like a friend. I was afraid that if I said something, I might be prevented from seeing him and . . . I couldn't bear that. That's when you came home. Dave and Chris had just seen him that morning. They were sure he wasn't wild but thought he might be valuable and that we should try to catch him. But then you were mad and seemed unhappy that I'd been riding horses, but I didn't know why, so I didn't say anything."

I was rambling again so waited for him to say something. He looked like he was trying to figure out how to feel about my confession.

Mom spoke up instead. "Tell him about Dr. Emory."

"Oh . . . right," I said, gathering my thoughts again. "Well, I was able to catch him in the corral . . . there's a corral down by the creek . . . and Dave and Chris brought hay over . . . but they didn't come anywhere *near* the house," this seemed an important point, "and Chris had told Dr. Emory about Gold and thought that—"

Dad was holding his hand up for me to stop. "What gold?" he asked.

I felt my face redden but couldn't help gushing a little as I admitted, "It's what I call the horse. He's really beautiful, Dad, and he's looking nicer and nicer since I've been brushing him and—"

"You've been *brushing* him?" Dad almost exploded.

"Yes. And he lets me halter and lead him and pick out his feet and he's so cute when I—"

Dad looked floored and it was Mom's turn to hold her hand up to halt me. "Dr. Emory?" she prompted gently.

"Um . . . right," I said, making myself get back on track. "Well, Chris thought it would be a good idea if he, Dr. Emory, saw Gold. That he'd be able to, you know, advise us."

I saw nothing unreasonable in this statement, but Dad's expression scared me. He looked like he was struggling to keep himself from *really* exploding. I looked at Mom nervously.

"You'd better tell him everything," she urged.

"Everything . . ." I repeated, searching my mind for relevant facts. "Well, Dr. Emory thinks he's probably valuable and someone's missing him. And he's going to try to find out who lost him. And he thinks he's Iberian . . . or something . . ." I still wasn't sure what this meant. "Oh, and he's going to test his manure for worms, but Chris says all horses have worms, it just depends on how many. . . ." I stopped for breath and was wracking my brains for any other important data.

"And. . . ." prompted Mom.

"And . . ." I felt like I was treading water in a stormy ocean. "And . . . Oh!" A rather pertinent point came to mind. "He doesn't like boys. Men. Guys. He doesn't like male people. At all."

Relief flooded me as I felt I had now said everything that needed to be said, but Dad's face was slightly red, his countenance dark. It seemed like both my mother and I held our breath waiting for the volcano to erupt.

Instead, Dad rose stiffly to his feet, said, "I'm going to go take a shower," very evenly, and then left the kitchen.

Mom and I both exhaled long, slow breaths, and I grimaced, looking at her inquiringly.

She looked relaxed and somewhat philosophical—more her normal self. "Well, I'm glad *that's* over. The bad news is, the last time I saw your father that mad, he fired two people."

"What's the good news?" I whispered, starting to feel nervous all over again.

"I doubt if he'll fire you."

I knew she was trying to lighten the mood, but my apprehension was growing with every passing minute. Normally Dad took quick showers, but he was taking *forever*; probably not a good sign. Plenty of time for me, and no doubt him, to realize that I had admitted to not only allowing Dave and Chris over when my parents weren't home—near the house or not—but also

to inviting an adult man that they didn't know. Though I knew in my heart that all had been completely safe and innocent, it was dawning on me now how my dad was going to view it. Then I started thinking about how Gold was going to behave when Dad went down to see him, which I knew he would. By the time my dad returned to the kitchen—clean, shaved, dressed, and calm but looking very awake and horribly serious—I was a wreck.

"You'd better show me this animal," he said, grimly, "and then we'll have to decide what to do."

"Decide what to do" could mean either "decide what to do with the horse," or "decide what to do with Allison." It probably meant both.

I ran after him as he headed out the back door. He walked so fast that it was hard to keep up. I wanted to ask him to slow down, to not approach Gold too abruptly, but I doubted he would listen to me right now. I guessed Dad was going to see him at his worst and there was nothing I could do about it.

Gold was already on the far side of the paddock, standing very alert and watching the road with eyes wide and ears pricked forward. He looked magnificent. I was watching Dad's face and saw surprise replaced quickly by a deep frown. He looked around, obviously taking note of the tarp-covered hay and other items the boys had brought.

He approached the fence and Gold leaped forward, jumping into a high-stepping trot I hadn't seen him do before, arching his powerful neck and shaking his beautiful head as if in annoyance. I couldn't suppress an ill-timed giggle. Dad gave me a quelling look, and the humor in the situation evaporated. Still, I couldn't help admiring Gold and felt my heart swell with pride as if he were somehow attached to me. He *was* starting to look a lot cleaner, his golden coat glowing in the late morning sun. At least I was sure my father would be able to see how I could have, at a far distance, mistaken him for a light or reflection of some kind.

I wish you'd calm down, though. You're doing nobody any good by putting on this show.

"Where did the poles come from?" asked Dad, looking at the gate.

"Chris brought them," I answered, and then realized that Dad must have been aware of this paddock all along to know that the poles were added. *Of course he was. Stupid me.*

Tight-lipped again, my dad turned away from the fence and began striding back to the house. I wished I could stay with Gold and work on his mane and tail but decided I had better follow my dad.

When he got to the house, he looked at Mom, still sitting at the table, and brusquely said, "I'll be back later."

Without breaking his stride, he ordered me to stay away from "the animal" and left the kitchen to go upstairs. He came straight back down and we heard him leave through the front door. Mom and I just looked at each other for a few moments, then I told her what had transpired at the corral. It wasn't much. A comprehending look crossed her face, then was gone, as if she would keep me from knowing—whatever it was.

I went to my room to work on homework, trying to keep my mind occupied. After a while, I picked up my phone and called Robin.

"My dad knows," I said darkly.

"Did he freak?" she asked.

"Pretty much. At least . . . I think so. It's kind of hard to tell. He's not talking to me, but he seemed really mad. I've never seen him like that."

"So, what's going to happen?"

"I don't know yet. He didn't say anything, but that's a bad sign. Then he left and all I know is that he's mad."

"Geez. I hope you don't get into too much trouble."

"Me too."

We said bye and I tried to go back to homework but just couldn't concentrate. I remembered that Brenda had called me, almost a week ago now, and I had been feeling bad for not returning her call. I wasn't exactly in the mood to deal with her but didn't want to ignore her either. I figured the distraction would be worth it.

"You didn't call me back," she said, sounding peevish.

"I'm sorry. I was really busy that day and didn't have my phone with me."

"You were busy on Labor Day?" she asked as if the notion was incomprehensible.

I hadn't meant to open the subject, but she *did* ask. "Yes, we were gone pretty much all day."

"Oh yeah? Where did you go?" This was unusual. Brenda, curious about *me?*

"We went to a barbecue," I said. Some internal devil prompted me to add, unnecessarily, "And horse show."

"Horse show," repeated Brenda. I could hear the disbelief in her voice. "Since when are you interested in horses?"

"Since all my friends here ride," I said, trying not to feel too smug. It didn't matter whether she understood or not. I was beyond that.

"Oh, so your friends were riding in it?" she asked.

"Yes." I considered letting it go at that, but it was the first time I could remember Brenda ever starting a conversation by sincerely asking me questions. "I got to ride most of the time, too, but I wasn't showing or anything. It was really fun."

"Hmm," she said. "So you know someone with an extra horse?"

Quite a few extra, no doubt. "Yes, the person who invited us. It was at their ranch."

"Oh," she said and was quiet. I half wanted her to ask, "At whose ranch?" but also still felt the less she knew about that the better. She was bound to assume too much, which would be embarrassing. And I didn't think she'd be able to understand the "just friends" concept. I was still having trouble with that myself, for different reasons.

"How are you doing?" I asked. Time to put the focus back on her. "How's school and everything?"

She said everything was great. She was having a fun time with her new friends, she had just gone shopping and had some cute clothes—which she described in meticulous detail—and her boyfriend was a *dream*. It occurred to me that this was pretty much the same conversation we'd had last time.

"That's great!" I said, sincerely. I really did want her to be happy, yet there had been something of a hollow tone to her words.

"Yeah," she said quietly as if she'd run out of things to say. That certainly wasn't like her.

I decided to tell her about Gold. She might not care about horses at all, but he wasn't a secret anymore.

"There was a horse wandering around on our property and I caught him. Nobody knows who he belongs to, but everyone seems to think he's special."

"Really," she said as if not knowing what else to say. Then, "Are you going to get to keep him?"

Get to keep him?

It's not that I hadn't thought *of* it, vaguely, but I hadn't thought *about* it. I couldn't afford to. Getting to keep Gold was as ridiculous as being Dave's *real* girlfriend. It wasn't going to happen. *Not in a million years.*

"No," I said decidedly. "People are looking for the owners right now, so it's just a matter of time. I'm just taking care of him."

"Oh," said Brenda. "I guess that's good. Right?"

"Yes." I didn't want to think that through either. We talked a few more minutes, but now we both seemed depressed. We promised to keep in touch and started to say our goodbyes, but something prompted me to say, "Brenda? I . . . just want to say thank you."

"For what?" she asked, sounding suspicious.

"Thanks for being my friend for so long. You were my friend when nobody else was." I felt a little awkward being this open with her—it was something we'd never acknowledged out loud before—but it suddenly seemed important for me to say it. "I . . . I appreciate what you did for me. And I'm glad you want to stay in touch."

She was silent for a moment but finally said, quietly, "You're welcome." But then she said, "Allison . . ."

"Yes?"

"You're still a dork."

"I know."

"Well . . . bye."

I laughed. "Bye."

It seemed useless to try to concentrate on homework after that, so I grabbed my sketchbook and pencil bag and wandered back downstairs. Mom was on the phone.

"So we can expect you about six?" she asked. "Yes . . . Thank you so much. I appreciate you taking the time and trouble . . . All right. Goodbye."

My heart leaped for some stupid, hopeful reason. *You really are a loser, you know that? As if she would invite* him.

"I'm going out on a limb here for you, Allison," said Mom. "I don't know what your father's going to say or do, so until we have a chance to talk, you won't say anything. Okay?"

"Okay," I said meekly.

"I looked up Dr. Emory's number—luckily it's in the phone book—and invited him to dinner. I'm hoping your dad won't be mad, but I think he should meet him as soon as possible."

I nodded, though I was unsure of her reasoning. Still, she knew Dad best. "Where do you think he went?" I asked.

I could tell she had an idea but, "I'm not sure," was all she'd say.

Wandering out to the back porch, I sat on the steps, partially in the shade. Our lawn was growing nicely now in spite of the seemingly never-ending late summer heat. It was going to be another very hot day. *Boring,* hot day. I gazed toward the hills and sighed heavily, knowing Gold was there at the foot of them, just out of sight. Did horses get bored? Probably. Gold always seemed happy to see me, even without food.

What was going to happen now? I had a horrible feeling Gold's days with me were numbered and my freedom to associate with Dave was highly in question. I wanted to go and call him just to hear his voice, even if I'd feel embarrassed at not having a real reason for calling. But he was probably nowhere near his phone, probably riding a wave, body wet, hair windswept. He'd be laughing. It was so easy to picture him that way. I doubted he'd have reason to think of me. My throat tightened, and I mentally kicked myself for allowing my mind to wander there, but it was too late. I hid my face in my arms and let tears slip down my cheeks.

By the time my dad came home, my face was dry but my heart hurt and I had a headache. It was only noon, but I already wanted the day to be over. The windows were still open and I could hear my parents talking; apparently Mom had asked a question before they entered the kitchen.

"Yes, that's where I went, but they weren't home. I left a message with the housekeeper and I *will* be talking to them."

Oh no! Please don't let them be talking about who I think they're talking about.

"Greg, don't jump to too many conclusions. I don't believe there was any intention of wrongdoing on anyone's part. I really don't."

"Perhaps not, but apparently I didn't outline the boundaries clearly enough for Allison. Maybe *they* will take me more seriously."

Ugh! They are *talking about who I think they're talking about.*

"Honey, that's not completely fair. I think she tried to do as you said, but she was also concerned about the horse. And the boys just tried to help."

It was quiet for a few moments, and I wondered if my dad could see things from her point of view. But then I could imagine that Dad had given her one of those "Are you sure?" looks, as Mom said, "Well, it won't hurt to talk to them, I suppose. But please don't approach them with assumptions. Make allowances for their motives to be . . . altruistic."

It was quiet again. Then Dad sighed loudly and said, "I'm not really doubting the intentions of either Allison or the boys . . . at this point . . . but there still needs to be some limits set and adhered to. I need to know I can trust them. She's growing up so fast, and I know that one of these days she's going to want to date someone. At that point, I'll probably never trust the boy. Whoever he is, I already don't trust him. But I want to be able to trust *her*. I need to know she'll do what's right, even if she doesn't understand it."

My cheeks were burning. I was beginning to hate the fact that I was growing up. It was mentally depressing, emotionally painful, and socially embarrassing. And that's without the physical aspects. And my parents! Well, Mom seemed to be more reasonable but Dad—what on earth was he going to say to the Calderas?

Just kill me now. How will I ever face Dave again after this? Oh, wait . . . that's right, I'm probably never going to be allowed to see him again anyway. And I certainly wouldn't blame him if he didn't want to see me.

My eyes started leaking again and I left the porch steps, not wanting to hear any more. I wandered to the front of the house and sat in the shade there until I felt calmer, then reentered the house, went upstairs, and fell asleep.

I never heard Mom tell Dad about Dr. Emory coming to dinner, but I supposed he must have at least acquiesced. Mom came to wake me up about five. I got up, washed my face, and approached my Dad cheerlessly to ask permission to go and feed Gold. He nodded, obviously making note of my attitude, but I didn't care. I was hurt and angry and very, very tired. I still just wanted the day to be over, though I was a little curious about what Dr. Emory would say and how Dad would react to him. If it hadn't been for that, I probably would have just gone back to bed again.

By the time Dr. Emory arrived, I was feeling resigned—for the moment— and very subdued. Neither Dad nor I seemed willing to break the silence, now tangible between us. I had nothing to say. I had a feeling he had too much and might open the floodgates if he spoke to me at all. I wasn't ready

for that so wanted to avoid it as long as possible. I assumed he was reserving final judgment until all the facts were in.

Mom had made a roast with mashed potatoes and gravy, one of Dad's favorites and likely to be appreciated by our masculine guest. When Dr. Emory arrived, he and my parents introduced themselves and exchanged pleasantries while I kept a low profile, already seated at the dining table. He joined me there while Mom and Dad went into the kitchen. I probably should have been helping instead of Dad, but I wasn't thinking about it.

"How are you holding up?" Dr. Emory whispered.

I looked at him, startled.

His good-humored face softened. "That bad, huh?"

I nodded but still didn't speak. Mom and Dad returned with serving dishes and set them on the table. Dad took his place while Mom returned to the kitchen for something.

"You know, I'm glad your wife called, Mr. Anderson," said Dr. Emory. "I would have called myself, and probably should have, but the circumstances were . . . unusual. I came over as a favor to a good friend. When I realized that Allison hadn't told you of her discovery, I urged her to tell you. From what Mrs. Anderson said, she did tell you that evening, but you only found out this morning."

Mom came back and sat down. "Please, call me Jen. Yes, I chose not to tell him. He was out of town until last night."

"Oh, I see," he said pleasantly.

"So . . . James, is it?" asked Dad, sounding polite but businesslike, "What do you make of this animal? And call me Greg, please."

I was annoyed that my dad kept calling Gold "animal"—as if he were some nondescript creature—but I kept quiet, my eyes on my plate.

"I think it's safe to say that he is, indeed, a very valuable animal, either Lusitano or Andalusian. From his general build and movement, I'd say he was a performance horse of some kind. Since he's a stallion, it's most likely that he was being kept as a breeding animal. If I could get close enough, I'd be able to see if he has a tattoo or perhaps a micro-chip. It would tell us who he is and who he belongs to, but the way things are, that's not going to happen without tranquilizers. I'd be very reluctant to do that." He shook his head and frowned. "He seems to be in pretty good health, though, considering he must have been lost for some time, perhaps months. He needs deworming and to have his weight built back up. I have a friend, Dr. Susan Welke, that I'd like to examine him, administer dewormer, and so forth. With your permission of course."

Dad was quiet for a few moments, chewing his food and looking at his plate. "How safe do you feel this animal is? Allison has been working fairly closely with him, apparently, and I'm very concerned for her safety. I'm not comfortable with keeping him here if she's the only one able to get near him. Would it be possible to move him to another location while you try to find his owners?"

I cried out at that. I couldn't help it. "Please, Dad! Please let him stay here! He's not dangerous. I swear! He just doesn't like guys. Chris thinks he's been hurt, and that's why he acts the way he does. It's all show anyway." I turned to Dr. Emory, who was quickly becoming Dr. James in my mind and a potentially strong ally. "He'd be better off here, right? Maybe your friend can make Dad feel more . . . comfortable . . . about him?"

"Allison," Dad said reproachfully.

"Actually, I think she'd be the perfect person to set your mind at ease. Animal behavior is her area of expertise. She would absolutely be able to tell you whether the horse is a danger . . . beyond the normal parameters of working with horses, of course. As for him remaining here," he said, looking at me, "there's no doubt that *he'd* probably prefer it, though it's a shame the paddock is so far from the house."

"If he doesn't stay here, where will he go?" I whispered.

"We have some facilities at the clinic, of course, but we're not set up to house animals indefinitely. He'd probably either go to the animal shelter or, given his apparent value, the sheriff's department might take custody of him and house him. It's hard to say. The fact that he's a stallion poses some problems that the shelter might not want to handle, but the sheriffs aren't equipped to handle them either. It would be nice to know he was getting better care and more attention than he'd get at any of these alternatives. All in all, the best solution would be for him to be kept by the people that found him." He looked at me. "The likelihood that you'll actually get to keep him is pretty slim, I'd say. Eventually, his owners are sure to be found. But you never know. And there might be a reward."

He was smiling at me, but my heart was still lodged somewhere near my stomach, making it impossible to feel happy, and impossible to eat. I

knew I couldn't afford to think about keeping Gold. But to consider taking a reward? *Bounty? Blood money?*

I shivered and looked pleadingly at my dad.

Dad regarded me levelly, then turned to Dr. James again. "If, and I'm only saying *if*, we were to keep him here, what would you suggest as far as care? I'm not happy about not being able to see Allison from the house when she's with the horse."

At least he's "the horse" now instead of "the animal."

"I'm sure something can be arranged. Perhaps our friends the Calderas can be of assistance." I knew he was trying to be helpful, but mentioning the Calderas right now was probably not the best timing. He seemed to pick up on tension in the air and added, "Regardless, I'm sure we can make it work. I'm willing to help in any way I can."

"That's very kind of you, James," said Mom, warmly. "I think it would be wonderful if your friend could give us her opinion. Don't you think so, Greg?" I could tell she was trying to keep a positive tone going and was thankful.

Dad nodded, looking not altogether happy but resigned, at least for the time being. "If she'll come, we'd be grateful." He looked at me again. "We'll see what she says and then talk about options. But I'm not making any promises." He sounded severe again. "There are quite a few things we need to work out."

I glanced at Dr. James. He smiled, his eyes twinkling a little. Then he winked at me as if we shared some kind of secret.

Mom brought out dessert—she'd made a peach cobbler, another of Dad's favorites—and the adults continued to talk, getting to know each other. Dad seemed to relax once the subjects of horses and Calderas were avoided, and Dr. James appeared to be carefully doing so; probably no mean feat in his position. He and Dad eventually found they shared interests in racquetball and golf and said perhaps they could play together sometime. This seemed promising, and Mom and I cleared the table, retiring to the kitchen to leave them to talk.

She was quiet for a while as we began washing dishes, but finally said, "Do you remember what I said earlier, Allison?"

I looked at her, unsure of what specific remarks she referred to.

"About accepting *whatever* Daddy decides?"

I gulped and nodded, my eyes starting to sting.

She nodded and smiled at me. "Just remember, nothing lasts forever. Nothing bad, anyway." She smiled again, but I wondered if she knew something I didn't.

I felt tired and wanted to be alone, so I excused myself. Mom looked at me sympathetically and nodded. I thanked Dr. James for coming and for all his help. I avoided looking at my dad.

Lately my life seemed to have, well, taken on a life of its own—it felt out of my control and left me wondering what would happen next. And I wouldn't have had it any other way, except for the being in trouble part. I was conscious of feeling alive and aware in a way I had never noticed before. It was rather amazing. And frightening. But I would never choose to have things back the way they had been before we moved here. Before Gold. Before my friends. Before Dave.

I spent the rest of the evening alone with music and candlelight.

Sunday was interminable. Dad insisted on going with me to feed Gold but wouldn't allow me to enter the paddock to brush him or anything. It would have been impossible anyway as he paced nervously on the far side of the paddock the whole time we were there. Dad tried to engage me in conversation as we returned to the house, asking about school and classes, but I returned monosyllabic answers and tried not to sound too surly.

Most of that day was spent quietly in my room, but I became more and more nervous as the day wore on. I hadn't forgotten about my dad's failed attempt at talking to the Calderas and was sure he hadn't forgotten it either. I wondered when they were likely to be home and hoped it would be too late for them to follow up on my father's contact. If I could only have one more day—if I could just talk to Dave *first*, maybe explain a little—he might not hate me.

The phone rang about five o'clock and I held my breath, listening from the top of the stairs. Apparently it was just Dr. James saying that his friend, Susan Welke, would be able to drive over tomorrow after her clinic hours, if that was okay. When ten o'clock came and went, I began to breathe a little easier. Surely they wouldn't call now.

The phone rang at ten-thirty. I stepped out onto the landing to listen and was hit with dismay.

"Alex . . . thank you for calling," my dad said, sounding very serious. "Well, yes . . . I would appreciate it if it's not inconveniencing you this late . . . I appreciate your understanding . . . Right . . . Very good, I'll see you shortly."

I ran halfway down the stairs and stared at my dad, just turning away from the phone. "Please . . . don't. . . ." I whispered.

He looked at me, then at Mom, said to her, "I'll be gone a little while," and left.

My world seemed to be coming apart at the seams. I ran back up the stairs, closed my door, and cried until I fell asleep.

Chapter Nineteen

Wish I Had A Clue

Waking up feeling exhausted is a terrible thing, especially on a Monday morning. Waking up also feeling betrayed, hurt, and angry at someone you've always trusted and loved, well, that's the worst. That's the way I felt. On top of that was the looming certainty that the only lights in my otherwise unremarkable life would soon be extinguished. I couldn't imagine much worse. Okay, nobody had *died*—that would definitely have been worse—and yet I felt I was grieving; for what, I wasn't sure yet.

I was allowed to go feed Gold by myself and he was happy to see me, but the lump in my throat made it hard to even say hello to him. He began eating as soon as I threw him his hay, but he watched me immediately walk away. I was sure I detected hurt and accusation in his expression. How much worse was it going to be if I saw Dave today?

He'll be avoiding you for sure after whatever Dad must have said to them. Why even worry about it? But I couldn't help it. Waves of dread kept washing over me and I found it difficult to remain calm and expressionless as Dad drove me to school.

"Don't forget you're taking the bus today," he said as I opened the door. "I won't be home until later. Then we'll have a talk."

I listened without looking at him. For just a moment, I considered that maybe, just *maybe*, I was being unfair. *Right. And everything that's hap-*

pening to you is fair? I got out of the car and tried to close the door without slamming it, then walked away.

Robin was waiting for me. I wished that she wasn't. She was going to her locker and I was determined to avoid that area. I said I'd meet her in class.

"So, what happened?" she asked eagerly on entering the room. So eagerly that it annoyed me.

"I don't know for sure yet," I answered.

"Can you come over after school?" she asked.

I shook my head. "Dad's home. I don't know if I'll be able to come over anymore. I don't know if I'll be allowed to ride anymore. I . . ." My throat was constricting already and the day had barely started. Not good. "I don't know anything," I whispered.

"But what about Gold? What did your dad say about him?" she persisted.

"I . . . don't want to talk about it. Is that okay?" I didn't want to be rude, but I also didn't want to get into details. That would be deadly.

"Okay," she said, but she continued to watch me closely.

When the bell rang, she said, "See you at lunch?"

I shook my head again. "There's something I need to do."

I had no idea what kind of reception I'd receive at the tables, but there was no way I was going to expose myself to the kids there. No matter how Dave treated me—or didn't—I was going to have a hard time. *If* he wanted to see me at all—and I thought that was a very big *if*—I didn't want a built-in audience. If he ignored me, it would kill me. If he'd been hurt by whatever my dad had said, it would kill me. If he was angry about whatever Dad said, it would still kill me. I preferred to not have such a public death.

I knew Melanie could tell something was wrong in PE, but she didn't ask any questions. She just remained her normal, unassuming self. It was somewhat comforting, but I wasn't looking for anyone to confide in. I was still feeling too hurt and angry—but mostly worried. I kept my gaze away from any boys visible on the field and went through the motions of lacrosse. Luckily Dave wasn't on my team or the team opposing us.

"Are you eating outside today?" Melanie asked lightly. I thought she was actually asking if I'd like to eat with her. After all, it was Monday.

"I have . . . something," I prevaricated. "I'll eat with you tomorrow, though. Okay?" It wasn't really a lie. I did have something to do—stay away from *everybody.*

"Okay. Then I'll see you tomorrow."

"Yes. Thanks," I said, trying to smile but feeling like a mask was plastered to my face.

I walked the long way around the school, away from the field and away from the cafeteria and quad, and made my way to the library, thankfully open during lunch. As I had hoped, there was hardly anybody there and nobody I recognized. I found a small, unoccupied table toward the back, took a random book off a shelf, and pretended to read.

I was sure to be left alone. It had become obvious that most people either automatically didn't like me or didn't want to get to know me enough to find out if they would. So far today I hadn't been maligned by anyone. At least not that I'd noticed, though I hadn't been paying attention.

I was sure it would soon be clear to all the fangirls that the Calderas were safe from my grasping ways and evil influence. It still seemed so bizarre that it had ever been an issue. Why would he—they—want to subject themselves to whatever abuse lay in store for them if they remained friends with me? Surely I'd already been way more trouble than my friendship was worth. After all, it wasn't as if he—they—*needed* me. They had loads of friends, and tons more people in line just waiting to be noticed. What did I have to offer? Serving as a female friend to Robin?

Yes, of course, but they . . . he . . . doesn't have to sacrifice himself for that. I want to be friends with Robin. Even if it'll be heartbreaking knowing that she gets to spend time with him while I—

"Whatcha doin'?"

The soft voice speaking directly behind me one moment took form solidly in front of me the next, sitting on the edge of the table and looking quizzically down at me.

"Oh, just . . . studying," I said, trying to find my breath, which had suddenly disappeared, and noticing that my face was wet. I hastily dabbed at it with the back of my hand, pretending to push my glasses further up on my nose. I couldn't bring myself to look up into his face. I could barely make myself breathe.

The book was gently removed from my hands. "Hmmm . . . *Applied Aeronautics*. Planning on building a plane?"

Startled, I looked at the title of the book. *Tales of Scandinavia*. Busted. I blushed furiously and fidgeted in my seat.

He laughed softly and stated, "You're doing it again, aren't you?"

"What?"

"Worrying. When are you going to trust me? I never turn my back on a real friend, you know."

I caught my breath again and my hands started shaking a little. So he wasn't mad? He wasn't hurt? He obviously wasn't ignoring me. I dared to glance at his face and gasped. His eyes were twinkling. *I thought they would be.* And he was smiling his most charming smile. *I was afraid he might be.* His skin looked darker, yet shone brightly as if polished by the sun and wind. And the highlights in his hair—those weird, pink highlights—glistened even in the fluorescent lighting of the library. *Right . . . surfing.*

Any one of these things would have been enough to make me forget my own name, but it was the barely scabbed over scrape on his cheek, just below his right eye, that had made me gasp. I couldn't help reaching out toward him, my hand still shaking. But I stopped just in time, pulled my hand back, and sat on it.

"What happened?" I breathed.

"What . . . this?" He touched the scrape. "Nothing. Surfing accident. I got careless and let my guard down." He looked at the ground and grinned broadly, as if the memory was extremely amusing. "Stupid board," he said, and flashed a wicked smile at me.

"Oh," I said quietly. I was still coming to grips with the fact that he was here—right here—*with me!* He had sought me out. Then it hit me—why I was so surprised about that.

"I'm so sorry!" I whispered harshly. I hadn't meant to whisper, but my throat wasn't behaving normally today at all and I was hanging on to my emotions by a thread. I would *not* cry. Not here and now anyway. *Never again in front of him.*

He frowned. "Sorry? For what?"

The shaking in my hands was echoing through my stomach and spreading outward. "My dad . . ." I whispered.

"You're worried about that?" he said, screwing up his face a little. "That's no big deal."

"But he shouldn't have! You've done nothing . . . nothing wrong!"

"It's okay," he said, seriously. "Really. I think it's totally cool that your dad cares so much about you. And that he respects us enough to want to talk to us. I totally get it. Really! I wouldn't want anyone messing with . . ." He left the rest of the thought unspoken, kicking his heel against the table leg. "My dad said that if he had a daughter, he'd probably shoot the first boy that got too close and ask questions later." He was laughing, but I was blushing all the more, a possible implication of all this striking me in a way it obviously wasn't striking him. "So, do you know what happens next?"

I gazed at him blankly. *You ask me out? You confess your undying love to me? You rescue me on your white . . . um . . . black horse and we ride off into the sunset together?*

His eyes started twinkling again. "About the horse?"

"Oh," I said, snapping back to reality. "I . . . I don't know. My dad said we'd talk tonight. I'm pretty sure there'll be discipline involved, but I don't really know. He's never been mad at me before." I looked into Dave's eyes worriedly, as a thought occurred to me. "You didn't get in trouble with *your* dad, did you?"

"Naw," he said. "We got a little fatherly lecture, but he knows we'd never do anything to hurt you. But *Angel* . . ." he said, laughingly, "she felt it her duty to repeat everything my dad had said, and then some. And then Henry . . ." He was shaking his head at the memory but again didn't finish the thought.

"Henry what?" I couldn't help being interested in anything concerning Henry, as if understanding him might give me insights into Dave's thoughts and life in general.

"Oh, nothing. Henry's just Henry. He wasn't even supposed to be up, let alone hear what was going on. But are *you* in trouble?" He was frowning now and looked concerned.

"I . . . don't know. A little, I think." I may as well be honest with him. He'd find out anyway.

"Hmm," he said, still frowning. "Well, call me later, okay?" The bell rang then and he stood up, slowly backing away from the table. "Let me know what happens."

I nodded and watched him until he was out of sight. I didn't feel like moving. I wanted to sit still and continue to soak up the warmth his presence had wrapped me in. The shaking I had fought to suppress was now a steady shivering, but I didn't care. My nerves were shot but my heart was full. I wondered if I'd get in too much trouble if I skipped class and stayed here, but I decided that getting into any more trouble knowingly probably wasn't a good idea. Better late than never. I left the library and took the most direct route to English.

I felt wrapped in a haze during class. On two separate occasions, Miss Sanders had to call my name multiple times before getting my attention. The other kids giggled and snorted with laughter, but I didn't care. They couldn't know; I was so much more pleasantly occupied.

He cares! He really does! He doesn't hate me and he's not mad! And he wants me to call him later. I was firmly fixated on *later*.

Miss Sanders asked me to stay after class.

"Is everything all right, Allison?" she asked. She seemed genuinely concerned.

"Yes, fine," I said, surprised by her question.

"You know, you turn in very good work, but you've seemed extremely distracted and unhappy, almost from the first day of school. You were late today and you're paying less and less attention in class. I'm pretty sure that sooner or later, no matter how good at English you are, that's going to affect your grades."

I tried to read her face, not sure how to respond.

"I'm not the only one of your teachers who's noticed. And we hear and see a lot of what is happening on campus . . . *and* off."

I stared at her wide-eyed, completely horrified. Now the teachers were talking about me? *What on earth?*

"I'm sorry, Miss Sanders. I don't mean to, you know, lose focus in class."

"Well, if you ever need an adult to talk to, I want you to feel free to talk to me. Okay?"

"Yes. Thank you," I said, trying to feel and sound sincere, but wary and a little creeped out.

"And," she said, trying to maintain my attention as I was trying to leave, "be careful of getting into . . . relationships . . . that you're not ready for. Don't let anyone take advantage of you. Okay?"

Now I was horrified *and* speechless. Wasn't anyone going to leave me alone? I was *nobody*. Why was everybody watching me? I smiled as best as I could—the mask again—and left the room as quickly as possible.

I was going to be late for study hall—again. Two classes in one day; the second time this semester for study hall and Mr. Payne kept track. Cutting across the quad was the quickest way, and my reason for avoiding it wasn't an issue anymore, so I did. The area was almost clear of students already. Then I went around the cafeteria and along the gravel service road where I normally wouldn't go, especially alone, but I thought it might save more time.

I rounded the back corner and came to an abrupt halt. A familiar figure leaned against the wall, smoking a cigarette. I tried to reverse silently, hoping to go undetected, but my ankle turned slightly on a rock and I made noise catching my balance. I froze.

The boy in the varsity jacket turned to look at me and I gasped in surprise for the second time today. The area around his left eye was almost completely black and blue. He regarded me calmly, exhaling smoke before pushing off the wall, and then walked toward me. I braced myself for whatever abuse might be aimed my way. But he just sneered nastily, took a last drag on the cigarette before flicking it away and then blew the smoke in my face as he passed me. I held my breath until he'd gone, then ran toward class, coughing a little in spite of my caution.

The bell rang just moments before I entered the room and I dreaded Mr. Payne's sarcasm. But all he said was, "Miss Anderson," nodding to me in exaggerated cordiality. I quickly took my seat next to Robin.

She wrinkled her nose and whispered, "You smell funny." Then, in disbelief, "Have you been smoking?"

I tried to emulate her own don't-be-an-idiot look and whispered, "Of course not."

I didn't want to explain it, but I recalled a question I'd had. When only five minutes of class remained—a time when Mr. Payne's rules relaxed considerably—I asked.

"Did you ever find out what Dave was doing Friday?" It didn't seem like too strange a thing to ask, but she looked at me warily.

"Nothing important," she said, trying to evade the question.

She wasn't getting off that easily. "I saw the scrape on his cheek." I regarded her steadily. "And that boy, the bully, has a black eye."

Robin looked really annoyed now. "So what?"

"I want to know!"

"Shhh!" she hissed at me, her eyes darting around the room. "Not here. Wait."

We waited for the bell to ring, my apprehension rising every moment. In spite of the warm afternoon, I was starting to feel decidedly chilled and the shivering was back.

When the bell had rung and the desks closest to ours had been evacuated, she said, "I'm not supposed to say anything, especially to you. I'm not even supposed to know, but Matthew told me."

"Ladies," Mr. Payne addressed us, "are we leaving today?" Obviously a rhetorical question so we didn't bother to answer; he'd already turned his back on us anyway.

We gathered our things and stepped outside, around the side of the building where Dave had talked to me before.

"When Dave heard what I said about those guys, and then Matthew said what had happened before, well, he got mad. I told you that. *Really* mad. You haven't seen him *really* mad. So they went over to Northfield and . . . well . . . picked a fight. Although," her brow wrinkled, "I guess you could say those other guys picked the fight. After all, they started it."

I suddenly felt bad. *Very* bad. Like I was going to cry, faint, throw up—all of the above. Physical violence was something I couldn't handle. I couldn't even watch movies that were too brutal or gory. The idea of Dave using violence against someone because of me was more than distasteful. The idea that he would subject himself to it was even worse. Intellectually, I knew it wasn't really my fault. After all, I hadn't wanted the attention of those other boys. I hadn't been "asking for it." I didn't even know them. And I wasn't to blame for Dave finding out about it, yet I still felt completely responsible. I was starting to feel a little mad myself. I was also feeling deathly ill.

"Where's Northfield?" I asked, my voice sounding rough.

"Northwest of here, towards Lowell. The country club and estates are there. Most of those kids go to Lowell High, but some come here. I guess those guys were from there. I didn't recognize them, but Dave seemed to know who I was talking about."

"How did he get there?" I asked, puzzled.

"Chris drove," she said, shrugging her shoulders, as if it was a given.

"What? I thought he watched out for his brother! He drove him to get in a fight?"

In spite of my nerves—already jangling and causing me to shake badly—and slight nausea, I was angry. *Very* angry. I bet I could give Dave a run for his money when it came to how angry I was. How *could* he?

"Are you okay? You've gone as white as a ghost again."

"I've got . . . I've got to go. I . . ." I couldn't think straight. These guys were going to be the death of me, I was sure of it. "I have to catch the bus."

"Yeah . . . okay," said Robin. "Guess I'll see you tomorrow."

"Tomorrow," I repeated absently. "Right. Okay."

She shook her head at me sadly and walked off toward the front of the school, which is what I should have been doing. My bus was due to leave, but there was something I felt compelled to do instead. Not because there was any coherent thought put into it, but something else had taken over—something fierce—and, apparently, I was going to obey it.

Instead of heading to my bus, I turned toward the parking lot close by, my heart and throat burning, my stomach and mind churning. In spite of his taciturn nature and dubious opinion of me, I had been impressed by Chris' insight and calm thoughtfulness. So far at least. And from what Robin had said and what I'd observed myself, he *did* seem to watch out for his brother. That's what older brothers *should* do, right? But apparently that was giving him too much credit. What kind of person would drive his friend, *especially* his brother, to engage in a fight?

Something else occurred to me which, while more selfish in nature, sent an equal wave of dread through me. What if my parents—what if my *dad*—found out about it? I couldn't imagine him finding this activity acceptable, even if it was for my sake. It wasn't defense, it was retaliation. Or something. That made me very confused. *Don't think about that. You're not thinking straight.*

Seething and still shaking from head to toe, I approached the parking lot, scanning the vehicles and students for the one I was looking for. Running on instinct and adrenaline—another first for me—I finally spotted my quarry, talking to a couple of other guys. He looked to be turning to go to his truck, several vehicles farther away from where he now stood. Even if I ran, which given my current unstable physical condition was not a good idea, I probably wouldn't catch him before he got in. So I did the only other thing I could think of.

"*Chris!*" I yelled, as loudly as possible.

Wow, yelling in public; another first. I really am all about new experiences lately. It also occurred to me that I wasn't feeling normal and wasn't entirely sure what I was doing.

I couldn't tell whether Chris had heard or not, but one of the guys near him got his attention and pointed to me. Chris' expression was unreadable as he looked my way. He turned back to say something to the guys before walking unhurriedly over to where I stood shivering at the edge of the sidewalk. I hadn't even considered what I was going to say, or whether I had a right to say anything at all. But as soon as he stepped close, I lit into him, my voice lowered just enough to try to keep our conflict private.

"How could you let Dave fight that guy?" I hissed at him. "What were you thinking? You actually *drove* him there? Did it occur to you that maybe if you *didn't* drive him, he couldn't go, and maybe, just *maybe*, he wouldn't get hurt?"

He was standing with his weight mostly on one leg and both thumbs hooked into his back pockets. He wasn't looking at me but off to the side, staring fixedly, as if something over there was much more worthy of his attention.

"Were you thinking at all?" My voice had risen in spite of my good intentions and I tried to rein it back in. "I thought you really cared about him. Aren't you supposed to watch out for your younger brother? What if he'd been seriously injured? How would you feel then? And I assume he could get into really bad trouble for it too, right? Does that matter? I guess you're not as smart or, or, or . . . caring as I thought." Perhaps it was unfair of me to vent entirely at Chris; I was mad at Dave, too, but Chris' attitude was making me even madder and my shaking was becoming hard to conceal. My voice rose again. "Do you even care? Do you care about *anything?*"

"I care," he said, emotionless and still looking away. "Are we done?"

I wanted to feel outraged and insulted, but I suddenly just felt very tired and sick to my stomach. My face was wet again, but I didn't care. Maybe it would do him good to see that at least *someone* cared about his brother. But the anger and adrenaline that had held me up and kept me going were spent. Now I just felt very light-headed.

"Completely," I said roughly.

I turned, intending to walk away with what dignity I could. Instead, I took two steps, my knees began to buckle, and I knew I was headed for the pavement. As my backpack slipped to the ground, a strong arm was suddenly around my ribcage, holding me still against a hard hip and chest while I tried to regain my feet.

"Damn it!" Chris swore harshly under his breath.

I felt I had every right to echo that sentiment, but his arm had knocked the breath right out of me and I was having a hard time just standing. When it became clear that my strength wasn't currently equal to the task, he grabbed my backpack, slung it over his own shoulder, and adjusted my arm to support me walking.

"When's the last time you ate?" he asked. It was such a random question that it completely distracted me. "Can you walk to my truck?"

I was still working on the first question. *When was the last time I ate? I remembered playing with my food—was that last night? Did I eat before that?*

Chris swore again as my knees buckled. The next thing I knew, his other arm had lifted my legs and he was carrying me.

No! This is so wrong! I'm mad at you! Don't you dare help me. . . .

Unfortunately, my communication skills were behaving as erratically as my physical functions.

"You don't have epilepsy, do you?" He asked this as he somehow opened the truck door without having to put me down, then lifted me impossibly high onto the seat. The question was conversational in tone, as if he might be mildly interested if I did.

I frowned, feeling extremely dizzy, but I looked at him and shook my head.

His expression barely acknowledged my response before he put my backpack at my feet and closed the door. A moment later, he was sitting beside me and starting the engine.

"Should I take you home?" he asked flatly.

I nodded, then said, "No . . . no. You'll . . . I'll . . . get in trouble."

"Let me worry about that," he said. "Is someone at home for you?" Then he startled me by reaching over and feeling my brow. He swore again, softer this time. "You've got a fever."

"Dad's not home. Mom's . . . working . . ." was all I was able to say. I closed my eyes and tried to remain conscious. That would be too humiliating if I were to pass out in his truck.

This is so not fair! You can't be the hero after I've abused you! You can't be all Mr. Thoughtfulness when I've accused you of not even caring about your brother! I wanted to still be mad but was too tired and dizzy for the effort.

He said no more but backed the truck and began to drive. It seemed only a couple of minutes later that we stopped and he jumped out. He had driven to the pool and was talking to my mother through the chain link fence. Mom looked worried and nodded her head. Chris came back to my side of the truck and opened the door.

"Think you can walk?" he asked.

Of course I can! I'm not going to let you carry me again! I just nodded and slid clumsily down from the seat. He caught and steadied me a little as I hit the ground, then let go. As I started to walk carefully toward the pool entrance, he grabbed my backpack and followed.

"She's just here to see her mom," Chris said to the lady attending the desk.

"Go right in, hon," she said.

We passed through a gate and out into the glare of the sun reflecting off the pool. Mom was waiting for me there.

"Let's bring her over into the shade. Here," she said, leading me to some chairs under a cabana. I sat down gratefully. Mom crouched beside me and felt my forehead while Chris stood nearby, impassive.

"You must be Chris," said Mom. "Thank you so much for bringing her here." She turned to me and said, "I'm glad you didn't take the bus. You could have collapsed on the walk home."

I hadn't thought of that, but then, I didn't know that I was actually sick. It explained a lot.

Chris mumbled something to the effect of, "Don't worry about it," but I still had a concern.

"Mom, please don't let him get in trouble for driving me. He was just trying to help."

She looked at me as if my concern were nonsensical. "Of course he won't, sweetheart. No need to worry about that."

I wasn't sure whether I was actually worried about him getting into trouble—I was mad at him after all—or about him becoming a martyr and getting some kind of perverse pleasure from it. *Not on my account! I think he might enjoy that too much. I just don't get him at all.*

Chris mumbled something else about going to work and left me with Mom, now watching the occupants of the pool with one eye and me with the other. Dad called her later, wondering where I was. She explained that I'd been taken ill and was driven to her, but she didn't say how or by whom. I assumed she would explain better later. As soon as the evening attendant arrived, Mom rushed me out to the car and drove home.

Inside the house, she said, "You'd better lie down unless you feel like eating a little?"

I remembered what Chris had asked, which just made me mad again— *how dare he pretend to care about me when he doesn't even care about his brother!* I declined anything. "What about the vet? I need to be awake."

"Don't worry. We'll be fine. I can take her to see Gold. It might even be best if you're not there. We'll see how he behaves around women in general."

I didn't like the idea at all but couldn't put up much of a fight. I went upstairs to lay down and it was completely dark in my room when I woke up. The clock said eight. The television was on with the volume low as I came downstairs, and Mom and Dad looked cuddly together on the couch.

"Allison!" said Mom, looking up. "How are you feeling, sweetheart?"

"I don't know," I said, rubbing my eyes. I hadn't bothered to put my glasses on which was never a good idea. Everything was blurry and misshapen. I walked the rest of the way down the stairs carefully.

Mom got up and felt my head. "You're very warm. Sit down and let me take your temperature."

She sat me on the couch close to the spot she'd vacated next to Dad, but I didn't look at him. I was still mad at him too. Mom had disappeared upstairs but returned after a few moments with a thermometer.

"Are you warm enough?" she asked.

I nodded. I wasn't feeling particularly well, or even awake, but I needed to know, so asked, "What happened?"

Mom put the thermometer in my mouth and said, "Well, Dr. Emory came over with Dr. Welke . . . she's *very* nice by the way. Anyway, since you were asleep, I thought we should go ahead and feed Gold. She agreed that it might be a good idea to see how he behaved with strangers when you weren't present. We walked down together and he was waiting at the fence . . . he really is so cute when he's waiting for you—"

Dad cleared his throat impatiently and she got back on track. "She was very impressed with him, not only by his looks . . . apparently he is a '*fine specimen*'." Mom said this with such attitude that it would have made me laugh if I'd not been feeling sick, and not had a thermometer in my mouth, and not still been mad at all the other important males in my life. "But she was also impressed with his nature. We didn't feed him right away. She wanted to see how gentle he'd remain with her in the corral when he was hungry, but he was a perfect gentleman. He let her halter and lead him, and then handle his feet and brush him, just as you had done. Then she gave him a paste dewormer. He was very sweet and she assured me that as far as she could see, there was no reason to worry over his temperament."

This was encouraging. I sneaked a glance at Dad to see how he felt about it, but his expression was neutral. He began to talk about the conversation he'd had with Dr. James while Mom and Dr. Welke had visited Gold.

"I have agreed to keep the horse, 'Gold,' as you've named him, here with certain provisions. This includes some disciplinary measures. But perhaps we should discuss it when you're feeling better. Tomorrow."

I pulled the thermometer out of my mouth and said, "No . . . no . . . I need to know. Now. Tonight." Now was *later*. I had a phone call to make.

Mom took the thermometer and frowned over it.

"James is going to talk to the Calderas—Chris in particular, I guess—about getting a paddock set up closer to the house. The horse can be fed and watered more carefully and we can make sure both he and you remain safe. We're also agreed that Chris is the best person to work with him, to try getting him accepting male handlers. That is, if he'll help."

I realized I was frowning disapprovingly. This no longer sounded like a reasonable idea.

"Now for the downside. Are you ready to deal with it?"

I looked briefly at him then at Mom and nodded.

"We've never had to do this before, and we hope we never have to again, but it's vital you understand how important it is—that when we give you rules or set limits on you or your involvement with friends, you obey them. You knew about the horse for about three weeks before telling us. And during that time, you also behaved irresponsibly in doing things and having people here without our knowledge, namely the Caldera boys and even Dr. James, who, thank God, obviously wouldn't dream of hurting you. But your actions demonstrated poor judgment that I can't ignore. Under different circumstances, with different people, the situation could also have become very different, and I can't disregard that."

I felt dirty and heavy from head to toe, knowing that what he was saying was, in fact, true. Even though I had never meant to do wrong, and on some points had even convinced myself that I hadn't, I had still done it willfully. This time the guilt weighed upon me; no shrugging it off. It was a nasty feeling, even though I still knew nothing really wrong had been done.

"So our decision is that you are grounded: three weeks for being secretive about your horse activities and three weeks for being irresponsible. No after school or weekend activities, no friends over, no cell phone, and no riding."

"Three weeks?" I asked weakly. It seemed a very long time, but I could probably do it.

"Three weeks for each offense. Six weeks."

"Six weeks!" I squeaked. That was *forever*. "No cell phone?"

"No cell phone. You can use our home line. Your friends can call and you can call them."

"No riding?" My heart dropped a little further at the thought.

"Not while you're grounded."

"What about Gold?" I whispered.

"You can take care of him as usual," said Mom, "and I'll help. Daddy and I have had a very long talk about this. We agreed that, if you're able to stay within the boundaries of this grounding, afterward, we'll arrange for riding lessons and there will be no unreasonable restrictions on your activities with horses, Gold or otherwise, or with your friends."

"As long as we know what you're doing and who you're with, of course," added Dad.

My mind was reeling a little. This was horrible; no riding, no friends. No life. Six weeks seemed an impossibly long time. Six weeks of school would be hard enough but six weekends? On the other hand, beyond that sounded good—if I could exist past the six weeks of my sentence.

Funny how you didn't have a life until a few weeks ago, and now you don't again. No . . . that's not exactly true. I still had a phone call to make.

"We're going to count the six weeks starting this past Saturday since that's when you told Daddy about everything, which means five more weekends and the following school week. All right?" asked Mom. "Now, you had

better get back to bed. You've got a fever and I think you'd better stay home tomorrow." I started to disagree, but Mom said, "You are not going to school sick. And don't worry, we'll take care of Gold."

I shut my mouth and nodded. I didn't have the strength to argue anyway. Only one thing burned with importance right now.

"I need to make a phone call," I said, my voice raspy.

"I think you need to get to bed," said my dad.

"I promised," I whispered. "I don't want . . . people . . . worrying if I don't go to school tomorrow."

Apparently this seemed reasonable. Dad nodded and Mom smiled, looking at Dad with what looked like a *"See!"* expression.

I went upstairs to retrieve my phone. It wasn't as if I used it that much anyway, but it had been an important link to Dave. I wrote the phone numbers of Dave, Melanie, and Robin on the back of my sketchbook. Then I quickly memorized Dave's before coming back downstairs and handing the phone to my mother. I would rather she had it than my dad. My anger had cooled somewhat, but I was feeling very bruised over the whole business. And my head hurt—though I supposed that wasn't my dad's fault.

"Not too long, okay?" said Mom.

I nodded and went to the phone, dialed the number, and held my breath. I hoped this wouldn't be one of those weird calls where it seemed like I was interrupting him from something else. He answered almost right away.

"Allie! Are you okay?" The sound of his voice, saying my name and sounding concerned, melted the remains of any fears or anger I had. How on earth could I be angry at him?

"I'm okay. I've got a fever, though. I guess I'm going to be staying home tomorrow."

"Okay. I'll call you," he said.

"Um . . ." I tried to think quickly. "Um . . . could you tell Robin that I won't be using my cell phone for a while? But she can call me at home."

"Hmmm . . . gotcha," he said. "So . . . are you grounded or something?"

"Yes, that's right," I said, not wanting to discuss details over the phone. Lowering my voice, I said, "Don't tell anyone else, though. Okay?" I couldn't bear the thought of everyone knowing my humiliation.

"Of course not. Just Robin, right?"

"Right," I agreed. It seemed pointless to mention Chris. He'd know soon enough anyway. At least I had no fears that he would blab it to anyone.

"Well . . . take care of yourself, okay?"

"Okay," I said softly.

"And Allie . . ." he said, almost too softly for me to bear.

"Yes?" I closed my eyes and imagined his face, so close on the other end of the phone. I felt a little breathless.

"Don't worry."

I forced myself to breathe in and out. "Okay," I whispered. I replaced the receiver and began walking toward the stairs.

"Allie?" said Mom. I roused from the fog I was in long enough to look at her. "Are you all right? Do you want something to help you sleep?"

I nodded, then shook my head. I might not have a real life for the next six weeks but, at this moment, all was right with my world. I fell straight to sleep and didn't wake until two the next afternoon.

Chapter Twenty

Clipped

I stayed home for three days. Dad stayed home with me for the first two, though I kept to my room most of the time. I was glad to have an excuse for not being lively or talkative around him. Not that I was holding a grudge anymore—okay, maybe a little—but more because I hadn't quite figured out what the appropriate attitude was for me to take.

On the one hand, I had to admit the judgment he'd made—he *and* Mom I suppose, but I suspected mostly *he*—was reasonable and fair in a certain light. On the other hand, I still knew I hadn't really done anything to deserve it and wasn't going to be hypocritical, acting like I was happy or overly contrite about it. I planned on being good from now on, I really did, and would pay more attention to the spirit of the law as well as the letter. But even if I could have gotten a do-over, I would have told my mom about the horse sooner and done everything else pretty much the same way. I definitely wouldn't have traded away one second of the time I'd spent with Dave.

I wasn't even sure about the bully situation. I realized I probably should have told someone, but what would I have said? *"Those boys scare me?"* They hadn't actually done anything. The boy that seemed to be the main problem looked like he might avoid me from now on—except when I accidentally interrupted his cigarette breaks, of course. Hopefully I wouldn't have to worry about it anymore.

On Wednesday, I came downstairs about noon. Dad was working in his office just off the living room, his door standing open, so he saw me go and sit on the couch.

From his doorway, he asked, "How are you feeling?"

I had turned the television on and was flipping through the channels. "Sick," I said, watching the stations flash by.

"I didn't get a chance to tell you yesterday . . . you were asleep most of the day . . . but I asked Dr. Emory and Chris to come over later. We'll be discussing what's best for the horse . . . and everybody. This closely concerns you too, so you might want to, you know, get dressed. Or something."

It sounded like a good idea so I nodded, but I honestly didn't care much at the moment. I just didn't feel well. About two-thirty I figured I should probably take a shower—if I *had* to see people, I'd best be clean—and, still feeling chilled afterward, dressed in sweats. I left my hair loose to dry and rested on the couch, glasses off, eyes closed, until I heard a truck drive up and the doorbell ring. Dad had closed himself back in his office sometime before, so I got up and answered the door.

It was Chris. I still didn't have my glasses on, but something in his expression looked wrong, as if I'd surprised him somehow. And I thought his face looked slightly pink, but it was probably just from all the sun he'd gotten over the weekend. Perhaps I'd been too sick or mad to notice it before.

"Hey," he said. His eyes had already slid away from me, as they always did. *Whatever. I don't like you much right now either.*

"Hi," I responded, then stepped back to let him in.

My dad came out of his office and nodded to Chris. "Glad you could make it," he said. "Can I get you something?" He looked and sounded like he felt awkward.

I was feeling dizzy so went back to the couch, not wanting to have to make small talk. I sat with my bare feet pulled up and my arms wrapped around my knees.

"No, thanks," said Chris. He sat in the chair closest to the front door and farthest away from me.

Luckily for all of us, another vehicle was heard outside almost immediately and Dr. James soon joined us. Both Chris and Dad seemed relieved. I rested my forehead on my knees and wished I could just go back to bed. They didn't talk long; everything was very businesslike. That's one thing I

had observed about most of the men I knew—they seemed to like to cut to the heart of a matter and move on. At the moment, that suited me just fine.

It was decided that a temporary paddock would be set up beyond the back lawn. It would be easily visible from the house, but far enough away to be safe and keep flies and vermin as far from our living space as possible.

Chris said his family had plenty of portable corral panels we could use for as long as we needed. He also suggested that, since I was sick and it was a job that needed to be done, he should take on the task of cleaning the paddock at least every couple of days. Especially while Gold was still down by the creek. Everyone now seemed to take it for granted that he originated from a traditional and probably affluent horse farm or ranch and assumed he would have experience with this. It was something necessary that Chris could do around him without having to get too close. He would figure out a schedule that worked around school, soccer, his job, and whatever duties he had at home. And he would only be here during evenings and weekends when at least one of my parents were home. This last point seemed unnecessarily particular but, for the sake of my future freedom, I was happy to go along with it. It wasn't like it would matter to either Chris or me.

When I was feeling better, I would resume feeding and grooming Gold and working with him in the corral with the halter and lead. Gradually, but as soon as possible, I would begin leading him outside the corral and eventually bring him up to his new enclosure.

"We can probably come on Saturday evening to set the paddock up," said Chris. "We're helping at a show during the day."

Hearing this, I perked up a little and actually looked at him. The word *we* stood out and sounded full of potential. Then I remembered—grounded. Allowing Chris to be around at all was probably already sitting uncomfortably with my dad. Allowing Dave here as well? Too much to hope for.

I had looked away but could tell Chris was still watching me. I was sure he'd read my thoughts; it had probably been obvious to anyone paying attention.

He surprised me though, when he said, "I'm not trying to bend your rules at all regarding . . . visitors . . . but would it be all right if my brother helped with the corral? We work well together and he's interested too . . . in the horse."

Was Chris really doing that? For me? Trying to get on my good side? *Like he cares. He must have his own motives.*

"Yes, that'll be all right . . . just for the corral. I'll be around to help too," said Dad. He looked like he was going to say more, but glanced at Dr. James and changed his mind. It was probably something that needed to be said in private.

I didn't care. I hid my face against my knees again and smiled. *Something in my otherwise bleak immediate future to look forward to!*

The guys continued to discuss Gold, including changing his feed to help build his weight back up, and conjectured concerning his story. Now that it was obvious he was special and very well-trained, the possibilities were more limited than I'd once considered. I lost interest when they started talking about potential legal issues.

"Dad," I said, addressing him personally for the first time in days, "I'm going back to bed."

He nodded.

I turned to Dr. James and tried to smile. "Thank you, Dr. James. For everything."

"My pleasure, Allison," he said, smiling.

I looked at Chris, but he was looking at a spot located somewhere under Dr. James' chair.

Fine. Whatever.

I turned to go, then stopped and sighed. I couldn't do it; like it or not, I owed him. Turning back, I stepped closer to Chris. It caused him to look up long enough for me to look him in the eyes and say, "Thanks."

"Yeah," he said softly, nodding his head slightly, then he looked back at the ground again. He looked different somehow, but I wasn't sure why. Younger or something.

I shrugged it off and went back to bed.

When Mom came home, I came back downstairs. She had a folder and some books for me.

"Robin and Dave stopped by the pool and brought homework for you. They are such considerate friends," she said, happily. "I guess Robin got the assignments from the classes you have together, but Dave got your English and Science assignments, and books in case you didn't have them. I was *very* impressed with their thoughtfulness."

This last remark was said pointedly and no doubt aimed at Dad. In spite of the fever still making me feel unwell, I managed to smile, though I wondered what Miss Sanders would make of Dave's "thoughtfulness." I also made myself eat something before returning to bed and then slept through the night.

By Thursday, my fever had gone down, though I was left with a cough. Dad went to work in Sacramento and Mom went to work at noon as usual. It was nice to be home alone. I got all my homework done and made myself eat, though I wasn't hungry at all. I was starting to feel a little more clear-headed and like myself again, but also a little embarrassed as I thought over what had happened Monday.

Did I really say all those things to Chris? And he actually *carried* me to his truck? If only I hadn't come down sick that particular day! If my body had been stronger, it would have saved me—and him—annoyance at the very least. All the more reason to continue riding, right? I could only get stronger, and surely I owed that to myself. Of course, I had been angry at the time, not embarrassed, but now I was thinking how odd it must have appeared to anyone watching us. Hopefully no one had been.

And the whole confrontation—thing. It was so unlike me. Then to hold a grudge against him? And my dad too? What was wrong with me? Maybe I was losing my mind. I was feeling normal enough now, though.

I still thought Chris was the weirdest person I'd ever known, but I wasn't mad at him anymore. Not that he'd care one way or the other, I was sure, but I didn't like feeling mad at people or feeling that they were mad at me. Not people I knew and cared about.

Those others, the ones who seemed to have a problem with me simply because I existed, well, I'd been dealing with their kind for a long time. I wasn't going to let them get me down too much now. Especially not since I was more and more convinced that Dave accepted me, was on my side, no matter what. He'd said so, and it was obviously important to him that I knew it and believed it too. So I would. I hoped that I would see him at school the next day, but if not, he was supposed to come on Saturday with Chris. It was enough.

About four o'clock I decided to call Melanie, just to let her know why I'd been gone and to see what I'd missed in Art. A woman with a slight accent answered the phone and I asked for my friend.

"May I ask who is calling, please?" she asked in a hushed voice.

"This is Allison . . . from school," I said.

"Oh . . . hello, Allison. I don't think I have met you. I am afraid Melanie is not well and is asleep right now. But I will tell her you called."

I thought about how my friends had been thinking of me and asked, "Would you like me to pick up any work for her?"

"No, thank you. She has a friend taking care of that already."

"Oh . . . okay," I said, wondering who her friend was. "May I call again this weekend?" I asked.

"That would be fine." She hung up the phone before I could say anything more, but I didn't think she had meant to be rude. She just sounded very worried. I wondered if Melanie had become sick when I did.

Next, I called Robin.

"Hey," she said. "How are you feeling?"

"Better. I think I can come to school tomorrow."

"Good. Hey, what happened between you and Chris?"

I suppose I should have expected that, but I had thought it water under the bridge. "Nothing really. We're cool . . . I think." I wasn't holding a grudge anymore. It hadn't even occurred to me to wonder whether Chris was. "Why?"

She was silent for a moment, then said, "He wouldn't say everything that happened, only that you were sick and he drove you to your mom. But the next day. . . ."

"The next day what?"

"Well . . . it was really funny, but you know how girls are always trying to get Chris' attention and hanging out so close to him, and he just ignores them and it drives them nuts?"

I couldn't help laughing a little; that's exactly what always happened. "Yes."

"Well, on Tuesday, Dave and Chris and a few of the other guys got called to the office. Someone had seen them over at Northfield and told the principal, and they had also been in touch with the principal over at Lowell. I guess some of the Northfield guys had got called in there and some here. There were bruises on all sides, but nobody would say anything so they got off with

warnings that if it happened again, they'd be suspended and kicked off their respective teams for the season. Maybe worse. Pretty serious. At lunch, all the guys were asking about what was going on and everything, but the girls were acting like Chris had the plague or something. Like they were afraid to approach him but even more obsessed with him, you know? It was creepy."

"Hmmm," I murmured, mostly to prove I was listening. The idiosyncrasies of the fangirls were beyond my desire or ability to comprehend.

"But then Jessie asked where *you* were . . . which I thought was weird because, you know, she hasn't exactly been missing you before now. So anyway, I said you were sick and asked her why she wanted to know. She said she'd heard you'd been in a big argument with Chris, like you were mad at him for ignoring you or something. Then he grabbed you and carried you to his truck and drove away, and nobody's seen you since."

"You've got to be kidding," I whispered.

I replayed that scene over in my mind. I'd kept my voice down, hadn't I? *No one was that close. Not close enough to hear. At least I didn't think so.*

"I was mad at him, about Dave and driving him so he could fight. I don't even know why I did it. I just wasn't feeling good at all. And then I just . . . I don't know . . . ran out of energy. I was walking away and almost fell. He caught me. Then I couldn't make my legs work and I was feeling really dizzy . . . I guess I had a fever . . . so he carried me to the truck. That's all. You know the rest."

I remembered Chris swearing in annoyance as he caught me. I hadn't thought too much about it, but I guess I'd assumed he swore because helping me that way was distasteful to him. Did he know people would jump to conclusions about us? Was *that* why? That was probably the last thing he wanted. *What a joke!*

"Man . . . you should hear some of the rumors," she said.

"What! Like what?"

"Just . . . stupid. You know. I feel sorry for Chris, though. Yesterday the girls had gone from being standoffish to being all over him. It was disgusting. Dave thought it was pretty funny, but it's really annoying. We haven't seen him much since then. The guys said he's been helping coach during lunch, just laying low. You'd probably better do the same when you come back."

This is getting old. Putting up with Dave's groupies is one thing, but now Chris' too? That's just not fair to either of us. I remembered how I'd thought Chris had told Dave to avoid me, to play down rumors that I was dating him or something—or at least, that was what I had assumed. *And now people are thinking Chris and I . . . ? Maybe that's poetic justice. And maybe* that's *why he swore.*

It would have been funny except that, well, it just wasn't. And hardly poetic justice for me. I felt like I was getting the raw end of the deal all the way around; grounded at home and *still* a pariah at school.

Friday was pretty much everything I thought it would be. Scandalized looks and lowered voices in the corridors: *"That's the girl that. . . ."* Curious stares in Algebra. Random blows from lacrosse rackets during PE that wounded my sensibilities more than my body. Whispers in English and grieved glances from Miss Sanders. Who knows what she was thinking. A raised eyebrow from Mr. Payne along with various other reactions from the students in study hall. These last, at least, were tempered by Robin's stalwart presence. The only highlight was lunch.

Melanie hadn't been in PE so I didn't think twice about heading directly to the library, though I took the long way to avoid the maximum number of people. I sat in the same place as before, at the back of the building, and pretended to work on an English assignment. About halfway through the lunch period, I heard steps behind me and Dave sat down across from me at the small table.

"How are you doing?" he asked in his softest voice.

That question could have referred to several different aspects of my life right now. But the only thing going through my head was how his voice, speaking that softly to me, always felt like a caress and tended to rob me of the ability to form . . . coherent . . . um. . . .

I realized I was staring when his brows rose inquiringly. "Are you feeling better?"

"Oh! Yes," I said. "Yes, much better, thanks."

"So . . . grounded," he scrunched up his face.

I nodded. "Six weeks."

"That's pretty harsh," he said. "And no phone?"

I nodded, then wanted to clarify, "But I can use the house phone. Just no cell phone. No—"

"Privacy," he finished for me.

"Yes."

"No scheming or plotting."

I looked up at that, startled.

His eyes were twinkling and he laughed. "After all, you're obviously such a devious person."

Maybe. I probably could be . . . for the right incentive.

I smiled, then frowned, remembering what Robin had told me. "I'm sorry you got in trouble."

He looked confused. "In trouble for what?"

I looked at his face, especially where the scrape had been. It was barely discernible now, but I touched the corresponding spot on my own face.

"You know. . . ." I didn't want to have to say it.

"Oh," he said. Then he shrugged and said, "No trouble."

"But there could have been!" I said, urgently but with my voice lowered. "You could have really been hurt. Or something terrible could have happened."

"You worry too much," he said, dismissively.

I felt a spark of the anger I'd felt earlier in the week and was surprised.

"Please," I said, looking him in the eye. I didn't know how much he'd care, but I wanted him to know I meant it. "Please, don't ever do that again."

He returned my gaze defiantly at first as if I'd annoyed him, but then the look softened, to the point that I was quickly becoming distracted by other thoughts. I broke eye contact.

"I can't promise that," he said softly, "but I doubt if those guys will bother you again. If they do, though, you have to tell me."

"If they do," I said, "I'll tell *somebody*."

He regarded me silently for a moment, then smiled and said, "Hmm."

We continued talking until the bell rang. I told him what my dad, Chris, and Dr. James had discussed about Gold. He told me about the show they would be going to over the weekend. It sounded like they were going to be very busy, and I felt a little bad for adding to their already full schedule. But not *too* bad. I couldn't be sorry when it meant I'd get to see him, for almost whatever reason—as long as he wasn't hurt or in trouble.

When the bell rang, he stood up and said, "Come on, I'll walk you."

"What?" I was surprised. I thought the object was for him to *not* be seen with me. "Are you sure?"

He gave me a baffled look and said, as if I was asking him the stupidest question ever, "Yeah."

I felt my cheeks go from whatever shade of pink they already were just from talking to him, to several shades darker at the sheer pleasure the gesture gave me. *Does he really have no idea how I feel about him?* If he did, he hid it well. He certainly never seemed to be purposely trying to make me feel anything for him. I just did.

A certain measure of harmony had resettled over my home and family relationships. I was trying very hard to act the way I always had, especially around Dad, but it was difficult. I just wasn't the same person, and I felt I was still changing; a work in progress.

On Saturday, I spent most of the morning with Gold. I took my CD player when I went to feed him and let it blast as I brushed his body and set to work again on his tail. Unfortunately, I had to start pretty much from scratch as, having lost most of the week, his tail had become almost as tangled as it was to start with. Luckily he didn't seem to mind the music and it helped to have a rhythm to work to.

When I finished, I practiced leading him around. He was very good, always stopping when I did and never trying to be the leader. I thought I'd experiment and began to run slowly; he lengthened his stride. I ran a little faster; he trotted politely next to me, still not trying to take the lead or go his own way. I was thrilled. I began to wonder how he would behave outside the corral but didn't feel ready to try it. What I really wanted to do was *ride* him. I was sure I could get him to stand quietly and close enough to the fence for me to boost myself up. But I had promised. No riding. It was frustrating, but I would have to be patient.

The rest of the day wore slowly on. Dave and Chris hadn't been sure when they'd be able to come. The stock show they were at was in the Central Valley somewhere and they'd have to go back to the ranch to pick up the panels first.

A little after six-thirty, the phone rang and Mom answered it; they were on their way.

Nothing had been said about where I should be or what I should be doing while they were here, and no specific limitations had been set. So I

figured I'd at least watch from the porch unless I was told I couldn't. That didn't seem too likely. My parents weren't prone to pettiness.

Chris drove his truck down the dirt road and stopped below the lawn. The boys jumped out and pulled on thick gloves as they walked. Chris kept his gaze ahead, but Dave flashed me a broad smile before turning his full attention to the contents of the trailer. Dad joined me on the back porch to watch.

He called to them, "Do you need any help?"

"Naw. We got it," Dave called back, nodding at my dad.

Dad watched for a moment then went back into the house. The guys soon had the panels and gate set up. They placed a large metal trough at the side closest to the house and were just securing a metal feeder near the gate when the porch light came on.

Dave came toward me, pulling off his gloves, then sat on the steps just below me. Chris walked to the back of the trailer and closed it up. He was walking back to where we sat as Dad stepped out onto the porch, followed closely by Mom.

"Looks good," said Dad. Probably a completely unnecessary comment, but I guess he wanted to show appreciation somehow.

"Thank you so much for doing this for us, boys," said Mom, making up for Dad's brevity.

Chris stood silently, but Dave said, "Our pleasure." He smiled at me, eliciting the usual reaction, then smiled up at Mom.

"Would you like to have dinner with us? We have plenty and you must be hungry," said Mom.

Yes . . . yes . . . yes!

Dave looked at Chris and something passed between them, though there was no change in their expressions.

"We'd love to," said Dave, "but we've got to get the trailer back to the ranch and rejoin my dad in Stockton, so we'd better get going. Thanks for the offer, though." He smiled winningly at my parents, then walked back toward the truck with Chris. Halfway to it, he turned to walk backward, looked at me and said, "See you Monday?"

I stuttered a little, "Ye . . . ye . . . yes!" and nodded my head.

He lifted his hand and I gave a wave back, feeling self-conscious in front of my parents.

The rest of the weekend passed quickly and I spent as much of it with Gold as I thought my parents would tolerate. Monday began what felt like the first real day of my grounded life and the days that followed took on something of a regular routine and rhythm. In many ways, life now felt similar to life before Dave in that every day seemed much the same as the one before, nothing unusual or particularly exciting happened, and weekends were long and lonely.

But life would never be the same—*I* would never be the same. And even though sometimes days would pass without having any direct contact with him, Dave seemed to be thinking of me and wanting to make sure I didn't "worry."

That first Monday, Robin had relayed a message from him that I should spend lunch with them as I had before. I'm sure that he would have meant it as a suggestion, but Robin repeated it in the form of an edict and, as a loyal subject, I obeyed. Tanner, Kyle, and even Shane nodded to me in a friendly fashion, and Jessie and Stacie smiled but kept their distance. Matthew actually paid more attention to me than Dave, expressing his satisfaction at my return and saying that he'd missed me. That was nice but hardly turned my head. The one real smile Dave shot my way meant more than anything Matthew could say or do, much as I appreciated him.

On the walk back toward classes, Dave appeared at my side and walked so close that several times we bumped shoulders slightly and his arm brushed against mine. He didn't even acknowledge it when we parted ways, but he didn't need to; he'd made enough of an impression.

I chose to resume eating in the cafeteria on Tuesdays and Thursdays although Melanie didn't return to school all week. It seemed best to act normal and as if everything was the same as it had been before all the stupid assumptions and rumors. Which it was—and wasn't. I certainly didn't feel the same. Nothing drastic had happened to my reflection in my mirror, yet I thought I detected something different. I just couldn't quite put my finger on it.

Melanie returned to school the following Thursday, after missing a full week of school, and I was very happy to see her. She didn't participate in PE but waited for me while I changed. She had dark rings under her eyes and coughed, seeming very self-conscious about it.

As we walked to the cafeteria together, I asked, "Are you all right?"

"Yes," she said, coughing again. "I'm fine."

"I tried to call a few times, but your Mom always said you were sleeping. I was . . . kind of worried about you."

"My mother is overly protective," she said. "I probably could have come back to school before, but she wouldn't let me. I just . . . just have a cough now. It's nothing." She was playing with her locket.

"Okay," I said, thinking that it didn't explain anything, but I figured she would tell me what she wanted me to know.

I still wondered which friend had been taking her school work to her. The only other person I'd ever seen her close to was the boy, Roger. What was the deal there?

Dave wasn't always at the tables when I was, and sometimes a couple of days would go by without my seeing him at all, but never longer than that. It was as if he knew I'd have trouble if I didn't have contact with him. The part of me that liked to dream about impossible things liked to think that *he* didn't like to go without the contact too, but I knew deep down that was just wishful thinking.

The contact we *did* have was usually very brief but always directed specifically at me. Sometimes he would come up behind me and gently tug or flip my braid, or if we were walking, he'd walk close enough to brush arms or shoulders with me a couple of times. A few times he managed to do this during PE or on the walk back toward the changing rooms. But otherwise, we watched for each other, making eye contact long enough for me to know he'd seen me.

It was enough—barely. A couple of times at the end of lunch he managed to pass notes to me—random but funny observations about things that had happened or that he'd seen. I tried to reply back as wittily as I could but always felt lame. I kept the notes though.

Robin sometimes told me of things that he'd said or done in the classes she shared with him, which I appreciated. I wondered if she told him things about me, though nothing of interest ever seemed to happen in our classes. About once a week I went to the library. He always met me there for at least a few minutes and we'd catch up with each other a little. I told him about Gold. He talked about everything going on his life, which always seemed ridiculously busy. His soccer team hadn't lost a game. He'd won some cash prizes at a horse show or rodeo. They'd been surfing or spent the day at a dirt bike course or a skateboard park. Always something.

On the days Dave wasn't at the tables, Matthew always made himself available for conversation and what seemed like just lending us his physical presence, as if for protection of some kind. I wondered if Dave had asked him to watch out for me—us. The other boys often gathered around us too.

Stacie and Jessie, while not going out of their way to draw me into conversation, seemed to accept my presence as *de rigueur*. Some of the other girls continued to glare or flash dirty looks my way, but nobody did anything overtly mean. I ignored them. Occasionally I would see one of the boys that I'd had run-ins with before but, except for Varsity Jacket, they never even acknowledged my presence. As for Varsity Jacket, I just walked in the opposite direction whenever I saw him, and he didn't go out of his way to find me.

Chris was never at the tables when I was, so I didn't know whether he was avoiding the area completely or just when I was there. I knew he was spending time with Gold because I saw the evidence: fresh loads of hay, manure-free paddock, and multiplying tire tracks near the corral. But he didn't draw attention to himself. He was obviously extremely busy—even more so than Dave—and I never wanted to get in his way anyway.

I continued to work with Gold on the lead and began to walk him outside the corral. The first day I did this I was very nervous. What if he got scared and pulled away from me? What if he *didn't* get scared and pulled away from me because he wanted to be free again? I tried to stay calm as I tied him to the fence rail with the quick-release knot that Dave had shown me, then walked to the gate. I pulled aside the lower pole first and kept an eye on Gold. He kept an eye on me too. Taking a deep breath and bracing myself for whatever might happen, I removed the top pole. Gold watched with interest but calmly swished his tail and waited for me to go back to him. I untied him, turned him, and headed toward the gate. He walked calmly beside me as if we did this every day. We didn't go far the first day. Gold wasn't nervous, but I was. I extended the walks a little more every day.

When I told Dave about it, during one of our rendezvous in the library, he suggested I begin bringing him closer to the house and then put him in the new paddock for short periods, just to get him used to it. This sounded like an excellent idea. I told my parents and did as he said.

Thick plywood appeared over a part of the cattle guard, which I assumed Chris had brought so that I could lead Gold over it. Apart from dropping his head to look more closely at it as we crossed, Gold's behavior remained impeccable, never giving me a moment of anxiety. He was extremely interested in exploring the new territory. When we finally got right up to the house, his eyes and ears were alert, his nostrils wide, but his body remained calm; no dancing or pulling as I'd seen other horses do when they were nervous.

The day after I told Dave about bringing Gold all the way up to the house, Chris appeared in the evening next to the steel paddock, filling the metal trough with the garden hose. I wandered out to the back porch to say hi. It seemed like ages since I'd seen him.

"How are you doing?" I asked, just trying to be polite.

He looked at me briefly but steadily, then nodded his head and went back to watching the water flow into the trough.

I felt awkward but figured I needed to be able to talk to him. I'd be bumping into him more once I'd brought Gold up here to stay.

"How is it going with Gold?" I asked. I hadn't seen him around Gold at all since those first visits and hadn't thought too much about it—until now.

"Making progress," he said, without looking at me. "He doesn't freak out when I clean the paddock. I'm giving him a supplement. It's good for his skin and coat. He looks forward to that. Right now I put it in the feeder, but I'll try and get him to take it out of the bucket while I hold it." He looked at me and shrugged. "We'll see."

I didn't know how I felt about that. I was convinced Chris only wanted what was best for Gold and that what he was doing was important for a lot of reasons. Yet it gave me an odd feeling. Jealousy? That was nonsensical.

"I brought alfalfa up," he said. "You might want to start feeding him here in the evening. It'll help him get used to it faster. And your dad should spend some time visible to him. That way he won't freak when he does see him."

This sounded reasonable and I shared the information with my parents.

Every evening during that school week, I walked Gold up to the house and put him in the paddock, feeding him the alfalfa that now resided on a wooden pallet under another tarp, just out of his reach. He quickly adapted to the new enclosure and I told my parents I planned to bring him up for good on Saturday.

This all went according to plan. Saturday evening Chris brought the remaining hay up from the corral, as well as the long-tined rake and shovel he used to clean it. Gold watched us with interest but seemed no more perturbed by Chris' proximity than mine. This was a good thing, yet I still had ambivalent feelings about it.

"Do you have a wheelbarrow?" Chris asked.

"A wheelbarrow? I'm . . . not sure. Why?"

"It'll make cleaning his paddock easier."

I asked my Dad. Apparently we had one in the garage and we could use it. He followed me outside to talk to Chris, and they picked a spot near the dirt road to start a manure dump. Then Chris said he'd be back in a couple of days and left.

The following Monday, the third week of my sentence, I joined Robin in going to the tables. Dave wasn't there, but Matthew came over immediately.

"So, are you coming?" he asked, looking expectantly back and forth between us.

"To what?" I asked.

"What are you talking about?" asked Robin.

"To my birthday, of course. Next Saturday. Well, my birthday's actually Thursday, but the party's Saturday. Don't tell me you forgot," he said, frowning.

"Oh yeah," said Robin. "No, of course I didn't."

"I . . . didn't know about it," I said, feeling a little guilty but sure I had never heard about it. I would have remembered being invited to a friend's party.

"What?" Matthew said, looking at me and grabbing his chest dramatically. "I'm grieved. I asked you guys to ask her! Oh well, I'll ask you now. My house, this Saturday, high noon to whenever."

"Thank you for inviting me," I said, feeling grateful but very awkward. "I'm afraid I don't think I can come." As far as I knew, Matthew didn't know about my current social activity status and I didn't want to have to explain it.

He didn't let it go that easily. "Why not?"

"You're being nosy," said Robin, annoyed.

"It's okay," I said. "I . . . did something my parents weren't happy about and I'm grounded . . . next weekend." There was no need to say how long I was grounded. That would certainly elicit too much curiosity.

"Bummer," he said, looking genuinely disappointed.

After school I told my mother about Matthew's birthday but didn't mention the party; there didn't seem to be much point. But I did want to get him something. He'd been a good friend, and I wanted him to know that I valued his friendship. I had no idea what to buy a boy, especially one I didn't know that well. But I remembered our time at the library and the way he talked in general, and I thought a book might be appropriate. I arranged to walk to the pool after school one day so Mom and I could shop a little. Unfortunately, it was a day that Dave had left early for a soccer game, but Robin walked with me. I ended up getting Matthew a birthday card and a gift card from a bookstore.

On Thursday, I explained to Melanie that I had to talk to a friend whose birthday it was, and then joined the kids at the table.

I gave Matthew the envelope and said, "Happy birthday. I'm sorry I can't come to the party, but I hope you have a good time."

He looked into my eyes and it occurred to me for the first time that perhaps he liked me a little more than I had realized.

Suddenly Dave was by his side, grinning at me, his arm slung over his friend's shoulders. "Of course he'll have a good time. We'll make sure of that."

Matthew grimaced back at him and tried to sock him in the ribs, but Dave was too quick and jumped out of the way, laughing.

Friday night the phone rang. Mom answered it and seemed overjoyed at who was on the other end. I didn't pay too much attention and wandered outside to watch Gold as the sun went down. He was settling in very well and seemed to enjoy having people nearby. Mom joined me on the porch shortly after.

"You didn't tell me Matthew was having a party," she said, accusingly. "That was Patricia Morris. I guess Matthew asked her to call to see if you could be let off for a while 'for good behavior.'" It sounded like something Matthew would say. She apparently thought it was funny as she laughed.

"I assumed I wouldn't be able to go, so I didn't bother to ask," I said.

"Well, I think *maybe* we can make an exception. Friends don't have birthdays every day, after all. I'll talk to Daddy, okay? I think you *have* been very good."

She smiled and kissed my forehead as she got up to go back in the house. Dad had been gone most of the week—Los Angeles again. I wondered what he would say. Maybe—*maybe . . . I might actually get to go. And if I get to go. . . .* I felt a little ashamed that I had an ulterior motive, knowing Dave would be there, but I did want to go for Matthew's sake too.

Dad agreed that I could attend the party for a couple of hours. I think I owed my boon more to the fact that Mom and Dad both liked the Morrises and thought Matthew a "very nice boy" than to any good behavior on my part, but I wasn't going to quibble about it.

Mom had left it up to me when I would like to go, so I decided, if the party started at twelve o'clock, *everyone* should be there by two, right? Just in case. The early October day was still very warm, so I decided to wear shorts and a nice t-shirt. And my Converse of course; I rarely wore anything else anymore.

"Do you have your bathing suit on?" asked Mom when I came downstairs, ready to go.

I probably looked at her as if I thought she was crazy.

"You know it's a pool party, right?" she asked, and I felt the color drain from my face.

"No, I didn't know," I almost whispered. This was awful. There was no way I was exposing myself to—well, *everybody*—in a bathing suit. I was likely to feel self-conscious as it was. "Well, I'm only staying a couple of hours. It's fine."

"Okay," said Mom, doubtfully. She knew how much I loved to swim.

I ran upstairs and exchanged my Converse for flip flops.

The Morrises lived on the west side of town, apparently closer to Northfield than to Douglas. Mom had some shopping she wanted to do, so she dropped me off and said she'd be back in a couple of hours. Feeling nervous as I walked to the front door, I could hear laughter and loud voices coming from somewhere behind the house.

A tall girl with dark hair answered the door. I'd seen her once before at the restaurant; one of Matthew's older sisters, I assumed. She looked me up and down rather insolently.

"Oh," she said in a bored voice. "They're out back." She walked away leaving the door open.

I felt uncomfortable entering a house I didn't know, but stepped in and closed the door. Mrs. Morris came around the corner just as I was wondering exactly where to go.

"Allison!" she gushed. "It *is* Allison, right? I'm so thrilled you could make it! Matthew was so afraid you wouldn't be able to come."

"Oh," I said, not sure what to say. "I'm . . . I'm glad I could come too."

"Well, come this way," she said, leading the way through a large, open and airy living room to a back wall that seemed mostly glass. The two center doors stood open to the outside, and sounds of boys laughing, girls squealing, and loud splashing invaded the room.

The large, covered patio had tables covered in serving dishes. The chairs were padded and comfy-looking, and a barbecue stood at one end, coals hot and ready. The enormous yard was occupied almost completely by a huge, oddly-shaped pool, a wide expanse of surrounding concrete, and more furniture, including a couple of canvas canopies.

"Allie!" I heard Robin's voice call. She was in the pool but pulled herself out, then walked to me, dripping. She looked very cute in a one-piece. "You made it!" She seemed really glad to see me.

"Hey!" said Matthew, making his way over as well. He looked like he *had* been wet but was already drying out. "I was glad your mom said you could come. Did you wear your suit? The water's nice and warm!"

He was trying to make it sound enticing, but I wasn't interested. I *was* feeling self-conscious again, though. I was obviously the only one not going in the water. I followed Robin and Matthew over to join another group near the pool. While listening to their chatter, I looked around to see if I knew anyone else. Some were kids I sometimes saw at the tables, but others I'd never seen before.

Robin noticed me looking around and said, "Most of the soccer team's here, and their girlfriends if they've got them. I don't know a lot of the others. Friends of his from different classes, I guess."

I recognized Jessie and Stacie, both in the pool and staying close to Dave. I'd noticed him almost right away but was trying not to be obvious in watching him.

After a short while, I noticed Matthew's dad was standing by the barbe-cue, and delicious aromas soon began to entice us in its direction. Kyle and Tanner, who had also been in the pool, got out and wandered over toward the patio. The girls around our table were looking that way as well.

"Hungry?" asked Matthew.

I admitted that I was and stood up to follow him, but at the same time, Dave was pulling himself out of the pool close by. So close, in fact, that I would have to pass by him to get to the patio. I couldn't ignore him—not that I wanted to. He looked amazing, just the way I had pictured him when I had imagined him surfing: his hair dark and curly from the water, small rivulets streaming down his chest and arms, his eyes sparkling happily. I felt suddenly more shy than usual.

"So you made it," he said, coming to stand right in front of me. "Where's your bathing suit?"

"I . . . I can't stay long." I mumbled. "I wasn't planning on swimming, so I didn't wear one."

He looked at me with narrowed eyes for a moment, then made a *hnh* kind of sound and walked past me.

Robin took his place and started to say something, but I was suddenly grabbed around the waist and plunged into the pool, held close by strong arms. My glasses fell off as soon as I hit the water, and if I hadn't been com-pletely sure it was Dave, I might have panicked. Instead, I turned around to face him when he finally let go. His face looked so funny under the water—looking so much younger and just like Henry—that I couldn't help laughing and had to force myself up, having lost all my air.

He broke the surface at the same time as me wearing a self-satisfied grin. He grabbed my flip-flops, floating nearby, then swam to the edge, still beating me there. Waiting until I'd reached the edge next to him, he got out quickly, then reached down to help me.

"You're lucky she can swim," scolded Robin. "What if she couldn't? What if that's why she didn't wear a suit?"

I was amazed at her outburst. *Is that what she'd been thinking?*

Dave looked at her indulgently. "Of course she can swim. Her mom works at the pool, doesn't she? Besides," he added, looking back at me and smirking a little, "I would have rescued her."

Robin rolled her eyes, stepped forward and pushed him hard, causing him to fall back into the pool. She then linked her arm in mine and said, "Come on, Allie. Food."

Mr. Morris had made delicious hamburgers as well as hot dogs, Polish sausage, and some kebab style vegetables which were wonderful. We all ate our fill on the patio, then sat around talking. Dave had retrieved my flip-flops again, as well as my glasses, and gave them back to me. He and Tanner were the first ones back in the pool. Robin soon followed and I went to sit on the edge with my feet dangling in the water. Whenever Dave came near, I pulled them out—just in case—which seemed to amuse him greatly, but he made no more moves to dunk me.

Matthew came and sat next to me for a while and made me laugh a lot. My parents were right; he really was a nice boy. I noticed Dave seemed to be keeping an eye on us, but he made no move to interfere. When my mother arrived, I got up to leave. Dave swam over and got out of the pool.

"It's my birthday at the end of the month," he said, sitting at the edge of the pool and looking at me steadily. "You'll come to the party."

I liked his confidence and was thrilled at the demand—er, invitation—to be there, but wasn't as assured.

"I . . . I hope I can," I said, sincerely.

He looked me in the eye for a long moment. Then he smiled his wicked smile. "You'll be there."

He watched as I said goodbye to Robin and Matthew. I thanked Mrs. Morris for inviting me and turned once more to look back at the pool. He was still sitting on the side, watching. Several people called goodbye and waved to me, causing several more, some I had just met today for the first time, to do likewise. I felt somewhat restored. My friends liked me if no one else did, and I thought the new people I'd met today were not likely to disavow the acquaintance in the future.

I was happy and content as we drove home, though I made up an accident to account for my damp clothes and hair. Not that Mom would have been angry about Dave pushing me in. She probably would have laughed. But the memory of him holding me close—much more intimate in retrospect than it had seemed at the time—was too personal for me to want to refer, even lightly, to the incident. I'd keep it to myself. And now I had another event to wonder about, perhaps look forward to—Dave's birthday.

Most of my thoughts for the rest of that weekend, however, revolved around a certain pair of strong arms and soft, brown eyes.

Chapter Twenty-One

So Close

Life, at least school life, continued in the same pattern and basic routines that it had before Matthew's birthday. That day, the first Saturday of October, had marked the beginning of the fourth week and the exact halfway point of my restricted status, so it was actually something of a milestone for me.

I thought I had done pretty well so far with the help of my friends, especially Dave of course, who continued to make sure we had contact at least every couple of days. I don't think it could have been obvious to anyone else except perhaps Robin, who seemed to accept my need for that contact without question or judgment. Even she might not have been completely aware of its extent, though, were the truth known, I suspected she had a similar need. And I never knew for sure *when* I'd see Dave, but I'd stopped fretting about *whether* I'd see him or hear from him. I knew I would.

I was still treated coldly or completely ignored by all the popular girls, but it seemed to be a sort of general animosity and not for any new, specific offenses.

That week I became aware of a slight buzz around school and soon posters began appearing to announce a fall dance. This took hold of my imagination a little too much. If others had known my mind, they might have thought, *"She's such a klutz and so* not *athletic. How could she even think of dancing?"* I sometimes asked myself the same question. But the fact was I did. Think of dancing that is. In spite of my general lack of coordination and athleticism, I had a great sense of rhythm, and when I put my mind to it, I could learn repetitive steps and moves and get into the music with the best of them. Okay, maybe not the best, but it was something I wasn't afraid to try and enjoy. It probably helped that my parents enjoyed dancing, and my dad had danced with me when I was younger.

Unfortunately, it wasn't something I'd ever had a chance to do socially or in any organized fashion. But I could boogie like nobody's business in the privacy of my bedroom, or once in a while when I was grooming Gold and was sure nobody would see. I had great tunes, too, though Robin had shaken her head over my eclectic collection of CDs, complaining she'd never heard of most of the bands.

Doing the math, I realized I would still be grounded on the day of the dance, but that didn't stop me from daydreaming about it and practicing behind my closed door. Of course, the only real reason I would want to go was if a *certain* someone asked me. And, of course, he knew the terms of the prohibition placed on me so, unless he forgot, which wouldn't be typical of him, he wouldn't ask. I didn't know if he even liked dancing anyway, but it was fun to fantasize about it and certainly helped pass the time.

Overhearing some of the other girls talking about it at lunch one day, I asked Robin, "Are you going to the dance?"

She screwed her face up and looked like I'd asked her if she were going to the moon. "Hardly." Then she frowned at me. "Do you want to go?"

"I don't know," I said, not wanting to admit the truth. "I've never been to a dance."

This was true. Dances had been organized for the junior and senior classes of my old school, but nothing for the lower grades or middle school. The fall dance here at Douglas High was open to freshmen through seniors; one of the advantages of being at a small school, I suppose. Dave wasn't around today, but the other boys were sitting close by and Matthew had overheard us.

"Remember the dances we had in middle school?"

The other boys groaned or laughed.

"Kinda lame," said Kyle.

"Yeah," said Tanner, "where's the fun in 'no contact'?"

They all muttered their agreement.

I must have looked puzzled so Matthew explained. "Our principal didn't allow physical contact while dancing, so you couldn't hold hands or waists

or anything at any time during the dance, and no one danced to slow songs at all. Very lame. She was just paranoid."

"Yeah, and parents had to drop you off and pick you up at the door. You couldn't get in or out otherwise," said Kyle.

"I don't remember you going to any of the dances," Tanner said to Robin.

"That's because I didn't," said Robin, crossly. "I don't dance."

That put a damper on the conversation and the topic changed.

Several days later Robin and I were sitting on the grass—it was one of those days when people had come out of the woodwork and the tables were overflowing—and the topic came up again. Dave was there this time. Though he was sitting on the table some distance away, we more or less faced each other which made eye contact easy.

Another boy came up and ventured to ask Robin if she was going to the dance, but she blushed and looked annoyed, repeating the claim that she didn't dance. Tanner and Kyle had apparently asked Jessie and Stacie, though I wasn't sure who was going with whom, and they were discussing whether they would dress up or go for a more casual look. Casual dress was acceptable at this dance, but students were expected to dress up for winter formal and the prom later in the year. While proms were reserved for juniors and seniors and their guests, the winter formal was also open to the lower grades. I was very interested in having another chance to go to a dance this year.

When the bell rang, we all stood up to go, said, "Bye," and went our separate ways. I found Matthew walking beside me.

"I wanted to ask if you'd consider going to the dance with me," he said.

He actually sounded shy and formal, unlike him, and I was taken by surprise—delighted but a little nonplussed. On the one hand, though I had started to feel that Matthew might like me, I hadn't even considered going to the dance with anyone besides Dave. On the other, I was extremely flattered that Matthew would ask and wasn't sure that, had it been possible, I wouldn't have accepted. I was trying to come up with a good reason why I couldn't go, without sounding like I didn't want to go with *him*, when Dave walked up and draped his arm over his friend's shoulder.

"She's not going, my friend," he said, as if consoling him.

"How do *you* know?" asked Matthew, frowning and looking annoyed at the interruption.

"Robin told me she doesn't like to dance," he said, looking steadily at me, his eyes glittering, a little dangerously I thought. "Right, Allie?"

I was already feeling off-balance from the invitation. This was pushing me over the edge. I didn't know what to do except agree with him.

"Oh. Right," I said. I had the presence of mind to add, "Thank you for asking me, though." I cared about Matthew and didn't want him to feel bad that I wouldn't go with him. At least it was true that I wasn't going at all.

Dave and Matthew walked off together, though Matthew had forcibly shed Dave's arm. I continued to class but was completely distracted all afternoon with thinking over the interaction.

I could have said no on my own. Was Dave really trying to be helpful? Or was he interfering for his own reasons? He had been very devious in what he'd said to his best friend, which I found disturbing. After all, *I* wasn't the one who didn't like dancing, but he'd made it sound like I was. In effect, Matthew hadn't just heard that I couldn't accept going to *this* dance, but that I wasn't likely to accept in the future either. Is that what Dave had intended? And if so, why? Just because he didn't want me doing anything with Matthew? And did that feeling extend to others or just Matthew? Did it mean that if he could have, Dave would have asked me to the dance himself and wanted a clear opportunity to ask me in the future? I liked this scenario, but it wasn't the only one I could think of. *He's probably just trying to keep me from having to say I'm still grounded.*

In the meantime, Gold had settled into his new surroundings very well. I could tell that he was beginning to regain weight, and my daily grooming and Chris' supplement seemed to be working magic on his coat. It glistened brilliantly in the sun: a deep, rich honey-topaz color. I was still distressed about his mane and tail which, in spite of my being able to finally get most of the tangles out, still looked a dull and dirty grayish-brown.

Dr. James was coming once a week to check on him and update us on the search status. They had thought they had a lead on a horse that had gone missing in Nevada, but nothing had come of it. At least, not so far. It had sent a cold stab to my heart, though. Intellectually, I knew the day would come when Gold's true owners would be found, but it hadn't been that real to me before. The thought that someone might soon be responding to a "found" notice was unsettling to say the least.

Chris had been coming several times a week, but I stayed out of his way. I had to admit, at least to myself, to some real feelings of jealousy; apparently Gold was something—some*one*—I didn't share well with others. Chris was able to not only move around in the paddock without Gold seeming to mind, but also to stroke and pet him as he fed him the supplement. I had watched through my bedroom window most of the time, but I finally had to go down and join them.

"You're doing really well with him," I admitted, grudgingly.

Something in Chris' expression told me right away that he knew. He *knew* that I was feeling jealous. How did he *do* that?

"He's tolerating me," he said a little gruffly. But I had been watching. I got the impression that they liked each other just fine. "You've got him looking pretty good."

"I'm sure the supplement you're giving him must be helping," I conceded.

"It wouldn't be that obvious if you weren't putting the muscle into grooming him. He's starting to look more the way I think he's supposed to." He was quiet again, watching Gold move around the paddock. "There are a couple of other things we could do that would help his health and appearance," he said.

"What's that?" I asked.

"We could lunge him. It would give him more exercise and help get him really fit. He's not able to move enough in this pen."

"What does 'lunge' mean?" I'd never heard of it, but it sounded painful.

He looked apologetic—or maybe annoyed—like he'd forgotten that I was equine illiterate. "It's working him on a long line. The old corral is big enough to make a perfect lunging area. I'll bring what we need and teach you." He said this matter-of-factly, reminding me strongly of his brother and how he seemed to give commands. But then he added, "If you want."

This sounded acceptable and I nodded. "What's the other thing?"

He *almost* half-smiled. "We give him a bath."

"A bath?" Doing such a thing had never occurred to me.

"Yeah. We've got some good stuff that'll clean his mane and tail really well and make them easier to brush out too."

This sounded excellent and I nodded enthusiastically.

"Okay," he said. "We'll do it soon."

I wasn't sure what that meant, but both ideas sounded great. I'm sure he couldn't have cared less, but Chris was officially back in my good graces. I guess I *could* share Gold—at least a little.

One other thing had started to bother me: Dave's birthday. I was able to find out that his actual birthday was October 21st, which fell on a school day, but he wouldn't say any more about the party. Whenever I tried to ask, which I tried to do without seeming too desperate to know, he just grinned and said I'd find out. Very frustrating. I neither knew where nor when it would be and, most importantly, whether I'd be allowed to go.

I wondered if it would be at his home. I hadn't seen the whole house, or anything approximating a back yard, but I didn't think they had a pool. So hopefully no pool party. And if my parents had bent the rules for Matthew's party, wouldn't they have to for Dave's? I sure hoped so.

The day of the fall dance came and I was brooding a little. Melanie had admitted that she would be going but only blushed and fiddled with her locket when I asked if she was going with someone. She didn't have to be—I knew that people were going on their own and if I hadn't been grounded, I suppose I could have too—but she *was* going with someone. It also occurred to me that Dave had never said that he *wasn't* going. I spent a little while feeling low about that but finally came to the conclusion that there was no reason why he shouldn't go and enjoy himself. It wouldn't mean that he didn't care about me.

Mid-afternoon I came downstairs as my mom was getting off the phone. "I've just been talking to Cheryl. You know, next Saturday you won't be grounded anymore, so I was talking to her about lessons for you. What do you think?"

My first reaction was elation. I knew, of course, that next Saturday I was free—comparatively—but hearing Mom say it made it seem more definite. And riding! It felt like *forever* since I had, and it was something I would certainly look forward to. But then I remembered Dave's birthday. I still didn't know anything about it. Not even enough to really tell Mom about it. *So* annoying.

It was almost dinner time and I was brooding again—knowing the dance was starting soon, wondering if Dave would be going and, for the millionth time, whether I'd get asked to the next dance by *anyone*—when the phone rang. Dad was home and answered it, and I could tell immediately by his

body language and general aura of tension that the last name of the person on the other end probably started with C.

My pulse sped up and my mind wrangled with the possibilities. It could be Chris talking to Dad about "the animal." I didn't think they'd spoken about him lately and Dad liked to be kept informed. Or it could have been Mr. Caldera talking about—anything. Who knows? Or it could be Dave. I hoped it was Dave.

Dad's side of the conversation consisted mostly of thoughtful "Hmmm"s and acknowledging "Uh-huh"s, so it was impossible to get an idea of what was being communicated to him. But he finally said, "How late will this be?" and, "We'll have to talk it over." There was silence for a few moments, then, "All right. Yes, we'll let you know." Doubt that it was Dave assailed me until he continued, "Yes, she's right here," and held the phone out to me, looking stern.

My hand was shaking a little as I took it and said, quietly, "Hello?"

"Allie," Dave's voice seemed to caress me.

I bet he hadn't used that tone of voice to talk to Dad.

"Hi," I said, turning my back to my father so he couldn't see how pleased I was.

"I was just asking your dad if you can come celebrate my birthday next Saturday."

"Oh," I said, trying to keep my voice calm but wanting to squeal.

"We're going to the movies in town, then back to my house for dinner and stuff. Your parents'll let you come, right?"

"Yes, I hope so," I said, not completely sure but not seeing why they wouldn't.

"Well, call me tomorrow and tell me, okay? But you'd better call later. I think we're gone until late afternoon."

"Okay," I said, barely able to contain my delight.

I helped Mom set the table and get the meal laid out, then looked at Dad expectantly.

He cleared his throat. "Allie's invited to David Caldera's birthday next Saturday," he said to Mom. "They're going to see a PG-13 movie escorted by Alex and at least one other parent, and then going to their home for dinner and to hang out. Alex and . . . Angel, is it?"

I nodded.

"Alex and Angel will both be there to chaperon. He said there would be a large group going to the movies, but just close friends going back to the house. The movie starts at two-fifty. There's apparently no specific ending time, but he said they'd be happy to drive her home any time we wanted."

Dad had spoken stiffly, as if relaying a message verbatim and careful not to change any part of it or betray his feelings about it.

"Can I go?" I asked, practically jumping out of my chair. "*Please?*" I hated pleading but needed them left in no doubt of how much I wanted to go. I'd been good and I'd held up my end of the deal. I felt prepared to argue my case and appeal if necessary, but Mom was smiling and looking pleased.

"Seems like everyone's having a birthday, doesn't it? You'll be having yours soon, too." She smiled at me, then looked at Dad. "I have no problem at all with her going. I'm convinced they'll take good care of her, and I'm sure you'll agree that her behavior has been exemplary."

Dad nodded his head slowly. "Yes, I think it has too. And I admit that the boys have impressed me with both their thoughtfulness and their restraint. As long as things continue this way, I have no problem with you associating with them." I couldn't believe my dad had just praised the Caldera brothers. "But," he added, looking at me seriously, "you are still too young to be dating or anything close to it. Group gatherings with adults present are acceptable, but anything else better have our express approval. Is it understood?"

I happily agreed, though "restraint" wasn't a word I thought of in conjunction with the brothers. At least, not with Dave. Of course, Dad hadn't dealt much with him. Chris was the one who came across as very self-controlled, though I had my doubts about him too.

"So, I can go?" I wasn't taking any chances that I had misunderstood; I wanted to hear him *say* it.

"Yes, you can go," he said and gave me what looked like a grudging smile.

"Thank you, Daddy!" I said, leaping out of my chair and running to kiss him on the cheek and hug his neck like the little girl I knew he still wanted me to be.

"Oh!" said Mom looking stricken. "Oh well, I suppose it will wait another week."

"What?" Dad and I said at the same time.

"Riding. I had set up lessons with Cheryl for Saturdays."

"Can't I still go?" I asked. "In the morning?"

Mom gave me an indulgent look. "We'll see," she said. "I'll give her a call tomorrow."

"I'll be out of the country—I fly out to Germany on Thursday—so Mom's in charge of that weekend and everything that's going on. Don't take any liberties, okay?" Dad sounded rather severe but he needn't have worried. I wasn't about to get grounded again.

"Yes," I agreed, trying to sound obedient and smiling as I hadn't smiled at him for quite some time.

He looked at us both sternly. "I mean it."

"I know, Daddy," I said, still smiling. I couldn't help it. I had so much to look forward to!

The rest of the weekend sped by and I dutifully tried to call Dave about eight o'clock Sunday night, but Angel answered the phone and said they weren't home yet. She sounded happy to talk to me, asked how I was and said she would let him know that I called. That would have to do, I supposed. He would either call me back or I'd probably see him the next day. He didn't call back.

On Monday, there was talk about the Fall Dance, the general consensus being that it had been very nice and reasonably well-attended, though the main complaint was that more students should have gone. Apparently the chaperon-to-student ratio had been depressingly high. Melanie said she enjoyed it but didn't have much to say otherwise. I was disappointed, having hoped for details, especially about who she had gone with.

The main topic among our group now was, of course, Dave's birthday. Speculation over which movie we'd be seeing combined with whispered confidences of what individuals were getting him. I'd put quite a bit of thought into this myself but hadn't been able to decide on anything. In spite of my undeniably deep feelings for him, I didn't know him as well as his other close friends did. At least I was able to number myself among these. Seeing how many people seemed to be going to the movie, that was saying a lot.

It was plain that all the freshmen who regularly hung out during lunch were invited and probably the sophomores too, most of whom counted themselves primarily as Chris' friends but claimed acquaintance with Dave since middle school. Friends from his classes who didn't necessarily hang out at the tables would be coming, and his whole soccer team, as well as friends from out of the area that he knew through the show circuits. There were apparently even some kids from Lowell High coming that he stayed in touch with through sports.

I wondered exactly how many people would be attending the movie and would the theater be able to accommodate all of us, as well as whatever regular customers they might have? I worried about stupid things like that sometimes. I was already feeling bad for those regular customers; I had a feeling we were going to be a noisy bunch.

Chris came on Wednesday, bringing a lunge line and a whip. I eyed the whip unhappily, but he assured me it was just an aid, a tool, and not an instrument of torture. I haltered Gold and we walked together down to the bigger corral. I had told my parents about our plans, of course, and they were fine with the activity as long as Chris was there, or at least until he thought I was competent doing it by myself.

When we got to the corral, I sat on the fence and watched him replace the lead rope with the lunge line. Then he walked Gold in a circle around himself, letting out the line until they were about ten feet away from each other. He explained everything he was doing, showing how the whip was held to keep the horse moving forward and not losing contact through the line. Gold tried to stop a couple of times and looked at Chris as if he was bored, but Chris told him to "walk on" and moved the whip just enough for him to move forward again.

"He's definitely done this before," he said. "Let's see what we can do."

He raised the whip slightly and tried several different commands until Gold broke into a nice trot, arching his neck and looking very impressive. Apparently he responded to "trot on" quite well but responded equally well to commands in Spanish. Chris then urged him into a lope, which caused Gold's muscles to ripple and his long mane and tail to wave and flip. He was so beautiful it took my breath away.

"Whoa," said Chris, letting the whip fall a little and stepping toward his head, gathering the line as Gold slowed and finally stopped. "He's very well-trained and mannered. He shouldn't give you any trouble." When I didn't

respond to his comment, he held the length of line in his hand out toward me and said, "Come on. Your turn."

I gladly joined him in the corral. Anything I could learn to do with Gold, I would. Chris showed me how to hold the end of the lunge line folded in my hand and to keep myself at the center of the circle as he gave Gold the command to walk on.

When I felt comfortable, he said, "Let's get him trotting." He came to stand right behind me, laying his left hand on my left shoulder and the other over my right hand on the whip.

I felt flustered at first, losing focus due to his touch and closeness and the sudden sensory memory of his strong arms carrying me to his truck. Getting a grip, I reminded myself that he certainly didn't mean anything by it and was just being my teacher. Gold, in the meantime, had sprung forward and it took all my concentration to keep myself facing him and remain steady on my own feet. Chris had now stepped back slightly, moving in the same circle behind me, and after a while showed me how to stop him. We turned and worked him in the opposite direction, eventually stopping to lead him back toward the house.

Chris had spoken to me no more than necessary to give instructions this whole time—nothing unusual there—but now said, "You want to ride him, right?"

My eyes went wide and I nodded enthusiastically. "Of course!"

"Well, don't," he commanded. "Not unless someone's with you."

I was mulling over the imperative nature of Calderas as a species when I felt him staring at me. Unusual, but I'd seen that look before.

"I promise," I assured him.

He seemed satisfied with that and left.

I didn't have an opportunity to talk with Dave until Thursday. He'd been so closely surrounded by friends so far this week that we hadn't bumped into each other, at least not literally, nor spoken since I'd talked to him on Saturday. I was feeling rather needy and decided to skip lunch with Melanie and try the library. I'd almost given up seeing him at all when he walked up and leaned against the table, just like he had the first day he'd met me there.

"What's up?" he asked, sounding a little irritated and looking at me too penetratingly, as if to cut through any nonsense.

"Nothing," I said, feeling awkward and wondering why he was asking. It wasn't like him to let his impatience with me show, even though I was sure he must have felt it before. Had I pulled him away from something he'd rather be doing? I hated feeling like I'd done that.

"So, you're coming on Saturday, right?" he asked, as if looking for something to say. I didn't think he really had any doubts about it.

"Yes," I said. Then, feeling like I needed to make conversation, I said, "I guess I'm going to Bar 8 in the morning first, though."

Now he looked interested and said, "Oh yeah? Why?"

"My first riding lesson with Cheryl is on Saturday."

"Really. That's good. Hey, ask your dad if you can hang out afterward for a while. Maybe me and Robin'll go."

"Really?"

"Maybe." He shrugged noncommittally but smiled as the bell rang and said, "Anything's possible." He got up and started walking away.

"Actually, Dad's gone for a while," I said, feeling the need to clarify. "Mom's in charge for the weekend."

He turned, still walking, grinned and said, "Even better," then continued walking away.

Feeling bewildered—his behavior sure kept me guessing—I gathered my things and headed to class, more or less appeased. I didn't see him for the rest of the week.

Not too surprisingly, I barely slept Friday night thinking of possibilities for the next day. Would Dave show up at Bar 8? Who'd get to sit next to him at the movie? The idea of sitting next to Dave in the dark kept my mind pleasantly, if also tortuously, occupied for a long time. After all, I knew there was going to be a great horde of people there, and the likelihood of sitting anywhere near him was pretty slim, but one could always hope. And fantasize. And what were we going to do at his house and how many people would be there? Many other questions and suppositions about the day occurred to me, but my mind always returned to sitting next to Dave in a darkened theater. I finally fell asleep with my head on his shoulder.

I woke up early feeling like it was Christmas or the first day of summer vacation, only better. I knew for sure, one way or another, I was spending

most of the day somewhere near Dave. What a great way to spend my first day of regained freedom! And even if I wasn't able to be near him all the time, I'd be with friends. That was truly wonderful in itself. I supposed there might be some people at the theater, girls, who would be unhappy that I'd been invited. But I was fairly sure they wouldn't be among the unknown number going to his house. They'd hardly try to pull anything mean at Dave's birthday anyway—I hoped.

I dressed quickly and then ran out to feed Gold. A little later Mom walked down to the corral with me to let him loose for the morning. He seemed happy to be there and frisked around quite a bit before kneeling down and rolling. I was glad I hadn't groomed him yet today. Mom watched him admiringly as he gamboled about and then laughed when he rolled. I could tell she was also growing attached to him.

When we arrived at Bar 8, a little early for my ten o'clock lesson, Tom was just heading out with a small group of riders and waved to us as we passed. There was no sign of Dave or Robin.

"Can I hang out for a while after my lesson, Mom?" I asked. Even if Dave didn't make it, I'd be happy to spend extra time there.

She considered for a moment. "I suppose so, but you don't want to be late this afternoon, right?"

"I won't," I assured her.

"Well, let's say that I pick you up around noon. Okay?"

"Thanks, Mom."

Cheryl had me brush and saddle Flash, then lead her out to one of the small arenas. I mounted and began walking her around. Cheryl asked me to walk and trot in both directions for a while, giving me instructions to keep my heels down, keep my seat forward, and keep my eyes on where I was going and not on the horse's ears, which I had a tendency to do.

"You seem much more relaxed and confident than the first time you were here," she said.

I realized she was right. I was.

"Well," I said, thinking of the real reasons for that, "Robin and Dave . . . and Chris too . . . have taught me so much, and given me opportunities to ride and learn about handling horses. It's really helped. I don't feel as nervous now." I realized that she probably didn't know about Gold, so I told her a little about him as I rode.

After a while, Cheryl asked me to stop and approached carrying a halter and lunge line. She adjusted the halter over Flash's bridle, attached the line, and asked me to walk on.

"You've got the basic skills down pretty well. Now we want to concentrate on your seat. Learning to feel how the horse moves and maintaining your balance and movement to correspond with theirs will enable you to ride well and safely. It's critical if you plan on doing anything more than just pleasure riding."

Since I was secretly interested in doing *much* more than just pleasure riding, I was glad to go along with whatever she had in mind.

She told me to loop the reins over the saddle horn and free my feet from the stirrups and then walk, concentrating on keeping my body relaxed, feeling the four beat movement of the horse and finding my center of balance within it. Next I had to stretch my arms out to my sides, as if I were an airplane, and try to concentrate on feeling the weight settle in my seat and heels. This didn't seem too bad until she made Flash trot and I immediately came to grief and had to start all over again.

"You're tensing up. That's normal," she said, making Flash walk again, "but don't allow your muscles to tighten. The rhythm of her gait has changed, that's all. Your seat remains basically the same but adjusts slightly. If you tense up, you'll be fighting her, bouncing and losing your balance easily. It's no fun for her either. Not to mention how much more you'll ache tomorrow than you otherwise would."

We worked like this for the remainder of my allotted time. I was starting to feel like I was getting it, though I also felt like a little kid playing airplane, when I heard a loud engine growl nearby. Soon after, both Dave and Robin were looking over the fence and watching me. I put my arms down, embarrassed.

"How's she doing?" Robin asked.

"Coming along nicely," said Cheryl, smiling. "I think we've done enough for today. If you'd like to keep Flash out a little longer, it would be fine. You can put her away when you're done."

"Thanks, Cheryl," I said, really grateful. The others echoed me.

"Want to go for a short ride?" Dave asked. "Or hang out here?"

"It's *your* birthday," I said, smiling.

"No, it *was* my birthday," he countered. "We're just acknowledging it today."

"Same difference," said Robin.

Much as I wanted to ride with them, just hanging out with them sounded even better right now. I didn't know how many people I'd be sharing them— him—with later. And there was something else I still wanted to do. "Can we just hang out? My mom's going to be here in about an hour, and I never really got to see the Shires."

"Oh yeah!" said Robin, smiling.

Dave agreed. He put Flash's tack away while Robin and I made a fuss over her, gave her an extra good brush, and led her back to her stall. Then we walked across the parking lot to the pasture where we'd seen the huge animals before. They were nowhere to be seen today.

Dave carried a halter, but it was huge, as if for a giant's mount. We entered the pasture and climbed up the first tree-studded hill to look across to the next hillside. There at the top were the three horses: two large, grayish-white and the smaller tan and white. I was expecting to walk all the way down this hill and up the next when Dave let out a shrill whistle between his teeth and tongue, just like he had when calling Merle the first day I'd seen him.

The horses had their heads down, grazing, but at his whistle they looked up at us. Nothing happened at first, as if they were ignoring us or perhaps deliberating between themselves. But then one of the big horses wheeled and charged down the hillside toward us, and the other two horses followed.

"Uh-oh," said Robin, her eyes growing wider. "Watch your feet."

Dave grinned and stood his ground while Robin and I prepared to move quickly out of the way if necessary. The first Shire loped up the hill, slowing near the top, while Dancing Medicine Girl easily overtook him and bounded past us. The first Shire came to a halt in front of Dave and the second lumbered up right behind him.

"You guys are out of shape," Dave laughed. He patted the huge horse and then stood on tiptoe to get the halter on. I couldn't help smiling; he looked so cute, like a perfectly proportioned mini-man next to a giant.

David and Goliath. Though Goliath couldn't have been as beautiful and obviously gentle, and I doubt even that David could have been as perfect.

"Come and say hello. This is Hector," he said, stroking the enormous head next to him. He indicated the only slightly smaller horse standing just beyond the gelding. "That's Holly."

I walked over nervously, conscious of Dave's nearness and attention as much as the amazing size of the horse. Robin was standing next to Holly, stroking her neck and talking to her while Girl walked around us in circles.

"Come here," said Dave. He moved to the horse's side. "Let me give you a boost up."

"What?" I exclaimed. "Oh . . . no . . . I don't think so. . . ."

"Scared?" he teased.

"Yes," I admitted. "He's huge. And I'm afraid of heights."

"Don't be stupid," he laughed. "I won't let go."

As usual, it was hard to completely say no to him. I reluctantly complied, moving toward the great horse's shoulder, stepping into Dave's interlocked hands, and allowing him to toss me onto Hector. His broad back wasn't exactly comfortable, but I felt oddly safe. Exhilarated, too, so high above the ground on an animal that in ancient times might have carried heavily armored knights into battle.

"Give me a boost, too!" said Robin.

"Hang onto his mane," Dave said to me, then led us near enough to Robin to boost her up onto Holly's back.

"You're going to ride her without a bridle or anything?" I asked, dismayed.

"We do it all the time," she laughed.

I wondered if Dave was going to jump up behind me and fervently hoped he would. But he just said, "Hold on," and began walking back down the hillside, this time zig-zagging to make the ride easier than going straight down. Robin followed us on Holly, laughing and trying to hang on as the mare jogged a little. Girl sped by all of us, running all the way down to the gate.

"How do you like him?" asked Dave as we reached the fence and stopped.

"He's wonderful!" I leaned forward, reaching down his neck as far as I could to hug him. He was so solid, strong, and calm. If I wasn't starting to feel uncomfortable sitting on his broad back, I would have wanted to ride him forever.

"Ready to get down?" Dave asked.

"I guess," I said, reluctantly.

I leaned forward again, swung my leg over and slithered down. Dave caught me, steadying me as my feet touched down. The morning was cool, but the touch of his arms once again, and the warmth of his body against mine, though brief, set my pulse racing immediately.

I wonder what it would feel like to really *be close to him—*

"Hey! A little help here would be nice," said Robin.

Though athletic, the drop to the ground was apparently intimidating even for her. Dave put Hector's lead rope into my hand and went to help her.

Dancing Medicine Girl had been circling the big horses and us again in much the same way a puppy might circle larger dogs, wanting to be noticed by them. Dave set Robin down and came back to take Hector's halter off. Girl followed Dave, bumping her head against his back a couple of times and almost knocking him over as he stood on tiptoe again.

"Girl wants some attention, too," said Robin, laughing.

"It's a shame she can't be ridden," I said without thinking.

"Of course she can," countered Dave, pushing her away and patting her shoulder.

"Maybe *you* can," I said, still not really thinking.

"'Maybe?' Are you doubting my abilities again?" He looked at me in mock surprise, but his voice held an edge, as if I had issued a challenge.

"N . . . no! No! Of course not!" I answered, completely flustered.

"Hmmm. I'll put this away," he said, indicating Hector's halter. "Meet you over by the big arena."

"Uh-oh," said Robin for the second time today. We left the field and headed toward a large structure on the far side of the bunk house. It was a full-size arena, roofed, but open on all sides.

"What?" I wondered if I'd done something wrong.

Robin just sighed in what sounded like resignation and said, "You'll see."

I guess I shouldn't have been surprised to see Dave walking toward us leading Girl and accompanied by Tom, who had apparently just got back from the ride. They were followed by a girl and a guy of college age.

"What are you doing?" I asked, my alarm growing.

"You never got to see me ride a bucking horse, right?" he said.

"That's okay!" I said, shaking my head. "You don't have to do this!"

He gave me a long-suffering look as if I didn't understand *anything*—which, of course, I didn't—and continued to walk around the long side of the large arena toward what I recognized as a bucking chute, followed by Tom. This activity apparently had his seal of approval so there seemed to be little I could do. I began hoping that, for whatever reason, Girl just wouldn't feel like bucking today.

No such luck. Robin and I climbed onto the lower rails of the arena fence and watched Dave pull gloves on while the others loaded Girl into the chute. When he seemed satisfied with the rigging, he adjusted his hat and looked over at us. The girl wrangler, now manning a stopwatch and a large bell near the chute, waited for his nod, then gave the bell a ring. The guy swung the gate open and Girl burst out, kicking and flailing like a cyclone.

They hadn't even put a flank strap on Girl and she was going berserk. My stomach was one huge knot and I held my breath as I watched, the memory of the bull ride flooding back. Robin was talking next to me, but I was unaware of specific words. It seemed an eternity before the bell rang again, very loudly, but Dave held on as if unable to let go.

"Why didn't he jump off?" I yelled, panicking.

Robin didn't answer, but when I glanced at her, she was frowning. Now I was really worried. A violent buck sent Dave into the air. He hit the ground and rolled, finally landing heavily on his back, not lightly on his feet the way he had before.

I cried out and without even thinking climbed the fence. Jumping down inside the arena, I ran to him and kneeled by his side, saying his name. He was laying still, his eyes closed, his face relaxed as if in sleep. I wanted to grab him, stroke his hair, shake his shoulder, but I was afraid to touch him in case something was broken.

Then several things occurred to me at once. First, that if he *were* badly hurt, I would never forgive him for being such an idiot—as if it mattered what I thought or felt. Second and most ridiculously, I was amazed his hat was still perfectly on his head. Third, I was wondering why I was the only one freaking out. Glancing back at Robin, I saw she was still on the fence looking irritated, not worried. None of the others had moved.

I looked back at Dave and was at first relieved, then infuriated to see a smirk slowly twist his lips, one eye opening to twinkle at me in amusement.

"Scare you?" he asked, laughing.

Far from wanting to stroke him, I'd never wanted to hit anyone as much as I wanted to slug him now, but I couldn't do it. I just wasn't the violent

type, even though he did seem to be bringing out something of that nature in me. Besides, I was sure if I did that, it would just make him laugh harder. Disgusted, as much at my own overreaction as with his deception, I stood up and stalked off, away from everybody. *Nobody* was going to see the stupid tears of relief I was fighting.

"What?" he called after me, still laughing. "I don't get any sympathy? It's my birthday!"

I ignored him—almost impossible to do—and walked to the guest house, and then to the restroom where I quickly regained control.

If he wants to kill himself for his birthday, I'm certainly no one to try to stop him!

I shuddered, washed my hands, and went to sit on the porch outside to wait for my mother. A motorcycle, a familiar dirt bike, was parked near the edge of the road. One helmet hung from a handlebar. I shuddered again. Dave, Robin, and Tom were just walking toward the house. I wasn't holding a grudge, exactly, but found I didn't trust myself to look at Dave.

It's too easy to think of what could have happened. What if he had fallen the wrong way?

What if his neck . . .

What if. . . .

Dave sat in the chair closest to me. "Were you really scared for me?" He sounded incredulous.

"You are *so* gullible," said Robin, not sympathetic at all. "He was so playing you, and you totally fell for it."

Having nothing worth saying on the subject, I held my peace, keeping my eyes focused on the hills far away. In my peripheral vision, I saw Dave turn to Robin and she responded to whatever he'd done with a shrug, but I refused to give them my attention. I still didn't trust myself. Mom drove up the road a few moments later and I was glad. I needed some time to completely regain my composure.

"My mom's here." I tried to say it lightly and jumped up to leave.

Dave was right behind me. "Hey!" he said sharply.

I stopped and faced him.

"I'm sorry if I really scared you." He looked almost embarrassed.

I tried to shrug it off again. "It's okay."

"See you a little later. Right?" He actually sounded unsure, as if he thought I might be so mad I wouldn't go.

"Yes, of course. I'll be there."

He nodded and I went to the car.

Mom looked at me oddly and said, "Is everything okay?"

"Of course," I said, still in my false, calm, everything-is-normal-and-fine voice.

She asked how my lesson went and I gladly related the relatively innocuous details of my actual lesson, leaving out everything that followed. When we got home, I ran down to see Gold and walked him back up to the house, happy to have someone nonjudgmental to discuss Dave with, even if the conversation was a little one-sided. I spent some time grooming Gold, filled his water, and set aside flakes of hay for Mom to feed him later, then went to get ready for the party.

By the time I had showered and changed, I was feeling calm but a little worried about whether I had alienated Dave. He didn't seem to get discouraged easily and nothing I had done before now had done it. I guessed I'd find out.

The theater was in Lowell and I was glad to see Tanner and Kyle were also early. I joined them among a group of kids I otherwise didn't know. Jessie and Stacie arrived soon after and joined our growing group. While they didn't exactly fall all over me, they treated my presence as something expected and didn't make me feel out of place. A man and woman had also arrived. I assumed they were chaperoning.

Soon a large, gray SUV arrived, and Jessie said, "Dave's here."

Chris had been driving the huge vehicle but stayed close by it while Dave joined the now very large group, laughing and talking with everyone he could. Mr. Caldera arrived with Robin in a much smaller hybrid—probably the quiet car he'd driven to our house. He said something to Cris, tossed him the keys, then walked with Robin to join the throng. I walked over to Robin and determined to sit beside her no matter what else might happen. A head count was taken and something negotiated at the theater door, and then we filed in.

"They've rented the whole theater. Well, one screen anyway. Pretty cool, huh?" said Robin, grinning.

I guessed that took care of the problem of annoying the other patrons! Once inside, we were treated to drinks and popcorn or candy if we wanted.

Then we entered the theater and found seats. I stayed close to Robin and found that Tanner and Kyle, and now Matthew too, were staying close to us. As I suspected, Dave sat nowhere near us. The movie was good, I think—an action/adventure film—but my mind wandered intolerably. I couldn't help wondering where he was and who he'd ended up sitting next to.

Robin and I sat together, with Matthew on my left and Tanner and then Kyle on her right. Stacie sat next to Kyle with Jessie on her other side. There was a lot of joking and interaction going on with the movie, but I was too preoccupied to participate. It didn't help that Matthew kept finding excuses to make observations to me or tried to get Robin's or the other boys' attention by leaning over me. He seemed to be finding excuses to be closer to me, but I couldn't help wishing he was someone else.

I noticed that he smelled really nice, but he didn't smell like Dave. Matthew smelled lightly of pleasant cologne. Dave smelled like plain soap, sunshine, and wild, open spaces.

When the movie was over, everyone was laughing and talking and seemed to have enjoyed it immensely. I felt like I was the only one who didn't have a clue what it had really been about.

We wandered back outside where the sun was low in the sky. People lingered, talking for a while before waving and saying goodbye to their close friends and Dave in particular. As the crowd thinned more and more, it became easier to keep an eye on him too. Our eyes connected a couple of times, enough to let me know he was aware of me. But he kept his distance until only twelve of us remained, plus Dave's dad and the parent couple, who turned out to be Jessie's folks.

When they'd said goodbye to Mr. Caldera, there were six girls to shepherd to his car while the boys went noisily to the SUV. Chris was already inside. I didn't think he had come into the theater. Two of the girls and two of the boys were strangers to me, but everyone else seemed on very good terms with them and they spent the ride catching up with each other. These kids apparently lived closer to Lowell and went to Lowell High.

I'd been able to remain quite stoic while at the theater, but during the ride to the ranch I felt more and more nervous. I didn't blame Dave for not talking to me at the theater—there had been so many people and I was sure he would be careful to spread himself around as he usually did—but would he ignore me at his house? Was he mad at me? Or was he just saving time with his best friends for last? After all, I hadn't seen him speak to Robin or Matthew either.

My question was answered and my heart set at ease as soon as I got out of the car in the front courtyard of his house. It was almost dark now, but motion lights had turned on as we drove up, flooding the area with light. Dave was at our car door and holding it open. I was the last one out.

"Are you still mad at me?" he whispered, just loud enough for me, and possibly Robin just ahead of me, to hear.

The sound of his voice, his words, and his closeness caused me to shiver. Everything else was forgotten. I turned to look at him and melted entirely. He really seemed to want to know.

"I'm not mad at you," I said, trying to keep my voice even.

"Good!" He grinned widely at me. "Come on, there're people that want to see you."

He led the way into the house and toward the kitchen and family room. It felt so wonderful to be back! I felt immediately at ease, as if I were used to coming here every day.

The huge family room, which had been rather dark when I'd been here in the middle of the day, was now brightly lit. Two long, deeply padded couches placed in a wide "V" faced a huge screen on the south wall. A very large fireplace was built into the opposite wall with two smaller couches facing it behind the others. A full-sized pool table stood at the far end of the room. That end was also partially open to the outside through a wide and currently open doorway. Whatever lay outside was also well-lit.

The room was paneled in dark wood and decorated with original land-scapes and Western scenes framed on the walls. Dark leaved plants, and small and medium-sized bronze statuary, similar to the piece in the entryway, served as accents. It was a masculine yet comfortable looking room. I loved it.

Angel was busy in the kitchen but greeted everyone and gave all the girls a hug. I was the last one in so the last to be hugged. She exclaimed over me and I thought she gave me an extra squeeze. She grabbed my hand and made me sit on a stool at the kitchen island where she was working, wanting me to talk to her. A little flustered at first—I didn't think of myself as an entertaining person—I remembered Gold and began to tell her about him. The guys had obviously told her something about him. She asked many questions and seemed truly fascinated.

I didn't notice at first, but almost all the other kids had disappeared. Voices from above us seemed to confirm that's where most of them were. Kyle and one of the boys from Lowell were playing pool, and I saw people moving outside beyond the open double doors. Dave came through these and approached us, smiling.

"This is called 'monopolizing,' Angel," he said, a laugh ready in his eyes.

"What do you mean?" she asked. "We are not 'monopolop' . . . *that* word. We are talking only."

"Well, it's my birthday and my turn to 'monopolop' Allie."

I couldn't help laughing.

Dave's eyes twinkled brightly, and he completely disarmed me by grabbing my hand long enough to pull me gently off the stool. I followed him into the family room. Music was coming from outside, and voices, different music, and what sounded like gunfire was coming from upstairs.

"I never got to show you around before. This is our family room . . . obviously." He looked around as if trying to see it as I might. "It's okay, I guess."

"I love the fireplace," I said. "It's so huge." I moved toward it, drawn by framed photos on the wide mantle.

"Yeah," he acknowledged. "It's nice when it's freezing outside, but it gives off too much heat to use most of the time."

The photos seemed to be typical family pictures with different groupings of the boys and their dad. I had hoped there might be a hint of a mother figure somewhere amongst them but saw none. One fairly large photo immediately arrested my attention. It was of two boys. The one that drew my eyes to him first was Chris, yet he looked so different—his face a little fuller, jaw more square, his hair blonder and cut very short. I assumed the other boy, the one with his arm slung around Chris' neck, must be Dave, but when I focused on him it was—Chris. A younger, happier Chris, but this one was most definitely Chris.

Questions as to who the other boy was were forgotten and replaced with questions about Chris. He looked so young in the picture yet was probably about Dave's age now, maybe a year younger. And his expression—open, happy, actually *mischievous*, as if something delightfully naughty had just occurred to him. I saw that expression fairly often on Dave. I'd never even imagined it on Chris.

I turned to Dave but didn't have to ask. The question must have been obvious.

"That's Ric, our older brother," he said, rather seriously. "He died about . . . mmm . . . two and half years ago."

"I'm so sorry!" I said, completely shocked.

First I learn that there is, indeed, yet another brother, but then that he's dead? And who is the stranger in the photo that is apparently now Chris?

"Come here," said Dave, gently pulling me after him again. He walked back out to the foyer and kept walking straight through to the north side of the house. "By the way, there's another bathroom here," he said, opening a door on the right to a small, nicely decorated restroom. The next door on the right opened into a large, darkened room occupying the front north corner of the house. "This is a guest room. And that's the garage," he said pointing to the door at the end of the hallway.

On our left were dark wood double doors, which he opened. He stepped inside and flipped a light switch. I caught my breath. It was a formal sitting room, smaller than the family room but richly and elegantly appointed in cream, dark rose, and burgundy satins, cherry wood furniture and molding, and bright brass fittings. A beautiful brass and glass chandelier hung from the center of the ceiling. A fireplace with brass accessories faced the doors we had come through, and a single door in the same wall stood open to a dark room beyond. Another set of double doors set under an archway were on the interior wall, and a huge, closed doorway, corresponding to that in the family room, were the only other openings. There were no windows.

The principal feature demanding my attention when we walked in, and I assumed the main reason Dave had brought me to this room, was a huge portrait in a heavy golden frame. It hung over a cherry wood mantle above the fireplace. It looked like one of those studio photographs that is retouched to look painted, but on closer inspection I could see it was indeed a real painting.

It was a conventional kind of family portrait, but the background, detail, and expressions of the subjects made it exquisite. Behind the figures, the setting looked like a gray stone wall partially covered in greenery with water running down it. From the sunny highlights on skin and hair, it must have been done outside. They all looked at least three or four years younger than they were now.

Mr. Caldera sat on what looked like a fancy wrought iron bench in his typical dressy but very Western attire, his hair completely dark without a hint of gray. Ric stood just behind and to the right of him, his hair much longer than in the previous picture. He had an open, self-assured countenance.

Chris stood to his father's left, his gaze intense and smoldering a little, a quirky smile playing around his lips. It made me wonder what he was thinking about, and I was impressed by how attractive it made him look. He was leaning on his father, one arm resting easily on his shoulder and, except for the hair color and slight difference in face shape, he looked amazingly like Dave. Just looking at him made me feel strange, like when you see someone you're sure you once knew but can't place where or when.

Dave, looking like himself but also a bit like Henry did now, stood to the right of his dad and in front of Ric, perhaps leaning back against his big brother. He had a sweet smile on his face but a characteristic twinkle in his eye. It was *very* Dave. Henry stood squarely, almost militantly, in front of Chris and looked like—Henry—just younger. Stevey sat on his daddy's lap, a very little boy with a serenely beautiful smile.

Though the likenesses had been taken so long ago, they all looked impossibly like themselves—except for Chris. His picture was so strange; so like him, and yet not like him at all. And, of course, I'd never met Ric so couldn't know.

"It's an amazing painting," I breathed, truly in awe. "I wish I could paint like that."

Dave gave me a funny look, as if he thought it was a very odd thing to wish, but just said, "I remember having to stand still for it. Even though the artist did a lot from photographs, when it came down to the faces, he insisted on having us sit for him. It was murder."

I could imagine how hard it must have been, even one at a time, to get five boys to sit still long enough to do anything, but to capture such definitive expressions was astonishing to me.

"What happened?" I finally asked. "To Ric?" He had shown me the portrait; hopefully he wouldn't mind me asking.

"Ric was supposed to go to college and then come home and help run the ranch. Oldest son and all." His mouth twisted a little bit. "He didn't want to, though. He wanted to see the world and meet people and do things, I guess. When he was old enough, he graduated early and enlisted in the army. Dad was so mad." He shook his head at the memory. "But he was really proud of him too. Ric figured he'd put in his term of service, maybe two, and then come home. But before he'd even finished training, he was in a car accident. Drunk driver hit him head on. The other guys survived, but he died."

"That's so sad," I whispered, blinking back tears. Not normally an outwardly emotional person, I was surprised at how readily they had sprung to my eyes. That had been happening a lot lately. I thought of the photo in the other room. "Were you close?"

"Yeah. Pretty close," he said, quietly. "You know, he was my big brother. He watched out for all of us. But Chris was closer. They were inseparable. I think Ric kept Chris out of trouble most of the time. It was really hard after he died. Things changed. A lot. And then . . . other stuff happened." He looked uncomfortable and apparently wasn't going to confide further about that. "Now Chris and I spend more time together, and we try to watch out for our little brothers." He shrugged, as if not sure what more to say.

I was thankful that he was talking so openly to me and didn't seem to mind that I had asked. Considering the Chris I knew, I tried to adjust my thinking with all the new insight and information but failed miserably.

A noise at the door made us both look around. Stevey stood looking in at us, as if waiting for permission to enter.

Dave smiled at him. "Hey, Stevey, look who came. You remember Allie, don't you?"

We walked back to the door and Stevey immediately reached out and took my hand, leading me away and back to the foyer. I looked at Dave, but he just shrugged again, smiling. Stevey led me through the tiled archway into the dining room beyond. Roughly square in shape, two long, rectangular tables and chairs occupied the center. At least thirty people could be seated there easily. The only other furniture were tables and sideboards along one side of the room, but the walls were alive with hanging plants, beautiful, brightly colored paintings, and more of the exquisite tile set in patterns around the room. It was a warmly beautiful, rather exotic room. Closed double doors on the north interior wall obviously led into the formal sitting room we'd just left.

The most amazing feature of the room was the seemingly nonexistent far wall. As in the family room, two heavy accordion-style doors were com-

pletely open to a covered patio and courtyard beyond. The sound of gurgling water came from here. I remembered hearing it before.

"Do you like it?" Dave asked.

"Are you kidding?" I breathed. Like that first time I'd been here, my experience was taking on a dreamlike quality. "It's amazing."

He seemed both pleased and very amused.

Stevey kept me moving forward, barely able to notice the food that had already been laid out on one of the tables and nearby sideboards, or even its aroma. I went willingly, stepping outside onto a flagstone patio completely covered by a canopy of green and illuminated by tiny white lights. The cool night air moved freely around me as I moved out from under the huge pergola and I looked around in wonder. To my right was a pond. The wall of the house here was covered in large gray stones to match the pond, partially covered in moss and various plants. Water trickled down in streams from bronze spouts at the top to the pond below.

The walled courtyard itself was huge; much larger than any room I'd seen in the house. Lavender, and what I assumed to be other aromatic herbs, grew in large clay planters set around the yard, as did larger flowering shrubs and trees. I noticed lemon and orange. The tops of more trees could be seen beyond the back wall. A real fountain was set in the far corner, adding to the calm trickling sound. In the center was a large rock and tile fire pit surrounded at a little distance by heavy wooden benches. Chris was currently feeding the flames.

After seeing the pictures, I couldn't help trying to look at him differently. My gaze might have been more intense than I realized as, after almost smiling at Stevey, he looked up at me briefly, as expressionless as ever, but then looked with a more searching expression. It reminded me of the way he'd made me feel the first time I'd met him, and I felt just as confused and disturbed. Then he looked annoyed and looked away. He got up wiping his hands on his jeans and walked toward the family room saying, "Everybody's been looking for you."

I don't get it. That can't be the same person as in those pictures! What makes him so irritable and distrusting? Or is he just sad? Was it just the losses? The loss of his brother? The loss of his girlfriend? Was it something done to him? Or did he do something that he can't forget or forgive himself for? What could that possibly be? After all, everyone makes mistakes. . . .

Now that I'd seen proof that he hadn't always been so gloomy, I couldn't help being more curious, especially since he was Dave's brother.

Chris must have told the other kids where we were as they began to join us, and Angel appeared, clucking her tongue and seeming put out.

"Where were you guys?" asked Matthew, looking from me to Dave and back again, making me feel as if I'd done something wrong.

"Geez," said Dave, exasperated. "I was just showing Allie the rest of the house. She's never seen it."

"Oh," Matthew said, not looking convinced.

A couple of other people were looking at us oddly too. *Oh brother, in trouble already. But this is Dave's house and I'm not going to ignore him here!*

We filed into the dining room to fill plates with the delicious food laid out there. There was, what seemed to me, an odd mixture of obviously Mexican dishes with other, less recognizable fare. I must have looked confused as Dave was soon at my side describing the dishes I wasn't familiar with. He explained that Miguel had helped Angel prepare the food, as he often did for large meals and parties. His specialty was Mexican while many of the other dishes were Spanish in origin. Several seemed to have fish or shellfish.

"I . . . I really don't like fish," I said, feeling apologetic when Dave tried to get me to take some paella.

"Really?" he asked, giving me one of those, "that's incomprehensible" looks again. He then proceeded to point out which ones I might want to avoid. I tried a little of several things—it had become clear that Dave's heritage was Spanish, and I wanted to be able to acknowledge Angel's culinary skills—but mostly took the more familiar Mexican entrées.

He waited for me to follow him back out to the courtyard and indicated I should sit next to him on one of the vacant benches. The benches were just barely big enough for two people, which meant sitting side by side with him. I was in heaven. It was worth not getting to sit next to him at the theater to be able to share this time with him at his home. It seemed even more intimate.

While we were eating, Dave opened the gifts his friends had brought. He was very gracious and seemed truly pleased with everything. I had ended up buying a CD gift card. I knew he liked music, especially classic hard rock, but had no idea what he owned. He acted as if he loved it, and I felt very embarrassed but happy too. Then something occurred to me.

"Where's Henry?" I asked him.

He rolled his eyes slightly and said, "Henry's spending the night with a friend." He didn't seem to want to elaborate.

I was comfortable for quite some time until Dave's closeness, the heat of the fire, and the spices in my food began to get to me, in spite of the cool evening air. The trouble was, I didn't want to move. Not for *anything*.

Robin sat next to Tanner across the fire pit from us. The two of them had kept us laughing with their bantering, egged on by Dave, Matthew, and Jessie, but Robin suddenly looked at me and said, "Are you okay?"

Startled, I answered, "Of course! I'm fine."

But the damage was done.

"We should go in," said Dave, standing up. "Let me take your plate."

Embarrassed again—as if I were the important one; it was *his* party, after all—I handed it to him and then followed him and the others into the house.

"What're we playing?" asked one of the boys from Lowell.

"Something we can play too!" whined one of the girls I didn't know.

"Rock Band or Guitar Hero?" asked Matthew.

"Rolling Stones or Beatles?" countered Tanner.

"Van Halen!" said Dave, grinning widely.

"Guitar Hero it is then, though I suppose we could set up both," said Matthew.

One of the Lowell girls was looking at me and talking to Robin, obviously asking a question about me.

I heard Robin say, "No, just friends, like us."

The girl looked at me again but seemed satisfied. I felt embarrassed but flattered, too.

Dave placed our plates in the sink—Angel wouldn't hear of us trying to wash them—and I followed closely behind him and Robin as they ascended the staircase.

At the top of the landing and around a dividing wall, a large room opened up. About as wide as the kitchen immediately downstairs but longer, the room was crowded with overstuffed couches and huge comfy chairs. I noticed the latter in particular and couldn't help wondering what the chances were of sharing one with Dave. Two large screens occupied the nearest corner of the room. A variety of gaming consoles and game cases littered the floor around them. Band posters and sports paraphernalia adorned the walls, and a desk with a computer stood near large French doors. These opened onto a small balcony.

I ended up sharing one of the oversize chairs with Robin. Stevey sat on our laps part of the time and sometimes disappeared for a while—I assumed to play in his room. Everyone took turns playing songs, including me. I acquitted myself pretty well with an easy Beatles song Mom had sung to me as a child, and aided by my decent dexterity and sense of rhythm. It was much more fun to watch the others, though, especially Dave. We were often laughing so hard there were tears streaming down our faces. Tanner was particularly goofy and when he and Dave got together it was one of the funniest things I'd ever seen or heard, both boys channeling rock stars and wailing the lyrics out at the top of their voices. Robin avoided playing as long as she could, saying she'd rather wait for a different game.

After a while, I asked Robin what the time was as there was no clock visible in the room.

"What time is it?" she asked the room at large, loudly.

"Why?" asked Dave.

Robin turned to me. "Why?"

"My mom's coming to pick me up at ten," I said.

"No, she's not," said Dave. "She's coming at twelve." He could tell I doubted him and added, "Really. I called and asked."

"You did?" I asked, floored.

He just grinned back and continued playing.

After a while they changed games, the girls commandeering one screen while the boys took the other. Kids came and went up and downstairs, sometimes bringing back food, sometimes staying downstairs to play pool or just hang out. Dave stayed upstairs, so I did too. He tried to get me to play something else, but gaming wasn't something I had much experience with or, apparently, aptitude for, and I quit to continue watching everyone else. I didn't like the shooting games and the others just made me feel dizzy. I thought it was probably just as much fun watching and listening to them anyway. Most of the time I seemed to be laughing. I didn't feel forgotten either, as everyone deferred to my judgment if, for some reason, a decision had to be made, even if it was just whether to turn left or right. And I was constantly being asked, "Did you see that?" or being told to, "Watch this!"

Once or twice I wondered what had become of Chris. I hadn't seen him since before we had eaten but assumed he was acting the part of big brother and staying out of the way. At ten o'clock the kids from Lowell had to leave, one of their parents having come to pick them all up. At that point, the remaining boys got bored and wanted to get down to what they had really been waiting to do: link systems and kill zombies and/or aliens. Robin and the boys were all sitting or lying on the carpet while I remained in the comfy chair, very content to watch or hide my face when it got too gory.

About ten-thirty, Chris appeared carrying a pajamaed Stevey. Maybe he'd been with his little brother most of the time. Stevey's hair was wet and I wondered if Chris had given him a bath.

"Say Goodnight, " he told him.

Stevey didn't say anything but opened and closed his hand a few times in farewell.

Everyone called out "Goodnight, Stevey!"

He smiled and hid his face against Chris' neck. Chris turned and walked back behind the corridor wall. Stevey's bedroom must be to the right of the stairs somewhere. I couldn't help wondering where Dave's was. Chris didn't come back to join us.

About eleven, I got up to go to the bathroom. I doubted whether anyone noticed as they were so intent on their game. I used the one downstairs, across from the mud room, and then came back into the family room. The doors to the courtyard were still open but most of the lights, inside and out, were off. I wandered back to the mantle, curious to look again at the photos.

I could see Chris and his father sitting outside by the fire. They were talking, though his dad was doing most of it. I couldn't quite make out what they were saying until Chris stood up quickly, almost violently. He raised his voice and said, "I *don't* want to talk about this right now," and then walked toward the house.

"Well, we had better talk about it *soon*," said his dad gruffly, causing Chris to stop in his tracks.

"Look," said Chris, his voice lower, "I'm tired of it. Can I just take this year off? There're other things I'd rather be doing right now."

"You know it doesn't work like that. You're in the homestretch. Don't quit now! Just think of what it will mean, how it can help you get into the right college—"

"*Dad!*" Then Chris swore angrily and said, "Not right now!"

I felt guilty, though I hadn't meant to spy or eavesdrop, and turned to leave but was surprised to see Angel asleep on one of the small couches facing the fireplace. I froze as Chris entered the wide doorway.

He raised his voice again, but not angrily, and said, "I'll lock up," then proceeded to close and bolt the multiple doors. When he turned and saw me, he paused for just a moment, expressionless, then walked past me toward the foyer. Merle trotted behind him, her nails clicking on the tile floor. I assumed he was locking the other doors and figured I'd make a break for it and get back up the stairs.

At the foot of the stairs, however, another surprise waited: Stevey— holding a DVD in his hands. As I approached him he held it up to me: *Lady and the Tramp.*

I love that movie!

"Stevey, I think you're supposed to be in bed," I said as gently as I could. I hated to say no but didn't want him getting in trouble.

"What's he got there?" asked Chris, coming back into the big room. He came over and squatted next to Stevey. "*Lady and the Tramp*, huh?" He couldn't completely stifle a smile, as if something funny had occurred to him. "You want to watch this?"

Stevey nodded solemnly, then reached for my hand.

"Do you mind?" asked Chris. "You don't have to. He's supposed to be in bed, but it *is* a special day."

"Sure," I said, feeling warm and fuzzy pink all over. "I'd love to watch it with him."

Stevey and I got comfortable on one of the big couches, and Chris started the movie for us, putting the controller in my hand and digging out a couple of warm throws from behind the couch. I saw him gently lay one over Angel too, apparently still asleep on the couch behind us. Then he went upstairs. I watched him walk across the opening to the game room and disappear into the corridor beyond. His room must have been somewhere over the north side of the house. Stevey snuggled close to me, and I breathed in the sweet scent of his clean hair, feeling impossibly content.

I was woken up by something insistently tickling my nose. My eyes opened to see Dave, his face no more than a few inches away from mine and sitting just on the other side of Stevey, who was asleep and snuggled under

my arm. Dave was holding the tail end of my braid and must have been tickling my nose with it. Merle was on the couch on the other side of me, her head resting in my lap. The movie was just reaching my favorite part, where Tramp and Lady eat spaghetti and inadvertently kiss. We watched in silence, my face burning until that part was over.

"I'd better put him to bed," whispered Dave, "and your mom'll be here soon too."

I nodded.

"Come on." He gathered Stevey up in his arms and headed upstairs where sounds of zombie massacre and laughter could still be heard.

I followed him into a large bedroom, obviously belonging to little boys. He laid Stevey gently on the lower mattress of a set of bunk beds, then covered him up. We retreated quietly, leaving the door ajar.

"He'll stay asleep for a while," whispered Dave, "but he wakes up a lot. I'll get him later. He sleeps with me if Henry's gone," he explained.

I gulped and shivered, not letting myself think too much about that.

"You want to watch the rest of the movie?" he asked.

My eyes must have lit up at the idea as he waved me to follow him. We crept back down the stairs and sat on the couch, not quite as close as we had been just moments before, but close enough. We were soon joined by Robin and Tanner, who had wondered where Dave had gone. Robin sat next to me and wriggled under the throw with me. Tanner grabbed another throw from what seemed like an inexhaustible supply between the sets of couches.

We were all snuggled under the cozy throws, in the dark and watching the movie, when the doorbell rang. Angel sat up abruptly, then muttered what sounded like self-censure in Spanish and bustled toward the foyer and front door.

"I've got it," Dave said, leaping up and racing ahead of her.

It was, as I had assumed, my mother at the door. I was a little sad to have to leave, but I had no complaints. Saying thanks to Angel and Dave, giving Angel a hug, and waving goodbye to them, I left with my mom. I had so much new information to think over and new experiences to remember. It had been another incredible day.

Chapter Twenty-Two

No Escape

Sunday, the day after Dave's party, Robin called and asked if she could come over. I thought it was a bit odd, but said I was sure it would be okay, and did she need a ride?

"No, Chris said he could take me before work and then pick me up later if it's all right with your folks."

"I'm sure it is but hold on. . . ."

Dad would be gone for several more days at least; Mom was still in charge. I ran and asked her and she seemed happy with the idea.

"Yes, it's fine," I told Robin. "Come on over. Wait till you see Gold! You're going to have to admit he's gorgeous now!"

She sounded dubious but said she'd be over in about an hour. I was downstairs waiting when I heard Chris' truck pull up on the road and went out to meet them. Robin hopped out of the cab and grabbed a large blue bucket that had been on the floor by her feet. Chris came around the front of the truck and joined us.

"It's probably best to do this in the driveway," he said.

"Do what?" I asked suspiciously, eyeing the bucket.

"Chris said we're going to give Gold a bath, so we brought the stuff." She held the bucket up as she said this and it rattled from whatever was inside.

I nodded agreement, happy with the proposed project but not yet sure how it would be accomplished. Chris took the bucket from Robin and said

he'd get "everything" ready, whatever that meant. We went into the house to tell my mom that Chris was out front and that we were going to give Gold a bath. She thought it was a splendid idea and said to let her know if we needed any help. I had taken Gold to the corral after his breakfast so he could run around if he wanted to, but when we walked down there to get him, we found he'd done more than that.

"Ugh! I guess it's a good thing we're doing this," I said. He'd obviously spent some time rolling and was filthy, and his lower legs and the end of his tail were black with fresh mud from the stream.

"Sorry," said Robin, shaking her head. "Gorgeous, he ain't."

"Well, he was," I assured her, "and we'll make him even prettier. You just wait and see."

"Mmhmm," she responded, obviously still doubting. "He's fattened up a bit. I'll agree to that."

Gold came over right away and let Robin pet him while I put his halter on. Then we walked him back up to the house.

"How exactly are we going to do this?" I asked. "And is he going to be . . . you know . . . okay with it?"

"The driveway's probably the best place. It's going to get very wet. We'll just make mud anywhere else. As for him, I guess we'll find out. I think that's why Chris is still here."

We led Gold around the house to the driveway. He remained reasonably calm but alert, his eyes, ears, and nostrils taking everything in. He'd never been in front of the house before. Chris had the hose unrolled and ready, and the bucket apparently filled, with Mom's help, with warm water and some of the shampoo they'd brought.

"Hopefully he'll stand still and won't spook at any traffic that comes along," he said. "I'll hold him. You get to wash him. And I don't want to get wet. I have to be at work soon."

His proposed plan seemed fair—at that particular moment—so I passed the lead rope to him. He moved Gold about halfway down the driveway and we followed with the hose and bucket. Robin turned the hose on and began reciting what sounded like a *CliffsNotes* version of "Horse Bathing 101." Chris concentrated on keeping Gold more or less in one spot as Robin hosed off the lower part of his legs to get him used to it. The water was obviously cold and he danced a little, trying to avoid the chilly spray, but he didn't pull away or do anything to make us nervous. Then we used the warm water from the bucket with sponges on the rest of his body. He was soon standing calmly, completely wet.

"Get some of that shampoo straight into his mane and tail," said Chris, "and let it sit there while you wash his body. It'll help get them cleaner."

This sounded like a great idea until we actually started to do it and began to get pretty wet ourselves in the process.

"Hey . . . look at this," said Robin, flipping his long mane, normally falling over the left side of his neck, to the right side.

I had been working on his tail but came to look, and Chris stepped over to see too. There was an ugly scar almost in the center of his neck, just below the crest. It had been hidden by his mane all this time, remaining undiscovered due to my inexpert grooming. Now it was plain to see that it had been a nasty wound and probably not too long ago, though certainly before I'd found him. His neck appeared slightly malformed, as if something had taken a chunk out of it.

"What could have caused that?" asked Robin. "Barbed wire? An animal?"

I had no idea and Chris just frowned, saying nothing.

Reaching out, I smoothed the area with my fingers. There were rough areas where the skin was still dry and slightly scabby, and the hair hadn't grown back, his dark skin showing through the pale surrounding coat.

There didn't seem to be much we could do about it, so I went back to work on his tail and Robin continued to work his mane into suds. When she was finished there, she went to work with the soapy sponge on his legs, and then his body, and I followed behind her with a stiff brush. We were soon as soaked as he was.

Over the past month, the weather had begun to cool compared to the blazing hot days of August and September. Now November was just days away and there was a very noticeable difference. Although the sun was out and the sky was clear, a slight breeze blew steadily. What had felt pleasant when we'd first started was now chilling us to the bone.

I was starting to be suspicious of Chris' strategy. I peeked at him a number of times, half expecting, even *hoping*, to catch something of the mischievous gleam in his eyes that I had seen in the pictures at his house. But his expression revealed nothing and he never betrayed whether he was aware of my observation. By the time Robin and I had Gold completely lathered up, our

teeth were chattering from the cold, our sneakers squelched as we walked, and I'm sure I looked at least as bedraggled as she did.

"I need to get to work," Chris said when we were about to rinse Gold off. "You'll need to take turns holding him."

"This is *so* not fair," said Robin, glaring at him. "We're freezing and you're still dry. Is that why you suggested *I* come and help do this?"

His eyes flashed from her to me for a split second, but he was unable to completely hide the slight quiver of his lips. He looked away to hide it, but I'd definitely seen it.

"Seriously," he said, as if ignoring her comment. "I gotta go."

I walked over and took the lead from him as Robin began rinsing Gold's legs with the hose.

"Yeah. Okay. See ya," said Robin, sounding disgruntled, a disgusted look on her face.

As Chris turned toward his truck, she stuck her tongue out at his back, then looked at me, a wicked gleam in her eye. She held the hose up and asked, "Should I?"

I couldn't help smiling broadly at her. I knew what I'd seen. "It's unfair for him to get away completely unscathed," I answered.

Chris didn't turn or stop walking but said, in his driest tone, "Don't even think about it."

That's all Robin needed to convince her. She ran several steps toward him with the hose, her thumb positioned tightly over the end of it, shoes squelching loudly as she went, and blasted him squarely in the back of the head. Water soaked his shoulders and back, then ran down the back of his jeans. She'd only let it hit him for a second, but it had done a satisfactory amount of damage.

Chris stopped in his tracks, his shoulders hunched from the shock. Robin and I looked at each other with wide eyes, both wondering how he would react.

He didn't turn, but in the same tone as before said, "You'll pay for that." He started walking again and added, "*Both* of you."

Robin and I exchanged looks again. She was grimacing. I probably did the same. Chris reached his truck, got straight in without looking back, and drove away. We both laughed uncertainly.

"Do you think he's really mad?" I asked, trying not to feel too concerned. I had no idea what payback from Chris would be like.

Robin raised her brows and shrugged, a smile still playing around her mouth. "No telling. It's Chris. But I couldn't resist."

We both laughed again. It *had* been pretty funny. It was frustrating, though, not being able to see his face. Had he smiled? Was he just ticked off? Was he *really* angry? If he truly meant to take revenge, I guessed we'd find out if the latter were true.

"I heard Chris leave. Could you use some more help?" Mom had come out and was surveying our handiwork so far. "His mane and tail are looking better, aren't they?" she said.

"Kinda hard to tell," said Robin making a face. "We need to rinse them out and maybe do a second shampoo."

"Could you hold him, Mom?" I asked. "Then Robin and I can both work on him again. I think we've done his body and legs pretty well."

She agreed and took the lead from me. We took turns rinsing Gold, getting soaked all over again. Another familiar engine sound caused us to watch the road coming from the south. Dave appeared on his dirt bike followed a moment later by Tom in his truck. They both came to a stop at the edge of the driveway.

"Is it okay for us to be here?" Dave asked.

"Of course," replied my mom, but she had a slight crease between her brows. I had a feeling this was due more to the motorcycle than anything else.

The guys walked slowly toward the end of the driveway. Gold kept a wide eye focused on them and I continued to stroke him.

"Have you got him, Mom?" I asked, just to be sure she was still comfortable holding him.

"Yes, I think so. We're fine," she said, stroking his face as the guys continued toward us slowly.

"You got a little wet," said Dave, grinning.

"Your powers of observation are stunning," said Robin, testily. "I notice you got here in time to stay dry."

"Hey! I was doing chores. I got done as fast as I could. I can leave again if you want . . ." He began to turn away.

"No!" I blurted, then felt embarrassed as everyone looked at me. I guess he was just kidding, but I didn't want him to leave for any reason. "No," I said again, calmly this time. "Why don't you take over for Mom?"

"Sure," he said, still grinning, and relieved my mother of the lead rope. Gold accepted the substitution with equanimity. I was thrilled.

"So this is the famous golden stallion I keep hearing about. He's quite something, isn't he," observed Tom.

"He's looking great!" said Dave, enthusiastically. "And he doesn't seem to have a male problem anymore."

"Thanks to Chris, I guess," I said, trying to be fair.

"Whatever the problem was, it must have been of relatively recent origin for him to have recovered his trust so quickly," said Tom. "He may have strong long-term associations with women handlers but some bad experiences with men."

We agreed this seemed possible. Whatever the reason for his distress before, he now stood calmly with his eyes closed, seeming to enjoy all the attention. Tom then left to continue to town.

Robin and I finished rinsing Gold and then added the special conditioner they'd brought, working as many snarls out with our fingers as we could. We let it sit on the hair for a while and talked with Mom about school, horses, and life in general. She was watching all of us with intense interest. I think she thoroughly enjoyed having my friends there. I was trying my hardest not to betray anything.

Gold seemed content to doze in the sun, now a little warmer than before, his back and flanks drying quite quickly. On Robin's instructions, I took a wet sponge and bathed his face carefully. He even let me sponge his ears a little bit, holding his head low enough for me to reach them easily.

"Wow. I wish Gali would do that for me. We always fight about me doing his face and especially his ears," said Robin. "Gold seems to really trust you."

"He's obviously a good judge of character," said Dave, smiling at me.

I smiled back, trying desperately not to blush but not sure of my success.

"The feeling's completely mutual," I replied to Robin.

I gave Gold a hug around the neck. His chest was still pretty wet, getting me damp again, but I didn't mind. I stepped back, stroking his face, and he nuzzled my stomach gently, making me laugh.

Mom sighed heavily and we all looked at her. She smiled wistfully. "I sure wish you could keep him, sweetheart," she said. "I'm afraid it's going to be hard for you to see him go."

I was sure she hadn't meant to depress me, but my day suddenly darkened and a cold chill, having nothing to do with the cool breeze or my dampness, shot down my spine. Dave was frowning and looked like he was biting the inside of his lower lip.

I gave Gold another, longer hug and said, "I know."

"Let's get him finished," said Robin brightly, not allowing us to mope. "I won't make a final judgment on his appearance until he's dry."

I laughed and agreed.

"Are you still having problems with the way he looks?" asked Dave.

"Well, let's put it this way," she said, looking at me, then Mom. "I hope she has better taste in guys than in horses."

I thought my eyes would pop out in surprise that she'd say such a thing, not just in front of Dave, but my mother! Dave acted as if he hadn't heard the remark, but I thought Mom looked—smug. There was no other way of describing it. I hoped the others hadn't noticed.

"Come into the house when you're done and I'll get you some lunch," she said, still smiling as she turned and walked back to the house.

We thoroughly rinsed Gold's mane and tail, keeping the rest of his body as dry as possible but getting completely soaked again ourselves. When we were done, we stood back to survey our handiwork. He looked a little patchy, his legs and stomach still quite wet and much darker than his head or his back. His mane and tail hadn't lightened as much as I'd hoped they would, but they were still wet too. In spite of these things, I thought he looked amazing.

"Wow. Big improvement," said Robin.

I nodded in agreement.

"You should walk him around until he's completely dry," said Dave.

"True," agreed Robin. "If we put him back in his paddock like this he's going to roll and get all muddy."

"Right," I said, glad they had the horse sense I lacked. "What about his tail?" I asked, frowning at this appendage. It was dragging on the ground.

"Hmm," murmured Robin. "That's a problem. It's going to get totally filthy again, at least until it's dry."

"You should braid it, like your hair," said Dave, looking at me. "It'll make it shorter. We sometimes do that with our horses, especially before a show."

Robin and I agreed it was an excellent idea. I took off my shoes and ran into the house to find hair bands while Robin began braiding his tail. I took over from her and finished it when I returned.

"Start walking him and I'll put the hose and stuff away," said Dave. "Deal?"

"Deal!" we both chimed, thrilled to be done with water and hose.

It seemed like a good time to lunge Gold, especially since I hadn't spent much time with him the day before, so we picked up the whip and lunge line by his paddock before continuing to the corral. Dave caught up as I was trading the lead rope for the lunge line and Robin was closing us into the corral.

I put Gold through his paces—walking, trotting, even coaxing a slow lope out of him. Dave and Robin sat on the fence and kept up a commentary imparting instruction, advice, and encouragement to me. Robin's comments tended to be critical while Dave's were more positive. I greatly appreciated both.

Gold looked magnificent. The late October sun made the golden hair of his coat and the more silvery hair of his mane sparkle and gleam. He had filled out a lot since I'd first found him, his densely muscled shoulders and hindquarters making his rather large head and thick, muscular neck look more balanced and proportionate to the rest of his body. His legs, by contrast, were slim and finely formed, strong enough to carry and propel his weight, yet capable of quick turns, beautiful suspension, and probably a good deal of speed were it ever required of him. That was something I would have liked to see: Gold at a flat out gallop. For now that wasn't possible, but his self-evident abilities were promising, even to my uninitiated understanding.

"We should let the braid out. The hair'll dry faster," said Robin. "And I want to see what he looks like."

Dave and I felt the same, so Robin got down from the fence and took the braid out of Gold's tail while I held him.

"You're not twins anymore," observed Dave, a slight smile on his lips. "Don't you ever wear your hair loose?" He added, a wicked gleam in his eye, "Besides when you're sleeping?"

Immediate blush. *Yes, I very well remember that day too, thank you.*

"Not too often. Mostly just around the house. It gets into mischief otherwise."

Dave's eyes danced and his smile broadened.

"Let's see," said Robin, moving behind me and grabbing my braid.

"Hey!" I objected, trying to turn to face her but hindered by the necessity of holding Gold.

"Stay still!" she commanded. "I just want to see what it looks like. Haven't you ever cut it?"

"Of course I cut it . . . sometimes . . . a little," I said defensively.

"No, like . . . *cut* it. You know. Short."

"No," I answered. "I've never thought much about it."

"Well, I would have strangled myself with it before now if my hair was this long," she said, freeing the last sections of mine. "Wow . . . you're twins again."

My straight hair, as usual when it had been in braids for a while, and especially if it had been damp, fell over my shoulders and down my back in narrow ripples. Although Mom kept it trimmed for me, I hadn't really cut it for quite a while—years in fact—and it reached well below my hips. Gold's tail looked similar, slightly wider ripples waving in the breeze, the air's movement keeping all but the longest strands off the ground. It hadn't attained the tight crimping my hair had, but both his mane and tail already had a natural, graceful wave of their own.

I set him walking again in the opposite direction and then trotting. He truly took my breath away. I was in awe; completely smitten—as if I hadn't been before! A feeling that was unfortunately becoming familiar sneaked up on me again, making my throat tighten and my stomach feel funny. I angrily tried to forget my mother's words from earlier and suppress the prickling behind my eyes.

Gold's bright, honey-colored coat glistened in the sun, waves of pure molten gold rippling as the muscles beneath the skin moved and changed the contours of his body. His long mane and tail, mostly silver and creamy white now with some darker brown and gray underneath, billowed out behind him as he moved. He was breathtakingly beautiful.

I couldn't resist allowing my imagination to go where I hadn't been allowing it to: what if nobody claimed him? What if the people who had lost him just never came looking for him? *What if I got to keep him? Forever?*

I sniffed and a couple of tears rolled down my cheeks before I could prevent them, my hands being otherwise occupied.

"Are you crying?" asked Robin, annoyingly observant and as implacable as ever.

Dave was looking at me more closely now too.

Thanks, Robin.

Not wanting to admit to my momentary lapse, and especially not wanting to transgress my own paramount commandment—*Thou shalt not cry in front of Dave*—I answered in as no-nonsense a voice as I could. "My eyes are just a little sensitive to the breeze, that's all."

"Oh, right," said Robin, clearly unconvinced.

Dave was still watching me, leaning forward on the fence, arms resting on his legs, his chin resting in his hand. I brought Gold to a halt and wiped my cheeks.

"I should probably take him back up," I said, hoping my voice sounded normal.

"Don't you want to ride him?" Dave's voice made me pause.

Are you kidding?

He still regarded me very closely. Now it made me feel uncomfortable.

"Of course," I answered, calmly, "but I have no saddle or bridle."

"That's okay," his voice, as smooth as I'd ever heard it, said. "Just get up on him, like you did with Hector. You want to, don't you?"

Didn't someone, once upon a time, get into big trouble heeding words like that?

I was sorely tempted. I remembered a certain promise, but I'd only promised not to ride him without someone else around, right?

"Yes," I admitted. I began shivering at the prospect of actually riding this gorgeous animal.

"Well, all right!" Dave said, jumping down from the fence.

Robin came and took the lunge line from me. The shivering had intensified, my teeth almost chattering like the first day I rode Flash. Dave noticed. Of course.

"Okay?"

"Yes!" I assured him. "I'm a little chilled, I guess."

This was true but not the cause of the shivering. Being with Dave, so close to him with his attention focused on me, and being about to ride this amazing creature—it was as close to Nirvana as I could at present imagine.

"Grab some mane, like you did with the Shire. Remember?" I did. Vividly. "This guy should be a much more comfortable ride."

He was. His back felt warm through my damp pants and certainly seemed more suited for human riders than Hector's, yet broader than the other horses I'd ridden. He was also a little slippery, his sleek, clean coat offering little traction to help keep me astride. I was going to have to really hang on. Dave took the line from Robin and began walking us around the corral. After several steps, I began to relax. Gold's strides were long, his motion beneath me smooth and comfortable in spite of the soreness I felt from my lesson the day before.

"How're you doing?" asked Dave.

"Amazingly!" I breathed, enraptured. "He feels incredible."

"He looked like he has a nice, smooth trot. Do you want to try?"

How could I say no? "Yes!"

"Okay," he said. "Remember what you learned with Cheryl: sit deep, keep your heels down, relax, and let your center of gravity move with him."

"Right," I said, trying to duplicate what I had done and felt while riding the day before.

Dave let the line lengthen until Gold was making a circle around him, then used his voice and the end of the lunge line to move him forward slightly into a slow, jogging trot. After a moment of panic, I forced myself to relax again and concentrate on Gold's movement. It remained even, not as bouncy as the other horses I had ridden. His mane tousled gently over my hand as he moved, and I found I wasn't gripping him as tightly as I thought I would. His gait felt smooth yet incredibly powerful and controlled, as if at my command he could leap into battle or jump the corral fence. I couldn't believe how balanced and safe I felt and wondered if he was extra careful just for me. *No, that's impossible. He's just a horse, after all.*

It had become very quiet. No one had spoken for some time, and I looked at the others, trying to guess what they were thinking. Robin looked approving and a little surprised. Dave was harder to read. He looked serious, more serious than I was used to him looking, especially when looking at me, and

a little intense too. I started to feel squirmy. If I hadn't known it to be highly unlikely, I might *almost* have thought he looked—admiring.

"What do you think?" I asked nervously, half laughing but wanting to break the silence. "Is he looking any better to you, Robin?"

She nodded slowly and said, "He looks great with you riding him."

Dave brought Gold to a walk, then caused him to stop, turned him, and set him going in the opposite direction. His eyes flitted from one point to another on both Gold and me, not diminishing my internal discomfort one bit but leaving me guessing his true thoughts.

After a few moments, he said, "I wish I had a camera."

"A camera?" I asked.

"Yeah. You need to see how amazing you look. You were made for each other. I think he brings out . . . I don't know. Something. Something in you. A confidence you don't usually have. Like you can be yourself with him."

I was very struck by what he said and realized he was right. I did always feel safe and confident with Gold. I had since the first time I'd met him.

I was on a high for days after that weekend. And when the high wore off and the everyday normality resumed, I found it easier to maintain my emotional equilibrium. Every time I doubted either my right to be in Dave's universe or his, let's call it "fondness" for me as I still didn't have a clue exactly what it was, all I had to do was recall certain events and feelings to be reassured. So far, every time I had doubted him, he'd gone out of his way to make me feel wanted and important. He seemed to constantly be showing me that he cared about me. There was no value I could attach to that; it was priceless to me. I couldn't help it if I still saw him very differently than he saw me. He *did* see me. And it was still enough.

Tuesday morning at the end of Algebra, our home room, we finally received our school photos. I was scared to look at mine and immediately slapped them onto my desk, cellophane down, wanting to know when the make-ups would be. Robin looked critically at hers through the clear window, then tore open the envelope and pulled them out for a closer look.

"They're great!" I said, catching a glimpse and reaching for them.

She pulled them away, apparently not done scrutinizing them herself. "Hmmm . . . not *too* bad . . . I guess. Better than last year's. Those were awful! I looked scrawny and sick." She finally passed them to me so I could have a better look.

I had been right about the photographer catching that expression Dave had provoked. Her eyes were sparkling, there was wonderful color in her face, her hair flamed and looked alive, and her head was tilted at such an angle, it made her look haughty and vulnerable at the same time. It looked like the kind of picture you'd see in a high style magazine.

"Wow," I breathed, impressed. "These are fantastic. Can I have one?"

"You really think so?" she asked, looking pleased. "Of course you can have one. Who else am I gonna give them to? Let me see yours, though."

I groaned and slowly turned the envelope over. I was shocked. I was expecting to see the gawky twelve-year-old I was sure I looked like. But I didn't look like that. I looked—good! My eyes looked bright and a little larger than I thought they really were, and my glasses gave me a slight air of sophistication that I knew wasn't truly me. There was a rosy pink to my cheeks and lips—that was thanks to Dave too—but it wasn't suffused over my whole face. My hair, while pulled back like normal, had a softer look. A few lighter colored wisps framed my face as if I'd done it like that on purpose. I wasn't smiling, but my lips were slightly parted and I looked—older.

"Wow," Robin said. "Yours turned out really good too."

I couldn't help laughing, thinking Dave could get a job as a photographer's assistant. He'd be worth his weight in gold if his influence made even me look this decent. Robin wanted to know what was so funny, but this seemed like one of those things it was wiser not to tell her. "I'm just surprised," I said. "My pictures *never* turn out this well." That was true enough.

"It looks just like you, though," said Robin.

"No, it doesn't, but that's a good thing," I argued.

"It absolutely does," she argued back.

"Right. Well, at least I don't think I need to do it over again. That's a relief."

She shook her head at me and dug a pair of scissors out of her backpack. We cut our sheets of wallet-sized photos and exchanged pictures, writing short phrases on the backs.

I wrote, *Thanks for being my friend! ~Allie~*. Kind of pathetic, but heartfelt.

She wrote, *You're weird, but I love ya! Robin*, with a little heart drawn beside her name.

I wondered what Dave's pictures looked like and could I get my hands on one? Would he ask for one of me? I almost felt I wouldn't be too embarrassed to give him one of these.

Melanie and I exchanged pictures too, at lunch. I had been interested to see what hers looked like, as Robin's and mine had turned out so well. She already looked like a model, so I was sure they would be beautiful. But I was surprised by what I saw. They looked like her with her lovely features and her luxurious hair. But there was a sallow tone to her skin that I'd never noticed before and slight dark smudges under her eyes, which I had noticed after she had the flu. What surprised me most was a look of sadness, an almost haunted look, especially in her eyes. Even so, it was still a beautiful image.

My mom was thrilled with my pictures, echoing Robin's "They look just like you!" But Dad seemed less pleased, asking if I'd been wearing makeup or had they retouched them to make us look older? Mom kept the larger ones, took two wallet-sized, and gave the rest back to me "for my friends." I resisted pointing out to her that these could be counted on the fingers of one hand. I was actually grateful. Not so long ago that would have been one finger.

The next day we sat at the tables during lunch and several people were still looking at and exchanging photos. Stacie and Kyle were shyly exchanging pictures and Tanner was bugging Robin for one when Matthew approached and sat next to me. As he sat, his arm reached around to hang across my shoulders, as one would do with a buddy. I was surprised but not particularly bothered by it. In fact, the physical contact was oddly validating. At least one guy seemed to *like* me.

"So . . ." he said, smiling. "May I have one of your pictures?"

I flushed with gratification. "Sure . . . I guess," I answered, now feeling a little shy.

He gave me one of his. It was a great picture.

I dug mine out of my backpack, giving him one. I didn't offer to write anything on the back. What would I have put? *'Thanks for being kind to me'*? Pathetic. *'You're nice'*? Patronizing and sounding like a Valentine heart candy.

I was still considering this when I became aware of Dave and Chris. It was still unusual for Chris to join the group, and Dave had continued to keep his distance from me at school. Dave was frowning slightly. Chris was scowling, but that was normal. Dave approached us slowly but never actually looked at me. Instead, he seemed intent on holding Matthew's eyes as if staring him down. As he got closer to the table, Matthew rather self-consciously removed his arm from my shoulders.

Dave nudged Kyle to move over when he reached the table and sat directly across from Matthew. The two of them began talking about the soccer finals coming up as if nothing had happened, but I felt funny. It seemed like something else was going on. Chris had lost interest and was talking to some of the older kids at the other table.

Weird! Both of them are just really weird!

I forgot about the pictures at that point, but Dave never asked for one of mine. The subject never came up again around him and I didn't feel comfortable, just out of the blue, asking for one of him.

The weather continued to change to not only quite chilly but precipitation, and I was glad that we had bathed Gold when we did. Chris brought over a blanket he said I should use on him, especially at night now that the temperature was dropping. He explained that, like most horses, Gold's body should respond to the cooling weather by growing in a shaggy, winter coat, but until then the blanket would help keep him warm. When the temperature remained cold all day, I should just leave it on him but still groom him as often as I could. The brief time of his shining golden coat was already past, and most of the time now he was a dull brown from dirt and mud. Even though I tried to keep him brushed, it felt like a losing battle.

Shorts and skirts were rarely seen at school anymore; jeans and sweatshirts were now the norm. There was another change in the air, too: a vibrancy and excitement that didn't seem to have a specific cause beyond the changing season. I noticed the difference in Dave especially, which I suppose wasn't remarkable since I certainly watched him more than anyone else. His eyes seemed to twinkle more readily. He was almost always smiling, and he seemed even more inclined to tease the girls and find opportunities for mischief with the guys.

On rainy days, our core group congregated in the Ag. Science room since almost everyone except me took this instead of regular science. Even Chris joined us on most rainy days. And I still met with Melanie in the cafeteria

twice a week. On fine days, Chris was nowhere to be seen and Dave was often missing too.

"Training," said Robin one day when curiosity and a certain longing had gotten the better of me, and I *had* to ask. A few of us stood around the tables disconsolately, the tables themselves being damp from morning rain, although the sun now shone brightly.

"Training?"

"On the clear days, the coaches have basketball training and track athletes are out on the track, keeping fit for spring. Chris'll be on the courts most of the time. He's like Douglas' star player, and he helps train the junior varsity team too. They expect him to get a good college scholarship next year. There's probably already been scouts watching him."

"Hmm," I acknowledged, thinking this might fill in a piece of a puzzle. Or maybe not.

"And Dave and the others run during lunch when it's dry enough. They'll start training hard once soccer is completely over. And some of the track people do basketball or football too, so we see less of them when winter comes, especially the guys."

"Does Dave play basketball?" I asked, thinking I wasn't going to be seeing him at all.

"No. Their dad only allows them to do two school sports per year. They both play soccer. Chris plays basketball, and Dave's going out for track and field."

"Mmm," I acknowledged again. That explained why so many people, including Dave and Chris, were wearing sports clothes as often as jeans and t-shirts these days and disappeared on sunny days. I guessed I was going to like rainy days best.

The second Sunday of November, I was awoken early by my phone buzzing on my nightstand. I had talked with Brenda just before going to sleep; no real news on her end and she hadn't been much interested in mine. It had been a short call.

The sound of the phone now startled me, sounding very loud against the table top in the otherwise silent dark. I glanced at my clock: six o'clock.

Groaning a little—why would anyone be calling me so early on a Sunday?—I looked at my phone and saw it was Dave. I was suddenly quite awake.

"Hello?" I whispered, not exactly on purpose, but my voice wasn't working yet.

"Snow day!" His voice was a raspy whisper too.

"Snow day?" I whispered back.

"Get your snow boots on," he said in his normal voice. "We'll be there in thirty."

"Wait. . . . What?"

"You can go, right? And you've got snow gear?"

"I don't know . . . and . . . no. What snow gear?"

Long-suffering sigh on the other end of the phone. "Go ask if you can go. We're all going; Dad and Robin too."

I hesitated a moment, then said, "Okay. Hang on, I'll be right back."

I crept out of bed—it was freezing!—and sneaked into my parents' room. Mom was the surest bet, so I gingerly touched her shoulder. She startled awake and almost woke Dad.

"Shhh . . ." I hushed her. "It's okay. There's snow . . . somewhere. Dave wants to know if I can go. His dad's taking them and Robin's going too." These seemed like important details.

Mom yawned and looked at the clock. "Good grief, it's early," she said. "I suppose so. You'd better feed The Animal before you go."

"I will," I whispered, stifling a giggle. Mom and I had taken to calling Gold "The Animal" like Dad had. Of course, we were much more affectionate about it. "Go back to sleep," I said. Then I crept back to my room and picked up my phone.

"Yes."

"Dress warm," said Dave. "You have boots, hat, gloves?"

"Um . . ."

"Never mind. Just dress as warm as you can. We're leaving right now."

"Okay."

"Bye."

"Bye."

Wide awake now, a growing excitement rousing me even more—*I'm going to the snow! With Dave!*—I dressed thoughtfully but quickly in jeans, a pullover sweater with a long-sleeved t-shirt underneath, a sweatshirt jacket over that, and two pairs of socks. I didn't have "snow" boots so pulled on the only ones I had, the one's I'd bought recently for riding. That was the best I could do. I washed my face, brushed my teeth, and braided my hair as quickly as I could, then went out to feed Gold. Just beyond the back door, I was brought to an abrupt halt by what, to me, was a very strange sight.

The world had gone gray; not completely colorless, but almost. At first I thought, *It's snow!* Then I realized there was no real substance to what I saw, just a thin veneer of white, muting the colors underneath and making the world look like a black and white photograph. I'd never seen anything like it in real life. We didn't get frost in West Los Angeles. I stepped down from the porch, my breath puffing in little misty clouds before my face and my feet leaving wet footprints that let the color beneath the frost bleed through.

"It's a good thing we've got that blankey, isn't it?" I said to Gold, stroking his nose as he blew wispy breaths of his own at me. I noticed there were little trails of steam rising from some of the edges of his blanket and laughed. "Do you have your own furnace on under there? I guess we leave this on for now."

I reached under the blanket near his shoulder and was surprised by how toasty he was. After feeding him and checking his water, I went back into the house to keep warm. I sat at the dining room window and kept watch until the big SUV arrived. Dave jumped out from a back seat and started running toward our porch, but he stopped and waited when I left the house.

"Hmm," he said, taking in my idea of dressing warmly. "We'll have to do something about you when we get there."

Not knowing how else to respond and just being thrilled to be along for the ride, I smiled and said, "Okay."

He waited as I climbed into the back seat next to Robin and then climbed in after me. Henry and Stevey were bundled up in thick jackets in the third seat. Stevey appeared cherubic and calm. Henry looked excited and ready for mischief, like his big brother.

"Hi Stevey," I said. Stevey continued to watch out the window. "Hi Henry," I said, smiling at the older boy. He grinned back, shrewdly I thought.

I'm going to have to keep an eye on him.

Chris was driving and Mr. Caldera was in the passenger seat.

"Good morning, Allison," said the latter, giving me his charming smile.

"Good morning," I replied, slightly shy. I still didn't know him very well.

Sitting in the middle of the second seat, I could see most of Chris' face in the rear view mirror, and when he moved his eyes to it, he could see me. He did so now, our eyes meeting briefly as he backed the vehicle into our driveway. He tipped his head up in a slight nod of acknowledgment.

"You're going to freeze," said Robin pessimistically, her version of greeting.

"I've got it covered," said Dave, grinning.

"Okay." Robin still sounded doubtful.

She looked bundled up enough for the North Pole. Both she and Dave wore thick insulated jackets and pants, gloves, knit hats, and sporty looking rubber boots obviously designed for snow. Everyone else was dressed similarly. Now I *did* feel underdressed, though I felt warm enough right now.

Chris was heading back to the main highway, but instead of turning left toward town, he turned right and headed deeper into the hills. Heavy frost lay on most of the roofs and the tops of other stationary objects we passed, and could be seen covering open areas of grass and road alike. In obviously warmer and more sheltered areas, nothing but threads of gently rising mist indicated how cold it was.

The conversation was lively, consisting mostly of past snow experiences the others had shared, and I listened with great interest if limited comprehension. I caught their excitement, however, and was looking forward to the treat to come just as much as I was already treasuring these moments sitting next to Dave and being with my other favorite people. After having been asked what winter had been like in Los Angeles—"just cooler and wetter than summer"—and admitting that it was true that I'd never been to the snow, I didn't have much to say. Just being able to sit and soak up the feelings that surrounded and filled me made me happy. I began to pay more attention to the music playing too: instrumental rock I didn't recognize at all. I liked it a lot.

"You're awfully quiet," said Robin, after a while.

Suddenly self-conscious, I looked at Dave. He just smiled.

"I really like this music," I said. It was the only thing in my head at that moment, apart from the random thoughts that plagued me in Dave's company, which couldn't be articulated anyway.

"Chris' choice," said Dave, nodding appreciatively, as if he also heartily approved. "Whoever drives gets to call the tunes. Well . . . *usually* gets to call

the tunes," he amended. "Just wait 'til next year, though," he said, smirking and nodding slyly, his eyes half closed.

"Rock out," said Robin, her eyes laughing. "We'd better carry ear plugs around in case we have to ride with him."

I laughed with the others but became instantly distracted.

Dave driving. Riding in the car with him. Only him? That's an interesting concept.

"You know it!" he agreed, still grinning. But he'd startled me; could he read my thoughts? He was looking at me, his eyes twinkling, and I knew I was blushing like mad.

Chris looked at me in the mirror again briefly, as if accepting my commendation of the music. Mostly upbeat, virtuosic playing, with elements of jazz and metal, it was unlike anything I'd heard before. It was different from the angsty alternative I usually heard coming from his truck, and not what I would have associated with him. *Just goes to show you. . . .*

Patches of pure white had been visible for some time, especially through breaks in the trees and hillsides where higher mountains could be seen. But after about thirty minutes Chris pulled to the side of the road and he and Dave put chains on the tires.

"Just in case," Mr. Caldera said. "We don't have too much farther to go, but we'll be leaving the main road and it might not have been plowed recently."

Continuing on, we eventually began climbing a smaller, winding road. At one point the road ran along an open hillside, and the prospect that opened up was amazing. We had climbed much higher than I had thought and I exclaimed in surprise at the incredible sight. Dave and Robin just grinned. The view was beautiful, but my eyes were drawn to one of the farther mountainsides. It stood out as different: gray and scarred. At first I thought there were no trees, then realized that what looked like dark sticks stuck vertically in the ground, *were* the trees—bare skeletons of trees.

"What happened there?" I asked. "Fire?"

"Yeah," said Dave. "It happens, mostly in the summer, especially if it's been a dry year. That's from a couple of years ago."

"Looks scary, huh?" said Robin.

It certainly did, but I just nodded.

"It's a lot scarier when it's close to home," Dave said seriously. Frowning, he looked away, out the other side of the vehicle.

We were passing through more forest now, the panorama left behind, but I couldn't help being curious.

"So, you've had a fire close to your ranch?"

"We have dealt with wildfires many times," said Mr. Caldera. "It usually starts farther away and is contained before it puts our livestock or home in real danger. It is just one of the realities of living where we do. There have only been three serious threats that I know of since my family has owned the property. Two happened before I was born and the house had to be partly rebuilt because of one of them. The last one happened when the boys were younger. It was . . . very frightening."

The mood had changed and I wished I hadn't said anything. I couldn't help being curious still, but could tell from the look on Dave's face that he didn't want to talk about it. It surprised me, as he was usually so open and at ease about everything.

The drive continued for a while in silence, but the mood quickly lightened again with Robin, Dave, Henry, and even Mr. Caldera talking and laughing together. Chris looked at me again in the rearview mirror, but he never said anything. We finally stopped in an open space, just under some tall pines. Although the sky above us was becoming lighter, it was still quite dark under the trees.

"Here we go," said Dave in an excited, heavy whisper, grinning from ear to ear. He turned around to unfasten Stevey's car seat, leaning on me as he did so, then he jumped out.

I looked back at the boys to see their expressions. Stevey looked vaguely interested in what lay outside the truck, but Henry was already climbing out, his cute countenance intense, expectant. He ran laboriously for a few steps, his relatively short legs sinking deeply into the foot and half or so of snow, then threw himself, whooping and laughing, into a deep bank of it.

"Come back here," said Dave, waving me to the rear of the SUV.

Chris already had the back doors open and was unloading snowboards, foam sleds and what looked like a small, plastic toboggan. There were a variety of boots and other items behind the rear seat. Dave was looking at my feet in a calculating manner, finally grabbing a rubber, fleece lined boot and wanting to match its sole to the boot I was wearing. It looked just a little bigger.

"I thought so," he said with evident satisfaction. "Try this on. I think it'll fit."

I leaned against the back bumper of the truck, Dave helping me keep my balance as I pulled my boot off and replaced it with the one he handed to me. It fit pretty well, in spite of looking too big. I put the other one on as Dave pulled out a down jacket for me to try. I stood up and took the hoodie off—I had already realized it was not going to keep me warm enough—and slipped into the coat. The sleeves were a little long, but it would do. I zipped it up as Dave pulled a few more items from the truck.

"These should work," he said, handing me insulated gloves. "They used to be mine, too. They're too small for me now but still too big for Henry."

I blushed furiously as it was clear he was dressing me in his own clothes. But he continued as unaffected as ever. Lastly, standing face to face, he pulled a knit beanie over my head and ears, almost knocking my glasses off but catching and setting them gently back in place. I was holding my breath and shivering, overwhelmed by his thoughtful care. Nobody but my parents had ever treated me the way he did and, as always, it moved me.

"There," he said, standing back to evaluate his work. "Perfect. Now you have to have fun. Sometimes I think you don't know how, or you're afraid to. Not today, okay?"

These last remarks surprised me. Is that what he honestly thought? And he *did* think of such things? *And is it true?*

I shivered violently and he looked concerned.

"Are you cold?" I shook my head quickly; I was already very cozy. "Come on," he said, his eyes dancing. He grabbed a snowboard and what looked like several pairs of goggles and led the way. "Wait 'til you see this. . . ."

I followed him, stepping carefully through the foreign substance in the unfamiliar boots and following in the tracks of the others who had gone on ahead. We walked through fairly dense trees for several minutes. I was enchanted by the pristine beauty of the white forest, the clarity of the air feeling almost sharp to my lungs and the exposed skin of my face. Every so often, a soft *thud* sounded close by when a large clump of snow became too heavy and fell off a pine branch onto the snow covered ground. The only other sounds were the powdery *crunch* our boots made as we stepped through the white blanket.

As the trees thinned, more of the sun reached us. We finally came to an open field surrounded on two sides by the forest. To our left was a fairly steep, treeless incline, but I gasped at the view spread out directly before us.

The others all appeared to be on the far side of the field, surveying the view and talking and laughing. Then they began walking with all the gear toward the steep hillside. Dave and I walked to where they had been moments before.

There was a gentle decline before us, but spreading out beyond that to the mountain-studded horizon was a panoramic view, tinged golden by the rising sun and unlike anything I'd ever seen. It was worthy of one of those huge picture books that grabs your attention at the front of bookstores. Almost everything was snow covered, but darker colors—rock, last year's shed needles, and patches of green—showed through in small sheltered patches. It was truly magical.

I stood gawking for quite some time until something hard, cold, and stinging hit the back of my head. Sure of my attacker, I turned around, ready to protest Dave's behavior. But I was brought up short.

Chris stood several yards away, coolly regarding me, expressionless as ever, and forming another snowball between gloved hands. My jaw dropped and my eyes popped wide realizing he'd not only circled back and hidden in the trees waiting for me to come out into the open, but he now prepared, very deliberately, to pelt me with another projectile. I began backing away as quickly as the snow and cumbersome boots allowed.

"Get her, Henry," he said, calmly.

What!

The next thing I knew, I'd been tackled by a robust eight-year-old, almost knocked off my feet, and was now held quite firmly, my arms pinned against my sides. I expected Chris to lob the snowball from where he stood, but he began walking very slowly toward me holding the large, firmly packed orb in his right hand.

"No . . ." I said, unbelieving and looking for a way out of the situation. I looked to Dave. He'd moved out of the way as soon as I'd gotten hit, probably thinking he was next. Now he watched, looking confused but apparently amused enough to allow his brothers to continue.

"Henry!" I said firmly, managing to extricate my arms. "Let . . . me . . . *go!*" I gasped, now ineffectively working to remove his arms from around my waist.

He just laughed. Now I was laughing too—nervously.

Chris continued his slow, deliberate progress toward me, torturing me with anticipation until he stood directly in front of me. He didn't look me straight in the eyes but took brief glances there. "What? You don't think I'd hit you square in the face with this, do you?"

I laughed nervously again. "I . . . don't . . . um . . ."

He scowled slightly as if hurt that I'd consider such a thing. "I'd never do that," he said, his voice deadly soft, and I felt a moment of relief. Perhaps he was content with just alarming me badly.

Nope. In the next instant, he slipped behind me, grabbed the back of my collar, and stuffed as much of the well-packed snow down it as he could before Henry's grip loosened and they both let me go. I squealed loudly, both from the cold of the attack and the absolute fright he'd given me. Henry was rolling on the ground laughing. I quickly unzipped my jacket and tried to remove as much of the offending ice from my back as I could.

"Consider us even," Chris said, a strange look in his eyes and a very slight smile on his lips.

I caught my breath in complete surprise. I couldn't tell whether he was just satisfied with his revenge or if he really thought it was funny. But *that* was the expression I had seen in the painting, the *"You'll never guess what I'm thinking"* look that had fascinated me. It was gone quickly and so was he, stopping just long enough to scoop up another large wad of snow. Then he walked away toward the hillside the others had climbed.

"One down," he said, quietly. "Come on, Henry."

Chapter Twenty-Three

Not Always

"I guess that's official initiation into the family," said Dave, watching his brothers hike up the hill. "Welcome to it!"

He gave me his most charming smile, the one that can melt anyone, especially me. But I couldn't help feeling funny about what he'd said. On the one hand, to really be a part of this wonderful family would be an amazing thing; I was already in love with all of them. Well, almost all of them. Those I didn't exactly love, I had a growing appreciation for, even if it was a little hard to recall it right now. *On the other hand. . . .*

"So . . . I guess that makes me your sister?" I said jokingly, hoping to be set straight.

He grinned widely, "Yeah, something like that."

From friend to sister, not exactly the relationship progression I'd been dreaming of.

Chris' retribution on Robin was not accomplished as quickly or quietly as it had been on me. She'd taken charge of Stevey on getting out of the SUV, but after seeing what happened to me, she'd put him safely into Mr. Caldera's custody so she could concentrate on evasion tactics. She managed this for a while, the whole time loudly threatening the boys with fates worse than death if they persisted. She eventually got caught between Chris and Henry, who took turns pelting her with small, hard-packed snowballs as they closed the distance between them. This escalated into a full-on war with Robin

throwing her own quickly made and ill-formed balls back at them, with a special concentration on Chris.

Finally apprehending her and pinning her by the elbows from behind, he allowed Henry to do the honors. She fell to her knees in her struggle and Henry gleefully stuffed as much snow as he could down her back before she wriggled free and started pelting them again, screaming and laughing at the top of her lungs as she did. Dave and I had been watching and laughing from below, but now felt it relatively safe to join them.

Everyone gathered about halfway up the hill where a narrow shelf split the hillside roughly in two. The upper half was steep. The lower was somewhat steep on one side but sloped more gently on the other, finally leveling out into the field below. I was exhausted when we reached them. Even Dave was a little winded, but he immediately joined his two brothers and Robin in sizing up the slope and discussing how they should descend it. They made note of a prominent hillock toward the center of the level area we stood on. Stevey and Mr. Caldera had begun making a snowman near the trees. I stood marveling at the view.

"Allie! Come on!" called Dave.

I shook my head.

"What?" He sounded incredulous. "You don't want to?" Then he looked thoughtful. "Oh . . . I guess you've never done anything like this before, right?"

"I'll just watch," I said, hoping he wasn't going to insist. He could be so darn persuasive and I already knew that I had little resistance to his will.

He regarded me silently for a moment, then smiled, skated to the edge, and prepared to descend. "I'll go first," he said, securing his free foot.

He maneuvered his board and began a leisurely descent down the steepest edge of the hillside in a somewhat start and stop fashion as if afraid to go too fast. I was pretty sure that wasn't true. Chris went down next, making a slow, wide sweep back and forth, mostly across the center and more gradually sloping side of the open hillside. He looked around constantly as if looking for something, but when he got to the bottom where Dave already was, he looked up to us and gave a thumbs up.

"Me next!" said Henry excitedly, pushing himself to the edge of the terrace, about the middle of the hill, and tightening his bindings.

He descended faster and not in as much of a zigzag pattern as Chris had done but without the stops in between like Dave. Robin followed next, just a little faster than Henry. When she reached the bottom, the four of them toiled back up to where I waited. Mr. Caldera and Stevey were still working on the snowman.

"Come on, didn't that look like fun?" asked Dave, a little out of breath as he gained level ground again. "I can teach you. . . ." he said, coaxing.

"I . . . I think I'll just watch." I was determined not to be tempted. He just didn't understand my balance issues.

Henry went down the hill first this time, faster and whooping all the way. Then Robin went, also looking more confident and even doing a one-eighty turn. Both began hiking back up as soon as they reached the bottom. Dave went down on the steepest side again, but fast this time and doing tricks similar to those I'd seen kids do on skateboards. Chris followed, looking more at ease but less exhilarated. Dave's expression had been one of pure joy, like Henry's on exiting the truck. Chris looked calm, almost serene, as if his mind were blank or transcended to some other plane. If his eyes had been closed, he could have been asleep. He made everything look so effortless. Except smiling. He definitely wasn't good at that. At least, not anymore.

As I watched him and Dave hike back up the hill together, I thought about his revenge strategy again and was very perplexed. Why did he choose to attack me first instead of Robin? She'd seen what happened to me, so he'd already lost the element of surprise. He could have used that to much greater advantage against Robin. Surely he would have known that?

Instead, he chose to attack me first, making sure *I* suffered the brunt of the first attack. Why? Because if he had attacked Robin first, yes, he would have gotten the element of surprise, but it would have been over more quickly and efficiently with both of us, and therefore probably not as satisfying? She certainly wouldn't have suffered the way I did in the same situation. And he wouldn't have been able to get me twice without completely terrorizing me. He probably knew I wouldn't put up a fight the way Robin would, but that the anticipation and uncertainty and then snow down my back would be a better punishment for me than a forced attack. He really *did* get me twice. He definitely got his money's worth, first out of me, and then her.

If he'd done the same to Robin, she would have just dealt with it right away and it would have been over. Because she saw what happened to me, she knew what was coming. She had to deal with that anticipation and then fight back, which Chris must have known she would do. He probably found

that satisfying as well. The fact that he had planned the whole thing with Henry proved it. *What kind of evil genius is he?*

Stevey and Mr. Caldera had finished their snowman and now approached me. The others were still hiking up the hill, to the very top this time.

"You must go down the hill," said Mr. Caldera, not scolding but obviously expecting it.

"Oh . . . I . . . I don't know," I replied nervously. "I'm not good at—"

"Look," he said, cutting me off brusquely, though I was sure he didn't mean to be rude. "Stevey and I will show you. Right, Stevey? We shall go down *this* side. It's not so steep. Come on, Stevey," he said, holding his hand out to his son. "Watch us and see how easy it is."

Robin had made it back up and walked over as Mr. Caldera pulled the toboggan into place at the edge of the plateau. He settled Stevey in the front then sat behind him, his hands on movable handles on the sides.

"We'll push you!" called Robin. "Come on!" she said to me, and we both ran and pushed them over the edge.

The sled began slowly then quickly picked up speed.

"Let's use the boards!" She grabbed my sleeve and dragged me to where the foam boards were.

"I don't think—" I started, eyeing the relatively steep drop.

"No, we'll go over there. The easier side," she said, grinning. "Special, just for you." She laughed and dragged her board over there. I followed with some trepidation, but game to try. "So," she continued, "snowboarding's kind of like skateboarding and surfing, but this is more like Boogie-boarding, only without the waves. You ride and steer pretty much the same way, by leaning your body. You've Boogie-boarded, right?"

I was relieved I could honestly say yes to that. You didn't grow up near the beach in Southern California without bodyboarding at least a little.

"So, instead of waves carrying you, you've got gravity pulling. Don't let the nose dig in and you should be fine. Bank to the sides to slow down. I'll go first!"

She laid the board down and pushed off as she flattened herself on it. She made it look so easy and fun. Standing up at the bottom, she laughed and waved for me to follow her down.

It was now or never. I didn't dare look to see where Dave was or if he was watching; I would have lost my nerve. I pushed myself forward on the board and panicked as it immediately slipped down the slope and picked up speed. I forgot to angle and concentrated on keeping my weight back on the back of the board. Near the bottom, I managed to turn slightly which probably saved me a nasty crash, but I still went tumbling off. I was laughing, though. Dave and Henry were whooping from the top of the hill, I assumed in approval.

"Okay," I said breathlessly, picking myself up off the ground. "That was *nothing* like Boogie-boarding."

"It was fun, though. Right?"

"Yes," I admitted, laughing. "It was fun."

"Watch out below!" called Dave, his voice echoing around us.

We stayed where we were as Dave, then Henry—less flamboyantly—and finally Chris boarded all the way down the hill. Dave and Chris both came down the top half very fast, seeming to aim for a precise spot on the level shelf, then became airborne briefly.

I caught my breath when Dave jumped. He grabbed and tweaked the board before he landed, then quickly turned near the bottom, sending up a rooster tail of snow. Henry did slow slalom movements down the top part of the hill, hit the terrace and caught the air after jumping at the edge. He tucked his little knees up close to his body and then landed nicely, gliding the rest of the way down. We applauded and cheered. Chris came down the hill so fast and low it scared me. When he jumped, he seemed to tumble in the air before landing. He hit the snow again going so fast he went most of the way sideways to keep from going too far into the open field.

"Show off! I can do that," Dave chided. He looked at me sheepishly, "I can do that, but it takes me a little longer to get warmed up to it, especially here. On the bigger slopes, it's easier."

We all walked back up the hill together, Dave teasing Chris, calling him a hotshot and an exhibitionist, and Chris trying to cuff him over the head. Chris finally threw down his board and attacked Dave, who just managed to drop his own board and run a few steps before being tackled to the ground and made to eat snow. Henry thought it was hilarious. It *was* pretty funny and Dave seemed to be laughing the hardest. The sound of his laughter was rich, warm, and very contagious. I had thought it would be.

When Chris was satisfied, they picked up their boards and caught up with us at the level area. The three older boys continued to the top while Stevey, Mr. Caldera, Robin, and I took our turns down the gentler side of the hill

again. We continued like this for quite a while, Robin and me taking turns with Stevey on the toboggan while Mr. Caldera snowboarded. He seemed a little embarrassed that he didn't go to the top of the hill with his sons.

"I prefer skiing," he said.

Henry kept his tricks to small jumps and board grabs while Dave and Chris seemed to try to jump as high as they could and fit in as many different moves as possible before hitting the ground. Chris managed this better than Dave, who seemed intent on outdoing his brother but more often ended up biting it, laughing the whole time. Both older brothers also took turns going down the hillside with Stevey on the toboggan. Several times Stevey came to me, taking my hand and wanting me to ride with him, which I did.

After a while, feeling extremely tired, I took a break by sitting on a large fallen tree to the side of the terrace. From here I could easily watch everyone and rest my already aching muscles.

"Are you okay?" asked Dave, coming over to check on me.

"I'm fine," I assured him. "Just taking a break."

He smiled, said, "Okay," and backed away before returning to his board and hiking up to the top again.

The truth was, not only was I already tired and a little sore but quite wet and cold, though I didn't want Dave worrying about it. I was trying to sit in the sun, which was drying my pants legs out a bit.

Chris eventually came over to where I sat. I watched him warily as he approached, but he held both hands up as if to show that he came in peace. He sat on the tree log with me, not too far away, and we remained silent for a while, watching the others and enjoying the magnificent view.

When I was finally fairly sure he had no ulterior motives in sitting with me, at least not detrimental to my general warmth and comfort, I defied danger and risked conversation. This had always been hit and miss with Chris, seeming to depend on his mood.

"This is such a gorgeous place. How do you know about it? Does your family own it?"

Chris shook his head, his eyes on the skyline. "It belongs to a friend of my dad. He's invited us here a lot and told us we could come whenever we want, so sometimes we do at the beginning of the season. There's usually good early snowfall right here and it stays sheltered from the wind and sun most of the day, so the snow remains longer. Sometimes we come later in the winter if we only have a few hours, but the conditions aren't always as good. Like today." He looked around appreciatively but frowned into the sun. "It's perfect, though the snow's not that deep. Otherwise we usually go to Tahoe or further north for a couple of days."

"You guys are really good at it, aren't you?" I commented. "Snowboarding, I mean."

He shrugged. "We've been doing it a long time, but we just play around. Dave and I prefer the bigger slopes and terrain parks, and Dad prefers skiing, but this is fun for everyone. When we go away, Angel and Stevey come too, but we go where there's a lodge and other stuff for them to do. Angel does *not* like snow." He *almost* smiled. "She likes the atmosphere at the lodges, though, and seems to enjoy her time there."

Dave made it to the top of the hill again and went flying down, doing a three-sixty as he took the jump, and even managing to flash us a huge, joyful grin as he turned our way.

"Nothing gets him down, does it?" I observed, thinking out loud. "I mean . . . he always seems so confident and happy. I really . . . admire that."

I suddenly felt uncomfortable and surprised at myself, speaking my thoughts aloud to Chris, but oddly relieved as well. In spite of my opinion on his lapse in judgment as far as a certain confrontation went, and though I never knew how he felt about me, I had no doubt that he loved his brothers. I trusted and respected that.

Chris' gaze followed his brother down the rest of the hill and the start of his ascent back up. "Mmm," he murmured but said nothing more.

What does that mean?

I was afraid I might regret it, going out on a limb like this, but now I wanted to know. "I mean, I've seen him annoyed by things, maybe even a little angry, but he most always seems happy, as if he doesn't have a care in the world. I've never seen him look worried or . . . or sad."

Chris was quiet for the longest time. I assumed either I had crossed too far over some family privacy line or he'd just lost interest. But he eventually sighed slightly, looking at the snow by his feet, and said, "Looks can be deceiving. People don't always show their true feelings." He glanced at me. "You should know that."

Very clever.

I thought this was his way of closing the subject, but he continued, "Someone might seem to be thinking or feeling a certain way but be feeling something completely different. Or even the opposite."

I, of course, knew this to be true, even prided myself on being good at it. Was Chris just rubbing it in, letting me know I didn't fool him? Or was he referring to Dave? Or someone else?

"Sometimes people only show what they want others to see. Don't you find that to be true?" He said this pointedly, pinning me with his eyes for all of about three seconds, almost a record for eye contact with him.

Squirm.

I thought it a very unfair rhetorical question, if it *was* rhetorical. I had to admit, I trusted Chris to a certain extent but wasn't anywhere near ready to share confidences. Then again, maybe he wasn't as sure of himself as he wanted to appear. I refused to take the bait. *I'd rather keep him guessing.*

He seemed to deliberate about something, glancing my way again before saying, "He has bad dreams." I was probably frowning. He assumed I didn't understand. "Nightmares."

I'd understood, but it took me completely by surprise, both the confidence and the content of it. *Dave has nightmares?*

"What about?" I asked, concerned. "Do you know why he has them?"

Chris was quiet again. I got the feeling he was letting me think about it just as much as he was considering how much more to tell me.

He finally said, "It's not for me to say, but he doesn't like to talk or even think about it, so you shouldn't mention it. I just thought that you should know." He stood up, looking at the horizon, then said, "By the way, it's Robin's birthday on Wednesday. She doesn't like people making a big deal, so she might not tell you, but I figured you should know that too. We'll be doing something on Saturday. You'll be invited. Just wanted to give you a heads up in case Dave forgets." With that, he walked away.

What the. . . ? What was all that supposed to mean?

I appreciated the warning about Robin's birthday—it would be just like her to tell me *after* her birthday to avoid too much attention—and about whatever was happening Saturday so I could ask my parents in advance. But what was that about Dave and nightmares? Did Robin know about it? Why did Chris think I should know? Because he knows how much I care for him? Or just because of the whole "sister" thing, which I assumed extended to Chris?

There was now a sensitive secret between Chris and me, and I wasn't sure I liked it. And I didn't want to get into trouble with Dave sometime in the future because I knew something he didn't want me to. At the same time, I was glad that Chris *had* told me. I never would have guessed. It shed a whole new light on the person I adored, and I wanted to know about everything that affected him.

Mr. Caldera called a halt to the activities just after Chris left me. Although it was barely noon, we were already mostly in shadow and it was much colder than it had been just a little while before. We gathered up the gear, made one last descent down the hill, and trekked back to the SUV. I froze even more as we walked back through the forest—my teeth were chattering and I shivered uncontrollably. I was happy once the heater in the big vehicle had kicked in.

"You should get some snow pants," observed Dave.

I glared at him. "Well, now that I know I might *need* them. . . ."

He looked a little wide-eyed and grinned hugely. "You sounded just like Robin!"

They both laughed and I joined them. Yes, they were definitely rubbing off on me.

"You had fun though, right?" he asked, his eyes dancing.

"Yes," I happily admitted. "I had a *ton* of fun."

"We'll have you snowboarding next time," he said.

"Next time?" I asked, half fearfully, half hopefully. I would love to do this again but still didn't think I wanted to snowboard. "I'll definitely have to get better clothing."

"Hmmm. Don't you have warmer clothes?"

I almost felt apologetic, as if I should have been better prepared. I shook my head. "I guess I'll have to go shopping soon if the weather's going to stay this cold for a while."

The others all looked at each other. Then Robin said, "This isn't even cold. January, February . . . *then* it's cold."

"And the snow is better," grinned Dave. "We'll hit the bigger slopes later when they're fully open."

"Bigger slopes?" I asked, my eyes wide.

Robin looked at me indulgently. "Where we were today would be considered barely more than a bunny slope, and that's only because it's not a long hill and you have to be able to stop quickly."

I nodded, hoping to look as if I understood. It was all right, though. It had been an amazing morning and I felt I'd learned a lot. A *lot.*

I was glad Chris had warned me about Robin's birthday. It gave me time to get her something. I deliberated over this for a long time. I still didn't feel I knew her that well but wanted to get her something more personal than a gift card. In the end, I bought a CD that was one of my favorites and I knew was unlike anything she already had. And Mom helped me pick out a green pullover sweater that we both thought would look great with her hair and eye color.

The activity on Saturday turned out to be a horse show that both Robin and Henry were riding in, and then we'd go for pizza afterward to celebrate Robin's birthday. We'd be getting up early the next day, so she asked if I could spend the night on Friday. My parents agreed without hesitation.

She also invited me to spend the afternoon of her birthday with her after school. We had a nice time, the whole crowd going for coffee, and then Dave walked back to her house with us. We spent most of the time outside playing with Gali and watching Robin put him through reining patterns. When it got dark, we went inside to keep Fiona company and talk about the upcoming show. Chris picked Dave up later when he was done with work.

I didn't get much sleep. It was funny because Robin had said she could never sleep the night before a show, but she slept soundly. I know because I was awake for most of it. Apart from just being excited about the show and getting to spend the whole day with friends again, I wasn't used to sleeping on the floor, and though I had plenty of blankets, it was very cold. And I'd never tell her, but Robin snored.

We were up well before sunrise to eat a hot breakfast, drink hot tea, and get Robin and Gali ready. Mr. Caldera pulled up with the long trailer about six-thirty and we reached the show grounds about an hour later. Chris, who'd apparently been taking a lot of time off work what with one thing and another, hadn't come, but Dave was there to help Robin and especially Henry. Angel and Stevey would come later to watch.

Robin's first class, a Western pleasure class, was at nine o'clock. She seemed nervous, which surprised me.

"Gali doesn't always behave himself in these classes," she said. "They're too ... pedestrian, or something. He doesn't like being held in. We don't have a chance anyway. So many people have showy, perfectly behaved horses. But I guess it's good for us to do something other than racing sports. The Calderas insist it is, anyway. But I still get nervous about it. We have a trail class later this morning. He does pretty well in those—they're interesting enough to keep him from getting bored. And then barrels and poles this afternoon." She paused and had a calm, quiet look on her face for just a moment, then turned to me and said, "I'm really glad you're here. I even slept well last night. And I feel really good today."

I flushed with pleasure. I hadn't done anything at all, yet Robin's words were heartfelt.

Henry, who looked very snazzy in his show attire, had been getting ready on the other side of the trailer with Dave's help. But now they both joined us to wait for our riders' first class. Henry had two horses for the day's events. The first seemed to be one of the pleasure horses Robin had mentioned, a pretty chestnut Quarter mare, rather small but well-mannered with nice gaits. The other was a taller—though still small compared to Gold—black horse looking a lot like Dave's Tee.

"Another brother," said Dave when I asked about him.

Henry's pleasure class was first. Dave and Robin kept up a discussion of all the riders' and horses' strengths and weaknesses from what they could see, including Henry of course. It was very educational. It was also encouraging when I realized that I could understand most of what they were saying, and I tried to store up the information. Dave especially made sure they explained anything I might not comprehend on my own, such as exactly what the judges were looking for.

"You'll be doing this soon," he said slyly, as if he knew something I didn't.

I wasn't going to argue with him, but I could have pointed out that I didn't exactly have a mount. Even thinking this brought me down a little. I was trying to avoid thinking of Gold's inevitable departure.

The day seemed to pass much too quickly, Henry's class followed immediately by Robin's, a short break, and then the trail classes. These took a long time as the riders went individually and there were a lot of entrants

in each division. Robin and Dave started seeing people they knew, and I even recognized some riding in the classes or just hanging out, like me. A few seemed to take special notice of my presence, but I tried to ignore the attention. Besides, I was officially there with Robin, not Dave.

We had time to eat lunch, then a quick change of clothes and mount for Henry, and changes of clothes for Robin and tack for Gali before the gym-khana events began. Henry and Robin were in separate divisions again, but these classes moved quickly, the large numbers of entrants offset by the speed of the events themselves.

The weather, which had been mostly sunny this morning, had completely clouded over, become a little windy and cold, and seemed to be threatening rain. I couldn't prevent myself from shivering which caused Dave to frown disapprovingly.

"Are you going to get some warm clothes? You know, it's not even cold right now." He seemed perfectly comfortable in a t-shirt, long-sleeved shirt, and denim jacket.

I laughed and looked apologetically at my sweat jacket. I had even layered underneath again. "I've never needed anything more than this before. We haven't had a chance to go shopping."

"Hmm," he said. "I forgot about it, but we'll get a group together for a foray into the city." He seemed to consider it further, then smiled and said, "Yeah. It'll be fun."

I smiled back. *Of course it will. Everything with you is fun!*

Our last event, Robin's pole bending, ended just as a light but steady rain began to fall. Dave helped get Henry's horses loaded in the trailer while I helped Robin unsaddle Gali. Then I put her tack away as she loaded him. In no time we were on the road for the drive back to Douglas, still relatively dry and very happy and talkative.

Angel, who had watched in the stands with Mr. Caldera and Stevey, met us at Robin's house where we unloaded Gali. Dave and his dad left with Henry to take his horses home and care for them. They would meet us back in town later. Angel enjoyed a cup of tea and probably a little gossip with Fiona while I helped Robin get Gali settled. Fiona had a warm mash ready for him which he dove into with relish. In spite of the misty rain, we spent some time rubbing him down while he ate.

Angel drove us to dinner while Robin regaled Fiona with all the details of our day. At one point Angel unaccountably said, "Dah-veed, he weel be driving soon." This seemed to be said with a deliberate look at me in the rearview mirror, but it was probably my imagination.

Dinner was noisy but fun. Angel ordered the pizza—lots of it—with much input from Robin, and it was ready just before Chris arrived. He'd come straight from work. Dave, Henry, and their dad rejoined us soon after that.

I mostly just observed and listened contentedly to the happy, rowdy group: Robin and Henry reliving their day, yet again, for Chris' benefit, and the adults enjoying lively conversation with each other. Only once in a while did they interrupt the conversation at our end of the table to interject something or, on several occasions, to tell me to eat more.

It occurred to me that I was really an outsider among them, not truly belonging to either family, yet feeling completely accepted by both. And not just accepted—*important*. They never treated me with the kind of deference that would have made me feel set apart from them, as you might treat someone you weren't sure of or didn't know well but wanted to make a good impression on. I always felt included. They always made me feel like I *did* belong though they never seemed to be trying to. And I still had no idea why they would even want to. For the dorky misfit I'd always felt I was, this was a huge thing. Wrapped in a feeling I couldn't even put a name to, I just knew I was grateful. Incredibly grateful.

When it was time to leave, I barely felt disappointed that Dave wouldn't be in the vehicle taking me home. He'd be taking the younger boys home with Mr. Caldera while Angel took Robin and Fiona home. That left Chris to drive me, but I was okay with that.

Dave bumped shoulders with me as we walked out into the mizzly rain. Before parting he softly said, "See ya," accompanied by my favorite smile, the gentle one I'd only seen him use for Stevey and me.

I smiled back, still feeling wrapped in warm fuzzies. "Bye."

Chris and I didn't talk much on the ride to my house, but I enjoyed listening to his music all the way there. When he dropped me off, he frowned deeply and observed, "You need a warmer coat."

I laughed.

I had my lesson with Cheryl the next day and rode in the covered arena since it was raining. She seemed pleased with my progress and started me "playing airplane," as Cody called it, at the lope which I managed to accomplish, more or less.

"I think we'll start you on Remmy next time," she said when the lesson was over.

I froze and gaped at her. Mom usually let me hang out for a while after my lessons before coming to pick me up, and I spent most of that time petting and talking to Remmy. He was very sweet and reminded me so much of Dave—the color of the hair of his coat, his friendly disposition, his brown eyes, sometimes bright and mischievous and at other times soft and gentle.

"What! Really? Is that all right?"

"Dave suggested it. He said you could use him as soon as I felt you were ready. Remmy's gaits are faster than Flash's and will be more challenging for you, but he's careful with new riders and very generous." She looked thoughtful for a moment and added, "Just like his owner. In fact," she paused and looked at me again, seeming to size me up in a way similar to the first time we met, "I think you'll be a good match."

She turned away then, but I was sure I saw her smirk.

What does that mean? Maybe I'm just being paranoid. I'm seeing and hearing things that just aren't there.

The weather remained changeable during the last weeks of the fall semester, which meant Dave was around quite a bit during lunchtimes. Chris was either in training himself or helping Coach with the younger players, both rain and shine, so we rarely saw him during school. And between work and basketball games after school, he was seldom around at all.

My parents let me walk home with Robin at least once a week on the dryer days so we could hang out and do homework together. We actually spent most of the time with Gali, Robin giving me supplemental lessons and I watching her work with him.

On rainy days, Mom picked us both up, either dropping Robin at her house or bringing her home with us. I enjoyed the latter more as I got to spend more time with her. She helped me groom Gold and gave me a chance to ride him a little if it wasn't too wet, me riding him bareback while she lunged him. His behavior was always exemplary, and while Robin hadn't changed her opinion of his appearance much, she was impressed by his wonderful temperament and beautiful movement.

On the dry days that I was home, I groomed and lunged Gold, walked him on the lead rope all over our property, and talked to him for hours. On Fridays, I was usually able to hang out after school, rain or shine, one place or another. The days seemed to be speeding by.

Our shopping trip was finally arranged and set for the second Sunday of December. There would be quite a group going and it was certainly something to look forward to. Dave said it would be "semi-chaperoned," but I didn't know what that meant. My parents again made no demur about the outing. I thought it was a little strange that they asked for no particulars and set no guidelines for me to follow, but I didn't want to think too hard— "gift horses" and all.

Mom had already taken me shopping for some warmer clothes. She had bought me two jackets: one was cute and warm enough for school, and another more practical and insulated for wearing around the horses or if I got to go to the snow again. She also bought me a couple of sweaters and another pair of jeans, but she said she'd give me some money for the mall trip so I could buy a couple more warm shirts or sweaters.

The only other things I bought before our shopping trip were acquired one day after school when Robin and I walked into town. At the hardware store, which also carried basic outerwear, Chris helped me find a pair of rubber boots suitable for taking care of Gold in wet weather. My Western boots were getting pretty gross from all the mud.

The guys got Dad's permission to add roof panels over about a third of Gold's paddock and siding around one corner. While apparently not really necessary, Chris was concerned that Gold should have some protection from wind and rain. That impressed me as very thoughtful.

Gold was almost solid brown now and his hair was becoming quite shaggy. Though I groomed him as much as I could and left the blanket on him most of the time, the general dampness of the weather plus his love of rolling guaranteed a dark, dull coat. Chris came by sometimes to work with

him, but I rarely actually saw him and never got to talk to him. He was so busy with sports and work these days that I don't think anybody saw him much.

I talked to Brenda on the phone a couple of times, but we seemed to have less and less to talk about. I told her about our snow trip, which she seemed interested in, and the horse show, which she didn't. When she told me of her most recent shopping trip, I responded by telling her about my big rubber boots. She didn't know what to say to that.

Thanksgiving came and went uneventfully, except for the actual trip to and from Los Angeles, my mother insisting that we spend the whole vacation time there. I felt guilty that I really hadn't missed our extended family at all. I'd thought of my grandparents and called them a couple of times, but I'd barely even thought of my cousins, except in comparison to the new children in my life: Henry, Stevey, Cody, and Cheryl's baby girl, Zoe. In contrast, I sorely missed my friends—my new family—very much, even though it was only a few days spent away.

Dave had asked what we were doing for Thanksgiving dinner and I told him about the trip down south. He had looked a little disappointed at first, but then he smiled, said he was sure we'd have a great time, and volunteered to make sure Gold got taken care of. I'd been concerned about that. Dad had figured we'd offer to pay Tom or one of the Bar 8 wranglers to stop by to feed and check on him or something. But Dave said they could take care of him as they'd be home the whole time.

It was the Calderas' tradition to have a huge Thanksgiving dinner with the families of their full-time employees, and also the Cowells; one big family gathering. Later, I wondered if Dave had been going to ask us to join them as well, but I never found out. I was extremely envious of Robin but happy and comforted too, knowing that both she and her grandmother would be well looked after during the holiday.

I was halfheartedly watching a movie with my cousins after the huge dinner on Thursday, trying not to be morose while thinking about how much more fun it would have been at Dave's house—and how he would *not* be thinking of me—when he called.

"Did you eat?" were his first words.

I laughed. "Of course. Nobody risks offending my grandmother. Not even me. Did you have a good dinner?"

He groaned. "I'm stuffed. Double stuffed. Like an Oreo cookie. And I haven't even had dessert yet. I don't think I'll eat again 'til Christmas."

At this point, Robin, who was apparently close by, started telling Dave to tell me things, and I told him things to reply to her, which got a little confusing, especially when he started interjecting his own comments. We all ended up laughing hard.

Finally Dave said, "Apparently I've got to go. See you Monday, I guess."

"Yes," I said, clinging to the softening sound of his voice.

"Bye."

"Bye."

Chapter Twenty-Four

I'll Find You

Semi-chaperoned, as far as our shopping trip went, meant that parents would be driving us to and from the mall, but otherwise we'd be left to our own devices. A wonderful concept. Mr. Caldera had arranged to take care of some business in Sacramento and then meet some friends for an early dinner. He was driving the hybrid and taking the girls: Robin, Jessie, Stacie, and me. Mrs. Morris was visiting a friend outside the city and bringing the boys: Matthew, Tanner, and Kyle. Chris wanted to drive himself so Dave went with him. Chris' friend, Shane, and a couple of the older girls were apparently coming too and would catch up with us there.

The weather was cloudy and threatening rain but not terribly cold, so I wore a new top and pair of jeans with my sweat jacket. The other girls dressed similarly. Robin wore the green sweater I'd gotten her and it looked perfect.

The trip there was actually fun. I had been concerned as I still wasn't completely comfortable around the other girls. Somehow Robin arranged for me to sit between them in the back seat while she sat in the front. At first I felt uneasy, but she turned around and talked to all of us most of the time, and the other girls, in talking back to her and each other, often included me in the conversation.

They mostly discussed what they were shopping for: Jessie was looking for clothes for herself, Stacie said, "Everything," and Robin said she just wanted to find something for her grandmother for Christmas. I had the money Mom had given me and some money of my own from past gifts and allowances that I hoped to purchase Christmas presents with, too. But something caused me to only mention the gift shopping. I rarely spent money—my only recent purchases being the pairs of Western and rubber boots—so I was looking forward to doing just that. It occurred to me that it might be difficult as at least one of the people I would be shopping for was here with me. I'd worry about that later.

"I bet you've been to some great malls, huh?" asked Jessie, surprising me with a direct question. "In LA?"

"I guess," I said. I'd never been the shopper Brenda had obviously become. "I didn't go shopping much. I got lost once when I was nine. It was in a really big mall and I was pretty scared, so. . . ." I shrugged.

"Well," said Robin, "this is a pretty big mall, I think, but we'll try not to lose you. Okay? But I'm *not* holding your hand!"

I did my best impression of not caring. "Well, fine!"

The other girls laughed.

Mr. Caldera dropped us off at the main entrance to the huge structure. I thought it looked like an enormous conservatory or botanical garden greenhouse from the outside. Dave and Chris were waiting there for us. They were dressed as they often were at school these days: Dave in a short sleeved collared shirt over a long sleeved thermal, and Chris wearing a T-shirt and sweat jacket. Both wore jeans and skate shoes.

We walked over to Dave to wait for the other boys to arrive. He nodded briefly to me and then had his attention claimed completely by the other three girls. I felt dorky just standing by myself, so went and sat on a low wall. Chris talked to his dad, or rather, his dad talked to him and he just nodded his head a lot. Then he walked back to us, fingers crammed in his front pockets, and stood kind of slouchy like normal. The other boys arrived with Matthew's mom soon after. They jumped out of the car, waved to her, and then entered the mall with us.

Inside was just as impressive as outside: bright, airy, and wide open with the central lobby area and main corridor between the two levels of stores open to the top of the transparent roof. It was a shame the day was gray and rainy as I'm sure sunlight would have streamed through. But inside was lit up just as much if not more by the gigantic festooned and lighted Christmas tree and the bright decorations and myriad tiny white lights throughout the

mall. It was beautiful—in a slightly gaudy, fantasy-land kind of way. I was relieved to hear familiar dance music playing fairly loudly in the background instead of the annoying holiday tune arrangements that usually dominated this time of year.

I guess I'd expected, or at least hoped, that I'd be able to stay near Dave from the beginning, but he hadn't looked at me since we'd entered the mall. Without even a backward glance in my direction, he urged Robin to follow him and seemed to hurriedly move away with her. Feeling a little slighted, both hurt and uncertain, I hoped I was just being too sensitive and started to follow them anyway. But my sleeve was plucked from behind, causing me to stop and turn to see who it was. I was expecting Matthew—I hadn't gotten to talk to him in a long time. But it was Chris. I was surprised.

"Let the others go ahead," he said in almost a whisper. "I need to talk to you."

My mind whirled. I hadn't really seen or talked to him either, not since the snow day over a month ago. Although he'd been at the pizza place the day of the horse show, and had even driven me home, I hadn't paid much attention to him. What was this about? Did it have to do with his confidences to me about Dave? Was it about Gold? His face was as solemn as ever, a slight crease between his brows that could turn into a scowl at any moment. Was I in trouble again?

The others had moved beyond us; we followed slowly, and at a slight distance. Robin looked around a couple of times, obviously looking for me, though Dave never did. She seemed to accept the fact that I was walking with Chris, for whatever reason, and then seemed to forget about me. The whole group was walking slowly too, looking in the windows they passed and talking together. When they stopped, we stopped.

"We need your help," Chris finally said.

"What?" I asked, startled. "How?" *What on earth could I possibly ever do for you? And at a mall?*

He kept his voice very low as he continued, "You've probably noticed, but Robin doesn't have much, materially at least. Her grandmother isn't able to buy her things. Especially clothes. She acts like it's no big deal, and she'd never say anything about it, but we figure, she's a girl, she must want clothes. Right? We . . . my family . . . want to get her some for Christmas. But it's not something we can easily do."

I stared at him in disbelief. *Really? You want me to help buy clothes for Robin? You guys are unreal!*

He looked a little concerned, like maybe it was asking too much of me. "Will you help?"

My heart beat faster and I felt like someone had lit me up like the huge Christmas tree in the center of the mall. *Are you kidding me?*

"I would *love* to!" I exclaimed, jumping up and down in excitement.

Chris tried to stifle a smile I had apparently surprised out of him. "Settle down or you're going to get everyone suspicious," he continued to whisper. "It's got to be a secret. She's really proud . . . doesn't like to appear needy or anything." I had come to that conclusion myself. "If she found out, she'd be really embarrassed and pissed off, and wouldn't let us do it. So—"

"We've got to be a little sneaky!" I whispered harshly, too excited to let him finish his own sentence.

"No," he corrected, frowning at me meaningfully, "a *lot* sneaky."

I controlled myself, not jumping up and down, wiggling, clapping my hands, or nodding my head too enthusiastically—none of the things I felt like doing—but was so excited I could barely stand it.

"So what do you want me to do? What's the plan?" I asked, ready for my assignment.

Chris seemed to be struggling to keep a straight face, obviously amused by my fervor and barely bottled up animation. My own smile was huge. This was going to be even more fun than I had imagined!

He cleared his throat and turned away to look elsewhere for a moment, then turned back to me. "We're going to have to make it up as we go along I guess," he answered, his expression controlled once more. "But mostly, get her to try on clothes and take note of what looks good on her. And what size. Stuff like that. But you've got to do it without her being suspicious. Nobody else knows about this, except Dave of course. And my dad. We'll figure out how to actually buy the stuff later. We're here all day. I'm sure we'll think of something. We'd better join the others before they think—"

I knew what he meant. I felt like saluting him but contented myself with an enthusiastic but whispered, "Yes, *sir!*"

He looked away again.

We tried to walk a little faster, though not so fast that we'd be noticed, and nonchalantly infiltrated the larger group, Chris walking ahead and me

falling into step next to Matthew. Dave turned, obviously noting my location and smiling slightly to let me *know. How could I have doubted him?* He seemed content for a while but eventually placed himself between Matthew and me. Matthew looked suspicious at first but was soon distracted by everyone else.

The aroma of food got the better of the boys right away. They stopped at every food concession and were constantly eating: pretzels, cookies, cinnamon rolls, smoothies—seemingly everything in sight. Dave insisted that Robin and I have a bite of a couple of things, and I had to admit the smells were delicious. But I was too excited to eat. I wanted to shop!

We'd been passing most of the shops without going in, but now that I had a definite objective, I wanted to get started. The guys were still eating when I insisted we go into one of the clothing stores. I wasn't an experienced shopper, but it was a franchise I liked and had found cute clothes in before. Jessie and Stacie were more than happy to follow my lead, and we practically dragged Robin in. The guys stayed outside and ate.

Robin mostly followed me around, which felt strange as she had always been the leader in everything else up until now. I tried to get her interested in a couple of things, but she almost refused to look at them. I was going to have to think up a good strategy. Deciding to try on a couple of things myself, I asked her to wait by the changing rooms so she could give me her opinion. The clothes themselves were nothing I actually planned to buy but hoped would spark an interest in her: a black skirt, a little on the long side, and a top with an interesting pattern. On someone else, it might have looked good—maybe. When I stepped out of the changing room, Robin started to giggle.

"I don't think so," she said, shaking her head and trying to recapture a straight face.

"You don't think so?" I asked, turning around as I looked in the mirror. "I thought it might look cute with my new rubber boots."

"Allie, you know you don't have to *try* to be a dork, right?" she said, but not unkindly.

"Well, then you'll just have to help me find something appropriate. Something . . . less dorky."

"Okay," she said. "Hurry up and change back. I'll be looking around."

I rejoined her as soon as I could. She had already picked out a few things, mostly in soft colors and washed denim which I admitted were the kind of thing I would have chosen myself. I had already scoped out some ideas for her and grabbed them quickly.

"Okay, I'll try them on, but you've got to try *these*. I don't want to try stuff on alone."

"But . . . I'm not really buying anything like that today."

She looked unsure, but I cajoled, "Come on . . . it'll be fun. I'm not buying anything either. Just seeing what different things look like. When's the last time you actually tried on clothes like this?"

She shrugged her shoulders and shook her head. I held my selection out to her and she grinned lopsidedly, taking them from me and following me toward the changing rooms again. This time we both came out to examine ourselves and each other in the long mirror. She looked adorable in a somewhat short red plaid skirt and a fuzzy red sweater. I wore a light blue denim skirt, also shorter than I would normally wear, with a soft pink top.

"Nice," we heard Matthew's voice. Dave and Matthew stood behind us, also looking into the mirror. We both blushed and turned to face them.

"That skirt's short," Dave said to me, frowning slightly.

I blushed harder, not sure if he was displeased.

"It looks cute," said Matthew, grinning and wagging his eyebrows at me. "Her legs are just long. You too," he said, looking at Robin with appreciation. "The skirts look *fine*." His eyebrows moved again, causing us to laugh self-consciously.

Dave shoved him away, but he moved back and leaned his arm on his friend's shoulder.

"We just wanted to let you know we're going to that game store across from here, so . . . take your time," Dave said, smirking.

Matthew was still grinning too. Robin turned away in chagrin, but I caught the conspiratorial look and pleased smile Dave gave me, and this time I flushed with pleasure.

We spent more time in that store, Jessie and Stacie joining us and giving us feedback, as we did for them. It was really fun. It was hard leaving everything in the dressing rooms as I actually would have bought a couple of things, but that was no longer my mission. I was going to focus on Robin.

Making a mental note of what looked nicest on her and which articles she seemed to like best, I left the store with her to enter the one right next to it. The same procedure was repeated here. Robin was starting to enjoy

looking for things for herself now and chose some things I would never have chosen for her. Some looked good on her and some, not so much. Jessie and Stacie had made some purchases and seemed very happy. We had been over an hour in just those two stores so decided we should check on the boys and rescue them if necessary.

Unnecessary. They were all either still checking out games on the shelves or playing on the consoles set up in the store.

Shane and the two other girls had arrived, the girls shadowing the two older boys as if they were couples. I'd seen both girls around before, the darker haired one often hanging on Shane one way or another. The other, I wasn't sure of. She hovered around Chris but I never actually saw her touch him. Not that I cared at all, of course, but I couldn't help being curious.

We wandered around looking at stuff for a while, then decided to hit one more clothing store nearby. We told Dave and he just nodded without looking at us, intent on beating a racing game he was playing. The two older girls decided to come with us.

I didn't find much I liked for myself in this store, but Robin tried on a couple of things that were very cute on her. By the time the boys found us, we were ready to go. I noticed they had all bought something. "For my brother(s)," seemed to be the case for all except Tanner, who surprised us by saying, "For my mom." We all laughed.

"What?" he asked defensively and shrugged. "She likes to play."

The boys continued their grazing through every concession stand we passed, and we took some detours through card, jewelry, and shoe stores. We eventually came to a lovely little carousel. The boys tried to goad the girls into going on it, but we refused. Actually, I would have gone on if Robin or Dave had, but I wasn't going to admit to it. I was sure it would have been too tame for even Dave's little brothers, let alone him. It was pretty though.

We continued past a lot of stores that held no interest for any of us, but our group seemed to attract quite a bit of attention, especially from other girls. They ogled the boys, sometimes openly flirting with them and, when it was clear that we were together, scrutinized or blatantly ignored us girls.

There was no denying the guys were good-looking. Throughout the day it became clear that a few different groups of girls were trailing them, giggling or even approaching them whenever the boys obviously noticed their presence, which was *always*. The other girls in our group acted annoyed by it. I just felt lucky. I was surprised I secretly felt proud of them and very gratified to be included in the group. And I felt less out of place than I would have thought. It was nice to be with them outside of school, where there were no negative elements making my flaws obvious or trying to keep me in my place.

When we did find stores of interest—the girls mostly checking out clothes and jewelry, the boys checking out the board stores, electronics, and anything sports related—we either waited for each other outside or found a store close by to spend our time in. Most of the time. Occasionally the boys just followed us into whatever store we went into. This happened when the other girls were pulled with a force like a tractor beam into a large cosmetics store. I was pulled along, just following the others' trajectory. The boys trailed in after us.

I followed Robin around—she was definitely the leader in this situation—and watched as she looked at different items and tried samples against her skin coloring. I supposed that one day I should mess around with makeup, but at present it didn't interest me much. Tanner and Kyle were pestering Jessie and Stacie, and Dave and Matthew were standing close to us. I couldn't help noticing that their attention was on something over our heads, though, and not on us at all. Matthew had a leering look on his face and was whispering something to Dave. Dave wore a definite smirk.

Looking up, I saw that pictures of apparently naked female models, positioned carefully to not expose *everything*, ran the length of this side of the store. The same was true with male models on the other side.

I blushed furiously. Both boys noticed *me* noticing *them* and looked half amused, half self-conscious. Robin noticed too and walked over to punch them—hard—calling them, "Perverts!"

Chris, who was walking by just at the right time, slapped both their heads. They complained and started laughing loudly. Robin tilted up her chin, grabbed my arm, and steered us out of the store. Dave and Matthew followed. Jessie and Stacie and the other boys saw us leaving and followed too. The other boys stayed behind with the older girls.

After that, the boys made a point of stopping at a couple of lingerie stores, commenting on things displayed in the windows and begging the girls to go in so they could have an excuse to go as well. We were sure they only did it to embarrass and annoy us. They were successful. Then we decided to sit for

a while and wait for the older kids to catch up. Dave took exception to our location, though, refusing to sit down and wanting to move somewhere else.

"Why?" we asked. The seats here seemed just fine.

"This store makes me mad," he answered, frowning.

We looked at each other, mystified. It was an upper-end clothing retailer. The store had a nice *façade* and looked really cool to me. I wouldn't have minded going inside, except that this particular store seemed to be specifically for guys and a heavy scent emanating from the store was already giving me a headache. A large picture of an attractive male model, clothed yet showing as much skin as possible, graced the entrance.

"You're just jealous," said Robin, wickedly. The other girls giggled.

Dave's eyes glittered. "Hardly. I can look like that." He indicated the picture.

"I don't know. . . ." she taunted, looking admiringly at the picture.

He swore, not angrily but obviously accepting the challenge. He began to unbutton his shirt.

"*Dave,*" said Robin, warningly.

He ignored her and took the shirt off, tossing it down onto the closest seat. He then proceeded to take the thermal off, exposing his still deeply tanned skin beneath. My blush was back with a vengeance and I couldn't help staring at him.

"Dave!" Robin sounded scandalized.

He smiled his dangerous smile and jammed one hand down hard, palm deep into a front pocket, causing his jeans to dip provocatively low and showing a waistband beneath, just like the picture. He picked up the short-sleeved shirt with his other hand and draped it over his shoulder. I had to remind myself to breathe. The other girls had gone quiet. Tanner felt inspired to take his jacket off and then lifted his t-shirt, not all the way off, but emulating the model a little more closely.

The boys struck nonchalant poses with bored expressions, looking so much like real models that I couldn't stifle a giggle. Dave looked at me with an only slightly less dangerous look in his eyes. I caught my breath again and mentally kicked myself. At this rate I'd be blushing all day, but it couldn't be helped; I thought he was simply the most perfect being in existence. I was completely convinced of it. Several other girls in our vicinity had stopped in their tracks and seemed to be enjoying the scenery also.

"Gentlemen!" a voice said with authority. We all turned to see a security officer glide over on a two-wheeled vehicle. "You will put your shirts on and behave appropriately or leave the mall." He wasn't nasty about it, but the uniform and tone of voice brooked no argument.

"We were just doing that," said Dave politely, slipping the collared shirt on. Tanner pulled the edge of his shirt back down.

"Are you kids actually shopping?" the security officer asked genially, looking at each of us.

Everybody held up their purchases and responded affirmatively, except Robin and me. We hadn't bought anything yet.

"Well, stay out of trouble," he said in a friendly way, then glided off.

"No problem, sir," called Dave.

He took the shirt off again for just a moment and pulled the thermal back on. I caught myself sighing.

Then four guys walked out of the store. Two carried bags from the store, but all of them looked like they could have been dressed by one of the store's sales associates. They were older than us, more like Chris and Shane's age, and carried themselves with great self-assurance.

"*That*, ladies, is *exactly* what the problem is," said Dave loudly, acid dripping from his voice. He looked disgusted and angry.

The guys stopped and looked over at us. I didn't think I'd ever seen them before.

"*Dave*," said Robin in a harsh whisper. "*Don't!*"

"What have we here?" said the one in front. "Oh . . . wait. . . ." He pretended to sniff the air and made a sour face. "Whew! Whatever it is smells *ripe*. The wind must be blowing in the wrong direction, guys. Smells like . . . cow shit."

Dave looked about to explode, pure hatred on his face. I'd never imagined his face could look that way. He took three determined steps towards the bigger, older guys before he was stopped. Chris and the others had just joined us, definitely in the nick of time. Chris grabbed Dave's arm tightly before putting himself between his brother and the other group of boys. Matthew, Tanner, and Kyle had jumped to their feet, obviously willing to back Dave up, but Shane stepped forward too, signaling them to keep their places.

The air hung tensely between the two groups. Then the apparent leader of the other boys snorted once, sneering, and motioned his group to move

on. And I realized I *did* recognize one of them—the last one with thick, curly blond hair. He was the guy that had pushed me into the arms of Varsity Jacket, that day with Robin. He looked straight at me as they walked by, but I couldn't read his expression.

"What are you thinking?" growled Chris, turning angrily on his brother when the threat had gone.

Dave pulled his arm violently out of Chris' grip but didn't say anything. His brother scowled at him for a moment longer, then reached out and cuffed his head for the second time today; this time harder.

"Ow!" complained Dave, rubbing his head and sounding and looking more his normal self. I was relieved. "Can we get away from here now?"

We continued our tour through the huge mall, ascending the escalator to the second floor again. There were a lot of stores we passed without even looking in. Sometimes we split up briefly to shop in different stores, agreeing to meet back at a specific place before continuing.

Robin and I entered a bookstore, not for anything in particular but because we apparently both liked books in general and were looking for gift inspiration. She wandered off toward the back while I stayed closer to the front where the bargain tables were. I loved looking through the large picture books, especially those of faraway places. I noticed that Dave and Matthew had stayed close by, just outside the store. After a while, Robin joined me in perusing the bargains. I had found a beautiful book I thought she might be interested in.

"Your grandmother's from Ireland, right?" I asked her.

"Her parents were," she said, coming over to look at the book with me. "She used to go back and visit family I guess, a long time ago. But she doesn't travel anymore."

"This is a nice book," I observed. "It has beautiful photography. Do you think she'd like something like this?"

Robin leafed through it for a moment. "It *is* really nice," she said, "but how much is it?"

"It's on sale," I showed her the original price and then pointed out the sticker saying sixty percent off. "It's a really good deal."

Robin agreed and hesitated only a moment before picking it up. "I think she'd really like it," she said softly and smiled. "I'll still have some money left over too."

She bought the book and we left the store together, the boys joining us just outside. The mall was much more crowded now than when we'd first come, and would pose more of a challenge for our little troupe to not get separated. We looked in a few more stores as a group, even clothing stores, the boys often coming in with us. They seemed to be subdued and keeping a closer eye on us, which both comforted and somewhat alarmed me.

Is that really necessary? Or are they just being protective?

I could deal with the latter. But memories of the recent encounters I'd had at school and what had apparently happened after, and what could have happened just a little while ago, had me wishing they didn't feel the need.

"So, what is the deal with those guys earlier?" I asked in an undertone when Robin and I were a little apart from the group.

She frowned. "Those guys are from Northfield. Rich kids. Country Club kids. They look down their noses at us and especially hate the Calderas and some of the others. I don't know all the reasons why, but I know there are issues between some of the ranchers and farmers around here and the developers of Northfield. Bad feelings trickle down, I guess. I don't know if *they* even know the reasons, but those kids act like they're so much better than us. It really makes Dave mad.

"A couple of years ago there was a bad incident. Some of our kids got into a fight with some of their kids; mostly eighth and ninth graders I think. There were bloody noses on both sides, but their side definitely got beat up worse. I think there were a couple of broken bones, like fingers or something. Sports people got benched and there were even a few suspensions, both over at Lowell and at the schools here. It was kind of a big thing."

She looked thoughtful for a moment, then said, "Actually, now I think of it, I think Chris was suspended and almost got expelled, but I don't know any of the details. He was already in high school. I never saw him much and didn't really know him. I just remember Dave saying something about it back then. Anyway, a few days after that, some young steers turned up dead at different locations, one of those being the Caldera Ranch. Some were shot and some were clubbed. It was horrible and sickening . . . and I didn't even see it. I mean, what kind of monster can just go out and kill a bunch of animals? They never did figure out exactly who did it, but we had a general idea."

I shivered and didn't want to think about the poor animals. It would certainly be a reason for animosity but didn't explain the source of the

problem. I wondered if the cattle incident had anything to do with Dave's bad dreams. I found myself watching him a little more closely than normal, even for me. He still seemed subdued, but he caught me watching him once and smiled gently.

We shopped a little more, but our group was becoming somewhat dull. We had been all the way around the mall, up and downstairs, and had at least tasted most of the wide variety of foods available outside the food court itself, but most of us still had several hours to wait before being picked up again. I don't think any of us actually wanted to leave, but we were beginning to wonder what we were going to do to keep ourselves occupied, "And out of trouble," whispered Robin. I couldn't imagine *who* she was referring to.

We were all carrying bags with our purchases by this time, and Chris offered to take and secure them in the box of his truck until we were ready to go. Everyone was grateful; some of them had bought quite a bit, including heavy things like shoes and books, and the bags were becoming a nuisance. Shane offered to help him carry everything out to the truck and the girls went with them, also helping to carry a few of the bags.

Shane and the dark-haired girl were definitely acting like a couple, walking with their arms around each other and even kissing, which made at least Robin and me feel embarrassed. I'd been watching Chris a little but barely ever saw him and the other girl even talk, let alone have physical contact; nothing demonstrative that would indicate anything more than acquaintance. Not that it mattered to me, of course, but Chris was still the object of curiosity on my part—just not as much or for the same reasons as his brother.

We had all settled on seats or on the ground near the huge Christmas tree. It felt good to sit down again for a while. Parents were lined up with their little children to see Santa, who sat on a huge chair near a large glass elevator. They were extremely noisy. And the mall was even more crowded now than just a short time ago. Along with dance music still playing in the background, there was Christmas music coming from Santa's area, the echoing sound of voices talking and laughing, the squeaking of tennis shoes, other muffled music probably coming from a nearby store, and the click of women's heels on the tile floor. The whole place was bustling and loud.

"So, what are we going to do now?" asked Kyle, yawning.

"We haven't been in the big department stores yet," said Jessie, so far the winner of the spend-the-most-money/buy-the-most-stuff award.

"We could check out the food court," suggested Tanner. Almost every-one groaned at that.

It was quiet for a few moments, but Dave had a mischievous look back in his eyes. "We could play mall manhunt."

Everyone looked at him as if they'd misheard.

"What's that?" asked Jessie.

"Basically," answered Dave, "hide and seek."

"Are you serious?" asked Stacie.

"Totally," said Dave.

Matthew grinned. "I've played that here with these guys, though it was a long time ago." He was still smiling as he considered. "That might be re-ally fun with everyone here."

He and Dave nodded, as if the more they thought of it, the more they liked the idea. "We'd better wait for the others to get here. See if they want to play."

It seemed to be decided, but when Chris arrived he was alone. The others had decided to go somewhere else for the rest of the day. When he was told of the projected plan, he looked uncertain then thoughtful, as if something had occurred to him.

"Okay," he said, finally, "but we need to establish the rules clearly so nobody gets in trouble. We're not little kids anymore, and there's a lot of us."

"Yeah, we've already had one brush with the law today," commented Tanner and then realized he should have kept quiet. Chris raised his brows at him and looked inquiringly at his brother.

Dave shrugged it off and refused to comment. Instead, he made us gather around closely so that he could be heard without raising his voice. We didn't want to attract any more attention than we already had.

The rules according to Dave (with interjections for clarification from Chris) went something like this:

The glass elevator in the middle of the mall is "home." The person who's "It" faces the elevator with their eyes closed and counts to fifty (as fast as they like), then goes in search of prey.

Anyone caught is subject to being the next It. When everyone is home, both caught and safe, the present It gets to choose the next It from the people they caught.

Stairs, escalators, and elevators are safe zones—you can't be followed onto them, but you can't loiter on them either. Once on
them, you have to continue, up or down, and then get off.

No running at all. (Walking sort of fast is okay.)

No using people to hide behind or as obstacles. (Immediate out
and we'll probably get kicked out of the mall.)

Security guards (or police) have a safe zone of ten feet around
them. Players can be within the ten feet, but It can't (unless
approached by said officers—try to avoid that.)

No going into stores unless you're actually buying something,
and then you have to come straight back out. Same with using
restrooms. It cannot go into stores, but there are no specific
"safe" rules for other players to exit. (Once outside, you're fair
game, so it's usually best to avoid going in or be sure you're
not spotted.)

Behind columns, palm trees, big potted plants, and platform stages
are all viable hiding places.

Watches are synchronized and games last no more than thirty
minutes. If you haven't been tagged within that time, you return home safe.

By the time he had finished explaining, there was a general hum of excitement throughout the group. I wasn't sure what to think, but I felt a little
nervous. It may have been stupid, but inexplicable fears of being chased
and childhood memories of being lost both interfered with the otherwise
growing sense of adventure I seemed to be developing. It must have been
evident as Dave approached me, a now familiar quizzical look on his face.

"You're looking worried," he scolded gently.

"She's afraid of getting lost," teased Robin, who had overheard. I was
sure she didn't realize how accurate her taunt was.

Dave looked at me and his eyes crinkled up at the corners as if it was
the funniest thing he'd heard in a while, but he didn't laugh out loud. He
said softly, "Don't worry. We won't lose you. I'll find you wherever you are."

I couldn't help but be distracted by the way "We" had become "I'll," but
my cheeks flushed anyway. This time, I almost felt he was watching for that
response, a slow, warm smile spreading over his face as he regarded me,
distracting me even more. Chris got his attention by hitting him lightly on

the shoulder and jerking his head, causing Dave to follow him a few steps away. The brothers had their heads together for a minute or two. Then they turned back to the group.

"Okay," said Dave, still speaking as the leader, though I was pretty sure Chris was really in charge. "We'll have a practice game first so you can see how we play. Chris will be It for the practice and the first real game. Is that acceptable?"

There was a general murmur of assent.

"I warn you, though," he said, grinning. "Watch your backs. Chris is merciless and deadly."

I shivered. *Yes. Yes, he is.*

Chris immediately faced the elevator, his eyes closed. Then he said, "One!" very loudly to let us know the count had begun.

Everybody scattered—except me.

I'd never been any good at tag or hide and seek, or any other type of chase game. Especially at school but even with my young cousins, the sensation I feel when I know someone will be chasing me absolutely terrifies and paralyzes me, so I'm always the first one caught. That means I'm either It forever, as I'm no good at running to catch other people either, or other players just ignore and pass over me knowing that, in the long run, the game is more fun without me. That no doubt added to my long list of other faults and apparent deficiencies that had always made me an outcast.

I stood frozen, knowing that Chris was capable of drawing out my terror beyond what I felt right now and was probably counting as fast as he could. Then again, maybe he would just tag me and move on to more challenging game. I was thinking these things, looking around and trying to make my feet move toward the nearest store, the escalator, the entrance to the mall— maybe I could just sit outside in the rain until the game was over—*anywhere* out of an immediate line of sight, when I was grabbed roughly from behind.

"What the hell are you doing?" Dave whispered harshly, sounding completely exasperated.

Relief and embarrassment flooded me in equal measure. I gladly let him drag me toward a huge potted plant and then pull me down behind it. The container was large enough to shield both Dave and me but only if he crouched closely behind me, which he did, one hand on my shoulder, his

body leaning slightly against my back, the sound of his breath not too far from my ear. He was almost hugging me.

"We'll just wait until he's gone," whispered Dave.

Or we can just stay like this for a while. It felt like the temperature in the building must have risen suddenly.

A few moments more and Dave was pulling me up; Chris had gone.

"What were you thinking?" he asked. "He would have *had* to tag you and that would mess up our plan."

Diverted, I asked, "What plan?"

"Chris is going to avoid you so you can go back to the stores where you found stuff for Robin."

I was beginning to understand.

"Where should we go first?" he asked.

Nonsensical fears forgotten and getting back into the original spirit of this trip, I led him to one of the stores where Robin and I had tried on clothes. Finding her size was easy as we wore the same sizes, although I was taller and the clothes fit her better. Dave stood by as I gathered the items that had been the most attractive on her and that she had liked the best. Then we asked a sales person to hold them behind the counter for Chris. He'd come later to pay for and take them. From here we moved on to the other stores we had visited. If I wasn't sure about something, I held it up and asked Dave's opinion. He always had one. He also constantly seemed amused.

"You're really having fun with this, aren't you?"

I couldn't help laughing and smiling openly—shyness, for the moment, forgotten. "I really am!"

He laughed and smiled widely in return.

Having set aside all the items of interest, I became concerned.

"That was a lot of clothes. Was it too much?"

Dave shrugged. "Chris'll only buy what he wants. Dad and Angel are chipping in too, so we can get a bunch of stuff." He looked at his watch. "Our time's up. Look, I might evade Chris, but nobody's likely to believe you did. Sorry." He sounded apologetic, as if afraid of hurting my feelings but having to state the truth.

"It's okay. I know," I said.

"Chris said he'd tag you by the chocolate store and bring you in when we were done. I'll pretend I evaded him. It wouldn't be a good idea for us to walk in together anyway because . . . well. . . ."

"I understand," I said quietly.

This seemed to be an unspoken agreement between us. He had let his guard down a lot lately at school—I seemed to finally be accepted as simply another member of the Caldera circle, nothing more—but even among his close friends, he appeared to be worried that his attention to me wasn't misunderstood. The same was true for Chris.

Dave regarded me with what looked like concern for a moment, but concern in what respect, I didn't know. I forced a laugh and said I'd go willingly to my fate, smiling and hoping to stave off any possible feelings of sympathy or remorse on his part or despondency on mine. He smiled back but still looked thoughtful. I turned my face away and willed myself to stay positive. It had been an awesome day and I could only imagine how Robin would respond when she received the clothes.

Chris was waiting for me near the appointed store. I gave him a small piece of paper that I'd written the names of the stores on. Then we walked back "home" together. Everyone was there, eager to play again. They were all expressing either surprise that it took Chris so long to catch them or that he hadn't caught them at all. But I noticed a sly look in his eyes and almost a smirk on his lips as he turned to count again.

"One!" he said loudly.

Okay, this time it's for real!

My hand was immediately grabbed and I found myself being pulled along by Dave again, this time walking fast and moving down one of the wide, center walkways. After a few steps, he let go of my hand as if just becoming conscious that he'd grabbed it. I knew I was blushing. He looked as unselfconscious as ever.

"Come on, or you'll make it too easy for him," he said.

We walked until we reached an escalator going up, ascended it quickly, and then started to double back toward the Christmas tree. We stayed close to the storefronts, Dave's eyes furtively scanning both the level we were on and what he could see of the one below. We took a risk crossing a bridge between the two sides of the upper level to get closer to the down escalator in the center of the mall. Then Dave pushed me back into a store's front alcove

while he stealthily scoped out the area below. I laughed. He reminded me of a little boy playing army, although I suppose he would have considered it more urban warfare. He looked back at me and frowned suspiciously for a moment, then beckoned for me to join him.

"What's so funny?" he whispered, descending the moving staircase as quickly as he could without leaving me behind.

"Nothing," I said, letting him know there *was* something, but I wasn't going to tell him.

He frowned again, but his eyes were bright with curiosity. I liked the expression and thought it would be fun to try to inspire that again sometime.

When we stepped off the escalator, somehow Chris was right in front of us. There had been no sign of him just a moment ago, but now he easily reached out, lightly tagging us both, and then turned and walked away, a smile barely a hint on his mouth.

We walked over to the seating area close to "home" expecting to be the first ones there. We weren't, Matthew apparently having been tagged even before us. We laughed and commiserated with each other, and hoped we wouldn't have to wait too long before Chris found the others. We didn't. As if his pride were injured by having to throw the first game, he seemed to outdo himself in hunting down and sending back our friends. They showed up by twos and threes within a few minutes of each other. Soon we were all gathered there. Chris sprawled indolently over several seats nearby. Only fifteen minutes had elapsed, and nobody had gotten home safely.

"That's crazy," said Robin, indignantly. "You must have cheated. How could you possibly have done that?"

Chris didn't move, lying on his back across the seats, but his eyes slipped over to us under barely open lids. "Crazy ninja skills," he said. "Dave's It. "

"I knew *that* was coming," said Dave and got up to go and count.

We all dispersed again. I started to follow Robin and Tanner, who seemed to be heading in the same direction for a few yards before they split up. In my indecision to follow one of them or try my luck alone, I hesitated just long enough to severely damage my chances of going undetected, and I knew it.

Ducking behind a pillar, I watched as Dave walked leisurely in my direction, then stopped close by, his back turned to me. My heart was pounding hard, but I also felt like laughing—just nerves I guess. He turned his head enough for me to see his profile and he was smiling slightly. Did he know I was there? Was he just giving me another chance to get away?

Instead of proceeding farther, he walked back and I slipped away. Had he done that to prevent me from getting home too quickly? As I moved through the mall, I kept finding him between myself and any route to permanent safety. And he always had that slight smile on his face as if he was up to something.

Finally looking down on the seating area, I saw that most of our group were there. Only Tanner and Stacie were missing. I crept quickly to the elevator, preparing to take it down, but was tapped on the shoulder as I waited for the doors to open.

"Sorry," said Dave, not sounding apologetic at all. "You knew I'd find you, right? I've let you go this long, but I can't let you get back without tagging you." He was shaking his head and smiling.

I smiled back and said, "That's fair."

It had been fun and I'd coped completely on my own, pathetic as that was. And he hadn't terrorized me in order to tag me. I appreciated that. We rode the elevator down together and I was added to his collection. Tanner had made it back safe while we were in the elevator, but Stacie was still gone.

"I'll be right back," said Dave, and he was. He'd seen Stacie through the glass walls of the elevator as we descended, hiding behind one of the palm trees. He went straight to her.

We played one more game, Dave choosing Matthew to be It and leaving me to my own devices this time. Robin grabbed my arm and we stuck together, even ducking into a store for Robin to purchase some tea for Fiona, until Matthew stepped out from behind a pillar and tagged us. He ended up getting everyone except Dave and Chris, which clearly annoyed him, but he was still good-humored about it.

We were all pretty hungry now so decided to find somewhere to eat while waiting for our rides home. We sat in a large booth and I was happy to sit next to Dave, but I ended up spending most of the time trying to catch Chris' eye. Had he been successful in retrieving the clothes for Robin? I was dying to know, but he steadfastly ignored me. He could be so maddening!

At about six o'clock Dave got a call from his dad, ready to take us home. Dave told him we'd be there in a few minutes. He and Chris would wait with the guys until Matthew's mother arrived, and then they would drive home too. We got up to pay for our meal, Chris insisting on paying for Robin's and mine, and went outside to find Mr. Caldera. Most of the kids followed Chris to his truck to retrieve their loot. I followed too, but for a different reason.

At the first opportunity I could without Robin hearing, I tugged on Chris' jacket and whispered, "Well? Did you get . . . everything?"

He looked at me a little sideways. "Of course."

"*Everything?*" I repeated, surprised. I assumed he would choose what he wanted and leave the rest.

"Yes."

I frowned. "What about wrapping? Are you going to do that?"

For the first time, he looked uncertain, frowning, as if he hadn't thought of that. "We'll figure something out. Angel can do it, I guess."

"I could do it," I offered. "Mom can help, too. She'd want to." I wanted to do more than just make the purchases possible.

He still frowned but seemed to consider. "Dad'll take you home last," he said quietly. "Call Dave when you're the last one."

I smiled and nodded. I got in the car with the other girls and we headed home. The return journey was even more pleasant than the trip there as the other girls seemed more accepting of me, making me feel that much more comfortable with them. We dropped Stacie off first, and then Jessie. Robin seemed very happy when she got home, clutching her bag to her chest and waving us off.

As we left her driveway, I pulled my phone out and called Dave. "We just left Robin's."

"Okay," he answered. "Chris says you offered to wrap the stuff for us, and I guess we'll take you up on that. We can meet you at your house."

"Okay," I replied, very happy.

When we reached my house, Chris' truck was already parked along the road. Dr. James' truck was also in the driveway. I hadn't seen him for quite a while. Taking the bags out of the box, the boys joined me at their dad's car.

"Thank you so much for the ride," I said to Mr. Caldera. "We had a lot of fun."

He smiled. "I'm very glad," he said. Then he looked past me to his sons and said, "Don't outstay your welcome."

"We won't, Dad," said Dave.

That would be impossible. . . .

I turned back to Mr. Caldera and said, "Would you like to come in too? I'm sure my parents would be happy to see you."

He considered for a moment, then agreed, "Just to say hello."

They followed me to the front door and into the house. I was prepared to see my parents and Dr. James sitting in the living room. But not the long faces they wore. Chris was the last one inside and closed the door. My parents and Dr. James rose from their seats and everyone greeted each other, but the atmosphere was tense. Something had happened.

"What is it?" I asked, alarmed. Had something happened to Gold? Was that why Dr. James was there? "Is Gold okay?" I asked, everything else forgotten.

"There's news, Allie," said my father. "His owner has been found."

Chapter Twenty-Five

If You Need A Friend

"What?" I said, hoping I'd heard wrong, misunderstood somehow. I waited for someone to confirm the statement.

"Gold's rightful owner has been found, sweetheart," my mom gently reaffirmed.

I had nothing to say. I wanted to remonstrate, but it was obviously pointless. I had known this day would come, though I'd refused to think of it any more than I could help. I began shaking a little and Dave and Chris both moved slightly closer as if to catch me if I fell. Mom signaled for me to sit on the couch near her and Dad came and sat on the back of it, behind us. Mr. Caldera and the boys looked indecisive.

"Please, come and sit down," Mom said to them. "James was just waiting for Allison to get home before telling us the details. I'm sure you're also interested."

They *did* look interested and eager to be included. Mr. Caldera sat in a chair near Dr. James. The boys sat close to me on the floor near the fireplace, the crackling of which was the only sound for a few moments. I had so many questions, but I dreaded them being answered and couldn't ask them.

Mom looked at everyone in turn. "Can I get anybody anything? Something to drink? Alex . . . a cup of coffee? I just made some."

He hesitated only a moment before saying, "Yes, thank you." The boys declined and I certainly didn't want anything.

"It's been rather confusing," said Dad as Mom went to the kitchen, "and we haven't heard the latest. Would you mind starting at the beginning, James? Allison and Alex and his sons won't know most, if any, of what we already know."

I looked at my father in surprise, but he avoided my gaze. Mom came back with a cup of coffee for Mr. Caldera and then sat next to me again.

Dr. James looked at me sympathetically. "It *has* been confusing," he admitted. "And just so you don't become alarmed at any point in this story, you need to know that Gold came from a very caring home. He'd been through some trouble in the weeks before you found him, but he'll be going to another excellent home. You have my word on that. I've looked into it personally, to the best of my abilities."

I swallowed and nodded, still shaking. Threatening tears tickled my nose.

"I'll start where I came into the story as it'll probably be easier to keep track that way. Most of what I'm going to tell you first, I've kept between your parents and myself. We didn't want you worrying about it needlessly."

I acknowledged this but wasn't sure how I felt about it. I looked toward Dave and Chris, but Dave shrugged and shook his head slightly with an open look that convinced me he hadn't known about it either. Chris was looking elsewhere, as usual. I looked back to Dr. James.

"After I left you that day, when I'd seen Gold for the first time, I filed a report with the local sheriff's department. It was important to let the authorities know that the horse had been found, and it was obvious, even in his rough state, that he was a valuable animal; someone would be missing him. I did some asking around locally for about a week and came up empty, as you know. So I tried searching a wider area: north, south, and west. This also yielded nothing. It seemed unlikely that he'd come from anywhere in the mountains, so I didn't focus east of here. Later, after you'd told your parents, I came back with your father's permission and took some pictures of him, hoping they might help us find his owners. In the meantime, we had asked Dr. Welke out and she scanned him for a microchip. She found none but did find evidence that he may have had one. You might have noticed the nasty scar on the crest of his neck, under his mane."

Yes, we had. I nodded.

"She only saw it because she was checking for a reading. She said it looked possible that he'd had one, but that it may have been removed by someone

in a hurry and not treated properly afterward. It's not supposed to be possible to remove them, so we still weren't sure. We didn't want to alarm you and thought it better to wait until we found out what the whole story was."

I shuddered and Dad laid his hand on my shoulder. Dave was watching me, obviously concerned. I wanted to run out to Gold, to assure myself that he was still there and that he was all right, though I knew he was.

"Then what happened?" I whispered.

"After a couple more weeks, I contacted law agencies in Nevada. It didn't seem likely that he could have come from so far away, or survived by himself through the dry summer in the mountains, but he had to have come from somewhere.

"Over a month went by before I was contacted by a deputy in western Nevada. He'd heard that we'd found a horse matching a vague description left at his branch by a Harry Franklin, back in mid-July. He had almost forgotten about it. The man had come in to ask if anyone had reported finding a palomino horse. He said that he'd been transporting the horse to a buyer and had been able to show the officer registration papers, but had not wanted to file an official report. He said he'd continue looking on his own, but left a contact number.

"The officer thought it odd but did a cursory search and inquiry to see if any horses had been reported found—*or* stolen—matching the sketchy description Harry had given. He found none. Harry had thanked the officer, only asking that if any word came to them, that they would contact him. He was assured they would. The officer logged in the visit and phone number, but after Harry left he did a much wider search focusing on horse theft. He still found nothing and eventually forgot about it until he had a conversation with his friend in another town, a town I had called, and the found stallion was mentioned.

"The officer became curious. A horseman himself, he knew a stallion would potentially be worth a lot of money. If it was the same horse, which seemed plausible, he now thought it even stranger that Harry hadn't wanted to file a report. Officer Ruiz obtained my cell number from his colleague and contacted me. This was about seven weeks ago."

I looked at my parents in amazement. They'd known about it all this time? Was that why they had been so easygoing about my activities and spending time with the Calderas? They'd just been happy to keep me distracted?

I wasn't sure whether to be thankful for the indulgence or angry about the withheld information. I was too numb right now to decide.

"At this point, the story takes a turn into undercover detective work," said Dr. James, not quite able to suppress his enjoyment in relating the story and his part in it. "Officer Ruiz and I were in contact for several weeks while we came up with a plan together. Then he tried to contact Harry.

"We both agreed that the circumstances seemed suspicious and decided to try to set up a meeting between Harry and me. It seemed he had disappeared for a while, not answering the number he'd given them. Ruiz ran a search on his name and the cell number but got no leads. We know now that Harry was out of the country, probably trying to avoid his client. He finally showed up again a couple of weeks ago. He answered Ruiz' call, saying he'd been doing business out of the country and hadn't had that cell phone with him.

"I flew out to Nevada to meet with Officer Ruiz, and the meeting with Harry was arranged." Dr. James' eyes were bright, this part of his story related with undisguised relish. "I'd meet him at a local diner. He'd been told that a palomino stallion had been found wandering the foothills on a rancher's property in Mineral County, Nevada. Ruiz told him that I wanted to see proof of ownership: papers, pictures, whatever he had. We figured he'd be more forthcoming with a regular guy than with the sheriff's department. We were also hoping he'd slip up somehow, do or say something to give himself away if it really was all a lie—and we were sure it was. Ruiz and his colleague, Officer Unger, would be nearby.

"I was waiting for Harry in a booth at the diner. He seemed confident and affable at first, but we had arranged for Unger to come in after him, in uniform, and sit in the booth behind him, facing me. Harry became uncomfortable right away.

"He had official-looking Spanish registration papers of a horse named 'Corona de Oro,' and one professional photograph like those advertising breeding programs or show successes. The horse in the picture was immaculately clean and groomed and in optimum health, but it was definitely Gold. I pulled out pictures I'd taken of Gold right before I left and showed them to Harry. He obviously knew right away it was the same horse, but he tried to play it cool, saying, 'It could be the same horse, but I'd need to see him myself.'

"I said that everything seemed in order, but that I'd been trying to imagine how the horse had escaped. And why hadn't he filed a report with local authorities? They could probably have devoted more resources to helping him if they'd had something official to act on.

"He became very agitated and his temper flared. He gave me some lame story about the horse escaping into the desert in the middle of the night when he was trying to change a flat on the trailer. He wasn't able to start looking for him until the next morning, but the horse was long gone by then.

"I said, 'We noticed a deep scar, obviously left from a serious, relatively recent wound. Do you know anything about that?'

"I could tell that he did, but he hesitated as if deciding what to say. After a moment, he reminded me that the horse had gone missing a few months before. Perhaps it was something that had happened to him after running away.

"I showed him another photo, but this time, it was one of the first I'd taken. I said, 'This is what he looked like when I found him . . . at the beginning of September. If your picture is anything close to what he looked like when you first lost him, he's been missing a lot longer than that.'

"Harry looked extremely uncomfortable and aware of the officer sitting behind him. He said, 'Look, I don't know what you're driving at, but I want my horse back. Are you going to take me to him?'

"I'd been watching Unger in my peripheral vision and saw him nod his head. Then he got up, left a tip on his table, walked to the register to pay, and left. Harry visibly relaxed and said that the horse in my pictures looked like his horse, but he wouldn't know for sure unless he actually saw him. If I refused to tell him where he was, then he would have to take the matter to the authorities.

"I couldn't help laughing since 'authority' had just been there and left. I told him, 'Well, then you should know that my name is James Emory and I'm actually a veterinarian. This horse was rescued by a teenage girl in California and we're sure he's been lost for at least five months.'

"I looked at him steadily to let him see that it was true. He showed signs of panic but held himself together long enough to say, 'Hey, I don't know what your game is, but we're done here,' and stormed out of the diner. He was apprehended right outside by Ruiz and Unger and taken into custody on suspicion of horse stealing."

Dr. James appeared slightly flushed, the memory of his detective work clearly enjoyable to him. He sipped his coffee for a moment. My shivering hadn't ceased and was making me feel even more tired and nervous. I was having a hard time wrapping my mind around the facts that Dr. James had told us.

"So . . . where had Gold come from?" My voice sounded harsh to my own ears. I was finding it almost impossible to correlate the animal in Dr. James' story to my magnificent friend outside. Had he really found his way here through the mountains?

"Unfortunately, Harry wasn't forthcoming with information about either the true owner of the horse or his client who, we presumed, he'd still been trying to procure the horse for. His prints were taken, however, yielding the information that Harry Franklin was actually Ernest Ward, wanted for embezzlement in Florida. All we had to go on to track Gold's owner were the papers from Spain. Nevada Bureau of Investigation took Harry . . . uh, Ernie . . . into custody and eventually got the whole story out of him. About the same time, with Officer Ruiz' help, we were able to track Gold back to the farm that bred him in Spain, and from there to Laura Dellender in eastern Oregon.

"When we contacted her, she was horrified by what had happened, as you can imagine, and her first concern was for Gold, though she calls him 'Coro.' I was able to assure her that he'd been well looked after, though perhaps not in the kind of surroundings he was used to. We talked at some length on the phone, and I told her the whole story from this end. She was able to fill in some of the gaps from the beginning. But it's getting rather late. Perhaps. . . ."

The word sounded like a question, but I needed to hear everything. I wasn't going to sleep anyway. I was pretty sure of that.

"No . . . please," I whispered. "Please tell us everything."

Dad nodded, so Dr. James continued.

"Gold was born in the south of Spain and purchased and brought to America as a two-year-old by Laura. Laura is a horse breeder specializing in PRE horses: pure Spanish breeds. She'd gone to Spain to find a new colt she could train that would eventually be suitable for her breeding program. She had expected to return with an older gray stallion, but when she saw Gold, she had to have him. She actually sold off several of her other horses just so she could buy him. She continued his training and showed him lightly

until he was five, then sent him back to Spain to receive advanced training . . . basically, horse high school."

I sat open-mouthed by this time. It had been so obvious he was very special, but I never would have guessed at *this* background. And Dr. James must have been speaking of dressage. That was one of the things that Melanie had told me of; the way *she* rode.

"He was there for six months, doing so well and impressing his original owners so much that they wanted to buy him back again. Apparently true palomino Andalusians are fairly rare, and one with his size, color, and temperament . . . well, he was worth a lot of money. Laura wasn't prepared to part with him at that time as the money wasn't important. So she brought him back, continued to show him successfully, and bred him to a few of her own mares. Apparently the foals proved he would be the sire she had hoped he'd be, and she proceeded to make plans for expanding her breeding program.

"Unfortunately, earlier this year her fortunes took a bad turn and several things forced her to put Gold up for sale. Her husband had been gambling deeply and made some very foolish business decisions. At the same time, they lost quite a bit of money in the stock market. She also found out he—" Dr. James paused and seemed to rethink how much detail he needed to relate, then continued, "Well, he'd been up to other things. She ended up filing for divorce and had to sell off whatever horses she could to keep her property and foundation stallions and mares. Although sure that she would eventually have made a lot of money through Gold, she couldn't risk it all, so chose to keep the older, more proven horses that she already had.

"About the same time she lost her stable manager, who had also been her agent. Apparently he was concerned about his job security because of her precarious financial situation and took another job offered to him.

"Enter Ernest Ward as Harry Franklin. Laura desperately needed someone who could both run her breeding program and deal with the sale of her horses. I'm not clear where he came from, but she was impressed with his references and the way he handled himself and his work. She felt free to concentrate on her personal life and finances. Harry seemed like a great guy. He worked hard and was able to sell off many of the younger horses and broodmares for a good price. But she wanted to be more involved in Gold's sale. Not only was he worth a great deal of money, she was also very fond of him.

"She had contacted the farm in Spain to see if they were still interested in purchasing him, but they were now themselves no longer able to buy him. At least, not for the price Laura needed. They did, however, put her in contact with a Señor Alvarez from Colombia, who had seen Gold while he was there observing the schooling of his own horses. He's a wealthy landowner who wanted to purchase Gold for his granddaughter's twenty-first birthday. She's an experienced horsewoman involved in showing and pageantry, and her family appreciates Spanish breeds, particularly Andalusians. Gold seemed like the perfect horse for her. Laura was thankful for the contact and got in touch with Señor Alvarez.

"At the same time, Harry told Laura that he knew of someone who would pay a great deal for Gold, even more than she was asking. Corona de Oro was exactly the kind of horse his contact had been looking for. Laura said she would consider any offers, of course, but it was also important to her that he went to a good home.

"Well, both men were extremely interested in him. Señor Alvarez and his agent came, as well as the agent of Señor Morales, the businessman from Chile that Harry had been in touch with. Señor Alvarez made the most generous offer he could, but Señor Morales' agent made a much higher offer, saying that he knew the horse would be a prized possession of his employer. Laura had a bad feeling about this Señor Morales and wasn't happy that Gold might end up as nothing more than some sort of status symbol."

Mom had brought Dr. James and Mr. Caldera more coffee, and Dr. James paused a few moments to thank her and drink. Mom, Dad, and Mr. Caldera asked a few questions I barely comprehended. The information Dr. James was recounting to us was the part of the story even they didn't know. I was finding it so hard to take it all in. Although it was easy to believe that Gold was a special, valuable animal, the fact that someone like me could be part of his story was bewildering. I was still shivering nervously but wanted Dr. James to continue. He took another sip of coffee and did so.

"Laura fears that part of the resulting trouble was her imperfect grasp of the Spanish language. The agents both spoke English quite well, and Harry spoke Spanish fluently, but she wonders if communication wasn't terribly clear between herself and the buyers. Both parties were under the impression that their offer had been favored, and they left to await further

communications and arrangements. Laura had already decided on the buyer from Colombia and felt it was safe to leave further arrangements to Harry.

"Unfortunately, Harry turned out to be unscrupulous. Señor Morales' agent made a deal to pay Harry a small fortune to procure the horse for his employer; they didn't care how it was accomplished. Harry contacted Señor Alvarez and expressed his regret that, due to his employer's financial distress, she had decided she must accept the more extravagant offer. Señor Alvarez was disappointed but accepted this and no more was said to him about it.

"Harry made his own arrangements, pretending to be handling Gold's sale and transportation to Colombia while actually conducting the illegal transaction with Señor Morales' agent and planning on getting him into Mexico. There Harry would be paid a large sum and the horse would be taken off his hands. The original selling price was wired to Laura's bank, which she had no reason to assume was from anyone other than Señor Alvarez.

"There was only one more thing she insisted on doing; having Gold micro-chipped. She knew she should have done it long before, but since he was going out of the country again and she wanted to make sure he remained safe, she wanted it done now. Harry tried to talk her out of it, of course, but she insisted. We assume he was present when the microchip was fitted, and that once all his vet checks and tests had been completed, he drugged Gold and removed it again as soon as possible. He must have removed quite a bit of flesh to be sure of extracting it and imperfectly closed and treated the wound himself. This must have been done while at the farm but would still have been healing at the time of his kidnapping. This is one of the things that Harry . . . Ernie . . . won't admit to, so we'll probably never know exactly what happened.

"Gold was loaded into a trailer and driven off to the airport, or so Laura supposed. After this, until Allison first saw him, the story is unclear, and Ernie isn't relating anything he doesn't have to. Apparently Gold never did like Ernie . . . Harry . . . which probably wouldn't have been too much of a problem if he'd just taken him to the airport. But to avoid the hassles and inquiries they'd have trying to get him on a different flight, they had arranged to meet near the Mexican border, we assume somewhere south of New Mexico from the route he must have taken.

"Obviously something happened somewhere in western Nevada and Gold got away. Either he really did have a flat on the trailer and had to take the horse out to fix it or he was doing something else; perhaps trying to treat the wound in his neck. Whatever it was, it certainly left an impression on Gold. He must have purposely stayed away from any men he saw and made his way into the Sierras.

"I'd been wondering how Gold could have survived for so long in the hills and mountains. But according to Laura, it would have been similar to where he was born and raised. As long as he could find water, he could survive for a while. And so he did. But if he hadn't been found by you, Allison," he said, looking at me kindly, "he may not have lasted too much longer."

I shuddered and felt the blood drain from my face. I could easily picture all this happening just as he described it. Far from feeling gratified at finding Gold, however, I was ashamed that I hadn't told somebody about him sooner. The shivering just wouldn't stop now and I was starting to feel sick.

Dave spoke up here. Both he and Chris had been listening silently, but frowns had gradually darkened both their faces throughout the story. "When did all this happen?"

"According to Laura, Gold left her farm on June twelfth."

"All that time and nobody else noticed he was missing?" Dave asked.

Dr. James shook his head. "Laura feels terrible that she didn't follow up to make sure he'd arrived at his new home safely, but she had no reason to suspect anything was wrong. Ernie had taken care of other, admittedly smaller sales perfectly well, and it had helped her out immensely. She had put her trust in him and thought he'd be staying on at her farm for quite a while.

"When he didn't come back, she was disappointed but had no reason to think he'd done anything wrong. When the money was wired to her account as arranged, she handed the remaining details over to Ernie. He was to make all the necessary arrangements, travel with Gold, make sure he made it to his new home, and then return. She had promised him a bonus when he came back. Apparently he told her he might take a vacation while he was in Columbia. She had confidence in him and accepted what he'd said.

"In the meantime, she'd been overwhelmed by divorce issues. She'd been glad to entrust the whole transaction to Ernie. Señor Alvarez was not expecting further communication and didn't contact her again.

"The actual buyer was in touch with Ernie, at least at first, and so knew of the horse's escape. There was no reason for him to contact Laura. He wouldn't have contacted her anyway. As long as he got the horse, one way or

another, he would be happy. So the burden was on Ernie to find him. And I got the impression that this Señor Morales is not the kind of man you want unhappy with you.

"When Ernie realized he wasn't going to be able to find Gold quickly, he notified Morales' agent and said he'd be in touch. The buyer wanted Ernie to keep a low profile, but after weeks without even one lead he finally started to inquire at individual sheriff's offices. He admitted that, at one of the offices, he recognized someone that he'd come into contact with in Florida. He couldn't afford to be recognized as Ernest Ward and disappeared for a while, we assume into Mexico.

"When he ventured back, he answered the call Ruiz had made to him. And here we are. The last I heard, Nevada Bureau of Investigation was talking to authorities in Florida, and the FBI might even get involved. They aren't as interested in Ernie as they are in Señor Morales and his agent, for some reason.

"Which brings us up to date," he said. He had told the tale with evident satisfaction and had obviously enjoyed the adventure. But now he looked apologetic, realizing what the final outcome would mean for me.

Nobody spoke for a few moments. Mr. Caldera looked thoughtful. I could tell the boys were both watching me, though I didn't look their way. My mouth had gone dry, but I was determined to hang on to my emotions.

"What happens now?" I asked evenly, though the words came out as almost a whisper.

"Señor Alvarez was overjoyed to learn that Gold was, indeed, still for sale and that Laura had intended him to have the horse all along, in spite of Señor Morales' better offer. He is preparing new paperwork and I'll be doing some retesting so that his country's import regulations are satisfied. Señor Alvarez will arrive next Saturday to take Gold to a stable closer to the airport where he'll await travel clearance to Colombia. That is, of course," he said, looking at Dad, "if you don't mind him staying here until then. Laura also plans on being here for the exchange. She'd like to personally thank Allison and to meet with Señor Alvarez again. And Gold, of course."

Dad indicated it was fine with him. I thought that he would be overjoyed to get rid of "the animal," but he actually looked a little sad.

"I was also hoping that Alex would consent to be present," Dr. James said, looking at Dave's dad, "and help interpret for us. I'm sure Señor Alvarez will have his agent with him, and I know he speaks some English, but I'm sure it would help."

"I would be pleased to," Mr. Caldera said, graciously.

Dave impulsively added, "Can we come too?"

"If Greg and Jen don't mind," his dad said.

Mom and Dad made it clear they were all very welcome to be here.

"Though, I believe Chris has commitments on Saturday," said Mr. Caldera. "He may not be able to come."

Nobody cared to deny or affirm this possibility, but I was hardly paying attention anyway. Even though Dave was sitting close by, our families in one accord, I was at that moment only really aware of the bright golden light going out of my life. I couldn't ignore it anymore; it was hitting me in the face and making my eyes water.

"We should be leaving," said Mr. Caldera, looking apologetic and nodding to his sons to follow his lead. He shook hands with Dr. James and then my dad, and gave slight, quaint bows to my mother and myself. "You can rely on my help with anything you may need. Please don't hesitate to ask."

Dave and Chris stood to leave also, but I couldn't bring myself to look into their faces in case they saw the tears threatening to spill over. Outwardly, I thought I was hanging on admirably well. Chris walked by, hesitating for a moment as if he would have said something, but then moved past me. Dave didn't pause but laid his hand on my shoulder, letting it linger and drag lightly across it as he slowly walked by. I drew comfort from both gestures. When they left, I felt both relieved and lonely. Excusing myself, I went upstairs.

I had thought I'd break down crying once I'd reached the privacy of my room, but I sat on the edge of my bed and felt oddly calm, though the tears that I hadn't allowed to fall before now slipped down my face. There were only a few, and then they were gone. I heard the sound of the front door closing again, then someone coming up the stairs to tap lightly on my door.

"Come in," I said, quietly.

My mother entered. She sat next to me and put her arms around me. I let her hold me for a few moments then leaned slightly away. I appreciated her love but didn't feel like being hugged.

"I'm sorry, sweetheart," she said, gently. "We knew this day would come, but it doesn't make it any easier, does it?"

I shook my head slowly, sadly, but had nothing to add.

"Can I get you anything?" she asked, softly.

I shook my head again, not even trusting myself to say no. I still felt numb but thought that if I actually spoke, it would shatter that numbness and bring the pain to the surface. And then—I'd lose it. For the present I preferred feeling numb.

She kissed me on the forehead and quietly withdrew.

I sat looking at the floor for some while until I heard my phone buzzing. It was in my small bag, still in place over my shoulder. I was pretty sure there was only one person that would contact me right now, and at any other time I would have been scrambling to answer. But I just didn't want to talk. Not even to him. I waited until the buzzing stopped, then slowly retrieved and looked at my phone.

One text message.

I know you're feeling sad. You can call me if you want to talk. Day or night, anytime. See you tomorrow.

A light in my darkness; I felt a little stronger. Much as I loved to hear his voice, I was glad he hadn't called to actually talk. I was sure to have cried and it would have made me feel weaker than I already did and embarrassed too. Knowing that he was just there was everything. At that moment, I felt that friendship was the best thing in the world and, as dissatisfied as I was with it at other times, right now it was perfect.

Although it was early, I got ready for bed, lit the candle Robin had given me, and turned off my light. I sat still on my bed, watching the flame flicker, my phone in my lap and open to Dave's message. I'd be keeping it for a long time. And this time the candlelight truly did soothe me.

I thought of Dave and Robin; I now considered them my closest friends. There were no lingering doubts left and, sad as I was, I didn't feel alone. Losing Gold was going to be hard to get over. I knew it would take time, but I had to look at how much I'd gained because of him. He had been the main catalyst drawing my friends and me close together; I was sure of it. It was now hard to think of life without them. I wondered if they felt the same way about me, but it didn't matter. They were there.

Comforted, I blew out the candle. I lay down kind of wishing I had Dave's hat to hold again, like a security blanket. Even having that memory comforted me, and I fell asleep quickly.

I awoke very early, troubled by dreams again: Gold leaving in a horse trailer; watching a plane fly overhead knowing Gold was on it; running to catch a train I thought Gold was on somewhere; trying to chase after someone leading Gold away but being held back by a firm grip on my arm. I showered to try to wash the memory of it away, then dressed quickly and was at Gold's side. I fed him then took his blanket off and groomed him. He was becoming a little shaggy, which was good for him but made the mud cling to him even more.

It seemed like it was going to be a fine, sunny day and I was disappointed. From the way I felt, it should have been pouring with rain. I waited for the last possible moment to leave Gold for the day, leaving the blanket off and giving him a big hug around his gorgeous, thick neck.

I felt calm though very distracted all day and had a hard time focusing when my friends or teachers addressed me. Of course, Dave had told Robin everything; she obviously knew but was actually sensitive enough to not bring the subject up. Under different circumstances that probably would have surprised me.

When I got home, I ran straight out to see Gold and did my homework outside on the back porch so I could watch him every second possible, even though the temperature was dropping quickly. I spent a long time grooming and just talking to him, trying to absorb and store up moments and memories of him. His sweet, warm smell. His silky, if somewhat shaggy coat. His soft, velvety nose. The prickly whiskers around his chin and nostrils. The smooth and rough hardness of his hooves. The low, rumbly greeting every time he saw me. His lithe walk and proud carriage. The way even the weak winter sunlight glanced off his rough winter coat.

When I finally came in to dinner, Mom said, "Are you doing all right, Allison?"

I was able to smile at her as I went to wash my hands at the sink. "Yes, Mom. I'm doing all right."

Not fantastic, not great, but all right. Let's not dwell on the topic, though. That climate is subject to abrupt change.

"It looks like you had a lot of luck yesterday," she said lightly as we were sitting down at the table to eat.

I looked at her blankly. *Luck? She couldn't be that cruel, surely.* I felt that yesterday had to be one of the most unlucky I would ever have.

Mom returned my gaze sympathetically and reached across the table to cover my hand with hers for a moment, rightly assessing my confusion. "It looks like your shopping was very successful," she said, with a nod toward the bags of clothes the guys had brought in yesterday.

I hadn't even noticed, but they had left them against the wall just inside our dining area. I'd forgotten all about them. My mother had probably been trying to be tactful in not mentioning them before, but she was obviously curious.

"You got much more than I thought you were going to. Which," she added hastily, "is fine. It's your money."

It was even easier to smile this time. She was going to *love* this.

"Actually, those are gifts the Calderas bought for Robin." I gave my parents a brief account of the day's activities as they related to Robin's clothes and my part in them. "I offered our services to wrap them. I thought you might want to help, so they met us here to drop them off."

Mom's reaction surprised me; her curious demeanor had crumpled and tears stood clearly in her eyes.

"That is so *wonderful!*" she breathed. "Here I'd thought you'd bought yourself a new wardrobe, and you'd actually bought one for Robin!"

"Dave and Chris bought the clothes, Mom," I corrected her sternly. "I just helped. It was their idea and they paid for it all."

Both my parents appeared to be speechless for the moment, but my mother finally said, "That was an extremely thoughtful and generous thing for them to do. For teenage boys to think of and do such a thing? I'd say very remarkable."

"Perhaps they had a little help in coming up with the idea," said Dad. I knew he was just trying to be realistic, the way he always was, and he didn't mean to sound so demeaning or skeptical. But it made me rise to their defense.

"I know Mr. Caldera was a part of the plan, but they're *always* doing things to help . . . people." I would have said more, but as I was only aware of how much they'd helped me, and *some* of how they helped Robin and her grandmother, and Tom and Cheryl too, I decided not to be specific. I thought of Dave's text message the night before and couldn't help adding, a little indignantly, "I don't think they need any *help* in being kind."

"Allison," said Mom, quietly but reproachfully. "You know Daddy didn't mean anything by that. It just seems," she paused, searching for the right word, "unusual."

I lapsed into slightly sullen silence for a while. I wasn't convinced that Dad hadn't meant anything by what he'd implied. Though he'd shown appreciation for the things they had helped with—the things that he knew of—and had also shown a somewhat grudging forbearance with my association with them, he still appeared uncomfortable when they were around, as if he didn't trust them. Especially Dave. I supposed he figured Chris was safer because he was older, more mature, and perhaps less likely to have evil designs on his younger, hopelessly dorky daughter. But it was too funny if he seriously thought Dave did. I couldn't help smiling grimly at myself over that. It was excruciatingly clear to me that Dave's interest was a kind of brotherly friendship, like with Robin.

And Chris? *Please! We're only just starting to tolerate each other . . . sort of . . . which is just fine.*

Tuesday was similar to Monday—perhaps more focused on my part. My thoughts were still centered mostly on Gold, though I was once again trying to avoid thinking of his physical departure. I didn't have to think of it; the implacable reality of it followed me around and rested oppressively on me like my own personal black cloud. I didn't dare acknowledge it, though, or there would be a downpour.

"Are you okay?" Robin asked in Algebra.

It startled me. "Yes! I'm . . . I'm fine."

She didn't look convinced but took her seat next to me, pulling her binder out of her backpack.

"Guess what," she said, as if I possibly could.

I raised my brows to indicate my interest. She dropped the binder loudly on the desk and pointed to it in dissatisfaction. I regarded her again, my eyes wide.

"Your picture," she said, exasperated. "It was right *there*, and now it's gone. I don't even know when I lost it."

I looked at the binder more closely. It had a clear front filled with an odd assortment of unused stickers, pictures cut out of magazines, and

photographs, which had included mine. Even she didn't have a photo of Dave. I guessed he must not have passed any out. Beyond that, and perhaps registering that it reminded me a little of her room, I hadn't paid too much attention to it. Now I saw that there was a small space, roughly in the center and toward the top, where my photo had been. A small, black rectangle where the binder color showed through the other pictures highlighted the loss.

"It must have fallen out somewhere. Do you have another?"

I couldn't help laughing at that. "I gave exactly four of them away. Yes, of course I have another. I'll bring one tomorrow."

"Okay," said Robin, smiling almost shyly. "Thanks."

I hadn't yet told Melanie about Gold's owner being found. I didn't want to risk breaking down as I had before. And I didn't mention it in PE either, just in case, but I was determined to tell her all about it at lunch. Even if I slipped a little bit then, it was just her and me, and any weakness on my part would be more likely to go unremarked.

"I'm really sorry for you," she said after I had told her. She looked truly sad. "I know you've become very attached to him. It's hard to lose such a good friend." It was obvious these weren't just words to her. I could see that tears stood in her eyes. She'd felt this way before too.

I nodded, trying not to let my resolve slip. "It's hard that he's going so far away . . . to know that I'll never see him again." Then I forced myself to laugh a little and said, "I suppose it's just as well, or I'd be a nuisance going to visit him all the time."

She smiled at that, but I wondered what pain I had caused her to remember.

There was still so much I didn't know about Melanie. I had ascertained that she was an only child, like me, and she lived on this side of Northfield. That allowed her to come to Douglas High instead of Lowell, where some of her other friends were. I knew she owned a chestnut mare named Copper Copycat that she called Kitty, and rode and evented another horse belonging to someone else. Beyond that, she didn't like to talk about herself but would turn the conversation onto other paths: art, books, movies, horses, and animals in general.

"Do you think you could come over or do something during winter break?" I asked, hopeful for the distraction. We would be off for two whole weeks—surely we could manage to get together somehow within that time.

"I don't know. Maybe. I'll ask my mother."

I tried to look positive, but her tone had sounded hollow. This had become a well-rehearsed answer.

After school that day, my mom suggested we get the clothes for Robin wrapped. "After all, it's Christmas next week."

Somewhere in the back of my mind I'd known that. But I'd been so intent on not thinking about the coming weekend that the actual holiday had completely crept up on me.

"We should write some cards as well, and get them in the mail before it's too late," added Mom. "We need to get everything done by Monday anyway."

"Why by Monday?" I asked, suspicious.

She gave me a longsuffering look as if I'd forgotten something we'd discussed many times. "We'll be leaving for Grandma's on Tuesday morning."

I'm sure horror registered on my face. "We're going away again?" I almost squeaked.

"Of course," she said, obviously trying to be patient with me. "You know we always spend Christmas with them. And we discussed it when we first moved here, remember? We had said that we'd at least spend Christmas with family, even if we didn't see them before."

I gulped. A vague memory stirred, but I couldn't have been paying close attention; I guess it hadn't registered as important at the time. Now it seemed crucial. I had hoped, *sincerely* hoped, that I'd spend a significant part of the break with friends.

"How long will we be staying?" I asked quietly, trying not to sound too unhappy.

"We'll stay at least until next Saturday, maybe Sunday. Daddy's let Rob cover most of the travel he'd normally have done for the past couple of months. With so much going on and so much unknown with Gold, he hasn't wanted to leave until everything is settled. He's been very concerned about you, you know. He knows this will be difficult for you."

She looked at me sympathetically again. "When we get back, he'll have to leave for a while, but you'll still have a week to hang out with your friends. Maybe we can arrange for some extra lessons with Cheryl. And you never know . . . getting away for a while might be a good thing."

I knew what she was referring to but still didn't want to actually talk or even think about it.

We wrapped Robin's gifts, pairing some items together to make it appear like fewer presents. The guys had been concerned about that, knowing how prickly she could be about anything she perceived as charity. We put the wrapped presents out of the way in Dad's office. Then Mom brought out boxes of greeting cards. She wrote the family cards and those to her and Dad's friends. She told me to take what I wanted for mine.

Brenda, Robin, and the Calderas were the only ones I was sure celebrated Christmas, so I picked out nice "Season's Greetings" cards for Melanie and Matthew. After a moment's thought, I wrote two more, one each for Jessie and Stacie. We might not be close, but they seemed to be warming up to me and I didn't think it could hurt. Mom had me write my name in cards to Dr. James and the Reid family. I saved the Calderas' for last, writing each name inside with great care:

To:

Dave, Chris, Henry, Stevey, Angel, and Mr. Caldera

Love, Allison

I thought the sentiment "Love" would be okay since it was to all of them. I could easily admit to the world that I loved the whole family. The fact that Dave's name came first had no special meaning.

No, none whatsoever.

That night I dreamed again: Gold leaving; me trying to run after him; being held back by a person unseen. When I awoke, it hit me hard: he was being taken from me in just three days. It was over.

For all the learning I was able to do at school or things I was able to remember during that time, I may as well have been a zombie from one of Dave's video games. Except for the whole eating people thing. I was numb again and going through the motions my normal self would have done, but *she* wasn't actually there. Afterward, I wondered if a brain scan would have revealed any higher function brain activity taking place at all. I kind of doubted it.

My closest friends bore with it and didn't make me feel bad for essentially ignoring them. My teachers looked worried or exasperated. Everyone else either shook their heads, became impatient, or rolled their eyes and seemed to accept it as normal. I overheard quite a lot of muttered comments similar to "space cadet" from people in my vicinity, but it didn't matter.

The weather remained fair but cold, which unfortunately meant the guys weren't around much. Even Tanner was playing basketball, and Kyle was often in the weight room keeping in shape for wrestling after a successful freshman football season. The older girls and groupies in general didn't hang out with us, whether they were involved in sports or not. Even Jessie was playing girl's JV basketball and was also sometimes missing.

I'm sure I was very dull company for poor Robin. I even forgot to meet with Melanie on Thursday; it just slipped my mind. When my friends were around me, they kept themselves entertained entirely and expected even less of me than normal. Though, looking back, I realized how protective of me everyone seemed. You'd think I had lost a family member or something, and perhaps that's what it felt like. I'd never had a person really close to me die or move that far away before, so I didn't know.

The Calderas were very supportive too and, though they couldn't be around much at school for one reason or another, were always physically checking on me, staying close before and after school, even if only for a couple of minutes. I didn't register any of this at the time, but afterward I remembered and was very grateful for them all.

Thursday after school, the phone rang. Mom answered it. I was shivering on the back porch, pencil in hand and supposedly doing homework. But in reality, I was watching Gold, hungrily storing up every movement and sound.

"Allison," said my mom, opening the back door just enough to stick her head out, "Dave is on the phone."

It took a moment for that to register. *That's nice.*

"He was wondering if he and Robin could come over after school tomorrow. They thought you might like some help."

There didn't appear to be anything strange about that. I might have smiled; I don't remember.

Mom had her "patient" face on. "Do you want to talk to him? Or would you like me to answer for you?"

It took another moment for that to sink in too, but I must have gone in and talked to him as Mom gave us all a ride back to my house Friday afternoon. Dave, who I rarely saw with a backpack, had actually brought one today.

"We'll help you get Gold cleaned up a little," he said tentatively, as if apologetic for something nasty that simply had to be dealt with.

When we got home, we went straight out to Gold. I haltered him and they took his blanket off. Then we led him to the back lawn where the grass was thicker and more even. Mom prepared a big bucket of warm water, and I held him while the others soaped and rinsed his tail and lower legs.

"It's too cold to do his whole body," Robin said.

I just nodded. Anything they wanted to do with him was fine as long as I got to hold and stroke and talk to him. When they were satisfied with his legs and tail, Robin braided his tail to keep it off the ground and Dave wrapped it up to keep it neat and clean. Then he went to work with the curry comb and then the dandy brush all over his body. Robin worked tangles out of his mane with her fingers, brushing it until it was smooth and then braiding it in sections. I saw her fingers linger over the area where the deep scar was, but she noticed me watching and continued without saying anything. Dave must have told her about that too. I used a soft brush gently around his face and forelock.

Gold seemed to enjoy all the extra attention, standing complacently with his eyes closed, often resting his nose or forehead lightly against my chest. When he was as clean as he was going to get, Dave pulled electric clippers and a big orange extension cord out of the backpack he'd brought. It was the first thing that had made me feel curious in days.

"What are you going to do with those?"

"Get rid of his 'grandpa' whiskers," he said, smiling at me and taking the lead rope from my hand. "Since he's been shown and stuff, he's probably used to these things." He gave Gold a pat on the neck and said affectionately, "Come on Hot Stuff. Let's make you more presentable."

When Gold was standing closer to the house, Dave gave the rope back to me and went to plug in the extension cord. With Robin's help in spotting long hairs and whiskers, he clipped around Gold's face, ears, jowl and throatlatch area, and his lower legs. When he was done, Gold looked much better, though still a little teddy-bearish.

"Thank you," I said quietly. "I wouldn't have been able to get him looking half as good as this." I was desperately *not* thinking about *why* we were getting him cleaned up.

"Well, we're not done yet," said Dave. I looked at him questioningly. "Grab the lunge line and let's take him down to the corral."

Since it had been dry all week, this seemed reasonable. The grass had been growing and it was very pleasant down there. Dave unplugged the clippers but left them there and grabbed his backpack. When we got down to the corral, he closed the rails behind us. From the backpack, he dramatically pulled a beautiful dark pierced leather bridle with a fringed browband, silver buckles, and a fancy looking silver bit. Then he laid his finger on his lips.

"Don't tell anyone," he said conspiratorially. "It's my dad's. He probably wouldn't mind anyway, but I didn't have a chance to ask him." He grinned, his eyes mischievous. "I don't know if it's the kind of bit he's used to, but it's from Spain. Let's lunge him a little, then we'll see if it works on him."

I felt a little uncomfortable with Dave's proposition but wasn't going to wimp out now. Experimenting with Gold as far as grooming, lunging, even riding him a little hadn't seemed to matter too much before; not knowing who his owner was made it almost as if he didn't have one. But he did. They were coming tomorrow. *Tomorrow!* I shuddered violently and the others noticed.

I shook it off and lunged Gold. Then Dave brought the bridle over to fit it to him. His head was apparently quite a bit larger than the last horse to wear it and all the buckles needed adjusting. Gold chomped the bit slightly, unused to it, but otherwise he remained calm.

When Dave had the bridle fitted over the halter to his satisfaction, he said, "Shall I try him first? I'm not sure how he'll respond to the bit."

I knew he was tactfully saying he wasn't sure if *I* could handle him bridled, but I didn't take offense. I knew the caution was for my benefit. I nodded and he led Gold close to the fence rail.

Gold seemed unsure about being ridden by him, but Dave was on his back before he could completely make up his mind. He jumped forward slightly, a high, suspended lunge, then settled into an extended trot that looked effortless. He seemed to glide forward, his neck arched, tail held out, his hindquarters propelling him powerfully as his front legs reached forward.

I could only imagine how smooth it must feel to ride him like that. Dave didn't appear to be causing this gait, his hands low and relaxed, the reins

slightly loose, his legs hanging away from Gold's sides. Gold soon settled into a more relaxed trot, then a walk, and finally came to a halt in the middle of the corral. He was breathing deeply and blowing through flared nostrils, looking around as if trying to see Dave on his back. Dave stroked his neck and murmured something to him. After a few moments, he slowly gathered the reins and let his legs hold Gold's sides more naturally. He continued to talk quietly to him, stroking his neck and making Gold move forward.

Dave rode him at a walk, trot, and very slow, relaxed canter both directions of the rough circle we'd worn into the ground over the past weeks. Then he brought him back to a walk. At first I thought he was stopping, but after coming to a halt, he held the reins firmly and continued to squeeze his legs. Gold obediently moved backward. Dave moved him forward again into a trot, then seemed to gather him up but kept his legs firm and back as if wanting him to move forward. Gold's movement seemed to compact, his neck arching, his hind legs barely moving forward but pushing his body up with great suspension as his front legs seemed to keep time in a silent dance. He only did it for a few moments before Dave relaxed the reins and urged him forward into a more natural trot, and then brought him back to a relaxed walk.

"That was amazing," said Robin, her eyes wide. She'd stated what I'd been thinking.

"Yeah," said Dave, smiling widely. "I had a feeling he could do that fancy shit."

"You mean *dressage?*" I asked, preferring the proper term.

"Yeah. How'd you know that word?" he asked, his eyes twinkling but looking slightly suspicious.

"You're not the only one who knows how to do research, you know," I said, trying to tilt my chin at him the way I'd seen Robin do.

Apparently Dave thought something about that was funny as he laughed loudly. It was true that I'd been doing research, but the fact that I knew about it at all was due to Melanie. But whenever I'd mentioned her to them, they'd responded oddly. I still hadn't figured that out, since they'd both said they didn't know her. I decided not to say anything else regarding my knowledge.

Dave jumped lightly down from Gold's back and brought him over to me. "Your turn," he said, clipping the lunge line to the halter. "You want just a little contact with his mouth. It's very soft. He's an incredible ride, just like I thought he would be."

He was standing slightly in front of Gold, stroking his neck as he talked to me. I could tell he'd made some kind of new connection with him and was glad.

"I wish we had more time. There's a lot I'd like to try with him," he said.

I was just thinking the same thing for different reasons, and the thought sent pain through my heart. A sudden, acute sense of loss washed over me, but I pushed it down, refused to acknowledge it.

"*Dave* . . ." hissed Robin.

He looked at me, remorse evident on his face; the first time I'd ever seen that expression on him. He looked so cute, distracting my thoughts just enough to regain my composure. I'd forgiven him way before he said, "Sorry. I wasn't thinking."

"It's okay," I said and did my best to smile at him.

He helped me mount and waited while I got comfortable. I closed my eyes as Gold started walking, feeling him move beneath me and trying to get a feel for his mouth without holding the reins too tightly. My right hand rested against his warm withers, smoothing the hair and feeling the strong muscles of his shoulder move.

"Okay?" asked Dave.

"Okay," I breathed.

More than okay. Heaven. I wish. . . .

I couldn't afford to go there. I opened my eyes and closed my calves slightly, urging Gold into a gentle, gliding trot. He felt so perfectly molded to not only to my physical shape but my own internal rhythm. Everything he did felt incredibly smooth, as if he had excellent built-in shock absorbers.

Kind of like Chris' truck . . . only so much better.

The analogy made me smile and when I looked at Dave, he was smiling too.

"Bring him back to a walk," he said.

He walked over to us, stopping Gold, and took the lunge line off.

"You need to ride him at least once completely by yourself," he said.

I took the opportunity to experiment, riding him all over the corral and even loping him, though, even with his comfortable gait, I was a little afraid

of slipping off. It was turning to dusk when Dave jumped off the fence and opened the pole gate so I could ride Gold through.

We walked together in silence back up toward the house, me riding Gold and Robin and Dave walking on either side of us. I don't know if they were feeling the same as me or if they were just being considerate, but I appreciated their quiet presence. I was still in "record" mode and any sound besides Gold's breathing and the clopping of his hooves might have corrupted the file.

Dave held the paddock gate open for us, and I ducked as I rode him in, stopping in the center. Not wanting to get down, I leaned forward, almost laying along his back and neck, my face against his braided mane, my arms reaching down toward his chest. He stood still as if he understood. I lay there soaking him in until Mom and Dad came out on the back porch, causing him to raise his head to look at them. I suddenly realized how cold it was.

"I think you'd better come in for the night," said Dad, gently.

"Okay," I said, but Gold was a little too tall for me to comfortably jump down from bareback, at least without help.

Dave noticed my hesitation and immediately came close, his strong hands and arms holding and steadying me as I slipped down from Gold's back. I wasn't aware of blushing this time, the response perhaps offset by my growing sense of sorrow.

Robin watched as we took the beautiful bridle off, fitted Gold's blanket for the night, and then took the halter off. Any talking was in hushed voices, like you would use around someone sleeping or ill. It felt very strange. I fed him then leaned against the metal rail of the paddock, just watching him with the others. My parents stood watching too, but they finally went in the house. We followed.

Mom had made spaghetti and Dave and Robin showed their appreciation by asking for seconds. I was still playing with firsts. Chris came to pick them up after work, and I retired for the night right after they left, sleeping immediately but troubled by the same dreams.

The morning dawned appropriately gray. Feeling lethargic, I dragged myself out of bed and looked out my window to watch Gold. He stood facing the back door as he did every morning, waiting for me to appear.

Waiting for his breakfast. This will be the last time. . . .

My throat began to constrict and I felt sick. Thinking a shower might restore me, I stood under the spraying water until I felt I could face the day and the hardships it would hold. Then I dressed carefully in clean jeans, sweater, boots, and my down jacket.

The early morning was spent mucking out Gold's paddock so that it would look decently clean, and filling his water, though I didn't allow myself to consider how unnecessary that was today. When he finished eating, I picked out his hooves then took his blanket off and brushed him until my arms ached. I took the braids out of his mane and set his tail free, brushing them smooth. The hair was all tight waves, cascading over his neck and down his rump. In spite of his coat being a little long and rough, he looked magnificent.

About nine-thirty, I heard Chris' truck pull up out on the road. A couple of minutes later the guys walked around the back corner of the house.

"Hey," said Dave, softly.

"Hi," I said softly in return.

Chris tipped his head in silent greeting. I noticed he was holding something in his hand, but I couldn't see what it was and then forgot about it. We solemnly went through similar motions to those we had the day before, but they now seemed reverent, as if part of an important ritual that had to be performed. None of us talked unless strictly necessary and even then, in hushed voices. The only differences today were that we didn't wash or clip him, Dave didn't take a turn riding him, and both Gold's and my hair were unbound. If I'd really been paying attention, it probably would have seemed creepy, but I could already tell this was going to be one of those surreal days. I was just going to have to go with it. If I could keep my emotions in check, I might feel some satisfaction about it later, but it was going to be difficult.

Dave had once again brought his father's Spanish bridle. "But I've got permission this time," he said, as if he thought I'd be impressed or thankful.

I didn't feel anything.

When I began to ride Gold on the lunge line, I saw that the item in Chris' hand was a small video camera. He was filming us.

Dave noticed me watching him. "Remember I said I wished I had a camera?" Dave asked quietly. "Chris had an even better idea. We'll give you a DVD when we're done."

That made an impression. I felt a threatening, prickly sensation in my nose and eyes and swallowed hard. *That was too thoughtful.* "Thank you," I said, meekly.

About ten-thirty, we went back up to the house to give Gold one final, good brush and an apple treat, and to await the inevitable. Within about half an hour, Laura Dellender had arrived followed soon after by Dr. James.

The end had come. From that time on, I felt in shock, like I was witnessing something awful that I had no control over or ability to stop. I don't remember much. Laura seemed like a nice lady: in her forties, slightly plump, and ecstatic that "Coro" was safe. She thanked me, and the Calderas too, for taking such good care of him. Apparently Dr. James had been in close contact with her and had told her everything he knew about our time with him. I think she might have asked me some questions, but I was so out of it that my parents or the guys must have answered for me. She seemed sympathetic.

Mr. Caldera arrived about one o'clock and had lunch with us. I noticed that he kept looking sternly at Chris. Chris ignored him. He was good at that.

I couldn't eat. The adults kept up a cordial conversation that didn't have to include me. I was aware of Dave sitting close beside me—close enough to bump elbows—and was comforted by his presence, but that's the only other thing I remember about lunch.

At two, we heard a low rumbling that heralded something was here. Dad got up to go see and by the time he came back with two gentlemen, I was shivering.

Doom.

The first was an older man with pure silver hair and a small mustache and beard, elegantly dressed in a plain but obviously expensive suit: Señor Alvarez. The second man was much younger, also dressed in a suit, and obviously Señor Alvarez' agent. Greetings and necessary introductions were exchanged all around in both Spanish and English, and Señor Alvarez warmly clasped my hand. He spoke to me in passionate tones that alarmed me slightly, but Dave whispered that he was simply expressing his warmest gratitude that Gold had been found by such a "worthy and beautiful young lady." Any other time I'm sure my cheeks would have been scarlet, especially hearing those words spoken with Dave's softest voice, but I felt nothing. I just continued to shiver.

Señor Alvarez and his agent were offered refreshment, and the adults continued to talk, conjecture, and exclaim over the strange story we were involved in and how amazing it all was. Mr. Caldera did most of the translating, though occasionally Dave would whisper something to me that he thought I might want to know. Nothing registered. When they finally all got up to head outside, I stood to follow and felt my knees wobble. Chris put his hand out as if he'd catch me, then moved in front of me, staying close. Dave took a position just beside and a little behind me.

Señor Alvarez exclaimed when he saw Gold, though I didn't know if it was in approval or dismay. I knew he must look very different from when he had seen him last, but he smiled and said something gracious.

A large horse transport, looking very much like a rock star's tour bus, had pulled down the dirt road that led to the hidden corral, had turned around, and now awaited its precious cargo. A man stood nearby as if awaiting a cue. The agent gave it, and the man walked forward carrying items that turned out to be a padded horse blanket, head covering, and padded tail and leg wraps. My shivering quickly turned into a steady shudder.

He's leaving. They're taking him away. This is really happening. We've really reached the end.

When he was all covered up and hardly recognizable, my father suggested I say goodbye. I could barely move but stepped forward to stroke the part of his nose not covered. I told him I loved him. I'd miss him. I told him to be good and not get into trouble. I told him to be safe. He nuzzled my chest and gave me his rumbly *hurhurhur* as if he knew it would be the last time we'd see each other.

Then the man started to lead him away. I watched, frozen, as he was led up a ramp and then disappeared inside the large vehicle. Not exactly like my dreams but horribly close enough. The engine of the huge van started up and it began to pull away. Crying out, I started to run after it but found my arm grabbed roughly from behind. I turned quickly, in desperation, to see who it was.

Dave.

Looking back, I saw the van just disappearing around the edge of the house. I shuddered again and Dave let go of me. This whole time I had managed to hold on to my emotions, but I couldn't anymore. I fled to the house.

By the time I reached my room, I was sobbing. I threw off my glasses and sprawled on my bed. The tears were not going to be held back now and my body was shaking uncontrollably. I heard someone coming up the stairs and looked up, assuming it was my mother. But it was Dave's concerned face that appeared. He must have run after me.

Darn. The one time I don't *want him near me.*

As he tapped lightly on the door frame, I sat up to face away from him, toward my window. Squeezing my eyes shut, I tried to stop crying but couldn't. I had held it back all week and now allowed the floodgates to open. They weren't going to be shut again so easily. I heard him hesitate on the threshold of my room then quietly step around the end of my bed to sit next to me, facing me with one knee bent, barely touching me. I couldn't avoid him seeing me crying without turning my back on him, so I covered my face with my hands instead.

He sat quietly while I struggled to calm myself. I tried to hold my head up and be brave about the whole thing, but it hurt too badly. All I could see was Gold being driven away, disappearing forever to places unknown, with people I knew nothing about. The sobbing started again and I couldn't prevent it.

"I'm sorry!" I gasped, horrified that, not only had I lost Gold, but I might finally scare off the person most important to me.

"Sorry about what?" Dave asked gently, his voice very soft. "Don't be an idiot. You're allowed to cry, you know. Hell, you love him. It hurts more than anything when people you love leave you, for whatever reason. But you'll find another horse to love. I just know it."

These comforting words only served to aggravate my raw emotions and I sobbed harder than ever. Was it that easy to replace someone? I didn't believe that. If I ever lost *him*. . . .

As Dave's arms encircled me and pulled me toward him, I heard someone else coming up the stairs, but I didn't care. He rested his chin on my head and I vented into his chest, practically sitting in his lap. I felt him lift his head for a moment to see who was at the door. But whoever it was must have gone away. He laid his head against mine again and held me in silence for what seemed like a very long, painful, blissful time.

Chapter Twenty-Six

Don't Let Go

If I'd had my way, I would have remained in Dave's arms all night—*much* more comforting than his hat. But there was no way that was going to happen. I had sobbed my heart out, leaving a damp patch on his coat where my cheek now rested, and he'd just silently and gently held me. When the sobbing was over, the tears continued to flow steadily but quietly as sad thoughts and images bombarded my mind. Gold being mistreated and wounded by the dastardly Ernest Ward, a.k.a. Harry Franklin. Gold wandering for weeks in the baking hot summer sun, searching the mountains for water and scraps of edible vegetation. Gold almost dying because he had avoided people, his only real hope of survival. Gold walking away from me—forever.

Then even darker, sadder thoughts assailed me from out of nowhere— thoughts of Dave, still patiently holding me. He had lost his beloved big brother to a terrible car accident. How devastating that must have been! And where was his mother? He must miss her terribly. *"It hurts more than anything when people you love leave you, for whatever reason."* He knew the pain of loss much better than me.

When the tears subsided, I remained still, exhausted and loath to relinquish the feel of Dave's arms around me, though I knew the embrace to be completely platonic on his part. But three things happened in close succession that interrupted and ultimately put a stop to it.

First, the leg I'd bent so I could sit comfortably against him had fallen asleep. The pins and needles hadn't started yet, but I was sure they were going to be vicious. It occurred to me that if *my* leg was asleep, then *his* probably was as well, as I was partially sitting on it and had been for quite some time. The second, immediately following these musings, was a loud rumble coming from Dave's stomach. He'd been here since nine-thirty this morning, and I didn't think he'd eaten much at lunch; I hadn't eaten a thing. It had to be at least three o'clock now. I was used to going without eating, but a metabolism like his probably needed constant attention.

I finally sat up and pulled away from him slightly, rubbing at my face and feeling like I'd just woken up.

"Sorry," he said, putting a hand on his stomach. Any awkwardness I might have felt in our situation was dispelled by the genuine concern for me I saw on his face.

At that moment the third circumstance, the sound of someone coming up the stairs again, put even more distance between us.

"Are you all right?" Dave asked, very softly.

I was still wiping my face with my jacket sleeve and trying to make my hair behave. Part of it was lingering, stuck to his jeans and booted foot.

"Yes, I'm all right," I answered, just as softly.

Mom was at the open door. I assumed it was her that had come up before, in which case she had seen his arms around me then, but I was glad we now had a foot or so of space between us.

"Dave," said Mom softly, seeming apologetic, "your father is leaving and says he'll give you a ride. Chris left a little while ago."

Dave nodded. "I'll . . . be right there."

He gently lifted the long strands of my hair still clinging to him and set them beside me with their fellows, a small smile on his lips.

"Has a mind of its own, doesn't it?" he observed.

Hmm . . . it's clinging to you the way I still want to, so . . . no, not really.
I sighed but tried to smile at him.

"I guess I'd better go. Don't want Dad coming up here. *Believe* me," he said, standing up to leave.

I tried to smile again and said, "Thanks. Thanks for being here and . . . and . . . not minding that I was crying. Thanks . . . for not turning away."

It took a lot for me to say that, to admit to that fear, and I was reluctant to look up into his face, into his eyes. But he was quiet for so long that I finally did. He was looking down at me with a puzzled look, but something else, too. It was as if he was trying to see something in me, to understand something.

"I'll never turn away from you, Allie," he said, very seriously.

He looked both concerned *and* confused; another new expression. I liked this one too. I felt extremely self-conscious, like the day he turned up on my doorstep and I was in my PJs. I looked down again, knowing that I was blushing, but as he still hesitated, I made myself look back.

He was still looking at me oddly, his eyes searching mine in a way they'd never done before. My whole body flushed warm and I held my breath, wondering what would happen next, wondering what he was thinking. I knew what *I* was thinking.

He smiled a little crookedly and stuck his thumbs in his back pockets, looking uncertain. "You going to be okay?"

Yes, I will.

I nodded and tried to smile again, but I really wasn't sure these recent efforts were making it from my brain to my mouth.

"I'll see you later. Okay?" he said, still seeming to hesitate.

My heart was beginning to thump, my psyche willing him to sit down with me again. And if he did. . . .

If he does. . . .

Instead, he slowly backed away, finally turning at the end of my bed to walk to the door. He looked back once before heading downstairs. I waited until I heard the front door close then got up, quietly closed my bedroom door, pulled off my coat and boots, and crawled beneath the comforter on my bed. Curling into a ball with the cover pulled over my head, I didn't allow myself to think of anything except how it felt to be held by Dave, how genuinely concerned he had seemed, and the sweet, bemused expression he'd had on his face. I didn't know what any of it meant—if it meant anything at all—except that I was more in love with him than ever.

After sleeping for a couple of hours, I got up, washed my face, found my glasses, and brushed and braided my hair. When I went downstairs, I felt calm, not numb like before but rather insulated, as if wrapped in thick fleece. I was aware of a sense of loss but wasn't going to face it right now. The physical memory of Dave's gestures and expressions of concern was

shielding me or perhaps just distracting me from it, and I was content with that. I was able to function through the evening and even made myself eat a little. When I slept later that night, I had no disturbing dreams and awoke feeling subdued and detached from reality—but okay.

"Cheryl called and wondered if you'd like to have a lesson today," said Mom lightly, as if nothing had happened the day before.

"Yes," I said quietly. "I'd like that." Anything to preoccupy myself. "Can I hang out for a while?"

Mom smiled. I was sure she understood. "If it's all right with Cheryl, it's all right with me. Oh, by the way . . . I gave Robin's presents to Dave and his dad to take home. I wanted to make sure they got them before we leave."

Oh yeah . . . Robin's presents . . . we're leaving. . . .

I was glad about the gifts, but the reminder that we were going out of town tomorrow did nothing to elevate my spirits. I buried the thought with the others I wasn't dealing with right now. Dad drove me to Bar 8 after lunch and dropped me off early, telling me to call when I was ready to come home.

"Thanks, Dad," I said. I'd stay as long as I could.

I went immediately to Remmy, who whickered gently when he saw me. He was inside his stall and, rather than take him out into the cold, I brought brushes in and groomed him there. His coat had remained fairly sleek in spite of the cold weather but was now a duller, darker brown than the pink-tinged bronze of the sunnier months.

More appropriate now to my state of mind, the sky was overcast, dark, and threatening to rain. I saddled Remmy inside the barn then led him out to the covered arena where Cheryl eventually joined us.

She worked with us for almost an hour, then said, "You've come a long way, Allison. A long way in a fairly short time. And I think Remmy there suits you."

I reached forward and stroked his neck. "He suits me perfectly," I said with as much conviction as I could.

Almost perfectly. As perfectly as is possible now . . . I think. . . .

Shaking off the menacing mopes, I tried to smile at her.

"How would you feel about entering your first show?" she asked.

My eyes flew wide. "Really? You think I'm ready?"

"Nobody's ever really ready for their first show. You've just got to do it. It's kind of like swimming. You just don't know what it's like until you've jumped in and done it once."

I'd been swimming as long as I could remember and wasn't sure of the comparison. "Kind of like riding itself," I said.

"Yes, I suppose," she replied.

"Can I learn how to barrel race?" I asked.

"Hmm," she pretended to consider. "I'm not sure you're ready for that. I was thinking more along the lines of Western pleasure and maybe trail classes. Basic skills."

That was a compromise I could make—for now. Cheryl left me then to rescue Tom from babysitting his own children, and Remmy and I worked a little longer. I was getting used to his stride and enjoying him immensely. What he lacked in grace, power of movement, and air of nobility—at least, compared to Gold—was amply made up for by seemingly endless energy and unflagging willingness to please. On the ground, he was considerate and manageable. Though not excitable, he always seemed very alert and vitally interested in anything happening around him.

He was extremely affectionate, loving to be stroked and talked to, and he seemed to desire physical contact: his shoulder, face, or nose touching me somewhere if we were standing still. Gold had remained slightly aloof as if he appreciated the attention but could happily live without it. He had seemed to enjoy making *me* feel better rather than seeking attention for himself. Remmy was incredibly sweet though, very fun to ride, and it was easy to feel great affection for him.

I'd brought my phone with me, ostensibly to call my dad when I wanted to be picked up, but mostly I was hoping to get a call from Dave. So far in our friendship he had checked up on me in similar circumstances. And if he did call or text me, I might just happen to mention that I was at Bar 8. Then he might think that being at Bar 8 himself for a while was a good idea.

It could happen.

I wanted to call Robin too, but I'd hoped to hear from Dave first. I knew she would want to hear about yesterday but might be waiting for me to be ready to talk about it. Sometimes she seemed conscious of these things and sometimes she didn't.

Finally taking Remmy back to the barn, I unsaddled him and took my time grooming him in the breezeway before returning him to his stall. The afternoon was disappearing fast and so was the light; dark storm clouds gathered outside and a strong, cold breeze began to bend and buffet the tree tops.

I called Robin.

"Hey," she said. "How're you doing?"

"Okay, I guess," I replied, trying not to sound too despondent.

"You're gonna miss him, huh?" she said, stating the obvious.

"Yes, I'm going to miss him a lot."

"Dave told me most of the story, but what were the people like? His owner and the person buying him? All Dave would say was 'some lady and an old dude.'"

I had to laugh at that and tried to describe the people a little better, including how nice and worthy they seemed, but that I hadn't really noticed details at the time.

"So . . . you're going out of town, right?" she said, changing from one painful subject to another.

"Yes," I admitted, finding it even harder to not sound depressed.

"What did Dave say? We were all hoping you could come to the party."

"Party?"

"He didn't tell you? The Calderas have a party on Christmas Eve."

Of course they do.

"Just close friends and neighbors . . . you know . . . but they decorate the house and it's really beautiful, and we just eat and hang out and have fun." She was quiet for a moment. "I can't believe he didn't tell you."

"Maybe he didn't think the time was right," I replied. "I was pretty upset yesterday."

"Yeah, probably. I'll tell him when he gets back," she said.

"Gets back?" I asked, suddenly feeling desolate.

"Yeah, they went somewhere today . . . Dave and Chris at least . . . dirt bikes I think, but I don't know where. They won't be back until tomorrow night."

"Oh," I said, any pretense of *not* feeling despondent abandoned. "They would ride in this weather?"

She laughed. "I've never known the weather to stop them from doing anything, though I didn't know they were going until last night. They often go on the spur of the moment. Especially when they're really stressed, you know?"

I thought I could understand that, though I wasn't sure how it applied at the moment. We talked a little more and promised to call each other later in the week. She said she had gotten me something and would give it to me next week when, hopefully, we could hang out. I said the same, having gotten her another CD I thought she'd like and a nice big candle.

"Have fun in LA," she said.

"Have fun at the party," I said, trying not to feel too envious. I had some new memories to hang onto and they should get me through the week. They would have to.

Knowing Dave wouldn't miraculously appear, I called my father to pick me up. I said farewell fondly to Remmy and went to say goodbye, thank you, and "Merry Christmas" to Cheryl and Tom. Then I went to the guest house porch to wait for Dad.

I kept the ringtone on my phone turned off but held it in my hand or pocket the rest of the day, just in case. No call ever came.

The next morning I dragged my feet getting ready until Dad got exasperated with me.

"We'll be hitting the worst LA traffic if we don't leave *now!*"

I took a lingering look around my room, closed my eyes for a moment, remembering Dave there, then reluctantly left it.

The journey to Los Angeles was tedious; eight hours of boredom interrupted by brief stops at nondescript hamlets for snacks and restrooms. I had brought my sketchbook and pencil case along but felt completely uninspired. Besides, the last drawings I'd done were of Gold, and I didn't feel ready to look at them again yet.

Most of the trip was spent listening to music through my headphones, but the songs now only reminded me of my friends—Dave in particular and Douglas in general. I also made sure I had physical contact with my phone at all times in case *someone* called or texted. I would have been thrilled either way.

Already homesick, I couldn't help tormenting myself, wondering if Dave had known yesterday that we'd be going away. And if he had, why hadn't he

said anything? And if he hadn't known, did he know now? Did it matter to him? These latter thoughts were always quickly followed by strong mental reprimands reminding myself that he was *not* my boyfriend, he *didn't* have those feelings for me, and there was *no* reason for us to keep track of each other beyond what normal friends did. Right? Did Robin and I keep track of each other that way? No.

But she always knows where he is and what he's doing.

That would start the whole process over, repeating all the way to my grandmother's house and then sporadically through the first few days there. It was going to be a very long week.

Christmas Eve came and went and, as had become my self-destructive habit, I spent most of it wondering if Dave had thought of me at all. I sure thought about him, though I suspected he was too busy and having too much fun to feel any curiosity about my activities.

On Christmas morning I didn't even want to get out of bed. But since I was sleeping on the convertible sofa in my grandmother's living room, I could already hear her puttering about in the kitchen, and aunts and uncles and a quantity of small cousins could be at the door at any moment, it seemed prudent just to go ahead and get the day started. Perhaps it would get it over with more quickly too. After showering and dressing, I picked up my phone, my heart leaping.

A text from Dave.

'Merry Christmas!'

I almost cried, relief warming and relaxing me through and through like a yummy cup of hot chocolate on a freezing cold day. *Sweet, chocolatey hot chocolate with thick, whipped cream on top.* I hadn't realized until that moment how tense I'd been feeling.

'Thank you! You too!' I replied, then added, *'See you soon?'*

'Of course,' was the immediate reply and anything still tense was converted to something like pudding—metaphorically speaking. And also probably chocolate.

You're pathetic.

True of course, but I couldn't have cared less. Hearing from him was the best present I got for Christmas, and I was able to be patient with even the brattiest of my little cousins, remaining content for the rest of the day.

The only cause of discomfort I felt was instigated by my grandmother then picked up and aggravated by my mother and aunts.

"You have a birthday coming up, don't you Allison?" Grandma asked. "What do you have planned?"

"I don't know," I answered honestly. With all the other events and preoccupations lately, it hadn't seemed important and the topic hadn't come up.

"Fifteen, isn't it? Fifteen," she repeated a little dreamily and looked into space as if it was something special, perhaps remembered with fondness.

I couldn't imagine why. *Too old to fully enjoy what others considered childish things, too young to be taken seriously.* I could think of no reason to look forward to it in particular. *Now, sixteen. . . .*

"Do you have a boyfriend yet?" Grandma asked out of the blue, then immediately turned to my mother and asked, "Does she have a boyfriend?" as if I weren't a reliable source for this information.

"No, Grandma!" I said quickly, feeling panicky. This was *not* a topic I wanted pursued.

My dad, sitting and reading a magazine close by, was pretending not to listen, but he really was. I can always tell when he's pretending. Mom's younger sister, Audrey, was unbraiding and playing with my hair.

"No dates yet?" Grandma said, as if this was a concern. "Nobody's asked you?"

I squirmed. Technically, I *had* been asked out; Matthew had asked me to the dance. It hadn't occurred to me before, but that would have been my *first* date—had I said yes and been allowed to go, that is.

Dad betrayed his state of awareness here, obviously as uncomfortable with the topic as I was. "Allison's not dating until she's at least sixteen," he said, gruffly.

"Well, I suppose things are different these days," said Grandma, sounding both uncertain and a little offended, "but your grandfather first asked me out when I was fifteen. And most of my friends had dated even earlier." This last was said to my mother, though it sounded more like a challenge thrown at my dad. "My mother was *married* at fifteen."

I wouldn't mind dating, but married!

While I might secretly agree with Grandma, at least the dating part, I knew I was scarlet and wished they would drop the subject. Mom leaned over and whispered into her older sister's ear. Aunt Kate's eyebrows rose,

and she turned an inquiring stare at me. I wanted to sink into the ground or turn invisible. I would have excused myself from the room if Aunt Audrey wasn't holding my hair. She seemed to sense my discomfort and changed the subject.

"Do you ever think about cutting your hair, Allie?"

I shook my head. "Not really," I replied. I really hadn't, though the topic seemed to be coming up a lot lately.

"It seems like it would get in the way a lot," she said, then seemed to feel bad for sounding negative. "It's really nice, though. Very . . . long. And soft."

Yes. Long. Soft. Those were about the best things you could say about it. Not pretty. Not wavy or luxurious or shiny. Just—long. But I could picture strands of it clinging to Dave, and the memory made me want to smile. I knew it wasn't registering on the outside, but inside it was huge and blissful.

I escaped soon after that; I didn't want to hear any more. I spent the remainder of the day actually enjoying my cousins' company and avoiding the conversation and inquisitive glances of the adults in the family; quite a reversal for me. I saw my young cousins in a different light now too. I tried not to compare them to the other children I'd become fond of, but I felt I could appreciate the younger members of my own family a little better because of them. It made it easier than ever to tap into the true dork in myself, allowing me to be silly and less self-conscious around them. All in all, it was a very nice day.

The following day I tried calling Robin three times, but she never answered. And in spite of my leaving two messages, she never called me back. I assumed she was too busy, having too much fun, or had gone somewhere and left her phone at home. I tried calling again the next day but still no reply.

It was Saturday and my mom had arranged for us to have lunch and go shopping with Brenda and her mom, Nicole. It was a trying day for me. Brenda kept making comments about how I hadn't changed.

"Didn't you wear that shirt all last year?"

"Your glasses still make your face look funny. You should try a different style or something."

"Still not wearing makeup, I see. You know, I think it would help . . ."

But I knew that I was completely different on the inside. It seemed to confuse her greatly because I looked the same but didn't respond to her in the same compliant, subservient way I always had before. If I didn't like something, I had no problem admitting to it, politely but firmly. Any time she tried to bully me into saying or doing anything I didn't agree with, I quietly but obstinately refused.

She, on the other hand, looked completely different: her hair cut short and styled attractively, her nails obviously done at a salon, and she wore makeup. A lot of makeup. It looked nice, not thick and overdone like that of some of the girls at school, but it made her look much older. I guess that was the point.

I knew her family was doing well financially. Mom and Nicole had been friendly when we were at school together and had kept in touch. Brenda's parents never understood why my parents chose to move to "the boondocks" instead of to a "nicer" neighborhood like they had. Brenda's mom had remonstrated with mine about the kind of school I'd be forced to go to if we moved to a small rural community. How could they deprive me of the benefits of a better school, more varied opportunities, and more affluent society?

I was so thankful that they had! While I was sure there were positive aspects to all of those other things, I never would have met Dave. Or Robin and Melanie. And I wouldn't have found Gold. I might have still felt like the hopeless, spiritless nobody I felt like before—before everything. Or worse.

Being accepted by the popular people at school had been vitally important to Brenda, and not quite accomplishing it had always chafed at her. It was, I think, one of the reasons she had often lost patience with me, and I had always felt bad for her and made allowances. I guess she was finally fitting into that crowd now, though. She made no secret about the labels she was wearing—her clothes were clearly expensive—and it reminded me of a certain scene with Dave at the mall. At that point, I escaped happily into my imagination to be with him until Brenda pulled me abruptly out.

"You haven't changed at all, have you?" she said with something of a superior air. "Still spacing out. . . ."

I had, of course, changed a great deal, but when it came to spacing out, I think I was far worse now than I had ever been before. I didn't see any point in correcting her, though. And although she appeared more stylish and outwardly mature, she didn't seem to have changed in essentials one bit.

"Dreaming about your cowboy?" she said archly and in an unnecessarily loud voice.

Now she *did* have my attention, as well as the attention of several passersby and both our mothers. The latter looked at us, her mom with blatant curiosity and mine, well, I'm not sure what her expression was but it made me feel uncomfortable. It was extremely likely that I was blushing, too. I was *really* going to have to do something about that.

"I don't own a cowboy," I muttered under my breath.

She laughed, pleased that she had succeeded in embarrassing me. I was afraid this was going to become a tool of torture toward me—friendly torture, of course. Realizing she hadn't once mentioned Trevor, her boyfriend, I asked if she was still dating him.

She looked peeved. "I'm not going out with *him* anymore," she said. "There's another guy I like, though, and he likes me."

"Oh," I said, not knowing what else to say. She didn't elaborate and I didn't ask.

Mom and I were subdued on our way back to my grandmother's house. I felt socially exhausted by both Brenda and her mother. Among other things that were incomprehensible to me, they seemed to have picked up namedropping as a hobby. Or perhaps I'd just never noticed it before. I guess we were supposed to be impressed. It was a shame that neither Mom nor I had a clue who all the people were that they were constantly talking about, but talking about them certainly seemed to make them happy.

I would have loved to go home and retreat to my own bedroom, but we had one more night of family togetherness to get through at Grandma's. Robin still hadn't called and I was starting to worry a little. I wanted to call Dave and ask what was going on, but since I doubted my motivation for doing so, I restrained myself.

It was with incredible though slightly guilty relief that I loaded my two bags into the car and said farewell to my grandparents, and with growing anticipation that I watched the miles slip by on the way home. My parents commented at least twice that I was being very quiet, which I thought strange as I was never exactly noisy. I stared out the window and couldn't have told you what I'd been thinking of that entire trip, but I was left with an impression of pink-tinged brown. There was another color my mind kept touching on, but I firmly redirected it. For now, bronze was much safer.

I tried calling Robin once from the car but lost the signal. When we finally got home, it was dark and the house was very cold. Dad started a fire but I went straight to my room and closed the door. Picking up my phone, I tried Robin again. She didn't answer. My hands shaking a little, I called Dave. His number wasn't available. Feeling even more nervous, I called the Caldera house. Answering machine. Very strange. I had no real reason to be worried, but I went to bed feeling uneasy. I would try again tomorrow.

In the morning, after Dad had left on his trip, I tried all the numbers again, but still had no luck. I left another message for Robin asking that she call me back, and I left one for Dave too. I didn't leave a message at the Caldera home. It certainly wasn't the way I'd hoped to start my last week of winter vacation.

About midday it occurred to me that my mother might have a number for Robin's house. She did. She also thought it a little odd that I couldn't get in touch with her. I tried not to show how concerned I was getting. When I called, Fiona answered.

"Hello, dear," she said. "Yes, Robin's here. Did you have a nice Christmas?"

"Yes, it was okay. We spent it in Los Angeles." I decided to not say whether I thought that was a good thing or not.

"Well, let me get Robin for you," she said, and must have gone off to find her.

It seemed a long time before Robin came on. "Hello?" she said, as if she wasn't sure who was on the other end.

"Robin," I said. "Hi. I've been trying to reach you for days. Are you all right?"

"Of course," she said.

Awkward pause.

"Did you have a nice Christmas? Was the party fun? I wish I could have been there," I said, trying to warm up the conversation.

There was another awkward pause before Robin said, "Yeah. It was fine. The party was fun."

Okay, something's wrong . . . but I don't have a clue what it is!

I couldn't ever remember feeling this way with her; at least, not since those first days of school when we didn't know each other at all.

"I tried calling Dave . . . to find out if you were okay. I was worried. He didn't answer either. Is . . . is something wrong?"

I was suddenly feeling sick, very *much* like those first days of school, or like when everybody was treating me badly after the Caldera's event and I thought my friends were angry at me too. People used to routinely treat me this way in elementary and middle school. Even Brenda. Had I done something to make them mad? Had I hurt them somehow? My brain was racing, but I just couldn't think of anything.

"They're all up in the mountains somewhere, up in the snow. They go after Christmas every year. He's probably not getting calls."

"Oh," I said, feeling oddly deflated instead of relieved.

Another thing she knew about him that I didn't. Why on earth would he have told me about that? *No reason I can think of.*

"I've got to go," she started, but I stopped her.

"Can you come over tomorrow?" I asked, feeling a little desperate. It immediately hit me that without Gold here, there wasn't much to do. "We could hang out at Bar 8 or something."

"I don't know," she said, sounding reluctant for some reason.

"Well . . . call me tomorrow, okay?" I hoped whatever the problem was would be cleared up by then.

"Yeah, okay," she said and hung up.

The rest of the day dragged by. Mom and I went into town to pick up our mail at the post office and do grocery shopping. I was tempted to go over to Robin's house, and might have if there wasn't this odd tension between us. In the stack of mail was an envelope, obviously a card, addressed to all of us from the Calderas. I opened it. In a strong, attractive print was written:

To Allison and the Anderson Family

Love,

Alex, Angel, Cris, Dave, Henry, and Stevey

The post date said December 20, two days before we went out of town. But of course, nothing is delivered on Sunday and my parents had had the mail held since the Friday before we left, about the same time we'd sent our card to them. That made me feel happy, even though I was assuming Mr.

Caldera had actually written the card. It certainly wasn't Dave's writing—I knew what that looked like—and it looked too masculine to be Angel's.

Then I frowned and looked at the names again. I thought I'd seen wrong, but there it was: C-r-i-s, not C-h-r-i-s.

Wow. All this time.

It wasn't as if it made any difference to the way I'd been using his name all along; it had come out sounding right at least. But I'd taken for granted that it was "Chris," short for "Christopher." I felt embarrassed by the mistake but knew it was an honest one. I'd never seen his name written down before. I hoped he didn't mind too much, if he'd even looked at the card I'd sent. It made me stop in my mental tracks and double check Dave's name, but I'd been thinking of it correctly. I knew for sure that it was short for David.

The next day I waited quite a while for Robin to call me, but finally broke down and called her. I felt like I was pestering her and I'd never felt that way before. It's not as if we lived constantly on the phone with each other the way some of our classmates did. I liked to talk only when I really had something to say, and that just wasn't that often. Dave and Robin both talked way more than I did, though I wouldn't have classified either of them as garrulous. Chris and I seemed to share the reticent gene. That is, *Cris*. It was funny how I felt the need to correct the spelling of his name in my head whenever I thought of him now. It was going to take a little getting used to.

"Can you come over or something?" I asked. I was glad she had actually answered her phone, but I felt nervous.

"I don't know," she said, sounding as hesitant but less severe than yesterday. "I'm not feeling too good."

I didn't believe her for a second but said, "I'm sorry. Maybe Mom and I can just come by to give you your present? I'm sure Mom would like to visit with Fiona."

"You already gave me enough." The words sounded dead, hollow somehow.

"I . . . I don't understand. I haven't given you anything yet," I said.

"Do you think that because we don't have money, that I'm stupid?" she asked heatedly. "Because I'm not!"

"Robin," I started, but she had ended the call.

Although I was stunned, I was starting to understand. There was only one thing she could be referring to: the presents from the Caldera family. She thought *I* had given them to her! What to do? My first impulse was to call her back immediately and explain, and if she wouldn't answer her phone—which I suspected she wouldn't—to call the house and explain to Fiona. I couldn't bear Robin being angry with me if there was any way I could make amends.

Then I realized I couldn't explain. Not only had I been in league with the whole scheme, but the Calderas had apparently given the gifts anonymously. To explain would feel like betraying them, or trying to pass the blame. I couldn't do that either. I thought about trying to call Dave again but decided not to. What would I say, even if I did get a call through? Nothing that wouldn't sound recriminating. Better to just wait and see, difficult though that would be.

In the meantime, I decided to call Melanie to see what she was up to. But her mother answered the phone, said Melanie wasn't home, and she didn't make me feel optimistic about a message being passed on. Maybe I'd try again later. I felt bad that I was only now thinking of her, but I'd been pretty preoccupied, what with one thing and another. In the end, I persuaded my mom to take me to Bar 8 and I hung out with Remmy, phone at the ready, while she visited with Cheryl. When I rejoined them, they asked if I wanted to take extra lessons this week and I leaped at the chance, as much to keep my mind occupied as to improve my riding.

It was the next day while riding that I felt my phone vibrate in my pocket, telling me someone had called. I fervently hoped it was Robin calling to forgive me and was unusually eager for my lesson to end. While leading Remmy back to the barn, I pulled out my phone.

'*1 missed call.*'

'*1 voice mail.*'

"Hey . . . it's Dave. Sorry, I didn't get your message before . . . mmm . . . mountains. And I let my battery die . . . you know. So . . . yeah . . . call me back."

I quickly unsaddled Remmy and returned him to his stall. I'd brush him later. My hands shaking, I called Dave.

"Hey," he said.

"Hi," I replied, afraid of what might come next.

"I need to apologize to you," he said.

That completely surprised me. "What? Why?"

"Because we didn't tell Robin who the presents were from. We figured she'd just know, so we labeled them 'From Santa.' It never occurred to us that she'd think you were the culprit. When I got your message, I called her first to see what was up. I'm really sorry."

I felt bad that *he* felt bad, but relieved, too; relieved that he wasn't mad at me for some reason and that now, hopefully, things would be normal again with Robin.

"You don't need to apologize," I said. "It was just a misunderstanding. Did you get it sorted out with her?"

"Yeah. She got mad at me for the presents, then I got mad at her for being stupid and proud about it. Then she got mad at me because it had seemed like you had given her everything, which," he sounded like he was trying to be fair, "I guess makes sense. But then I got mad at her for getting mad at you. But she was obviously already feeling pretty bad about it, so . . . I think we both forgave each other, but I kind of lost track."

I laughed. He always made everything seem all right. Just one of many reasons why I loved him.

"So . . . do you think I should call her?"

"Definitely," he said.

"Okay." Then I just *had* to ask him. I couldn't stop myself. "Are you coming home soon?"

"Mmm . . . not sure. The snow's been pretty amazing, but there've been some problems too, so . . . I don't know. We'll be back before school starts, though. Why? Miss me?"

I caught my breath at the way the question sounded—as if, perhaps, he *wanted* me to miss him. I forced myself to breathe and think clearly, then answered him, trying to sound as nonchalant as he had. "Of course."

He laughed. "Good. See you later."

"Okay. Is everything all right?" I wondered what the "some problems" meant.

"Yeah. Call Robin."

"Okay."

"Bye."

"Bye."

I groomed Remmy—rather dreamily and feeling heart-warmed and happy—then went to find my mother. She was having coffee with Cheryl and Gloria, Tom's aunt who lived in and managed the guest house. Though

Christmas week was always a busy time for them, there was no one staying there now for a couple of days and they were enjoying the quiet.

"See you tomorrow?" asked Cheryl as we were leaving.

"Yes, please," I said happily. "Can I bring Robin?"

Mom's brows rose slightly, but she indicated both the lesson and guest would be acceptable.

"Of course," said Cheryl. "You and Robin are welcome here anytime. Just don't go riding unless we're home and know you're here."

That went without saying; I wouldn't have dreamed of riding without permission. It seemed like a strange thing to say, but I supposed she had to make sure it was understood.

Mom agreed to stop at home so we could pick up Robin's gift, and then drive to her house. She also said it would be fine to ask her to spend the night, but didn't I want to call her first? Had I already asked her? I admitted that I had not, but didn't say I preferred to arrive unannounced or why. The truth was, I didn't want Robin to have an opportunity to wriggle out of the proposition. She'd have to deal with me if I was at her house, and I was sure I'd have an ally in Fiona.

It was a testimony to my friends, and probably to Dave in particular, that I was so proactive in this situation. Robin had once said I was rubbing off on Dave, but I was sure it was far more the opposite. Some of his impulsive nature must be rubbing off on me as, not so long ago, I would have waited timidly to hear from Robin instead of actually confronting her. Now I just wanted to clear the air and get back to normal as quickly as possible.

When we reached Robin's, Fiona answered the door looking surprised but pleased to see us.

"I'm sorry if we're disturbing you, Fiona," said Mom. "We . . . just thought we'd drop by." I hadn't explained anything to my mother, but she had apparently picked up vibes.

"That's fine! It's lovely to see you! Come in, come in!"

Fiona shooed us into the house as Robin appeared at the hallway corner, her eyes looking larger than normal and her face pale.

"Why don't you come right into the kitchen with me, Jen, and we'll make tea," said Fiona. She took Mom's arm and walked with her down the hallway toward the kitchen.

I looked at Robin and tried to smile; I was still having difficulty with it. Hoping my expression was at least benign, I walked forward, holding out the wrapped box with the CD and candle inside, the real present from me. She looked embarrassed and didn't want to look me in the eye. I felt awkward too.

She took the gift, then said in a rush, "Allie, I'm so sorry! I shouldn't have gotten mad at you. Even if you *had* bought me all those things, which of course you *didn't*, but even if you *had*, I shouldn't have gotten so mad or felt hurt."

"It's okay," I said quietly. "I think . . . I think I can understand, a little, how you felt. For a long time my parents struggled, maybe for different reasons, but . . . I remember. My clothes weren't always new and didn't always fit right, and I got laughed at because of it. I got made fun of for other reasons too. I still do. Apparently . . ." I said, trying to grin, "apparently I'm a dork, among other things."

Robin smiled crookedly at that. "Yeah, I used to get made fun of a lot too when I was little. Until Dave decided he didn't want to make fun of me anymore. Then he didn't let anyone else make fun of me either. You've met Henry. He should give you an idea of what a terror Dave was. Never one to back down from a fight."

We both laughed a little and then she looked serious again. "I'm really sorry. I was . . . a jerk . . . and you were just trying to be kind."

I noticed tears were standing in her eyes and didn't want her to feel bad anymore. "You've got to admit, though," I said. "We did pretty well, right?"

She grinned reluctantly and nodded. "For one stupid moment I actually believed in Santa Claus. Every really cute thing I had tried on was there. Then I got mad." Her face crumpled again. "Now I see I just have amazing friends."

"That love you," I added.

"Yeah," she said quietly, and now her face was flooded with color.

She walked suddenly forward and hugged me tightly, her head resting on my shoulder. It was the first time she'd ever done anything demonstrably affectionate toward me. Grateful, I hugged her tightly back.

"Allie?"

"Yes?"

"Thanks."

Chapter Twenty-Seven

Getting Nowhere

Fiona seemed overjoyed to allow us to kidnap Robin for the night. Robin protested at first, not because she had changed her mind about forgiving me, but because she was unhappy about leaving Fiona alone with her chores. Her Gran insisted she'd be fine if Robin left Gali's food ready.

Robin and I retreated to her room so she could grab some things for overnight, and she also gave me the gift she had gotten me. I wanted her to open hers first, but she insisted on me doing mine. We compromised by opening them together. She looked pleased with my gift. The CD was one that I challenged her to *not* want to dance to. And, since I hadn't noticed any obvious color scheme in her bedroom, I gave her a large but pretty, multi-colored, marble-patterned, vanilla-scented candle.

When I opened my gift, I gasped then exclaimed. Not only had she given me a pretty frilly pink scrunchy with gold threads through it, and a lovely dusky rose scented and colored candle that would match the paint trim in my room, she had also given me the exact switchplate cover that I had admired at the hardware store. I couldn't get over it. Though it seemed silly to be that tickled over getting such a thing, it really was one of the most thoughtful gifts I could remember ever receiving and I told her so. She seemed very gratified. I realized, of course, that Chris—*Cris*—might have told her about it, but she was the one who actually gave it to me. I thanked her profusely.

We stopped on the way home to pick up pizza for dinner and later watched *The Princess Bride*; just us girls. Robin had never seen it, and Mom and I agreed that had to be rectified. We stayed up pretty late and, although my mom had prepared the guest room for Robin, she said she would rather sleep on the floor in my room—if that was okay. It was, and we stayed up even later talking and giggling quietly, mostly about the boys at school and especially about Dave, of course.

It was mid-morning when I awoke. The sun was well up and I panicked for a moment, thinking that I'd forgotten an important chore. Then I relaxed again, sadly, and noticed that Robin wasn't in the room. I waited, thinking she might have just gone to the bathroom, but she didn't come back and I heard no noise of movement beyond my door. After putting a sweatshirt, some thick socks, and my glasses on, I crept downstairs. She wasn't watching television and she wasn't in the kitchen. Perplexed, I finally looked out the back window. I hadn't done that since Gold went away.

My eyes were drawn immediately to the empty corral and I felt a sharp stab of grief. Then I saw Robin sitting on the back steps and my heart was eased somewhat. I opened the back door and joined her on the steps.

"It's so pretty here," she whispered, smiling. "I woke up and couldn't go back to sleep. I guess I'm just too used to having to wake up early all the time. I didn't want to wake anyone with the TV or anything, so I came out here. I love the way the hills look in the morning. We don't have a view like this at my house."

I didn't respond right away. I loved the way the hills looked in the morning too, but it had been quite a while since I'd noticed them. While Gold was here, he had held my attention captive, making everything else pale in comparison, with one notable exception. Now when I looked out across to the hills, I thought of when I first caught glimpses of him; how I would scan the then dry, brown hillsides for the glimmer of his tawny coat. The hillsides were emerald green now and I tried to appreciate the way the pale sunlight glistened on the wet grass close to us, the way late morning mist still clung to the treetops in shadows farther away. But it was hard to see past the empty paddock.

Enough moping! You have things to celebrate!

"Wait here a minute," I said and went back to the kitchen.

I got everything out that I needed for hot chocolate, heated the milk, used extra chocolate, and poured it out into large mugs. I was thrilled we still had a can of whipped cream left from Thanksgiving. After topping off the mugs with swirls of the fluffy cream, I rejoined Robin and handed her one.

"A toast," I said, holding my mug up toward her.

"A toast? With hot chocolate?" asked Robin, her eyes merry.

"Yes," I said, decidedly. "Here's to friendship."

Robin smirked and looked her normal self again. "To friendship," she echoed, and then added, "forever!"

I drew my mug back and frowned, pretending to hesitate. "Forever?"

She laughed. "Yeah! Forever. You got a problem with that?"

I smiled. "No. That sounds pretty good to me." We clinked our mugs together.

We enjoyed our hot chocolate then went inside, had something more substantial for breakfast, and got ready for the rest of the day. Coming back to my room after using the bathroom, I overheard Robin talking to Fiona on her phone.

"I just wanted to make sure you're okay . . . Yeah . . . Had pizza and watched movies . . ." She laughed gently. "Okay . . . We're going to Tom and Cheryl's. Could Allie come over tonight? Thanks . . . Yeah . . . Okay. Bye, Gran." She turned to me and smiled, looking slightly sheepish. "I worry about her, you know?"

I nodded.

"So . . . do you want to come spend the night tonight?"

"Of course!" I said happily.

My mother was up by then, and she was fine with the overnight exchange plan. Though we could have had a ride and I knew it would be a long way, I asked Robin if she wanted to try walking to Bar 8. She looked unsure at first, but it was a cool, dry day and we had no better way to kill time. We started out earlier than necessary so that, even though we were walking, we'd get there before Cheryl expected me. It took a lot longer than I thought it would and we were pretty tired when we got there. We stopped to rest on the bleachers under the covered arena. The arena floor seemed littered with random apparatus, much like an obstacle course.

"Looks like Cheryl's going to start trail class training with you," said Robin, grinning widely, her eyes bright. "You're moving up in the world."

We went to Cheryl's house to let her know we were there. She admitted, "Yes, we'll work on general pleasure and trail class skills today. Robin, go ahead and ride Fritz. You can help demonstrate."

Robin cheered, beaming, and I caught her excitement, both of us racing to the barn to groom and saddle our respective mounts. Robin won. For the next hour Cheryl had us navigate the trail course she had set up, Robin first so that I could observe her, and then she followed me closely to demonstrate and help me out of jams. Remmy was so patient—I would have loved to know what his thoughts on his clumsy rider were. At the end of the lesson, I felt I'd reached a new level, like in a video game. *"You have reached Equitation Level Three. You should now rest and meditate on your accomplishments."* I just wished I felt that way about other aspects of my life.

Mom picked us up a little later and we stopped at home just long enough for me to pack overnight things and for Robin to make sure she had all her stuff. I also grabbed the scrunchy she'd given me and slipped it on my wrist. Another lesson had been arranged for Saturday, but tomorrow we'd be free to do what we wanted. I already had something in mind.

Fiona was happy to see us and Robin was touchingly solicitous to her. I was certainly seeing a much softer side of her these past couple of days and felt honored she felt comfortable enough with me to let her guard down. When we went out back, Gali neighed loudly and trotted up to the fence. Robin giggled.

"Did you miss me?" she said happily, and I felt a twinge of sadness that I would never again hear the throaty *hurhurhur* of my lovely Gold greeting me. My eyes were tearing up a little, but I was able to brush them away before Robin turned to me, smiling. "It's nice to know I'm more than just the hand that feeds him. Do you mind if I ride?"

"Of course not," I said. I enjoyed watching other people ride and now paid close attention to details.

"We could go for a walk up the street," she said, "if you don't mind actually walking. He sometimes gets a little nervous on the road, but I'd love to get him out of the paddock for a while."

This sounded like an excellent idea, so we spent the rest of the afternoon taking turns riding Gali in a large, open field quite a way up the street Robin lived on. Apparently a couple of years before, she and Dave had spent days clearing the field of large stones and debris and filled in holes so that it could

be ridden in fairly safely. We still walked around it when we first got there, making mental notes of where the larger ground squirrel holes were so we could avoid them and removing any large rocks that had worked their way to the surface. Then we took turns exercising Gali.

Robin pulled several small branches from the sides of the open area and laid them out in different formations for me to practice some maneuvers. We backed through them, stepped over them, trotted through, and I tried to get Gali to sidestep around, which I wasn't very good at.

Riding Gali was so different from riding Remmy. It was good for me to work on a horse not as responsive to my aids. When it started getting dark, we made our way back to the house and settled Gali for the night. Then we helped Fiona with dinner and watched television with her until bedtime.

We awoke very early. Robin went out to feed Gali then cooked us all breakfast while I made hot chocolate. We took our time, enjoying the cold quiet of the morning. When it was a little warmer, we went to hang out with Gali.

"What do you want to do?" asked Robin.

I had already thought this through and was surprised Robin hadn't suspected.

"I want you to teach me how to barrel race."

Robin looked surprised then indecisive. "I'm not sure Cheryl would approve."

"Cheryl doesn't need to know," I said, playing with Gali's forelock.

"Hmmm . . . I think you're going to get me into trouble, but . . . okay. Let me ride him first. Okay?"

"Of course," I said happily.

Robin saddled and worked Gali in both directions of her corral, and then let me mount.

"Okay . . . we won't do too much. You're not ready and I don't want Gali getting sick of barrels, but we can make a start. It would be better if Cheryl, or even Dave, worked with you."

In my mind, I agreed wholeheartedly that it would be *best* if Dave worked with me, but I happily went along with what she thought. First we worked on my cues for lead changes, which were very rough. Not only was I not too clear in my mind on exactly how it worked, but Gali's lope was also hard for me to sit into. I tended to bounce; not conducive to using my seat and legs effectively. After doing this for a while, Robin had us walk the barrel pattern, showing me just where the stopping point was before turning into the barrels.

"I think that's enough for one day," she said after a while. "You need to take it slow. There are still some basic things you need to work on before you'd be able to run them anyway."

I knew what she was saying was true, but in the days following Gold's departure I had made a decision: nerves or fear would no longer keep me from trying new things, especially when it came to horses and riding. I was going to work as hard as I could and as hard as I was allowed to in order to excel. Being especially good at any one thing had never really mattered to me before, but I had finally found something I felt truly passionate about. Well, two things, of course, but only one I could pursue and act on.

We unsaddled Gali, gave him another brush, and made sure he was content before leaving him to play in the corral. The day was chilly and gray but perfect for walking, so we decided to walk into town. Fiona wanted to make dinner for Mom and me, so she gave Robin a small list and some money and said we could help later. For now, we planned to just walk around and get a snack for lunch before buying the items and returning home.

First things first, we headed down to the coffee shop. Having hot drinks to sip as we walked seemed like a good idea. Unfortunately, the grocery store we needed was also nearby so we'd have to walk all the way back again before going home. We laughed and agreed that we'd certainly get enough exercise between yesterday and today.

There was activity at the abandoned gas station. No vehicles, but two kids on skateboards. My stomach flipped at the prospect of Dave being there. I couldn't see clearly enough, but before I could distinguish that it was not him, Robin enlightened me.

"Hmm . . . Matthew and Tanner."

Apparently we had hesitated long enough for them to notice us, for both raised arms in greeting and Robin returned it. We entered the store and by the time we had bought our drinks, the boys had joined us.

"What are you girls doing on this fine day?" asked Matthew, smiling in his calm, friendly way.

"Just hangin'," said Robin. "Gettin' hot beverages to keep us warm. We're just going to walk around."

"Can we come with you?" asked Tanner, his eyes bright.

Robin looked at me and shrugged her shoulders. "It's fine." She said it as if she didn't care, but I thought she seemed pleased.

I didn't mind one way or the other. I only wished someone else was there too.

In no hurry as we walked back toward the center of town, the boys sometimes took detours to investigate the boarding potential of various obstacles and structures along the way. But they mostly walked alongside us, trying to make us laugh. They succeeded most of the time, though I still wasn't sure my expressions were accurately portraying what I was supposed to be feeling.

It was then that I realized that I wasn't—feeling those emotions, that is. I hadn't really noticed until now—I guess I was too new at analyzing my own feelings—but there was definitely something missing. Though the general numbness had mostly worn off, whatever that emotional element is that translates to real smiles and laughter seemed to still be slumbering. I could fake it and that was the best I could do.

This troubled me, preoccupying me to the extent that the others had to keep rousing me from abstraction, telling me I was too quiet, and causing me to fake smile and apologize. And I did feel bad about it. I should have been happy in their company. I liked all three of them immensely. Tanner was his usual goofy, happy self. Matthew was observant and witty, appealing to my literary and artistic side as he always did. Robin was just Robin and I was comfortable and content to simply be in her company. But something was missing. Something inside. Something *vital*.

When we got downtown, my stomach flipped for a second time today. Cris' truck was parked down the street from the hardware store.

They're back? Dave's back?

Robin must have noticed my intense attention as she followed my line of sight. She frowned. "They're back?" she said, echoing my thought exactly. "I didn't know they were back."

She made a bee-line for the hardware store and I eagerly followed. The guys stayed outside with their skateboards. Cris was nowhere to be found inside and we escaped out the back to the lumber yard before the zealous clerk could descend on us. We found Cris—aproned, gloved, and goggled—ripping wood on a huge table saw. Not wanting to distract him, we waited until he'd finished the plank he was working on and stepped forward when he was done. He switched the saw off and removed the goggles before turning toward us.

"Hey," he said roughly. Hardly a greeting. I couldn't tell if he was annoyed at being interrupted or embarrassed for some reason. His eyes slid to me for a moment, then back to Robin. He seemed—distant—as if we were people he didn't know very well or didn't like. It made me feel funny, but I wasn't sure how, and definitely didn't know why.

"You guys are back?" Robin asked.

He shook his head. "No. Just me. I came back Monday . . . need the work. One of the other guys is on vacation this week and I was offered his hours, so. . . ." He shrugged as if that was all he needed to say. I guess it was. His attention was caught then by Tanner and Matthew, doing flip tricks in the parking lot. Apparently they were already bored. "You'd better get them out of here before they get in trouble," he said, dully.

"Okay," said Robin, looking at him speculatively. I wondered if she thought him as weird as I did. "When's Dave coming back?"

"Probably tomorrow. For sure on Sunday," he added unnecessarily.

Of course they'll be back before school.

"I've got to get back to work."

I thought his voice sounded cold. He turned away, back to what he'd been doing, without another glance at us. We rejoined Matthew and Tanner and proceeded to draw them away from the parking lot.

Then it hit me. In that moment, I felt sure I was the most insensitive, ungrateful person on the planet.

"I just remembered something," I said a little breathlessly to the others. "You go ahead. I'll . . . I'll catch up."

Without another word, I left them on the sidewalk in front of the hardware store and made my way back through the parking lot. I tried to be careful about distracting Cris again, but he had seen me coming and turned the saw off as I approached. He took the goggles off once more, then the rather heavy gloves he was wearing. There was a question in his eyes. He looked concerned but guarded.

There was no easy way to do this, so I just blurted it out. "Thank you!"

He looked truly surprised and very confused.

"For everything you did to help with Gold. I don't think I ever said thank you. It meant—" My mind wouldn't even wrap around exactly what it had meant, but I felt a heavy debt suddenly weighing me down. I took the scrunchy off my wrist and twisted it around my fingers. "It meant *so* much."

Now my eyes were tearing up and I got angry with myself. Not that I cared whether he saw me cry or not, but I wanted to get past this raw, easily provoked pain. "And I'm sorry," I continued, trying to pull my mind away from the still open wound. At that point, I accidentally dropped the scrunchy.

He looked bewildered again, frowning deeply and actually staring at me as I self-consciously picked the scrunchy up. He *never* stared at me.

"For what?" he asked.

"For spelling your name wrong."

The fact that he didn't look confused now told me that he *had* seen the Christmas card. He half turned away, then turned back but didn't meet my eyes. I would have thought he was angry or at least impatient, except for the tiniest of twitches near the corner of his mouth. Yes, it was definitely there.

"You're forgiven," he said evenly, as if he were being very magnanimous.

That might have irked me a little if he hadn't allowed himself to glance at me again. The expression on his face didn't seem patronizing or irritable. I'm not sure what it was, being one of those fleeting here-one-second-gone-the-next things. But I felt better.

"Thanks," I said softly, trying to smile, but still not sure if the impulse was reaching my lips. I turned to go.

"And," his voice stopped me and I turned back to face him, "you're welcome." He looked away before continuing, "But you don't owe me anything."

I couldn't tell if he would notice, but I nodded anyway then walked away. I didn't hear the saw start up right away and turned to look back once. I thought he might have been watching me go, but he'd turned away again by the time I looked back. Feeling much lighter in heart and spirit, I put the scrunchy in my hair and rejoined the others, who had apparently decided to just wait for me. It had been almost two weeks since I'd seen Dave. I had thought another two days would be impossible to stand, but I *did* feel better and was very glad I had gone back and talked to his brother. I think my day would have been ruined if I hadn't.

We walked around Old Town for a while, mostly just looking in the windows as our presence in the stores, especially the antique stores, seemed to make the proprietors nervous. It was fun anyway, Robin and I exclaiming over and admiring the jewelry and china pieces. The guys did the same with knives, guns, old cartoon and superhero paraphernalia, and seemingly anything made of metal or leather.

We stopped for a sandwich in the old ice cream parlor, the boys each getting their own, and Robin and me splitting one. When we were done, Matthew wanted to pay for everything, but I didn't feel right about that for some reason. I insisted on paying for myself and planned on paying for Robin too—after all, we had split a sandwich—but she glared at me with a *haven't-you-learned-anything-recently* look, and I let it go. But Tanner was grateful that Matthew paid for his.

We took our time making our way back to the center of town. There Matthew left us saying that he was meeting his dad at the fire station to go home with him. He said goodbye very sweetly and made me feel he had enjoyed spending the time with us, maybe even me in particular, and that he was a little sad to have to leave. We all agreed that we'd see each other Monday. Tanner continued on with us, he and Robin joking with each other the rest of the way back to the grocery store.

I was lost in thought most of the time: thoughts of Dave, of course—*all* kinds of thoughts; thoughts of Cris and his enigmatic and sometimes infuriating ways; thoughts of Matthew.

Matthew never made me feel uncomfortable, but I did feel that he liked me. *Like* liked me. If not for the fact that my heart was already well and truly occupied by someone else, I might have been interested. Now that I knew him better, I could recognize that he was a very good-looking guy and truly seemed *nice* in the best sense of the word. I was thankful for his friendship and wanted him to know it, but I also didn't want to give him any false hopes or ideas. It almost seemed conceited to think that way, but I was quite sure any attraction he had toward me was due more to his kind nature and not any real ability to fascinate on my part.

I thought about my grandmother's question, whether I had dated at all. I had a feeling that, had I told my parents I'd been asked to go to the dance by Matthew and if I hadn't been grounded, they would have approved and given their permission. I felt equally confident that if Dave had asked, they, or at least Dad, would have said no without hesitation. He always had that not-until-she's-sixteen card to play, too. And to be honest, I wasn't sure even my mother would be on my side in that situation. I sighed. *It doesn't matter anyway. Nothing like that's going to happen.*

Tanner followed us around the grocery store, carrying his board and mostly behaving himself. Then he insisted on carrying the bag of groceries

for us. Apparently he lived one street over from Robin, not terribly close but close enough to cut through some fields and come out on his own street. Robin looked mulish about his offer at first, but then shrugged and handed him the bag. Later, we enjoyed fixing shepherd's pie with Fiona and then eating it with Mom before she took me home.

Over the weekend Dad came home and I had another lesson with Cheryl. We concentrated on negotiating trail obstacles and worked on my backing and sidestep aids. It felt good to be on Remmy again. Although he and his half-brother were so similar in build, I found Remmy much more comfortable than Gali; a better fit in many ways.

The rest of the time dragged by. Vacations had always been enjoyable to me before, even when I'd had no friends and nothing much to do. But now I couldn't wait to get back to school. I wondered how I would feel the next time I saw Dave. I missed him so much! The last time I'd seen him was the day Gold left; the day he had comforted me and held me in his arms. Would I feel awkward? Would he act weird?

The answers to those questions were yes and no, respectively. My cheeks grew warm as soon as I approached the tables and caught sight of him on Monday. The tables themselves and the ground around them were dry, and *everyone* seemed gathered there. Dave was talking to the kids surrounding him, but he watched me steadily as I walked toward them as if ascertaining that I was all right, all my limbs intact, still attached to my body at the appropriate locations and functioning properly. I had a feeling he probably inspected his horses and cattle in much the same way. But then he smiled adorably and looked happy to see me.

He probably doesn't smile at his horses quite like that.

There seemed to be no awkward feelings on his part, which was simultaneously a relief and something of a disappointment. Still, none from him meant I didn't have to worry about mine.

Just continue to hide them.

He was sitting on the table as he usually did, and Robin sat on the bench right next to him. She had saved a spot for me on her other side which meant, while I wasn't right next to him, we could easily see each other—if we wanted to. As was his natural inclination, his attention was fairly divided between those of us on each side of him, those standing in front of him, and those sitting at our table, but behind him.

Although most of my senses were occupied, dealing with his relatively close proximity and the recent memories it evoked, I was partially aware of the surrounding conversations. These ranged from how the holiday itself and general vacation were spent, to the scope of impending athletic training for the current and, especially, upcoming seasons. It looked like today would prove to be a rare occurrence; we wouldn't be able to look forward to too many gatherings with the entire group.

Dave, Tanner, and Jessie would be running and training in earnest for the track season. Matthew was on the swim team. Most of the girls were either in softball or soccer. Even Robin was playing softball. I'd have to figure out what to do with myself if everyone else was busy at lunch. Melanie might be seeing a lot more of me. During PE, I mentioned that I had called over the holiday break. Had she gotten the message? She blushed slightly and apologized, saying her mom didn't always remember to tell her things. I was starting to think something more than that was wrong but kept it to myself. I hoped one day she would tell me what it was.

At the tables, somebody groaned that summer vacation seemed a long way off, and someone else asked when the next holiday was.

"Martin Luther King Junior Day, right? In a couple of weeks?" said Tanner.

"Yeah," answered a few people, including Robin. Then she said, "Speaking of *birthdays*, yours is coming up soon, right Allie?"

Immediate blush. Everyone's eyes, friendly and otherwise, were on me. I seemed to remember her asking me when my birthday was after we had celebrated hers. Unfortunately, she had a good memory.

"Yeah, when *is* your birthday?" asked Matthew from the other side of the table.

I'd been trying not to look directly at Dave too much, without seeming to ignore him—a tricky skill at the best of times—but couldn't help glancing at him now. His eyes rested on me gently, perhaps fondly. I could tell he already knew. Either Robin had told him or he had asked, and I wondered which it was.

"Allie?" Matthew's voice roused me.

"Oh . . . um," I faltered, knowing my cheeks were still pink. "In a couple of weeks. It's a Saturday."

"What are you doing?" he asked.

"Are you having a party?" asked Tanner, obviously wanting the answer to be yes.

This was embarrassing. I'd never had a real party before. Not with *real* friends. I vaguely recalled something when I was very small. I think my mother had invited all the neighborhood kids. It was noisy and chaotic and I hadn't understood what was happening or who all the people in my home were. After that, I guess my parents decided that inviting the neighbors just so I could have a party was defeating the purpose, and I never had to endure it again. Then when I got older—well, I just didn't make friends easily.

"What do you *want* to do?" asked Dave's voice, softly.

That was easy. "I want to ride," I said decidedly. "Or go watch another show."

Robin and Dave smiled at each other and then at me, indulgently it seemed, as if proud of their *protégée*.

"Hey, isn't that when the Bar 8 thing is?" asked Stacie.

"Oh yeah!" said several voices, and I looked to Robin, surprised I hadn't heard anything about it. She and Dave exchanged glances again.

Then Dave said, "We were supposed to try to keep it a surprise for as long as we could, but . . ." he shrugged and grinned. "Oh well."

I was still confused. "There's a thing? At Bar 8?"

"They're holding a schooling show." I looked at him questioningly, and he explained. "It's just kind of like practice for the bigger shows later. There's usually not too much going on around this time of year, so they like to hold little events for locals and their guests. It gives new riders like you, or people who don't get to ride much, a chance to get used to showing. It also gives people an opportunity to train new horses without the pressure of hard competition. It's really low-key, you know? When we found out when your birthday was, things just kind of fell together."

I'm sure I was sitting with my mouth hanging open. They had arranged this? For me? Then a possible impediment occurred to me. I lowered my voice and asked, "My parents?"

"They know all about it," said Dave, shrugging again. "I think they're helping."

I was blown away. Everything else in the intervening days was colored by my equal dread and excitement for this coming event. Dread because it was my birthday and I loathed the thought of possible concentrated attention on myself. Excitement because—it was my first show! I didn't care about winning or losing anything. I had no competitive spirit, and Dave had intimated there was no real competition. But to challenge myself, prove to myself that I could do something well, especially something I really cared about—that had become very important to me. I also felt I had something to prove to others. Just participating in such an event would be a major accomplishment for me.

Though the days that followed were cold, the weather remained mostly fair and dry. That meant that, beyond that first day back at school, we saw even less of the people involved in track than we did before Christmas. They spent almost every lunch time either running or practicing their various skills. After school they were either involved in other sports or ran through town and back. I found myself honestly wishing I could really run. Robin and I often sat in the bleachers during lunch so we could at least watch our friends, though Dave and the others rarely got a chance to talk to us.

One such rare day, Dave frowned at me and said, "Is something wrong?"

Startled, I shook my head vigorously. I hadn't thought about it for a while, but I was happy enough. Wasn't I?

"Everything okay?" he persisted, his expression a little intense and making me feel uncomfortable. "You're not getting bothered by anyone again, are you?"

I hadn't even thought of those incidences. Well, not much. Every once in a while I'd see one of those guys but be able to avoid them, or hear something mean-spirited but block it out. It hadn't been too bad; not for quite some time.

I shook my head again. "No, I'm fine. Why?"

He looked at Robin, then back at me. "You're so quiet all the time. Even more than normal. And I haven't seen you really smile since . . . a while."

My heart sank a little and loss leaped to the forefront of my mind. So it was still there, lurking, waiting for me to let my guard down. I'd thought I was recovering. And I thought I was acting normally. I'd even made con-

certed efforts to do so and had thought I was succeeding. Apparently my acting skills were slipping and the only person I was fooling was myself.

"I'm fine," I said, wanting to convince everyone present. "Really!"

Not looking convinced at all, he and Robin exchanged glances again.

"Okay," he said, but I think he was just being considerate in not pushing me.

Besides a heavier load of homework and more infrequent glimpses of and time spent around Dave, only one other thing occurred between finding out about the show and the actual day itself to distract my thoughts from it: Winter Formal notices. It would take place the Friday following my birthday and I couldn't help wishing. I had no realistic hope of being asked by the person I wanted to go with, but would anybody? And if they did, what would my answer be?

My birthday dawned chilly but remained dry. I felt like I hadn't slept well and had a familiar nightmare in my mind when I awoke. It was good that I was up extra early, though, as Mom had agreed to help Phyllis in the kitchen at Bar 8. Although they had extra wrangler help over this long weekend from the college students, they would be kept busy assisting guests who were riding in the show. I was confident Dave and Robin would be there early as well and was too excited to want to hang around at home anyway. Dad would come along later to help out at the arena. That had surprised me a little; not that he'd want to help in general but in this specific situation. I knew he still wasn't completely resigned to the whole "Allison riding" thing. Today, I hoped, might change that.

Cheryl had given me several lessons over the two weeks since I had found out about the show and had told me there would be two difficulty levels of trail class. She made sure I understood that I wouldn't have to do anything I hadn't already been practicing, but I was still extremely nervous.

When I'd learned about the show and had time to think about it, I had timidly asked Dave if I could ride Remmy, as I'd become rather used to him. The one calming factor I had in all this was the thought of being able to ride him and not a horse I was less accustomed to.

Dave had looked at me strangely, then smiled and said simply, "Of course," as if there had never been any other possible arrangement to consider.

Cheryl had assured me I needed no special clothes to wear, so I just wore clean jeans, my boots, and a decent, long-sleeved, buttoned shirt that was skulking in the back of my closet. Not exactly something I'd wear for every day but it looked oddly appropriate now. I also wore my warm jacket as the mornings had been frosty.

When we got to the ranch, I was thrilled to see Cris' truck with a trailer hitched to it parked in the dirt lot closest to the barns. Hopefully Dave was there too. Mom parked the car at the far end of the paved guest lot and I walked with her to the big house, scanning the grounds for evidence of him.

"Happy birthday, Allie!" said Cheryl, beaming at me as soon as she saw me.

The sentiment was echoed by other people, known and unknown to me, and I felt my face redden. Phyllis and Gloria were there and seemed to look at me fondly, and several guests and wranglers watched me with interest.

"Thank you," I said, feeling extremely shy and uncomfortable. I was flattered but sincerely hoped that we'd gotten that out of the way and there'd be no further reference to it. My nerves were rattling enough as it was.

"Are you ready?" Cheryl asked.

I tried to smile. I honestly didn't know.

"I think you'll find the boys out in the home barn. They brought in a couple of green horses to ride today. And I believe Robin's coming soon with Angel."

"Green?" I asked, diverted.

Cheryl laughed. "It just means they're inexperienced. They're usually young horses that need exposure to different things like trailering and crowds and the whole showing experience. But it can also be older horses that haven't done those things much."

"Oh," I said, unsure what else to say. "Thanks."

I backed away and out of the house as calmly as I could and as quickly as I dared, but I couldn't wait to see Dave. And the new horses, of course.

I found them on the far side of the second barn. Cris was brushing a small bay mare and Dave was saddling a horse that looked similar to Tee at first, but even I could tell it wasn't him. This horse was slightly bigger all over and looked a little nervous. As I got closer, I could also see that it was a mare, and actually built quite differently than Dave's gelding.

"Hey!" He was smiling. "Happy birthday!"

Cris stopped what he was doing for a moment and said, "Happy birthday, Allison."

Blush. Again. I was hoping it wasn't going to be one of *those* days.

"Hi," I said, trying to include both Cris and Dave in my greeting, but looking mostly at the latter. "Thanks."

"You nervous?" Dave asked.

"Um . . ." I stalled. *Is there a wrong answer?* I decided honesty was probably best in this situation, so admitted, "Yes."

He laughed gently and said, "Don't worry. You'll do fine. And Remmy'll take care of you. You should go get him ready. I'm taking this one into the small arena to warm up," he said, indicating the black mare. "Why don't you join us there?"

I nodded enthusiastically and ran off to brush and saddle Remmy. Going through the motions of getting him ready soothed my nerves immensely. I felt almost calm by the time I rejoined Dave.

He chatted softly and didn't ask too many questions, making me feel even calmer about the upcoming classes but more acutely aware of his nearness and attention. He explained that the mares they had brought weren't used to trailering or showing, so this was perfect practice for them. They were born on their ranch but would be sold when they had more training. The mare he was riding was a half-sister to Tee, sharing a mother but having a different father; both dam and sire were quarter horses. I guessed that explained the difference in body build, as Tee's sire's offspring, from what I'd seen so far, had very similar conformation.

"Oh, by the way," he said lightly, "I've got a present for you. But I'll give it to you later, okay? Like . . . after the show?"

I held my breath, blushing furiously, but nodded. *Dave got me something? What could it be?* Winter Formal tickets had been on sale for a week now. *Is it possible. . . ?*

"You ready for this?" His voice rescued me from manic suppositions. He stopped the mare and looked at me, his brows raised in question, his eyes crinkling in a familiar expression of speculative humor.

Ready or not. . . .

I nodded but knew I probably looked panic-stricken. He laughed gently again and invited me to open the gate. I hadn't practiced on real gates, just the trail class dummy we used in the arena, but I was able to manage it due to Remmy's talent. I was feeling better again already. Dave beamed at me—making me feel, again, like a favored child of a proud parent—and closed the gate behind us. He actually had much more trouble than I'd had opening it, the mare being rather temperamental. He turned it into a lesson for her and I was impressed anew by his patience and gentleness.

Turning his mount to ride up beside me, he said, "Hey . . . here . . ." and took off his hat—his *black* hat—and settled it on my head. "Why don't you wear it for luck today? We still need to get you one of your own, right?"

I was speechless. The gesture seemed so thoughtful, but he couldn't possibly know exactly how comforting or meaningful it was to me. I tried to smile, not sure if I was accomplishing it, but my heart was full.

As we made our way toward the covered arena, we were joined by quite a few people. Robin had arrived with Mr. Caldera, Angel, and Dave's little brothers, and she had brought Gali to try him in the cutting class. Stacie had a tall, rangy looking sorrel gelding she was apparently rehabilitating. Dave told me he had been a racehorse but had suffered injuries. Then he was sold to someone who didn't treat him well, leaving him both mentally as well as physically scarred. It was a very sad story and I marveled that such a thing could happen.

Dave assured me it was unfortunately too common. "Someone buys a horse not knowing what they're really committing to and then abuses it, either intentionally through meanness or more often unintentionally through fear, ignorance, and neglect. Stacie's been working with him for a long time, just trying to make him a happy, healthy pleasure horse. She originally planned to just get him back into shape. Responsive, you know? Then she'd sell him to a good home. But now she's becoming too attached to him. Her goal today is just to have him around small crowds and keep him calm in the arena with the other horses. He still has a tendency to think everything is a race."

I'd been oblivious to the growing number of people arriving with their horses and milling about the barns and arenas, but now noticed how busy and crowded the usually open spaces were. Both parking lots were full.

In case of rain, the covered arena would be used for most events, but the other large arena had numbered cattle milling about and would be used first for a green horse and rider cutting event. Robin, who had never entered this kind of event before, was going to give it a try.

Gali had some training from Dave and Cris before they'd given him to her, so he wasn't afraid of cattle, but he hadn't had any practice in years. Robin's experience was mostly visual and theoretical, though Dave had worked with her during the summer a little. Dave, Cris, and the wranglers occasionally called encouragement and instructions to her and the other riders.

I was happy to see my dad hanging out with Tom, Mr. Caldera, Mr. Morris, and Dr. James. They watched and helped with physical work when appropriate, but seemed happy to leave the verbal coaching to the younger folks. Jessie was there schooling a horse for her little sister. Matthew, Tanner, and Kyle had just come to watch. They all wished me a happy birthday and I did, indeed, feel happy.

Robin seemed pleased with her round. When the cutting class was over, the focus shifted to the covered arena, which was already set up for the first trail class. I was nervous when it was my turn, but the apparatus and surroundings were familiar, I'd memorized the course order, and Remmy was so calm and confident that it felt like I was just going through the motions. He was doing all the work and making me look good. Of course, I had to have him moving in the right direction and communicate speed and the order of the obstacles, but he was so accommodating and made it easy for me.

We finished the course satisfactorily and a little cheering section in the stands and on the side of the arena erupted into loud applause and whistling for me. My cheeks flamed, but I didn't mind. I'd never been applauded for anything before and I was proud of me too!

A couple of times during my ride I'd felt a swell of pride in Remmy's talent and behavior. Not for anything I had done, but because Dave's training and influence were so evident in him. With his experience, he could have behaved completely bored with the simple course, like many of the other green riders' horses who plodded around rather apathetically. But he went through the course with his ears pricked forward as if intensely interested in everything, and he moved around and lifted his feet over obstacles very conscientiously. I patted and praised him profusely as I joined my friends, then dismounted. He rubbed his face on me gently and seemed happy that I was pleased.

The advanced trail class followed, with more experienced horses and riders as well as people like Stacie, Dave, and Henry riding their green mounts. Then my dad, Cris, and a few others helped to clear the arena for the pleasure class.

I had thought this would be the easiest, but when I saw that Dave was also riding the mare, my brain decided to take a vacation. I had no idea what I was doing or what was happening around me but was very aware of his position in the class at all times. It was comforting to know that he normally wouldn't be entered in that kind of class. At regular shows, I probably wouldn't have to deal with that distraction. I was glad when it was over but also glad I had ridden. And I had two "participant" ribbons to show for it!

We got some lunch while the arena was set up for gymkhana events. We let our horses have a drink then tied them at the long rail where we could keep an eye on them. I suggested that I should take Remmy back to his stall since I wasn't riding in any more classes. But Dave quickly vetoed the idea and even Cris, who I'd hardly heard a word from all day, asked if I wouldn't rather still ride.

"Of course!" I answered. *What a silly question.*

Lunch had been laid out on the huge porch of the guest house and was wonderful, as usual, and included barbecue cooked by Miguel and Mr. Caldera. I was congratulated over and over for my "good rides" until I was well and truly embarrassed again—after all, it wasn't like I'd done anything amazing or anything—but I knew everyone meant well and I felt very content. Now I could just relax and enjoy watching the rest of the classes.

None of our school group rode in any of the afternoon events, but Henry rode the black mare, and Cris led Stevey through a couple of courses. We clapped like crazy for him and called his name when he was done. He looked our way but wore his usual slight dreamy smile, as if he wasn't completely aware of what was happening or why, but seemed content all the same.

All too soon the show was over and everyone began loading their horses into trailers, putting them in the guest barn, or leaving the ranch horses for the wranglers to lead back to pasture. Our group lingered near the arena until one by one our friends left and only my family, Robin, the Calderas, and the Reids were left. It was starting to get dark and rather chilly, and the adults were starting to move toward the guest house.

"You should go put the horses away, then come back to the guest house," said Cheryl.

She seemed to be talking mostly to me, so I nodded and began to lead Remmy away. Dave and Robin followed leading their horses until Cheryl called Robin to help her in the kitchen. Robin looked mutinous as if she might argue, but then handed Gali's reins to Dave. I thought it a little strange—surely Cheryl had all the help she could need—and I turned to look back. Mom had a strange expression on her face as if she wanted to come with us too, but I was surprised to see a similar look on Cris' face. Then he turned and led Stevey by the hand toward the house.

What's going on? I wasn't going to argue, though. As nervous as alone time with Dave made me, I wouldn't trade those moments for anything. *Not anything!*

"You did really well today," he said.

"What!" I blurted, tearing my mind away from the possible motives of the others and the rabbit trails of various scenarios my mind was already galloping down: Dave and me . . . *alone . . . in the barn. . . .*

He looked at me sideways, narrowing his eyes a little, and shook his head with a slight smile and frown. "Where do you go?"

I glanced at him, completely embarrassed. I knew what he was referring to but couldn't answer. It seemed reasonable to fantasize about the person I adored when I wasn't around him, but why did my mind insist on taking little excursions when I was actually with him? And I certainly couldn't tell him about it!

"Did you have fun today?" he tried again, as if he were being patient with a child.

"Yes!" I said enthusiastically. "It was wonderful! I don't think I'll be as nervous next time."

"Hmm," he said, stopping me and seeming to inspect my face. "No, that's not it . . ."

"What?" I asked, now really confused.

"It's not the right smile. Not the *real* one. I can tell, you know."

I didn't know what to say and he gave me that look again, the one that says he wants to know what's going on in my head.

"I said, a minute ago, that you rode really well today," he said, trying to get our conversation back on track.

"Oh . . . thanks . . . but Remmy's the one who did everything. I felt like I was just along for the ride, letting him do all the work. He makes it so easy."

"You really like him, don't you?" he observed.

"He's wonderful!" I said passionately. There were all kinds of reasons why I was starting to love Remmy, and not all of them were directly related to Dave. "I love working with him," I admitted, "and even just being with him. And I think . . ." here I hesitated because I thought it might sound silly or conceited, then decided to say it anyway, "I *think* he likes me too."

"Well, that's good," Dave said as we entered the home barn and I caught sight of the colored balloons and banner above Remmy's stall door. "Because he's yours. Happy birthday!"

Chapter Twenty-Eight

Smile On My Face

I was sure I must have heard wrong, but instead of saying, "What!" like an idiot again, I said, very loudly, "No!"

He looked like I had slapped his face.

"I mean . . . you can't. You can't give him to me."

"Why not?" he frowned.

I shivered. "Because . . . because . . . it's too much and . . . and . . . it's *Remmy!*"

He shrugged as if it were no big deal. "We gave Robin a horse. She didn't say no." He didn't sound accusing, just very puzzled.

"That's different," I said, shaking even more. "You've known her forever and she's practically family and . . . she's *Robin!*"

I realized that this didn't sound sensible, but *I* understood what I meant. I didn't know if he would, however, and my eyes were starting to water. *Great . . . what a time to get emotional. I wasn't going to do this anymore, remember?*

"And you're Allie and we're giving you a horse too." His voice was becoming softer and another shiver ran down my spine. "I know he can't make up for . . . you know. But he's a really good horse."

"But I didn't even get you anything for Christmas."

"I didn't get you anything for Christmas either."

"No . . . you're giving me a horse for my birthday. A *horse!*"

"Think of him as from the whole family. It was a joint decision. You needed a horse, and we had one that was perfect for you."

"But he's *your* horse," I insisted.

"Well, now he's yours. For as long as you want him anyway. Don't sell him or anything, though. Okay?"

Horrified that he could think I would ever do that, I said, "Of course not!"

I felt myself coming undone. The recurring bad dream of this morning, Gold disappearing out of my life forever, was still relatively fresh in my mind. This generous gift and being here with Dave seemed like an unbelievably *good* dream, like when he had held me after Gold was gone.

With all my heart I wanted to hug him, but I didn't want to freak him out. He might think I was trying to force myself on him. I just couldn't do it. My shaking increased and I had to take my glasses off with my free hand, wiping my eyes to prevent tears spilling over. When I looked back at Dave, into his eyes, there was only one thing I could think of.

I wish . . . I want . . . I want him to . . . to hold me again. I want . . . want him to kiss me. . . .

It was the first time I had actually said the words to myself.

He'd been standing very close, holding the reins of the other horses in one hand. Now he dug the fingers of his free hand into his front pocket and took a step back looking, I thought, a little wary. Was it because of the shaking? The threatening tears? Or had he read my thought somehow?

Ugh . . . you are such an idiot!

I felt myself blush wildly, making my discomfort complete. I said, "Thank you," but it came out huskily and I turned away toward Remmy to release us both from further awkwardness. I put my arm around *my* horse's neck and laid my cheek against him.

"You're welcome, Allie," Dave answered, very softly. Then I heard him move away with the other horses.

The rest of the afternoon passed in a blur. I still felt rather awkward as we walked back to the guest house, but he acted as he always did and kept up a gentle, mostly one-way conversation until we reached the house. Once there, he seemed to purposely fade into the background with Cris.

There was a cake, homemade by Phyllis—chocolate with raspberry frosting—and presents from my family and friends. Mom and Dad had bought me my own saddle and bridle for Remmy. Robin gave me a red halter and

lead rope for him. Tom and Cheryl gave me my own new grooming kit. There was also a beautiful photograph in a gold colored frame of me riding Gold, captured somehow from the video Cris had taken. A DVD copy of that video was wrapped with it from "The Caldera Family."

I spent most of the time shaking; I'd never had so much concentrated, positive attention on me and I felt very overwhelmed. Everything was truly wonderful and greatly appreciated, but nothing could compare to the gift standing out in the barn or the person who had given it. And though he repeated that Remmy was a gift from his whole family, I couldn't help it if my heart insisted on receiving the gift from him alone.

Mr. Caldera put a folded paper into my hands.

"This is a copy of Remmy's papers, so you can use them for showing if you need to. He is crossbred, of course, but his pedigree is very good. Your name has been added to David's as owner."

Still feeling overwhelmed, I couldn't say a word, but opened the paper and stared at my name following Dave's, then noticed Remmy's official name: Caldera Remington Bronze.

I was disappointed that there was no sign of Dave at Bar 8 over the remainder of the long weekend. I thought, hoped, he might show up at some point. But the barrels had been left up in the covered arena, which I made use of. I practiced with Remmy, just at a walk and trot. I think I confused him a lot, but I also felt I was starting to get a sense of space and distance. Robin called on Sunday to see how I was getting along with him and also informed me that the Calderas were out of town at a Quarter Horse show. I couldn't help sighing. They were always so busy! But I was happy, too; at least I knew Dave wasn't avoiding me.

There were details to work out, of course. We would board Remmy at Bar 8, at least until the season changed and dryer weather could be counted on. The Calderas said that we could keep the pipe corral until we had something more permanent, and they offered to help with that, too. Right now that whole area was nothing but mud most of the time, and it would be better to have Remmy where I could ride him, rain or shine. Whether or not I got to see him on school days would depend on me getting my homework done, which was becoming even harder and more abundant.

The week following the show, I was very distracted. Winter Formal would be on that Friday night. I heard it mentioned—it would be decorated, have a live band, and sounded like fun—but no one even hinted at asking me to it. Not that I was surprised, but I couldn't help hoping. That week the rain started, too. It had rained on and off before, but now it was almost every day and when it rained, it poured.

On Monday, we found out we'd be dancing in the gym for PE. Since it was much too wet to be outside and we'd already spent a lot of time on basketball—a sport I especially failed at, being too timid to block and having lousy aim—our coaches had the brilliant idea of "killing two birds with one stone." Not only did they want to keep us dry and have us all doing the same thing, but they hoped to spark more interest and enthusiasm for Winter Formal. I thought it was a great idea. It seemed like everyone else was groaning and making faces; the general atmosphere was mutinous.

The worst part was that we were dressed in our PE clothes. When it was explained that profits from Winter Formal went to school sports scholarships, at least there was a murmur of acceptance.

My primary concern, of course, was Dave's location in the crowd of students gathered in the gym. We would be doing line dancing, which sounded like fun, but I was going to be very self-conscious if he was somewhere he could see me. Though complacent with the actual activity, knowing that Dave might be near was not a good thing. Melanie and I stuck together and, like most of the girls, we somehow ended up in one of the front lines. Most of the boys managed to secure places in the back rows and, as unfair as it seemed, the coaches were apparently okay with it. Most of the boys, but not all.

Dave was in the row behind us, at the other side of the gym, flanked by some of the prettiest girls in the school. While I was glad he wasn't right behind *me*, I was a little bothered by his situation and wondered whether he had placed himself there or the girls had maneuvered themselves next to him. Either way, I couldn't help stealing glances in his direction. The girls were always laughing, obviously enjoying his company. Worse, he seemed to enjoy theirs in return.

And why shouldn't he? Are you forgetting something? Like . . . he's attractive and popular. And you're . . . not!

I tried to stay focused on the rhythm and the steps and, for the most part, thought I did okay. Although not the most athletic or coordinated of

people, I had a good sense of rhythm and ability to remember patterns, which aided me immensely. Melanie, next to me, had an easy grace and seemed to find it all simple and enjoyable. That helped me too.

Everyone seemed relieved when the class was over, but there was a lot of laughter and, though they acted as if it was all done under protest, it seemed like most people had had fun.

I didn't have an opportunity to be close to Dave again until the next PE period on Wednesday. Robin and I had eaten in the Ag. Science room on Monday, but the track people had been missing, and I ate with Melanie as usual on Tuesday. I hadn't seen Dave before or after school either and was starting to suffer from a familiar anxiety, but I was also determined to be firm and not allow it to get the better of me. How many times had he told me not to worry? And he'd just given me a horse. *His* horse. Dave was Dave, and I wasn't truly his friend if I didn't accept him the way he was, and accept every aspect of him.

Keyword here, "friend," not "boyfriend." Maybe "sister" at best. Why is it so hard to remember that? Be content!

PE on Wednesday was much the same as Monday except that I had a little more eye contact with Dave; a glance and a smirk assured me all was well. He was still in the midst of a group of girls who took great delight in telling him what to do. He seemed to find the steps difficult, but I couldn't help wondering if it was an act. I made the difficult decision to ignore whatever was happening behind me and ended up enjoying myself again with Melanie. Boys had intermingled more with the girls today and the mixed group of people closest to us were having a good time. Soon it seemed like everyone was enjoying the class and laughing a lot.

I was still having a hard time with that—laughing—but I was trying. Ever since Dave had made me aware of my deficiency, I'd been even more self-conscious about what I was actually feeling and whether I was smiling at appropriate times. I still didn't know, but I thought it was getting better.

Friday, as we gathered in the gym, we were told we'd be doing partnered dancing. There were several wolf whistles and whoops and my heart beat faster. Dave wasn't too far from where Melanie and I stood and my hopes soared. I'd given up on wishing he would ask me to Winter Formal. It was tonight, after all; much too late to find the right clothes or anything. But dancing with him now would sure make up for not going to the real dance. Would he ask me to be his partner?

I never found out. Coach Schmidt told us to partner up, preferably boy/girl, at which there was some snickering. My heart leaped when I saw Dave looking and moving in my direction, but he was ambushed by a pretty, brown-haired Asian girl who pleaded with him to be her partner. Several other girls whined, "No fair!" and similar sentiments, but the brown-haired girl had pounced first and won.

I was disappointed, of course. I wished he had insisted on being *my* partner—*if* he had truly been moving toward me—and I beat myself up a little for not being the type of girl to try to take what she wants. But that just wasn't me. I couldn't imagine throwing myself at him or being bossy or whiny like the other girls. It just wasn't who I was. Not to mention my fear of rejection.

Just one more reason you'll get nowhere with him. . . .

Melanie had been claimed quickly by a tall, good-looking boy who seemed to know her, but I didn't really know any of the other boys in our class. Just Dave. I was resigning myself to end up with another girl, or worse, not have a partner at all, when Coach Schmidt grabbed my hand and dragged me over to a boy quite a bit taller than myself, who hadn't found a partner either.

"Anderson, partner with Larsen," she said brusquely, then moved off quickly to pair up other stragglers.

I recognized him as someone from my English class though we'd never acknowledged each other before. He looked at me and turned red to the roots of his fair hair.

Could it be possible? Someone who blushes more easily than me? Amazing!

I didn't feel embarrassed at all and was the more outgoing of the two of us; a very unusual position to find myself in.

"Hi, I'm Allison," I said, holding my hand out for him to shake. I suppose it was a weird thing to do, but I didn't know how else to break the ice.

He smiled and seemed set at ease by my cordial action. Apparently he knew what to do with my outstretched hand as he shook it vigorously and said, "Hi, I'm Gerald."

"Have you ever . . . done this before?" I asked.

He snorted a little, saying, "Not really." I understood him to mean, "No, never."

"Then we're on equal footing," I said, trying to smile.

He looked confused and I clarified, "I haven't really danced this way either, except with my dad when I was little. I don't think that counts."

He still looked unsure but he smiled and his color seemed to even out again.

The coaches began instruction, from where to put our hands—an important consideration—to the actual steps. The dance was a swing version and we practiced for quite a while until the coaches thought we could handle putting the steps to music. That's when it got really funny. Some pairs took to it right away; I suspected they'd done it before. Most of us seemed more inclined to get tied up in knots and bump into each other and other couples, but we had great fun while doing it.

I caught sight of Dave and his pretty partner some distance away, and he saw me too. He seemed to inspect Gerald then looked back at me, a smirk on his face. I wasn't sure what that look meant, but it had been all mine. *Still so pathetic.*

At the end of the period, the other coach, Coach Barry, reminded us about the dance that night and encouraged us—well, more like *ordered* us—to go. But it didn't seem likely that anyone would if they hadn't already planned on it unless they just happened to have a tux or gown handy. I certainly didn't and I definitely wasn't holding out any hope of Dave asking me. I was wondering if he'd be going himself when Gerald turned to me.

"Are you going?" he asked, starting to color up again. "To the dance?"

"Oh!" I said, surprised and pulling my attention back to him. "No, I . . . I don't think so."

"Would you like to go?" he asked shyly. "With me?"

Now he had my full attention. I looked at his hopeful expression and felt bad. He seemed like a really nice guy, and it had certainly cost him something to be brave enough to ask me. A part of me wanted to say yes, just because he *was* a nice guy, and I did want to go. *We could probably have a lot of fun together, but. . . .*

"I'm sorry," I said, trying to let him down gently. I couldn't bring myself to consider it. "I . . . I really can't," I said. "My dad . . . he . . . he won't let me go out with anyone until I'm sixteen."

Gerald looked a little disappointed.

Feeling flattered, I reached for his hand and said, "But I appreciate you asking me. Thanks!" I tried to genuinely smile at him, but I don't think I quite achieved what I was aiming for.

He looked appeased, though, perhaps even relieved, and smiled back at me. We said goodbye and went our separate ways to change.

I wondered what Dave might be up to over the weekend. For the rest of the day, I lingered in those places I thought I might catch a glimpse of him or, even better, actually bump into him. But I didn't see him again. In Study Hall, Robin sighed loudly and looked glum, so I quietly asked her what the matter was.

"It's gonna be a boring weekend," she whispered back. When I looked at her questioningly, she added, "I hate it when Dave goes out of town."

So did I, but this was news to me. She always knew more about what he was doing than I did, though; nothing unusual in that. "Where are they going?" I tried not to sound too interested.

"Rodeo, somewhere up north." She sighed again. "I usually only get to go with them if it's just a day trip, unless Angel's going. But they left just before study hall and'll be gone for the whole weekend. It's a qualifier . . . and I wish I was riding! Gran's pretty lenient about letting me go places like that with them, especially for rodeo and shows, but she's not lenient about grades and homework. My English grade wasn't so good and I have a paper to write this weekend, so. . . ." She shrugged, then sighed again.

I sighed too. It sounded like there would be no chance of seeing Dave around this weekend. I tried to look at the bright side; at least I knew he wouldn't be at the Winter Formal with someone else tonight.

I spent as much of the weekend with Remmy as my parents would allow, but I had homework to do, too, and Dad would be going on a trip again for at least a couple of weeks. He said it would be nice if both Mom and I were around, so we were.

The track students spent lunchtime with us on Monday, Dave and others recounting their rodeo adventures of the weekend. Jessie, Stacie, Matthew, and Kyle had all gone and competed in the multi-district qualifying event. Jessie and Kyle scored high enough in their events to go to the state cham-

pionships. Robin looked disgruntled and complained about not getting to go. Dave patted her head and looked sympathetic.

On Tuesday, we were dancing again but most of the track people, including Dave, were conspicuously absent. There was some murmuring about this as they'd been seen changing, and even more when it became known that they'd been given the option of working out in the weight room instead of dancing. This was viewed by almost everyone else as a huge cop out, not to mention a great loss of desirable dancing partners.

Gerald was still there, however, and found me. I was pleased to be his partner again and let him know it. Feeling more at ease with each other, we found things to talk about quietly as we learned new steps; some kind of Latin dance. It was a little embarrassing, but everyone was suffering the same plight. Everyone except the students in the weight room, of course. Several of them stepped out into the corridor for a moment to watch us, including Dave. He had a thoughtful look on his face and I wondered what he was thinking. Then Coach Barry herded them back in.

Thursday we did more line dancing, and I was able to stay near Melanie again. Gerald positioned himself close enough to talk to us and I was glad. I felt I'd made another friend in this otherwise challenging and rather hostile class. I also thought I'd acquitted myself well; as well as most people in the class I think, though I hadn't been watching other people dance very much. I'd been minding my own steps and actually enjoyed PE for the first time this year. It would be back to regular physical torment next week.

The weekend was a drag except for the time I spent with Remmy. The Calderas went to a motocross event on Saturday and took Robin with them. Dave had invited me, too, as they'd be back the same day, but Dad was out of the country and Mom was unable to get in touch with him. She didn't feel comfortable letting me go without his permission, ". . . under the circumstances."

That troubled me at first then made me a little mad. The only "circumstances" I could imagine she meant was that it happened to be the Calderas, and Dave in particular, that had asked me. I wondered how the circumstances would have been viewed if someone else had asked, but I held my peace. I knew she wasn't going to budge without Dad's okay, and it reminded me that I was truly going to have to pick my battles very carefully.

I had already figured out that being allowed to accept Remmy as a gift from them was a huge concession on the part of my parents. I had probed a little into the particulars surrounding this agreement, Mom giving me the basics, and Dave filling in a few details.

Mr. Caldera had called Dad soon after Gold's departure and voiced their desire to help me have my own horse to ride. He'd said Dave seldom rode Remmy anymore and was loaning him to Bar 8 to keep the horse happy and exercised. Dad had offered to buy Remmy, but Dave was reluctant to completely relinquish him. Then Dad thought it might be better just to buy me my own horse. Perhaps the Calderas had another horse that would be suitable? Dad appreciated the sentiment but didn't want "anybody to feel obligated." This last statement wasn't clarified and, much as I wanted to know, I didn't dare ask. I already had some idea about *who* he thought might feel obligated, and in what way. But he was so wrong.

But now, and in this situation, wouldn't be the best time to challenge him. Dave didn't seem to find anything amiss with Dad's scruples, and I didn't want to indicate that I did. One way or another, in the end they had allowed it.

In the meantime, I had a lesson with Cheryl on Saturday and Tom invited me to go on a trail ride with some guests on Sunday. I hadn't had much chance to ride outside the arenas as I'd been warned not to wander off on my own outside the ranch grounds, at least not yet. Remmy was reliable, but my skills and judgment were apparently questionable.

The weather was cool and a little windy, but Remmy was well-behaved and seemed to enjoy getting beyond the arena for a change. I sure did and tried to commit the trails we took to memory. One of these days I wanted to be able to take him out by myself, without getting lost. I also had an idea of exactly where I wanted to eventually go.

The following week crawled by. The weather was still cold but mainly dry so PE was outside. I saw little of Dave, but Robin had assured me they were planning on being at Bar 8 on Saturday for the work day.

On Saturday, I dressed in older clothes that I didn't mind getting dirty or even ruined, as Cheryl had indicated I should. The day was breathtakingly beautiful; one of those crisp, crystal-aired days with rays of sunshine streaming through brilliant white, fluffy clouds, rimming them with gold.

Everything looked more clearly defined than normal and colors seemed more saturated: the greens greener, browns browner, blue sky bluer. I stopped often just to breathe and gaze about.

"Are you okay?" Dave asked at one of these times. I guess he'd noticed my little breaks.

"Yes!" I answered. "It's just so gorgeous today!"

He and Robin looked around as if they were only just noticing, which perhaps they were, but they agreed with my pronouncement.

"I wish I could paint it," I said absently.

Dave's forehead creased and he gave me a funny look. "Paint it?"

We'd been painting arena fences all morning with some of the wranglers who had come to help for the weekend. We were now in the covered arena giving new coats of paint to the equipment.

"On a canvas," I said, realizing he'd missed my meaning. "I haven't done much painting before, and I've never done a landscape, but I hope to have a chance next year in art."

"Hnh," he kind of grunted. I don't think it was something he understood. But that was okay.

When we'd finished painting, we ate the sandwiches prepared for us by Phyllis and then got permission to go for a short ride. Realizing I now possessed his usual mount, I offered Remmy to Dave. I said I was fine riding Flash, but Dave insisted he could ride a different horse. He and Robin walked off toward one of the pastures, where all the horses except Remmy and the Reid's personal mounts were kept, while I got Remmy ready.

Since he was fairly clean from being kept in a stall much of the time, we were ready long before the others, so I helped brush their horses. It was so relaxing to just hang out with my friends, but as I brushed I could already tell I would be pretty sore the next day from all the painting we'd done. It was completely worth it.

We had a nice ride, starting off down the dirt road we'd ridden on before, then cutting through pastures and taking a trail through more wooded areas until we arrived back at the ranch. A chilly breeze had sprung up, which felt good after our morning toil. The clouds had begun to move more quickly across the sky, too, and it was now noticeably darker. We hadn't been gone long, but we'd had some good runs and I'd seen my first coyotes—exciting for me, but Robin rolled her eyes at my wide-eyed wonder. Dave's eyes just twinkled.

When we got back and put the horses away, Cheryl came and asked if we would work on cleaning tack. It hadn't been done since the year before and most of the saddles and bridles were pretty dry and dusty. This turned out to be quite arduous work even though we sat to do most of it. Tom found a couple of sawhorses we could use to hold saddles. Then he spread a clean tarp out on the floor of the barn breezeway for us to sit on.

That was fun too, listening to the radio blare country music and sitting on the tarp while I cleaned bits and oiled bridles, breastplates, and leather girths. The others worked mostly on the saddles. Tom started the barbecue when he got home from a job. After a couple of hours, heavenly aromas wafted all the way to the barn. We were so hungry! When all our stomachs started growling noticeably, we gave up and headed for the house. Picnic tables behind the guest house were ready, though the paper plates and napkins had to be weighted down so they didn't blow away. Tom kept looking suspiciously at the sky and shaking his head.

The food was great, as it always was, and all the better for our ravenous state, but soon after we sat down to eat the first drops of rain hit us. It wasn't heavy, but if we had stayed there, sooner or later we might be soaked. The wranglers took their food and headed back to the bunkhouse, but we weren't supposed to go there. Phyllis and Gloria retreated to the guest house kitchen with as many things as they could carry, and the rest of us, including little Cody, helped carry everything else. The three of us didn't want to stay in the house so took our food back to the barn.

It had gotten much darker just in the few minutes since we'd sat down to eat, but the breeze had died away and it now actually felt warmer. Sitting on the tarp in the barn, watching the light fade through a steady but very light rain, and listening to the radio with my trusted friends; it couldn't get much better. Or so I thought.

Cris found us when he came to the ranch after work. We sent him back to the house to get food then he joined us again. But he seemed subdued, even for him. Robin and Dave bantered and I tried to join in the conversation when I had something to say, but I was content to just be there with them. Dave frowned slightly at me a couple of times and seemed to be keeping an eye on me but didn't bug me with solicitous questions.

After a while, Tom and Cheryl came out to sit with us. Tom pulled a folding chair out for Cheryl and sat on a bale of straw himself. Both were very appreciative of our help. We felt the same way about the food and for just having a fun day. I think I was the most appreciative of all; they'd done so much for me, and there weren't many places or opportunities outside of Bar 8 for me to spend quality time with Dave. Yes, I was very thankful for Tom and Cheryl, for many reasons.

We had finished eating, had cleared away our plates, and were watching how the light from inside the barn illuminated the drizzle falling just outside when Tom started singing along to a song on the radio. I was surprised by how good his voice was, but he sang with an exaggerated twang that had Robin giggling and Dave putting his fingers in his ears, begging him to stop.

"Only if someone dances with me," he said, wagging his eyebrows at Cheryl. "Come on, babe. Let's show 'em how it's done."

"Not me," she laughed, warding off any advances with her upraised hands. "I'm beat. Get one of these young 'uns to do it."

Robin shrank away but I was betrayed by curiosity. "How can you dance to this?" I asked. It wasn't what I thought of as dance music.

"Ah! A volunteer!" he exclaimed, grabbing my hand and grinning as he pulled me to my feet.

"Um . . ." I wanted to get out of the situation, but Tom was already in control and began leading me through movements similar to the swing dance I'd learned with Gerald. Before I knew it, I was following him pretty closely and amazed that I was keeping up.

"Aw," he said, letting me go and frowning as the music ended. "That wasn't long enough." Then, "Wait a minute!" His eyes grew brighter again and a slow smile spread across his face.

The radio DJ had started another song immediately, saying something about it being a special request on this rainy evening.

"I *love* this song!" Tom exclaimed in a harsh whisper, a huge smile lighting up his face. He grabbed my hand again before I could sit down and swung me back into a dance. The rhythm was slightly different and slower, which made it much easier to follow him.

I was having fun but feeling embarrassed too, pretty sure everyone was watching us. Not my favorite situation. A quick glance at the others confirmed this. Robin and Cheryl were smiling widely. Cris wasn't smiling but was certainly watching, though he looked reluctant as if he'd rather not. I figured he was just trying not to appear too anti-social. Dave's expression was easier to read. I could see his grin and could imagine the twinkle in his eyes. He was watching intently which made me even more self-conscious.

Back and forth I went with Tom a couple of times more, then suddenly it was *his* hand holding mine and *his* arm wrapping around my waist as the dance brought me close to him. As he pushed me out again, I stared at him in surprise, momentarily forgetting to breathe until I really had to.

"What? You didn't think I could dance?" Dave asked, looking at me in a mock superior way.

I remembered how the girls in PE had enjoyed instructing him. He'd acted as if he wasn't sure what to do, and I had wondered if it had just been an act for their benefit. From the way he danced now, it seemed highly probable. He wasn't as sure of his movements as Tom was, and I suspected he'd been watching intently to study the steps, but he was surprising me. We hesitated and fumbled a little, especially when I wasn't sure what to do next, and he wasn't as adept at leading either, but it was incredible fun.

It vaguely registered that, when Tom had relinquished me to Dave, he'd immediately pulled Robin up into action. In spite of her initial vocal opposition to this, she was soon giggling like crazy. But my attention was mostly held by Dave, his smile and the laughter in his eyes. Something bubbled up inside me, an overwhelming thrill of joy that I could barely contain. Then he maneuvered us out into the rain, still falling lightly, his smile even broader than before. And I was laughing. *Really* laughing.

As the song came to an end, he turned me under his arm one last time, both of us breathing a little faster than normal. He looked at me and nodded, still smiling widely.

"Yeah . . . that's it," he said.

It didn't surprise me that I didn't understand him. I was too busy just soaking him in and listening to my quickened heartbeat. But I asked anyway. "What?"

"Your smile," he said. "That's the *real* one."

Chapter Twenty-Nine

Going Under

A couple of days after the work day, Cris approached me right after school. He must have been waiting, which seemed odd. He held out a piece of paper and I looked at him in question.

"This is Estephanie's e-mail address," he said. "The granddaughter of the man who bought Gold. She owns him now. I thought you might want to keep in touch."

I was so surprised I think my jaw actually dropped. I didn't reach for it right away, which obviously made him feel uncomfortable.

"How . . . ?" I started to ask.

He tried to shrug it off. "The day they left, I asked Señor Alvarez if they'd keep in touch. You know . . . let us know how Gold was. I gave him my e-mail." Now he looked *really* uncomfortable. "Maybe I should have told you before, but," he looked at the ground, "you seemed . . . unhappy. I . . . we . . . didn't want to remind you of him."

I tried to grasp what he was saying but was having a hard time comprehending both what he'd done and why. He'd been there that day—had made a point of being there, actually. I reached out slowly for the piece of paper, my hand shaking a little.

"Señor Alvarez let me know when they'd gotten him home safely. He was still here . . . well, closer to Sacramento . . . for almost three weeks before they got his medical papers sorted out. If I'd known—"

I gasped at hearing that and looked up into his face, but he avoided my eyes and didn't finish what he was saying.

"Then Estephanie e-mailed me a couple of weeks ago and suggested you might want to stay in touch with her."

I felt my face flush with pure pleasure. I could write to the lady who now had Gold?

"Thank you!" It came out as a rather passionate whisper, and I could have sworn his tanned cheeks darkened.

He nodded curtly, said, "You're welcome," a little gruffly, and walked away.

I was left standing there, the piece of paper in my trembling hand.

Dad picked me up that day. I still had the piece of paper clutched in my hand and silently held it out to him as I got into the car.

"What's this?" he asked.

I'd been on my best behavior for some time now, in spite of several rebellious thoughts when it came to my parents' obvious, or even suspected, prejudice against Dave and his family. I was determined to be as up front about everything as I could. Not that I had ever been troublesome, but I was careful not to stir the calm that had settled since Gold had gone.

"It's the e-mail address of Señor Alvarez' granddaughter. Cris gave it to me. She said I could keep in touch . . . if I want." I looked at him hopefully. He was kind of strict about Internet stuff. "May I?"

He made a face as if he was considering, then said, "That would probably be all right. Let's ask Mom, okay?"

I nodded and crossed my fingers. If Dad was inclined to be favorable, Mom was sure to be amenable.

She was. She actually seemed more thrilled with the prospect than I was.

When I'd finished my homework, Dad drove me to ride Remmy for a little bit. I much preferred it when Mom drove me there as she would use the time to visit with "the neighbors," as she enjoyed calling the Reids. This arrangement worked well for me as, while Mom and Cheryl kept each other occupied at the house aided by Cody and Zoe, who Mom adored, I practiced barrel racing with Remmy. Well, not barrel racing *precisely*, but skills I knew I needed to be able to do it. I had a long way to go but was anxious to do more than just sit on Remmy's back. I wanted to really *ride*. I wanted to

show my parents that I wasn't made of glass, too; that I could do this. And I wanted Dave and Robin to be proud of me.

We worked on lead changes, quick stops from a trot and canter, and turns at a walk and trot. I was concentrating on my reining, making my leg aids clear and firm, using my seat effectively, and staying balanced. It was a lot to think of all at the same time and my success was negligible, but I *did* feel I was accomplishing something.

If Dad drove me instead of Mom, I worked more on basic gait changes and just exercising Remmy. Doing anything more might have sparked curiosity, even suspicion. I wasn't quite ready to deal with that yet. He usually sat and watched us, which was a little disconcerting, but I didn't mind too much. After all, he had allowed me to not only take up riding but to now have my own horse. And at least he didn't try to coach me, as I was sure he was capable of doing.

On this day I rode in the arena for about half an hour while Dad sat in the stands and talked to Tom, who had just come home. I quit a little earlier than normal as I was anxious to get home and write to Estephanie.

On the way home, Dad said, "I'm talking to Tom about building a small barn for your horse."

"Really?" I said, very excited at first, but then certain implications occurred to me.

On the one hand, I would love to have Remmy that close, to be able to feed him and care for all his needs by myself, to have him handy to ride whenever I wanted, and just to be able to talk to and be with him. On the other hand, Bar 8 was where the arena and equipment were to practice and have my lessons with. Even more importantly, it was the most likely place for me to spend time, *quality* time, with Dave—and other friends, of course. So far my parents hadn't demurred at all about me hanging out there, even when they knew Dave would be there. True, they always knew or asked if Robin would be there too, but that was okay. And it was looking like unless there was something special going on, such as on my birthday or the work day, he wasn't likely to be there anyway. *So* busy!

Over dinner, my mom and dad discussed the projected stable plan, which probably wouldn't be started until summer vacation, but my mind was already composing an e-mail. When I'd helped clear the dishes, I got on the computer and wrote:

"Dear Estephanie, (it seemed weird to be prefacing it 'Dear' when I'd never even met her, but Mom assured me it was okay)

"My name is Allison Anderson and I am the one who found Corona de Oro. (It was hard to not write 'Gold'; I had to consciously think of his legal name.) *Cris Caldera gave me your e-mail address and said I could write to you. Thank you for thinking of me. I hope Corona de Oro is well and being good for you. Do you have a nickname for him? I miss him very much, but I am learning to ride and have my own horse now.* (I stopped and savored the delicious feeling of knowing that I not only had a horse of my own, but that it was Remmy, and that it was Dave who had given him to me!) *I even rode in my first show on my birthday.* (I realized this would probably sound lame to an experienced horsewoman such as she was supposed to be, but I didn't have much else to write about.) *I hope to be able to do barrel racing one day and maybe pole bending too. Please write back and tell me how Corona de Oro is. Thank you for letting me write to you.*

"Sincerely,

"Allison"

I was a little unsure of my letter and asked Mom to read it over, but she said she thought it was fine. I hit "send" and got ready for bed.

Valentine's Day came and went with little attention and absolutely no expectations on my part, but it did seem to serve as a catalyst for new phenomena at school. It's not that I hadn't seen it happen at all before, but now that the weather was remaining fairly dry and was definitely warming up, it certainly seemed more prevalent. Robin put our feelings on the subject best. We had walked across the quad and gone around the end of the science building on our way to our health class, almost bumping into a couple lip-locked in the shadow of the building.

"Ugh!" she exclaimed loudly to make sure they heard. She sounded disgusted, like she'd accidentally put her hands in something nasty. "*So* annoying!"

Yes, it was. Very. And rather disturbing. And interesting. And I was a little envious. But really, only a *very* little. I was glad that I never knew any of the kids; that would have just made me feel awkward around them. They all seemed to be sophomores or older, at least the ones I'd seen. They also seemed completely oblivious to everyone else around them. I'm sure they were enjoying their activity, but those of us running across them were just bugged.

The fan girls became more prevalent and aggressive too. We still saw little of the track team, but when we did, there was sure to be a horde of obvious groupies gathered around. They vied with each other for the boys' attention and seemed to use any excuse to physically touch their idols somehow, especially Dave, and especially his hair.

I had to look away whenever this happened or it would make me feel sick. The only thing keeping the situation bearable was the long-suffering look often evident on his face or the droll expression he'd occasionally turn to us. I sometimes wondered, if he disliked the attention so much, why did he put up with it? The answer was simple and always followed quickly: because he was Dave. He was, after all, obviously used to this kind of thing, and I could no more imagine him being mean to these girls than I could imagine him being mean to me.

The other boys, while not quite as favored, appeared to bask in the attention, though Matthew seemed content to forgo their expressions of regard and focus on us if Dave wasn't nearby. Cris was rarely around. When he was, the girls were cautious, as if wanting to express their admiration but a little afraid of his reaction.

Robin and I, and even Jessie and Stacie, were often relegated to sitting on the grass, though Kyle never seemed far from Stacie these days. If Dave and the others came to sit with us, they were most often followed by a retinue of at least the most tenacious devotees. It was more than annoying; it was disheartening to the nth degree.

It was just as well that I had a store of memories that could remind me of Dave's particular attention to me. And if those memories had been made of tangible material, I'm sure they would have been worn and frayed from my taking them out to look at them so often. I'd even retrieved my "Dave List" from the bottom drawer of my desk and added, without too much detail in case my mom ever saw it, just enough information to prompt my memory of every special moment that had happened since the last time I'd tossed it in there:

Days in the library
Snow day
Shopping—hide and seek
The day Gold left
Birthday and Remmy
Workday dance

I continued to keep the list in the drawer under a pile of other papers and books. It would have been the end of me if it were ever found by friend or foe at school, so I never carried it with me. But whenever it felt like a long time since reasonably close contact or attention, I could retreat to my room and reassure myself. I never knew of Dave doing *any* of those kinds of things with or for any of the fan girls that stalked him. It was a little easier to imagine him doing them with Stacie or Jessie, but I'd never been aware of any such interaction with them.

It seemed reasonable to assume that I was, indeed, special to him in some way, and I drew strength and confidence from that. To read more into it was very tempting, though. I couldn't help indulging my imagination sometimes. But all I had to do was remind myself of the things he *hadn't* done—the things I was trying to *not* let myself fantasize about—and that everything on that list I *could* imagine him doing for Robin also, to bring me back to a sense of reality. I was quite sure there were no romantic inclinations between them at all.

One afternoon Robin joined me in Study Hall looking embarrassed—very unusual for her. "What's the matter?" I asked right away.

Instead of answering, she showed me her binder, the black one with the clear front. The black one with the clear front that she'd put my picture in. The picture that had fallen out that I had given her another of. Which apparently had fallen out again. There was a small black square showing through the clear cover where my picture had been. Again.

"I'm starting to think you don't really want it," I said, jokingly. "You've been very irresponsible with my picture."

"I don't know what happened. I'm pretty sure it was there this morning, but I did drop it in Ag. Science. I guess it got knocked loose and then fell out

somewhere." She looked apologetic and said, "Can you bring me another? I'll use stronger glue this time, I promise!"

I laughed, thinking it odd that my photos couldn't stay in her binder, but I was touched that she wanted to replace it again. I'd want to replace hers also, if I ever lost it.

I'd been thinking of Estephanie quite a bit, but I had never been one to check my e-mail on a daily basis because I rarely received any. Even Brenda preferred to call me if she wanted to tell me anything. I resisted checking every day though I was sorely tempted to. Estephanie finally replied to my message and I read it a few days after Valentine's Day:

"Dear Allison,

"I am so glad you wrote to me. Please forgive my English as I am still learning, but this is good practice. Yes? You ask about Corona de Oro's name. This is a very big name, is it not? I believe you called him 'Gold.' I am calling him that also. Except sometimes when he is acting very proud I call him 'Señor Oro.' He has often a distant look in his eyes as if he sees far away. I think that perhaps he thinks of you. Or perhaps he thinks of the world's problems. I do not know. But sometimes he is very serious. And sometimes he looks as if he knows a good joke, but he will not share it with me. He is kind, however, at all times. He likes to work very hard. I am sending you some pictures of Gold and me dressed up for Festival. He dances beautifully. I will write again soon.

"Your New Friend,

"Estephanie"

The pictures were amazing. Most were of Estephanie riding Gold, both of them dressed in festive finery. One was a posed portrait of Gold, like something for a magazine, looking the cleanest and healthiest I'd ever seen him. Magnificent. Another was a close up of Estephanie and Gold from her waist and his shoulders up, and standing close together. Estephanie was incredibly beautiful.

There was much in the e-mail for me to conjecture over, and I did. I also printed it out with the pictures so I could show my friends. They all agreed that Gold looked well taken care of and that Estephanie was pretty. I couldn't help noticing Dave's eyes grow a little bigger when he looked at the close up of her, obviously admiring.

When I had the opportunity to show Cris, he exhibited no emotion at all, but just said, "He looks good," and handed the pages back to me.

By the beginning of March, it wasn't just the track team who were often missing. It seemed like everybody—everybody except me—was involved in sports that kept them busy both during and after school and even sometimes on weekends. Cris, who had finished the basketball season leading his team to the playoffs, continued to be absent at lunch and worked every day after school. In fact, Cris was noticeably missing even when the others weren't. When he was with us he seemed, not just distant, but really depressed. I was somewhat worried about him but felt awkward expressing it.

I was glad that Robin looked around one day when most of our core group of friends were together and said, "What's up with Cris? He's never around."

Dave shrugged as if to make an excuse for him. "He's just busy. I think he's still helping Coach with stuff. And I think he might be doing extra course work too, to get ahead, but I'm not sure. He hasn't been talking about things much."

A shadow had passed across Dave's face as if he'd been reminded of something he'd rather not think about, and I wondered what troubled him.

Cris seemed like such a smart guy. It was hard to imagine him—or Dave for that matter—having trouble keeping up at school. But they were so in-credibly busy all the time. I had often wondered when they found time to get their homework done. There had always been that question in my mind about exactly where the guys stood with school.

Cris would probably be one of the oldest students at Douglas High soon, as he would already be eighteen starting his senior year. Had he gotten behind and was now trying to catch up? It would make sense and be applaudable if he were using his spare time at school to get back on track. After all, he'd be graduating next year. I had to admit to myself, a little reluctantly, that I

kind of missed him. It just wasn't quite the same without him brooding in the background somewhere.

Between exams and homework I was kept busy, too. I was determined to keep my grades at least decent or my parents would limit my time with Remmy and any time I could potentially spend with friends.

So far this year I'd earned "A"s in Health, English, Art, and Computer Lab. Those were my easy classes, the ones I was good at and enjoyed, though I had probably only done well and enjoyed Health because Robin was in the class with me. I had scraped by with "B"s in Algebra, History, and Biology and was surprised to get a "C" in PE. I hadn't expected to do that well. My parents were okay with the PE grade; I had sometimes gotten worse in middle school. They observed that my horse activities kept me more active and seemed pleased about it.

Math and Science were different cases; they'd be keeping a close eye on those subjects. I was glad that Robin and I had Algebra together. She was much better at it than I was. I'd probably done as well as I had because we worked on it together a lot, especially in Study Hall. And now that Health was over, we were in Geography together. I didn't think I'd have any problems with that.

Melanie and I still ate lunch together at least twice a week. I tried hinting that I'd like to see her on a weekend sometime, but she seemed to be busy with her horses every time I brought it up. I would have loved to have tagged along and helped or just watched, but I didn't feel comfortable asking. I think I was just afraid of her saying no outright or making excuses. She seemed to sidestep every attempt to see her outside of school. Not that I doubted her friendship was genuine, but the few interactions I'd experienced with her mother were so odd and discouraging. I couldn't imagine what she could possibly have against me. She didn't even know me!

One Friday, right before Spring Break, Melanie surprised me by suggesting we eat outside. It was such a pleasant day—warm, but not hot—that I was more than happy to agree. I figured we could eat at the tables where my other friends usually ate, near the field, as I doubted anyone would be there today anyway. She blushed slightly and said she'd rather not eat there if I didn't mind.

"Could we eat just outside the cafeteria, in the quad?" she asked as if she were a huge bother.

"Of course," I said. "Wherever you want."

We found a spot in the sun—at the end of a table where I didn't recognize anyone—and talked of horses and art as we usually did. We also touched on how some of our friends—in my case, all except her—were involved in school sports.

"Do you do any sports? Besides riding, that is?" I asked.

She shook her head slowly and looked like she might say something more, but the look disappeared as if she'd changed her mind. At that moment Roger walked up.

He spoke to Melanie, I assumed, but he looked at me severely the whole time. "You're sitting outside." It seemed like an inane observation, but since he was glaring at *me*, I felt discomposed and vaguely guilty.

"Yes, I'm sitting outside," said Melanie, evenly but firmly, as if unrepentant for some great sin. She looked calm, but there was a pink to her cheek that hadn't been there a moment before.

Roger, dressed and groomed impeccably as always, seemed ruffled by her chilly answer. "So . . . remember I've got a game, so I'm leaving early." His stern gaze shifted from me to Melanie.

He still looked disapproving as he looked at her, but I thought there was also a look of real concern for some reason. Although his expression hadn't really changed, there was a definite softening to his eyes as he regarded her, a look I'd sometimes thought I'd seen in Dave's eyes when he looked at me.

"I remember," she said quietly but not raising her eyes to his.

"So you'll meet Mom out front?" he persisted.

If I had been him, I would have noticed that the slight pinkness in her cheeks was deepening and that I must be either embarrassing her cruelly or making her really angry. Either way, I was surprised at the indication of strong emotion from her and would have been on my guard.

Melanie finally raised her eyes to his and said, in an overly controlled manner, "I will be there." Then she dropped her gaze again, the picture of meekness.

Roger glanced at me, still looking as if he disapproved of my presence, and then walked away. After he'd gone, she looked a little unhappy and fiddled with her silver locket.

"Is . . . is everything all right?" She was such a private person, I didn't really expect her to tell me, but it seemed wrong not to at least ask.

She looked at me and smiled, a little self-consciously I thought, though her placid façade quickly reasserted itself. "Yes, I'm fine," she said gently.

"Is he your brother?" I asked.

This seemed like a reasonable assumption to make and question to ask, but she looked startled for a moment and gave me an unequivocal, "No!" Her eyes had gone wide, but now she smiled. "He's . . . a friend."

"Oh," I said, completely unsatisfied with her answer.

She changed the subject.

So he wasn't her brother. At least I knew that much now. But was he *just* a friend? Or was he a "friend" to her in the way Dave was a "friend" to me—a relationship more heavily invested in on one side than the other? Well aware that I knew very little about her, I now thought she must be much more complicated than I'd ever imagined. "Still waters run deep" seemed to apply well to her. I remembered once thinking the same might be true about Cris. Melanie continued to play unconsciously with her locket and said no more on the subject. But I thought I could detect a slight—a very slight—smile on her lips, even during lulls in our conversation.

Spring Break was fun, Robin and I spending much of it at each others' houses and as much at Bar 8 as we could. She still helped me practice riding but began to balk at using Gali. While I just trotted him in loose cloverleaf patterns, he was fine, but I wanted to start going faster. I hadn't tried it on my own with Remmy at a lope yet, caution insisting that I have someone watching out for me and my clumsy ways. I also knew I needed someone to watch and tell me what I was doing right and, more importantly, wrong. When she finally let me urge Gali into a lope, I immediately came to grief around the first barrel, almost losing my seat and not maintaining control of him. We weren't even going that fast yet.

When I got him back under control, she said, "I don't think this is such a good idea. Gali's used to going really fast around the barrels. I don't want him soured from doing this too much. You need to have Cheryl coaching you. Or Dave. Or Cris even. On a different horse."

Unhappily, I agreed with her but was far from giving up. Cris was out of the question. I doubted he would have agreed to help, but he was never around anyway; he always seemed to be working and rarely hung out with us at school. And though I had learned to trust him, pretty much, I still felt cautious around him. I didn't think I could just come out and ask him to do something like that. No, Dave was the only obvious choice. So one day during the break, when we were all at Bar 8, I asked him.

He frowned and looked appraisingly at me for a few moments, then had me hold the horses while he and Robin moved barrels in one of the small arenas. Then he said, "Okay, show me what you know."

I hadn't had much opportunity to try Remmy around real barrels and decided to play it safe by just taking them at a quick trot. He began to be a handful, obviously wanting to go faster, but kept his head and listened to me—mostly.

Dave narrowed his eyes as Remmy and I rode back up to where he and Robin were. He was still frowning. "I think you should ask Cheryl," he said decidedly.

My heart plummeted. *Am I that hopeless? Pathetic? Or does he not want to waste time on me?* I wanted to ask but found I couldn't. I didn't really want to hear the answer.

Cheryl's response was at least direct. "Hun, you're not quite ready for anything like that. It probably looks easy, but I've seen more people get into trouble over barrel racing than almost anything else. Except maybe bull and bronc riding," she added with a smile. "You just keep on riding and you'll get there, don't you worry. You're riding really well, and you've got all the time in the world."

The trouble was, I didn't *feel* like I had all the time in the world. All my friends had been riding for years and years, and I was such a newb. It felt like, unless I could make major strides quickly, I was never going to really fit in or be taken seriously by them. At least, not where horses were involved. I'd already figured out that Dave only seriously competed at rodeos and cutting horse events, and Robin only competed where they had advanced level classes and girls' rodeo events. I felt I needed to do something extreme to show that I was determined to do whatever it took if someone would just help me. Just riding around was fun, but I wanted to do *more*. It's not like I was asking to ride bucking horses!

Disappointed as I was, I was happy when Cheryl said we would slowly start working on pole bending and gymkhana games. She helped with the local chapter of gymkhana riders, and while she said it wasn't usually the same intensity as rodeo, the riding took skill and control and she thought I was capable of starting. She showed me how to set the poles up in a line and

pace off the approximate distance between each, then let me trot a slalom pattern through them. That had me using reining, my legs and seat, and was great for working on my balance. It was fun—for now. Mostly, I could see how it would benefit me in the future for real timed events.

During the break, I also got to go shopping with Mom and Robin to buy me clothes more suited to showing. I appreciated Robin's input but had my own ideas too. I ended up with black pants, a soft pink shirt, and my most important purchase, a black hat. For now my black boots, already scuffed and worn, would suffice. Robin tried to talk Mom into chaps and a vest for me too, but they were expensive. Mom insisted on conferring with my dad about them.

The Saturday before school started again, Cheryl took another of her students and me to a small show. Mom came along for the ride and to help watch Cody and Zoe. It was great fun and although I missed the presence of my friends, it was probably better that they weren't there. I felt quite relaxed and focused, acquitting myself well in the classes I was entered in—according to Cheryl anyway. I finally felt like I was, perhaps, getting somewhere. It still wasn't exactly what I wanted to do, though. I brought the subject up at dinner that night as my dad made an opening.

"So, how'd it go today?" he asked complaisantly. He'd become slightly more open about discussing horsey matters but didn't seem completely resigned to it either. I felt caution was still necessary.

"Great!" I beamed at him. "It was so much fun! And Remmy was perfect!"

Innocent enough admissions and they *were* true, but I was also trying to use a little psychology on him. I didn't want to think of it like that, though. I suspected that, deep down, my dad was still hoping I'd change my mind. He hoped I'd decide that horses were too scary, too much trouble, or too hard to ride or handle, and go back to the puppy offer. Puppies were small and safe, were less likely to get me physically hurt, and didn't have built-in ties to a certain family that he was still reserved about, to say the least. He liked Tom Reid a lot, but Bar 8 held those same ties so his reserve extended to Tom's family and their ranch.

He pretended like everything was cool, but I knew better. I knew my dad. I also knew he truly loved me and wanted what was best for me, but I was starting to have my own ideas about what that was. For now, he was trying to be content for me to be happy, and I was determined to leave him in no doubt about how I felt about riding and horses in general. I'd never been as happy or actively involved in anything in my life.

It was helpful that Mom was having a good time with it too, though. She enjoyed the connection to the whole Bar 8 family and thought that the physical aspects of riding and taking care of horses were very good for me. I agreed.

"Cheryl says she's progressing quickly," Mom said. "She actually said that she's never had such an adept pupil."

"She did?" I asked, really surprised. She hadn't said anything like that to me.

"Yes, she did," said Mom, an obvious note of pride in her voice.

"Hmm," said Dad, taking another bite of dinner.

Now or never. . . .

"Dad . . . Mom . . . I want to barrel race. Can I learn? Please?"

This was a gamble. I was hoping they either didn't know enough about it to have a strong opinion or would be encouraged enough by Cheryl's praise and my enthusiasm to let me go for it. I should have known better. *Dad . . . horses . . . history. . . .*

He regarded me seriously as he continued to chew and finally said, "I don't think so."

Deflation.

"But—" I quickly tried to compose an argument in my head. But he held up his hand and raised his eyebrows at me, a sure signal that I didn't want to push him any further right now.

And I didn't. So right now wasn't the time. I was hardly giving up, but I was too aware of all the concessions he had already made. Large concessions: riding, having my own horse, who gave me that horse, the projected stable. I silently gave thanks for these things. And determined to wait.

After Spring Break, school life fell into a similar pattern to before it. Homework was horrendous and more exams loomed, but preoccupation with one boy's existence still took up most of my mental and emotional energy. I spent as much time as I could around Dave, and he paid attention to me—or not—in varying degrees of intensity. When he was close, and especially if I had his undivided attention, I basked in it and hoarded each little memory, every nuance of expression that could barely be construed as affection, and

every action that made me feel singled out in any particular way. It didn't happen very often, though, and almost never at school anymore. There still was never any word or overt gesture to make me think that he felt anything more than friendly or brotherly toward me. And I continued to tell myself that was okay.

On the plus side, I had apparently ceased to be any threat to the female population of Douglas High and was left alone—for the most part. Occasional glares and overheard mean words had little more effect on me now than they had in junior high. It wasn't their opinion that was important to me.

Matthew continued to be a considerate friend but, in hindsight, his proximity seemed determined by Dave's presence or absence.

On the rare occasions that the track team had meets at Douglas High, I stayed after school with Robin and we worked on homework as we watched. Those were fun days and Dave always looked for us and was happy to find us in the bleachers. He usually managed to come and talk after and sometimes even during the event.

Most of the time the meets were somewhere else, and once Robin had a softball game on the same day and couldn't make it. Mom had offered to stay and watch the meet with me, but I thought that would seem weird and I went home miserable instead. Mom and I went to watch Robin play several times when her game was nearby, though. It was so much fun to root for her and we were able to give her a ride home, too.

One day in early April there was a little buzz, mostly among the juniors of our group. They were talking about a camping trip that the seniors took for a few days between exam times; kind of a stress-reducing, bonding thing. I wasn't terribly interested as I didn't know any seniors and I wasn't especially aware of their absence while they were gone, but the others made it sound like a big thing. I'd never even been camping, but I kept that to myself.

I got to participate in two more shows, even earning a yellow ribbon for a trail class. At my level that might not be impressive, but it served to make me much more confident in my own potential. It also gave me tangible proof of competency to show my dad. Somehow Dave found out about it and went out of his way between classes to congratulate me. It meant more to me than he could ever know.

I hadn't given up my primary goal, however. If the barrels were left out at Bar 8, I made use of them if no one was watching. When they weren't set out, I moved some of the pole bending poles, approximating the distance between them and pretending they were barrels. I often wondered if I was completely confusing Remmy, but he was always sweetly patient and co-operative whether he understood or not. I was doing more real galloping now too, just for short stretches, and practicing coming to faster and faster halts and turns. I did this mostly in the covered arena where the footing was good but also sometimes on the dirt road, and still only when I was sure I wasn't observed.

As the weather continued warm and dry, even having some hot days in early May, the atmosphere at school changed yet again. Though there was a lot of distraction with sports, exams, and continuing PDAs, there was also a growing sense of anticipation—summer vacation was coming. I looked forward to the long school-free days and planned to spend as much of it around my friends—yes, Dave in particular—as possible.

One Friday our whole group were together after school. I hadn't seen Dave much that week and had been suffering my normal withdrawal, so I was extremely happy when he positioned himself beside me on the walk into town.

"Can you hang out tomorrow?" he asked.

I immediately shuddered and felt myself flush. I wanted to say, "Of course!" but decided to play it safe. Dad was home and I never knew what he'd say where the Calderas were concerned. "I can ask," I said. Then, wanting to leave him in no doubt of my own sentiments, "I hope so. Why?"

"Picnic." He said it innocently enough, but his eyes were glittering and his mouth twitched.

Obviously not *just a picnic.*

"I'll have Angel call. She says she misses you." His smile was wide this time and I felt warmed down to my toes, both by his smile and the thought that Angel was thinking of me.

He was true to his word. Just before dinner, the phone rang and Dad answered it. He spoke politely to the person on the other end and handed the phone to Mom. It became clear that it was Angel and Mom was very happy to talk to her. They talked for some time before the conversation obviously turned to the next day's plans.

"Tomorrow? Yes, I'm sure she can go. Hold on just a minute." Mom looked at Dad and said, "A picnic. With the Calderas. Angel and Robin will be there too." These last words were important additions, of course.

He nodded and went back to his paper.

"It sounds lovely . . . Yes, of course . . . All right . . . Oh, yes, she's right here."

She offered the phone to me.

"Hello?"

"Hey." Dave's voice. Angel must have passed the phone off to him as Mom passed ours to me. "So, just be ready pretty early, okay? You might want to bring sunscreen or something. Angel will pick you and Robin up."

"Where are we going?" I couldn't help wondering, though it truly didn't matter.

"Secret," he said. "See you tomorrow. Okay?"

"Okay."

I wasn't sure what to wear to this "picnic," so I called Robin.

"Where is it we're going?" I asked as if I'd been told but couldn't remember.

"Uh-uh," she said, laughing. "He didn't tell you, did he? You'll just have to wait to find out."

A little frustrated but even more intrigued, I asked, "So, what are you wearing?"

"It's going to be hot. Probably shorts. Don't wear sandals, though. You'll be better off with shoes."

I was glad I'd called.

Angel picked me up early with Stevey and really did seem happy to see me. Then we picked Robin up and drove for over an hour, eventually turning down a narrow dirt road that seemed to have traffic disproportionate to the size and location of the road. I wondered what was going on until Angel parked and we stepped out of the car. What had been a low humming from inside the vehicle was now a very loud whining and buzzing that I recognized immediately. Motorcycles.

Robin grinned at me as we helped Stevey out of the car, then we walked toward a hillside dotted with people in different stages of setting up day camps. Near the top, under a canopy shading a blanket-covered tarp, waved

Mr. Caldera. They must have gotten there early and set up before the boys took off to do—whatever it was they were doing. Robin held Stevey's hand and Angel took my arm as we made our way up the hill. Mr. Caldera met us half way to escort Angel the rest of the way up and offered her a fairly comfy looking folding chair to sit in.

"Where are they?" asked Robin, looking down across the landscape before us.

This was acre after acre of open space scored by hilly, winding dirt tracks. Here and there groups of people stood or riders congregated. Farther away there seemed to be a smaller, mostly flat, self-contained track where people were riding, though it didn't look like any kind of organized race. Beyond these was another separately enclosed track that didn't look like it would be used. It was a little hard to tell, as much of it appeared to be set lower than the surrounding grounds, though the hills looked even bigger. Closer to us, a line of riders waited for the start signal.

"Cris has ridden two heats already," said Mr. Caldera. "David, I believe, is riding in one right now."

Robin and I each held one of Stevey's hands as we went back down the hill and walked to a vantage point closer to the action. At first I didn't recognize him, but Robin pointed to a rider roughly in the middle of the group waiting to start, and I recognized the green and black bike. The rider I wasn't sure about, his face completely shielded by a large helmet. They all looked similar in their protective gear—like brightly colored spacemen.

The riders took off at the signal and I watched *my* rider eagerly as the group negotiated the track, hills, and jumps. Apart from getting bogged down on a turn, Dave kept toward the front of the field of riders, flying off the hills and tearing around the flat. A couple of people crashed into each other but picked themselves up and got out of the way of the others, apparently unhurt. I wasn't even aware when the race was over.

"What happened? Who won?" I asked, confused.

"I don't know, but Dave wasn't in the first three. They ride two races at the same class level, but I don't know which that was."

I was starting to wonder if this was going to test my fortitude like the bull riding had.

"Come on," said Robin. "Let's go find Cris and Henry."

We walked around for a while, making sure to stay off the tracks and away from moving motorcycles until we found the Calderas' big SUV and trailer. Cris was helping Henry adjust his helmet as he sat on what looked like a smaller version of the bigger bikes.

"Henry rides too?" I asked. Knowing the Calderas, I shouldn't have been surprised, but he seemed too young.

"This is his first year to race," Cris said as we approached. He was dressed similarly to his brothers, though in mostly black with some yellow, and not at present wearing a helmet.

"He's been riding with us for years at home, though." Then he said to Henry, "Go warm up."

We left them and wandered back toward where we'd last seen Dave. He was watching for us and waved, still astride his bike, his helmet under his arm.

"You made it!" he yelled above the surrounding noise. He smiled widely as we walked toward him.

My pulse sped up and I had to swallow; I couldn't help it. Though dusty and scruffy-looking, his hair sweaty and mussed from the helmet, he was still gorgeous to me.

"Yeah," Robin yelled back.

He focused on me. "So, what do you think?"

I tried to do my best impression of his smirk and said, "So . . . this is your idea of a picnic?"

He laughed loudly. Then he said, "The picnic's real enough. You just get free entertainment while you eat!"

This was true. They had brought a huge cooler packed full of goodies, but it still wasn't my idea of a picnic. That's not to say I wasn't happy to be there, but my vision of sitting down together on a blanket surrounded by greenery and the quiet beauty of nature was quite shattered. It was more like grab a sandwich and go on to the next race amid hundreds of other people, loud motorcycles, and increasingly hot and dusty conditions. I *was* happy to be there, and extremely gratified that Dave had asked me to come—really, I was—but I had a feeling it was going to be a long, trying day.

It was. Mr. Caldera divided his time between keeping Angel company in the shade, rooting loudly for his sons on the sidelines, and helping them with their gear and motorcycles. Robin and I took turns with Angel taking care of Stevey, though when he indicated he needed to go to the bathroom we tracked down an older brother. One thing was certain—we got plenty of exercise!

From what I could tell, nobody had actually placed in a race yet, but they were all happy with their rides so far, except for one of Henry's where his bike had stalled twice. They talked together at some length about what could have caused it and what they should do to fix it when they got home, but Robin and I just looked at each other and shrugged.

I have to admit, the races themselves were exciting, the riders negotiating hills and turns and some man-made jumps of various sizes along the course. And there never seemed to be a break; just one race after another. Many riders fell, but our guys all managed to stay upright and on their bikes, though a few times I felt myself cringing from close calls or quailing at the height and breadth of some of the jumps. Still, it wasn't as bad as I had feared at first; not as bad as watching them ride bucking animals. But very noisy. I felt I could probably become a fan. Anything that Dave—or any friend—was into, I wanted to at least be a fan of.

As the afternoon wore on, I started getting a headache, probably as much from the sun as from the noise. I also realized I hadn't eaten much, which might have contributed to it. We'd done a lot of walking around: from the hill where Angel seemed content to read a book and watch the action from her chair in the shade; to the portable restrooms with Stevey or for ourselves as we didn't like to go off alone; to the bike trailer where the guys hung out with people they knew and changed motorcycles for different races; or closer proximity to finish lines, especially when any of our guys were racing. And it seemed like one of them was racing almost all the time in different age groups or bike sizes.

Finally, it seemed as if the event was winding down; the crowds had thinned out and a lot of the riders appeared to be loading their bikes for travel. I began to feel sad that the day was over. Even though I hadn't spent much of it actually with Dave, it had been the kind of day that I had been missing—a family day with him. Being included like this made me feel incredible—necessary and special. Loved, I guess. Not that my own family didn't love me, of course, but this was different.

Everyone except Cris—and Angel, who was already there—climbed up the hill to grab a bite to eat. I expected that it would also signal the end of the day and cause us to pack up to leave, but instead everyone began talking

about the next event: Freestyle. I was confused again. More racing around the track? How was that different? Dave said he should get back to Cris, who was staying with the bikes. He grabbed a couple of sandwiches from the cooler for his brother, smiled at us—a little too wickedly for my peace of mind—and sauntered back down the hill toward the cars and trailers.

"Let's go, shall we?" said Mr. Caldera after a few more minutes.

"Go?" I asked, confused again. Weren't we staying with them? Watching—something?

"It's a short course and we want to get closer," said Robin. "We could see a little from up here, just barely, but it's more exciting closer. The stunts are pretty wild."

Stunts. Wild. Oh boy.

Mr. Caldera and Angel walked together, and Robin and I followed with Stevey and Henry, who was apparently not taking part in this particular event. Although the crowds had dwindled, a lot of people had done what the Calderas had—packed up most of their stuff and moved to a different part of the park to watch. We stood on another hillside looking down at the third, shorter track. This one had monster hills and man-made ramps with wide, deep spaces between them.

I had a really bad feeling about this.

"So . . . this is a competition? A race?" I couldn't see how this was going to work.

"No, not a race," Robin answered. "There *are* Freestyle competitions, but this is just a demonstration. Local riders and some who have come from farther away just do their jumps and see what others are doing."

"To show off," I said.

Robin looked at me oddly, as if she wouldn't have thought of calling it that, then laughed. "Yeah . . . when you get right down to it, I guess so. Some are interested in going pro and competing, but a lot of them mostly do freeriding locally and get together at events like this to . . . show what they can do."

"Freeriding?" I hadn't heard the term before. Then again, I'd never heard of any of this. I wasn't so sure I was going to be a fan of this aspect of Dave's dirt bike riding.

"Yeah, just using the lay of the land to do tricks and stunts and stuff. The Calderas do it a lot on the ranch. Speed is only important in getting the air that they need. In competition, riders are judged by the difficulty and style of their tricks, not speed."

"Oh," I said as an announcer's voice came out of nowhere and named the first rider. I hadn't been aware of an announcer earlier, but perhaps it had just been too noisy.

Watching the first rider was enough to confirm my worst fears. This was at least as bad as bull riding. What was wrong with these guys? Had I fallen in love with someone completely self-destructive, or what? I was more sure than ever this family was, one way or another, going to do me in. Everything that I thought I knew was constantly challenged by them. *Sometimes I feel like I don't know anything!*

The announcer explained that there were fifteen riders ranked according to competition experience. The more experienced riders were expected to do more difficult tricks toward the end of the demo. The first two riders scared me badly enough. Just the height they achieved with their bikes was frightening. Dave was third. According to Mr. Caldera, he'd been riding for years and freeriding for the past two, but didn't have much opportunity to compete. *So busy . . . go figure.*

My heart was thumping in my throat from the moment he ascended the first ramp. Angel crossed herself, her lips moving silently. On the first jump, Dave and his bike laid out almost completely sideways. It took a moment for me to realize that he'd done it on purpose; I thought, at first, that he had lost control of the bike. He wobbled a little on touching down and I think we all caught our breath, but he straightened out and sped into the next ramp. This time, he kicked his feet straight out behind him, regaining his seat well before hitting the ground again. The last jump seemed easier, as he straightened his body to lie horizontally face first along his bike before regaining his seat, but I didn't know enough to judge. I was just glad when he was done and safe on the ground again.

I was hoping that he'd come to join us right away, but there was no sign of him. I also hoped Cris would be next and then the people I cared about most would be done and I could relax again. But he wasn't.

While watching the other riders, I tried to think of what the allure was; what made these guys—the Calderas and the others—do these crazy things? I'd heard of adrenaline junkies before; was that it? I tried to imagine what it must feel like to hang that high in the air. It must feel like flying!

That would be an understandable incentive, but this seemed so dangerous. Surely there were safer ways of recreating that sensation? Maybe that was the whole point, though. I couldn't imagine Dave or Cris doing anything simply because it was safe.

Cris was the tenth rider and I steeled myself. The announcer was saying something about competition results and professional interest, but I didn't really understand. I got the gist: Cris was pretty good at this, which didn't surprise me. He was good at everything, apparently, except maybe social skills. And school? I still didn't know, but I was starting to have my doubts.

He started with some kind of handstand, his body almost vertical to his bike, which, again, I feared he'd lost control of. Of course not. He and his bike came back together, clearing the gap and landing safely. My heart throbbed in my throat again and I was determined to not hold my breath on the next jump, but my effort was wasted. I couldn't help it. He executed a similar move to the horizontal trick of his brother, only laying flat on his back, his feet extending over the handlebars.

He's older. He's more experienced. He knows what he's doing.

None of these thoughts helped. There was something about Cris that worried me even more than Dave did. Something dark and disturbing. *Something fatal. . . .*

He sped into the last jump and it was huge, he and his bike doing a complete somersault in mid-air. My heart felt like it performed the stunt with him and I felt a little dizzy. He landed in one piece but came to grief a moment later for some reason. Momentum made his body fly through the air and hit the dirt wall at the side of the track. We all gasped and I felt like crumpling to the ground. But Cris sat up right away, wriggled his back as if straightening a kink, and got to his feet even as people ran to his side to make sure he was okay. He took his helmet off as if to prove that he was indeed all right, slung his arm through it, and retrieved his fallen bike.

I needed to get away. Plucking at Robin's sleeve, I said, "I'm going to the bathroom."

She raised her brows—it hadn't been that long since we'd gone—and said, "Want me to come?"

"No." I shook my head. "I'll be fine. Stay with Stevey. I kind of just want to sit quietly for a minute. Headache." I had mentioned it earlier and she nodded.

I didn't need to use the restroom but found a picnic bench in the general vicinity, within sight of the parking area. I assumed that the others would stay to watch the remaining riders and hoped it would give me time to regain a more positive perspective. Right now, I was just mad.

I saw Cris walking his bike to the trailer and was surprised that he'd left the others. He loaded and tied the bike down next to the others on the trailer, not seeming to notice me at all, but when he was done, he walked over to where I sat. He hadn't looked at me once but sat down close by. Still feeling overwhelmed, I couldn't bring myself to talk at first. He sat silently as if waiting for me to initiate—whatever.

"Do you have a death wish or something?" I asked finally, a little more heatedly than I meant to. "I can understand Dave wanting to do bigger and more difficult stunts, tricks . . . whatever . . . and being competitive with you. You're his big brother. He looks up to you. But you . . . you act like you don't even care . . . like you're oblivious to what you're doing all the time. As if it doesn't matter."

He glanced at me with a wary, possibly hostile look in his eyes, then looked away but said nothing.

"You know that it would kill your dad and your brother if anything happened to you, right? Do you ever think of them? Doesn't anything scare you?"

This was taking a big gamble. He could totally give me the cold shoulder and walk away. He could verbally put me in my place. It wouldn't have surprised me if he did both. Perhaps I didn't have the right to remonstrate with him, but for all his apparent insight into others, I wondered if he ever thought of how his own actions affected the people who loved him and counted on him.

"It matters," he muttered.

"What?" I asked, confused.

"What I'm doing. It matters. It matters to me."

I stared at him, unbelieving. Was he really that selfish? That arrogant? He seemed to read my mind and, for whatever reason, wanted to clarify.

"I'm not suicidal, if that's what you're thinking. I don't plan on dying anytime soon. And, yeah . . . I feel scared sometimes. But not by jumping a dirt bike, or riding a bull, or whatever. Pushing myself . . . willing myself to do these things; it's the only time I feel . . . anything."

He was quiet for a few moments and the quiet allowed his words to sink in. I was shocked.

"*Almost* the only time," he added, as if the correction was important. "It's the only time I'm free," he said, softly.

I frowned, not understanding at all. "Free of what?"

He stared at the ground by his feet but didn't answer.

After a short silence, I ventured, "You'll be graduating next year."

"Yeah," he said, then snorted softly, derisively.

"Don't you have plans? Things you want to do? You know . . . with your life? You're going to college, right?"

I was staring at him now, trying to catch any glimmer of expression in his face, but it was lifeless. Blank. Hopeless? An oppressive cloud seemed to hang over us in spite of the beautiful day and noisy, exuberant life taking place all around us.

"Don't you have a dream?" I asked more softly, starting to feel wounded but not sure why.

After a few moments, he replied, "I used to. It's gotten hard to remember, and . . . seems too impossible. It's easier to not think about it. It just . . . brings me down. I sometimes feel like I'm drowning, like I can't breathe."

I swallowed hard. Hearing the pain, what sounded like despair in his voice, was really getting to me.

"How can any worthy dream be impossible?" I asked, not understanding the particulars but angry that anyone should feel this way. "How can you just give up on it? Isn't it worth fighting for?"

He scowled at the ground. I didn't know if it meant he was angry or just thinking. You never knew with Cris.

"Some things are worth fighting for. And some things . . ." here he scowled even more and tightened his lips, "some things are worthwhile, but you can't fight for them."

"I don't understand," I admitted, willing to be enlightened.

He sighed heavily. He had picked up a small branch, fallen from a nearby oak, and was stripping the bark from it with his fingers. "I believe there are things that are right and things that are wrong. But things can be right at the right time, and wrong if it's not the right time."

He paused for a moment and I was glad; trying to follow his train of thought was challenging for me.

"I believe that people have choices and that sometimes making the right choice is the most difficult thing. Sticking by those choices, especially when you *want* to make the wrong ones, and the rest of the world would make the right ones *seem* like the wrong ones, is the hardest of all."

I had no idea what he was talking about and I was beginning to think that he had forgotten who he was talking to. But his expression had evened out, softened, as if talking out loud had helped to confirm something in his own mind.

He continued in a softer voice, frowning only slightly again. "People around you can ridicule you and lie about you, but you stick to your decision because you know that it's right, if not for everybody else, then at least . . ." his lips tightened again and he nodded his head, still looking at the ground by his feet, "at least for yourself."

He'd completely lost me, but the scowl had disappeared and he turned back to me, a much lighter though somewhat searching expression on his face. His eyes met and held mine in a way he never allowed—not since the first day we'd met. I was hit with a barrage of feelings, just like that first time, and my heartbeat inexplicably quickened.

What the heck are you talking about? You are the weirdest guy. And I have no idea what just happened!

He seemed suddenly conscience-stricken and looked away, but his mood had definitely lightened.

"Sorry," he said, seeming apologetic as if he had, truly, forgotten who he was talking to. He stood up to leave.

I was left speechless except for one overwhelming question. It had been in the back of my mind for a long time, but the day's activities had brought it closer to the front. The pain I felt from him now made it seem important to know.

"Cris," I called as he began to walk away.

He stopped dead in his tracks and turned back slowly, looking wary again.

His confidences had given me courage, so I asked softly, "Where is your mother?"

He looked surprised and a little pained at the question. I didn't think he was going to answer as it looked like he was turning away, but he turned back long enough to reply colorlessly and equally softly, "My mother is dead."

Then he walked away.

Cris' admission, confession, whatever it was, haunted me for days. There was so much I wanted to know but now felt, even more than before, that I couldn't ask. His tone of voice and expression while answering my last question assured me of that, and I would have felt even worse asking Dave. Was *that* what his nightmares were about? I had tried asking Angel that one time but she evaded the question. Not much point in trying that source again. I thought about asking Robin but resisted the impulse. It seemed like the kind of thing one of the Calderas should explain. Otherwise, I'd feel like I was gossiping or something. And I still didn't know about Robin's parents. I didn't want to ask questions that might inadvertently hurt her too.

Cris remained elusive at school and when I did see him he gave no indication that he remembered our conversation at all. *Business as usual, I guess.*

It hadn't made an impression on me before, but I knew that the day of the motocross event was also the day of Junior Prom. Now I wondered if Cris had gone. If he hadn't, which seemed likely considering the day's activities, had he wanted to go? It was none of my business, of course, but I found myself hoping that he did. Did he have a girlfriend? What about the girl from our mall trip? She had obviously felt something for him. I began wishing he had *someone.*

Concerns for other people were soon banished from my mind, however, and all it took was one phone call. Less than a month until school was out, my hopes and plans for the summer went crashing into oblivion.

"Hi, Allison!" Brenda's voice sounded very happy on the other end. Unfortunately, not usually a good sign. "How are you?"

"Hi!" I replied, a little surprised. I had called her recently, just to stay in touch, but she usually only called when she had something she thought exciting to share, or when she was depressed and needed to feel better. Apparently talking to me somehow did that for her. "I'm fine. You?"

"Great!" she said. "I'm *totally* looking forward to summer now. Most of my friends are spending most of the summer somewhere else. It was going to be *so* boring."

"So, what's happening now? Are you going away too?"

"Silly. I get to visit you. Then you'll be here for the summer, right?"

Wait . . . What? I had heard what she'd said, but it didn't make sense. "What are you talking about?"

"You know," she insisted. "I'm going to visit you there while my parents are in Cabo. Then you'll come to LA" It went quiet on her end of the phone for a moment, then she swore. "Don't tell me you didn't know yet? Mom said not to say anything until your parents told you, but that was a *week* ago!"

I don't remember any more of what she said or how I responded. It *couldn't* be true. For her to come here would be bad enough—I didn't even want to think through any possible scenarios of *that*—but I would have to go to Los Angeles? Why? For how long?

"We didn't want to say anything until we were sure," said Mom when I confronted her about it.

Dad wasn't home yet. He'd been leaving early every morning, working in Sacramento at the new main office and coming home late.

"Daddy is lining up some very important trips to Asia for the summer. He's hoping he can take me too. You know," she said, taking my hand and looking into my eyes, "we would take you too, if we could. But Daddy's not even sure he can swing the trip for me. We haven't had a real vacation in," she blew gently through her lips, "six years or so. We were hoping you wouldn't mind too much. That's why we contacted Nicole, to see if you could spend a part of the time with them. They were all for it but wondered if Brenda could stay with us while they took a short vacation too."

It felt like ice water was coursing through my veins. I couldn't believe this was happening.

"How long?" I asked, quietly.

"Just a week, sweetheart." She rubbed my arm. The shock probably registered on my face. "It's just a week's cruise and then they'll be back."

She had misunderstood. "No," I said, my throat constricting. My voice sounded rough. "How long will *you* be gone?"

"Oh. I'm not sure. If everything goes well, five or six weeks."

My eyes felt like they'd pop out of my head. "Six *weeks?*" I squeaked. "That's too long!"

"I'm sorry, Allison. We'd bring you if we could. Really!"

"No . . . no . . . I . . . don't want to go. I want to stay here!" *This is not happening.*

My mother looked at me sadly as if she thought she understood how I felt. "You can't stay here by yourself, sweetheart. That's just not realistic."

I didn't care. Not one bit.

"What about Remmy? What about . . . about . . ." I was trying not to let my lips tremble as I thought of it. "What about my friends? I won't get to spend time with them?"

She looked steadily at me, seriously and rather searchingly. It made me feel uncomfortable. "Remmy will stay at Bar 8. Tom has already agreed to make sure he's exercised and given plenty of attention. And the stable should be finished by the time we get back."

I didn't care about the stable. I could live without the stable. I wasn't sure how I was going to survive the whole summer without Remmy. Without riding. Without Dave.

I wasn't sure what to say to my friends and didn't see Dave until a couple of days later, but as soon as he saw me, he asked what was wrong. It startled me. Was I that transparent?

"I'm going to be in Los Angeles for most of the summer," I said miserably, wondering if my news would affect him at all.

"That's cool," he said. "You can visit your friend . . . what's her name?"

"Brenda," I said.

"Yeah . . . Brenda . . . and your family. Right?"

I nodded. *No, obviously not affected.*

Robin made a face and said, "I have to go stay with my aunt for a few weeks."

"Really?" I asked, diverted. I'd never heard mention of any other family besides Fiona.

She nodded but then looked self-conscious, as if she hadn't meant to say anything. "What about you?" she asked, nudging Dave. "Where are you guys off to this year?" She looked at me and continued, "They travel every year. Sickening."

Dave grinned. "We have family here and there," he explained to me. "We don't travel all over. Usually just where we have family. It's Hawaii this year."

"Give me a break," huffed Robin.

"You have family in Hawaii?" I asked, now completely distracted.

"Yeah," he smiled widely. "It's great. My uncle owns a small ranch on Oahu. We get to surf all the time! About every three years we go to Spain. We have a lot of family there."

"Like I said," said Robin. "Sickening!"

I still wasn't happy that I was going away, but I felt somewhat better knowing that my friends weren't going to be around much either. Maybe it was just as well that I was leaving after all. It might be worse to be here in Douglas with my friends gone. I was still going to miss them though. And Remmy.

The following Saturday, after my regular lesson, Cheryl gave me an entry form for an open horse show that would be held the first weekend of summer vacation. She pointed out several classes she thought I could enter, including a novice pole bending class. I took the form home and went over it with Mom. She agreed that, as it might be the only chance I'd have to compete this summer, that I could enter it.

I chose my classes carefully and Mom signed it, writing a check to cover the entry fees. I got the envelope ready but didn't seal it. There was one more thing I was going to add. I also added the cost of the extra class in cash. Then I sealed it and took it out to the mailbox. I didn't want to think about it too much, but I didn't feel guilty about it either. No, not one little bit.

The last couple of weeks of school felt very strange. Even though my closest friends seemed more available, hanging out in the hot sun at the tables that had become peculiarly our own, the time went by so fast. I would have done almost anything to prolong the days. Even Cris seemed to hang around as if he actually wanted to. He didn't appear any happier but seemed more interested in the conversations. I wondered what he was feeling. Was he looking forward to Hawaii, as Dave obviously was? Or was he going to miss us, even though he seemed to have avoided us for much of the year?

One thing happened to lighten my heart and gave me even more reason to look forward to fall and the start of the new school year. Miss Sanders called me over after English a couple of weeks before the end of school.

"Allison, I've enjoyed your work this year. You've seemed much happier lately than you did at the beginning of school. Have things . . . been better?"

she asked. I wasn't sure whether she had a reason for probing or was just being solicitous.

"Yes, thank you. Fine. Everything is . . . fine."

"Well, I'd like to suggest that you join my advanced class in the fall. The students in that class have to work hard, and there's a lot of extra reading and more written assignments. But it will prepare you to take advanced placement exams in a year or two."

I didn't know what to say. I was flattered that she thought I was good enough to participate in it but wasn't sure if I wanted to do the extra work. I didn't want to jeopardize any extra time I might have for friends and riding.

"Um . . . thank you, Miss Sanders. I'll . . . I'll think about it," I said and turned to go.

"There's just one thing," she said, and I turned back to face her. She hesitated, looking concerned, then said, "David Caldera will also be in that class. He was in it this year. Would that be a problem?"

I think I finally consciously controlled my blush response. It was the first time I was really aware of being able to do it, especially since it had become such a nuisance.

Breathing slowly and staying focused on her face, I replied, "No . . . no, that's fine. We're . . . friends."

"Well, I'll make the recommendation," she said. "I look forward to it." She smiled pleasantly.

"Yes . . . thank you . . . I . . . I look forward to it too."

That was putting it mildly! Advanced English—with Dave? He was in *advanced* classes? I left the room and steadied myself against the wall just outside. The tenuous control I'd had evaporated and I started shaking a little, laughing to myself.

The absolute end of me!

The last week of school sped by crazily, each day feeling strange as our schedules were disrupted and shortened due to finals. I would have loved to have hung out after school earlier in the week—my time left to spend with friends was growing short and increasingly precious. But my dad insisted I come home and study for any finals I had. I didn't think it would help. I figured either I knew stuff or I didn't and cramming wasn't going to do me much good now. But I tried to be content anyway. Being sullen about it wouldn't have helped either, and I was so thankful for the time that I'd been allowed to spend with them.

Yearbooks had been given out early in the week and, of course, the first person I had to look up was Dave. Sure enough, his picture was there, trademark grin in place and a twinkle *almost* visible in his eyes. It was easy to imagine it there anyway. Next, I found my own, though I already knew what it looked like. I had still wanted to redo it but everybody, including my parents, had said they liked it, so I let it go. I had no problem getting everybody to sign my book, which was gratifying, and even somehow received "Have a fun summer" type comments from people I didn't even know.

I was furious with Dave, though. He ruined his picture, drawing heavy eyebrows and a mustache and beard on it. Luckily there were plenty of other pictures of him participating in sports. He was also voted "Best Smile" along with the pretty brown-haired girl he'd danced with during PE. It was a great picture of him; I just wished she wasn't in it too, especially as they were cheek to cheek with their arms around each other.

In the back of the book, Dave wrote, *"Your butt's gonna hurt so bad in August—ha ha!"* I'd probably have to explain to my parents that it wasn't a threat or an intimate observation but simply the truth considering I wouldn't be able to ride all summer. I'd be sore once I started again! My other friends all wrote more unexceptional comments. Except Cris. I flipped through quickly, just to see if he had at least signed it, but he hadn't.

Oh well. . . .

The last day of school wasn't as sad as it could have been. We all went for coffee after school, the boys alternately skating ahead and then falling back to be with us again. It reminded me so much of those first weeks, when I'd just met Robin and Dave and Cris and Matthew—and the rest. Now they were all so dear to me. And we'd be together tomorrow too, everybody having agreed to meet near the fairground's barns first thing in the morning, whether they were riding or not. I couldn't wait.

Dave, Cris, and Henry had ridden in a couple of early cutting classes by the time I arrived with Mom and Dad. We had gone early to Bar 8 to get Remmy ready, then loaded him in Cheryl and Tom's trailer. They were also

taking a horse for another student who was meeting Cheryl at the show. Then we followed them to the fairgrounds. I unloaded Remmy and tied him to the trailer, then went to find the others.

I'd forgotten that Dave hadn't seen my new clothes. He looked appreciative, complimenting me, and I couldn't control the blush this time. He was looking handsome in dark jeans, a black and white striped shirt, and my favorite black hat. He playfully swapped his with mine for a short while, though mine was obviously too small for him and his still rode low over my ears.

"I always said you had a big head," laughed Robin. He just grinned back.

He gave mine back before my first class, a Western Pleasure class in which I took third. I was ecstatic and everyone seemed proud of me. Robin and Henry did well in their classes also, and the morning passed quickly. We watched each others' classes whenever possible and cheered each other on.

I checked in with Mom and Dad during a break between classes around lunchtime, but they were happy, talking to acquaintances and walking around. They said they'd be there to watch the pole bending and I was thankful they walked in the opposite direction, away from the main arena. I didn't want an audience for what I was about to attempt. I hoped to accomplish my goal, then explain myself and deal with the fallout later.

I reluctantly avoided my friends, who were hanging out by the barns and trailers, and made my way toward the large arena. Remmy, who had always been well-behaved for me before, began to prance and pull against my hand as soon as we neared the gate as if he knew what was coming up. Several other horses nearby were behaving the same way, which didn't help, and it was taking all my concentration just to contain him. I struggled briefly with the idea of just walking away, forfeiting the race without even trying, but as I heard the contestant before me called, I steeled my mind against it. I would never forgive myself if I chickened out now. This was something I had to do for myself, and it didn't matter if no one else understood.

I tried to stay calm without much success and forced myself to breathe slowly through my nose, mentally running the cloverleaf pattern and stroking Remmy's neck trying to trick him into calming down too. This was also unsuccessful. Walking him away from the entrance gate worked, but we couldn't go too far, and as soon as we turned back toward it, he pulled and pranced again.

I was wishing I'd used the restroom a little more recently and debating with myself again about chickening out, my heartbeat racing, when our full names were called over the loudspeaker. Time to put critical thought on hold and hope my practicing and instincts would come through for me.

We almost had a false start, Remmy was so anxious to go, but I turned him once more and then set him through the gate. I thought I heard someone shout my name as we entered the arena but couldn't think about it as Remmy bolted, the way he must have entered arenas hundreds of times with Dave riding him.

With Dave riding him . . . of course.

Remmy might have been manageable during our practices at Bar 8, but this was completely different. He obviously knew this was the real thing, a competition, and I was sure he was used to running to win. I couldn't even gulp at the realization.

Just sit deep, hang on, and ride!

I was so distracted that I failed to rein properly, causing Remmy to run almost a straight line into the arena and very wide of the course I should have followed. I managed to pull him up and cue a lead change to get to the first barrel, but now that he had an actual target, he jumped forward again, fighting me as I tried to slow and straighten up. If we didn't, we were going to slam into the arena railing.

My heart beat so fast and sounded so loud in my ears; I was aware of little else. I suppose there must have been noise from the crowd in the stands, and the announcer might have narrated my nightmare ride. But all I was aware of was my heartbeat thumping in my ears, Remmy's pounding hooves, his heavy breathing, and his grunts of impatience every time I tried to hold him back. We negotiated the first barrel, overshooting too far and making me pull him up to straighten him out again. Then he charged the second barrel. This one I felt a little more in control of and was able to stay reasonably close to it, exiting the turn in a good position to approach the third and last barrel.

I knew we weren't going anything like as fast as the other competitors, and I hadn't thought that I'd care. Winning wasn't the point. But I didn't want to crawl either. I shouldn't have worried. I *should* have been concentrating on holding Remmy in and finishing the course as safely and with as much

dignity as possible. Instead, I was thinking about how badly I'd ridden so far and how horrendously long my time was going to be.

I gave Remmy his head a little and ended up not being able to slow him again in time to turn. Approaching actual barrels at this speed was never figured into my practice, and I had no points of reference. He almost collided with the third barrel, sat back on his hindquarters, and then sprang forward and slightly away. I tried to go with him but didn't even think to grab the saddle horn. Momentum and my lousy balance were against me. I fell off.

The barrel was hard. *Very* hard. I suppose it could have been worse. They *could* have been metal. Luckily for me, they were a heavy duty plastic or something, weighted so they wouldn't get knocked over easily, but they were still harder than me. *Much* harder. As I hit the barrel and then the ground, pain like I'd never experienced before shot through my side like lightning, then radiated outward until I felt like I was drowning. Dark waves closed in over me and everything went black.

As I became aware of the world again, I tried to move.

A voice I knew very well spoke urgently. "Stay still. The paramedics are coming. Let them make sure you're okay."

A sharp stab of pain in my side convinced me to do as I was told. I opened my eyes to see two dark silhouettes bowed over me and blocking out the sun, glows like halos outlining their heads: one a light pinkish-gold, the other a pale silvery-yellow.

"Are you okay, Allie?" asked Dave, concern becoming apparent on his face as my eyes struggled to focus on it.

My glasses. . . .

A searing pain burned through my side again. I could feel tears pouring down from the corners of my eyes into my hairline and ears for some reason, though I didn't feel like crying. I laughed. Absurdly, a similar event popped into my head and I couldn't resist.

"Scare you?" I said. Then I was out again.

Chapter Thirty

Tangled Up

What had seemed like a great idea a few weeks ago was going to be biting me in the, um—*ribs*—for quite some time. And it's funny how words don't have much meaning or you think you know what they mean until you experience it for yourself. Kind of like love. A year ago I would have said that I knew what love was. Now I knew that I was just beginning to find out; that it was a more powerful thing than I had ever imagined. Well, that's what the phrase "dazed and confused" was to me now. I actually *knew* what it meant.

Convinced I was physically fine, I tried to sit up again just as the emergency medical technicians reached me. Dave and Cris were kneeling, one on either side of me, and a third person, a man I didn't recognize, knelt close to where my head had been. I caught a glimpse of Remmy standing nearby, looking dejected with his head hanging low, right before pain pierced through my side and I passed out for the third time.

When I regained consciousness again, I'd been moved to a tent and one of the medics—thankfully female—was examining my chest, ribs, and stomach area. She covered me with a blanket and called out to whoever was outside, "You can come in now."

Dave was the only one who entered the tent, coming to stand next to me.

"You're an idiot. You know that, right?" His expression was the most severe I'd ever seen it, at least when directed at me, and I could tell he really meant what he said. "And yes, you scared me. Are we even now?"

I tried to smile, but I was in a lot of pain. I was hoping that they'd give me something for it or knock me out again when my parents rushed into the tent and Dave stepped out of the way.

In an unusual role reversal, my mother was the one wigging out and asking frustrated-sounding questions like, "What were you thinking? Are you trying to get yourself killed?" Why? How? What? I couldn't answer anything; it hurt too much and my brain didn't seem to be working properly.

Dad came forward and looked at me anxiously but said nothing, his lips tight. Then I noticed that Cris had come in behind him. It was obvious that *everyone* was mad at me.

The EMT reassured them that my life wasn't in danger. There didn't seem to be any major fractures, head injury, or internal damage, but my ribs were already bruising and my blood pressure was very low. I should be taken to a hospital for better examination. They had called for another team to replace them at the show and they would take me by ambulance.

Dad faced the boys for a moment, his back toward me, then turned and stepped away from them. Cris, after seeming to ascertain that I'd live, looked furious and left. Mom was still fretting, but she seemed a little calmer—and a little angrier—now that she knew I'd probably be more or less all right.

"Didn't it occur to you that you might get hurt? And you did this against our decision. You could have broken your neck! Did you even stop to think about it?"

No, I hadn't, but that was pretty much everything I was saying to myself now and hauntingly similar to the things I'd said to Cris not too long ago. Maybe that was why he was so mad. *See? You're a hypocrite! It'll serve you right if they finally give up on you. You're more trouble than you're worth!*

When everyone stopped talking, I said the one word that was distressing me most. "Remmy?"

Dave looked at my parents, then shoved his hands into his front pockets and came to stand next to me again, his face solemn and unsmiling. "He's fine, though I think he thinks the accident was *his* fault. He looked sorry and worried."

I could picture Remmy exactly as he said and tears slid from the corners of my eyes again. "Where—" I started to ask, but Dave interrupted me.

"Someone was holding him. Cris went to get him. He'll make sure he's taken care of and tell Cheryl what happened. Don't worry about him."

I was silent, trying to gather my thoughts and feelings, but I couldn't. I hurt too badly—though it wasn't quite as bad as it had been at first—and my brain was feeling fuzzy. I wondered if they had given me something and I didn't even know it.

"I guess I'm in trouble," I stated. I didn't really need to ask.

Dave didn't turn his head, but the motion of his eyes indicated he was thinking of my parents when he lifted his brows and said, "Probably."

I knew I should be feeling something emotionally: contrition, fear, guilt, embarrassment. Something. But nothing seemed to be working except pain receptors.

The second emergency team arrived and strapped me to the gurney I was apparently on.

I looked toward my mom and croaked out, "Hospital?" Now I was feeling dizzy and nauseous. "I don't want to go to the hospital!" I had a fear of hospitals. Just one of those things.

"It'll be okay, we'll be there," she said.

Dad still hadn't said a word but moved closer so his back was toward Dave, blocking my vision of him. I thought perhaps Dave had made his getaway, but when they moved me from the tent to the ambulance, I saw that he was still close by. I wished I could say something to him, but they moved me too fast and my brain was working too slowly. I just saw his face. It was very blurry at this distance without my glasses, but I could tell his usual lighthearted demeanor was absent.

The ride to the hospital was the only thing that seemed to happen quickly. The rest of the afternoon and early evening dragged by as I lay in the emergency room for what seemed like days, being poked and prodded and peered at by several different doctors and nurses. I couldn't remember if they had given me anything at the fairgrounds—my senses were certainly dull—but now they gave me something that really helped with the pain. It made me drowsy, too, and I drifted in and out of sleep or consciousness; I'm not sure which but I hardly cared. I was diagnosed with three cracked and badly bruised ribs and scrapes to the flesh covering them. I would be very sore for quite a while but otherwise was fine. I was told I couldn't do any sports or exercise except walking; maybe swimming in a few weeks when I felt up to it and the wounds were healed.

"Riding?" I asked, alarmed.

"Definitely no riding," the doctor said, a stern frown on his face. "Not for at least six to eight weeks. And then you should take it slowly. No more racing, jumping, galloping of any kind. Just take it easy. Give your bones a chance to mend completely."

"Six weeks!" I forced out. Even though my brain wasn't working right, I knew that was impossible. It was being grounded all over again.

I was finally allowed to go home that evening and was thankful that they didn't think it necessary to keep me overnight. My blood pressure had stabilized and I was able to sit up, painfully, for the ride home.

In one of my more lucid moments, I realized that my dad hadn't said a word since the accident, and not just to me directly but within my hearing. He didn't even seem to be allowing any emotion to cross his face. I was sure this meant he was too angry to trust himself with speaking. My mother just looked tired and unhappy. As the medication they gave me at the hospital began to wear off, my side began to throb dully, but my mind started to clear too. The seriousness of what I'd done and what would probably result from it began to hit me.

Mom helped me straight to my room when we got home. I was glad that the lateness of the hour, my physical condition, and their probable assumption that my mind was foggy from medication postponed whatever repercussions I was going to have to deal with. I just wanted this day to end.

When I awoke, my ribs hurt horribly but my thoughts were coherent enough, though there was a high-pitched whining I hoped was coming from outside the house and not inside my head. I played yesterday's mishap over and over again in my mind, and each time some new aspect of willfulness, selfishness, and yes, foolishness occurred to me. Yesterday I was sorry I'd ridden so badly that I'd gotten hurt. Now I saw that there was so much more to it than that.

I had falsified the entry form. While perhaps not exactly a legal paper, it was a document of trust—and I had chosen to break it. I hadn't looked at it that way, of course, but I hadn't been allowing myself to think of it at all. If I'd made myself really think things through I was sure, or at least I would have liked to think, that many if not all of the flaws in my plan would have occurred to me.

As it was, I'd been determined to *not* think about it. I could have easily talked myself out of it based on fear alone. But I had already decided earlier in the year that I wouldn't allow fear to keep me from doing anything, especially where horses were concerned. So I purposefully hadn't thought about it, except in rather abstract terms of something I was going to do in the future. I had thought through none of the possible consequences. Until now, that is. Now they were crashing in on me like waves, almost overwhelming me. Running and hiding from what I'd done wasn't an option.

Not only had I falsified the entry form, I'd put Remmy into an impossible situation. A more skillful rider would have been able to control and maneuver him optimally—but not me. It was crystal clear to me now why nobody had wanted me doing it. Poor Remmy; he had just been trying his best for me, or at least doing what he'd been trained to do to the best of his ability. It wasn't his fault. A horrible thought crossed my mind. What if Dave now thought me completely unworthy of Remmy? *What if he wants to take him back?*

I started feeling really sick to my stomach. I wasn't sure which would be worse, the loss of another horse I loved, or the loss of his good opinion, perhaps even his friendship. The thought of losing either didn't help my growing nausea at all, might even have been causing it. But I felt like I deserved it.

More consequences forced themselves into my mind and I didn't resist them. The emergency people had been standing by in case of accidents such as mine, of course, but I now felt bad that it had been *me* taking up their time. I mean, it would have been one thing for an accident to have happened to someone who at least really knew what they were doing, someone competent, a real athlete. But for someone like me? Someone just—stupid? Even Dave had called me an idiot. That hadn't hurt too much at the time, but now? Now I was feeling acutely embarrassed and guilty. It hurt, but I knew it was true. One more reason for him to want nothing more to do with me. *But please don't hate me . . . don't give up on me. . . .*

Finally, and most importantly, I'd made everybody worry about me. *Really* worry. I was sure it had been Dave or Cris that I'd heard call out my name, but as they were both at my side as soon as I fell, I assumed they'd both seen the whole disastrous thing. I could recall the helpless, sick feeling I'd had while watching them in dangerous situations, especially when Cris had come off his motorcycle and hit the dirt wall. Had I made them feel the same way? I'd certainly never wanted to do that.

And what about my parents? I knew they couldn't have seen my fiasco, for which I was extremely thankful, but how did they find out? And I must have really made them worry. Not my intention at all. I vaguely remembered thinking that once I'd finished the event, they'd know how seriously I intended to pursue riding and would see that I was capable. That was now "blown to kingdom come," as Grandpa might say. Worse—it wasn't true; I obviously wasn't capable at all. What was their reaction going to be? Would I be grounded again? Worse? Maybe *they* would make me give Remmy back, and I felt it would be no more than I deserved. *But I hope not! Please, please, please, don't let it be so. . . .*

Yes, I was probably in a lot of trouble. I tried to get up, feeling the need to explain immediately to my parents and ask for their forgiveness too, but pain stabbed at me sharply and I cried out.

"Mom?" I called as loudly as I could and then cried out again at the wave of pain and light-headedness it caused. I hoped she'd heard me.

After a moment, my mother came in with a glass of water and some tablets for me.

"Mom!" I exclaimed. I noticed my face was wet.

Her face had looked drawn and stern as she came in, as if she hadn't slept, but now she looked concerned. "Does it hurt?"

It hurt to breathe. It hurt to move. It hurt to think. But I'd already decided I wasn't going to complain. I deserved this. "Yes, but I've got to talk to you. To you and Daddy."

Her face softened a little. She put the water and pills down to help me prop myself up. Then she sat on the side of my bed. "Take this first," she said calmly, handing me glass and pills.

I meekly did as I was told, then handed her back the glass. "Mom, I'm so sorry!"

She didn't say anything but nodded her head. She looked terribly tired and sad, and I got a horrible feeling in the pit of my stomach.

"Is Dad *very* angry?" I whispered.

"He was very worried," she said, seriously. "Now he's just very concerned. And yes, I'd say he's pretty angry, but I think Dave bore the brunt of that for you."

"Dave?" I asked, confounded. "What does Dave have to do with this? What happened?"

"Before we left to follow the ambulance, Dave asked if he could come along. Cris had just returned to give me your glasses. He must have gone back looking for them. Your father rounded on both of them. He said he didn't want them having anything more to do with you, that he'd gone against his intuition in letting them have any kind of influence on you at all, and this was what had come of it."

"What?" I squeaked, and then moaned as pain stabbed again.

"Daddy blamed them . . . their influence on you . . . for entering the race. Especially Dave. He blames him that you've been barrel racing at all when we had expressly told you no. Then Dave stepped toward your dad. Daddy says he thought he was going to strike him, but Cris intervened, stopping him. I'm afraid this whole incident has only confirmed his fears for you and his distrust of them."

"No," I said softly. It felt like the breath had been sucked from my body. My world was shifting, cracking, falling in on itself. "No, no, no . . . that's wrong! He doesn't understand. He didn't—" I tried to swallow, but my throat was burning, closing, my side and head throbbing in spite of the medication. "Dave didn't . . . he didn't know! He had nothing to do with it! *Nothing!*"

My mother looked concerned but skeptical.

"I have to talk to him!" I said.

Mom looked stern again as if steeling herself against softer inclinations, an unnatural expression for her. "I don't think that right now is a good time to test your father's patience, Allison. I'd say, at this moment, he's determined you'll never see or talk to Dave again."

"No . . . no . . . I don't mean that," I said desperately, shaking my head but not letting myself react to the horrifying words she'd just spoken. "I need to talk to *Daddy!*" I couldn't stand the thought of him continuing one more minute with these false perceptions. "I *need* to talk to him," I said, trying to sound more reasonable. "Now!" I attempted to force myself up, determined to get out of bed.

"He's outside," said Mom. "I'll go get him."

"I want to come downstairs," I said, firmly. I wasn't sure why, but I didn't want to look any more pathetic than I could help when I talked to him. I needed him to take me seriously.

With my mother's help, I got out of bed and down the stairs. It was painful, but I struggled to not moan or whimper; it was penance as far as I was

concerned, and I didn't want anyone to think that I wanted sympathy. At all. Mom helped me onto the couch and wanted me to lie down, but I refused. Perhaps it was just more stupidity on my part, but I wasn't going to allow myself *any* comfort until the record was set straight and my friends were exonerated for *my* wrongdoing. Mom walked off to find Dad and I wiped my face dry. I hadn't meant to cry, but my face was wet again so apparently I had. That wasn't allowed either.

The high whining sound came to an abrupt stop and after a few moments I heard my parents enter the house through the kitchen, my dad obviously stopping at the sink to wash his hands first. When he stepped to the edge of the stairs, I tried to turn fully to look at him, but the pain was too great.

"I need to talk to you, Daddy, but it hurts to turn that way," I said, trying to stay—and sound—very calm.

I heard him take his shoes off before stepping onto the living room carpet, then clear his throat as if readying himself for a confrontation. He went and sat in the chair closest to him, which also happened to be the one farthest from me. He had bits of grass stuck to him and looked hot and sweaty.

"How's it feel?" he asked, pointing in the direction of my side.

"It hurts, but that's okay. I deserve it."

His eyebrows went up, clearly surprised at my contrite attitude.

"It was completely stupid of me to even try what I did. Even Dave called me an idiot and he was right." Dad's face darkened at Dave's name so I hurried on. "I didn't mean to cause trouble. It just . . . it didn't occur to me that anything bad would happen." I realized it sounded lame, but it was the truth.

"It didn't occur to you that you were disobeying us? That you could get hurt? *Badly* hurt? You know it could have been much worse. What if—"

"I know!" I exclaimed, not meaning to interrupt rudely, but needing to explain. "I know . . . but I didn't think of it before. Really! I didn't let myself. If I had let myself think about it, I wouldn't have had the guts to go through with it. And it seemed so important. But now all I can think of is how it's affected everyone else, and how much trouble I caused, and I'm so sorry! Really, *really* sorry! But you're wrong if you blame the Calderas, Dad. They had nothing to do with it!"

"I think they had everything to do with it," he said angrily. "Your good sense and behavior in general seem to have deteriorated ever since you met them. I can't allow it to continue, Allie. I just can't! You're not to see them anymore. That's all there is to it."

"Dad! That's not—"

"I made allowances before, Allie," he almost shouted, interrupting me in turn, "I cut them slack, and against my better judgment too. But this is too much. I won't allow them to lead you to disobey us or to put you in danger. It's unforgivable, and I'm not going to discuss it anymore. No more second chances!"

He got up to walk out, his face rather red and obviously controlling himself with great effort. I had already started shaking—I couldn't help it—and it was causing my side to throb horribly, but I remained as calm as I possibly could. I *had* to make him understand, and that wasn't going to happen if I was crying or incoherent.

"Please, Daddy. Please listen for just a minute?" I was able to keep my voice steady—not whining—and was a little surprised when Mom added her voice to mine.

"Greg, you haven't given her a chance to say anything. That's not fair."

Dad looked as if the air had been taken out of his sails, so to speak. Obviously not expecting to change his mind, he sat back down again.

"Well?" he said, looking impatient.

"The Calderas had nothing to do with what I did. *Nothing!* I had asked Robin to help me learn to barrel race a long time ago. I've wanted to do it ever since I saw it for the first time. I don't know why. It just looked so fun and like . . . to be able to ride that well . . . to be able to do *something* that well . . . just became incredibly important to me. And I wanted to be able to do something that my friends did . . . something that they'd be proud of me for. Robin said she didn't feel comfortable with it . . . that I should ask Cris or Dave or Cheryl.

"So I asked Dave a while ago if he would train me, but he wouldn't. He said to wait until Cheryl thought I was ready. Cheryl said I wasn't ready. I never even asked Cris. I was sure he wouldn't do it. Didn't you see how mad at me he was? I'm sure he never even knew anything about my wanting to barrel race, Daddy. And nobody knew that I'd entered the race. I did it on my own. No one influenced me at all. It was my own stupid idea. I wanted to do it for myself, to prove to myself that I could."

I stopped for breath and to change position. My side was killing me. I expected Dad would have something to say now, but he just sat staring at me and looked like he was processing what I'd said.

I took the opportunity to continue. "I've always felt like such a loser, but it never really bothered me . . . until we moved here. I'd felt that way before because . . . I guess that's how other people saw me and treated me, and it was easier to just accept it. I just didn't deal with it. But after we moved here and I met such amazing people, it *did* start to bother me."

I looked at Mom, hoping that at least she would understand. I was surprised to see tears in her eyes.

"My friends here, they didn't see me that way at all. At least," I couldn't help smiling a little at the memory, "I think maybe Robin did at first, but Dave never did. Or if he did, he never let it show. Both he and Cris have never been anything but thoughtful and careful with me. They treat me like . . ." I smiled again, wryly this time, "like family. I'm sure they would never encourage me or even allow me to do anything they thought would harm me or make you mad at me." I looked squarely at my father and allowed a pleading tone to enter my voice. "*Please*, Daddy. I *trust* them, and you can too. Please don't forbid us to be friends. They are . . . so important to me. I . . . I don't think I could stand it."

My last words were whispered and tears were freely streaming down my face. I couldn't do anything to stop them and now didn't even want to try. I'd been in a similar position before, but now it was different. If I had been denied Dave's friendship earlier in the year, it would have been hard enough. But now? Now it just didn't bear thinking of. I wasn't going to blubber or beg, but being separated from the most important person in my life was more than I could contemplate without feeling an overwhelming sadness. This time, I needed my dad to know that.

He was still regarding me seriously, thoughtfully, a frown on his brow. Without a word he got up and walked toward the kitchen, picking his shoes up on the way.

"I . . . need to lie down," I gasped painfully, trying to move into a position to do so.

Mom was at my side in a heartbeat, wiping her cheeks and looking even more tired than before. After she had helped me stretch out on the couch, she ran up the stairs and returned with pillows.

The whining noise resumed outside and I soon fell asleep.

I awoke to the phone ringing. I had no idea what time it had been when I'd first come downstairs, but from the light filling our living room, it now appeared to be early afternoon. On the second ring, I looked around and saw my mom rousing from her position, curled up in one of the chairs. I managed to sit up and was going to try to get up, but Dad stepped through from the kitchen and answered it.

"Hello?" he queried, rather gruffly. Then his tone changed. "Oh, yes. Hi, Tom." His voice dropped a little, his tone softening and sounding weary. "Yes, I think she's going to be okay. Just bruised and banged up a little . . . They say about four to six weeks. They didn't do an x-ray but are sure a few ribs are cracked. She'll just have to be careful until then . . . Oh, that's right, I'd completely forgotten . . . No, no. Let's go ahead. Why don't you come on over and we can talk about it."

He was quiet for a minute; Tom must have been telling him something at length. Finally he answered, "Well, that's true but . . . Oh, you did? I see . . ." I watched Dad comb his fingers back through his hair the way he did when he was uncomfortable with having to do something. "Uh huh . . . Oh, no, that's okay. Why don't you both come on over . . . Yes, that would be fine. All right . . . Yeah, see you then."

He hung up the phone and looked over at Mom and me. He looked a little sheepish and uncertain and said, "Tom's coming over. I forgot we had arranged to discuss the building of the barn today." Then he left the room again.

This was surprising. I had expected there to be talk of no more horses, or that, with Dad's prejudices, Remmy would be returned to the Calderas. But they were going to talk about the stable? I wasn't going to be forbidden to ride? I could keep Remmy? Or did Dad just want to talk to Tom face to face? Perhaps he felt too bad denying him the work to let him down over the phone.

Mom got up and followed Dad out of the room. She returned with more water and pills for pain, which I took and then drifted in and out of sleep until the doorbell rang. Mom answered it.

"Hello, Tom," she said, holding the front door open for him. He stepped through as Dad entered from the kitchen, striding forward to warmly clasp hands with him.

"So how's the girl?" Tom asked, nodding toward me.

"We think she'll live, but she's going to hurt for a while," said Mom.

"Could you please tell Cheryl how sorry I am?" I asked him.

Tom put his hands out as if to ward off a blow. "I'm not getting in the middle of that," he laughed. "You'll have to tell her yourself . . . when you're feeling better, of course."

I smiled, agreeing, and they all left the room. I started feeling nauseous again, thinking of how I'd made such a mess of things, of my relationships. Cheryl was probably really mad. And Dave—was he finally regretting complicating his life with someone like me?

I must have dozed again, but it seemed only a minute or two later when Mom woke me, saying, "Allison, you have a visitor."

I opened my eyes to see Dave standing just behind the couch, toward the end, looking down at me. Mom went back to the kitchen, leaving us alone.

"Hey," he said, softly. Then, "How are you feeling?"

At the same time, I blurted, "I'm so sorry . . ." but caught my breath at the broad smile he gave me, his eyes dancing. He didn't look like someone holding a grudge.

"I rode Remmy down, so you can at least spend some time with him before you leave," he said.

Before I leave. . . .

"I'll be around, working with Tom, so I'll exercise him until you can at least lunge him or something. Are you okay?" he asked.

I smiled weakly, but it was a real smile. "I guess I'm going to live to do something stupid again another day."

His smile was broad again, but he narrowed his eyes at me as he said, "Yeah, that really *was* stupid."

I flushed, but not with embarrassment or shame. I was *so* happy he was here. He could call me stupid whenever he wanted.

"Don't ever do anything like that again, okay?"

"Um . . . I can't promise," I said, just being honest. I hardly knew myself anymore. Last year, I would never have dreamed of doing anything remotely like what I'd just done. Who could tell what would happen tomorrow?

He still looked stern, so I added, "I'll try."

"Why *did* you do it?" he asked.

I shrugged my left shoulder—the side that didn't hurt as much—and picked at the throw Mom had covered me with. I wasn't sure how much

I wanted to tell him. It would be difficult. There was too much I couldn't explain; not to anybody, but especially not to him.

"I guess . . . I guess I was just afraid of being left out . . . getting left behind."

He looked confused—definitely one of my favorite expressions of his. When he raised his eyebrows at me, I realized that I hadn't satisfied his curiosity.

"You know," I said, embarrassed by my lapse into admiration, "not being able to keep up with you . . . and the others. I wanted you . . . everybody . . . to, you know, see I was serious . . . about riding."

He was still narrowing his eyes at me and I started to feel that odd squirmy sensation. I hadn't felt that way around him for a while. A look of comprehension came over his face. Then he looked really annoyed.

"So you still don't trust me? Don't you know me at all? What am I gonna do with you?"

If I'd been a more brazen sort of girl, I would have loved to make some suggestions. But at that moment my dad made his presence known anyway, walking into the room and clearing his throat. Wondering how much he had heard and trying to remember what had just been said, I reminded myself that he couldn't read thoughts—at least I didn't think so. I could tell Dave felt as tense as I did and Dad was obviously already tense too, clearing his throat again and running his hand through his hair.

"I need to apologize to you, young man," he started, looking uncomfortable, then added, "*Dave.*" Dad emphasized the name as if he realized he was going to have to get used to saying it. "And your brother, too. I jumped to conclusions, made assumptions, that were wrong. I was wrong. Allie has explained, mostly, what happened. And didn't happen. And . . . well," Dad was looking extremely uncomfortable now, "I'm sorry. I accused you, and now I believe you've actually been watching out for her. So . . . thank you."

I was floored but pleased, too. Dave nodded, acknowledging my dad's apology and looking as if a huge weight had been lifted from him, though still wary.

"I've got to ask you, though," Dad said, concern edging his voice and creasing his brow. "At one point yesterday, I thought you were going to try to plant your fist in my face, but your brother stopped you. It has me . . . uneasy."

Dave looked shocked. "No, sir! Definitely not! I—"

"And it's not the first time it's happened. I thought the same thing the first time we . . . er, met . . . in my kitchen."

Dave looked completely confounded and I was sure his face darkened, actually blushing, but his skin was already so tanned again it was hard to be sure.

"We'd just met Allie," he explained, "and for some reason, we assumed she didn't have a dad, at least not living here." He looked self-conscious at the memory. "We were surprised and thought, maybe, you were an intruder. We were just ready to, you know, defend her."

"Well, that's good to know . . . I think," said Dad, looking uncertain.

"Yesterday, I just wanted to explain that I hadn't encouraged her at all . . . to do what she did. I guess, because of the circumstances, I seemed threatening. I really apologize."

"But why didn't you? Explain that is. Why did you let me assume the worst about you?" asked Dad.

"Cris stopped me," he said, looking embarrassed again. "We've been taught not to react to blame or accusations, deserved or not, especially if the other person is really mad. My dad says he's never known it end well if you do. Better to let the other person calm down and hope the truth comes to light. And better to take the blame for someone and be innocent, than be guilty and let someone else be blamed. I'm not as good at it as Cris is. He . . . tends to think more clearly . . . so he had to remind me. I was glad he stopped me."

He glanced at me, obviously still embarrassed, and I caught my breath realizing what he was saying. They—*he*—took the blame, or at least the initial force of it, for me, just like Mom had said. I wondered if she knew at the time that they had done it on purpose.

"So you would have fought me if I'd been an intruder, but you'll take the blame for something you didn't do?" Dad's expression had lightened considerably; he found this amusing.

Dave thought about it for a moment, then said, "I guess it depends on the circumstances. But yeah, mostly. Taking blame's not the same as defending or standing up for someone else." His eyes drifted to me and rested there long enough to provoke the usual response. *That* memory would always be indelibly etched in my mind: his grazed cheek, the other boy's black eye. It was probably best if Dad didn't know about that.

"And do those situations happen often?" Dad was sounding serious once more, and I was feeling nervous and a bit indignant. Why was he giving Dave the third degree?

"Not often, sir," Dave said, looking unsure and glancing at me again.

I tried to shake my head slightly and warn him with my eyes without Dad noticing.

He turned back to my Dad and laughed lightly. "Things usually don't come to a fight."

I think he was trying to put my dad more at ease, but my father was looking solemn and thoughtful again.

The next few days were difficult. The doctor had said that I needed to breathe very deeply as much as possible and cough at least once a day to keep my lungs clear, but Mom insisted I do it twice. It hurt so badly it brought tears to my eyes, but I didn't complain about it.

Tom drove his tractor down on Monday to level a site and then began work on the stable's foundation. Dave came as well to help him, but I didn't see much of him. It would have been tempting to watch from the back porch, but I resisted. Not only did it seem like it would be kind of creepy for him, I didn't want my parents looking for reasons to limit my contact with him. I'd rather do it myself. And in a twisted, self-flagellating way, I didn't think I deserved the pleasure and comfort it would give me just to see him.

By Tuesday, I could sit up more comfortably, for longer periods, and allowed myself to visit outside for a little while—purely to check on Remmy, of course. I still got tired easily, however, and returned to my room to rest.

Brenda came on Wednesday and would stay for a week. I had originally planned to go with my mother to the airport to pick her up, but Mom felt the long trip to Sacramento and back would be too tiring. I called Brenda the night before just to tell her I wouldn't be able to be there, and why.

"You did *what?*" she asked, sounding both incredulous and actually interested.

"I fell on a barrel," I repeated. "I was barrel racing . . . sort of," I amended. I hadn't earned the right to call myself a barrel racer. "I shouldn't have done it, and I cracked some ribs because I was stupid." I was very determined to do some kind of voluntary penance for my idiocy, and owning up to it

seemed the least I could do—along with enduring the infernal pain I was constantly in, of course.

"Wow," she said, sounding impressed anyway. "I can't even imagine you doing anything like that."

This was understandable. The old me would have shrunk away from doing anything that drew attention solely to myself, and I certainly would have quailed at the thought of riding or racing of any kind, let alone doing them together. I didn't say anything about that.

"I'm not sure what we're going to do while you're here," I said, truly apologetic for many reasons. "I was hoping to at least go riding with you, but I'm not going to be able to."

"Hmm. Well, maybe that cowboy of yours can take me for a ride." I knew she was just playing around, but there was something about the way she said it that I really didn't like. "I'm going to at least get to see him, right?"

This was such a *bad* idea. I was almost starting to wish for some natural disaster to prevent her trip. Something really deterrent—like an erupting volcano or something.

"Oh, I'm so sorry Brenda, but our house is right in the path of the lava flow. Now's not the best time to visit. Maybe in, like, three years?"

I sighed. "Brenda, you have to *promise* me not to call him that. And he's not *my* anything, except my friend."

"Well, that's good," she said, cryptically.

I was *really* not happy about this.

Late Wednesday afternoon, I was waiting rather nervously in the living room, sincerely hoping that Brenda would arrive after Tom and Dave had left for the day. I knew that not only was Dave still here but Cris had stopped by as well, probably just curious as to the progress on the barn. I wasn't sure if he was still around, though; I was avoiding him.

The only reason I knew Cris had been here at all was because Dad had come in and told Mom and me that he had apologized to him and that he'd been surprised to find out that Cris had blamed Dave for my accident too. That made me feel even worse. I felt like I'd been nothing but a burden to Dave ever since we'd met and wondered if I'd ever get a chance to somehow make it up to him. *Before he gets completely tired of me and the trouble I seem to cause him.*

Finally, I heard our car pull into the driveway. Dad had apparently heard the car too and must have gone through the garage to carry in any luggage since he now came through the front door with it. I didn't know whether to be amused or dismayed that Brenda had brought two large suitcases, a garment bag, and a large duffel bag with her. I was glad we had a spare room; she hadn't seemed to have changed much in essentials from what I'd been able to tell, and she had always been really messy.

In spite of a certain amount of foreboding, I was happy to see her. I had hoped we could stay in the house, though, at least for today—maybe just watch television or something—but she immediately wanted a grand tour.

"Living room," I said, indicating the room we stood in. "Dining room." I pointed past her to the other side of the entry way. "Through there is Dad's office. And that's a bathroom." I wanted to avoid the kitchen, the direct route to the back where, as far as I knew, the guys were still working. "Come on and I'll show you your room."

We left her bags—I couldn't carry any because of my ribs—and went upstairs. To the immediate left was my room and farther down a short hallway was our spare bedroom.

"You're the first one to stay in it."

"Really?" She seemed happy with the bright room. "Let me see your room."

I pointed out the bathroom she'd share with me and where my parents' room was on the other side of the landing, then led her into mine. I loved my room with its pale gray walls and dusky pink and white trim.

"Is it this neat all the time?" she asked, making a face as if it were a bad thing.

"Pretty much," I confessed. "I sometimes don't pick my clothes up right away . . . or make my bed."

Brenda rolled her eyes at me and said, "You don't even have a TV or computer in here?" Then she walked over to the back window and looked out before I could answer or distract her. "Wow. I guess this really is in the country," she said. "Who's that on the tractor? Is that where—" She gasped loudly. "Who's *that*?"

Darn. She must have seen Dave.

I went to stand next to her, but she turned and pulled me after her, back toward the door.

"Ow!" I cried as the abrupt change in direction caused me pain. "Not so fast! Please?"

"Oh! Sorry!" She looked truly conscience-stricken. "I forgot! I'll try to remember . . . but come on! It must be your . . . *friend*." She lifted an eyebrow.

I couldn't help laughing, though I was dreading this encounter.

"Be good," I tried to growl menacingly but failed.

She just laughed. I didn't think she'd purposely try to hurt me, but I also didn't think she knew what would. She was like someone on a mission and I tried to keep up, saying "Hi," to Mom as we passed quickly through the kitchen and out the back door. I looked around, but Dave was nowhere to be seen. Either was Remmy.

"Who's *that*?" Brenda whispered. Tom had moved slightly and I could now see that it was Cris, not Dave, that had excited her attention. I was relieved for a moment but no more than that. This could be even worse. Nonsense on Brenda's part wasn't going to improve Cris' opinion of me at all. I was surprised that I even cared, but I did.

"Is that *him*?" she asked. The way she was looking at him didn't bode well.

Oh, botheration. "No, that's Cris, Dave's brother. He's almost *eighteen*." I tried to put a warning tone in my voice.

It backfired; her eyes lit up even more. "Does he have a girlfriend? He must have a girlfriend, right?"

"*Brenda!*" I warned through gritted teeth.

Cris obviously noticed us come out onto the porch and was just as obviously ignoring us. I was glad. I trusted Dave to be fairly patient with my friend, if only because she *was* my friend. I didn't hold out the same hope for Cris.

"That's Tom Reid," I said, trying to distract her and indicating the older man. "He and his wife own Bar 8. She's the one I've been taking riding lessons from."

Brenda nodded, looking mildly interested, but her eyes went straight back to Cris. I noticed movement at the far end of the dirt road, just before it dipped out of sight toward the cattle guard and stream, and I tried to get Brenda to follow me back into the house. But it was too late. She resisted my redirection and watched as Dave came fully into view, riding Remmy bareback slowly up the road. His black hat left her in little doubt as to who he was.

"That's Dave?" she said in a hushed tone. As he continued to move toward us and his features became clearer, she turned wide, unbelieving eyes on me. "Nice going, Allie!"

"*Shhh.*" I knew I was blushing furiously by the time Dave reached us but couldn't help feeling a certain satisfaction in her obvious approval.

He jumped down from Remmy and led him over to the porch, smiling his most charming smile as he took off his hat and looked up at us. He looked rather scruffy—dirty from work and dusty from his ride. His hair lay close to his head where his hat had been. Then he tousled it with his fingers, making it stick out in all directions like he'd just woken up. Adorable. I couldn't help being distracted for a moment and noticed that his hair was getting kind of long.

He smiled at Brenda, then looked at me. He seemed to be stifling a laugh and his eyes twinkled with amusement as he asked, "How are you feeling today? Still hurt?"

I smiled back, wondering what was so funny. The past few days I hadn't talked to him much, even though he'd been right outside. Apart from my self-imposed punishment, I felt shy and nervous around him again and still self-consciously tried to hide my obsession with him. When he was on my mind twenty-four-seven, it felt like it must be blatantly evident to the world. Hiding it was much harder to do when he was around and I was afraid it was obvious to anyone watching each time I looked at him. I couldn't help wishing, before I had to leave for Los Angeles, that we could be more than just friends. Nothing too specific, just—*more.*

His grin grew wider and he raised his eyebrows when I didn't respond right away.

"Oh! Better . . . thanks," I finally answered, still embarrassed. "It still hurts . . . just a little." *No sympathy!*

He nodded and looked at Brenda, then back at me.

"This is Brenda, my friend from LA," I said. Then, looking at Brenda, "This is Dave . . . Dave Caldera."

I was afraid they would shake hands—Dave seemed to be a hand-shaker—but he just said, "Hey," in a friendly, nonchalant way.

"Hi," replied Brenda, not so nonchalantly and exhibiting no shyness at all. In fact, she was looking at him in much the way I was afraid she would, the same way most of the girls at school did.

This is going to be a really long week. I can tell already.

"Thanks for exercising Remmy," I said to him. "Where did you go?"

"Back there," he answered, indicating eastward. "I gave him a good workout, up and down hills and stuff. Did you know there's a road back there? It's dirt, a fire road I guess, but I was thinking it might connect further up with the road leading to Tom's. It could be a way to get to Bar 8 without having to go on the paved road. A lot safer."

"Mmm," I mused, genuinely thankful for the tip and consideration. I'd been wondering about that. I certainly wanted to have a way of getting to Bar 8 with Remmy once the stable was built. "I'll have to check it out when I can ride again."

"I'll put him up," Dave said, patting Remmy's neck. "I think Cris is here to give me a ride home. We're leaving tonight and we'll be gone for a couple of days, but I'll see you when I get back." He said this while looking intently at me and I was thankful again, this time for what appeared to be consideration for my tendency to worry. Was he as aware of the dwindling time as I was? *Couldn't be . . . must be something else.*

He smiled at both of us, settled his hat back on his head, then turned Remmy and walked over to the other guys. Tom had packed up for the day and was just standing, talking to Cris. Cris was now obviously waiting for Dave, turning his back on us again to talk to him. Getting to properly meet Remmy would have to wait for another time; a time without distractions. I dragged Brenda back into the house.

"No wonder you're so smug and like it here so much," she said slyly. "I think there's a *lot* you haven't been telling me."

I glared at her, knowing my mother was hearing everything, and rushed her out of the kitchen and into the living room where Dad was watching television. Apparently he had taken Brenda's luggage up to her room as it was no longer in the entryway. I could tell she wanted to discuss the brothers immediately, but to her credit, she controlled herself until we went to my room after dinner.

Unfortunately Mom only fueled the fire by bringing up certain occasions—the mall trip, the "picnic," and Matthew's *and* Dave's birthdays—which I hadn't told Brenda about at all, confirming her earlier accusation. I'd had good reasons—selfish reasons perhaps, but *good* reasons—for not telling her, but now she had a million questions and I couldn't ignore all of them.

Fielding them the best I could, I made light of the circumstances and stressed the fact that I was never the only person invited. They weren't "dates" by any stretch of the imagination. I had already told her a little about my birthday but no details, and nothing about how I'd come into the possession of Remmy. Luckily, as her interest in horses was minimal, she wasn't likely to ask.

I also thought I'd figured out what Dave was laughing at earlier. My glasses had been broken somehow during my accident, perhaps stepped on by Remmy. I was due for an appointment anyway and would be seeing my old ophthalmologist when I went to Los Angeles. But, until I caught sight of myself in the mirror and realized what Dave had seen, I'd forgotten that the glasses I wore now were really old. The prescription wasn't quite right anymore and the frames were kind of big and dorky-looking. They made me look like a twelve-year-old nerd but were better than nothing.

The next day we spent partially at the pool in town. The weather was hot and Mom wanted to visit everyone there. They had asked her to come back and work now that the pool was open longer hours and was much busier, but she couldn't because of the trip with Dad.

Brenda had brought attire for every conceivable occasion so was prepared with her bathing suit: a bikini exposing every curve she had, and she had quite a few. Convinced that she would be bored, she brought a stack of magazines, a paperback novel of dubious content, and her MP3 player and headphones. She ended up flirting happily the whole time with several boys that she thought were cute. They looked vaguely familiar; I might have seen them around school, but they weren't Dave so I didn't mind. I was happy that she was happy.

I couldn't go into the water yet. Though my ribs hadn't been wrapped, my side was still lightly bandaged to cover the shallow lacerations from my encounter with the barrel. And I still hurt. The idea of actually swimming wasn't appealing, though I wouldn't have minded cooling off. As it was, I was content to sit in the shade, drawing and listening to my own music.

Robin called later to find out how things were going, and we arranged to pick her up the next day and hang out at Bar 8. I was looking forward to it but was nervous also. I still had an apology to make.

I told Brenda to wear comfortable clothes, jeans and sneakers at least. But her jeans fit her very tightly and the only shoes she'd brought with her

were hardly practical for wearing around large, heavy animals. My jeans wouldn't have fit her, but I convinced her to wear my Converse. She also hadn't brought what I would consider normal tops, just flimsy girly shirts and tank tops, but she laughed and refused to wear anything of mine.

"No offense," she said.

There was none taken.

"This is fine, right?" she asked, looking at herself in the antique mirror.

"I guess," I answered, knowing nothing I said was likely to sway her anyway. I grabbed my sunscreen, though, just before we left.

"Why don't you see if Robin wants to spend the night?" asked Mom out of the blue. "Daddy's out of town. We can have a girl's night."

Mom seemed very eager about it, but I would have preferred to see how Robin and Brenda got along first. Robin was such a no-nonsense person. I hoped she wouldn't want to kill Brenda within the first hour or so.

Robin was ready when we got to her house. She liked the overnight idea too, so I followed her back into the house while she got her things. The two girls looked each other over critically when we got back to the car, but neither was shy and both said, "Hi," openly, as if willing to think the best of the other. That seemed like a good start.

When we got to Bar 8, the others went and sat on the guest house porch to be out of the way while a large group of riders got ready to hit the trail. If I'd been allowed to ride, we might have tried to go with them, but I wasn't sure Brenda would even want to.

I sought Cheryl out, not looking forward to facing her but wanting to get it out of the way as quickly as possible. She wasn't in the guest house, but I didn't dare interrupt Phyllis to ask questions. She was flustered and busy, directing her helpers as they rushed to transition between the late breakfast people and getting ready for lunch. Instead, I slipped out the side door and over to the bungalow. Knocking first, I stepped into the cool house.

Cody sat in the middle of the living room floor building with large fit-together blocks. He looked up as I came in and held a block out to me in invitation.

"Hi, Cody," I smiled, stooping down next to him to fit the block onto his creation. Apparently I didn't put it in the right spot as he immediately removed it and put it somewhere else.

"Cheryl?" I raised my voice slightly.

A rapid, light thumping preceded Zoe tottering around the corner, following my voice. She looked adorable, still dressed in her footy pajamas, her fair hair tousled.

"Just a minute, hun," Cheryl's voice called from the kitchen.

Zoe teetered where she stood and I continued putting proffered blocks from Cody in wrong places until Cheryl came into the room.

"Well, how are you doing?" she asked, much more warmly than I thought I deserved.

"Okay, I guess. I'll live." Then, because I didn't want to appear to be avoiding the issue, I blurted out, "Cheryl, I'm so sorry. I shouldn't have tried to do what I did."

"Darn right, you shouldn't have!" she said decidedly. "Almost gave me a heart attack when I saw Cris looking all worried and leading Remmy back to the trailer. I couldn't believe it when he told me what you'd done. And I can't imagine what your parents must have felt. What on earth were you thinking, honey?"

I wasn't about to go into a long explanation. "Apparently, I wasn't," I said. "I just wanted to see if I could do it."

Cheryl blew out through her teeth and said, "Well, I'm sure you got in plenty of trouble with everyone else. And I have to admit, when I first heard of it, I was ready to drop you."

I stared at her, panic-stricken. "Drop me?" I almost squeaked.

"Listen, if people think I'm putting green riders like you in competitions they're not ready for, my reputation is shot to hell . . . pardon my French. It may not be a large part of our income, but that lesson money helps to pay the bills."

I felt the color drain from my face as this new repercussion of my selfish action sank in. "I'm sorry!" I breathed. "I . . . I just never thought!"

"Well, that's pretty obvious," she said, frankly. "But I'm also convinced that you'd never hurt anyone on purpose, so I'll let it go if . . ." she paused dramatically, making sure she had my attention, "*if* you promise to never do it again. Not without permission anyway."

I readily agreed.

"And I think you'll need to make it up to me," she said, a mischievous look in her eyes.

"Anything!" I said.

"Babysitting."

Cheryl had us doing just that while she went to visit with my mom for a minute and then help at the guest house. We kept the kids out back in the shade of the *pergola* most of the time while we weeded the flower beds and borders. For a few minutes, Brenda looked offended, as if pulling weeds and digging in the dirt were beneath her. But after whining a little about dirt under her nails and her manicure being ruined, she plopped down next to us and actually did a lot.

I was glad I'd brought the sunscreen and helped Brenda cover her bare arms and partially exposed torso. I also had the dubious good fortune of learning diaper changing, a skill I had so far successfully avoided learning but now looked like I would need. Robin knew how to do it and showed me as often as the opportunity presented itself, which it did a couple of times during the morning. Luckily Cody was already potty-trained.

Getting Brenda to help with the horses later however, when the trail riders returned, proved too much to expect. While Robin and I enjoyed helping to unsaddle and put the horses away, she watched from the shade and safety of the big porch. We purposefully left Flash saddled and just about dragged Brenda over to her.

"But I *really* don't want to," she whined.

"You have to," said Robin, implacably. "You have to do it once, then we'll leave you alone."

Brenda groaned pathetically, but after many assurances that Flash was calm and safe and that we wouldn't leave her alone for a second, she allowed us to help her mount. I remembered how awkward and ignorant I had been when Dave and Robin first started working with me. They had been so patient! Brenda looked scared and refused to take the reins or let go of the saddle horn, like some of the small children I'd seen here at the ranch. She grudgingly allowed us to walk her around though, which we did until she complained of her backside hurting.

We spent the rest of the afternoon tidying the tack rooms, raking the barn area, and mucking out some of the stalls. Well, Robin and I spent our time doing that while Brenda watched and talked to us. When we were done, we hung out on the big porch talking to guests, to the wranglers, and to each other. Brenda tried to flirt with the college guys, but they obviously had no real interest in her and she finally gave up.

Mom picked us up just as a group was leaving for an evening ride. Many were people we'd interacted with throughout the day and we waved to each other. I felt somewhat restored to the order of my life and place in the world—perhaps not redeemed in full, but granted clemency. I could live with that for now.

We left by the exit closest to town and, before heading home, picked up pizza and some movies to watch. The latter proved tricky as Robin wanted to watch horror movies and Brenda wanted chick flicks, but Mom vetoed most of them.

Finally, Robin said, "I don't really mind. Just no sad movies, okay?"

"And no *Princess Bride*," said Brenda.

We laughed. Apparently we'd made her watch it one too many times.

The evening was spent eating, watching movies, and letting Brenda oversee manicures and pedicures; she insisted and my mother was a very willing accomplice. When she suggested it, Robin and I groaned. It was her retaliation, I think, for our making her ride and pull weeds, but it seemed only fair to let her torture us with nail polish. She had brought a ton of it with her and was actually very good at it. We went to bed really late and ended up feeling like we'd had a great day.

And Robin hadn't murdered Brenda. Yes, an excellent day.

Chapter Thirty-One

Upside Down

Robin got a call at breakfast the next day. We were all still in our pajamas and feeling a bit groggy—too late a night and too much pizza—but she seemed to perk up right away.

"Hey," she answered. "I'm at Allie's house . . . You are? Hmmm . . . I'll see . . . Yeah, okay. See ya." She looked at me and said, "Dave."

My heart leaped, but I tried to sound nonchalant as I asked, "What's he up to?"

Brenda looked blatantly curious.

"He's at my house, mowing grass and stuff. He was wondering what we were doing today."

I wanted to say, "Whatever his heart desires," but instead looked toward my mother and shrugged my shoulders. We hadn't discussed the day's plans and I assumed we'd just hang out around the house.

Mom looked up briefly but said nothing.

"He wants to know if we want to hang out. You know, like, in town."

"That sounds great," said Brenda, her eyes lighting up.

I had mixed feelings. I desperately wanted to see him; my opportunities and time around him were dwindling so fast! I did worry about Brenda, though. It was embarrassing, how she seemed to feel the need to flirt and also the way she sometimes talked; not at all like my other friends. Her interests and values were just so dissimilar to theirs—and, apparently, mine.

Not feeling in a position to ask for anything, I looked at my mother again. "Can we, Jen?" asked Brenda.

"I guess that would be all right," said Mom, looking at me, "but you can't stay too late. Your dad's coming home today and he'll want to have dinner together."

I smiled at her gratefully and we went to get ourselves ready. Robin and I dressed as we usually did, and I suppose Brenda did too but very differently from us. In spite of the warm weather, we wore jeans, t-shirts, and our faithful sneakers. Brenda wore short shorts, a skimpy confection of a blouse, and sandals. Even Mom looked askance at her attire but again said nothing. I doubted that she would ever let me leave the house showing that much skin! I assumed she didn't feel she had the authority to object so didn't. I was glad. So far Brenda had been in a pretty good mood, but we still had five days to go until she went home.

"Are those going to be comfortable to walk in?" asked Robin, looking skeptically at her footwear.

"Of course," she said as if it were a silly question.

We shrugged our shoulders.

Robin called Dave back and arranged for us to meet him at the coffee shop. For reasons known only to herself, she didn't want to meet at her house, though that's where he was now. I didn't inquire into the matter.

We got to the coffee shop about ten o'clock but had to wait another hour before Dave got there. He'd said he would come as soon as he had finished everything that Fiona needed doing, and apparently she had thought of a couple of more things. He arrived with Tanner, both of them on skateboards, and we finally ordered drinks.

"Matthew wants to come," said Dave. I thought I detected slight annoyance, but I could have been wrong. "He said he'd be here soon."

"Okay," we all acknowledged.

We had nowhere special to be, and most of the day in which to get there. While we waited for him, we caught up with each other—what we'd been doing since school got out.

"You, of course, have been busy breaking bones," said Tanner to me, grinning and giving me two thumbs up. "You're way ahead of everyone else for summer injuries."

Everyone laughed, but I knew I was blushing. I wasn't too happy with this particular claim to fame.

Matthew soon arrived. After he'd bought a cold drink, I introduced him to Brenda and we all left the store. Brenda had already checked Tanner out thoroughly. I don't think he was her type, but she seemed happy to flirt with him, and he with her. Her preference still seemed to lie with Dave, which I felt was to be expected but was disheartening all the same. When Matthew arrived, however, her eyes widened and she looked truly surprised. I wondered whether she thought that he, in particular, was good looking, whether she was surprised to find more than one cute guy in "Hicksville," as she'd once called my new home, or whether she was just surprised that they could be my friends. Probably all three.

The boys all had their skateboards but were content to walk with us while they had drinks in their hands. Dave seemed quieter than usual, not that he was ever exactly noisy. He seemed content to let everyone else carry the conversation, as I was, but he kept his attention fairly divided between everyone as usual. I know, because I kept track, *my* attention not fairly divided at all. I knew why *I* felt subdued—my side still hurt constantly and we'd be leaving in about a week for the rest of the summer—but I didn't know what was bothering Dave. And something certainly was, though he seemed to be trying to hide it.

Brenda did her best to keep both Dave and Matthew engaged in whatever she was saying. Dave was always polite, though he appeared absentminded; not like himself at all. Matthew energetically participated with her but seemed to look at me a lot of the time. I got a strong impression that he wanted me to realize he was entertaining Brenda for *my* sake, as if it was a sacrifice and he'd rather be talking to me. I was extremely grateful for his efforts and smiled my thanks. Resisting the desire to stay close to Dave, I tried to follow conversation the best I could, but I was tiring quickly and my side really did hurt. The day was beginning to feel a little surreal; so similar in many ways to the day Robin, Matthew, Tanner, and I had spent together but very different too. Just—weird.

We ended up in the small park downtown. Other kids the guys knew were there and we hung out with them for a while. The boys messed around on their boards most of the time while Brenda, Robin, and I sat in the shade of the central gazebo. It felt good to sit down as I was tired already and hurting more, but I didn't say anything. I didn't want sympathy.

After a while the other kids began to leave, and for a moment I thought our guys were going to go with them, but they returned to us. I have a feeling my relief was evident as, when leaving the gazebo, Dave came close and bumped shoulders gently with me, just like he used to. It had been a while since he'd done anything like that. It was extremely comforting.

We continued to walk toward Old Town and had reached the hardware store when Dave said, "You guys go ahead and I'll catch up. I'm just telling Cris to pick me up later at Robin's."

Everyone nodded and kept walking. I would have liked to have gone in with him if it wouldn't have looked odd. Instead, I hung back a little, bringing up the rear of our group. I hadn't seen Cris' truck around but assumed he must have parked off the main street. When I saw Dave approaching us again, I could tell something was wrong and fell back a little farther.

"Is everything okay?" I asked quietly.

"Yeah . . . I guess," he said but didn't look convinced of it. "Cris wasn't there."

"Did he leave early?" I asked.

"Yeah, something like that. I'll call him later." That's all he would say, but he seemed even more distracted the rest of the day.

"So . . . that's Douglas, huh?" said Brenda when we'd walked back through town again and settled at the taco place.

I hadn't kept track of most of the day's conversations, but a lot of what I *had* heard had sounded comparative in nature on Brenda's part, and half apologetic, half defensive on the part of Tanner, Robin, and even Matthew. Robin was looking weary and annoyed now, though the others still seemed concerned with Brenda's opinions.

"Where do you go to, you know, *really* shop? Like clothes and stuff. And what do you do for fun?"

I wanted to tell her that just hanging out with friends was fun enough but thought that I might be the only one that felt like that.

"Well, there's the theater and arcade over at Lowell," said Tanner. "If you can get there."

"And there's always Northfield," said Robin, making a sour face.

"What's at Northfield?" asked Brenda, curious in spite of, or maybe even because of the others' expressions.

"Snobs," said Robin immediately.

"Jerks," said Tanner.

Dave said nothing but was frowning. I wondered whether it was at the thought of what lay at Northfield or whatever else was bothering him.

Matthew, ever the diplomat, explained, "Northfield's a community surrounding a country club. You know . . . golf course, fancy community center with huge swimming pools. Stuff like that. I'm on a swim team and we sometimes have meets there. They have a youth center too, but . . ." he drew out the word, "we wouldn't exactly be welcome there. And they have a huge equestrian complex. It's cool, but we don't really go there either."

Everyone except Brenda turned to Dave as if needing some kind of validation for this statement, but he didn't appear to be paying attention.

"I'm gonna go call Cris," he said, getting up and walking outside.

I looked at Robin and she shrugged her shoulders. I wondered if she was as aware of his distraction as I was. If she didn't know what was going on with him, I was sure there was no way I would.

Brenda looked impatient and said, as if to clarify a point, "So there's, like, no mall or anything?"

Everyone else suddenly had the same expression. It was almost comical.

Finally, Matthew said, "Most people go to Sacramento if they're serious about shopping."

"Sacramento. Why have I heard of that before?" asked Brenda.

"Uh . . . it's the state capital," said Robin sarcastically, her eyes wide in disbelief.

"Oh yeah, huh. But no, that's not it." Brenda shook her head, oblivious to Robin's tone.

Tanner turned his head to hide a smile while Robin still looked incredulous. I felt a little bad for Brenda. She wasn't dumb at all; her interests and priorities were just very different.

"I know what it was!" she said, turning to me, her eyes lighting up. "That's where your mom said you went shopping at Christmas. Right?"

At that moment Dave walked back in. I'd kept an eye on him through the window and he looked agitated while talking on the phone. Now he just seemed distracted again. I wanted to ask him what was up, but as he hadn't told me before, I doubted he would tell me now.

"Can we go?" asked Brenda brightly, as if Sacramento were just a stroll down the street.

"Go where?" asked Dave, sitting down next to Robin.

"The mall," said Robin, trying to keep a straight face. "In Sacramento."

"Oh," said Dave, looking confused and obviously wondering what he'd missed. "I don't know. I can see if someone can drive some of us. If Dad drove the SUV, we'd probably all fit, but Angel won't drive it. When are you here until?"

Brenda brightened even more at the attentive question. "I have to leave Wednesday. At least, that's when my plane ticket's for." This last remark seemed like an odd thing to add and I wondered what was going on in her head.

"Hmm," he said and then looked around at us. "What do you think? Everyone in?"

"What about your brother?" asked Brenda, looking coy. "He can drive, can't he?"

Dave's expression noticeably changed, but I couldn't read it. "I'm not going to ask Cris to take us," he said, evenly but firmly.

Brenda looked disappointed but turned to me again and said, "Maybe Jen would want to take us."

Maybe she would, but I'm not going to ask her. "I don't know," I said.

My mother called shortly after this saying she was on her way, for us to stay where we were and she'd pick us up there. We said goodbye to the boys and I tried not to let panic well up. Surely I'd see Dave again before we left. Apart from the impending separation, there was something just—wrong. It had me on edge.

Please, let me see Dave again before we leave. . . .

As we got into the car, Mom asked, "Did you have a good day?"

Without missing a beat, Brenda said, "There's not a lot to do around here, is there? We were talking about how cool it would be to go to Sacramento. You know, to go shopping or something."

Robin looked flabbergasted and I felt myself turning red at her audacity. Leave it to Brenda to go straight for what she wanted.

"Shopping in Sacramento?" asked Mom. I looked away from her, out the window, not wanting any part of this plan. "I suppose we can see what we can do," she said uncertainly.

We dropped Robin at her house and continued home. Dad was there and would continue to be home, at least in the evenings, until we left for Los Angeles. He said he had no qualms about a proposed shopping trip.

"I'm going to the office on Monday or Tuesday anyway. I guess I could play chauffeur for the day. Who all's going?"

I figured I'd better speak up here. "We're not sure but maybe Matthew, Tanner, and Dave. And Robin, of course."

"Hmm," he hummed, looking stern as he considered.

My feelings on the matter were tangled. I didn't care for the plan—at least, not now and under these circumstances. It felt like my fault that everyone was trying so hard to keep Brenda, *my* guest, happy. It seemed forced and unnatural. On the other hand, it was another chance to hang out with Dave before being banished to Los Angeles.

"Well, I can't take everybody, but I can certainly take you and Robin." Brenda looked pleased, but I had a feeling Dad was hoping the boys wouldn't go.

After dinner, Brenda bugged me into calling Dave to tell him what was going on. Supremely embarrassed, I did.

"Hey," he answered quietly, as if he was thinking of or doing something else. "What's up?"

Feeling even more awkward in having to explain my reason for calling, I stumbled over my tongue a little. "Um . . . shopping . . . Sacramento . . . Dad says he can't drive everybody. I mean, he can drive, but not everybody can go. I mean . . . he doesn't mind . . . I don't think . . . but not everybody would fit. In our car. If everyone wanted to go, that is. . . ."

Brenda rolled her eyes at me.

"Yeah . . . about that. Dad's busy all week," said Dave. "And Angel's visiting family down south until Thursday."

"Oh . . . Brenda leaves on Wednesday, so Dad said Monday or Tuesday."

"Hmm. I'll see what Matt's up to. We might not be able to go."

I felt that wouldn't necessarily be a bad thing. "That's okay. You guys would probably be bored anyway. Right?"

Brenda kicked me hard in the shin, pointed to me, then pretended to shoot herself in the head.

"I'll call you back when I find out anything, okay?"

"Okay," I said, rubbing my leg.

"See ya."

"Bye," I said, ending the call. "*Ow!*"

The next day was Father's Day. We just hung around the house and Dad barbecued. I lunged Remmy in the lower corral while Brenda watched, but she was bored. I hadn't heard from Dave by early evening and felt relieved and sad. Brenda was good about not bugging me to call him again, but I could tell it was on her mind from her rather petulant behavior all day and the way she kept looking at me accusingly. Dad didn't bring it up at all and I'm sure he was hoping the whole plan had been dropped.

Dave called about nine o'clock.

"So, I guess we can go tomorrow. If you want," he said.

He didn't sound enthusiastic and I wished I had a good excuse to veto the whole idea. For a second, I thought about pleading fatigue and pain from my injuries, but I was actually feeling much better. It would be too hard to lie, especially to Brenda.

"Okay," I said, not sure what else to say.

"Yeah . . . so . . . we'll meet you there, I guess. Same place as last time. I'm not too sure when, though. I'll call when we get there, okay?"

"Okay," I said again, feeling lame.

Dad needed to leave early, "To make it worth going in," he said, and Mom decided at the last minute to go as well. That really threw me as, awkward as I already felt about this excursion, having my mother escorting us certainly wasn't going to make it any better. I suspected my dad had something to do with her decision.

We picked Robin up and got to the mall before the stores were even open. So we wasted time getting coffee and then wandered around with Mom for a while. That wasn't bad, but when Dave finally called saying they had arrived, she followed us toward the main entrance.

I thought she was planning on accompanying us all day, but when we got close, she said, "I'll go my own way and meet up with you girls later. Okay? Have fun."

I gave her a grateful look. "Thanks, Mom." Perhaps I would survive this day after all.

The guys were sitting on the low wall outside, waiting for us. I was surprised to see Cris; he'd obviously been prevailed on to drive but didn't look happy about it. Then again, I'd never seen him look happy about anything.

The day turned out to be a very different experience than my first mall trip with them. And it was a very different group, too—much smaller with no real purpose in being there except, I suppose, to entertain Brenda.

Tanner and Matthew were the only ones who appeared to be in a good mood throughout the day. Cris was even more withdrawn and sullen-looking than usual. He trailed some distance behind us most of the time, looking depressed, and disappeared altogether from time to time. I probably wouldn't have noticed as much if Dave had been his normal, upbeat self, but he still seemed distracted and was obviously keeping an eye on his brother.

Brenda was whiny and seemed to be in a mood to find fault with everything, comparing the mall, the stores, the merchandise, and even sales people and other shoppers to what she was "used to." It was a mood I was quite familiar with. It was also obvious to me, though I hoped not to the others, that she was peeved by both Dave and Cris' lack of attention and response to her.

Robin looked progressively more dangerous as time passed. I guessed she was running out of patience with Brenda's current demanding and snooty behavior. I was uncomfortable the whole time, feeling or at least imagining everyone else's dissatisfaction with the day so far and anything else bothering them, and wishing my friends weren't being subjected to Brenda's dark side.

Tanner maintained his usual level of goofiness, if anything acting even more silly than normal. Matthew was the hero of the day, as far as I was concerned, by being unstintingly good-natured with Brenda and even purposefully finding things to ridicule with her or ask her opinion on, simply to distract her. I knew he was doing it deliberately by the droll looks he gave me, making me wonder if he was, in fact, doing it just for me.

When we'd been there a few hours, I found him walking next to me. The others had moved ahead, except for Cris. I didn't know where he had gone.

"Thank you!" I whispered to him. "I don't think she means to be so . . ."
I tried to think of the right word.

"Needy? Peevish? Despotic?" he offered lightly.

I laughed quietly. "All of the above."

We walked in silence for a moment, then he said, "Are you all right? You
look really tired. Is your side hurting?"

My side had been bothering me for at least an hour and I already felt
tired, but I hadn't wanted to say anything. "Yes, a little," I admitted.

"Hey, you guys," said Matthew loudly, startling me. The others stopped
and looked back at us. "We should go and sit down for a while," he said,
pointing toward a seating area.

I blushed hotly. Dave looked at me intently, his expression at first concerned then irritated. Definitely irritated. Was he upset with me?

"Why don't we go get something to eat?" said Cris' voice from behind me.

I hadn't noticed where he had come from. Everyone thought it was an
excellent idea, especially Robin and Tanner. Somehow along the way Dave replaced Matthew next to me while Cris walked slightly ahead on my other side.

"Are you okay?" Dave asked quietly as we walked along.

"I'm a little tired," I admitted to him also. It seemed pointless not to.

"I'm sorry," he said, frowning. "I kind of forgot."

"No . . . no," I said, not wanting him, of all people, to feel bad. "I'm fine.
Really!"

He's not mad at me! Was he annoyed with himself? Not for the first
time, I wished I could read him better.

"You should have said something," he said, then seemed to be frowning
at the back of Matthew's head.

Maybe he thought I *had* said something to his friend. Had he been mad
that he wasn't the one to notice that I wasn't feeling great? Or just annoyed
that it was Matthew? Or something else altogether? I'd probably never know.
There was so much I just didn't *get* about him but fervently wanted to.

When we reached the food court, we purchased our favorite snacks and
found a place to sit together. Except Cris. I didn't see him buy anything to
eat, but he wandered a short distance away and was talking on his phone. It
occurred to me that he was looking thinner. He hadn't looked at me or said
anything directly to me all day, either, but there probably wasn't anything
in that. I did wonder if he was still mad at me for the barrel racing incident.

Probably. He'd already proven he had a long memory and was capable of being vengeful. I shivered at the memory.

Oh well . . . if I get a chance, I'll apologize. Again.

Dave made a point of staying by my side as we got our food and then sat next to me while we ate. Those moments of being close to him were the best I had all day. When everyone had finished eating, we all got up to go. All except Dave.

"Maybe you should sit a little longer," he said to me, obviously planning on staying too.

I felt a thrill of pleasure at the thought and probably turned red again. But before I had a chance to sit back down, Brenda threw herself into the closest seat.

"Well, *fine*. I guess I'll just stay too."

The others stood around looking indecisive.

Before anyone else could say anything, I said, "No, really. I'm fine now. Let's go." I smiled at Dave and moved away from the table. The last thing I wanted was a scene over a situation I had caused.

A moment later Brenda moved too, but she didn't look happy. I realized that it must appear as if I was getting a certain amount of unfair attention. I wished she could understand that it wasn't like that, but I doubted that she could and there was no way I could say anything about it with everyone else there. I'd just have to try to avoid these situations from now until she was gone. Very disheartening.

Dave remained expressionless but stood and followed us. I hoped to find him walking next to me again but, except for brief moments, it didn't happen. I couldn't help wondering, if we'd been able to stay and sit together alone, would he have confided in me? Was that one of the reasons he had wanted to stay? He was usually so open and seemed so confident; it troubled me that *he* was troubled.

Robin planted herself next to me as we walked, letting the boys deal with Brenda. "What's *with* her?" she asked, sounding exasperated. "She's *really* starting to get on my nerves."

"She's a little . . ." I still wasn't sure what to say. Saying anything negative about a friend just felt wrong, even if it was true.

"Self-absorbed?" asked Robin.

"Yes, I guess she is a little," I admitted. After a moment, I asked, "What's up with Dave?" If anyone would know, she would.

She frowned at me. "What about him?"

"Do you know if something's bothering him?" I asked. "He seems so . . . distracted lately."

She shook her head dismissively. "No, I don't think so. He hasn't said anything. You're probably imagining it. You worry too much. Even Dave says so."

"Yes, I know," I said, laughing a little. But I knew what I'd observed, and though he hadn't said much, what he *had* said lately, and the way he'd said it, reinforced my opinion.

The afternoon dragged by and I was relieved when my mom called to see if we were ready to go. I didn't even ask the others, I just said, "Yes!"

Dave, Matthew, and Brenda were the only ones who had bought anything besides food, Dave buying a poster for Tanner that he had geeked over, and Matthew buying a video game. Brenda made several purchases but didn't seem satisfied with any of them when we got home. I ignored her attitude and looked forward to Wednesday.

There was only one more day to get through, but it seemed like an eternity. I went out to feed and groom Remmy early and then we hung out around the house. I was even glad that Dave hadn't arrived with Tom, but about ten o'clock I heard his motorcycle come up the street and then behind the house. Dad frowned and went outside to see who it was. He came back in looking disapproving. I wondered if Dave had worn his helmet, but there was no way I was going to go and check.

After Dave arrived, Brenda decided that it was a perfect day for sunbathing. Perhaps it was, but I mistrusted her motives. Figuring it wouldn't hurt to get a little start on a tan, and not having anything better to suggest, I followed her upstairs to change. I put on some shorts and a tank top from the previous summer, surprised that they seemed to fit differently now. Brenda emerged from her room wearing a bikini similar to the one she'd worn to the pool, with a sarong barely covering her hips and thighs.

She's wearing that? Here? Now?

I thought I'd been pretty patient with her, but now she was pushing the boundaries of my good will. Still, she was my guest. And she'd be leaving

tomorrow. I felt guilty that I was looking forward to it so much and decided not to object. I did, however, try to convince her that sunbathing in the front of the house made more sense than the back.

"We can use the driveway," I pointed out.

"But people would see us from the road," she objected.

"Nobody ever goes down our road," I exaggerated, sure that had nothing to do with her motives anyway.

She thought for a moment. "It'll probably be dustier there, too."

"It's more likely to be dustier in the back," I insisted. "Remmy kicks up a lot of dirt." *Not to mention whatever Tom and Dave are doing.* But it wouldn't be wise to say that. "Not to mention the flies."

"But the driveway is hard. I'd rather lie on the grass."

She had me there. I had to agree that our hard-won back lawn would be much more comfortable. Conceding to her superior logic, I gritted my teeth—in spirit, at least—grabbed a couple of our big beach towels and my sketchbook, and followed her downstairs.

Twenty-four hours. I can do this!

Dave looked up as we descended the back porch steps, did a noticeable double-take and paused before turning his back slightly and continuing his work. From that moment on we might not have been there for all the notice he gave us. I was glad and kind of proud of him. Brenda was, if not beautiful, quite attractive and definitely had a figure I was envious of. She positioned her towel so she could look in the direction of "the construction" whenever she opened her eyes. I enjoyed looking at him too and couldn't keep from smiling every time I did.

After about half an hour, I moved to the shade of the porch. I was sketching: Brenda, Remmy, the unfinished barn, Tom and Dave. After another half hour, Brenda was noticeably pink.

"You'd better put some sunscreen on," I said.

She sat up, squinted at me, and sighed heavily. "I'm going inside," she said, getting up.

She tromped into the kitchen and I followed, still smiling. The rest of the day passed in a mundane manner, which I didn't mind at all. I could handle a few more hours and hoped the boredom was making Brenda anxious to go back to her supposedly more appealing life in the city.

At dinner, Dad looked at Brenda and said, "So, this is pretty different than LA, isn't it?"

She nodded. "It sure is."

"I expect you're looking forward to getting home," observed my mom.

Brenda shrugged her shoulders. "Actually, I was wondering if I could just stay here with you? Since you're going to LA on Sunday anyway."

I almost choked on my chicken and my eyeballs felt like they would burst out of their sockets, sudden pain in my side bringing tears to them. I turned them on Mom hoping she'd at least prevaricate.

She did. Looking first at me in concern, then back to Brenda, she said, "Well, honey, you've got your plane ticket already and I'm sure your parents will be expecting you."

"Oh, they won't mind," she said as if that was all there was to say on the matter.

I couldn't shake my head without Brenda seeing, but continued to plead "No!" to my mother with my eyes. Since I was wearing my old, chunky-rimmed glasses, I wasn't sure how effective it was. I had no expectations of spending more time with Dave before we left, but it certainly wouldn't happen if Brenda stayed. I wouldn't allow it. I would do whatever she wanted while staying with her this summer but, selfish or not, I didn't want to give up my last few days here to her.

Dad looked like he was going to offer his opinion, but Mom prevented him by saying, "If it were Allison in the same situation, I'd be wanting to see her, even after only a week. I know I'm going to miss her terribly this summer when we're gone. I'm sure your mother's anxious to see you too."

Brenda looked like she would contradict this, but Mom jumped in again. "You know, we won't be seeing Allison for quite a while too, and we have some family things to take care of, so I think it's best if we keep to the original plan."

Dad seemed to accept this reasoning and I tried not to be too obvious in my relief. Brenda didn't look like she understood but could tell it was the final word.

I slept well that night, happily got up early to feed Remmy and help Brenda pack, and then put extra effort into conversation and general attention to her until we parted company at the airport later that day. Exhausted, I let out a deep sigh when we reached the car again.

"Has it been very trying?" asked my mom, her eyes laughing with understanding.

"A little," I grinned. "Thanks, Mom."

She smiled, not needing to ask for what. "I didn't know whether you were going to try to see your friends again . . . before we go."

"Oh . . . um . . . I don't have any plans." Which was true. *Hopes, but no plans.*

I hoped we'd be home before Dave left the house—I hadn't seen him that day at all—but we weren't. I spent the evening lunging Remmy and enjoying his company. I groomed him the best I could, especially his tail as it didn't take as much effort, but it was difficult as I couldn't put much strength into it without hurting. I was just wondering, again, if I'd see Dave anymore at all before we left when he called.

"Hey." His soft voice sent a thrill through me as it always did.

"Hi," I said, feeling shy.

"Tom's going to be busy for a few days working at another job, so I probably won't get over there until you leave." My heart fell, dismayed. "But we're talking about a beach trip on Friday. Do you want to see if you can come?" The same pathetic heart rose again. "Robin's going . . . maybe Jessie and Stacie. I'm not sure. We'll be camping before that, but Angel volunteered to drive you guys . . . I mean, girls."

My heart thumped hard at the prospect and I said, a little breathlessly, "I'll ask. I . . . I'd like to . . ."

"Call me back," he said.

"Okay."

When I asked my parents during dinner, my dad had his negative expression firmly in place as he said, "I don't think so Allie. We're leaving in just a few days. Besides," his expression softened, "I'm not going to see you for a while. I'm going to miss you."

And I'm going to miss Dave . . . my friends. . . .

I hadn't thought much about missing my parents, but I supposed I would. I'd just miss someone else more. I was glad I didn't voice this. It sounded much better coming from Mom.

"She's going to miss her friends, honey," she said gently. "It'll probably be the last time she sees them until . . . well, until school starts."

Ugh! That's forever! Tears sprang readily to my eyes and I battled to subdue them before they became noticeable. I think I was successful.

Dad frowned and ate in silence for a couple of minutes. I picked at my food and held my breath. *No pleading. Remember?*

"I don't know," he said, finally. "The beach?"

I wondered if he was thinking along a similar thought line to me. I was remembering what Dave looked like dressed in nothing but board shorts and water. But I doubted if Dad was thinking of *Dave's* appearance.

"Do you think she should be going in the water yet?" he asked Mom, pretty much confirming what I suspected.

"I won't swim," I offered. "Maybe just go in up to my knees. That way I don't even have to wear a bathing suit, just shorts. Much more comfortable."

There. That should help.

Apparently it did. "Who else is going? Not just kids, right? Somebody besides Cris is driving?"

"They're already going to be there . . . camping and surfing, I think. Robin's going, and maybe some other girls. Angel will take us."

"And bring you home?"

"Yes, Dad." *Honestly!*

After another few moments, he said, "Okay, but don't make plans for Saturday, all right? You're mine!" He said this last in his "monster" voice that used to make me squeal when I was little.

I tried to laugh as I thought it was what he wanted, but I really just felt relieved. "Okay, Daddy. Thank you!"

When I called Dave a little later and told him my good news, he took it in stride, sounding happy that I could go, but I was sure it wouldn't have been the end of his world if I'd said I couldn't. I could barely sleep that night, though. I hadn't been so excited about seeing him or doing anything since the barbecue and rodeo at his home. It felt like I'd come full circle in many ways, yet so much had changed! Things were so different from when I'd first met Dave—completely topsy-turvy and unpredictable. And not just my day-to-day life. *I* was different.

I was thinking exactly the same thing as we stood on a cliff overlooking the ocean, waves rolling and crashing, sometimes carrying their riders

safely all the way in toward shore, sometimes flipping them sideways or upside down, then crashing on and engulfing them. That's what Dave had done to me, to my heart and my life. It was a constant thrill ride, exciting me in ways I'd never imagined, except for those times when the whole world seemed to crash around me because of him. Because of my feelings for him.

"There's Dave!" yelled Jessie, pointing toward the water south of where we stood.

Robin squinted in that direction. "No, that's not him. Maybe that . . ." she said, pointing somewhere else. "No, that's not him either."

If they couldn't recognize him from this distance, I was sure I wouldn't be able to at all, even squinting through my glasses. Then I saw a surfer riding a wave as if he no more than skateboarded down a sidewalk. I'd seen enough surfing in my life to know that these waves were not very large. Still, it would take skill to ride them to their fullest potential. The surfer I watched cut effortlessly back through the wave a couple of times, then rode it toward shore as close as he could without getting off his board. I couldn't make out his features, but his general height and build, and the easy grace with which he maneuvered his board was so familiar.

"Is that Cris?" I hazarded, pointing slightly north.

The others all peered in that direction.

"I think you're right," said Robin slowly. "And there's Dave! For sure! Yes, there's Henry. And Tanner! And that must be Mr. Caldera!"

The five of them were paddling back out to the lineup during the lull, and we jumped and waved whenever one of them seemed to be facing our direction. Dave finally caught sight of us and pointed to the cliffs where we stood. They all waved and we squealed and yelled like demented fans demanding the notice of celebrities.

We stood and watched from the cliff for a long time. In the acquiring of new interests this year, I'd almost forgotten how much I loved the ocean. The sun and off-shore wind in my face and the sound of the waves in my ears; I knew and loved it so well. Until this past year, I would have said it was my favorite place in the world. Now, that was wherever Dave happened to be. To be watching him in my favorite element, to be able to be with him in my favorite environment, was my idea of perfect bliss.

Angel eventually got tired of standing and suggested we continue to the beach where we'd spend the rest of the day. The guys would meet us there soon. The town and beach were very different from the areas I was used to in Los Angeles, although the boardwalk did remind me a little of the pier and ocean fronts I had grown up around.

After we'd parked, Robin and Jessie went ahead to stake our claim with beach chairs, Frisbees, and a large umbrella. Angel and I carried a couple of big blankets and as many towels as we could. Stevey carried plastic buckets, spades, and rakes. Unfortunately, he kept dropping things but wouldn't let me help him, which made our progress rather slow. The others had the umbrella set up by the time we got to the chosen site and together we spread out the blankets.

I wouldn't have minded exploring the boardwalk, but we'd found a decent spot on the beach and Stevey and I were determined to protect and defend the territory against pirate and sea monster alike until the menfolk joined us. Angel settled into the shade and, not wanting to leave her completely alone, we stayed fairly close by, along the water's edge, just letting the shallow surf chase our bare feet.

After a while, Stevey wanted to return to Angel so I walked back to her with him. The guys arrived and found us soon after, and Robin and Jessie came back up from the surf to greet them. Mr. Caldera joined Angel under the large umbrella, and the older boys returned to Angel's car to bring the coolers and body boards. They broke into the food immediately on their return, obviously famished.

"So, how do you like it?" asked Dave after a few bites of a sandwich. "How does it compare to your LA beaches?"

I gazed at him; I'd barely been able to keep my eyes off him since he'd arrived. He and the others had shed their wetsuits, their tanned bodies making me feel pale and sickly by comparison. His hair was almost dry already, glowing slightly pink around the edges.

Do you even know about those highlights?

Dave's grin became a smirk, his eyes twinkling as he waved a hand in front of me, his brows raised in question.

"Oh . . . um . . . perfect." I couldn't help that it came out as a whisper. "It's . . . perfect." Blushing furiously, I was glad Stevey was nearby for me to redirect my attention to.

"So, Brenda left on Wednesday?" Dave asked, conversationally.

"Who's Brenda?" asked Jessie.

"Allie's friend from Los Angeles," said Robin, without a trace of rancor. "Or Beverly Hills," said Tanner, rolling his eyes.

"Not exactly," I said gently, though I guess she was living closer to that lifestyle now than she used to. From what she'd said, some of her friends were actually wealthy enough to shop Rodeo Drive, but it didn't impress me the way it did her. I decided not to share any of that, though.

"How did you guys ever get to be friends, anyway?" asked Robin. "You're so nothing alike."

It was one of those inexplicable things there was really no answer for.

"We've been friends a long time," I said. Then knew I needed to defend her. "I didn't really have any other friends . . . before I moved here. People . . ." I felt uncomfortable admitting this but felt it had to be said. "People used to pick on me . . . a lot. Brenda always stood up to them. She was always there."

"Why did people pick on you?" asked Tanner, frowning.

I just shrugged. Did I have an answer for that? Nobody else seemed to need an explanation. I thought Robin and Jessie could probably remember how they felt about me at the beginning of the year. I wasn't sure about Dave; I'd known him almost a year now and still couldn't figure out what he saw or felt when he looked at me. A goofy sister? A dorky friend? Someone less physically gifted than himself that he felt needed protection? As for Cris, no one ever seemed to know what he was thinking. I decided not to attempt an answer.

When Dave, Tanner, and Henry finished eating, they grabbed the Frisbees and ran toward a relatively unpopulated section of sand not too far from our day camp.

"Don't go sweeming for a hour!" Angel called after them. "Quique especially!" They all called back to let her know they'd heard. Cris rose up leisurely from where he'd been sitting in the sand and followed them.

"Come on, let's go!" said Robin excitedly, finishing some chips and brushing her hands off on her thighs.

She looked so cute in her bathing suit; not quite as skinny as I was, just more proportionate. Jessie, on the other hand, was certainly more well-endowed than either of us but seemed unselfconscious about it, unlike most of the other shapely girls in our year. I sure wished I could fill out a bathing suit the way she did, but I'd probably be too shy to let much show anyway. True to my word to my dad, I didn't have a bathing suit on, just shirt and shorts. It had been a simple choice to make anyway; I didn't want to waste the time I had left with Dave being overly concerned about the way I looked.

Not quite able to run or throw Frisbees, I held Stevey's hand as we walked to the wet sand with the buckets and utensils. Digging in wet sand was more my speed anyway. *Weak ankles . . . klutzy tendencies . . . firm, wet sand definitely much safer.*

We had built and rebuilt several lopsided edifices when Dave joined us, apparently thinking we needed help. He began constructing a several-storied palace before a wave made it up the beach far enough to demolish part of it. Both he and Stevey laughed and began to repair the damage. Soon Henry and Tanner had joined in, helping to race against the incoming waves. I was happy to sit back and watch. Robin and Jessie were in the water with body boards and appeared to be having a blast. Cris dove into waves near the girls for a while, then walked back to lay in the sand near the blankets and umbrella where Angel and his dad relaxed.

"Where's your bathing suit?" Dave asked, narrowing his eyes at me.

Henry immediately reached out and pulled my shirt up a little, happening to lift it on my injured side.

"Henry!" growled Dave, warningly. But he reached out toward my side all the same. The wounds were healing nicely and were no longer bandaged, but they were very noticeable. "Ow," he said, frowning. "Does it still hurt?"

"No, the scrapes don't hurt much," I said. I gently liberated my shirt from Henry's hand and covered my side again. "But my ribs still hurt . . . if I do too much."

He nodded, then went back to his construction.

It had been about an hour since we'd gotten there and I started to feel like I needed another layer of sunscreen. I figured Stevey did too. He was looking sleepy, yawning and almost rubbing sand in his eyes.

"I'm going to take Stevey back up," I said.

Dave looked up briefly and nodded to acknowledge what I'd said, but went right back to building.

"Stevey, let's go. Okay?"

Stevey ignored me. I held my hand out to him, but he crammed his hands between his crossed legs, out of my reach, and looked away. I sat quietly for a moment, wondering what to do next. I thought about how I'd seen Dave and

Cris interact with their brother and finally said, "I'm going to go see Angel. Do you want to come, Stevey?"

He gave no indication that he'd heard me but stood and began walking toward the blankets and big umbrella. I walked with him. When we got there, Angel put sunscreen on him while I liberally dosed myself. I was going to try to avoid getting burned this summer, especially today.

It was such a beautiful day: warm, but a steady breeze kept the sun bearable. Stevey found some snacks and ate for a little while but eventually lay down and fell asleep under the umbrella near Angel. Cris lay on his stomach in the sand close by and seemed to be fast asleep. I was thinking of going back toward the water when Dave came and spread a towel out between his big brother and me.

He sat down, smiled at me, and asked, "Okay?"

"Mmhmm," I assented, feeling so much more than just okay.

We sat for a while in companionable silence, watching our friends romping and Boogie-boarding in the water. Then Dave lay back, his arm under his head. Mr. Caldera had been lying, perhaps sleeping, under the umbrella. But now he got up and ran down to the surf near Henry, diving into a wave and reappearing just beyond his son.

Angel, who had been browsing through a magazine, said in a whisper, "I theenk I weel go een the water alsoh. You are staying here?"

Dave is here? I am here! I nodded.

"*Bueno.* You weel watch Esteban. *Si?*"

"*Si,*" I whispered back and smiled.

Her eyes crinkled up as she smiled back and reached over to gently pat my arm. Then she quietly got up and walked toward the water. I looked back at Dave to find him observing me from under half-closed eyelids, a calm, reflective expression on his face. Something about it instantly made me feel strange. Then he smiled the most amazing smile at me: beautiful in its contentment. Sighing deeply, he closed his eyes and was still.

Blissfully watching over the sleeping boys—most of my vigilance given to Dave, of course—I felt almost overwhelmed with thankfulness at the opportunity to be here with him, able to gaze at him to my heart's content.

I remembered the day I first saw him, how much older than myself he'd seemed and a little wild, dangerous. I thought that he had changed somewhat in appearance, though it was hard to define exactly how. Slightly taller, a little broader through the shoulders perhaps. And familiarity had certainly informed my perception of him in general. But he was still very much the same. Gorgeous. Unreachable. Untouchable—for someone like me.

And I still felt like I didn't really know him, but I wanted to; to know who he was inside and not just see him as some kind of perfect, unattainable idol. There were more things I knew *about* him, to be sure, but I had even more questions now than at the start. He still surprised me all the time and when it came right down to it, he was right; I didn't trust him. Not that I thought he'd ever purposely do me harm, but I continued to doubt his motivation, his true feelings, or whether he had any at all—for me at least. It was plain that he cared for me, but it was in such an easy-going, complaisant manner that sometimes it hurt almost as much as feeling ignored by him.

Sometimes.

And sometimes he *did* seem to forget about me as if I truly were his sibling; someone he cared about, perhaps felt an obligation to watch out for, but with no other emotions attached. I kept telling myself that it was enough, and a part of me wished it was. But it never really had been.

The breeze blew his hair gently around his face, across his forehead and around his cheeks. He was so close I could see the fine hair of his forearm ruffled by it, and occasionally grains of sand danced across the smooth skin of his chest and stomach. I wished I could take pictures of him—as creepy as that would probably seem to him—or that I had brought my sketchbook so that I could try to permanently record his appearance and these moments. Instead, I had to memorize them. The line of his jaw and chin. The curve of his dark lashes and eyebrows. His hands—nicely shaped yet already scarred and calloused from years of hard work and even harder play. His intriguing lips. I couldn't help a certain amount of musing over them. *What would it be like—?*

And then he groaned. Not a weak moan as if slightly uncomfortable, but a harsh, strangled, scared-sounding groan that startled me badly. His whole body twitched, his head jerking to the side, and he groaned again.

Cris propped himself up on an elbow and reached out to gently but firmly grab his brother's shoulder.

"Hey!" he said quietly, a tender tone to his voice as if speaking to a child.

Dave sat up with a start and looked around as if disoriented, breathing a little heavily. Then he squinted out to sea. After a moment, he pulled his knees up and wrapped his arms around them. Cris got up and rummaged in the coolers, pulling out several items.

"Hey," he said again, this time in his normal voice. When Dave finally looked at him, he said, "Catch," and threw him bottled water and a sandwich. "Do you want anything?" he asked me, coldly I thought.

I shook my head. "No . . . thanks."

He went back to sit where he'd been lying before and the brothers ate in silence. Stevey awoke and sat up soon after, yawning and looking adorable. I helped him find something he wanted to eat and then sat back where I had been before. Well, maybe just a *little* closer to Dave.

He looked at me and smiled, seeming reassured and content once again. Then his smile widened and the mischievous look came into his eyes. "Hey Cris, what do you think?" He looked at his brother and then back at me. "I think she looks really cute in those glasses."

Cris looked briefly at me, saying nothing, but shook his head and looked back out to the water. Then he stood up unhurriedly and walked toward it.

Déjà vu. Except Cris had called Dave an idiot for some reason on that first day.

Dave shrugged his shoulders at me. "*I* think they look cute. You should keep 'em." He got up and ran after his brother, tackling him as they both reached the waves.

I felt like my whole body was blushing. Full circle indeed. And upside down, inside out, head over heels. Completely. Soon the guys were playing with their younger brother and Tanner, the girls joining in the fun. I dosed Stevey and myself with more sunscreen, then walked with him back toward the water to paddle. Every moment of this day seemed so precious. The memory of it was going to have to sustain me for a long time.

The next morning, the morning before we would leave for Los Angeles, Dave called.

"Are you at home?"

"Yes, I—"

"Have you seen Cris?"

"No, not since—"

"I'm coming over."

"Okay—"

"See you in a minute."

"O—"

. . . .

Perplexed but excited, I made sure I wasn't looking any weirder than normal—nothing stuck in my teeth, not too much hair sticking out at right angles to my head—then went to wait on the front porch. After a few minutes but much quicker than should have been possible, I heard and then saw Dave approaching fast along our road. He came from the direction of Bar 8. I walked out to meet him and he came to an abrupt and dusty halt just off the road, right in front of the house.

"He's gone," he said, sounding a little choked. The sound of his voice matched the anguished expression on his face.

"What do you mean, 'He's gone'? Gone where? Why?"

He sighed heavily and pounded his fist angrily and repeatedly against his thigh. He didn't answer me right away, looking down the street in the direction of the highway, as if Cris might have gone that way. I wanted to reprimand him for not wearing his helmet again but thought better of it. He looked terribly worried and like he hadn't slept much. Trying to soothe his fears somehow and just listening to him seemed more important right now.

"I'm sure he's not really *gone*. Why would he go? And where?"

"You don't understand," he said, a little impatiently. "He and my dad, they haven't been getting along. Not for a long time. Ever since . . . well . . . things happened a while ago. My brother, Ric . . . and then other . . . stuff. This year's been the worst between them. Dad has plans, and Cris was pretty much going along with them. But recently . . . I don't know . . . he's been even more unhappy than before. He and Dad got into it bad late last night. I thought it was just about basketball, but it's not."

"Basketball?" I asked, confused. I knew Cris was supposed to be really good at it, but the season had been over for a long time.

"He's supposed to play basketball. There are scholarships in it. *Big* scholarships if you're good enough. And everyone says that Cris is. We knew there were scouts already interested in him, and that was confirmed this year even though Cris wasn't playing his best. His heart just wasn't in it, you know? So that's one thing Dad's been on him for . . . his attitude toward it . . . and other stuff too. He's supposed to go for a big scholarship. Dad's hoping for

UCLA because that's where he went, but he thinks Cris could even get into Berkeley or Stanford. He mostly just wants to make sure he goes to a really good school, I think, and hopes that he can stay in California to do it. The scholarship would help pay for it. And he's supposed to major in business, but Cris says it's not what he wants to do."

"What does he want to do?" I asked quietly, fragments of conversations nagging at me but affording no illumination.

"Dad . . . Dad never gives him a chance to say. Like he doesn't want to hear it. Then Cris gets mad and clams up. He won't even talk to me about it. I think he just doesn't want me getting in the middle of it, you know? Things usually calm down and even out again, but this time. . . ."

Dave looked so worried, I wanted to reach out and smooth the creases above his nose, the exaggerated curve in his eyebrows.

"I woke up last night . . ." He swallowed, as if at a bad memory. "I heard something so I got up. I thought maybe it was Stevey . . . he doesn't always sleep through the night . . . but it was coming from Cris' room. So I went over there to see what he was doing."

Now he looked very upset, his hands working the handlebars of his motorcycle as if he could wring the concern out of his mind.

"He was packing Ric's old army kit bag as if he was going somewhere. So I asked him, but he denied it. Said he couldn't sleep and was just getting his laundry together. But then he was gone this morning. I went looking for him, but there was no sign of him; no note in his room, truck's gone and the kit bag too. And he's turned his phone off. I can't even leave him a message."

He looked so distressed it made my heart hurt. I resisted the impulse to try to say something placating. I didn't know how he felt and wasn't going to pretend I did. But right now I felt less concern for Cris than anger at what appeared to be selfishness on his part and at how that was hurting Dave.

Finally, trying to turn his thoughts a little, I said, "Maybe he just needs time alone. Don't you think he'll come home when he's ready?"

He swallowed and his eyes were starting to look a little red and bright. I could hardly stand it anymore and fervently wished he was my boyfriend just so I wouldn't feel so awkward; wanting so badly to comfort him but afraid to even touch his hand.

"Remember when we walked downtown the other day, and Cris wasn't at work?"

I nodded.

"Well, his boss said he'd quit. He hadn't worked there in over a month, but he never told anybody. He's been going somewhere else when we thought he was at the hardware store. Dad doesn't even know about that. But he thinks he's doing drugs or something. He's even asked him a few times if that's why he's so depressed, why he doesn't care about anything. But then they just argue again. And Cris doesn't tell him anything. I don't believe it . . . it can't be possible. I'd know, I'm sure of it."

I was shocked, but couldn't say anything. It didn't seem likely, but I had little knowledge and no experience of that subject. Could it be possible? I'd have to think about it later.

"When Ric was alive," Dave continued in a low voice, "Dad wanted him to go to college, too . . . to learn business and management, and then help him run the ranch so he could take it over some day. Ric always said he would, but he wanted to do other things first. He wanted to go places, meet people, and Cris knew what he was planning all along. They were really close. Ric figured he'd join the army, travel, get some college while he was in there, maybe put in a couple of tours, then get out, finish college, and settle down at the ranch. Dad wasn't happy about it, but . . . well . . . you'd have to have known Ric. He was really easy-going, you know? Everybody loved him, and he'd do anything for you, but once he'd made up his mind about something, there was no turning him from it. He was always good-natured about it, but firm.

"So Dad eventually gave in . . . even became really proud of his decision. What we didn't know until after the accident is that Cris had planned on doing the same thing, so he could join him. Shit. They probably don't even allow that. But that's what Cris' plan had been."

His jaw was working hard again, a look of concentrated effort on his face. He appeared to be holding back tears then confirmed it by angrily wiping an arm across his eyes. "*Damn it,*" he swore softly.

It finally dawned on me why he was so concerned. I almost blurted it out but realized Dave didn't need to hear it spoken out loud.

Cris . . . why would you do this? Why this way?

"Can he do that?" I asked quietly.

Dave blew out through his mouth, obviously trying to control his emotions, and then wiped at his eyes again. "He's almost eighteen. Then he can

do what he wants. And I haven't kept track, but he's probably got enough units to graduate. I know he's taken exams early and took extra courses, did extra work. Why else would he do that?"

I stood quietly, not knowing what to say but willing to wait as long as he needed me to. My hands had found their way to the handlebar closest to me and rested lightly there. I guess I just wanted to feel physically connected to him somehow. I watched the sunlight dance off his hair, the slight pinkish tint on the ends glowing in its magical way, until I realized he was staring at my hands. I removed them from the handlebar self-consciously and he looked up into my face. The creases between his brows were gone, and his eyes had almost cleared, but they searched mine until I felt myself blushing and trying to regulate my breathing.

"You really have to leave tomorrow?" he asked softly, and my heart began to thud heavily at his tone of voice.

I nodded unhappily. I had almost—*almost*—become reconciled to going away. But now *my* eyes were tearing up. It felt like I was abandoning him; I so badly wanted to stay.

"I guess I'd better head back," he said, sounding reluctant but looking determined. "I don't know what's going to happen when Dad finds out he's gone, but I'd better be there."

I nodded again but hated for him to leave already, especially as troubled as he obviously was. I thought about inviting him in but had some suspicions about why I was being shuttled off to Los Angeles in the first place. The fact that Dave had ridden the motorcycle here wouldn't help matters at all, so I decided it wasn't a good idea. It made me just *that* much more unhappy, though.

"See you . . . tomorrow. Okay?" he said somberly.

"I could ride Remmy to Bar 8, you know. You don't have to come if you don't want to. I mean," I realized that might sound like I didn't want him to, which of course I did, "you might be busy or something."

He stared at me seriously for a moment as if to read the intent of my comment, then smiled slightly and said, "No, I want to."

He started his bike, but I reached out to touch the handlebar again. He looked up into my face.

"Be careful, okay?" I said, wanting desperately to leave him in no doubt that I *did* care. "You're not wearing your helmet again."

He snorted lightly and grinned a little. "Yeah . . . okay."

I stepped back toward the low fence and he rode in a semi-circle, still smiling slightly, and then took off. I sat on one of the posts, waiting for my heart to calm down before going back into the house.

I had hoped to get a call from Dave that evening saying that Cris was home, or that he had called and everything was all right, but I didn't. I wasn't sure how to feel about Cris. Angry at his seemingly callous disregard for his family? Sorry that, whatever he was doing, I hadn't felt on very good terms with him before he left? Hopeful that it was all just a misunderstanding and he'd be home again today, tomorrow—soon? Or just really worried? I felt bad that I hadn't gotten around to apologizing again but doubted Cris would care anyway.

We would be leaving fairly early in the morning, so I spent the evening second-guessing and double-checking what I had packed for my summer away and thinking through everything that had happened the past couple of days. Then I tried to go to bed early, but I probably would have been better off just staying up really late for all the sleep I got.

Though I kept waking up all night, I could never ascertain what had awoken me, dream or otherwise. As soon as I detected light through my window, I got up and went out to feed Remmy. I was going to miss him so much, but at least I knew he'd be here when I got back and that he'd be looked after very well. I groomed him for the last time while he ate, then went back inside to shower and get ready to go. Dave knew we were leaving at nine, so at eight-thirty I made sure the things I needed were loaded in the car and then went back to my room one last time.

I was going to miss it too. I'd never felt this way about a room before, but the soft gray walls had been witness to my most vulnerable moments, my deepest anxieties, and my most intimate interlude with Dave. It was like a silent best friend; unable to help, perhaps, but always a refuge.

I double-checked my backpack for all my most important and necessary possessions: cell phone, music player and earbuds, pencil case, sketchbook. The candles Robin had given to me wrapped carefully in a plastic shopping bag. The framed picture of me riding Gold from the Calderas and the pictures

of him I had printed from Estephanie's e-mails. And my yearbook, a valuable visual aid and link to my most precious possessions of all—my friends.

Then I dug out my "Dave List" from the bottom drawer of my desk. I would have to be zealous in guarding it against prying eyes this summer, especially from younger cousins and maybe aunts and friends as well. But it was another vital link to the memories that would keep me going until I returned home. Besides, I had some more things to add to it. I hid it in the blank pages of the journal Aunt Audrey had given to me two Christmases before, then zipped my backpack closed. Then I went downstairs, set it by the door, and went to talk to Remmy while I waited for Dave.

I heard his motorcycle coming from the road and my stomach turned to butterflies at the thought of seeing him this last time. Yesterday he'd seemed so forlorn, though he'd left with a smile. That's just the way he was. I wondered if it was a struggle for him to stay positive and confident most of the time or if he just couldn't help it. I wished again with all my heart that, somehow, I could stay with him and not leave.

The engine sound stopped before the motorcycle rolled into view behind the house. I was pleased to see he'd worn his helmet. He even held it up briefly, to make sure I noticed, and I nodded my approval. He looked really tired as if he hadn't slept much again, his hair mussed badly and a worried look still in his eyes. In spite of this, he smiled as he approached me.

"So, are you all ready to go?" he asked enthusiastically, as if the trip were a treat for me and something to look forward to.

I tried to reflect his positive attitude and smiled as best I could. "Yes, I think so—"

"Allie," my dad's voice came from the back door, but he regarded Dave steadily, "we want to leave soon. Say, fifteen minutes?"

I looked at Dave. He returned my dad's steady stare. It felt like something was passing between them; something unspoken but acknowledged, though Dave's demeanor was hardly submissive. One of those troubling, fascinating "male" moments that I kind of wished I understood and was kind of glad I didn't.

"Okay, Dad," I said meekly, hoping to lessen any tensions, if there *were* any.

Dad moved to go back into the house but paused and said, "And thank you . . . Dave . . . for everything." They nodded at each other and Dad went back into the house.

Everything? What on earth does that mean? They gave the impression that they had some kind of understanding between them, but words and appearances seemed to contradict each other. *Men!*

"I better get Remmy saddled," said Dave, and walked toward the porch where I kept Remmy's tack. Then he turned back, taking a piece of folded paper out of his back pocket. "I found this on the seat of my truck early this morning. Sunday's one of Miguel's days off and I usually do his morning chores, feeding the livestock and horses near the house. I use my truck, so Cris knew I'd find this by today." He handed the paper to me, then continued to the porch, the worried look back on his face.

Opening the paper, I read the few words written there:

Feed Merle for me

Remember to give these to Allison and Robin

I looked at him in question as he walked back toward me with a tight-lipped smile on his lips but no smile in his eyes. He steadied the saddle on the rail of the paddock and dug a small black device out of his front jeans pocket—an MP3 player.

"We put a bunch of stuff on there when we first heard you'd be gone all summer. You know, so you don't forget us." He smirked a little more naturally.

I blushed hotly. *As if that could ever happen.*

"I put my favorite stuff on there and Cris put some that he thought you'd like. We did one for Robin too. She'll be gone for a few weeks, but we'll be gone too . . . probably until school starts." He was quiet and serious for a moment. Then he laughed and said, "This year's gone by pretty fast, huh?"

I smiled and nodded, not trusting my voice at all and trusting my brain to say something comprehensible even less. I watched as he saddled Remmy and led him out of the paddock.

"I'll come by and get my bike later," he said. "It'll be safe here until then. And don't worry about Remmy. He'll be fine."

"I know," I said. My throat was closing up and my heart was picking up speed, sadness at odds with hope. If anything was going to happen between Dave and me, it would be now.

"Well . . ." he said softly, seeming to feel a little awkward. Then he stepped toward me.

My stomach flipped and I thought my heart would stop, ready to return the embrace I hoped he was in the act of giving me, and anything else he might offer. Instead of encircling me with his arms, however, he touched my arm, almost like tagging me; a brotherly gesture.

"Call me when you get there, okay?"

Disappointed but not hurt, I smiled. "Okay."

"I'll . . . meet you around front."

I smiled again and nodded, then watched him walk backward away from me several steps, leading Remmy. I closed the paddock gate and went into the house. Dad was already outside, loading the last of our luggage and locking the garage door. Mom was doing a final check through the house, making sure all the lights were off—except the upstairs hallway and stairs—and unplugging almost everything. I picked up my backpack and left the house. Dave had led Remmy to the road via the dirt drive. After putting my backpack in the back seat of the car, I walked over to meet him by the edge of the driveway.

"You're going to have a lot of fun this summer," he said, the epitome of positive attitude. He was standing so close that I could feel Remmy's breath on my arm. "And it'll go by fast. We'll keep Remmy in shape for you, and he'll be happy 'cause he'll see a lot of people and get ridden and pet and spoiled."

My eyes were tearing up as I reached out toward the brown head. "I'm going to really miss him," I said quietly, caressing Remmy's cheek, but looking into Dave's eyes.

"He'll miss you too," he said, smiling gently, his voice deadly soft. "And he'll be waiting for you to come home."

The recorder was on and I was going to remember and replay those words in my mind all summer. I knew he was being completely literal, but the recording of the words was mine and I could put any meaning I wanted to them.

"Allie?" My dad's voice cut through the close atmosphere.

We both took a step back from each other and it might have been my imagination, but Dave looked as suddenly self-conscious as I felt.

I lifted my hand slightly in parting salute and Dave returned it. Then I walked to the waiting car, my parents already inside. As I opened the door I looked back, lifting the music player still in my hand.

"Thanks!" I said and tried to smile brightly at him.

He grinned back.

Dad backed the car out of the driveway and waved slightly at Dave. Mom smiled and waved more vigorously. I couldn't resist turning to watch him out the back window as we began to move away down the road. He swung up easily into the saddle and gave chase along the side of the road all the way to where we turned onto the highway. Then he reined up in a cloud of dust, smiling, and waved once. I waved back, not sure if he could even see me. That was probably the last vision I would have of him until school started. The last *real* vision anyway. I was sure I'd see him constantly in my mind.

When he was out of sight, I settled back against the seat and dug my earphones out of my backpack, attaching them to the new MP3 player. The first track was familiar, and as I listened I recalled the day Cris drove us to the snow and the music we had listened to. *Cris'* music. He'd remembered I'd said I liked it!

Listening to the music track by track as the miles put growing distance between us, I thought constantly of my new friends and the new experiences I'd had this year; nothing short of amazing! As far as school went, especially on a social level, I felt I'd scraped by pretty well. *Very* well compared to previous years, though this year I had definitely cared more about what other people thought of me than ever before.

As for the rest, the whole year had been an emotional roller-coaster ride of ridiculous highs that made my heart soar with pleasure and hope, and devastating crashes that made me question everything I thought I knew about myself and the meaning of my life. And, except for one terribly painful loss, I wouldn't have changed a thing. Well, unless I could change someone else's heart, that is. The world as I knew it had truly been shaken up, upended, unhinged; I hardly recognized it. Things that had once mattered to me held little or no meaning anymore, or that meaning had drastically changed. My heart and head were full of things that I had barely even imagined before.

In fact, it was hard to remember anything being *really* important or meaningful to me before this year, and it seemed to be all *his* fault. Dave's existence had changed my entire outlook on life. Having the amazing good fortune to be included in his life, to be counted as his friend—as chafing as that often seemed—was truly magical; it had changed the very nature of my world. I was unaware of changing much on the outside, but I felt quite sure that if there *had* been a spell keeping me from growing, from changing into something different and new, it was now broken. The curse was lifted.

Nothing would ever be the same because of Dave, and I was going to miss him terribly until school started again.

It was going to be a very, *very* long summer.

The Glister Journals

Copper

"We're friends, right? Nothing's going to change that."
Yes. Of course. Whatever you say.

That was last year, full of surprise and change for Allison Anderson. The biggest surprise of all was Dave Caldera's friendship.

This year, she's starting with changes of her own, but they're nothing compared to those waiting back at school. New people and distractions keep her busy as distance grows between her and the boy she loves. Revelations pose more challenges and draw her closer to other friends.

And Dave?

Only time will tell.

Visit theglisterjournals.com or follow B B Shepherd
for news and updates.